BEST OF
Children's Classics

CLASSICS

Published 2022

FINGERPRINT! CLASSICS

An imprint of Prakash Books India Pvt. Ltd.

113/A, Darya Ganj,
New Delhi-110 002
Tel: (011) 2324 7062 – 65, Fax: (011) 2324 6975
Email: info@prakashbooks.com/sales@prakashbooks.com

facebook www.facebook.com/fingerprintpublishing
twitter www.twitter.com/FingerprintP
www.fingerprintpublishing.com

ISBN: 978 93 5440 574 7

Processed & printed in India

"Would you tell me, please, which way I ought to go from here?"

"That depends a good deal on where you want to get to," said the Cat.

"I don't much care where—" said Alice.

"Then it doesn't matter which way you go," said the Cat.

"—so long as I get SOMEWHERE," Alice added as an explanation.

"Oh, you're sure to do that," said the Cat, "if you only walk long enough."

—Lewis Carroll, *Alice in Wonderland*

Children have been listening to stories for thousands of years, but children's literature solidified as a genre only three centuries ago. John Newbery, a bookseller in England, published *A Little Pretty Pocket-Book* and *The History of Little Goody Two-Shoes* in the middle of the eighteenth century. He thereafter came to be known as 'the father of children's literature', since he was the first one to realise that children had no stories of their own. Before this time period, children's literature was didactic in nature, aimed at educating and refining young minds. After Newbury's publications, books that focused on stories that will bring pleasure and happiness to children, began to circulate in Europe and America.

The canon of children's literature is filled with fables, fairy tales, picture-books, short fiction, novels, and even retellings of classics in an easy-to-read format. Short fiction and novels, in particular, were critically appreciated and widely read, so much so that they have earned the status of classics. From adventures of mischievous kids, some of whom tumble into strange, magical lands, to relaying goings-on of talking animals and fantastical kids who never grow up—classic stories for children are many. And what a fascinating thing these stories are. Even though they are crafted keeping children in mind, they are read by adults with equal excitement. Many adults go back to the comfort such books offer, relishing the nostalgia and diving deep into the emotions they felt when they had first read them.

We have compiled four such classics that have made their mark in the history of English literature, making their writers distinguished in literary circles and immensely popular in the masses, and their works timeless. Entertaining yet informative, packed with wonder and magic, these are four classics that every child will cherish.

About this Edition

In this hardbound edition, with gilded edges and beautiful endpapers, are four classics that every child should read. These books are canonical in children's literature and have been adapted into various art forms. Follow the yellow brick road with Dorothy and Toto in *The Wizard of Oz*, read how the seven-year-old imaginative Sarah Crewe deals with the death of her father in *A Little Princess*, discover the private walled garden which has been locked for years with Mary Lennox in *The Secret Garden*, and go on an adventure with a boy who never grows up and lives with the fairies in *Peter Pan*.

Contents

A LITTLE PRINCESS

THE SECRET GARDEN

PETER PAN

The Wizard of OZ

by L. Frank Baum

Introduction

Folk lore, legends, myths and fairy tales have followed childhood through the ages, for every healthy youngster has a wholesome and instinctive love for stories fantastic, marvellous and manifestly unreal. The winged fairies of Grimm and Andersen have brought more happiness to childish hearts than all other human creations.

Yet the old-time fairy tale, having served for generations, may now be classed as "historical" in the children's library; for the time has come for a series of newer "wonder tales" in which the stereotyped genie, dwarf and fairy are eliminated, together with all the horrible and blood-curdling incident devised by their authors to point a fearsome moral to each tale. Modern education includes morality; therefore the modern child seeks only entertainment in its wonder-tales and gladly dispenses with all disagreeable incident.

Having this thought in mind, the story of "The Wonderful Wizard of Oz" was written solely to pleasure children of today. It aspires to being a modernized fairy tale, in which the wonderment and joy are retained and the heart-aches and nightmares are left out.

L. Frank Baum.
Chicago, April, 1900.

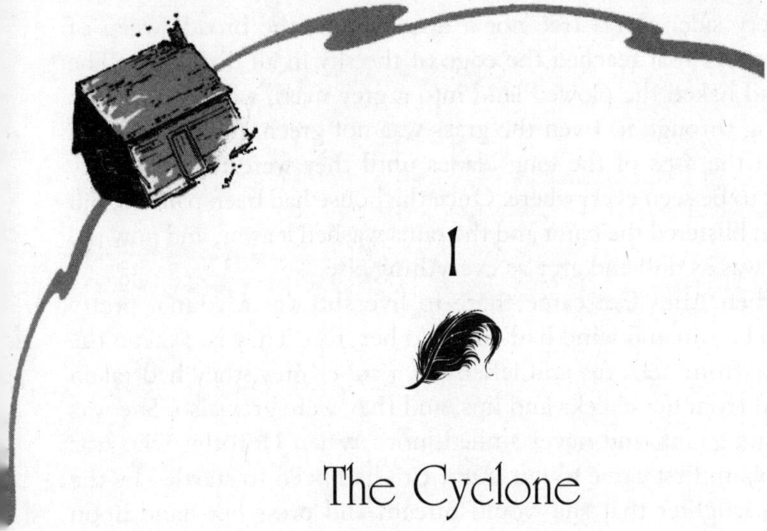

1

The Cyclone

Dorothy lived in the midst of the great Kansas prairies, with Uncle Henry, who was a farmer, and Aunt Em, who was the farmer's wife. Their house was small, for the lumber to build it had to be carried by wagon many miles. There were four walls, a floor and a roof, which made one room; and this room contained a rusty looking cooking stove, a cupboard for the dishes, a table, three or four chairs, and the beds. Uncle Henry and Aunt Em had a big bed in one corner, and Dorothy a little bed in another corner. There was no garret at all, and no cellar—except a small hole, dug in the ground, called a cyclone cellar, where the family could go in case one of those great whirlwinds arose, mighty enough to crush any building in its path. It was reached by a trapdoor in the middle of the floor, from which a ladder led down into the small, dark hole.

When Dorothy stood in the doorway and looked around, she could see nothing but the great grey prairie on every side. Not a tree nor a house broke the broad sweep of flat country that reached the edge of the sky in all directions. The sun had baked the plowed land into a grey mass, with little cracks running through it. Even the grass was not green, for the sun had burned the tops of the long blades until they were the same grey colour to be seen everywhere. Once the house had been painted, but the sun blistered the paint and the rains washed it away, and now the house was as dull and grey as everything else.

When Aunt Em came there to live she was a young, pretty wife. The sun and wind had changed her, too. They had taken the sparkle from her eyes and left them a sober grey; they had taken the red from her cheeks and lips, and they were grey also. She was thin and gaunt, and never smiled, now. When Dorothy, who was an orphan, first came to her, Aunt Em had been so startled by the child's laughter that she would scream and press her hand upon her heart whenever Dorothy's merry voice reached her ears; and she still looked at the little girl with wonder that she could find anything to laugh at.

Uncle Henry never laughed. He worked hard from morning till night and did not know what joy was. He was grey also, from his long beard to his rough boots, and he looked stern and solemn, and rarely spoke.

It was Toto that made Dorothy laugh, and saved her from growing as grey as her other surroundings. Toto was not grey; he was a little black dog, with long, silky hair and small black eyes that twinkled merrily on either side of his funny, wee nose. Toto played all day long, and Dorothy played with him, and loved him dearly.

Today, however, they were not playing. Uncle Henry sat upon the doorstep and looked anxiously at the sky, which was even greyer than usual. Dorothy stood in the door with Toto in her arms, and looked at the sky too. Aunt Em was washing the dishes.

From the far north they heard a low wail of the wind, and Uncle Henry and Dorothy could see where the long grass bowed in waves before the coming storm. There now came a sharp whistling in the air from the south, and as they turned their eyes that way they saw ripples in the grass coming from that direction also.

Suddenly Uncle Henry stood up.

"There's a cyclone coming, Em," he called to his wife; "I'll go look after the stock." Then he ran towards the sheds where the cows and horses were kept.

Aunt Em dropped her work and came to the door. One glance told her of the danger close at hand.

"Quick, Dorothy!" she screamed. "Run for the cellar!"

Toto jumped out of Dorothy's arms and hid under the bed, and the girl started to get him. Aunt Em, badly frightened, threw open the trapdoor in the floor and climbed down the ladder into the small, dark hole. Dorothy caught Toto at last, and started to follow her aunt. When she was halfway across the room there came a great shriek from the wind, and the house shook so hard that she lost her footing and sat down suddenly upon the floor.

A strange thing then happened.

The house whirled around two or three times and rose slowly through the air. Dorothy felt as if she were going up in a balloon.

The north and south winds met where the house stood, and made it the exact centre of the cyclone. In the middle of a cyclone the air is generally still, but the great pressure of the wind on every side of the house raised it up higher and higher, until it was at the very top of the cyclone; and there it remained and was carried miles and miles away as easily as you could carry a feather.

It was very dark, and the wind howled horribly around her, but Dorothy found she was riding quite easily. After the first few whirls around, and one other time when the house tipped badly, she felt as if she were being rocked gently, like a baby in a cradle.

Toto did not like it. He ran about the room, now here, now there, barking loudly; but Dorothy sat quite still on the floor and waited to see what would happen.

Once Toto got too near the open trapdoor, and fell in; and at first the little girl thought she had lost him. But soon she saw one of his ears sticking up through the hole, for the strong pressure of the air was keeping him up so that he could not fall. She crept to the hole, caught Toto by the ear, and dragged him into the room again; afterward closing the trapdoor so that no more accidents could happen.

Hour after hour passed away, and slowly Dorothy got over her fright; but she felt quite lonely, and the wind shrieked so loudly all

She caught Toto by the ear.

about her that she nearly became deaf. At first she had wondered if she would be dashed to pieces when the house fell again; but as the hours passed and nothing terrible happened, she stopped worrying and resolved to wait calmly and see what the future would bring. At last she crawled over the swaying floor to her bed, and lay down upon it; and Toto followed and lay down beside her.

In spite of the swaying of the house and the wailing of the wind, Dorothy soon closed her eyes and fell fast asleep.

2

The Council with the Munchkins

She was awakened by a shock, so sudden and severe that if Dorothy had not been lying on the soft bed she might have been hurt. As it was, the jar made her catch her breath and wonder what had happened; and Toto put his cold little nose into her face and whined dismally. Dorothy sat up and noticed that the house was not moving; nor was it dark, for the bright sunshine came in at the window, flooding the little room. She sprang from her bed and with Toto at her heels ran and opened the door.

The little girl gave a cry of amazement and looked about her, her eyes growing bigger and bigger at the wonderful sights she saw.

The cyclone had set the house down, very gently—for a cyclone—in the midst of a country of marvelous beauty. There were lovely patches of green sward all about, with stately trees bearing rich and luscious fruits. Banks of gorgeous flowers were on every hand, and birds with rare and brilliant plumage sang and fluttered in the trees and bushes. A little way off was a small brook, rushing and sparkling along between green banks, and murmuring in a voice very grateful to a little girl who had lived so long on the dry, grey prairies.

While she stood looking eagerly at the strange and beautiful sights, she noticed coming towards her a group of the queerest people she had ever seen. They were not as big as the grown folk she had always been used to; but neither were they very small. In fact, they seemed about as tall as Dorothy, who was a well-grown child for her age, although they were, so far as looks go, many years older.

Three were men and one a woman, and all were oddly dressed. They wore round hats that rose to a small point a foot above their heads, with little bells around the brims that tinkled sweetly as they moved. The hats of the men were blue; the little woman's hat was white, and she wore a white gown that hung in plaits from her shoulders; over it were sprinkled little stars that glistened in the sun like diamonds. The men were dressed in blue, of the same shade as their hats, and wore well-polished boots with a deep roll of blue at the tops. The men, Dorothy thought, were about as old as Uncle Henry, for two of them had beards. But the little woman was doubtless much older: her face was covered with wrinkles, her hair was nearly white, and she walked rather stiffly.

When these people drew near the house where Dorothy was standing in the doorway, they paused and whispered among themselves, as if afraid to come farther. But the little old woman walked up to Dorothy, made a low bow and said, in a sweet voice:

"You are welcome, most noble Sorceress, to the land of the Munchkins. We are so grateful to you for having killed the wicked Witch of the East, and for setting our people free from bondage."

Dorothy listened to this speech with wonder. What could the little woman possibly mean by calling her a sorceress, and saying she had killed the wicked Witch of the East? Dorothy was an innocent, harmless little girl, who had been carried by a cyclone many miles from home; and she had never killed anything in all her life.

But the little woman evidently expected her to answer; so Dorothy said, with hesitation, "You are very kind; but there must be some mistake. I have not killed anything."

I am the Witch of the North.

"Your house did, anyway," replied the little old woman, with a laugh, "and that is the same thing. See!" she continued, pointing to the corner of the house. "There are her two toes, still sticking out from under a block of wood."

Dorothy looked, and gave a little cry of fright. There, indeed, just under the corner of the great beam the house rested on, two feet were sticking out, shod in silver shoes with pointed toes.

"Oh, dear! Oh, dear!" cried Dorothy, clasping her hands together in dismay. "The house must have fallen on her. Whatever shall we do?"

"There is nothing to be done," said the little woman calmly.

"But who was she?" asked Dorothy.

"She was the wicked Witch of the East, as I said," answered the little woman. "She has held all the Munchkins in bondage for many years, making them slave for her night and day. Now they are all set free, and are grateful to you for the favour."

"Who are the Munchkins?" enquired Dorothy.

"They are the people who live in this land of the East, where the wicked Witch ruled."

"Are you a Munchkin?" asked Dorothy.

"No, but I am their friend, although I live in the land of the North. When they saw the Witch of the East was dead the Munchkins sent a swift messenger to me, and I came at once. I am the Witch of the North."

"Oh, gracious!" cried Dorothy. "Are you a real witch?"

"Yes, indeed," answered the little woman. "But I am a good witch, and the people love me. I am not as powerful as the wicked Witch was who ruled here, or I should have set the people free myself."

"But I thought all witches were wicked," said the girl, who was half frightened at facing a real witch.

"Oh, no, that is a great mistake. There were only four witches in all the Land of Oz, and two of them, those who live in the North and the South, are good witches. I know this is true, for I am one of them myself, and cannot be mistaken. Those who dwelt in the East and the West were, indeed, wicked witches; but now that you have killed one of them, there is but one wicked Witch in all the Land of Oz—the one who lives in the West."

"But," said Dorothy, after a moment's thought, "Aunt Em has told me that the witches were all dead—years and years ago."

"Who is Aunt Em?" enquired the little old woman.

"She is my aunt who lives in Kansas, where I came from."

The Witch of the North seemed to think for a time, with her head bowed and her eyes upon the ground. Then she looked up and said, "I do not know where Kansas is, for I have never heard that country mentioned before. But tell me, is it a civilized country?"

"Oh, yes," replied Dorothy.

"Then that accounts for it. In the civilized countries I believe there are no witches left, nor wizards, nor sorceresses, nor magicians. But, you see, the Land of Oz has never been civilized, for we are cut off from all the rest of the world. Therefore we still have witches and wizards amongst us."

"Who are the Wizards?" asked Dorothy.

"Oz himself is the Great Wizard," answered the Witch, sinking her voice to a whisper. "He is more powerful than all the rest of us together. He lives in the City of Emeralds."

Dorothy was going to ask another question, but just then the Munchkins, who had been standing silently by, gave a loud shout and pointed to the corner of the house where the Wicked Witch had been lying.

"What is it?" asked the little old woman and looked, and began to laugh. The feet of the dead Witch had disappeared entirely and nothing was left but the silver shoes.

"She was so old," explained the Witch of the North, "that she dried up quickly in the sun. That is the end of her. But the silver shoes are yours, and you shall have them to wear." She reached down and picked up the shoes, and after shaking the dust out of them handed them to Dorothy.

"The Witch of the East was proud of those silver shoes," said one of the Munchkins, "and there is some charm connected with them; but what it is we never knew."

Dorothy carried the shoes into the house and placed them on the table. Then she came out again to the Munchkins and said:

"I am anxious to get back to my aunt and uncle, for I am sure they will worry about me. Can you help me find my way?"

The Munchkins and the Witch first looked at one another, and then at Dorothy, and then shook their heads.

"At the East, not far from here," said one, "there is a great desert, and none could live to cross it."

"It is the same at the South," said another, "for I have been there and seen it. The South is the country of the Quadlings."

"I am told," said the third man, "that it is the same at the West. And that country, where the Winkies live, is ruled by the wicked Witch of the West, who would make you her slave if you passed her way."

"The North is my home," said the old lady, "and at its edge is the same great desert that surrounds this Land of Oz. I'm afraid, my dear, you will have to live with us."

Dorothy began to sob at this, for she felt lonely among all these strange people. Her tears seemed to grieve the kind-hearted Munchkins, for they immediately took out their handkerchiefs and began to weep also. As for the little old woman, she took off her cap and balanced the point on the end of her nose, while she counted "one, two, three" in a solemn voice. At once the cap changed to a slate, on which was written in big, white chalk marks:

"Let Dorothy Go To The City of Emeralds."

The little old woman took the slate from her nose, and, having read the words on it, asked,

"Is your name Dorothy, my dear?"

"Yes," answered the child, looking up and drying her tears.

"Then you must go to the City of Emeralds. Perhaps Oz will help you."

"Where is this City?" asked Dorothy.

"It is exactly in the centre of the country, and is ruled by Oz, the Great Wizard I told you of."

"Is he a good man?" enquired the girl anxiously.

"He is a good Wizard. Whether he is a man or not I cannot tell, for I have never seen him."

"How can I get there?" asked Dorothy.

"You must walk. It is a long journey, through a country that is sometimes pleasant and sometimes dark and terrible. However, I will use all the magic arts I know of to keep you from harm."

"Won't you go with me?" pleaded the girl, who had begun to look upon the little old woman as her only friend.

"No, I cannot do that," she replied, "but I will give you my kiss, and no one will dare injure a person who has been kissed by the Witch of the North."

She came close to Dorothy and kissed her gently on the forehead. Where her lips touched the girl they left a round, shining mark, as Dorothy found out soon after.

"The road to the City of Emeralds is paved with yellow brick," said the Witch, "so you cannot miss it. When you get to Oz do not be afraid of him, but tell your story and ask him to help you. Goodbye, my dear."

The three Munchkins bowed low to her and wished her a pleasant journey, after which they walked away through the trees. The Witch gave Dorothy a friendly little nod, whirled around on her left heel three times, and straightway disappeared, much to the surprise of little Toto, who barked after her loudly enough when she had gone, because he had been afraid even to growl while she stood by.

But Dorothy, knowing her to be a witch, had expected her to disappear in just that way, and was not surprised in the least.

3

How Dorothy Saved the Scarecrow

When Dorothy was left alone she began to feel hungry. So she went to the cupboard and cut herself some bread, which she spread with butter. She gave some to Toto, and taking a pail from the shelf she carried it down to the little brook and filled it with clear, sparkling water. Toto ran over to the trees and began to bark at the birds sitting there. Dorothy went to get him, and saw such delicious fruit hanging from the branches that she gathered some of it, finding it just what she wanted to help out her breakfast.

Then she went back to the house, and having helped herself and Toto to a good drink of the cool, clear water, she set about making ready for the journey to the City of Emeralds.

Dorothy had only one other dress, but that happened to be clean and was hanging on a peg beside her bed. It was gingham, with checks of white and blue; and although the blue was somewhat faded with many washings, it was still a pretty frock. The girl washed herself carefully, dressed herself in the clean gingham, and tied her pink sun bonnet on her head. She took a little basket and filled it with bread from the cupboard, laying a white cloth over the top. Then she looked down at her feet and noticed how old and worn her shoes were.

"They surely will never do for a long journey, Toto," she said. And Toto looked up into her face with his little black eyes and wagged his tail to show he knew what she meant.

At that moment Dorothy saw lying on the table the silver shoes that had belonged to the Witch of the East.

"I wonder if they will fit me," she said to Toto. "They would be just the thing to take a long walk in, for they could not wear out."

She took off her old leather shoes and tried on the silver ones, which fitted her as well as if they had been made for her.

Finally she picked up her basket.

"Come along, Toto," she said, "we will go to the Emerald City and ask the great Oz how to get back to Kansas."

She closed the door, locked it, and put the key carefully in the pocket of her dress. And so, with Toto trotting along soberly behind her, she started on her journey.

There were several roads nearby, but it did not take her long to find the one paved with yellow brick. Within a short time she was walking briskly towards the Emerald City, her silver shoes tinkling merrily on the hard, yellow roadbed. The sun shone bright and the birds sang sweet and Dorothy did not feel nearly as bad as you might think a little girl would who had been suddenly whisked away from her own country and set down in the midst of a strange land.

She was surprised, as she walked along, to see how pretty the country was about her. There were neat fences at the sides of the road, painted a dainty blue colour, and beyond them were fields of grain and vegetables in abundance. Evidently the Munchkins were good farmers and able to raise large crops. Once in a while she would pass a house, and the people came out to look at her and bow low as she went by; for everyone knew she had been the means of destroying the wicked witch and setting them free from bondage. The houses of the Munchkins were odd-looking dwellings, for each was round, with a big dome for a roof. All were painted blue, for in this country of the East blue was the favourite colour.

Towards evening, when Dorothy was tired with her long walk and began to wonder where she should pass the night, she came to a house rather larger than the rest. On the green lawn before it many men and women were dancing. Five little fiddlers played as loudly as possible and the people were laughing and singing, while a big table nearby was loaded with delicious fruits and nuts, pies and cakes, and many other good things to eat.

The people greeted Dorothy kindly, and invited her to supper and to pass the night with them; for this was the home of one of the richest Munchkins in the land, and his friends were gathered with him to celebrate their freedom from the bondage of the Wicked Witch.

Dorothy ate a hearty supper and was waited upon by the rich Munchkin himself, whose name was Boq. Then she sat down upon a settee and watched the people dance.

When Boq saw her silver shoes he said, "You must be a great sorceress."

"Why?" asked the girl.

"Because you wear silver shoes and have killed the Wicked Witch. Besides, you have white in your frock, and only witches and sorceresses wear white."

"My dress is blue and white checked," said Dorothy, smoothing out the wrinkles in it.

"It is kind of you to wear that," said Boq. "Blue is the colour of the Munchkins, and white is the witch colour; so we know you are a friendly witch."

Dorothy did not know what to say to this, for all the people seemed to think her a witch, and she knew very well she was only an ordinary little girl who had come by the chance of a cyclone into a strange land.

When she had tired watching the dancing, Boq led her into the house, where he gave her a room with a pretty bed in it. The sheets were made of blue cloth, and Dorothy slept soundly in them till morning, with Toto curled up on the blue rug beside her.

She ate a hearty breakfast, and watched a wee Munchkin baby, who played with Toto and pulled his tail and crowed and laughed in

You must be a great sorceress.

a way that greatly amused Dorothy. Toto was a fine curiosity to all the people, for they had never seen a dog before.

"How far is it to the Emerald City?" the girl asked.

"I do not know," answered Boq gravely, "for I have never been there. It is better for people to keep away from Oz, unless they have business with him. But it is a long way to the Emerald City, and it will take you many days. The country here is rich and pleasant, but you must pass through rough and dangerous places before you reach the end of your journey."

This worried Dorothy a little, but she knew that only the great Oz could help her get to Kansas again, so she bravely resolved not to turn back.

She bade her friends goodbye, and again started along the road of yellow brick. When she had gone several miles she thought she would stop to rest, and so climbed to the top of the fence beside the road and sat down. There was a great cornfield beyond the fence, and not far away she saw a Scarecrow, placed high on a pole to keep the birds from the ripe corn.

Dorothy leaned her chin upon her hand and gazed thoughtfully at the Scarecrow. Its head was a small sack stuffed with straw, with eyes, nose and mouth painted on it to represent a face. An old, pointed blue hat, which had belonged to some Munchkin, was perched on this head, and the rest of the figure was a blue suit of clothes, worn and faded, which had also been stuffed with straw. On the feet were some old boots with blue tops, such as every man wore in this country, and the figure was raised above the stalks of corn by means of the pole stuck up its back.

While Dorothy was looking earnestly into the queer, painted face of the Scarecrow, she was surprised to see one of the eyes slowly wink at her. She thought she must have been mistaken at first, for none of the scarecrows in Kansas ever wink; but presently the figure nodded its head to her in a friendly way. Then she climbed down from the fence and walked up to it, while Toto ran around the pole and barked.

"Good day," said the Scarecrow, in a rather husky voice.

"Did you speak?" asked the girl, in wonder.

"Certainly," answered the Scarecrow. "How do you do?"

Dorothy gazed thoughtfully at the Scarecrow.

"I'm pretty well, thank you," replied Dorothy, politely. "How do you do?"

"I'm not feeling well," said the Scarecrow, with a smile, "for it is very tedious being perched up here night and day to scare away crows."

"Can't you get down?" asked Dorothy.

"No, for this pole is stuck up my back. If you will please take away the pole I shall be greatly obliged to you."

Dorothy reached up both arms and lifted the figure off the pole, for, being stuffed with straw, it was quite light.

"Thank you very much," said the Scarecrow, when he had been set down on the ground. "I feel like a new man."

Dorothy was puzzled at this, for it sounded queer to hear a stuffed man speak, and to see him bow and walk along beside her.

"Who are you?" asked the Scarecrow, when he had stretched himself and yawned, "and where are you going?"

"My name is Dorothy," said the girl, "and I am going to the Emerald City, to ask the great Oz to send me back to Kansas."

"Where is the Emerald City?" he enquired. "And who is Oz?"

"Why, don't you know?" she returned, in surprise.

"No, indeed; I don't know anything. You see, I am stuffed, so I have no brains at all," he answered sadly.

"Oh," said Dorothy. "I'm awfully sorry for you."

"Do you think," he asked, "If I go to the Emerald City with you, that the great Oz would give me some brains?"

"I cannot tell," she returned. "But you may come with me, if you like. If Oz will not give you any brains you will be no worse off than you are now."

"That is true," said the Scarecrow. "You see," he continued confidentially, "I don't mind my legs and arms and body being stuffed, because I cannot get hurt. If anyone treads on my toes or sticks a pin into me, it doesn't matter, for I can't feel it. But I do not want people to call me a fool, and if my head stays stuffed with straw instead of with brains, as yours is, how am I ever to know anything?"

"I understand how you feel," said the little girl, who was truly sorry for him. "If you will come with me I'll ask Oz to do all he can for you."

"Thank you," he answered gratefully.

They walked back to the road. Dorothy helped him over the fence, and they started along the path of yellow brick for the Emerald City.

Toto did not like this addition to the party, at first. He smelled around the stuffed man as if he suspected there might be a nest of rats in the straw, and he often growled in an unfriendly way at the Scarecrow.

"Don't mind Toto," said Dorothy, to her new friend. "He never bites."

"Oh, I'm not afraid," replied the Scarecrow, "he can't hurt the straw. Do let me carry that basket for you. I shall not mind it, for I can't get tired. I'll tell you a secret," he continued, as he walked along. "There is only one thing in the world I am afraid of."

"What is that?" asked Dorothy. "The Munchkin farmer who made you?"

"No," answered the Scarecrow. "It's a lighted match."

4

The Road Through the Forest

After a few hours the road began to be rough, and the walking grew so difficult that the Scarecrow often stumbled over the yellow brick, which were here very uneven. Sometimes, indeed, they were broken or missing altogether, leaving holes that Toto jumped across and Dorothy walked around. As for the Scarecrow, having no brains he walked straight ahead, and so stepped into the holes and fell at full length on the hard bricks. It never hurt him, however, and Dorothy would pick him up and set him upon his feet again, while he joined her in laughing merrily at his own mishap.

The farms were not nearly so well cared for here as they were farther back. There were fewer houses and fewer fruit trees, and the farther they went the more dismal and lonesome the country became.

At noon they sat down by the roadside, near a little brook, and Dorothy opened her basket and got out some bread. She offered a piece to the Scarecrow, but he refused.

"I am never hungry," he said. "And it is a lucky thing I

am not. For my mouth is only painted, and if I should cut a hole in it so I could eat, the straw I am stuffed with would come out, and that would spoil the shape of my head."

Dorothy saw at once that this was true, so she only nodded and went on eating her bread.

"Tell me something about yourself, and the country you came from," said the Scarecrow, when she had finished her dinner. So she told him all about Kansas, and how grey everything was there, and how the cyclone had carried her to this queer Land of Oz. The Scarecrow listened carefully, and said, "I cannot understand why you should wish to leave this beautiful country and go back to the dry, grey place you call Kansas."

"That is because you have no brains," answered the girl. "No matter how dreary and grey our homes are, we people of flesh and blood would rather live there than in any other country, be it ever so beautiful. There is no place like home."

The Scarecrow sighed.

"Of course I cannot understand it," he said. "If your heads were stuffed with straw, like mine, you would probably all live in the beautiful places, and then Kansas would have no people at all. It is fortunate for Kansas that you have brains."

"Won't you tell me a story, while we are resting?" asked the child.

The Scarecrow looked at her reproachfully, and answered:

"My life has been so short that I really know nothing whatever. I was only made day before yesterday. What happened in the world before that time is all unknown to me. Luckily, when the farmer made my head, one of the first things he did was to paint my ears, so that I heard what was going on. There was another Munchkin with him, and the first thing I heard was the farmer saying,

"'How do you like those ears?'

"'They aren't straight,' answered the other.

"'Never mind,' said the farmer. 'They are ears just the same,' which was true enough.

"'Now I'll make the eyes,' said the farmer. So he painted my right eye, and as soon as it was finished I found myself looking at him and at everything around me with a great deal of curiosity, for this was my first glimpse of the world.

'I was only made day before yesterday,' said the Scarecrow.

"'That's a rather pretty eye,' remarked the Munchkin who was watching the farmer. 'Blue paint is just the colour for eyes.'

"'I think I'll make the other a little bigger,' said the farmer; and when the second eye was done I could see much better than before. Then he made my nose and my mouth; but I did not speak, because at that time I didn't know what a mouth was for. I had the fun of watching them make my body and my arms and legs; and when they fastened on my head, at last, I felt very proud, for I thought I was just as good a man as anyone.

"'This fellow will scare the crows fast enough,' said the farmer; 'he looks just like a man.'

"'Why, he is a man,' said the other, and I quite agreed with him. The farmer carried me under his arm to the cornfield, and set me up on a tall stick, where you found me. He and his friend soon after walked away and left me alone.

"I did not like to be deserted this way; so I tried to walk after them, but my feet would not touch the ground, and I was forced to stay on that pole. It was a lonely life to lead, for I had nothing to think of, having been made such a little while before. Many crows and other birds flew into the cornfield, but as soon as they saw me they flew away again, thinking I was a Munchkin; and this pleased me and made me feel that I was quite an important person. By and by an old crow flew near me, and after looking at me carefully he perched upon my shoulder and said:

"'I wonder if that farmer thought to fool me in this clumsy manner. Any crow of sense could see that you are only stuffed with straw.' Then he hopped down at my feet and ate all the corn he wanted. The other birds, seeing he was not harmed by me, came to eat the corn too, so in a short time there was a great flock of them about me."

"I felt sad at this, for it showed I was not such a good Scarecrow after all; but the old crow comforted me, saying: 'If you only had brains in your head you would be as good a man as any of them, and a better man than some of them. Brains are the only things worth having in this world, no matter whether one is a crow or a man.'

"After the crows had gone I thought this over, and decided I would try hard to get some brains. By good luck, you came along and pulled me off the stake, and from what you say I am sure the great Oz will give me brains as soon as we get to the Emerald City."

"I hope so," said Dorothy earnestly, "since you seem anxious to have them."

"Oh, yes; I am anxious," returned the Scarecrow. "It is such an uncomfortable feeling to know one is a fool."

"Well," said the girl, "let us go." And she handed the basket to the Scarecrow.

There were no fences at all by the road side now, and the land was rough and untilled. Towards evening they came to a great forest, where the trees grew so big and close together that their branches met over the road of yellow brick. It was almost dark under the trees, for the branches shut out the daylight; but the travellers did not stop, and went on into the forest.

"If this road goes in, it must come out," said the Scarecrow, "and as the Emerald City is at the other end of the road, we must go wherever it leads us."

"Anyone would know that," said Dorothy.

"Certainly; that is why I know it," returned the Scarecrow. "If it required brains to figure it out, I never should have said it."

After an hour or so the light faded away, and they found themselves stumbling along in the darkness. Dorothy could not see at all, but Toto could, for some dogs see very well in the dark; and the Scarecrow declared he could see as well as by day. So she took hold of his arm, and managed to get along fairly well.

"If you see any house, or any place where we can pass the night," she said, "you must tell me; for it is very uncomfortable walking in the dark."

Soon after the Scarecrow stopped.

"I see a little cottage at the right of us," he said, "built of logs and branches. Shall we go there?"

"Yes, indeed," answered the child. "I am all tired out."

So the Scarecrow led her through the trees until they reached the cottage, and Dorothy entered and found a bed of dried leaves in one corner. She lay down at once, and with Toto beside her soon fell into a sound sleep. The Scarecrow, who was never tired, stood up in another corner and waited patiently until morning came.

5

The Rescue of the Tin Woodman

When Dorothy awoke the sun was shining through the trees and Toto had long been out chasing birds and squirrels. She sat up and looked around her. There was the Scarecrow, still standing patiently in his corner, waiting for her.

"We must go and search for water," she said to him.

"Why do you want water?" he asked.

"To wash my face clean after the dust of the road, and to drink, so the dry bread will not stick in my throat."

"It must be inconvenient to be made of flesh," said the Scarecrow, thoughtfully, "for you must sleep, and eat and drink. However, you have brains, and it is worth a lot of bother to be able to think properly."

They left the cottage and walked through the trees until they found a little spring of clear water, where Dorothy drank and bathed and ate her breakfast. She saw there was not much bread left in the basket, and the girl was thankful the Scarecrow did not have to eat anything, for there was scarcely enough for herself and Toto for the day.

When she had finished her meal, and was about to go back to the road of yellow brick, she was startled to hear a deep groan nearby.

"What was that?" she asked timidly.

"I cannot imagine," replied the Scarecrow, "but we can go and see."

Just then another groan reached their ears, and the sound seemed to come from behind them. They turned and walked through the forest a few steps, when Dorothy discovered something shining in a ray of sunshine that fell between the trees. She ran to the place, and then stopped short, with a cry of surprise.

One of the big trees had been partly chopped through, and standing beside it, with an uplifted axe in his hands, was a man made entirely of tin. His head and arms and legs were jointed upon his body, but he stood perfectly motionless, as if he could not stir at all.

Dorothy looked at him in amazement, and so did the Scarecrow, while Toto barked sharply and made a snap at the tin legs, which hurt his teeth.

"Did you groan?" asked Dorothy.

"Yes," answered the tin man, "I did. I've been groaning for more than a year, and no one has ever heard me before or come to help me."

"What can I do for you?" she enquired softly, for she was moved by the sad voice in which the man spoke.

"Get an oilcan and oil my joints," he answered. "They are rusted so badly that I cannot move them at all; if I am well-oiled I shall soon be all right again. You will find an oilcan on a shelf in my cottage."

Dorothy at once ran back to the cottage and found the oilcan, and then she returned and asked, anxiously, "Where are your joints?"

"Oil my neck, first," replied the Tin Woodman. So she oiled it, and as it was quite badly rusted the Scarecrow took hold of the tin head and moved it gently from side to side until it worked freely, and then the man could turn it himself.

"Now oil the joints in my arms," he said. And Dorothy oiled them and the Scarecrow bent them carefully until they were quite free from rust and as good as new.

The Tin Woodman gave a sigh of satisfaction and lowered his axe, which he leaned against the tree.

"This is a great comfort," he said. "I have been holding that axe in the air ever since I rusted, and I'm glad to be able to put it down at last. Now, if you will oil the joints of my legs, I shall be all right once more."

So they oiled his legs until he could move them freely; and he thanked them again and again for his release, for he seemed a very polite creature, and very grateful.

"I might have stood there always if you had not come along," he said, "so you have certainly saved my life. How did you happen to be here?"

"We are on our way to the Emerald City, to see the great Oz," she answered, "and we stopped at your cottage to pass the night."

"Why do you wish to see Oz?" he asked.

"I want him to send me back to Kansas; and the Scarecrow wants him to put a few brains into his head," she replied.

The Tin Woodman appeared to think deeply for a moment. Then he said:

"Do you suppose Oz could give me a heart?"

"Why, I guess so," Dorothy answered. "It would be as easy as to give the Scarecrow brains."

"True," the Tin Woodman returned. "So, if you will allow me to join your party, I will also go to the Emerald City and ask Oz to help me."

"Come along," said the Scarecrow, heartily; and Dorothy added that she would be pleased to have his company. So the Tin Woodman shouldered his axe and they all passed through the forest until they came to the road that was paved with yellow brick.

The Tin Woodman had asked Dorothy to put the oilcan in her basket. "For," he said, "if I should get caught in the rain, and rust again, I would need the oilcan badly."

It was a bit of good luck to have their new comrade join the party, for soon after they had begun their journey again they came to a place where the trees and branches grew so thick over the road that the travellers could not pass. But the Tin Woodman set to work with his axe and chopped so well that soon he cleared a passage for the entire party.

'This is a great comfort,' said the Tin Woodman.

Dorothy was thinking so earnestly as they walked along that she did not notice when the Scarecrow stumbled into a hole and rolled over to the side of the road. Indeed, he was obliged to call to her to help him up again.

"Why didn't you walk around the hole?" asked the Tin Woodman.

"I don't know enough," replied the Scarecrow, cheerfully. "My head is stuffed with straw, you know, and that is why I am going to Oz to ask him for some brains."

"Oh, I see," said the Tin Woodman. "But, after all, brains are not the best things in the world."

"Have you any?" enquired the Scarecrow.

"No, my head is quite empty," answered the Woodman. "But once I had brains, and a heart also; so, having tried them both, I should much rather have a heart."

"And why is that?" asked the Scarecrow.

"I will tell you my story, and then you will know."

So, while they were walking through the forest, the Tin Woodman told the following story:

"I was born the son of a woodman who chopped down trees in the forest and sold the wood for a living. When I grew up I too became a wood-chopper, and after my father died I took care of my old mother as long as she lived. Then I made up my mind that instead of living alone I would marry, so that I might not become lonely.

"There was one of the Munchkin girls who was so beautiful that I soon grew to love her with all my heart. She, on her part, promised to marry me as soon as I could earn enough money to build a better house for her; so I set to work harder than ever. But the girl lived with an old woman who did not want her to marry anyone, for she was so lazy she wished the girl to remain with her and do the cooking and the housework. So the old woman went to the wicked Witch of the East, and promised her two sheep and a cow if she would prevent the marriage. Thereupon the Wicked Witch enchanted my axe, and when I was chopping away at my best one day, for I was anxious to get the new house and my wife as soon as possible, the axe slipped all at once and cut off my left leg.

"This at first seemed a great misfortune, for I knew a one-legged man could not do very well as a woodchopper. So I went to a tinsmith and had him make me a new leg out of tin. The leg worked very well, once I was used to it; but my action angered the wicked Witch of the East, for she had promised the old woman I should not marry the pretty Munchkin girl. When I began chopping again my axe slipped and cut off my right leg. Again I went to the tinner, and again he made me a leg out of tin. After this the enchanted axe cut off my arms, one after the other; but, nothing daunted, I had them replaced with tin ones. The Wicked Witch then made the axe slip and cut off my head, and at first I thought that was the end of me. But the tinner happened to come along, and he made me a new head out of tin.

"I thought I had beaten the wicked Witch then, and I worked harder than ever; but I little knew how cruel my enemy could be. She thought of a new way to kill my love for the beautiful Munchkin maiden, and made my axe slip again, so that it cut right through my body, splitting me into two halves. Once more the tinner came to my help and made me a body of tin, fastening my tin arms and legs and head to it, by means of joints, so that I could move around as well as ever. But, alas! I had now no heart, so that I lost all my love for the Munchkin girl, and did not care whether I married her or not. I suppose she is still living with the old woman, waiting for me to come after her.

"My body shone so brightly in the sun that I felt very proud of it and it did not matter now if my axe slipped, for it could not cut me. There was only one danger—that my joints would rust; but I kept an oilcan in my cottage and took care to oil myself whenever I needed it. However, there came a day when I forgot to do this, and, being caught in a rainstorm, before I thought of the danger my joints had rusted, and I was left to stand in the woods until you came to help me. It was a terrible thing to undergo, but during the year I stood there I had time to think that the greatest loss I had known was the loss of my heart. While I was in love I was the happiest man on earth; but no one can love who has not a heart, and so I am resolved to ask Oz to give me one. If he does, I will go back to the Munchkin maiden and marry her."

Both Dorothy and the Scarecrow had been greatly interested in the story of the Tin Woodman, and now they knew why he was so anxious to get a new heart.

"All the same," said the Scarecrow, "I shall ask for brains instead of a heart; for a fool would not know what to do with a heart if he had one."

"I shall take the heart," returned the Tin Woodman, "for brains do not make one happy, and happiness is the best thing in the world."

Dorothy did not say anything, for she was puzzled to know which of her two friends was right, and she decided if she could only get back to Kansas and Aunt Em it did not matter so much whether the Woodman had no brains and the Scarecrow no heart, or each got what he wanted.

What worried her most was that the bread was nearly gone, and another meal for herself and Toto would empty the basket. To be sure neither the Woodman nor the Scarecrow ever ate anything, but she was not made of tin nor straw, and could not live unless she was fed.

6

The Cowardly Lion

All this time Dorothy and her companions had been walking through the thick woods. The road was still paved with yellow brick, but these were much covered by dried branches and dead leaves from the trees, and the walking was not at all good.

There were few birds in this part of the forest, for birds love the open country where there is plenty of sunshine; but now and then there came a deep growl from some wild animal hidden among the trees. These sounds made the little girl's heart beat fast, for she did not know what made them; but Toto knew, and he walked close to Dorothy's side, and did not even bark in return.

"How long will it be," the child asked of the Tin Woodman, "before we are out of the forest?"

"I cannot tell," was the answer, "for I have never been to the Emerald City. But my father went there once, when I was a boy, and he said it was a long journey through a dangerous country, although nearer to the city where Oz dwells the country is beautiful. But I am not afraid so long as I have my oilcan, and nothing can hurt the Scarecrow, while you bear upon your forehead the mark of the Good Witch's kiss, and that will protect you from harm."

"But Toto!" said the girl, anxiously, "what will protect him?"

"We must protect him ourselves, if he is in danger," replied the Tin Woodman.

Just as he spoke there came from the forest a terrible roar, and the next moment a great Lion bounded into the road. With one blow of his paw he sent the Scarecrow spinning over and over to the edge of the road, and then he struck at the Tin Woodman with his sharp claws. But, to the Lion's surprise, he could make no impression on the tin, although the Woodman fell over in the road and lay still.

Little Toto, now that he had an enemy to face, ran barking towards the Lion, and the great beast had opened his mouth to bite the dog, when Dorothy, fearing Toto would be killed, and heedless of danger, rushed forward and slapped the Lion upon his nose as hard as she could, while she cried out:

"Don't you dare to bite Toto! You ought to be ashamed of yourself, a big beast like you, to bite a poor little dog!"

"I didn't bite him," said the Lion, as he rubbed his nose with his paw where Dorothy had hit it.

"No, but you tried to," she retorted. "You are nothing but a big coward."

"I know it," said the Lion, hanging his head in shame. "I've always known it. But how can I help it?"

"I don't know, I'm sure. To think of your striking a stuffed man, like the poor Scarecrow!"

"Is he stuffed?" asked the Lion, in surprise, as he watched her pick up the Scarecrow and set him upon his feet, while she patted him into shape again.

"Of course he's stuffed," replied Dorothy, who was still angry.

"That's why he went over so easily," remarked the Lion. "It astonished me to see him whirl around so. Is the other one stuffed, also?"

"No," said Dorothy, "he's made of tin." And she helped the Woodman up again.

You ought to be ashamed of yourself!

"That's why he nearly blunted my claws," said the Lion. "When they scratched against the tin it made a cold shiver run down my back. What is that little animal you are so tender of?"

"He is my dog, Toto," answered Dorothy.

"Is he made of tin, or stuffed?" asked the Lion.

"Neither. He's a—a—a meat dog," said the girl.

"Oh. He's a curious animal, and seems remarkably small, now that I look at him. No one would think of biting such a little thing except a coward like me," continued the Lion sadly.

"What makes you a coward?" asked Dorothy, looking at the great beast in wonder, for he was as big as a small horse.

"It's a mystery," replied the Lion. "I suppose I was born that way. All the other animals in the forest naturally expect me to be brave, for the Lion is everywhere thought to be the King of Beasts. I learned that if I roared very loudly every living thing was frightened and got out of my way. Whenever I've met a man I've been awfully scared; but I just roared at him, and he has always run away as fast as he could go. If the elephants and the tigers and the bears had ever tried to fight me, I should have run myself—I'm such a coward; but just as soon as they hear me roar they all try to get away from me, and of course I let them go."

"But that isn't right. The King of Beasts shouldn't be a coward," said the Scarecrow.

"I know it," returned the Lion, wiping a tear from his eye with the tip of his tail. "It is my great sorrow, and makes my life very unhappy. But whenever there is danger my heart begins to beat fast."

"Perhaps you have heart disease," said the Tin Woodman.

"It may be," said the Lion.

"If you have," continued the Tin Woodman, "you ought to be glad, for it proves you have a heart. For my part, I have no heart; so I cannot have heart disease."

"Perhaps," said the Lion, thoughtfully, "if I had no heart I should not be a coward."

"Have you brains?" asked the Scarecrow.

"I suppose so. I've never looked to see," replied the Lion.

"I am going to the great Oz to ask him to give me some," remarked the Scarecrow, "for my head is stuffed with straw."

"And I am going to ask him to give me a heart," said the Woodman.

"And I am going to ask him to send Toto and me back to Kansas," added Dorothy.

"Do you think Oz could give me courage?" asked the cowardly Lion.

"Just as easily as he could give me brains," said the Scarecrow.

"Or give me a heart," said the Tin Woodman.

"Or send me back to Kansas," said Dorothy.

"Then, if you don't mind, I'll go with you," said the Lion, "for my life is simply unbearable without a bit of courage."

"You will be very welcome," answered Dorothy, "for you will help to keep away the other wild beasts. It seems to me they must be more cowardly than you are if they allow you to scare them so easily."

"They really are," said the Lion, "but that doesn't make me any braver, and as long as I know myself to be a coward I shall be unhappy."

So once more the little company set off upon the journey, the Lion walking with stately strides at Dorothy's side. Toto did not approve this new comrade at first, for he could not forget how nearly he had been crushed between the Lion's great jaws; but after a time he became more at ease, and presently Toto and the Cowardly Lion had grown to be good friends.

During the rest of that day there was no other adventure to mar the peace of their journey. Once, indeed, the Tin Woodman stepped upon a beetle that was crawling along the road, and killed the poor little thing. This made the Tin Woodman very unhappy, for he was always careful not to hurt any living creature; and as he walked along he wept several tears of sorrow and regret. These tears ran slowly down his face and over the hinges of his jaw, and there they rusted. When Dorothy presently asked him a question the Tin Woodman could not open his mouth, for his jaws were tightly rusted together. He became greatly frightened at this and made many motions to Dorothy to relieve him, but she could not understand. The Lion was also puzzled to know what was wrong. But the Scarecrow seized the oilcan from Dorothy's basket and oiled the Woodman's jaws, so that after a few moments he could talk as well as before.

"This will serve me a lesson," said he, "to look where I step. For if I should kill another bug or beetle I should surely cry again, and crying rusts my jaw so that I cannot speak."

Thereafter he walked very carefully, with his eyes on the road, and when he saw a tiny ant toiling by he would step over it, so as not to harm it. The Tin Woodman knew very well he had no heart, and therefore he took great care never to be cruel or unkind to anything.

"You people with hearts," he said, "have something to guide you, and need never do wrong; but I have no heart, and so I must be very careful. When Oz gives me a heart of course I needn't mind so much."

7

The Journey to the Great Oz

They were obliged to camp out that night under a large tree in the forest, for there were no houses near. The tree made a good, thick covering to protect them from the dew, and the Tin Woodman chopped a great pile of wood with his axe and Dorothy built a splendid fire that warmed her and made her feel less lonely. She and Toto ate the last of their bread, and now she did not know what they would do for breakfast.

"If you wish," said the Lion, "I will go into the forest and kill a deer for you. You can roast it by the fire, since your tastes are so peculiar that you prefer cooked food, and then you will have a very good breakfast."

"Don't! Please don't," begged the Tin Woodman. "I should certainly weep if you killed a poor deer, and then my jaws would rust again."

But the Lion went away into the forest and found his own supper, and no one ever knew what it was, for he didn't mention it. And the Scarecrow found a tree full of nuts and filled Dorothy's basket with them, so that she would not be hungry for a long time. She thought this was very kind and thoughtful of the Scarecrow, but she laughed heartily at the awkward way in which the poor creature picked up the nuts. His padded hands were so clumsy and the nuts were so small that he dropped almost as many as he put in the basket. But the Scarecrow did not mind how long it took him to fill the basket, for it enabled him to keep away from the fire, as he feared a spark might get into his straw and burn him up. So he kept a good distance away from the flames, and only came near to cover Dorothy with dry leaves when she lay down to sleep. These kept her very snug and warm and she slept soundly until morning.

When it was daylight the girl bathed her face in a little rippling brook and soon after they all started towards the Emerald City.

This was to be an eventful day for the travellers. They had hardly been walking an hour when they saw before them a great ditch that crossed the road and divided the forest as far as they could see on either side. It was a very wide ditch, and when they crept up to the edge and looked into it they could see it was also very deep, and there were many big, jagged rocks at the bottom. The sides were so steep that none of them could climb down, and for a moment it seemed that their journey must end.

"What shall we do?" asked Dorothy despairingly.

"I haven't the faintest idea," said the Tin Woodman; and the Lion shook his shaggy mane and looked thoughtful. But the Scarecrow said: "We cannot fly, that is certain; neither can we climb down into this great ditch. Therefore, if we cannot jump over it, we must stop where we are."

"I think I could jump over it," said the Cowardly Lion, after measuring the distance carefully in his mind.

"Then we are all right," answered the Scarecrow, "for you can carry us all over on your back, one at a time."

"Well, I'll try it," said the Lion. "Who will go first?"

"I will," declared the Scarecrow, "for, if you found that you could not jump over the gulf, Dorothy would be killed, or the Tin Woodman badly dented on the rocks below. But if I am on your back it will not matter so much, for the fall would not hurt me at all."

"I am terribly afraid of falling, myself," said the Cowardly Lion, "but I suppose there is nothing to do but try it. So get on my back and we will make the attempt."

The Scarecrow sat upon the Lion's back, and the big beast walked to the edge of the gulf and crouched down.

"Why don't you run and jump?" asked the Scarecrow.

"Because that isn't the way we Lions do these things," he replied. Then giving a great spring, he shot through the air and landed safely on the other side. They were all greatly pleased to see how easily he did it, and after the Scarecrow had got down from his back the Lion sprang across the ditch again.

Dorothy thought she would go next; so she took Toto in her arms and climbed on the Lion's back, holding tightly to his mane with one hand. The next moment it seemed as if she was flying through the air; and then, before she had time to think about it, she was safe on the other side. The Lion went back a third time and got the Tin Woodman, and then they all sat down for a few moments to give the beast a chance to rest, for his great leaps had made his breath short, and he panted like a big dog that has been running too long.

They found the forest very thick on this side, and it looked dark and gloomy. After the Lion had rested they started along the road of yellow brick, silently wondering, each in his own mind, if ever they would come to the end of the woods and reach the bright sunshine again. To add to their discomfort, they soon heard strange noises in the depths of the forest, and the Lion whispered to them that it was in this part of the country that the Kalidahs lived.

"What are the Kalidahs?" asked the girl.

"They are monstrous beasts with bodies like bears and heads like tigers," replied the Lion, "and with claws so long and sharp that they could tear me in two as easily as I could kill Toto. I'm terribly afraid of the Kalidahs."

"I'm not surprised that you are," returned Dorothy. "They must be dreadful beasts."

The Lion was about to reply when suddenly they came to another gulf across the road; but this one was so broad and deep that the Lion knew at once he could not leap across it.

So they sat down to consider what they should do, and after serious thought the Scarecrow said:

"Here is a great tree, standing close to the ditch. If the Tin Woodman can chop it down, so that it will fall to the other side, we can walk across it easily."

"That is a first-rate idea," said the Lion. "One would almost suspect you had brains in your head, instead of straw."

The Woodman set to work at once, and so sharp was his axe that the tree was soon chopped nearly through. Then the Lion put his strong front legs against the tree and pushed with all his might, and slowly the big tree tipped and fell with a crash across the ditch, with its top branches on the other side.

They had just started to cross this queer bridge when a sharp growl made them all look up, and to their horror they saw running towards them two great beasts with bodies like bears and heads like tigers.

"They are the Kalidahs!" said the Cowardly Lion, beginning to tremble.

"Quick!" cried the Scarecrow, "let us cross over."

So Dorothy went first, holding Toto in her arms; the Tin Woodman followed, and the Scarecrow came next. The Lion, although he was certainly afraid, turned to face the Kalidahs, and then he gave so loud and terrible a roar that Dorothy screamed and the Scarecrow fell over backwards, while even the fierce beasts stopped short and looked at him in surprise.

But, seeing they were bigger than the Lion, and remembering that there were two of them and only one of him, the Kalidahs again rushed forward, and the Lion crossed over the tree and turned to see what they would do next. Without stopping an instant the fierce beasts also began to cross the tree, and the Lion said to Dorothy:

"We are lost, for they will surely tear us to pieces with their sharp claws. But stand close behind me, and I will fight them as long as I am alive."

"Wait a minute!" called the Scarecrow. He had been thinking what was best to be done, and now he asked the Woodman to chop away the end of the tree that rested on their side of the ditch. The Tin Woodman began to use his axe at once, and, just as the two

The tree fell with a crash into the gulf.

Kalidahs were nearly across, the tree fell with a crash into the gulf, carrying the ugly, snarling brutes with it, and both were dashed to pieces on the sharp rocks at the bottom.

"Well," said the Cowardly Lion, drawing a long breath of relief, "I see we are going to live a little while longer, and I am glad of it, for it must be a very uncomfortable thing not to be alive. Those creatures frightened me so badly that my heart is beating yet."

"Ah." said the Tin Woodman, sadly, "I wish I had a heart to beat."

This adventure made the travellers more anxious than ever to get out of the forest, and they walked so fast that Dorothy became tired, and had to ride on the Lion's back. To their great joy the trees became thinner the further they advanced, and in the afternoon they suddenly came upon a broad river, flowing swiftly just before them. On the other side of the water they could see the road of yellow brick running through a beautiful country, with green meadows dotted with bright flowers and all the road bordered with trees hanging full of delicious fruits. They were greatly pleased to see this delightful country before them.

"How shall we cross the river?" asked Dorothy.

"That is easily done," replied the Scarecrow. "The Tin Woodman must build us a raft, so we can float to the other side."

So the Woodman took his axe and began to chop down small trees to make a raft, and while he was busy at this the Scarecrow found on the river bank a tree full of fine fruit. This pleased Dorothy, who had eaten nothing but nuts all day, and she made a hearty meal of the ripe fruit.

But it takes time to make a raft, even when one is as industrious and untiring as the Tin Woodman, and when night came the work was not done. So they found a cosy place under the trees where they slept well until the morning; and Dorothy dreamed of the Emerald City, and of the good Wizard Oz, who would soon send her back to her own home again.

8

The Deadly Poppy Field

Our little party of travellers awakened next morning refreshed and full of hope, and Dorothy breakfasted like a princess off peaches and plums from the trees beside the river.

Behind them was the dark forest they had passed safely through, although they had suffered many discouragements; but before them was a lovely, sunny country that seemed to beckon them on to the Emerald City.

To be sure, the broad river now cut them off from this beautiful land; but the raft was nearly done, and after the Tin Woodman had cut a few more logs and fastened them together with wooden pins, they were ready to start. Dorothy sat down in the middle of the raft and held Toto in her arms. When the Cowardly Lion stepped upon the raft it tipped badly, for he was big and heavy; but the Scarecrow and the Tin Woodman stood upon the other end to steady it, and they had long poles in their hands to push the raft through the water.

They got along quite well at first, but when they reached

the middle of the river the swift current swept the raft downstream, farther and farther away from the road of yellow brick; and the water grew so deep that the long poles would not touch the bottom.

"This is bad," said the Tin Woodman, "for if we cannot get to the land we shall be carried into the country of the Wicked Witch of the West, and she will enchant us and make us her slaves."

"And then I should get no brains," said the Scarecrow.

"And I should get no courage," said the Cowardly Lion.

"And I should get no heart," said the Tin Woodman.

"And I should never get back to Kansas," said Dorothy.

"We must certainly get to the Emerald City if we can," the Scarecrow continued, and he pushed so hard on his long pole that it stuck fast in the mud at the bottom of the river, and before he could pull it out again, or let go, the raft was swept away and the poor Scarecrow left clinging to the pole in the middle of the river.

"Goodbye!" he called after them, and they were very sorry to leave him; indeed, the Tin Woodman began to cry, but fortunately remembered that he might rust, and so dried his tears on Dorothy's apron.

Of course this was a bad thing for the Scarecrow.

"I am now worse off than when I first met Dorothy," he thought. "Then, I was stuck on a pole in a cornfield, where I could make-believe scare the crows, at any rate; but surely there is no use for a Scarecrow stuck on a pole in the middle of a river. I am afraid I shall never have any brains, after all!"

Down the stream the raft floated, and the poor Scarecrow was left far behind. Then the Lion said:

"Something must be done to save us. I think I can swim to the shore and pull the raft after me, if you will only hold fast to the tip of my tail."

So he sprang into the water and the Tin Woodman caught fast hold of his tail, when the Lion began to swim with all his might towards the shore. It was hard work, although he was so big; but by and by they were drawn out of the current, and then Dorothy took the Tin Woodman's long pole and helped push the raft to the land.

They were all tired out when they reached the shore at last and stepped off upon the pretty green grass, and they also knew that the stream had carried them a long way past the road of yellow brick that led to the Emerald City.

"What shall we do now?" asked the Tin Woodman, as the Lion lay down on the grass to let the sun dry him.

"We must get back to the road, in some way," said Dorothy.

"The best plan will be to walk along the river bank until we come to the road again," remarked the Lion.

So, when they were rested, Dorothy picked up her basket and they started along the grassy bank, back to the road from which the river had carried them. It was a lovely country, with plenty of flowers and fruit trees and sunshine to cheer them, and had they not felt so sorry for the poor Scarecrow they could have been very happy.

They walked along as fast as they could, Dorothy only stopping once to pick a beautiful flower; and after a time the Tin Woodman cried out, "Look!"

Then they all looked at the river and saw the Scarecrow perched upon his pole in the middle of the water, looking very lonely and sad.

"What can we do to save him?" asked Dorothy.

The Lion and the Woodman both shook their heads, for they did not know. So they sat down upon the bank and gazed wistfully at the Scarecrow until a Stork flew by, which, seeing them, stopped to rest at the water's edge.

"Who are you, and where are you going?" asked the Stork.

"I am Dorothy," answered the girl, "and these are my friends, the Tin Woodman and the Cowardly Lion; and we are going to the Emerald City."

"This isn't the road," said the Stork, as she twisted her long neck and looked sharply at the queer party.

"I know it," returned Dorothy, "but we have lost the Scarecrow, and are wondering how we shall get him again."

"Where is he?" asked the Stork.

"Over there in the river," answered the girl.

"If he wasn't so big and heavy I would get him for you," remarked the Stork.

"He isn't heavy a bit," said Dorothy, eagerly, "for he is stuffed with straw; and if you will bring him back to us we shall thank you ever and ever so much."

"Well, I'll try," said the Stork, "but if I find he is too heavy to carry I shall have to drop him in the river again."

So the big bird flew into the air and over the water till she came to where the Scarecrow was perched upon his pole. Then the Stork with her great claws grabbed the Scarecrow by the arm and carried him up into the air and back to the bank, where Dorothy and the Lion and the Tin Woodman and Toto were sitting.

When the Scarecrow found himself among his friends again he was so happy that he hugged them all, even the Lion and Toto; and as they walked along he sang "Tol-de-ri-de-oh!" at every step, he felt so gay.

"I was afraid I should have to stay in the river forever," he said, "but the kind Stork saved me, and if I ever get any brains I shall find the Stork again and do it some kindness in return."

"That's all right," said the Stork, who was flying along beside them. "I always like to help anyone in trouble. But I must go now, for my babies are waiting in the nest for me. I hope you will find the Emerald City and that Oz will help you."

"Thank you," replied Dorothy, and then the kind Stork flew into the air and was soon out of sight.

They walked along listening to the singing of the bright-coloured birds and looking at the lovely flowers which now became so thick that the ground was carpeted with them. There were big yellow and white and blue and purple blossoms, besides great clusters of scarlet poppies, which were so brilliant in colour they almost dazzled Dorothy's eyes.

"Aren't they beautiful?" the girl asked, as she breathed in the spicy scent of the flowers.

"I suppose so," answered the Scarecrow. "When I have brains I shall probably like them better."

"If I only had a heart I should love them," added the Tin Woodman.

"I always did like flowers," said the Lion. "They seem so helpless and frail. But there are none in the forest so bright as these."

They now came upon more and more of the big scarlet poppies, and fewer and fewer of the other flowers; and soon they found themselves in the midst of a great meadow of poppies. Now it is

The Stork carried him up into the air.

well known that when there are many of these flowers together their odour is so powerful that anyone who breathes it falls asleep, and if the sleeper is not carried away from the scent of the flowers he sleeps on and on forever. But Dorothy did not know this, nor could she get away from the bright red flowers that were everywhere about; so presently her eyes grew heavy and she felt she must sit down to rest and to sleep.

But the Tin Woodman would not let her do this.

"We must hurry and get back to the road of yellow brick before dark," he said; and the Scarecrow agreed with him. So they kept walking until Dorothy could stand no longer. Her eyes closed in spite of herself and she forgot where she was and fell among the poppies, fast asleep.

"What shall we do?" asked the Tin Woodman.

"If we leave her here she will die," said the Lion. "The smell of the flowers is killing us all. I myself can scarcely keep my eyes open and the dog is asleep already."

It was true; Toto had fallen down beside his little mistress. But the Scarecrow and the Tin Woodman, not being made of flesh, were not troubled by the scent of the flowers.

"Run fast," said the Scarecrow to the Lion, "and get out of this deadly flower bed as soon as you can. We will bring the little girl with us, but if you should fall asleep you are too big to be carried."

So the Lion aroused himself and bounded forward as fast as he could go. In a moment he was out of sight.

"Let us make a chair with our hands, and carry her," said the Scarecrow. So they picked up Toto and put the dog in Dorothy's lap, and then they made a chair with their hands for the seat and their arms for the arms and carried the sleeping girl between them through the flowers.

On and on they walked, and it seemed that the great carpet of deadly flowers that surrounded them would never end. They followed the bend of the river, and at last came upon their friend the Lion, lying fast asleep among the poppies. The flowers had been too strong for the huge beast and he had given up, at last, and fallen only a short distance from the end of the poppy bed, where the sweet grass spread in beautiful green fields before them.

"We can do nothing for him," said the Tin Woodman sadly, "for he is much too heavy to lift. We must leave him here to sleep on forever, and perhaps he will dream that he has found courage at last."

"I'm sorry," said the Scarecrow. "The Lion was a very good comrade for one so cowardly. But let us go on."

They carried the sleeping girl to a pretty spot beside the river, far enough from the poppy field to prevent her breathing any more of the poison of the flowers, and here they laid her gently on the soft grass and waited for the fresh breeze to waken her.

9

The Queen of the Field Mice

"We cannot be far from the road of yellow brick now," remarked the Scarecrow, as he stood beside the girl, "for we have come nearly as far as the river carried us away."

The Tin Woodman was about to reply when he heard a low growl, and turning his head (which worked beautifully on hinges) he saw a strange beast come bounding over the grass towards them. It was, indeed, a great, yellow wildcat, and the Woodman thought it must be chasing something, for its ears were lying close to its head and its mouth was wide open, showing two rows of ugly teeth, while its red eyes glowed like balls of fire. As it came nearer the Tin Woodman saw that running before the beast was a little grey field mouse, and although he had no heart he knew it was wrong for the wildcat to try to kill such a pretty, harmless creature.

So the Woodman raised his axe, and as the wildcat ran by he gave it a quick blow that cut the beast's head clean off from its body, and it rolled over at his feet in two pieces.

The field mouse, now that it was freed from its enemy, stopped short; and coming slowly up to the Woodman it said, in a squeaky little voice, "Oh, thank you! Thank you ever so much for saving my life."

"Don't speak of it, I beg of you," replied the Woodman. "I have no heart, you know, so I am careful to help all those who may need a friend, even if it happens to be only a mouse."

"Only a mouse!" cried the little animal, indignantly. "Why, I am a Queen—the Queen of all the field mice!"

"Oh, indeed," said the Woodman, making a bow.

"Therefore you have done a great deed, as well as a brave one, in saving my life," added the Queen.

At that moment several mice were seen running up as fast as their little legs could carry them, and when they saw their Queen they exclaimed:

"Oh, your Majesty, we thought you would be killed! How did you manage to escape the great Wildcat?" and they all bowed so low to the little Queen that they almost stood upon their heads.

"This funny tin man," she answered, "killed the Wildcat and saved my life. So hereafter you must all serve him, and obey his slightest wish."

"We will!" cried all the mice, in a shrill chorus. And then they scampered in all directions, for Toto had awakened from his sleep, and seeing all these mice around him he gave one bark of delight and jumped right into the middle of the group. Toto had always loved to chase mice when he lived in Kansas, and he saw no harm in it.

But the Tin Woodman caught the dog in his arms and held him tight, while he called to the mice: "Come back! Come back! Toto shall not hurt you."

At this the Queen of the Mice stuck her head out from a clump of grass and asked, in a timid voice,

"Are you sure he will not bite us?"

"I will not let him," said the Woodman, "so do not be afraid."

One by one the mice came creeping back, and Toto did not bark again, although he tried to get out of the Woodman's arms, and would have bitten him had he not known very well he was made of tin. Finally one of the biggest mice spoke.

"Is there anything we can do," it asked, "to repay you for saving the life of our Queen?"

"Nothing that I know of," answered the Woodman; but the Scarecrow, who had been trying to think, but could not because his head was stuffed with straw, said, quickly, "Oh, yes; you can save our friend, the Cowardly Lion, who is asleep in the poppy bed."

"A Lion!" cried the little Queen. "Why, he would eat us all up."

"Oh, no," declared the Scarecrow. "This Lion is a coward."

"Really?" asked the Mouse.

"He says so himself," answered the Scarecrow, "and he would never hurt anyone who is our friend. If you will help us to save him I promise that he shall treat you all with kindness."

"Very well," said the Queen, "we will trust you. But what shall we do?"

"Are there many of these mice which call you Queen and are willing to obey you?"

"Oh, yes; there are thousands," she replied.

"Then send for them all to come here as soon as possible, and let each one bring a long piece of string."

The Queen turned to the mice that attended her and told them to go at once and get all her people. As soon as they heard her orders they ran away in every direction as fast as possible.

"Now," said the Scarecrow to the Tin Woodman, "you must go to those trees by the riverside and make a truck that will carry the Lion."

So the Woodman went at once to the trees and began to work; and he soon made a truck out of the limbs of trees, from which he chopped away all the leaves and branches. He fastened it together with wooden pegs and made the four wheels out of short pieces of a big tree-trunk. So fast and so well did he work that by the time the mice began to arrive the truck was all ready for them.

They came from all directions, and there were thousands of them: big mice and little mice and middle-sized mice; and each one brought a piece of string in his mouth. It was about this time that Dorothy woke from her long sleep and opened her eyes. She was greatly astonished to find herself lying upon the grass, with thousands of mice standing around and looking at her timidly.

Permit me to introduce to you her Majesty, the Queen.

But the Scarecrow told her about everything, and turning to the dignified little Mouse, he said:

"Permit me to introduce to you her Majesty, the Queen."

Dorothy nodded gravely and the Queen made a courtesy, after which she became quite friendly with the little girl.

The Scarecrow and the Woodman now began to fasten the mice to the truck, using the strings they had brought. One end of a string was tied around the neck of each mouse and the other end to the truck. Of course the truck was a thousand times bigger than any of the mice who were to draw it; but when all the mice had been harnessed, they were able to pull it quite easily. Even the Scarecrow and the Tin Woodman could sit on it, and were drawn swiftly by their queer little horses to the place where the Lion lay asleep.

After a great deal of hard work, for the Lion was heavy, they managed to get him up on the truck. Then the Queen hurriedly gave her people the order to start, for she feared if the mice stayed among the poppies too long they also would fall asleep.

At first the little creatures, many though they were, could hardly stir the heavily loaded truck; but the Woodman and the Scarecrow both pushed from behind, and they got along better. Soon they rolled the Lion out of the poppy bed to the green fields, where he could breathe the sweet, fresh air again, instead of the poisonous scent of the flowers.

Dorothy came to meet them and thanked the little mice warmly for saving her companion from death. She had grown so fond of the big Lion she was glad he had been rescued.

Then the mice were unharnessed from the truck and scampered away through the grass to their homes. The Queen of the Mice was the last to leave.

"If ever you need us again," she said, "come out into the field and call, and we shall hear you and come to your assistance. Goodbye!"

"Goodbye!" they all answered, and away the Queen ran, while Dorothy held Toto tightly lest he should run after her and frighten her.

After this they sat down beside the Lion until he should awaken; and the Scarecrow brought Dorothy some fruit from a tree nearby, which she ate for her dinner.

10

The Guardian of the Gates

It was some time before the Cowardly Lion awakened, for he had lain among the poppies a long while, breathing in their deadly fragrance; but when he did open his eyes and roll off the truck he was very glad to find himself still alive.

"I ran as fast as I could," he said, sitting down and yawning; "but the flowers were too strong for me. How did you get me out?"

Then they told him of the field mice, and how they had generously saved him from death; and the Cowardly Lion laughed, and said:

"I have always thought myself very big and terrible; yet such small things as flowers came near to killing me, and such small animals as mice have saved my life. How strange it all is! But, comrades, what shall we do now?"

"We must journey on until we find the road of yellow brick again," said Dorothy, "and then we can keep on to the Emerald City."

So, the Lion being fully refreshed, and feeling quite himself again, they all started upon the journey, greatly enjoying the walk through the soft, fresh grass; and it was not long before they reached the road of yellow brick and turned again towards the Emerald City where the great Oz dwelt.

The road was smooth and well paved, now, and the country about was beautiful, so that the travellers rejoiced in leaving the forest far behind, and with it the many dangers they had met in its gloomy shades. Once more they could see fences built beside the road; but these were painted green, and when they came to a small house, in which a farmer evidently lived, that also was painted green. They passed by several of these houses during the afternoon, and sometimes people came to the doors and looked at them as if they would like to ask questions; but no one came near them nor spoke to them because of the great Lion, of which they were much afraid. The people were all dressed in clothing of a lovely emerald green colour and wore peaked hats like those of the Munchkins.

"This must be the Land of Oz," said Dorothy, "and we are surely getting near the Emerald City."

"Yes," answered the Scarecrow. "Everything is green here, while in the country of the Munchkins blue was the favourite colour. But the people do not seem to be as friendly as the Munchkins and I'm afraid we shall be unable to find a place to pass the night."

"I should like something to eat besides fruit," said the girl, "and I'm sure Toto is nearly starved. Let us stop at the next house and talk to the people."

So, when they came to a good-sized farm house, Dorothy walked boldly up to the door and knocked. A woman opened it just far enough to look out, and said, "What do you want, child, and why is that great Lion with you?"

"We wish to pass the night with you, if you will allow us," answered Dorothy; "and the Lion is my friend and comrade, and would not hurt you for the world."

"Is he tame?" asked the woman, opening the door a little wider.

"Oh, yes," said the girl, "and he is a great coward, too; so that he will be more afraid of you than you are of him."

"Well," said the woman, after thinking it over and taking another peep at the Lion, "if that is the case you may come in, and I will give you some supper and a place to sleep."

So they all entered the house, where there were, besides the woman, two children and a man. The man had hurt his leg, and was lying on the couch in a corner. They seemed greatly surprised to see so strange a company, and while the woman was busy laying the table the man asked:

"Where are you all going?"

"To the Emerald City," said Dorothy, "to see the Great Oz."

"Oh, indeed!" exclaimed the man. "Are you sure that Oz will see you?"

"Why not?" she replied.

"Why, it is said that he never lets any one come into his presence. I have been to the Emerald City many times, and it is a beautiful and wonderful place; but I have never been permitted to see the Great Oz, nor do I know of any living person who has seen him."

"Does he never go out?" asked the Scarecrow.

"Never. He sits day after day in the great throne room of his palace, and even those who wait upon him do not see him face to face."

"What is he like?" asked the girl.

"That is hard to tell," said the man, thoughtfully. "You see, Oz is a great Wizard, and can take on any form he wishes. So that some say he looks like a bird; and some say he looks like an elephant; and some say he looks like a cat. To others he appears as a beautiful fairy, or a brownie, or in any other form that pleases him. But who the real Oz is, when he is in his own form, no living person can tell."

"That is very strange," said Dorothy; "but we must try, in some way, to see him, or we shall have made our journey for nothing."

"Why do you wish to see the terrible Oz?" asked the man.

"I want him to give me some brains," said the Scarecrow, eagerly.

"Oh, Oz could do that easily enough," declared the man. "He has more brains than he needs."

"And I want him to give me a heart," said the Tin Woodman.

"That will not trouble him," continued the man, "for Oz has a large collection of hearts, of all sizes and shapes."

"And I want him to give me courage," said the Cowardly Lion.

"Oz keeps a great pot of courage in his throne room," said the man, "which he has covered with a golden plate, to keep it from running over. He will be glad to give you some."

"And I want him to send me back to Kansas," said Dorothy.

"Where is Kansas?" asked the man, in surprise.

"I don't know," replied Dorothy, sorrowfully, "but it is my home, and I'm sure it's somewhere."

"Very likely. Well, Oz can do anything; so I suppose he will find Kansas for you. But first you must get to see him, and that will be a hard task; for the great Wizard does not like to see anyone, and he usually has his own way. But what do you want?" he continued, speaking to Toto. Toto only wagged his tail; for, strange to say, he could not speak.

The woman now called to them that supper was ready, so they gathered around the table and Dorothy ate some delicious porridge and a dish of scrambled eggs and a plate of nice white bread, and enjoyed her meal. The Lion ate some of the porridge, but did not care for it, saying it was made from oats and oats were food for horses, not for lions. The Scarecrow and the Tin Woodman ate nothing at all. Toto ate a little of everything, and was glad to get a good supper again.

The woman now gave Dorothy a bed to sleep in, and Toto lay down beside her, while the Lion guarded the door of her room so she might not be disturbed. The Scarecrow and the Tin Woodman stood up in a corner and kept quiet all night, although of course they could not sleep.

The next morning, as soon as the sun was up, they started on their way, and soon saw a beautiful green glow in the sky just before them.

"That must be the Emerald City," said Dorothy.

As they walked on, the green glow became brighter and brighter, and it seemed that at last they were nearing the end of their travels. Yet it was afternoon before they came to the great wall that surrounded the City. It was high, and thick, and of a bright green colour.

In front of them, and at the end of the road of yellow brick, was a big gate, all studded with emeralds that glittered so in the

The Lion ate some of the porridge.

sun that even the painted eyes of the Scarecrow were dazzled by their brilliancy.

There was a bell beside the gate, and Dorothy pushed the button and heard a silvery tinkle sound within. Then the big gate swung slowly open, and they all passed through and found themselves in a high arched room, the walls of which glistened with countless emeralds.

Before them stood a little man about the same size as the Munchkins. He was clothed all in green, from his head to his feet, and even his skin was of a greenish tint. At his side was a large green box.

When he saw Dorothy and her companions the man asked, "What do you wish in the Emerald City?"

"We came here to see the Great Oz," said Dorothy.

The man was so surprised at this answer that he sat down to think it over.

"It has been many years since anyone asked me to see Oz," he said, shaking his head in perplexity. "He is powerful and terrible, and if you come on an idle or foolish errand to bother the wise reflections of the Great Wizard, he might be angry and destroy you all in an instant."

"But it is not a foolish errand, nor an idle one," replied the Scarecrow, "it is important. And we have been told that Oz is a good Wizard."

"So he is," said the green man, "and he rules the Emerald City wisely and well. But to those who are not honest, or who approach him from curiosity, he is most terrible, and few have ever dared ask to see his face. I am the Guardian of the Gates, and since you demand to see the Great Oz I must take you to his palace. But first you must put on the spectacles."

"Why?" asked Dorothy.

"Because if you did not wear spectacles the brightness and glory of the Emerald City would blind you. Even those who live in the City must wear spectacles night and day. They are all locked on, for Oz so ordered it when the City was first built, and I have the only key that will unlock them."

He opened the big box, and Dorothy saw that it was filled with spectacles of every size and shape. All of them had green glasses in them. The Guardian of the gates found a pair that would just fit Dorothy and put them over her eyes. There were two golden bands fastened to them that passed around the back of her head, where they were locked together by a little key that was at the end of a chain the Guardian of the Gates wore around his neck. When they were on, Dorothy could not take them off had she wished, but of course she did not want to be blinded by the glare of the Emerald City, so she said nothing.

Then the green man fitted spectacles for the Scarecrow and the Tin Woodman and the Lion, and even on little Toto; and all were locked fast with the key.

Then the Guardian of the Gates put on his own glasses and told them he was ready to show them to the palace. Taking a big golden key from a peg on the wall he opened another gate, and they all followed him through the portal into the streets of the Emerald City.

11

The Wonderful Emerald City of Oz

Even with eyes protected by the green spectacles Dorothy and her friends were at first dazzled by the brilliancy of the wonderful City. The streets were lined with beautiful houses all built of green marble and studded everywhere with sparkling emeralds. They walked over a pavement of the same green marble, and where the blocks were joined together were rows of emeralds, set closely, and glittering in the brightness of the sun. The window panes were of green glass; even the sky above the City had a green tint, and the rays of the sun were green.

There were many people, men, women and children, walking about, and these were all dressed in green clothes and had greenish skins. They looked at Dorothy and her strangely assorted company with wondering eyes, and the children all ran away and hid behind their mothers when they saw the Lion; but no one spoke to them. Many shops stood in the street, and Dorothy saw that everything in them was green. Green candy and green popcorn were offered for sale, as well as green shoes, green hats and green clothes of all sorts. At one place a man was selling green lemonade, and when the children bought it Dorothy could see that they paid for it with green pennies.

There seemed to be no horses nor animals of any kind; the men carried things around in little green carts, which they pushed before them. Everyone seemed happy and contented and prosperous.

The Guardian of the Gates led them through the streets until they came to a big building, exactly in the middle of the City, which was the Palace of Oz, the Great Wizard. There was a soldier before the door, dressed in a green uniform and wearing a long green beard.

"Here are strangers," said the Guardian of the Gates to him, "and they demand to see the Great Oz."

"Step inside," answered the soldier, "and I will carry your message to him."

So they passed through the Palace gates and were led into a big room with a green carpet and lovely green furniture set with emeralds. The soldier made them all wipe their feet upon a green mat before entering this room, and when they were seated he said, politely:

"Please make yourselves comfortable while I go to the door of the Throne Room and tell Oz you are here."

They had to wait a long time before the soldier returned. When, at last, he came back, Dorothy asked:

"Have you seen Oz?"

"Oh, no," returned the soldier; "I have never seen him. But I spoke to him as he sat behind his screen, and gave him your message. He says he will grant you an audience, if you so desire; but each one of you must enter his presence alone, and he will admit but one each day. Therefore, as you must remain in the Palace for several days, I will have you shown to rooms where you may rest in comfort after your journey."

"Thank you," replied the girl; "that is very kind of Oz."

The soldier now blew upon a green whistle, and at once a young girl, dressed in a pretty green silk gown, entered the room. She had lovely green hair and green eyes, and she bowed low before Dorothy as she said, "Follow me and I will show you your room."

So Dorothy said goodbye to all her friends except Toto, and taking the dog in her arms followed the green girl through seven passages and up three flights of stairs until they came to a room at the front of the Palace. It was the sweetest little room in the world, with a soft, comfortable bed that had sheets of green silk and a green velvet counterpane. There was a tiny fountain in the middle of the room that shot a spray of green perfume into the air, to fall back into a beautifully carved green marble basin. Beautiful green flowers stood in the windows, and there was a shelf with a row of little green books. When Dorothy had time to open these books she found them full of queer green pictures that made her laugh, they were so funny.

In a wardrobe were many green dresses, made of silk and satin and velvet; and all of them fitted Dorothy exactly.

"Make yourself perfectly at home," said the green girl, "and if you wish for anything ring the bell. Oz will send for you tomorrow morning."

She left Dorothy alone and went back to the others. These she also led to rooms, and each one of them found himself lodged in a very pleasant part of the Palace. Of course this politeness was wasted on the Scarecrow for when he found himself alone in his room he stood stupidly in one spot, just within the doorway, to wait till morning. It would not rest him to lie down, and he could not close his eyes; so he remained all night staring at a little spider which was weaving its web in a corner of the room, just as if it were not one of the most wonderful rooms in the world. The Tin Woodman lay down on his bed from force of habit, for he remembered when he was made of flesh; but not being able to sleep he passed the night moving his joints up and down to make sure they kept in good working order. The Lion would have preferred a bed of dried leaves in the forest, and did not like being shut up in a room; but he had too much sense to let this worry him, so he sprang upon the bed and rolled himself up like a cat and purred himself asleep in a minute.

The next morning, after breakfast, the green maiden came to fetch Dorothy, and she dressed her in one of the prettiest gowns—made of green brocaded satin. Dorothy put on a green silk apron and tied a green ribbon around Toto's neck, and they started for the Throne Room of the Great Oz.

First they came to a great hall in which were many ladies and gentlemen of the court, all dressed in rich costumes. These people had nothing to do but talk to each other, but they always came to wait outside the Throne Room every morning, although they were never permitted to see Oz. As Dorothy entered they looked at her curiously, and one of them whispered:

"Are you really going to look upon the face of Oz the Terrible?"

"Of course," answered the girl, "if he will see me."

"Oh, he will see you," said the soldier who had taken her message to the Wizard, "although he does not like to have people ask to see him. Indeed, at first he was angry, and said I should send you back where you came from. Then he asked me what you looked like, and when I mentioned your silver shoes he was very much interested. At last I told him about the mark upon your forehead, and he decided he would admit you to his presence."

Just then a bell rang, and the green girl said to Dorothy, "That is the signal. You must go into the Throne Room alone."

She opened a little door and Dorothy walked boldly through and found herself in a wonderful place. It was a big, round room with a high arched roof, and the walls and ceiling and floor were covered with large emeralds set closely together. In the centre of the roof was a great light, as bright as the sun, which made the emeralds sparkle in a wonderful manner.

But what interested Dorothy most was the big throne of green marble that stood in the middle of the room. It was shaped like a chair and sparkled with gems, as did everything else. In the centre of the chair was an enormous Head, without body to support it or any arms or legs whatever. There was no hair upon this head, but it had eyes and nose and mouth, and was bigger than the head of the biggest giant.

As Dorothy gazed upon this in wonder and fear the eyes turned slowly and looked at her sharply and steadily. Then the mouth moved, and Dorothy heard a voice say:

"I am Oz, the Great and Terrible. Who are you, and why do you seek me?"

It was not such an awful voice as she had expected to come from the big Head; so she took courage and answered:

"I am Dorothy, the Small and Meek. I have come to you for help."

The eyes looked at her thoughtfully for a full minute. Then said the voice:

"Where did you get the silver shoes?"

"I got them from the Wicked Witch of the East, when my house fell on her and killed her," she replied.

"Where did you get the mark upon your forehead?" continued the voice.

"That is where the Good Witch of the North kissed me when she bade me goodbye and sent me to you," said the girl.

Again the eyes looked at her sharply, and they saw she was telling the truth. Then Oz asked:

"What do you wish me to do?"

"Send me back to Kansas, where my Aunt Em and Uncle Henry are," she answered, earnestly. "I don't like your country, although it is so beautiful. And I am sure Aunt Em will be dreadfully worried over my being away so long."

The eyes winked three times, and then they turned up to the ceiling and down to the floor and rolled around so queerly that they seemed to see every part of the room. And at last they looked at Dorothy again.

"Why should I do this for you?" asked Oz.

"Because you are strong and I am weak; because you are a Great Wizard and I am only a helpless little girl," she answered.

"But you were strong enough to kill the Wicked Witch of the East," said Oz.

"That just happened," returned Dorothy, simply; "I could not help it."

"Well," said the Head, "I will give you my answer. You have no right to expect me to send you back to Kansas unless you do something for me in return. In this country everyone must pay for everything he gets. If you wish me to use my magic power to send you home again you must do something for me first. Help me and I will help you."

"What must I do?" asked the girl.

"Kill the Wicked Witch of the West," answered Oz.

The Eyes looked at her thoughtfully.

"But I cannot!" exclaimed Dorothy, greatly surprised.

"You killed the Witch of the East and you wear the silver shoes, which bear a powerful charm. There is now but one Wicked Witch left in all this land, and when you can tell me she is dead I will send you back to Kansas—but not before."

The little girl began to weep, she was so much disappointed; and the eyes winked again and looked upon her anxiously, as if the Great Oz felt that she could help him if she would.

"I never killed anything, willingly," she sobbed; "and even if I wanted to, how could I kill the Wicked Witch? If you, who are Great and Terrible, cannot kill her yourself, how do you expect me to do it?"

"I do not know," said the Head; "but that is my answer, and until the Wicked Witch dies you will not see your uncle and aunt again. Remember that the Witch is Wicked—tremendously Wicked—and ought to be killed. Now go, and do not ask to see me again until you have done your task."

Sorrowfully Dorothy left the Throne Room and went back where the Lion and the Scarecrow and the Tin Woodman were waiting to hear what Oz had said to her.

"There is no hope for me," she said, sadly, "for Oz will not send me home until I have killed the Wicked Witch of the West; and that I can never do."

Her friends were sorry, but could do nothing to help her; so she went to her own room and lay down on the bed and cried herself to sleep.

The next morning the soldier with the green whiskers came to the Scarecrow and said:

"Come with me, for Oz has sent for you."

So the Scarecrow followed him and was admitted into the great Throne Room, where he saw, sitting in the emerald throne, a most lovely lady. She was dressed in green silk gauze and wore upon her flowing green locks a crown of jewels. Growing from her shoulders were wings, gorgeous in colour and so light that they fluttered if the slightest breath of air reached them.

When the Scarecrow had bowed, as prettily as his straw stuffing would let him, before this beautiful creature, she looked upon him sweetly, and said:

"I am Oz, the Great and Terrible. Who are you, and why do you seek me?"

Now the Scarecrow, who had expected to see the great Head Dorothy had told him of, was much astonished; but he answered her bravely.

"I am only a Scarecrow, stuffed with straw. Therefore I have no brains, and I come to you praying that you will put brains in my head instead of straw, so that I may become as much a man as any other in your dominions."

"Why should I do this for you?" asked the lady.

"Because you are wise and powerful, and no one else can help me," answered the Scarecrow.

"I never grant favours without some return," said Oz; "but this much I will promise. If you will kill for me the Wicked Witch of the West I will bestow upon you a great many brains, and such good brains that you will be the wisest man in all the Land of Oz."

"I thought you asked Dorothy to kill the Witch," said, the Scarecrow, in surprise.

"So I did. I don't care who kills her. But until she is dead I will not grant your wish. Now go, and do not seek me again until you have earned the brains you so greatly desire."

The Scarecrow went sorrowfully back to his friends and told them what Oz had said; and Dorothy was surprised to find that the great Wizard was not a Head, as she had seen him, but a lovely lady.

"All the same," said the Scarecrow, "she needs a heart as much as the Tin Woodman."

On the next morning the soldier with the green whiskers came to the Tin Woodman and said:

"Oz has sent for you. Follow me,"

So the Tin Woodman followed him and came to the great Throne Room. He did not know whether he would find Oz a lovely lady or a Head, but he hoped it would be the lovely lady. "For," he said to himself, "if it is the Head, I am sure I shall not be given a heart, since a head has no heart of its own and therefore cannot feel for me. But if it is the lovely lady I shall beg hard for a heart, for all ladies are themselves said to be kindly hearted."

But when the Woodman entered the great Throne Room he saw neither the Head nor the Lady, for Oz had taken the shape of a most terrible Beast. It was nearly as big as an elephant, and the green throne seemed hardly strong enough to hold its weight. The Beast had a head like that of a rhinoceros, only there were five eyes in its face. There were five long arms growing out of its body and it also had five long, slim legs. Thick, woolly hair covered every part of it, and a more dreadful looking monster could not be imagined. It was fortunate the Tin Woodman had no heart at that moment, for it would have beat loud and fast from terror. But being only tin, the Woodman was not at all afraid, although he was much disappointed.

"I am Oz, the Great and Terrible," spoke the Beast, in a voice that was one great roar. "Who are you, and why do you seek me?"

"I am a Woodman, and made of tin. Therefore I have no heart, and cannot love. I pray you to give me a heart that I may be as other men are."

"Why should I do this?" demanded the Beast.

"Because I ask it, and you alone can grant my request," answered the Woodman.

Oz gave a low growl at this, but said, gruffly:

"If you indeed desire a heart, you must earn it."

"How?" asked the Woodman.

"Help Dorothy to kill the Wicked Witch of the West," replied the Beast. "When the Witch is dead, come to me, and I will then give you the biggest and kindest and most loving heart in all the Land of Oz."

So the Tin Woodman was forced to return sorrowfully to his friends and tell them of the terrible Beast he had seen. They all wondered greatly at the many forms the great Wizard could take upon himself, and the Lion said:

"If he is a beast when I go to see him, I shall roar my loudest, and so frighten him that he will grant all I ask. And if he is the lovely lady, I shall pretend to spring upon her, and so compel her to do my bidding. And if he is the great Head, he will be at my mercy; for I will roll this head all about the room until he promises to give us what we desire. So be of good cheer my friends for all will yet be well."

The next morning the soldier with the green whiskers led the Lion to the great Throne Room and bade him enter the presence of Oz.

The Lion at once passed through the door, and glancing around saw, to his surprise, that before the throne was a Ball of Fire, so fierce and glowing he could scarcely bear to gaze upon it. His first thought was that Oz had by accident caught on fire and was burning up; but, when he tried to go nearer, the heat was so intense that it singed his whiskers, and he crept back tremblingly to a spot nearer the door.

Then a low, quiet voice came from the Ball of Fire, and these were the words it spoke:

"I am Oz, the Great and Terrible. Who are you, and why do you seek me?"

And the Lion answered, "I am a Cowardly Lion, afraid of everything. I come to you to beg that you give me courage, so that in reality I may become the King of Beasts, as men call me."

"Why should I give you courage?" demanded Oz.

"Because of all Wizards you are the greatest, and alone have power to grant my request," answered the Lion.

The Ball of Fire burned fiercely for a time, and the voice said:

"Bring me proof that the Wicked Witch is dead, and that moment I will give you courage. But so long as the Witch lives you must remain a coward."

The Lion was angry at this speech, but could say nothing in reply, and while he stood silently gazing at the Ball of Fire it became so furiously hot that he turned tail and rushed from the room. He was glad to find his friends waiting for him, and told them of his terrible interview with the Wizard.

"What shall we do now?" asked Dorothy sadly.

"There is only one thing we can do," returned the Lion, "and that is to go to the land of the Winkies, seek out the Wicked Witch, and destroy her."

"But suppose we cannot?" said the girl.

"Then I shall never have courage," declared the Lion.

"And I shall never have brains," added the Scarecrow.

"And I shall never have a heart," spoke the Tin Woodman.

"And I shall never see Aunt Em and Uncle Henry," said Dorothy, beginning to cry.

"Be careful!" cried the green girl, "the tears will fall on your green silk gown, and spot it."

So Dorothy dried her eyes and said, "I suppose we must try it; but I am sure I do not want to kill anybody, even to see Aunt Em again."

"I will go with you; but I'm too much of a coward to kill the Witch," said the Lion.

"I will go too," declared the Scarecrow; "but I shall not be of much help to you, I am such a fool."

"I haven't the heart to harm even a Witch," remarked the Tin Woodman; "but if you go I certainly shall go with you."

Therefore it was decided to start upon their journey the next morning, and the Woodman sharpened his axe on a green grindstone and had all his joints properly oiled. The Scarecrow stuffed himself with fresh straw and Dorothy put new paint on his eyes that he might see better. The green girl, who was very kind to them, filled Dorothy's basket with good things to eat, and fastened a little bell around Toto's neck with a green ribbon.

They went to bed quite early and slept soundly until daylight, when they were awakened by the crowing of a green cock that lived in the back yard of the palace, and the cackling of a hen that had laid a green egg.

12

The Search for the Wicked Witch

The soldier with the green whiskers led them through the streets of the Emerald City until they reached the room where the Guardian of the Gates lived. This officer unlocked their spectacles to put them back in his great box, and then he politely opened the gate for our friends.

"Which road leads to the Wicked Witch of the West?" asked Dorothy.

"There is no road," answered the Guardian of the Gates. "No one ever wishes to go that way."

"How, then, are we to find her?" enquired the girl.

"That will be easy," replied the man, "for when she knows you are in the country of the Winkies she will find you, and make you all her slaves."

"Perhaps not," said the Scarecrow, "for we mean to destroy her."

"Oh, that is different," said the Guardian of the Gates. "No one has ever destroyed her before, so I naturally

The Soldier with the green whiskers led them through the streets.

thought she would make slaves of you, as she has of all the rest. But take care; for she is wicked and fierce, and may not allow you to destroy her. Keep to the West, where the sun sets, and you cannot fail to find her."

They thanked him and bade him goodbye, and turned towards the West, walking over fields of soft grass dotted here and there with daisies and buttercups. Dorothy still wore the pretty silk dress she had put on in the palace, but now, to her surprise, she found it was no longer green, but pure white. The ribbon around Toto's neck had also lost its green colour and was as white as Dorothy's dress.

The Emerald City was soon left far behind. As they advanced the ground became rougher and hillier, for there were no farms nor houses in this country of the West, and the ground was untilled.

In the afternoon the sun shone hot in their faces, for there were no trees to offer them shade; so that before night Dorothy and Toto and the Lion were tired, and lay down upon the grass and fell asleep, with the Woodman and the Scarecrow keeping watch.

Now the Wicked Witch of the West had but one eye, yet that was as powerful as a telescope, and could see everywhere. So, as she sat in the door of her castle, she happened to look around and saw Dorothy lying asleep, with her friends all about her. They were a long distance off, but the Wicked Witch was angry to find them in her country; so she blew upon a silver whistle that hung around her neck.

At once there came running to her from all directions a pack of great wolves. They had long legs and fierce eyes and sharp teeth.

"Go to those people," said the Witch, "and tear them to pieces."

"Are you not going to make them your slaves?" asked the leader of the wolves.

"No," she answered, "one is of tin, and one of straw; one is a girl and another a Lion. None of them is fit to work, so you may tear them into small pieces."

"Very well," said the wolf, and he dashed away at full speed, followed by the others.

It was lucky the Scarecrow and the Woodman were wide awake and heard the wolves coming.

"This is my fight," said the Woodman, "so get behind me and I will meet them as they come."

He seized his axe, which he had made very sharp, and as the leader of the wolves came on the Tin Woodman swung his arm and chopped the wolf's head from its body, so that it immediately died. As soon as he could raise his axe another wolf came up, and he also fell under the sharp edge of the Tin Woodman's weapon. There were forty wolves, and forty times a wolf was killed; so that at last they all lay dead in a heap before the Woodman.

Then he put down his axe and sat beside the Scarecrow, who said, "It was a good fight, friend."

They waited until Dorothy awoke the next morning. The little girl was quite frightened when she saw the great pile of shaggy wolves, but the Tin Woodman told her all. She thanked him for saving them and sat down to breakfast, after which they started again upon their journey.

Now this same morning the Wicked Witch came to the door of her castle and looked out with her one eye that could see afar off. She saw all her wolves lying dead, and the strangers still travelling through her country. This made her angrier than before, and she blew her silver whistle twice.

Straightway a great flock of wild crows came flying towards her, enough to darken the sky. And the Wicked Witch said to the King Crow:

"Fly at once to the strangers; peck out their eyes and tear them to pieces."

The wild crows flew in one great flock towards Dorothy and her companions. When the little girl saw them coming she was afraid. But the Scarecrow said, "This is my battle; so lie down beside me and you will not be harmed."

So they all lay upon the ground except the Scarecrow, and he stood up and stretched out his arms. And when the crows saw him they were frightened, as these birds always are by scarecrows, and did not dare to come any nearer. But the King Crow said:

"It is only a stuffed man. I will peck his eyes out."

The King Crow flew at the Scarecrow, who caught it by the head and twisted its neck until it died. And then another crow flew at him, and the Scarecrow twisted its neck also. There were forty crows, and forty times the Scarecrow twisted a neck, until at last all were lying dead beside him. Then he called to his companions to rise, and again they went upon their journey.

When the Wicked Witch looked out again and saw all her crows lying in a heap, she got into a terrible rage, and blew three times upon her silver whistle.

Forthwith there was heard a great buzzing in the air, and a swarm of black bees came flying towards her. "Go to the strangers and sting them to death!" commanded the Witch, and the bees turned and flew rapidly until they came to where Dorothy and her friends were walking. But the Woodman had seen them coming and the Scarecrow had decided what to do.

"Take out my straw and scatter it over the little girl and the dog and the lion," he said to the Woodman, "and the bees cannot sting them." This the Woodman did, and as Dorothy lay close beside the Lion and held Toto in her arms, the straw covered them entirely.

The bees came and found no one but the Woodman to sting, so they flew at him and broke off all their stings against the tin, without hurting the Woodman at all. And as bees cannot live when their stings are broken that was the end of the black bees, and they lay scattered thick about the Woodman, like little heaps of fine coal.

Then Dorothy and the Lion got up, and the girl helped the Tin Woodman put the straw back into the Scarecrow again, until he was as good as ever. So they started upon their journey once more.

The Wicked Witch was so angry when she saw her black bees in little heaps like fine coal that she stamped her foot and tore her hair and gnashed her teeth. And then she called a dozen of her slaves, who were the Winkies, and gave them sharp spears, telling them to go to the strangers and destroy them.

The Winkies were not a brave people, but they had to do as they were told; so they marched away until they came near to Dorothy. Then the Lion gave a great roar and sprang towards them, and the poor Winkies were so frightened that they ran back as fast as they could.

When they returned to the castle the Wicked Witch beat them well with a strap, and sent them back to their work, after which she sat down to think what she should do next. She could not understand how all her plans to destroy these strangers had failed; but she was a powerful Witch, as well as a wicked one, and she soon made up her mind how to act.

There was, in her cupboard, a Golden Cap, with a circle of diamonds and rubies running round it. This Golden Cap had a charm. Whoever owned it could call three times upon the Winged Monkeys, who would obey any order they were given. But no person could command these strange creatures more than three times. Twice already the Wicked Witch had used the charm of the Cap. Once was when she had made the Winkies her slaves, and set herself to rule over their country. The Winged Monkeys had helped her do this. The second time was when she had fought against the Great Oz himself, and driven him out of the land of the West. The Winged Monkeys had also helped her in doing this. Only once more could she use this Golden Cap, for which reason she did not like to do so until all her other powers were exhausted. But now that her fierce wolves and her wild crows and her stinging bees were gone, and her slaves had been scared away by the Cowardly Lion, she saw there was only one way left to destroy Dorothy and her friends.

So the Wicked Witch took the Golden Cap from her cupboard and placed it upon her head. Then she stood upon her left foot and said, slowly, "Ep-pe, pep-pe, kak-ke!"

Next she stood upon her right foot and said, "Hil-lo, hol-lo, hel-lo!"

After this she stood upon both feet and cried in a loud voice, "Ziz-zy, zuz-zy, zik!"

Now the charm began to work. The sky was darkened, and a low rumbling sound was heard in the air. There was a rushing of many wings; a great chattering and laughing; and the sun came out of the dark sky to show the Wicked Witch surrounded by a crowd of monkeys, each with a pair of immense and powerful wings on his shoulders.

One, much bigger than the others, seemed to be their leader. He flew close to the Witch and said, "You have called us for the third and last time. What do you command?"

"Go to the strangers who are within my land and destroy them all except the Lion," said the Wicked Witch. "Bring that beast to me, for I have a mind to harness him like a horse, and make him work."

"Your commands shall be obeyed," said the leader; and then, with a great deal of chattering and noise, the Winged Monkeys flew away to the place where Dorothy and her friends were walking.

Some of the Monkeys seized the Tin Woodman and carried him through the air until they were over a country thickly covered with sharp rocks. Here they dropped the poor Woodman, who fell a great distance to the rocks, where he lay so battered and dented that he could neither move nor groan.

Others of the Monkeys caught the Scarecrow, and with their long fingers pulled all of the straw out of his clothes and head. They made his hat and boots and clothes into a small bundle and threw it into the top branches of a tall tree.

The remaining Monkeys threw pieces of stout rope around the Lion and wound many coils about his body and head and legs, until he was unable to bite or scratch or struggle in any way. Then they lifted him up and flew away with him to the Witch's castle, where he was placed in a small yard with a high iron fence around it, so that he could not escape.

But Dorothy they did not harm at all. She stood, with Toto in her arms, watching the sad fate of her comrades and thinking it would soon be her turn. The leader of the Winged Monkeys flew up to her, his long, hairy arms stretched out and his ugly face grinning terribly; but he saw the mark of the Good Witch's kiss upon her forehead and stopped short, motioning the others not to touch her.

"We dare not harm this little girl," he said to them, "for she is protected by the Power of Good, and that is greater than the Power of Evil. All we can do is to carry her to the castle of the Wicked Witch and leave her there."

So, carefully and gently, they lifted Dorothy in their arms and carried her swiftly through the air until they came to the castle, where they set her down upon the front door step. Then the leader said to the Witch:

"We have obeyed you as far as we were able. The Tin Woodman and the Scarecrow are destroyed, and the Lion is tied up in your yard. The little girl we dare not harm, nor the dog she carries in her arms. Your power over our band is now ended, and you will never see us again."

The Monkeys wound many coils about his body.

Then all the Winged Monkeys, with much laughing and chattering and noise, flew into the air and were soon out of sight.

The Wicked Witch was both surprised and worried when she saw the mark on Dorothy's forehead, for she knew well that neither the Winged Monkeys nor she, herself, dare hurt the girl in any way. She looked down at Dorothy's feet, and seeing the Silver Shoes, began to tremble with fear, for she knew what a powerful charm belonged to them. At first the Witch was tempted to run away from Dorothy; but she happened to look into the child's eyes and saw how simple the soul behind them was, and that the little girl did not know of the wonderful power the Silver Shoes gave her. So the Wicked Witch laughed to herself, and thought, "I can still make her my slave, for she does not know how to use her power." Then she said to Dorothy, harshly and severely:

"Come with me; and see that you mind everything I tell you, for if you do not I will make an end of you, as I did of the Tin Woodman and the Scarecrow."

Dorothy followed her through many of the beautiful rooms in her castle until they came to the kitchen, where the Witch bade her clean the pots and kettles and sweep the floor and keep the fire fed with wood.

Dorothy went to work meekly, with her mind made up to work as hard as she could; for she was glad the Wicked Witch had decided not to kill her.

With Dorothy hard at work the Witch thought she would go into the courtyard and harness the Cowardly Lion like a horse; it would amuse her, she was sure, to make him draw her chariot whenever she wished to go to drive. But as she opened the gate the Lion gave a loud roar and bounded at her so fiercely that the Witch was afraid, and ran out and shut the gate again.

"If I cannot harness you," said the Witch to the Lion, speaking through the bars of the gate, "I can starve you. You shall have nothing to eat until you do as I wish."

So after that she took no food to the imprisoned Lion; but every day she came to the gate at noon and asked, "Are you ready to be harnessed like a horse?"

And the Lion would answer, "No. If you come in this yard I will bite you."

The reason the Lion did not have to do as the Witch wished was that every night, while the woman was asleep Dorothy carried him food from the cupboard. After he had eaten he would lie down on his bed of straw, and Dorothy would lie beside him and put her head on his soft, shaggy mane, while they talked of their troubles and tried to plan some way to escape. But they could find no way to get out of the castle, for it was constantly guarded by the yellow Winkies, who were the slaves of the Wicked Witch and too afraid of her not to do as she told them.

The girl had to work hard during the day, and often the Witch threatened to beat her with the same old umbrella she always carried in her hand. But, in truth, she did not dare to strike Dorothy, because of the mark upon her forehead. The child did not know this, and was full of fear for herself and Toto. Once the Witch struck Toto a blow with her umbrella and the brave little dog flew at her and bit her leg, in return. The Witch did not bleed where she was bitten, for she was so wicked that the blood in her had dried up many years before.

Dorothy's life became very sad as she grew to understand that it would be harder than ever to get back to Kansas and Aunt Em again. Sometimes she would cry bitterly for hours, with Toto sitting at her feet and looking into her face, whining dismally to show how sorry he was for his little mistress. Toto did not really care whether he was in Kansas or the Land of Oz so long as Dorothy was with him; but he knew the little girl was unhappy, and that made him unhappy too.

Now the Wicked Witch had a great longing to have for her own the Silver Shoes which the girl always wore. Her Bees and her Crows and her Wolves were lying in heaps and drying up, and she had used up all the power of the Golden Cap; but if she could only get hold of the Silver Shoes they would give her more power than all the other things she had lost. She watched Dorothy carefully, to see if she ever took off her shoes, thinking she might steal them. But the child was so proud of her pretty shoes that she never took them off except at night and when she took her bath. The Witch was too much afraid of the dark to dare go in Dorothy's room at night to take the shoes, and her dread of water was greater than her fear of the dark, so she never came near when Dorothy was bathing. Indeed, the old Witch never touched water, nor ever let water touch her in any way.

But the wicked creature was very cunning, and she finally thought of a trick that would give her what she wanted. She placed a bar of iron in the middle of the kitchen floor, and then by her magic arts made the iron invisible to human eyes. So that when Dorothy walked across the floor she stumbled over the bar, not being able to see it, and fell at full length. She was not much hurt, but in her fall one of the Silver Shoes came off, and before she could reach it the Witch had snatched it away and put it on her own skinny foot.

The wicked woman was greatly pleased with the success of her trick, for as long as she had one of the shoes she owned half the power of their charm, and Dorothy could not use it against her, even had she known how to do so.

The little girl, seeing she had lost one of her pretty shoes, grew angry, and said to the Witch, "Give me back my shoe!"

"I will not," retorted the Witch, "for it is now my shoe, and not yours."

"You are a wicked creature!" cried Dorothy. "You have no right to take my shoe from me."

"I shall keep it, just the same," said the Witch, laughing at her, "and some day I shall get the other one from you, too."

This made Dorothy so very angry that she picked up the bucket of water that stood near and dashed it over the Witch, wetting her from head to foot.

Instantly the wicked woman gave a loud cry of fear; and then, as Dorothy looked at her in wonder, the Witch began to shrink and fall away.

"See what you have done!" she screamed. "In a minute I shall melt away."

"I'm very sorry, indeed," said Dorothy, who was truly frightened to see the Witch actually melting away like brown sugar before her very eyes.

"Didn't you know water would be the end of me?" asked the Witch, in a wailing, despairing voice.

"Of course not," answered Dorothy. "How should I?"

"Well, in a few minutes I shall be all melted, and you will have the castle to yourself. I have been wicked in my day, but I never thought a little girl like you would ever be able to melt me and end my wicked deeds. Look out—here I go!"

With these words the Witch fell down in a brown, melted, shapeless mass and began to spread over the clean boards of the kitchen floor. Seeing that she had really melted away to nothing, Dorothy drew another bucket of water and threw it over the mess. She then swept it all out the door. After picking out the silver shoe, which was all that was left of the old woman, she cleaned and dried it with a cloth, and put it on her foot again. Then, being at last free to do as she chose, she ran out to the courtyard to tell the Lion that the Wicked Witch of the West had come to an end, and that they were no longer prisoners in a strange land.

13

The Rescue

The Cowardly Lion was much pleased to hear that the Wicked Witch had been melted by a bucket of water, and Dorothy at once unlocked the gate of his prison and set him free. They went in together to the castle, where Dorothy's first act was to call all the Winkies together and tell them that they were no longer slaves.

There was great rejoicing among the yellow Winkies, for they had been made to work hard during many years for the Wicked Witch, who had always treated them with great cruelty. They kept this day as a holiday, then and ever after, and spent the time in feasting and dancing.

"If our friends, the Scarecrow and the Tin Woodman, were only with us," said the Lion, "I should be quite happy."

"Don't you suppose we could rescue them?" asked the girl, anxiously.

"We can try," answered the Lion.

So they called the yellow Winkies and asked them if they would help to rescue their friends, and the Winkies said that they would be delighted to do all in their power for Dorothy, who had set them free from bondage. So she chose a number of the Winkies who looked as if they knew the most, and they all started away. They travelled that day and part of the next until they came to the rocky plain where the Tin Woodman lay, all battered and bent. His axe was near him, but the blade was rusted and the handle broken off short.

The Winkies lifted him tenderly in their arms, and carried him back to the yellow castle again, Dorothy shedding a few tears by the way at the sad plight of her old friend, and the Lion looking sober and sorry. When they reached the castle Dorothy said to the Winkies:

"Are any of your people tinsmiths?"

"Oh, yes. Some of us are very good tinsmiths," they told her.

"Then bring them to me," she said. And when the tinsmiths came, bringing with them all their tools in baskets, she enquired:

"Can you straighten out those dents in the Tin Woodman, and bend him back into shape again, and solder him together where he is broken?"

The tinsmiths looked the Woodman over carefully and then answered that they thought they could mend him so he would be as good as ever. So they set to work in one of the big yellow rooms of the castle and worked for three days and four nights, hammering and twisting and bending and soldering and polishing and pounding at the legs and body and head of the Tin Woodman, until at last he was straightened out into his old form, and his joints worked as well as ever. To be sure, there were several patches on him, but the tinsmiths did a good job, and as the Woodman was not a vain man he did not mind the patches at all.

When, at last, he walked into Dorothy's room and thanked her for rescuing him, he was so pleased that he wept tears of joy, and Dorothy had to wipe every tear carefully from his face with her apron, so his joints would not be rusted. At the same time her own tears fell thick and fast at the joy of meeting her old friend again, and these tears did not need to be wiped away. As for the Lion, he wiped his eyes so often with the tip of his tail that it became quite wet, and he was obliged to go out into the courtyard and hold it in the sun till it dried.

The Tinsmiths worked for three days and four nights.

"If we only had the Scarecrow with us again," said the Tin Woodman, when Dorothy had finished telling him everything that had happened, "I should be quite happy."

"We must try to find him," said the girl.

So she called the Winkies to help her, and they walked all that day and part of the next until they came to the tall tree in the branches of which the Winged Monkeys had tossed the Scarecrow's clothes.

It was a very tall tree, and the trunk was so smooth that no one could climb it; but the Woodman said at once:

"I'll chop it down, and then we can get the Scarecrow's clothes."

Now while the tinsmiths had been at work mending the Woodman himself, another of the Winkies, who was a goldsmith, had made an axe-handle of solid gold and fitted it to the Woodman's axe, instead of the old broken handle. Others polished the blade until all the rust was removed and it glistened like burnished silver.

As soon as he had spoken, the Tin Woodman began to chop, and in a short time the tree fell over with a crash, when the Scarecrow's clothes fell out of the branches and rolled off on the ground.

Dorothy picked them up and had the Winkies carry them back to the castle, where they were stuffed with nice, clean straw; and, behold! here was the Scarecrow, as good as ever, thanking them over and over again for saving him.

Now they were reunited, Dorothy and her friends spent a few happy days at the Yellow Castle, where they found everything they needed to make them comfortable. But one day the girl thought of Aunt Em, and said,

"We must go back to Oz, and claim his promise."

"Yes," said the Woodman, "at last I shall get my heart."

"And I shall get my brains," added the Scarecrow joyfully.

"And I shall get my courage," said the Lion thoughtfully.

"And I shall get back to Kansas," cried Dorothy, clapping her hands. "Oh, let us start for the Emerald City tomorrow!"

This they decided to do. The next day they called the Winkies together and bade them goodbye. The Winkies were sorry to have them go, and they had grown so fond of the Tin Woodman that they begged him to stay and rule over them and the Yellow Land of the West. Finding they were determined to go, the Winkies gave Toto and the Lion each a golden collar; and to Dorothy they presented a beautiful bracelet, studded with diamonds; and to the Scarecrow they gave a gold-headed walking stick, to keep him from stumbling; and to the Tin Woodman they offered a silver oilcan, inlaid with gold and set with precious jewels.

Every one of the travellers made the Winkies a pretty speech in return, and all shook hands with them until their arms ached.

Dorothy went to the Witch's cupboard to fill her basket with food for the journey, and there she saw the Golden Cap. She tried it on her own head and found that it fitted her exactly. She did not know anything about the charm of the Golden Cap, but she saw that it was pretty, so she made up her mind to wear it and carry her sunbonnet in the basket.

Then, being prepared for the journey, they all started for the Emerald City; and the Winkies gave them three cheers and many good wishes to carry with them.

14

The Winged Monkeys

You will remember there was no road—not even a pathway—between the castle of the Wicked Witch and the Emerald City. When the four travellers went in search of the Witch she had seen them coming, and so sent the Winged Monkeys to bring them to her. It was much harder to find their way back through the big fields of buttercups and yellow daisies than it was being carried. They knew, of course, they must go straight east, towards the rising sun; and they started off in the right way. But at noon, when the sun was over their heads, they did not know which was east and which was west, and that was the reason they were lost in the great fields. They kept on walking, however, and at night the moon came out and shone brightly. So they lay down among the sweet smelling yellow flowers and slept soundly until morning—all but the Scarecrow and the Tin Woodman.

The next morning the sun was behind a cloud, but they started on, as if they were quite sure which way they were going.

"If we walk far enough," said Dorothy, "we shall sometime come to some place, I am sure."

But day by day passed away, and they still saw nothing before them but the yellow fields. The Scarecrow began to grumble a bit.

"We have surely lost our way," he said, "and unless we find it again in time to reach the Emerald City I shall never get my brains."

"Nor I my heart," declared the Tin Woodman. "It seems to me I can scarcely wait till I get to Oz, and you must admit this is a very long journey."

"You see," said the Cowardly Lion, with a whimper, "I haven't the courage to keep tramping forever, without getting anywhere at all."

Then Dorothy lost heart. She sat down on the grass and looked at her companions, and they sat down and looked at her, and Toto found that for the first time in his life he was too tired to chase a butterfly that flew past his head; so he put out his tongue and panted and looked at Dorothy as if to ask what they should do next.

"Suppose we call the Field Mice," she suggested. "They could probably tell us the way to the Emerald City."

"To be sure they could," cried the Scarecrow; "why didn't we think of that before?"

Dorothy blew the little whistle she had always carried about her neck since the Queen of the Mice had given it to her. In a few minutes they heard the pattering of tiny feet, and many of the small grey mice came running up to her. Among them was the Queen herself, who asked, in her squeaky little voice:

"What can I do for my friends?"

"We have lost our way," said Dorothy. "Can you tell us where the Emerald City is?"

"Certainly," answered the Queen; "but it is a great way off, for you have had it at your backs all this time." Then she noticed Dorothy's Golden Cap, and said, "Why don't you use the charm of the Cap, and call the Winged Monkeys to you? They will carry you to the City of Oz in less than an hour."

"I didn't know there was a charm," answered Dorothy, in surprise. "What is it?"

"It is written inside the Golden Cap," replied the Queen of the Mice. "But if you are going to call the Winged Monkeys we must run away, for they are full of mischief and think it great fun to plague us."

"Won't they hurt me?" asked the girl anxiously.

"Oh, no; they must obey the wearer of the Cap. Goodbye!" And she scampered out of sight, with all the mice hurrying after her.

Dorothy looked inside the Golden Cap and saw some words written upon the lining. These, she thought, must be the charm, so she read the directions carefully and put the Cap upon her head.

"Ep-pe, pep-pe, kak-ke!" she said, standing on her left foot.

"What did you say?" asked the Scarecrow, who did not know what she was doing.

"Hil-lo, hol-lo, hel-lo!" Dorothy went on, standing this time on her right foot.

"Hello!" replied the Tin Woodman calmly.

"Ziz-zy, zuz-zy, zik!" said Dorothy, who was now standing on both feet. This ended the saying of the charm, and they heard a great chattering and flapping of wings, as the band of Winged Monkeys flew up to them. The King bowed low before Dorothy, and asked:

"What is your command?"

"We wish to go to the Emerald City," said the child, "and we have lost our way."

"We will carry you," replied the King, and no sooner had he spoken than two of the Monkeys caught Dorothy in their arms and flew away with her. Others took the Scarecrow and the Woodman and the Lion, and one little Monkey seized Toto and flew after them, although the dog tried hard to bite him.

The Scarecrow and the Tin Woodman were rather frightened at first, for they remembered how badly the Winged Monkeys had treated them before; but they saw that no harm was intended, so they rode through the air quite cheerfully, and had a fine time looking at the pretty gardens and woods far below them.

Dorothy found herself riding easily between two of the biggest Monkeys, one of them the King himself. They had made a chair of their hands and were careful not to hurt her.

"Why do you have to obey the charm of the Golden Cap?" she asked.

The Monkeys caught Dorothy in their arms and flew away with her.

"That is a long story," answered the King, with a laugh; "but as we have a long journey before us I will pass the time by telling you about it, if you wish."

"I shall be glad to hear it," she replied.

"Once," began the leader, "we were a free people, living happily in the great forest, flying from tree to tree, eating nuts and fruit, and doing just as we pleased without calling anybody master. Perhaps some of us were rather too full of mischief at times, flying down to pull the tails of the animals that had no wings, chasing birds, and throwing nuts at the people who walked in the forest. But we were careless and happy and full of fun, and enjoyed every minute of the day. This was many years ago, long before Oz came out of the clouds to rule over this land.

"There lived here then, away at the North, a beautiful princess, who was also a powerful sorceress. All her magic was used to help the people, and she was never known to hurt anyone who was good. Her name was Gayelette, and she lived in a handsome palace built from great blocks of ruby. Everyone loved her, but her greatest sorrow was that she could find no one to love in return, since all the men were much too stupid and ugly to mate with one so beautiful and wise. At last, however, she found a boy who was handsome and manly and wise beyond his years. Gayelette made up her mind that when he grew to be a man she would make him her husband, so she took him to her ruby palace and used all her magic powers to make him as strong and good and lovely as any woman could wish. When he grew to manhood, Quelala, as he was called, was said to be the best and wisest man in all the land, while his manly beauty was so great that Gayelette loved him dearly, and hastened to make everything ready for the wedding.

"My grandfather was at that time the King of the Winged Monkeys which lived in the forest near Gayalette's palace, and the old fellow loved a joke better than a good dinner. One day, just before the wedding, my grandfather was flying out with his band when he saw Quelala walking beside the river. He was dressed in a rich costume of pink silk and purple velvet, and my grandfather thought he would see what he could do. At his word the band flew down and seized Quelala, carried him in their arms until they were over the middle of the river, and then dropped him into the water.

"'Swim out, my fine fellow,' cried my grandfather, 'and see if the water has spotted your clothes.' Quelala was much too wise not to swim, and he was not in the least spoiled by all his good fortune. He laughed, when he came to the top of the water, and swam in to shore. But when Gayelette came running out to him she found his silks and velvet all ruined by the river.

"The princess was very angry, and she knew, of course, who did it. She had all the Winged Monkeys brought before her, and she said at first that their wings should be tied and they should be treated as they had treated Quelala, and dropped in the river. But my grandfather pleaded hard, for he knew the Monkeys would drown in the river with their wings tied, and Quelala said a kind word for them also; so that Gayelette finally spared them, on condition that the Winged Monkeys should ever after do three times the bidding of the owner of the Golden Cap. This Cap had been made for a wedding present to Quelala, and it is said to have cost the princess half her kingdom. Of course my grandfather and all the other Monkeys at once agreed to the condition, and that is how it happens that we are three times the slaves of the owner of the Golden Cap, whomsoever he may be."

"And what became of them?" asked Dorothy, who had been greatly interested in the story.

"Quelala being the first owner of the Golden Cap," replied the Monkey, "he was the first to lay his wishes upon us. As his bride could not bear the sight of us, he called us all to him in the forest after he had married her and ordered us to always keep where she could never again set eyes on a Winged Monkey, which we were glad to do, for we were all afraid of her.

"This was all we ever had to do until the Golden Cap fell into the hands of the Wicked Witch of the West, who made us enslave the Winkies, and afterward drive Oz himself out of the Land of the West. Now the Golden Cap is yours, and three times you have the right to lay your wishes upon us."

As the Monkey King finished his story Dorothy looked down and saw the green, shining walls of the Emerald City before them.

She wondered at the rapid flight of the Monkeys, but was glad the journey was over. The strange creatures set the travellers down carefully before the gate of the City, the King bowed low to Dorothy, and then flew swiftly away, followed by all his band.

"That was a good ride," said the little girl.

"Yes, and a quick way out of our troubles." replied the Lion. "How lucky it was you brought away that wonderful Cap!"

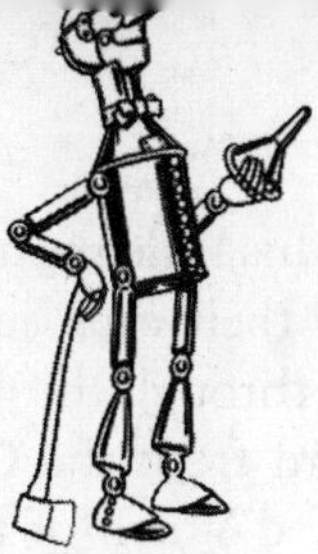

15

The Discovery of Oz, the Terrible

The four travellers walked up to the great gate of the Emerald City and rang the bell. After ringing several times it was opened by the same Guardian of the Gate they had met before.

"What! Are you back again?" he asked in surprise.

"Do you not see us?" answered the Scarecrow.

"But I thought you had gone to visit the Wicked Witch of the West."

"We did visit her," said the Scarecrow.

"And she let you go again?" asked the man, in wonder.

"She could not help it, for she is melted," explained the Scarecrow.

"Melted! Well, that is good news, indeed," said the man. "Who melted her?"

"It was Dorothy," said the Lion gravely.

"Good gracious!" exclaimed the man, and he bowed very low indeed before her.

Then he led them into his little room and locked the spectacles from the great box on all their eyes, just as he had done before. Afterward they passed on through the gate into the Emerald City, and when the people heard from the Guardian of the Gate that they had melted the Wicked Witch of the West they all gathered around the travellers and followed them in a great crowd to the Palace of Oz.

The soldier with the green whiskers was still on guard before the door, but he let them in at once and they were again met by the beautiful green girl, who showed each of them to their old rooms at once, so they might rest until the Great Oz was ready to receive them.

The soldier had the news carried straight to Oz that Dorothy and the other travellers had come back again, after destroying the Wicked Witch; but Oz made no reply. They thought the Great Wizard would send for them at once, but he did not. They had no word from him the next day, nor the next, nor the next. The waiting was tiresome and wearing, and at last they grew vexed that Oz should treat them in so poor a fashion, after sending them to undergo hardships and slavery. So the Scarecrow at last asked the green girl to take another message to Oz, saying if he did not let them in to see him at once they would call the Winged Monkeys to help them, and find out whether he kept his promises or not. When the Wizard was given this message he was so frightened that he sent word for them to come to the Throne Room at four minutes after nine o'clock the next morning. He had once met the Winged Monkeys in the Land of the West, and he did not wish to meet them again.

The four travellers passed a sleepless night, each thinking of the gift Oz had promised to bestow upon him. Dorothy fell asleep only once, and then she dreamed she was in Kansas, where Aunt Em was telling her how glad she was to have her little girl at home again.

Promptly at nine o'clock the next morning the green whiskered soldier came to them, and four minutes later they all went into the Throne Room of the Great Oz.

Of course each one of them expected to see the Wizard in the shape he had taken before, and all were greatly surprised when they looked about and saw no one at all in the room. They kept close to the door and closer to one another, for the stillness of the empty room was more dreadful than any of the forms they had seen Oz take.

Presently they heard a Voice, seeming to come from somewhere near the top of the great dome, and it said, solemnly:

"I am Oz, the Great and Terrible. Why do you seek me?"

They looked again in every part of the room, and then, seeing no one, Dorothy asked, "Where are you?"

"I am everywhere," answered the Voice, "but to the eyes of common mortals I am invisible. I will now seat myself upon my throne, that you may converse with me." Indeed, the Voice seemed just then to come straight from the throne itself; so they walked towards it and stood in a row while Dorothy said:

"We have come to claim our promise, O Oz."

"What promise?" asked Oz.

"You promised to send me back to Kansas when the Wicked Witch was destroyed," said the girl.

"And you promised to give me brains," said the Scarecrow.

"And you promised to give me a heart," said the Tin Woodman.

"And you promised to give me courage," said the Cowardly Lion.

"Is the Wicked Witch really destroyed?" asked the Voice, and Dorothy thought it trembled a little.

"Yes," she answered, "I melted her with a bucket of water."

"Dear me," said the Voice, "how sudden! Well, come to me tomorrow, for I must have time to think it over."

"You've had plenty of time already," said the Tin Woodman angrily.

"We shan't wait a day longer," said the Scarecrow.

"You must keep your promises to us!" exclaimed Dorothy.

The Lion thought it might be as well to frighten the Wizard, so he gave a large, loud roar, which was so fierce and dreadful that Toto jumped away from him in alarm and tipped over the screen that stood in a corner. As it fell with a crash they looked that way, and the next moment all of them were filled with wonder. For they saw, standing in just the spot the screen had hidden, a little, old man, with a bald head and a wrinkled face, who seemed to be as much surprised as they were. The Tin Woodman, raising his axe, rushed towards the little man and cried out, "Who are you?"

"I am Oz, the Great and Terrible," said the little man, in a trembling voice, "but don't strike me—please don't!—and I'll do anything you want me to."

Our friends looked at him in surprise and dismay.

"I thought Oz was a great Head," said Dorothy.

"And I thought Oz was a lovely Lady," said the Scarecrow.

"And I thought Oz was a terrible Beast," said the Tin Woodman.

"And I thought Oz was a Ball of Fire," exclaimed the Lion.

"No; you are all wrong," said the little man, meekly. "I have been making believe."

"Making believe!" cried Dorothy. "Are you not a great Wizard?"

"Hush, my dear," he said; "don't speak so loud, or you will be overheard—and I should be ruined. I'm supposed to be a Great Wizard."

"And aren't you?" she asked.

"Not a bit of it, my dear; I'm just a common man."

"You're more than that," said the Scarecrow, in a grieved tone; "you're a humbug."

"Exactly so!" declared the little man, rubbing his hands together as if it pleased him. "I am a humbug."

"But this is terrible," said the Tin Woodman; "how shall I ever get my heart?"

"Or I my courage?" asked the Lion.

"Or I my brains?" wailed the Scarecrow, wiping the tears from his eyes with his coat sleeve.

"My dear friends," said Oz, "I pray you not to speak of these little things. Think of me, and the terrible trouble I'm in at being found out."

"Doesn't anyone else know you're a humbug?" asked Dorothy.

"No one knows it but you four—and myself," replied Oz. "I have fooled everyone so long that I thought I should never be found out. It was a great mistake my ever letting you into the Throne Room. Usually I will not see even my subjects, and so they believe I am something terrible."

Exactly so! I am a humbug.

"But, I don't understand," said Dorothy, in bewilderment. "How was it that you appeared to me as a great Head?"

"That was one of my tricks," answered Oz. "Step this way, please, and I will tell you all about it."

He led the way to a small chamber in the rear of the Throne Room, and they all followed him. He pointed to one corner, in which lay the Great Head, made out of many thicknesses of paper, and with a carefully painted face.

"This I hung from the ceiling by a wire," said Oz. "I stood behind the screen and pulled a thread, to make the eyes move and the mouth open."

"But how about the voice?" she enquired.

"Oh, I am a ventriloquist," said the little man, "and I can throw the sound of my voice wherever I wish; so that you thought it was coming out of the Head. Here are the other things I used to deceive you." He showed the Scarecrow the dress and the mask he had worn when he seemed to be the lovely Lady; and the Tin Woodman saw that his Terrible Beast was nothing but a lot of skins, sewn together, with slats to keep their sides out. As for the Ball of Fire, the false Wizard had hung that also from the ceiling. It was really a ball of cotton, but when oil was poured upon it the ball burned fiercely.

"Really," said the Scarecrow, "you ought to be ashamed of yourself for being such a humbug."

"I am—I certainly am," answered the little man, sorrowfully; "but it was the only thing I could do. Sit down, please, there are plenty of chairs; and I will tell you my story."

So they sat down and listened while he told the following tale:

"I was born in Omaha—"

"Why, that isn't very far from Kansas!" cried Dorothy.

"No; but it's farther from here," he said, shaking his head at her, sadly. "When I grew up I became a ventriloquist, and at that I was very well trained by a great master. I can imitate any kind of a bird or beast." Here he mewed so like a kitten that Toto pricked up his ears and looked everywhere to see where she was. "After a time," continued Oz, "I tired of that, and became a balloonist."

"What is that?" asked Dorothy.

"A man who goes up in a balloon on circus day, so as to draw a crowd of people together and get them to pay to see the circus," he explained.

"Oh," she said, "I know."

"Well, one day I went up in a balloon and the ropes got twisted, so that I couldn't come down again. It went way up above the clouds, so far that a current of air struck it and carried it many, many miles away. For a day and a night I travelled through the air, and on the morning of the second day I awoke and found the balloon floating over a strange and beautiful country.

"It came down gradually, and I was not hurt a bit. But I found myself in the midst of a strange people, who, seeing me come from the clouds, thought I was a great Wizard. Of course I let them think so, because they were afraid of me, and promised to do anything I wished them to.

"Just to amuse myself, and keep the good people busy, I ordered them to build this City, and my palace; and they did it all willingly and well. Then I thought, as the country was so green and beautiful, I would call it the Emerald City, and to make the name fit better I put green spectacles on all the people, so that everything they saw was green."

"But isn't everything here green?" asked Dorothy.

"No more than in any other city," replied Oz; "but when you wear green spectacles, why of course everything you see looks green to you. The Emerald City was built a great many years ago, for I was a young man when the balloon brought me here, and I am a very old man now. But my people have worn green glasses on their eyes so long that most of them think it really is an Emerald City, and it certainly is a beautiful place, abounding in jewels and precious metals, and every good thing that is needed to make one happy. I have been good to the people, and they like me; but ever since this Palace was built I have shut myself up and would not see any of them.

"One of my greatest fears was the Witches, for while I had no magical powers at all I soon found out that the Witches were really able to do wonderful things. There were four of them in this country, and they ruled the people who live in the North and South and East and West. Fortunately, the Witches of the North and South were good, and I knew they would do me no harm; but the Witches of the East and West were terribly wicked, and had they not thought I was more powerful than they themselves, they would surely have destroyed me. As it was, I lived in deadly fear of them for many years; so you can imagine how pleased I was when I heard your house had fallen on the Wicked Witch of the East. When you came to me I was willing to promise anything if you would only do away with the other Witch; but, now that you have melted her, I am ashamed to say that I cannot keep my promises."

"I think you are a very bad man," said Dorothy.

"Oh, no, my dear; I'm really a very good man; but I'm a very bad Wizard, I must admit."

"Can't you give me brains?" asked the Scarecrow.

"You don't need them. You are learning something every day. A baby has brains, but it doesn't know much. Experience is the only thing that brings knowledge, and the longer you are on earth the more experience you are sure to get."

"That may all be true," said the Scarecrow, "but I shall be very unhappy unless you give me brains."

The false wizard looked at him carefully.

"Well," he said, with a sigh, "I'm not much of a magician, as I said; but if you will come to me tomorrow morning, I will stuff your head with brains. I cannot tell you how to use them, however; you must find that out for yourself."

"Oh, thank you—thank you!" cried the Scarecrow. "I'll find a way to use them, never fear!"

"But how about my courage?" asked the Lion anxiously.

"You have plenty of courage, I am sure," answered Oz. "All you need is confidence in yourself. There is no living thing that is not afraid when it faces danger. True courage is in facing danger when you are afraid, and that kind of courage you have in plenty."

"Perhaps I have, but I'm scared just the same," said the Lion. "I shall really be very unhappy unless you give me the sort of courage that makes one forget he is afraid."

"Very well; I will give you that sort of courage tomorrow," replied Oz.

"How about my heart?" asked the Tin Woodman.

"Why, as for that," answered Oz, "I think you are wrong to want a heart. It makes most people unhappy. If you only knew it, you are in luck not to have a heart."

"That must be a matter of opinion," said the Tin Woodman. "For my part, I will bear all the unhappiness without a murmur, if you will give me the heart."

"Very well," answered Oz, meekly. "Come to me tomorrow and you shall have a heart. I have played Wizard for so many years that I may as well continue the part a little longer."

"And now," said Dorothy, "how am I to get back to Kansas?"

"We shall have to think about that," replied the little man. "Give me two or three days to consider the matter and I'll try to find a way to carry you over the desert. In the meantime you shall all be treated as my guests, and while you live in the Palace my people will wait upon you and obey your slightest wish. There is only one thing I ask in return for my help—such as it is. You must keep my secret and tell no one I am a humbug."

They agreed to say nothing of what they had learned, and went back to their rooms in high spirits. Even Dorothy had hope that "The Great and Terrible Humbug," as she called him, would find a way to send her back to Kansas, and if he did that she was willing to forgive him everything.

16

The Magic Art of the Great Humbug

Next morning the Scarecrow said to his friends: "Congratulate me. I am going to Oz to get my brains at last. When I return I shall be as other men are."

"I have always liked you as you were," said Dorothy simply.

"It is kind of you to like a Scarecrow," he replied. "But surely you will think more of me when you hear the splendid thoughts my new brain is going to turn out." Then he said goodbye to them all in a cheerful voice and went to the Throne Room, where he rapped upon the door.

"Come in," said Oz.

The Scarecrow went in and found the little man sitting down by the window, engaged in deep thought.

"I have come for my brains," remarked the Scarecrow, a little uneasily.

"Oh, yes; sit down in that chair, please," replied Oz. "You must excuse me for taking your head off, but I shall have to do it in order to put your brains in their proper place."

"That's all right," said the Scarecrow. "You are quite

welcome to take my head off, as long as it will be a better one when you put it on again."

So the Wizard unfastened his head and emptied out the straw. Then he entered the back room and took up a measure of bran, which he mixed with a great many pins and needles. Having shaken them together thoroughly, he filled the top of the Scarecrow's head with the mixture and stuffed the rest of the space with straw, to hold it in place.

When he had fastened the Scarecrow's head on his body again he said to him, "Hereafter you will be a great man, for I have given you a lot of bran-new brains."

The Scarecrow was both pleased and proud at the fulfilment of his greatest wish, and having thanked Oz warmly he went back to his friends.

Dorothy looked at him curiously. His head was quite bulging out at the top with brains.

"How do you feel?" she asked.

"I feel wise, indeed," he answered earnestly. "When I get used to my brains I shall know everything."

"Why are those needles and pins sticking out of your head?" asked the Tin Woodman.

"That is proof that he is sharp," remarked the Lion.

"Well, I must go to Oz and get my heart," said the Woodman. So he walked to the Throne Room and knocked at the door.

"Come in," called Oz, and the Woodman entered and said, "I have come for my heart."

"Very well," answered the little man. "But I shall have to cut a hole in your breast, so I can put your heart in the right place. I hope it won't hurt you."

"Oh, no," answered the Woodman. "I shall not feel it at all."

So Oz brought a pair of tinner's shears and cut a small, square hole in the left side of the Tin Woodman's breast. Then, going to a chest of drawers, he took out a pretty heart, made entirely of silk and stuffed with sawdust.

"Isn't it a beauty?" he asked.

"It is, indeed!" replied the Woodman, who was greatly pleased. "But is it a kind heart?"

"Oh, very!" answered Oz. He put the heart in the Woodman's

'I feel wise, indeed,' said the Scarecrow.

breast and then replaced the square of tin, soldering it neatly together where it had been cut.

"There," said he, "now you have a heart that any man might be proud of. I'm sorry I had to put a patch on your breast, but it really couldn't be helped."

"Never mind the patch," exclaimed the happy Woodman. "I am very grateful to you, and shall never forget your kindness."

"Don't speak of it," replied Oz.

Then the Tin Woodman went back to his friends, who wished him every joy on account of his good fortune.

The Lion now walked to the Throne Room and knocked at the door.

"Come in," said Oz.

"I have come for my courage," announced the Lion, entering the room.

"Very well," answered the little man; "I will get it for you."

He went to a cupboard and reaching up to a high shelf took down a square green bottle, the contents of which he poured into a green-gold dish, beautifully carved. Placing this before the Cowardly Lion, who sniffed at it as if he did not like it, the Wizard said:

"Drink."

"What is it?" asked the Lion.

"Well," answered Oz, "if it were inside of you, it would be courage. You know, of course, that courage is always inside one; so that this really cannot be called courage until you have swallowed it. Therefore I advise you to drink it as soon as possible."

The Lion hesitated no longer, but drank till the dish was empty.

"How do you feel now?" asked Oz.

"Full of courage," replied the Lion, who went joyfully back to his friends to tell them of his good fortune.

Oz, left to himself, smiled to think of his success in giving the Scarecrow and the Tin Woodman and the Lion exactly what they thought they wanted. "How can I help being a humbug," he said, "when all these people make me do things that everybody knows can't be done? It was easy to make the Scarecrow and the Lion and the Woodman happy, because they imagined I could do anything. But it will take more than imagination to carry Dorothy back to Kansas, and I'm sure I don't know how it can be done."

17

How the Balloon was Launched

For three days Dorothy heard nothing from Oz. These were sad days for the little girl, although her friends were all quite happy and contented. The Scarecrow told them there were wonderful thoughts in his head; but he would not say what they were because he knew no one could understand them but himself. When the Tin Woodman walked about he felt his heart rattling around in his breast; and he told Dorothy he had discovered it to be a kinder and more tender heart than the one he had owned when he was made of flesh. The Lion declared he was afraid of nothing on earth, and would gladly face an army of men or a dozen of the fierce Kalidahs.

Thus each of the little party was satisfied except Dorothy, who longed more than ever to get back to Kansas.

On the fourth day, to her great joy, Oz sent for her, and when she entered the Throne Room he said, pleasantly:

"Sit down, my dear; I think I have found the way to get you out of this country."

"And back to Kansas?" she asked eagerly.

"Well, I'm not sure about Kansas," said Oz, "for I haven't the faintest notion which way it lies. But the first thing to do is to cross the desert, and then it should be easy to find your way home."

"How can I cross the desert?" she enquired.

"Well, I'll tell you what I think," said the little man. "You see, when I came to this country it was in a balloon. You also came through the air, being carried by a cyclone. So I believe the best way to get across the desert will be through the air. Now, it is quite beyond my powers to make a cyclone; but I've been thinking the matter over, and I believe I can make a balloon."

"How?" asked Dorothy.

"A balloon," said Oz, "is made of silk, which is coated with glue to keep the gas in it. I have plenty of silk in the Palace, so it will be no trouble for us to make the balloon. But in all this country there is no gas to fill the balloon with, to make it float."

"If it won't float," remarked Dorothy, "it will be of no use to us."

"True," answered Oz. "But there is another way to make it float, which is to fill it with hot air. Hot air isn't as good as gas, for if the air should get cold the balloon would come down in the desert, and we should be lost."

"We!" exclaimed the girl, "Are you going with me?"

"Yes, of course," replied Oz. "I am tired of being such a humbug. If I should go out of this Palace my people would soon discover I am not a Wizard, and then they would be vexed with me for having deceived them. So I have to stay shut up in these rooms all day, and it gets tiresome. I'd much rather go back to Kansas with you and be in a circus again."

"I shall be glad to have your company," said Dorothy.

"Thank you," he answered. "Now, if you will help me sew the silk together, we will begin to work on our balloon."

So Dorothy took a needle and thread, and as fast as Oz cut the strips of silk into proper shape the girl sewed them neatly together. First there was a strip of light green silk, then a strip of dark green and then a strip of emerald green; for Oz had a fancy to make the balloon in different shades of the colour about them. It took three days to sew all the strips together, but when it was finished they had a big bag of green silk more than twenty feet long.

Then Oz painted it on the inside with a coat of thin glue, to make it air-tight, after which he announced that the balloon was ready.

"But we must have a basket to ride in," he said. So he sent the soldier with the green whiskers for a big clothes basket, which he fastened with many ropes to the bottom of the balloon.

When it was all ready, Oz sent word to his people that he was going to make a visit to a great brother Wizard who lived in the clouds. The news spread rapidly throughout the city and everyone came to see the wonderful sight.

Oz ordered the balloon carried out in front of the Palace, and the people gazed upon it with much curiosity. The Tin Woodman had chopped a big pile of wood, and now he made a fire of it, and Oz held the bottom of the balloon over the fire so that the hot air that arose from it would be caught in the silken bag. Gradually the balloon swelled out and rose into the air, until finally the basket just touched the ground.

Then Oz got into the basket and said to all the people in a loud voice:

"I am now going away to make a visit. While I am gone the Scarecrow will rule over you. I command you to obey him as you would me."

The balloon was by this time tugging hard at the rope that held it to the ground, for the air within it was hot, and this made it so much lighter in weight than the air without that it pulled hard to rise into the sky.

"Come, Dorothy!" cried the Wizard. "Hurry up, or the balloon will fly away."

"I can't find Toto anywhere," replied Dorothy, who did not wish to leave her little dog behind. Toto had run into the crowd to bark at a kitten, and Dorothy at last found him. She picked him up and ran towards the balloon.

She was within a few steps of it, and Oz was holding out his hands to help her into the basket, when, crack! went the ropes, and the balloon rose into the air without her.

"Come back!" she screamed. "I want to go, too!"

"I can't come back, my dear," called Oz from the basket. "Goodbye!"

"Goodbye!" shouted everyone, and all eyes were turned upward to where the Wizard was riding in the basket, rising every moment farther and farther into the sky.

And that was the last any of them ever saw of Oz, the Wonderful Wizard, though he may have reached Omaha safely, and be there now, for all we know. But the people remembered him lovingly, and said to one another:

"Oz was always our friend. When he was here he built for us this beautiful Emerald City, and now he is gone he has left the wise Scarecrow to rule over us."

Still, for many days they grieved over the loss of the Wonderful Wizard, and would not be comforted.

18

Away to the South

Dorothy wept bitterly at the passing of her hope to get home to Kansas again; but when she thought it all over she was glad she had not gone up in a balloon. And she also felt sorry at losing Oz, and so did her companions.

The Tin Woodman came to her and said:

"Truly I should be ungrateful if I failed to mourn for the man who gave me my lovely heart. I should like to cry a little because Oz is gone, if you will kindly wipe away my tears, so that I shall not rust."

"With pleasure," she answered, and brought a towel at once. Then the Tin Woodman wept for several minutes, and she watched the tears carefully and wiped them away with the towel. When he had finished he thanked her kindly and oiled himself thoroughly with his jewelled oilcan, to guard against mishap.

The Scarecrow was now the ruler of the Emerald City, and although he was not a Wizard the people were proud of him. "For," they said, "there is not another city in all the world that is ruled by a stuffed man." And, so far as they knew, they were quite right.

The morning after the balloon had gone up with Oz the four travellers met in the Throne Room and talked matters over. The Scarecrow sat in the big throne and the others stood respectfully before him.

"We are not so unlucky," said the new ruler, "for this Palace and the Emerald City belong to us, and we can do just as we please. When I remember that a short time ago I was up on a pole in a farmer's cornfield, and that I am now the ruler of this beautiful City, I am quite satisfied with my lot."

"I also," said the Tin Woodman, "am well pleased with my new heart; and, really, that was the only thing I wished in all the world."

"For my part, I am content in knowing I am as brave as any beast that ever lived, if not braver," said the Lion modestly.

"If Dorothy would only be contented to live in the Emerald City," continued the Scarecrow, "we might all be happy together."

"But I don't want to live here," cried Dorothy. "I want to go to Kansas, and live with Aunt Em and Uncle Henry."

"Well, then, what can be done?" enquired the Woodman.

The Scarecrow decided to think, and he thought so hard that the pins and needles began to stick out of his brains. Finally he said:

"Why not call the Winged Monkeys, and asked them to carry you over the desert?"

"I never thought of that!" said Dorothy joyfully. "It's just the thing. I'll go at once for the Golden Cap."

When she brought it into the Throne Room she spoke the magic words, and soon the band of Winged Monkeys flew in through an open window and stood beside her.

"This is the second time you have called us," said the Monkey King, bowing before the little girl. "What do you wish?"

"I want you to fly with me to Kansas," said Dorothy.

But the Monkey King shook his head.

"That cannot be done," he said. "We belong to this country alone, and cannot leave it. There has never been a Winged Monkey in Kansas yet, and I suppose there never will be, for they don't

The Scarecrow sat on the big throne.

belong there. We shall be glad to serve you in any way in our power, but we cannot cross the desert. Goodbye."

And with another bow the Monkey King spread his wings and flew away through the window, followed by all his band.

Dorothy was almost ready to cry with disappointment.

"I have wasted the charm of the Golden Cap to no purpose," she said, "for the Winged Monkeys cannot help me."

"It is certainly too bad!" said the tender-hearted Woodman.

The Scarecrow was thinking again, and his head bulged out so horribly that Dorothy feared it would burst.

"Let us call in the soldier with the green whiskers," he said, "and ask his advice."

So the soldier was summoned and entered the Throne Room timidly, for while Oz was alive he never was allowed to come further than the door.

"This little girl," said the Scarecrow to the soldier, "wishes to cross the desert. How can she do so?"

"I cannot tell," answered the soldier, "for nobody has ever crossed the desert, unless it is Oz himself."

"Is there no one who can help me?" asked Dorothy earnestly.

"Glinda might," he suggested.

"Who is Glinda?" enquired the Scarecrow.

"The Witch of the South. She is the most powerful of all the Witches, and rules over the Quadlings. Besides, her castle stands on the edge of the desert, so she may know a way to cross it."

"Glinda is a good Witch, isn't she?" asked the child.

"The Quadlings think she is good," said the soldier, "and she is kind to everyone. I have heard that Glinda is a beautiful woman, who knows how to keep young in spite of the many years she has lived."

"How can I get to her castle?" asked Dorothy.

"The road is straight to the South," he answered, "but it is said to be full of dangers to travellers. There are wild beasts in the woods, and a race of queer men who do not like strangers to cross their country. For this reason none of the Quadlings ever come to the Emerald City."

The soldier then left them and the Scarecrow said:

"It seems, in spite of dangers, that the best thing Dorothy can do is to travel to the Land of the South and ask Glinda to help her. For, of course, if Dorothy stays here she will never get back to Kansas."

"You must have been thinking again," remarked the Tin Woodman.

"I have," said the Scarecrow.

"I shall go with Dorothy," declared the Lion, "for I am tired of your city and long for the woods and the country again. I am really a wild beast, you know. Besides, Dorothy will need someone to protect her."

"That is true," agreed the Woodman. "My axe may be of service to her; so I, also, will go with her to the Land of the South."

"When shall we start?" asked the Scarecrow.

"Are you going?" they asked, in surprise.

"Certainly. If it wasn't for Dorothy I should never have had brains. She lifted me from the pole in the cornfield and brought me to the Emerald City. So my good luck is all due to her, and I shall never leave her until she starts back to Kansas for good and all."

"Thank you," said Dorothy gratefully. "You are all very kind to me. But I should like to start as soon as possible."

"We shall go tomorrow morning," returned the Scarecrow. "So now let us all get ready, for it will be a long journey."

19

Attacked by the Fighting Trees

The next morning Dorothy kissed the pretty green girl goodbye, and they all shook hands with the soldier with the green whiskers, who had walked with them as far as the gate. When the Guardian of the Gate saw them again he wondered greatly that they could leave the beautiful City to get into new trouble. But he at once unlocked their spectacles, which he put back into the green box, and gave them many good wishes to carry with them.

"You are now our ruler," he said to the Scarecrow, "so you must come back to us as soon as possible."

"I certainly shall if I am able," the Scarecrow replied, "but I must help Dorothy to get home, first."

As Dorothy bade the good-natured Guardian a last farewell she said:

"I have been very kindly treated in your lovely City, and everyone has been good to me. I cannot tell you how grateful I am."

"Don't try, my dear," he answered. "We should like to keep you with us, but if it is your wish to return to Kansas I hope you will find a way." He then opened the gate of the outer wall and they walked forth and started upon their journey.

The sun shone brightly as our friends turned their faces towards the Land of the South. They were all in the best of spirits, and laughed and chatted together. Dorothy was once more filled with the hope of getting home, and the Scarecrow and the Tin Woodman were glad to be of use to her. As for the Lion, he sniffed the fresh air with delight and whisked his tail from side to side in pure joy at being in the country again, while Toto ran around them and chased the moths and butterflies, barking merrily all the time.

"City life does not agree with me at all," remarked the Lion, as they walked along at a brisk pace. "I have lost much flesh since I lived there, and now I am anxious for a chance to show the other beasts how courageous I have grown."

They now turned and took a last look at the Emerald City. All they could see was a mass of towers and steeples behind the green walls, and high up above everything the spires and dome of the Palace of Oz.

"Oz was not such a bad Wizard, after all," said the Tin Woodman, as he felt his heart rattling around in his breast.

"He knew how to give me brains, and very good brains, too," said the Scarecrow.

"If Oz had taken a dose of the same courage he gave me," added the Lion, "he would have been a brave man."

Dorothy said nothing. Oz had not kept the promise he made her, but he had done his best, so she forgave him. As he said, he was a good man, even if he was a bad Wizard.

The first day's journey was through the green fields and bright flowers that stretched about the Emerald City on every side. They slept that night on the grass, with nothing but the stars over them; and they rested very well indeed.

In the morning they travelled on until they came to a thick wood. There was no way of going around it, for it seemed to extend to the right and left as far as they could see; and, besides, they did not dare change the direction of their journey for fear of getting lost. So they looked for the place where it would be easiest to get into the forest.

The Scarecrow, who was in the lead, finally discovered a big tree with such wide-spreading branches that there was room for the party to pass underneath. So he walked forward to the tree, but just as he came under the first branches they bent down and twined around him, and the next minute he was raised from the ground and flung headlong among his fellow travellers.

This did not hurt the Scarecrow, but it surprised him, and he looked rather dizzy when Dorothy picked him up.

"Here is another space between the trees," called the Lion.

"Let me try it first," said the Scarecrow, "for it doesn't hurt me to get thrown about." He walked up to another tree, as he spoke, but its branches immediately seized him and tossed him back again.

"This is strange," exclaimed Dorothy. "What shall we do?"

"The trees seem to have made up their minds to fight us, and stop our journey," remarked the Lion.

"I believe I will try it myself," said the Woodman, and shouldering his axe he marched up to the first tree that had handled the Scarecrow so roughly. When a big branch bent down to seize him the Woodman chopped at it so fiercely that he cut it in two. At once the tree began shaking all its branches as if in pain, and the Tin Woodman passed safely under it.

"Come on!" he shouted to the others. "Be quick!"

They all ran forward and passed under the tree without injury, except Toto, who was caught by a small branch and shaken until he howled. But the Woodman promptly chopped off the branch and set the little dog free.

The other trees of the forest did nothing to keep them back, so they made up their minds that only the first row of trees could bend down their branches, and that probably these were the policemen of the forest, and given this wonderful power in order to keep strangers out of it.

The four travellers walked with ease through the trees until they came to the further edge of the wood. Then, to their surprise, they found before them a high wall, which seemed to be made of white china. It was smooth, like the surface of a dish, and higher than their heads.

"What shall we do now?" asked Dorothy.

"I will make a ladder," said the Tin Woodman, "for we certainly must climb over the wall."

The branches bent down and twined around him.

20

The Dainty China Country

While the Woodman was making a ladder from wood which he found in the forest Dorothy lay down and slept, for she was tired by the long walk. The Lion also curled himself up to sleep and Toto lay beside him.

The Scarecrow watched the Woodman while he worked, and said to him:

"I cannot think why this wall is here, nor what it is made of."

"Rest your brains and do not worry about the wall," replied the Woodman. "When we have climbed over it we shall know what is on the other side."

After a time the ladder was finished. It looked clumsy, but the Tin Woodman was sure it was strong and would answer their purpose. The Scarecrow waked Dorothy and the Lion and Toto, and told them that the ladder was ready. The Scarecrow climbed up the ladder first, but he was so awkward that Dorothy had to follow close behind and keep him from falling off. When he got his head over the top of the wall the Scarecrow said, "Oh, my!"

"Go on," exclaimed Dorothy.

So the Scarecrow climbed further up and sat down on the top of the wall, and Dorothy put her head over and cried, "Oh, my!" just as the Scarecrow had done.

Then Toto came up, and immediately began to bark, but Dorothy made him be still.

The Lion climbed the ladder next, and the Tin Woodman came last; but both of them cried, "Oh, my!" as soon as they looked over the wall. When they were all sitting in a row on the top of the wall they looked down and saw a strange sight.

Before them was a great stretch of country having a floor as smooth and shining and white as the bottom of a big platter. Scattered around were many houses made entirely of china and painted in the brightest colours. These houses were quite small, the biggest of them reaching only as high as Dorothy's waist. There were also pretty little barns, with china fences around them, and many cows and sheep and horses and pigs and chickens, all made of china, were standing about in groups.

But the strangest of all were the people who lived in this queer country. There were milkmaids and shepherdesses, with bright-coloured bodices and golden spots all over their gowns; and princesses with most gorgeous frocks of silver and gold and purple; and shepherds dressed in knee breeches with pink and yellow and blue stripes down them, and golden buckles on their shoes; and princes with jewelled crowns upon their heads, wearing ermine robes and satin doublets; and funny clowns in ruffled gowns, with round red spots upon their cheeks and tall, pointed caps. And, strangest of all, these people were all made of china, even to their clothes, and were so small that the tallest of them was no higher than Dorothy's knee.

No one did so much as look at the travellers at first, except one little purple china dog with an extra-large head, which came to the wall and barked at them in a tiny voice, afterwards running away again.

"How shall we get down?" asked Dorothy.

These people were all made of china.

They found the ladder so heavy they could not pull it up, so the Scarecrow fell off the wall and the others jumped down upon him so that the hard floor would not hurt their feet. Of course they took pains not to light on his head and get the pins in their feet. When all were safely down they picked up the Scarecrow, whose body was quite flattened out, and patted his straw into shape again.

"We must cross this strange place in order to get to the other side," said Dorothy; "for it would be unwise for us to go any other way except due South."

They began walking through the country of the china people, and the first thing they came to was a china milkmaid milking a china cow. As they drew near the cow suddenly gave a kick and kicked over the stool, the pail, and even the milkmaid herself, all falling on the china ground with a great clatter.

Dorothy was shocked to see that the cow had broken her leg short off, and that the pail was lying in several small pieces, while the poor milkmaid had a nick in her left elbow.

"There!" cried the milkmaid, angrily. "See what you have done! My cow has broken her leg, and I must take her to the mender's shop and have it glued on again. What do you mean by coming here and frightening my cow?"

"I'm very sorry," returned Dorothy. "Please forgive us."

But the pretty milkmaid was much too vexed to make any answer. She picked up the leg sulkily and led her cow away, the poor animal limping on three legs. As she left them the milkmaid cast many reproachful glances over her shoulder at the clumsy strangers, holding her nicked elbow close to her side.

Dorothy was quite grieved at this mishap.

"We must be very careful here," said the kind-hearted Woodman, "or we may hurt these pretty little people so they will never get over it."

A little farther on Dorothy met a most beautiful dressed young princess, who stopped short as she saw the strangers and started to run away.

Dorothy wanted to see more of the Princess, so she ran after her; but the china girl cried out:

"Don't chase me! Don't chase me!"

She had such a frightened little voice that Dorothy stopped and said, "Why not?"

"Because," answered the Princess, also stopping, a safe distance away, "if I run I may fall down and break myself."

"But couldn't you be mended?" asked the girl.

"Oh, yes; but one is never so pretty after being mended, you know," replied the Princess.

"I suppose not," said Dorothy.

"Now there is Mr. Joker, one of our clowns," continued the china lady, "who is always trying to stand upon his head. He has broken himself so often that he is mended in a hundred places, and doesn't look at all pretty. Here he comes now, so you can see for yourself."

Indeed, a jolly little clown now came walking towards them, and Dorothy could see that in spite of his pretty clothes of red and yellow and green he was completely covered with cracks, running every which way and showing plainly that he had been mended in many places.

The Clown put his hands in his pockets, and after puffing out his cheeks and nodding his head at them saucily he said:

"My lady fair,
Why do you stare
At poor old Mr. Joker?
You're quite as stiff
And prim as if
You'd eaten up a poker!"

"Be quiet, sir!" said the Princess; "can't you see these are strangers, and should be treated with respect?"

"Well, that's respect, I expect," declared the Clown, and immediately stood upon his head.

"Don't mind Mr. Joker," said the princess to Dorothy; "he is considerably cracked in his head, and that makes him foolish."

"Oh, I don't mind him a bit," said Dorothy. "But you are so beautiful," she continued, "that I am sure I could love you dearly. Won't you let me carry you back to Kansas and stand you on Aunt Em's mantleshelf? I could carry you in my basket."

"That would make me very unhappy," answered the china Princess. "You see, here in our own country we live contentedly, and can talk and move around as we please. But whenever any of us are taken away our joints at once stiffen, and we can only stand straight and look pretty. Of course that is all that is expected of us when we are on mantleshelves and cabinets and drawing room tables, but our lives are much pleasanter here in our own country."

"I would not make you unhappy for all the world!" exclaimed Dorothy. "So I'll just say goodbye."

"Goodbye," replied the Princess.

They walked carefully through the china country. The little animals and all the people scampered out of their way, fearing the strangers would break them, and after an hour or so the travellers reached the other side of the country and came to another china wall.

It was not as high as the first, however, and by standing upon the Lion's back they all managed to scramble to the top. Then the Lion gathered his legs under him and jumped on the wall; but just as he jumped he upset a china church with his tail and smashed it all to pieces.

"That was too bad," said Dorothy, "but really I think we were lucky in not doing these little people more harm than breaking a cow's leg and a church. They are all so brittle!"

"They are, indeed," said the Scarecrow, "and I am thankful I am made of straw and cannot be easily damaged. There are worse things in the world than being a Scarecrow."

21

The Lion Becomes the King of the Beasts

After climbing down from the china wall the travellers found themselves in a disagreeable country, full of bogs and marshes and covered with tall, rank grass. It was difficult to walk far without falling into muddy holes, for the grass was so thick that it hid them from sight. However, by carefully picking their way, they got safely along until they reached solid ground. But here the country seemed wilder than ever, and after a long and tiresome walk through the underbrush they entered another forest, where the trees were bigger and older than any they had ever seen.

"This forest is perfectly delightful," declared the Lion, looking around him with joy; "never have I seen a more beautiful place."

"It seems gloomy," said the Scarecrow.

"Not a bit of it," answered the Lion; "I should like to live here all my life. See how soft the dried leaves are under your feet and how rich and green the moss is that clings to these old trees. Surely no wild beast could wish a pleasanter home."

"Perhaps there are wild beasts in the forest now," said Dorothy.

"I suppose there are," returned the Lion; "but I do not see any of them about."

They walked through the forest until it became too dark to go any farther. Dorothy and Toto and the Lion lay down to sleep, while the Woodman and the Scarecrow kept watch over them as usual.

When morning came they started again. Before they had gone far they heard a low rumble, as of the growling of many wild animals. Toto whimpered a little but none of the others was frightened and they kept along the well-trodden path until they came to an opening in the wood, in which were gathered hundreds of beasts of every variety. There were tigers and elephants and bears and wolves and foxes and all the others in the natural history, and for a moment Dorothy was afraid. But the Lion explained that the animals were holding a meeting, and he judged by their snarling and growling that they were in great trouble.

As he spoke several of the beasts caught sight of him, and at once the great assemblage hushed as if by magic. The biggest of the tigers came up to the Lion and bowed, saying:

"Welcome, O King of Beasts! You have come in good time to fight our enemy and bring peace to all the animals of the forest once more."

"What is your trouble?" asked the Lion, quietly.

"We are all threatened," answered the tiger, "by a fierce enemy which has lately come into this forest. It is a most tremendous monster, like a great spider, with a body as big as an elephant and legs as long as a tree trunk. It has eight of these long legs, and as the monster crawls through the forest he seizes an animal with a leg and drags it to his mouth, where he eats it as a spider does a fly. Not one of us is safe while this fierce creature is alive, and we had called a meeting to decide how to take care of ourselves when you came among us."

The Lion thought for a moment.

"Are there any other lions in this forest?" he asked.

"No; there were some, but the monster has eaten them all. And, besides, they were none of them nearly so large and brave as you."

"If I put an end to your enemy will you bow down to me and obey me as King of the Forest?" enquired the Lion.

"We will do that gladly," returned the tiger; and all the other beasts roared with a mighty roar: "We will!"

"Where is this great spider of yours now?" asked the Lion.

"Yonder, among the oak trees," said the tiger, pointing with his forefoot.

"Take good care of these friends of mine," said the Lion, "and I will go at once to fight the monster."

He bade his comrades goodbye and marched proudly away to do battle with the enemy.

The great spider was lying asleep when the Lion found him, and it looked so ugly that its foe turned up his nose in disgust. Its legs were quite as long as the tiger had said, and it's body covered with coarse black hair. It had a great mouth, with a row of sharp teeth a foot long; but its head was joined to the pudgy body by a neck as slender as a wasp's waist. This gave the Lion a hint of the best way to attack the creature, and as he knew it was easier to fight it asleep than awake, he gave a great spring and landed directly upon the monster's back. Then, with one blow of his heavy paw, all armed with sharp claws, he knocked the spider's head from its body. Jumping down, he watched it until the long legs stopped wiggling, when he knew it was quite dead.

The Lion went back to the opening where the beasts of the forest were waiting for him and said, proudly, "You need fear your enemy no longer."

Then the beasts bowed down to the Lion as their King, and he promised to come back and rule over them as soon as Dorothy was safely on her way to Kansas.

22

The Country of the Quadlings

The four travellers passed through the rest of the forest in safety, and when they came out from its gloom saw before them a steep hill, covered from top to bottom with great pieces of rock.

"That will be a hard climb," said the Scarecrow, "but we must get over the hill, nevertheless."

So he led the way and the others followed. They had nearly reached the first rock when they heard a rough voice cry out, "Keep back!"

"Who are you?" asked the Scarecrow.

Then a head showed itself over the rock and the same voice said, "This hill belongs to us, and we don't allow anyone to cross it."

"But we must cross it," said the Scarecrow. "We're going to the country of the Quadlings."

"But you shall not!" replied the voice, and there stepped from behind the rock the strangest man the travellers had ever seen.

He was quite short and stout and had a big head, which was flat at the top and supported by a thick neck full of wrinkles. But he had no arms at all, and, seeing this, the Scarecrow did not fear that so helpless a creature could prevent them from climbing the hill. So he said, "I'm sorry not to do as you wish, but we must pass over your hill whether you like it or not," and he walked boldly forward.

As quick as lightning the man's head shot forward and his neck stretched out until the top of the head, where it was flat, struck the Scarecrow in the middle and sent him tumbling, over and over, down the hill. Almost as quickly as it came the head went back to the body, and the man laughed harshly as he said, "It isn't as easy as you think!"

A chorus of boisterous laughter came from the other rocks, and Dorothy saw hundreds of the armless Hammer-Heads upon the hillside, one behind every rock.

The Lion became quite angry at the laughter caused by the Scarecrow's mishap, and giving a loud roar that echoed like thunder he dashed up the hill.

Again a head shot swiftly out, and the great Lion went rolling down the hill as if he had been struck by a cannon ball.

Dorothy ran down and helped the Scarecrow to his feet, and the Lion came up to her, feeling rather bruised and sore, and said, "It is useless to fight people with shooting heads; no one can withstand them."

"What can we do, then?" she asked.

"Call the Winged Monkeys," suggested the Tin Woodman; "you have still the right to command them once more."

"Very well," she answered, and putting on the Golden Cap she uttered the magic words. The Monkeys were as prompt as ever, and in a few moments the entire band stood before her.

"What are your commands?" enquired the King of the Monkeys, bowing low.

"Carry us over the hill to the country of the Quadlings," answered the girl.

"It shall be done," said the King, and at once the Winged Monkeys caught the four travellers and Toto up in their arms and flew away with them. As they passed over the hill the Hammer-

The Head shot forward and struck the Scarecrow.

Heads yelled with vexation, and shot their heads high in the air; but they could not reach the Winged Monkeys, which carried Dorothy and her comrades safely over the hill and set them down in the beautiful country of the Quadlings.

"This is the last time you can summon us," said the leader to Dorothy; "so goodbye and good luck to you."

"Goodbye, and thank you very much," returned the girl; and the Monkeys rose into the air and were out of sight in a twinkling.

The country of the Quadlings seemed rich and happy. There was field upon field of ripening grain, with well-paved roads running between, and pretty rippling brooks with strong bridges across them. The fences and houses and bridges were all painted bright red, just as they had been painted yellow in the country of the Winkies and blue in the country of the Munchkins. The Quadlings themselves, who were short and fat and looked chubby and good-natured, were dressed all in red, which showed bright against the green grass and the yellowing grain.

The Monkeys had set them down near a farm house, and the four travellers walked up to it and knocked at the door. It was opened by the farmer's wife, and when Dorothy asked for something to eat the woman gave them all a good dinner, with three kinds of cake and four kinds of cookies, and a bowl of milk for Toto.

"How far is it to the Castle of Glinda?" asked the child.

"It is not a great way," answered the farmer's wife. "Take the road to the South and you will soon reach it."

Thanking the good woman, they started afresh and walked by the fields and across the pretty bridges until they saw before them a very beautiful Castle. Before the gates were three young girls, dressed in handsome red uniforms trimmed with gold braid; and as Dorothy approached one of them said to her:

"Why have you come to the South Country?"

"To see the Good Witch who rules here," she answered. "Will you take me to her?"

"Let me have your name and I will ask Glinda if she will receive you." They told who they were, and the girl soldier went into the Castle. After a few moments she came back to say that Dorothy and the others were to be admitted at once.

23

Glinda Grants Dorothy's Wish

Before they went to see Glinda, however, they were taken to a room of the Castle, where Dorothy washed her face and combed her hair, and the Lion shook the dust out of his mane, and the Scarecrow patted himself into his best shape, and the Woodman polished his tin and oiled his joints.

When they were all quite presentable they followed the soldier girl into a big room where the Witch Glinda sat upon a throne of rubies.

She was both beautiful and young to their eyes. Her hair was a rich red in colour and fell in flowing ringlets over her shoulders. Her dress was pure white; but her eyes were blue, and they looked kindly upon the little girl.

"What can I do for you, my child?" she asked.

Dorothy told the Witch all her story; how the cyclone had brought her to the Land of Oz, how she had found her companions, and of the wonderful adventures they had met with.

"My greatest wish now," she added, "is to get back to Kansas, for Aunt Em will surely think something dreadful has happened to me, and that will make her put on mourning; and unless the crops are better this year than they were last I am sure Uncle Henry cannot afford it."

Glinda leaned forward and kissed the sweet, upturned face of the loving little girl.

"Bless your dear heart," she said, "I am sure I can tell you of a way to get back to Kansas." Then she added:

"But, if I do, you must give me the Golden Cap."

"Willingly!" exclaimed Dorothy; "indeed, it is of no use to me now, and when you have it you can command the Winged Monkeys three times."

"And I think I shall need their service just those three times," answered Glinda, smiling.

Dorothy then gave her the Golden Cap, and the Witch said to the Scarecrow, "What will you do when Dorothy has left us?"

"I will return to the Emerald City," he replied, "for Oz has made me its ruler and the people like me. The only thing that worries me is how to cross the hill of the Hammer-Heads."

"By means of the Golden Cap I shall command the Winged Monkeys to carry you to the gates of the Emerald City," said Glinda, "for it would be a shame to deprive the people of so wonderful a ruler."

"Am I really wonderful?" asked the Scarecrow.

"You are unusual," replied Glinda.

Turning to the Tin Woodman, she asked:

"What will become of you when Dorothy leaves this country?"

He leaned on his axe and thought a moment. Then he said:

"The Winkies were very kind to me, and wanted me to rule over them after the Wicked Witch died. I am fond of the Winkies, and if I could get back again to the country of the West I should like nothing better than to rule over them forever."

"My second command to the Winged Monkeys," said Glinda, "will be that they carry you safely to the land of the Winkies. Your brains may not be so large to look at as those of the Scarecrow, but you are really brighter than he is—when you are well polished—and I am sure you will rule the Winkies wisely and well."

Then the Witch looked at the big, shaggy Lion and asked,

"When Dorothy has returned to her own home, what will become of you?"

"Over the hill of the Hammer-Heads," he answered, "lies a grand old forest, and all the beasts that live there have made me their King. If I could only get back to this forest I would pass my life very happily there."

"My third command to the Winged Monkeys," said Glinda, "shall be to carry you to your forest. Then, having used up the powers of the Golden Cap, I shall give it to the King of the Monkeys, that he and his band may thereafter be free for evermore."

The Scarecrow and the Tin Woodman and the Lion now thanked the Good Witch earnestly for her kindness, and Dorothy exclaimed:

"You are certainly as good as you are beautiful! But you have not yet told me how to get back to Kansas."

"Your Silver Shoes will carry you over the desert," replied Glinda. "If you had known their power you could have gone back to your Aunt Em the very first day you came to this country."

"But then I should not have had my wonderful brains!" cried the Scarecrow. "I might have passed my whole life in the farmer's cornfield."

"And I should not have had my lovely heart," said the Tin Woodman. "I might have stood and rusted in the forest till the end of the world."

"And I should have lived a coward forever," declared the Lion, "and no beast in all the forest would have had a good word to say to me."

"This is all true," said Dorothy, "and I am glad I was of use to these good friends. But now that each of them has had what he most desired, and each is happy in having a kingdom to rule beside, I think I should like to go back to Kansas."

"The Silver Shoes," said the Good Witch, "have wonderful powers. And one of the most curious things about them is that they can carry you to any place in the world in three steps, and each step will be made in the wink of an eye. All you have to do is to knock the heels together three times and command the shoes to carry you wherever you wish to go."

You must give me the Golden Cap.

"If that is so," said the child joyfully, "I will ask them to carry me back to Kansas at once."

She threw her arms around the Lion's neck and kissed him, patting his big head tenderly. Then she kissed the Tin Woodman, who was weeping in a way most dangerous to his joints. But she hugged the soft, stuffed body of the Scarecrow in her arms instead of kissing his painted face, and found she was crying herself at this sorrowful parting from her loving comrades.

Glinda the Good stepped down from her ruby throne to give the little girl a goodbye kiss, and Dorothy thanked her for all the kindness she had shown to her friends and herself.

Dorothy now took Toto up solemnly in her arms, and having said one last goodbye she clapped the heels of her shoes together three times, saying:

"Take me home to Aunt Em!"

Instantly she was whirling through the air, so swiftly that all she could see or feel was the wind whistling past her ears.

The Silver Shoes took but three steps, and then she stopped so suddenly that she rolled over upon the grass several times before she knew where she was.

At length, however, she sat up and looked about her.

"Good gracious!" she cried.

For she was sitting on the broad Kansas prairie, and just before her was the new farm house Uncle Henry built after the cyclone had carried away the old one. Uncle Henry was milking the cows in the barnyard, and Toto had jumped out of her arms and was running towards the barn, barking joyously.

Dorothy stood up and found she was in her stocking-feet. For the Silver Shoes had fallen off in her flight through the air, and were lost forever in the desert.

24

Home Again

Aunt Em had just come out of the house to water the cabbages when she looked up and saw Dorothy running towards her.

"My darling child!" she cried, folding the little girl in her arms and covering her face with kisses. "Where in the world did you come from?"

"From the Land of Oz," said Dorothy gravely. "And here is Toto, too. And oh, Aunt Em! I'm so glad to be at home again!"

A Little Princess

by Frances Hodgson Burnett

1

Sara

Once on a dark winter's day, when the yellow fog hung so thick and heavy in the streets of London that the lamps were lighted and the shop windows blazed with gas as they do at night, an odd-looking little girl sat in a cab with her father and was driven rather slowly through the big thoroughfares.

She sat with her feet tucked under her, and leaned against her father, who held her in his arm, as she stared out of the window at the passing people with a queer old-fashioned thoughtfulness in her big eyes.

She was such a little girl that one did not expect to see such a look on her small face. It would have been an old look for a child of twelve, and Sara Crewe was only seven. The fact was, however, that she was always dreaming and thinking odd things and could not herself remember any time when she had not been thinking things about grown-up people and the world they belonged to. She felt as if she had lived a long, long time.

At this moment she was remembering the voyage she had just made from Bombay with her father, Captain Crewe.

She was thinking of the big ship, of the Lascars passing silently to and fro on it, of the children playing about on the hot deck, and of some young officers' wives who used to try to make her talk to them and laugh at the things she said.

Principally, she was thinking of what a queer thing it was that at one time one was in India in the blazing sun, and then in the middle of the ocean, and then driving in a strange vehicle through strange streets where the day was as dark as the night. She found this so puzzling that she moved closer to her father.

"Papa," she said in a low, mysterious little voice which was almost a whisper, "papa."

"What is it, darling?" Captain Crewe answered, holding her closer and looking down into her face. "What is Sara thinking of?"

"Is this the place?" Sara whispered, cuddling still closer to him. "Is it, papa?"

"Yes, little Sara, it is. We have reached it at last." And though she was only seven years old, she knew that he felt sad when he said it.

It seemed to her many years since he had begun to prepare her mind for "the place," as she always called it. Her mother had died when she was born, so she had never known or missed her. Her young, handsome, rich, petting father seemed to be the only relation she had in the world. They had always played together and been fond of each other. She only knew he was rich because she had heard people say so when they thought she was not listening, and she had also heard them say that when she grew up she would be rich, too. She did not know all that being rich meant. She had always lived in a beautiful bungalow, and had been used to seeing many servants who made salaams to her and called her "Missee Sahib," and gave her her own way in everything. She had had toys and pets and an ayah who worshipped her, and she had gradually learned that people who were rich had these things. That, however, was all she knew about it.

During her short life only one thing had troubled her, and that thing was "the place" she was to be taken to some day. The climate of India was very bad for children, and as soon as possible they were sent away from it—generally to England and to school. She had seen other children go away, and had heard their fathers and mothers talk about the letters they received from them. She had known that she would be obliged to go also, and though sometimes her father's stories of the voyage and the new country had attracted her, she had been troubled by the thought that he could not stay with her.

"Couldn't you go to that place with me, papa?" she had asked when she was five years old. "Couldn't you go to school, too? I would help you with your lessons."

"But you will not have to stay for a very long time, little Sara," he had always said. "You will go to a nice house where there will be a lot of little girls, and you will play together, and I will send you plenty of books, and you will grow so fast that it will seem scarcely a year before you are big enough and clever enough to come back and take care of papa."

She had liked to think of that. To keep the house for her father; to ride with him, and sit at the head of his table when he had dinner parties; to talk to him and read his books—that would be what she would like most in the world, and if one must go away to "the place" in England to attain it, she must make up her mind to go. She did not care very much for other little girls, but if she had plenty of books she could console herself. She liked books more than anything else, and was, in fact, always inventing stories of beautiful things and telling them to herself. Sometimes she had told them to her father, and he had liked them as much as she did.

"Well, papa," she said softly, "if we are here I suppose we must be resigned."

He laughed at her old-fashioned speech and kissed her. He was really not at all resigned himself, though he knew he must keep that a secret. His quaint little Sara had been a great companion to him, and he felt he should be a lonely fellow when, on his return to India, he went into his bungalow knowing he need not expect to see the small figure in its white frock come forward to meet him. So he held her very closely in his arms as the cab rolled into the big, dull square in which stood the house which was their destination.

It was a big, dull, brick house, exactly like all the others in its row, but that on the front door there shone a brass plate on which was engraved in black letters:

MISS MINCHIN
Select Seminary for Young Ladies

"Here we are, Sara," said Captain Crewe, making his voice sound as cheerful as possible. Then he lifted her out of the cab and they mounted the steps and rang the bell. Sara often thought afterward that the house was somehow exactly like Miss Minchin. It was respectable and well-furnished, but everything in it was ugly; and the very armchairs seemed to have hard bones in them. In the hall everything was hard and polished—even the red cheeks of the moon face on the tall clock in the corner had a severe varnished look. The drawing room into which they were ushered was covered by a carpet with a square pattern upon it, the chairs were square, and a heavy marble timepiece stood upon the heavy marble mantel.

As she sat down in one of the stiff mahogany chairs, Sara cast one of her quick looks about her.

"I don't like it, papa," she said. "But then I dare say soldiers—even brave ones—don't really *like* going into battle."

Captain Crewe laughed outright at this. He was young and full of fun, and he never tired of hearing Sara's queer speeches.

"Oh, little Sara," he said. "What shall I do when I have no one to say solemn things to me? No one else is as solemn as you are."

"But why do solemn things make you laugh so?" inquired Sara.

"Because you are such fun when you say them," he answered, laughing still more. And then suddenly he swept her into his arms and kissed her very hard, stopping laughing all at once and looking almost as if tears had come into his eyes.

It was just then that Miss Minchin entered the room. She was very like her house, Sara felt: tall and dull, and respectable and ugly. She had large, cold, fishy eyes, and a large, cold, fishy smile. It spread itself into a very large smile when she saw Sara and Captain Crewe. She had heard a great many desirable things of the young soldier from the lady who had recommended her school to him. Among other things, she had heard that he was a rich father who was willing to spend a great deal of money on his little daughter.

"It will be a great privilege to have charge of such a beautiful and promising child, Captain Crewe," she said, taking Sara's hand and stroking it. "Lady Meredith has told me of her unusual cleverness. A clever child is a great treasure in an establishment like mine."

Sara stood quietly, with her eyes fixed upon Miss Minchin's face. She was thinking something odd, as usual.

"Why does she say I am a beautiful child?" she was thinking. "I am not beautiful at all. Colonel Grange's little girl, Isobel, is beautiful. She has dimples and rose-colored cheeks, and long hair the color of gold. I have short black hair and green eyes; besides which, I am a thin child and not fair in the least. I am one of the ugliest children I ever saw. She is beginning by telling a story."

She was mistaken, however, in thinking she was an ugly child. She was not in the least like Isobel Grange, who had been the beauty of the regiment, but she had an odd charm of her own. She was a slim, supple creature, rather tall for her age, and had an intense, attractive little face. Her hair was heavy and quite black and only curled at the tips; her eyes were greenish gray, it is true, but they were big, wonderful eyes with long, black lashes, and though she herself did not like the color of them, many other people did. Still she was very firm in her belief that she was an ugly little girl, and she was not at all elated by Miss Minchin's flattery.

"I should be telling a story if I said she was beautiful," she thought; "and I should know I was telling a story. I believe I am as ugly as she is—in my way. What did she say that for?"

After she had known Miss Minchin longer she learned why she had said it. She discovered that she said the same thing to each papa and mamma who brought a child to her school.

Sara stood near her father and listened while he and Miss Minchin talked. She had been brought to the seminary because Lady Meredith's two little girls had been educated there, and Captain Crewe had a great respect for Lady Meredith's experience. Sara was to be what was known as "a parlor boarder," and she was to enjoy even greater privileges than parlor boarders usually did. She was to have a pretty bedroom and sitting room of her own; she was to have a pony and a carriage, and a maid to take the place of the ayah who had been her nurse in India.

"I am not in the least anxious about her education," Captain Crewe said, with his gay laugh, as he held Sara's hand and patted it. "The difficulty will be to keep her from learning too fast and too much. She is always sitting with her little nose burrowing into books. She doesn't read them, Miss Minchin; she gobbles them up as if she were a little wolf instead of a little girl. She is always starving for new books to gobble, and she wants grown-up books—great, big, fat ones—French and German as well as English—history and biography and poets, and all sorts of things. Drag her away from her books when she reads too much. Make her ride her pony in the Row or go out and buy a new doll. She ought to play more with dolls."

"Papa," said Sara, "you see, if I went out and bought a new doll every few days I should have more than I could be fond of. Dolls ought to be intimate friends. Emily is going to be my intimate friend."

Captain Crewe looked at Miss Minchin and Miss Minchin looked at Captain Crewe.

"Who is Emily?" she inquired.

"Tell her, Sara," Captain Crewe said, smiling.

Sara's green-gray eyes looked very solemn and quite soft as she answered.

"She is a doll I haven't got yet," she said. "She is a doll papa is going to buy for me. We are going out together to find her. I have called her Emily. She is going to be my friend when papa is gone. I want her to talk to about him."

Miss Minchin's large, fishy smile became very flattering indeed.

"What an original child!" she said. "What a darling little creature!"

"Yes," said Captain Crewe, drawing Sara close. "She is a darling little creature. Take great care of her for me, Miss Minchin."

Sara stayed with her father at his hotel for several days; in fact, she remained with him until he sailed away again to India. They went out and visited many big shops together, and bought a great many things. They bought, indeed, a great many more things than Sara needed; but Captain Crewe was a rash, innocent young man and wanted his little girl to have everything she admired and everything he admired himself, so between them they collected a wardrobe much too grand for a child of seven. There were velvet dresses trimmed with costly furs, and lace dresses, and embroidered ones, and hats with great, soft ostrich feathers, and ermine coats and muffs, and boxes of tiny gloves and handkerchiefs and silk stockings in such abundant supplies that the polite young women behind the counters whispered to each other that the odd little girl with the big, solemn eyes must be at least some foreign princess—perhaps the little daughter of an Indian rajah.

And at last they found Emily, but they went to a number of toy shops and looked at a great many dolls before they discovered her.

"I want her to look as if she wasn't a doll really," Sara said. "I want her to look as if she *listens* when I talk to her. The trouble with dolls, papa"—and she put her head on one side and reflected as she said it—"the trouble with dolls is that they never seem to *hear*." So they looked at big ones and little ones—at dolls with black eyes and dolls with blue—at dolls with brown curls and dolls with golden braids, dolls dressed and dolls undressed.

"You see," Sara said when they were examining one who had no clothes. "If, when I find her, she has no frocks, we can take her to a dressmaker and have her things made to fit. They will fit better if they are tried on."

After a number of disappointments they decided to walk and look in at the shop windows and let the cab follow them. They had passed two or three places without even going in, when, as they were approaching a shop which was really not a very large one, Sara suddenly started and clutched her father's arm.

"Oh, papa!" she cried. "There is Emily!"

A flush had risen to her face and there was an expression in her green-gray eyes as if she had just recognized someone she was intimate with and fond of.

"She is actually waiting there for us!" she said. "Let us go in to her."

"Dear me," said Captain Crewe, "I feel as if we ought to have someone to introduce us."

"You must introduce me and I will introduce you," said Sara. "But I knew her the minute I saw her—so perhaps she knew me, too."

Perhaps she had known her. She had certainly a very intelligent expression in her eyes when Sara took her in her arms. She was a large doll, but not too large to carry about easily; she had naturally curling golden-brown hair, which hung like a mantle about her, and her eyes were a deep, clear, gray-blue, with soft, thick eyelashes which were real eyelashes and not mere painted lines.

"Of course," said Sara, looking into her face as she held her on her knee, "of course papa, this is Emily."

So Emily was bought and actually taken to a children's outfitter's shop and measured for a wardrobe as grand as Sara's own. She had lace frocks, too, and velvet and muslin ones, and hats and coats and beautiful lace-trimmed underclothes, and gloves and handkerchiefs and furs.

"I should like her always to look as if she was a child with a good mother," said Sara. "I'm her mother, though I am going to make a companion of her."

Captain Crewe would really have enjoyed the shopping tremendously, but that a sad thought kept tugging at his heart. This all meant that he was going to be separated from his beloved, quaint little comrade.

He got out of his bed in the middle of that night and went and stood looking down at Sara, who lay asleep with Emily in her arms. Her black hair was spread out on the pillow and Emily's golden-brown hair mingled with it, both of them had lace-ruffled nightgowns, and both had long eyelashes which lay and curled up on their cheeks. Emily looked so like a real child that Captain Crewe felt glad she was there. He drew a big sigh and pulled his mustache with a boyish expression.

"Heigh-ho, little Sara!" he said to himself "I don't believe you know how much your daddy will miss you."

The next day he took her to Miss Minchin's and left her there. He was to sail away the next morning. He explained to Miss Minchin that his solicitors, Messrs. Barrow & Skipworth, had charge of his affairs in England and would give her any advice she wanted, and that they would pay the bills she sent in for Sara's expenses. He would write to Sara twice a week, and she was to be given every pleasure she asked for.

"She is a sensible little thing, and she never wants anything it isn't safe to give her," he said.

Then he went with Sara into her little sitting room and they bade each other goodbye. Sara sat on his knee and held the lapels of his coat in her small hands, and looked long and hard at his face.

"Are you learning me by heart, little Sara?" he said, stroking her hair.

"No," she answered. "I know you by heart. You are inside my heart." And they put their arms round each other and kissed as if they would never let each other go.

When the cab drove away from the door, Sara was sitting on the floor of her sitting room, with her hands under her chin and her eyes following it until it had turned the corner of the square. Emily was sitting by her, and she looked after it, too. When Miss Minchin sent her sister, Miss Amelia, to see what the child was doing, she found she could not open the door.

"I have locked it," said a queer, polite little voice from inside. "I want to be quite by myself, if you please."

Miss Amelia was fat and dumpy, and stood very much in awe of her sister. She was really the better-natured person of the two, but she never disobeyed Miss Minchin. She went downstairs again, looking almost alarmed.

"I never saw such a funny, old-fashioned child, sister," she said. "She has locked herself in, and she is not making the least particle of noise."

"It is much better than if she kicked and screamed, as some of them do," Miss Minchin answered. "I expected that a child as much spoiled as she is would set the whole house in an uproar. If ever a child was given her own way in everything, she is."

"I've been opening her trunks and putting her things away," said Miss Amelia. "I never saw anything like them—sable and ermine on her coats, and real Valenciennes lace on her underclothing. You have seen some of her clothes. What *do* you think of them?"

"I think they are perfectly ridiculous," replied Miss Minchin, sharply; "but they will look very well at the head of the line when we take the schoolchildren to church on Sunday. She has been provided for as if she were a little princess."

And upstairs in the locked room Sara and Emily sat on the floor and stared at the corner round which the cab had disappeared, while Captain Crewe looked backward, waving and kissing his hand as if he could not bear to stop.

2

A French Lesson

When Sara entered the schoolroom the next morning everybody looked at her with wide, interested eyes. By that time every pupil—from Lavinia Herbert, who was nearly thirteen and felt quite grown up, to Lottie Legh, who was only just four and the baby of the school—had heard a great deal about her. They knew very certainly that she was Miss Minchin's show pupil and was considered a credit to the establishment. One or two of them had even caught a glimpse of her French maid, Mariette, who had arrived the evening before. Lavinia had managed to pass Sara's room when the door was open, and had seen Mariette opening a box which had arrived late from some shop.

"It was full of petticoats with lace frills on them—frills and frills," she whispered to her friend Jessie as she bent over her geography. "I saw her shaking them out. I heard Miss Minchin say to Miss Amelia that her clothes were so grand that they were ridiculous for a child. My mamma says that children should be dressed simply. She has got one of those petticoats on now. I saw it when she sat down."

"She has silk stockings on!" whispered Jessie, bending over her geography also. "And what little feet! I never saw such little feet."

"Oh," sniffed Lavinia, spitefully, "that is the way her slippers are made. My mamma says that even big feet can be made to look small if you have a clever shoemaker. I don't think she is pretty at all. Her eyes are such a queer color."

"She isn't pretty as other pretty people are," said Jessie, stealing a glance across the room; "but she makes you want to look at her again. She has tremendously long eyelashes, but her eyes are almost green."

Sara was sitting quietly in her seat, waiting to be told what to do. She had been placed near Miss Minchin's desk. She was not abashed at all by the many pairs of eyes watching her. She was interested and looked back quietly at the children who looked at her. She wondered what they were thinking of, and if they liked Miss Minchin, and if they cared for their lessons, and if any of them had a papa at all like her own. She had had a long talk with Emily about her papa that morning.

"He is on the sea now, Emily," she had said. "We must be very great friends to each other and tell each other things. Emily, look at me. You have the nicest eyes I ever saw—but I wish you could speak."

She was a child full of imaginings and whimsical thoughts, and one of her fancies was that there would be a great deal of comfort in even pretending that Emily was alive and really heard and understood. After Mariette had dressed her in her dark-blue schoolroom frock and tied her hair with a dark-blue ribbon, she went to Emily, who sat in a chair of her own, and gave her a book.

"You can read that while I am downstairs," she said; and, seeing Mariette looking at her curiously, she spoke to her with a serious little face.

"What I believe about dolls," she said, "is that they can do things they will not let us know about. Perhaps, really, Emily can read and talk and walk, but she will only do it when people are out of the room. That is her secret. You see, if people knew that dolls could do things, they would make them work. So, perhaps, they have promised each other to keep it a secret. If you stay in the room,

Emily will just sit there and stare; but if you go out, she will begin to read, perhaps, or go and look out of the window. Then if she heard either of us coming, she would just run back and jump into her chair and pretend she had been there all the time."

"*Comme elle est drôle!*" Mariette said to herself, and when she went downstairs she told the head housemaid about it. But she had already begun to like this odd little girl who had such an intelligent small face and such perfect manners. She had taken care of children before who were not so polite. Sara was a very fine little person, and had a gentle, appreciative way of saying, "If you please, Mariette," "Thank you, Mariette," which was very charming. Mariette told the head housemaid that she thanked her as if she was thanking a lady.

"*Elle a l'air d'une princesse, cette petite,*" she said. Indeed, she was very much pleased with her new little mistress and liked her place greatly.

After Sara had sat in her seat in the schoolroom for a few minutes, being looked at by the pupils, Miss Minchin rapped in a dignified manner upon her desk.

"Young ladies," she said, "I wish to introduce you to your new companion." All the little girls rose in their places, and Sara rose also. "I shall expect you all to be very agreeable to Miss Crewe; she has just come to us from a great distance—in fact, from India. As soon as lessons are over you must make each other's acquaintance."

The pupils bowed ceremoniously, and Sara made a little curtsy, and then they sat down and looked at each other again.

"Sara," said Miss Minchin in her schoolroom manner, "come here to me."

She had taken a book from the desk and was turning over its leaves. Sara went to her politely.

"As your papa has engaged a French maid for you," she began, "I conclude that he wishes you to make a special study of the French language."

Sara felt a little awkward.

"I think he engaged her," she said, "because he—he thought I would like her, Miss Minchin."

"I am afraid," said Miss Minchin, with a slightly sour smile, "that you have been a very spoiled little girl and always imagine that things are done because you like them. My impression is that your papa wished you to learn French."

If Sara had been older or less punctilious about being quite polite to people, she could have explained herself in a very few words. But, as it was, she felt a flush rising on her cheeks. Miss Minchin was a very severe and imposing person, and she seemed so absolutely sure that Sara knew nothing whatever of French that she felt as if it would be almost rude to correct her. The truth was that Sara could not remember the time when she had not seemed to know French. Her father had often spoken it to her when she had been a baby. Her mother had been a French woman, and Captain Crewe had loved her language, so it happened that Sara had always heard and been familiar with it.

"I—I have never really learned French, but—but—" she began, trying shyly to make herself clear.

One of Miss Minchin's chief secret annoyances was that she did not speak French herself, and was desirous of concealing the irritating fact. She, therefore, had no intention of discussing the matter and laying herself open to innocent questioning by a new little pupil.

"That is enough," she said with polite tartness. "If you have not learned, you must begin at once. The French master, Monsieur Dufarge, will be here in a few minutes. Take this book and look at it until he arrives."

Sara's cheeks felt warm. She went back to her seat and opened the book. She looked at the first page with a grave face. She knew it would be rude to smile, and she was very determined not to be rude. But it was very odd to find herself expected to study a page which told her that "*le père*" meant "the father," and "*la mère*" meant "the mother."

Miss Minchin glanced toward her scrutinizingly.

"You look rather cross, Sara," she said. "I am sorry you do not like the idea of learning French."

"I am very fond of it," answered Sara, thinking she would try again; "but—"

"You must not say 'but' when you are told to do things," said Miss Minchin. "Look at your book again."

And Sara did so, and did not smile, even when she found that "*le fils*" meant "the son," and "*le frère*" meant "the brother."

"When Monsieur Dufarge comes," she thought, "I can make him understand."

Monsieur Dufarge arrived very shortly afterward. He was a very nice, intelligent, middle-aged Frenchman, and he looked interested when his eyes fell upon Sara trying politely to seem absorbed in her little book of phrases.

"Is this a new pupil for me, madame?" he said to Miss Minchin. "I hope that is my good fortune."

"Her papa—Captain Crewe—is very anxious that she should begin the language. But I am afraid she has a childish prejudice against it. She does not seem to wish to learn," said Miss Minchin.

"I am sorry of that, mademoiselle," he said kindly to Sara. "Perhaps, when we begin to study together, I may show you that it is a charming tongue."

Little Sara rose in her seat. She was beginning to feel rather desperate, as if she were almost in disgrace. She looked up into Monsieur Dufarge's face with her big, green-gray eyes, and they were quite innocently appealing. She knew that he would understand as soon as she spoke. She began to explain quite simply in pretty and fluent French. Madame had not understood. She had not learned French exactly—not out of books—but her papa and other people had always spoken it to her, and she had read it and written it as she had read and written English. Her papa loved it, and she loved it because he did. Her dear mamma, who had died when she was born, had been French. She would be glad to learn anything monsieur would teach her, but what she had tried to explain to madame was that she already knew the words in this book—and she held out the little book of phrases.

When she began to speak Miss Minchin started quite violently and sat staring at her over her eyeglasses, almost indignantly, until she had finished. Monsieur Dufarge began to smile, and his smile was one of great pleasure. To hear this pretty childish voice speaking his own language so simply and charmingly made him feel almost as if he were in his native land—which in dark, foggy days in London sometimes seemed worlds away. When she had finished, he took the phrase book from her, with a look almost affectionate. But he spoke to Miss Minchin.

"Ah, madame," he said, "there is not much I can teach her. She has not *learned* French; she is French. Her accent is exquisite."

"You ought to have told me," exclaimed Miss Minchin, much mortified, turning to Sara.

"I—I tried," said Sara. "I—I suppose I did not begin right."

Miss Minchin knew she had tried, and that it had not been her fault that she was not allowed to explain. And when she saw that the pupils had been listening and that Lavinia and Jessie were giggling behind their French grammars, she felt infuriated.

"Silence, young ladies!" she said severely, rapping upon the desk. "Silence at once!"

And she began from that minute to feel rather a grudge against her show pupil.

3

Ermengarde

On that first morning, when Sara sat at Miss Minchin's side, aware that the whole schoolroom was devoting itself to observing her, she had noticed very soon one little girl, about her own age, who looked at her very hard with a pair of light, rather dull, blue eyes. She was a fat child who did not look as if she were in the least clever, but she had a good-naturedly pouting mouth. Her flaxen hair was braided in a tight pigtail, tied with a ribbon, and she had pulled this pigtail around her neck, and was biting the end of the ribbon, resting her elbows on the desk, as she stared wonderingly at the new pupil. When Monsieur Dufarge began to speak to Sara, she looked a little frightened; and when Sara stepped forward and, looking at him with the innocent, appealing eyes, answered him, without any warning, in French, the fat little girl gave a startled jump, and grew quite red in her awed amazement. Having wept hopeless tears for weeks in her efforts to remember that "*la mère*" meant "the mother," and "*le père*," "the father,"—when one spoke sensible English—it was almost too much for her suddenly to find herself listening to a child her own age who seemed not only quite familiar with these words, but apparently knew any number of others, and could mix them up with verbs as if they were mere trifles.

She stared so hard and bit the ribbon on her pigtail so fast that she attracted the attention of Miss Minchin, who, feeling extremely cross at the moment, immediately pounced upon her.

"Miss St. John!" she exclaimed severely. "What do you mean by such conduct? Remove your elbows! Take your ribbon out of your mouth! Sit up at once!"

Upon which Miss St. John gave another jump, and when Lavinia and Jessie tittered she became redder than ever—so red, indeed, that she almost looked as if tears were coming into her poor, dull, childish eyes; and Sara saw her and was so sorry for her that she began rather to like her and want to be her friend. It was a way of hers always to want to spring into any fray in which someone was made uncomfortable or unhappy.

"If Sara had been a boy and lived a few centuries ago," her father used to say, "she would have gone about the country with her sword drawn, rescuing and defending everyone in distress. She always wants to fight when she sees people in trouble."

So she took rather a fancy to fat, slow, little Miss St. John, and kept glancing toward her through the morning. She saw that lessons were no easy matter to her, and that there was no danger of her ever being spoiled by being treated as a show pupil. Her French lesson was a pathetic thing. Her pronunciation made even Monsieur Dufarge smile in spite of himself, and Lavinia and Jessie and the more fortunate girls either giggled or looked at her in wondering disdain. But Sara did not laugh. She tried to look as if she did not hear when Miss St. John called "*le bon pain*," "*lee bong pang*." She had a fine, hot little temper of her own, and it made her feel rather savage when she heard the titters and saw the poor, stupid, distressed child's face.

"It isn't funny, really," she said between her teeth, as she bent over her book. "They ought not to laugh."

When lessons were over and the pupils gathered together in groups to talk, Sara looked for Miss St. John, and finding her bundled rather disconsolately in a window-seat, she walked over to her and spoke. She only said the kind of thing little girls always say to each other by way of beginning an acquaintance, but there was something friendly about Sara, and people always felt it.

"What is your name?" she said.

To explain Miss St. John's amazement one must recall that a new pupil is, for a short time, a somewhat uncertain thing; and of this new pupil the entire school had talked the night before until it fell asleep quite exhausted by excitement and contradictory stories. A new pupil with a carriage and a pony and a maid, and a voyage from India to discuss, was not an ordinary acquaintance.

"My name's Ermengarde St. John," she answered.

"Mine is Sara Crewe," said Sara. "Yours is very pretty. It sounds like a storybook."

"Do you like it?" fluttered Ermengarde. "I—I like yours."

Miss St. John's chief trouble in life was that she had a clever father. Sometimes this seemed to her a dreadful calamity. If you have a father who knows everything, who speaks seven or eight languages, and has thousands of volumes which he has apparently learned by heart, he frequently expects you to be familiar with the contents of your lesson books at least; and it is not improbable that he will feel you ought to be able to remember a few incidents of history and to write a French exercise. Ermengarde was a severe trial to Mr. St. John. He could not understand how a child of his could be a notably and unmistakably dull creature who never shone in anything.

"Good heavens!" he had said more than once, as he stared at her, "there are times when I think she is as stupid as her Aunt Eliza!"

If her Aunt Eliza had been slow to learn and quick to forget a thing entirely when she had learned it, Ermengarde was strikingly like her. She was the monumental dunce of the school, and it could not be denied.

"She must be *made* to learn," her father said to Miss Minchin.

Consequently Ermengarde spent the greater part of her life in disgrace or in tears. She learned things and forgot them; or, if she remembered them, she did not understand them. So it was natural that, having made Sara's acquaintance, she should sit and stare at her with profound admiration.

"You can speak French, can't you?" she said respectfully.

Sara got on to the window-seat, which was a big, deep one, and, tucking up her feet, sat with her hands clasped round her knees.

"I can speak it because I have heard it all my life," she answered. "You could speak it if you had always heard it."

"Oh, no, I couldn't," said Ermengarde. "I *never* could speak it!"

"Why?" inquired Sara, curiously.

Ermengarde shook her head so that the pigtail wobbled.

"You heard me just now," she said. "I'm always like that. I can't *say* the words. They're so queer."

She paused a moment, and then added with a touch of awe in her voice, "You are *clever*, aren't you?"

Sara looked out of the window into the dingy square, where the sparrows were hopping and twittering on the wet, iron railings and the sooty branches of the trees. She reflected a few moments. She had heard it said very often that she was "clever," and she wondered if she was—and *if* she was, how it had happened.

"I don't know," she said. "I can't tell." Then, seeing a mournful look on the round, chubby face, she gave a little laugh and changed the subject.

"Would you like to see Emily?" she inquired.

"Who is Emily?" Ermengarde asked, just as Miss Minchin had done.

"Come up to my room and see," said Sara, holding out her hand.

They jumped down from the window-seat together, and went upstairs.

"Is it true," Ermengarde whispered, as they went through the hall—"is it true that you have a playroom all to yourself?"

"Yes," Sara answered. "Papa asked Miss Minchin to let me have one, because—well, it was because when I play I make up stories and tell them to myself, and I don't like people to hear me. It spoils it if I think people listen."

They had reached the passage leading to Sara's room by this time, and Ermengarde stopped short, staring, and quite losing her breath.

"You *make up* stories!" she gasped. "Can you do that—as well as speak French? *Can you*?"

Sara looked at her in simple surprise.

"Why, anyone can make up things," she said. "Have you never tried?"

She put her hand warningly on Ermengarde's.

"Let us go very quietly to the door," she whispered, "and then I will open it quite suddenly; perhaps we may catch her."

She was half laughing, but there was a touch of mysterious hope in her eyes which fascinated Ermengarde, though she had not the remotest idea what it meant, or whom it was she wanted to "catch," or why she wanted to catch her. Whatsoever she meant, Ermengarde was sure it was something delightfully exciting. So, quite thrilled with expectation, she followed her on tiptoe along the passage. They made not the least noise until they reached the door. Then Sara suddenly turned the handle, and threw it wide open. Its opening revealed the room quite neat and quiet, a fire gently burning in the grate, and a wonderful doll sitting in a chair by it, apparently reading a book.

"Oh, she got back to her seat before we could see her!" Sara explained. "Of course they always do. They are as quick as lightning."

Ermengarde looked from her to the doll and back again.

"Can she—walk?" she asked breathlessly.

"Yes," answered Sara. "At least I believe she can. At least I *pretend* I believe she can. And that makes it seem as if it were true. Have you never pretended things?"

"No," said Ermengarde. "Never. I—tell me about it."

She was so bewitched by this odd, new companion that she actually stared at Sara instead of at Emily—notwithstanding that Emily was the most attractive doll person she had ever seen.

"Let us sit down," said Sara, "and I will tell you. It's so easy that when you begin you can't stop. You just go on and on doing it always. And it's beautiful. Emily, you must listen. This is Ermengarde St. John, Emily. Ermengarde, this is Emily. Would you like to hold her?"

"Oh, may I?" said Ermengarde. "May I, really? She *is* beautiful!" And Emily was put into her arms.

Never in her dull, short life had Miss St. John dreamed of such an hour as the one she spent with the queer new pupil before they heard the lunch-bell ring and were obliged to go downstairs.

Sara sat upon the hearth-rug and told her strange things. She sat rather huddled up, and her green eyes shone and her cheeks flushed. She told stories of the voyage, and stories of India; but what fascinated Ermengarde the most was her fancy about the dolls who walked and talked, and who could do anything they chose when the human beings were out of the room, but who must keep their powers a secret and so flew back to their places "like lightning" when people returned to the room.

"*We* couldn't do it," said Sara, seriously. "You see, it's a kind of magic."

Once, when she was relating the story of the search for Emily, Ermengarde saw her face suddenly change. A cloud seemed to pass over it and put out the light in her shining eyes. She drew her breath in so sharply that it made a funny, sad little sound, and then she shut her lips and held them tightly closed, as if she was determined either to do or *not* to do something. Ermengarde had an idea that if she had been like any other little girl, she might have suddenly burst out sobbing and crying. But she did not.

"Have you a—a pain?" Ermengarde ventured.

"Yes," Sara answered, after a moment's silence. "But it is not in my body." Then she added something in a low voice which she tried to keep quite steady, and it was this: "Do you love your father more than anything else in all the whole world?"

Ermengarde's mouth fell open a little. She knew that it would be far from behaving like a respectable child at a select seminary to say that it had never occurred to you that you *could* love your father, that you would do anything desperate to avoid being left alone in his society for ten minutes. She was, indeed, greatly embarrassed.

"I—I scarcely ever see him," she stammered. "He is always in the library—reading things."

"I love mine more than all the world ten times over," Sara said. "That is what my pain is. He has gone away."

She put her head quietly down on her little, huddled-up knees, and sat very still for a few minutes.

"She's going to cry out loud," thought Ermengarde, fearfully.

But she did not. Her short, black locks tumbled about her ears, and she sat still. Then she spoke without lifting her head.

"I promised him I would bear it," she said. "And I will. You have to bear things. Think what soldiers bear! Papa is a soldier. If there was a war he would have to bear marching and thirstiness and, perhaps, deep wounds. And he would never say a word—not one word."

Ermengarde could only gaze at her, but she felt that she was beginning to adore her. She was so wonderful and different from anyone else.

Presently, she lifted her face and shook back her black locks, with a queer little smile.

"If I go on talking and talking," she said, "and telling you things about pretending, I shall bear it better. You don't forget, but you bear it better."

Ermengarde did not know why a lump came into her throat and her eyes felt as if tears were in them.

"Lavinia and Jessie are 'best friends,'" she said rather huskily. "I wish we could be 'best friends.' Would you have me for yours? You're clever, and I'm the stupidest child in the school, but I—oh, I do so like you!"

"I'm glad of that," said Sara. "It makes you thankful when you are liked. Yes. We will be friends. And I'll tell you what"—a sudden gleam lighting her face—"I can help you with your French lessons."

4

Lottie

If Sara had been a different kind of child, the life she led at Miss Minchin's Select Seminary for the next few years would not have been at all good for her. She was treated more as if she were a distinguished guest at the establishment than as if she were a mere little girl. If she had been a self-opinionated, domineering child, she might have become disagreeable enough to be unbearable through being so much indulged and flattered. If she had been an indolent child, she would have learned nothing. Privately Miss Minchin disliked her, but she was far too worldly a woman to do or say anything which might make such a desirable pupil wish to leave her school. She knew quite well that if Sara wrote to her papa to tell him she was uncomfortable or unhappy, Captain Crewe would remove her at once. Miss Minchin's opinion was that if a child were continually praised and never forbidden to do what she liked, she would be sure to be fond of the place where she was so treated. Accordingly, Sara was praised for her quickness at her lessons, for her good manners, for her amiability to her fellow pupils, for her generosity if she gave sixpence to a beggar out of her full little purse; the simplest thing she did was treated as if it were a virtue, and if she had not had a disposition and a clever little brain, she might have been a very self-satisfied young person. But the clever little brain told her a great many sensible and true things about herself and her circumstances, and now and then she talked these things over to Ermengarde as time went on.

"Things happen to people by accident," she used to say. "A lot of nice accidents have happened to me. It just *happened* that I always liked lessons and books, and could remember things when I learned them. It just happened that I was born with a father who was beautiful and nice and clever, and could give me everything I liked. Perhaps I have not really a good temper at all, but if you have everything you want and everyone is kind to you, how can you help but be good-tempered? I don't know"—looking quite serious—"how I shall ever find out whether I am really a nice child or a horrid one. Perhaps I'm a *hideous* child, and no one will ever know, just because I never have any trials."

"Lavinia has no trials," said Ermengarde, stolidly, "and she is horrid enough."

Sara rubbed the end of her little nose reflectively, as she thought the matter over.

"Well," she said at last, "perhaps—perhaps that is because Lavinia is *growing*." This was the result of a charitable recollection of having heard Miss Amelia say that Lavinia was growing so fast that she believed it affected her health and temper.

Lavinia, in fact, was spiteful. She was inordinately jealous of Sara. Until the new pupil's arrival, she had felt herself the leader in the school. She had led because she was capable of making herself extremely disagreeable if the others did not follow her. She domineered over the little children, and assumed grand airs with those big enough to be her companions. She was rather pretty, and had been the best-dressed pupil in the procession when the Select Seminary walked out two by two, until Sara's velvet coats and sable muffs appeared, combined with drooping ostrich feathers, and were led by Miss Minchin at the head of the line. This, at the beginning, had been bitter enough; but as time went on it became apparent that Sara was a leader, too, and not because she could make herself disagreeable, but because she never did.

"There's one thing about Sara Crewe," Jessie had enraged her "best friend" by saying honestly, "she's never 'grand' about herself the least bit, and you know she might be, Lavvie. I believe I couldn't help being—just a little—if I had so many fine things and was made such a fuss over. It's disgusting, the way Miss Minchin shows her off when parents come."

"'Dear Sara must come into the drawing room and talk to Mrs. Musgrave about India,'" mimicked Lavinia, in her most highly flavored imitation of Miss Minchin. "'Dear Sara must speak French to Lady Pitkin. Her accent is so perfect.' She didn't learn her French at the Seminary, at any rate. And there's nothing so clever in her knowing it. She says herself she didn't learn it at all. She just picked it up, because she always heard her papa speak it. And, as to her papa, there is nothing so grand in being an Indian officer."

"Well," said Jessie, slowly, "he's killed tigers. He killed the one in the skin Sara has in her room. That's why she likes it so. She lies on it and strokes its head, and talks to it as if it was a cat."

"She's always doing something silly," snapped Lavinia. "My mamma says that way of hers of pretending things is silly. She says she will grow up eccentric."

It was quite true that Sara was never "grand." She was a friendly little soul, and shared her privileges and belongings with a free hand. The little ones, who were accustomed to being disdained and ordered out of the way by mature ladies aged ten and twelve, were never made to cry by this most envied of them all. She was a motherly young person, and when people fell down and scraped their knees, she ran and helped them up and patted them, or found in her pocket a bonbon or some other article of a soothing nature. She never pushed them out of her way or alluded to their years as a humiliation and a blot upon their small characters.

"If you are four you are four," she said severely to Lavinia on an occasion of her having—it must be confessed—slapped Lottie and called her "a brat;" "but you will be five next year, and six the year after that. And," opening large, convicting eyes, "it takes sixteen years to make you twenty."

"Dear me," said Lavinia, "how we can calculate!" In fact, it was not to be denied that sixteen and four made twenty—and twenty was an age the most daring were scarcely bold enough to dream of.

So the younger children adored Sara. More than once she had been known to have a tea party, made up of these despised ones, in her own room. And Emily had been played with, and Emily's own tea service used—the one with cups which held quite a lot of much-sweetened weak tea and had blue flowers on them. No one had seen such a very real doll's tea set before. From that afternoon Sara was regarded as a goddess and a queen by the entire alphabet class.

Lottie Legh worshipped her to such an extent that if Sara had not been a motherly person, she would have found her tiresome. Lottie had been sent to school by a rather flighty young papa who could not imagine what else to do with her. Her young mother had died, and as the child had been treated like a favorite doll or a very spoiled pet monkey or lap dog ever since the first hour of her life, she was a very appalling little creature. When she wanted anything or did not want anything she wept and howled; and, as she always wanted the things she could not have, and did not want the things that were best for her, her shrill little voice was usually to be heard uplifted in wails in one part of the house or another.

Her strongest weapon was that in some mysterious way she had found out that a very small girl who had lost her mother was a person who ought to be pitied and made much of. She had probably heard some grown-up people talking her over in the early days, after her mother's death. So it became her habit to make great use of this knowledge.

The first time Sara took her in charge was one morning when, on passing a sitting room, she heard both Miss Minchin and Miss Amelia trying to suppress the angry wails of some child who, evidently, refused to be silenced. She refused so strenuously indeed that Miss Minchin was obliged to almost shout—in a stately and severe manner—to make herself heard.

"What *is* she crying for?" she almost yelled.

"Oh—oh—oh!" Sara heard; "I haven't got any mam—ma-a!"

"Oh, Lottie!" screamed Miss Amelia. "Do stop, darling! Don't cry! Please don't!"

"Oh! Oh! Oh! Oh! Oh!" Lottie howled tempestuously. "Haven't—got—any—mam—ma-a!"

"She ought to be whipped," Miss Minchin proclaimed. "You *shall* be whipped, you naughty child!"

Lottie wailed more loudly than ever. Miss Amelia began to cry. Miss Minchin's voice rose until it almost thundered, then suddenly she sprang up from her chair in impotent indignation and flounced out of the room, leaving Miss Amelia to arrange the matter.

Sara had paused in the hall, wondering if she ought to go into the room, because she had recently begun a friendly acquaintance with Lottie and might be able to quiet her. When Miss Minchin came out and saw her, she looked rather annoyed. She realized that her voice, as heard from inside the room, could not have sounded either dignified or amiable.

"Oh, Sara!" she exclaimed, endeavoring to produce a suitable smile.

"I stopped," explained Sara, "because I knew it was Lottie—and I thought, perhaps—just perhaps, I could make her be quiet. May I try, Miss Minchin?"

"If you can, you are a clever child," answered Miss Minchin, drawing in her mouth sharply. Then, seeing that Sara looked slightly chilled by her asperity, she changed her manner. "But you are clever in everything," she said in her approving way. "I dare say you can manage her. Go in." And she left her.

When Sara entered the room, Lottie was lying upon the floor, screaming and kicking her small fat legs violently, and Miss Amelia was bending over her in consternation and despair, looking quite red and damp with heat. Lottie had always found, when in her own nursery at home, that kicking and screaming would always be quieted by any means she insisted on. Poor plump Miss Amelia was trying first one method, and then another.

"Poor darling," she said one moment, "I know you haven't any mamma, poor—" Then in quite another tone, "If you don't stop, Lottie, I will shake you. Poor little angel! There—! You wicked, bad, detestable child, I will smack you! I will!"

Sara went to them quietly. She did not know at all what she was going to do, but she had a vague inward conviction that it would be better not to say such different kinds of things quite so helplessly and excitedly.

"Miss Amelia," she said in a low voice, "Miss Minchin says I may try to make her stop—may I?"

Miss Amelia turned and looked at her hopelessly. "Oh, *do* you think you can?" she gasped.

"I don't know whether I *can*," answered Sara, still in her half-whisper; "but I will try."

Miss Amelia stumbled up from her knees with a heavy sigh, and Lottie's fat little legs kicked as hard as ever.

"If you will steal out of the room," said Sara, "I will stay with her."

"Oh, Sara!" almost whimpered Miss Amelia. "We never had such a dreadful child before. I don't believe we *can* keep her."

But she crept out of the room, and was very much relieved to find an excuse for doing it.

Sara stood by the howling furious child for a few moments, and looked down at her without saying anything. Then she sat down flat on the floor beside her and waited. Except for Lottie's angry screams, the room was quite quiet. This was a new state of affairs for little Miss Legh, who was accustomed, when she screamed, to hear other people protest and implore and command and coax by turns. To lie and kick and shriek, and find the only person near you not seeming to mind in the least, attracted her attention. She opened her tight-shut streaming eyes to see who this person was. And it was only another little girl. But it was the one who owned Emily and all the nice things. And she was looking at her steadily and as if she was merely thinking. Having paused for a few seconds to find this out, Lottie thought she must begin again, but the quiet of the room and of Sara's odd, interested face made her first howl rather half-hearted.

"I—haven't—any—ma—ma—ma-a!" she announced; but her voice was not so strong.

Sara looked at her still more steadily, but with a sort of understanding in her eyes.

"Neither have I," she said.

This was so unexpected that it was astounding. Lottie actually dropped her legs, gave a wriggle, and lay and stared. A new idea will stop a crying child when nothing else will. Also it was true that while Lottie disliked Miss Minchin, who was cross, and Miss Amelia, who was foolishly indulgent, she rather liked Sara, little as she knew her. She did not want to give up her grievance, but her thoughts were distracted from it, so she wriggled again, and, after a sulky sob, said, "Where is she?"

Sara paused a moment. Because she had been told that her mamma was in heaven, she had thought a great deal about the matter, and her thoughts had not been quite like those of other people.

"She went to heaven," she said. "But I am sure she comes out sometimes to see me—though I don't see her. So does yours. Perhaps they can both see us now. Perhaps they are both in this room."

Lottie sat bolt upright, and looked about her. She was a pretty, little, curly-headed creature, and her round eyes were like wet forget-me-nots. If her mamma had seen her during the last half-hour, she might not have thought her the kind of child who ought to be related to an angel.

Sara went on talking. Perhaps some people might think that what she said was rather like a fairy story, but it was all so real to her own imagination that Lottie began to listen in spite of herself. She had been told that her mamma had wings and a crown, and she had been shown pictures of ladies in beautiful white nightgowns, who were said to be angels. But Sara seemed to be telling a real story about a lovely country where real people were.

"There are fields and fields of flowers," she said, forgetting herself, as usual, when she began, and talking rather as if she were in a dream, "fields and fields of lilies—and when the soft wind blows over them it wafts the scent of them into the air—and everybody always breathes it, because the soft wind is always blowing. And little children run about in the lily fields and gather armfuls of them, and laugh and make little wreaths. And the streets are shining. And people are never tired, however far they walk. They can float anywhere they like. And there are walls made of pearl and gold all round the city, but they are low enough for the people to go and lean on them, and look down onto the earth and smile, and send beautiful messages."

Whatsoever story she had begun to tell, Lottie would, no doubt, have stopped crying, and been fascinated into listening; but there was no denying that this story was prettier than most others. She dragged herself close to Sara, and drank in every word until the end came—far too soon. When it did come, she was so sorry that she put up her lip ominously.

"I want to go there," she cried. "I—haven't any mamma in this school."

Sara saw the danger signal, and came out of her dream. She took hold of the chubby hand and pulled her close to her side with a coaxing little laugh.

"I will be your mamma," she said. "We will play that you are my little girl. And Emily shall be your sister."

Lottie's dimples all began to show themselves.

"Shall she?" she said.

"Yes," answered Sara, jumping to her feet. "Let us go and tell her. And then I will wash your face and brush your hair."

To which Lottie agreed quite cheerfully, and trotted out of the room and upstairs with her, without seeming even to remember that the whole of the last hour's tragedy had been caused by the fact that she had refused to be washed and brushed for lunch and Miss Minchin had been called in to use her majestic authority.

And from that time Sara was an adopted mother.

5

Becky

Of course the greatest power Sara possessed and the one which gained her even more followers than her luxuries and the fact that she was "the show pupil," the power that Lavinia and certain other girls were most envious of, and at the same time most fascinated by in spite of themselves, was her power of telling stories and of making everything she talked about seem like a story, whether it was one or not.

Anyone who has been at school with a teller of stories knows what the wonder means—how he or she is followed about and besought in a whisper to relate romances; how groups gather round and hang on the outskirts of the favored party in the hope of being allowed to join in and listen. Sara not only could tell stories, but she adored telling them. When she sat or stood in the midst of a circle and began to invent wonderful things, her green eyes grew big and shining, her cheeks flushed, and, without knowing that she was doing it, she began to act and made what she told lovely or alarming by the raising or dropping of her voice, the bend and sway of her slim body, and the dramatic movement of her hands. She forgot that she was talking to listening children; she saw and lived with the fairy folk, or the kings and queens and beautiful ladies, whose adventures she was narrating. Sometimes when she had finished her story, she was quite out of breath with excitement, and would lay her hand on her thin, little, quick-rising chest, and half laugh as if at herself.

"When I am telling it," she would say, "it doesn't seem as if it was only made up. It seems more real than you are—more real than the schoolroom. I feel as if I were all the people in the story—one after the other. It is queer."

She had been at Miss Minchin's school about two years when, one foggy winter's afternoon, as she was getting out of her carriage, comfortably wrapped up in her warmest velvets and furs and looking very much grander than she knew, she caught sight, as she crossed the pavement, of a dingy little figure standing on the area steps, and stretching its neck so that its wide-open eyes might peer at her through the railings. Something in the eagerness and timidity of the smudgy face made her look at it, and when she looked she smiled because it was her way to smile at people.

But the owner of the smudgy face and the wide-open eyes evidently was afraid that she ought not to have been caught looking at pupils of importance. She dodged out of sight like a jack-in-the-box and scurried back into the kitchen, disappearing so suddenly that if she had not been such a poor little forlorn thing, Sara would have laughed in spite of herself. That very evening, as Sara was sitting in the midst of a group of listeners in a corner of the schoolroom telling one of her stories, the very same figure timidly entered the room, carrying a coal box much too heavy for her, and knelt down upon the hearth rug to replenish the fire and sweep up the ashes.

She was cleaner than she had been when she peeped through the area railings, but she looked just as frightened. She was evidently afraid to look at the children or seem to be listening. She put on pieces of coal cautiously with her fingers so that she might make no disturbing noise, and she swept about the fire irons very softly. But Sara saw in two minutes that she was deeply interested in what was going on, and that she was doing her work slowly in the hope of catching a word here and there. And realizing this, she raised her voice and spoke more clearly.

"The Mermaids swam softly about in the crystal-green water, and dragged after them a fishing-net woven of deep-sea pearls," she said. "The Princess sat on the white rock and watched them."

It was a wonderful story about a princess who was loved by a Prince Merman, and went to live with him in shining caves under the sea.

The small drudge before the grate swept the hearth once and then swept it again. Having done it twice, she did it three times; and, as she was doing it the third time, the sound of the story so lured her to listen that she fell under the spell and actually forgot that she had no right to listen at all, and also forgot everything else. She sat down upon her heels as she knelt on the hearth rug, and the brush hung idly in her fingers. The voice of the storyteller went on and drew her with it into winding grottos under the sea, glowing with soft, clear blue light, and paved with pure golden sands. Strange sea flowers and grasses waved about her, and far away faint singing and music echoed.

The hearth brush fell from the work-roughened hand, and Lavinia Herbert looked round.

"That girl has been listening," she said.

The culprit snatched up her brush, and scrambled to her feet. She caught at the coal box and simply scuttled out of the room like a frightened rabbit.

Sara felt rather hot-tempered.

"I knew she was listening," she said. "Why shouldn't she?"

Lavinia tossed her head with great elegance.

"Well," she remarked, "I do not know whether your mamma would like you to tell stories to servant girls, but I know *my* mamma wouldn't like *me* to do it."

"My mamma!" said Sara, looking odd. "I don't believe she would mind in the least. She knows that stories belong to everybody."

"I thought," retorted Lavinia, in severe recollection, "that your mamma was dead. How can she know things?"

"Do you think she *doesn't* know things?" said Sara, in her stern little voice. Sometimes she had a rather stern little voice.

"Sara's mamma knows everything," piped in Lottie. "So does my mamma—'cept Sara is my mamma at Miss Minchin's—my other one knows everything. The streets are shining, and there are fields and fields of lilies, and everybody gathers them. Sara tells me when she puts me to bed."

"You wicked thing," said Lavinia, turning on Sara; "making fairy stories about heaven."

"There are much more splendid stories in Revelation," returned Sara. "Just look and see! How do you know mine are fairy stories? But I can tell you"—with a fine bit of unheavenly temper—"you will never find out whether they are or not if you're not kinder to people than you are now. Come along, Lottie." And she marched out of the room, rather hoping that she might see the little servant again somewhere, but she found no trace of her when she got into the hall.

"Who is that little girl who makes the fires?" she asked Mariette that night.

Mariette broke forth into a flow of description.

Ah, indeed, Mademoiselle Sara might well ask. She was a forlorn little thing who had just taken the place of scullery maid—though, as to being scullery maid, she was everything else besides. She blacked boots and grates, and carried heavy coal-scuttles up and down stairs, and scrubbed floors and cleaned windows, and was ordered about by everybody. She was fourteen years old, but was so stunted in growth that she looked about twelve. In truth, Mariette was sorry for her. She was so timid that if one chanced to speak to her it appeared as if her poor, frightened eyes would jump out of her head.

"What is her name?" asked Sara, who had sat by the table, with her chin on her hands, as she listened absorbedly to the recital.

Her name was Becky. Mariette heard everyone below-stairs calling, "Becky, do this," and "Becky, do that," every five minutes in the day.

Sara sat and looked into the fire, reflecting on Becky for some time after Mariette left her. She made up a story of which Becky was the ill-used heroine. She thought she looked as if she had never had quite enough to eat. Her very eyes were hungry. She hoped she should see her again, but though she caught sight of her carrying things up or down stairs on several occasions, she always seemed in such a hurry and so afraid of being seen that it was impossible to speak to her.

But a few weeks later, on another foggy afternoon, when she entered her sitting room she found herself confronting a rather pathetic picture. In her own special and pet easy-chair before the bright fire, Becky—with a coal smudge on her nose and several on her apron, with her poor little cap hanging half off her head, and an empty coal box on the floor near her—sat fast asleep, tired out beyond even the endurance of her hard-working young body. She had been sent up to put the bedrooms in order for the evening. There were a great many of them, and she had been running about all day. Sara's rooms she had saved until the last. They were not like the other rooms, which were plain and bare. Ordinary pupils were expected to be satisfied with mere necessaries. Sara's comfortable sitting room seemed a bower of luxury to the scullery maid, though it was, in fact, merely a nice, bright little room. But there were pictures and books in it, and curious things from India; there was a sofa and the low, soft chair; Emily sat in a chair of her own, with the air of a presiding goddess, and there was always a glowing fire and a polished grate. Becky saved it until the end of her afternoon's work, because it rested her to go into it, and she always hoped to snatch a few minutes to sit down in the soft chair and look about her, and think about the wonderful good fortune of the child who owned such surroundings and who went out on the cold days in beautiful hats and coats one tried to catch a glimpse of through the area railing.

On this afternoon, when she had sat down, the sensation of relief to her short, aching legs had been so wonderful and delightful that it had seemed to soothe her whole body, and the glow of warmth and comfort from the fire had crept over her like a spell, until, as she looked at the red coals, a tired, slow smile stole over her smudged face, her head nodded forward without her being aware of it, her eyes drooped, and she fell fast asleep. She had really been only about ten minutes in the room when Sara entered, but she was in as deep a sleep as if she had been, like the Sleeping Beauty, slumbering for a hundred years. But she did not look—poor Becky—like a Sleeping Beauty at all. She looked only like an ugly, stunted, worn-out little scullery drudge.

Sara seemed as much unlike her as if she were a creature from another world.

On this particular afternoon she had been taking her dancing lesson, and the afternoon on which the dancing master appeared was rather a grand occasion at the seminary, though it occurred every week. The pupils were attired in their prettiest frocks, and as Sara danced particularly well, she was very much brought forward, and Mariette was requested to make her as diaphanous and fine as possible.

Today a frock the color of a rose had been put on her, and Mariette had bought some real buds and made her a wreath to wear on her black locks. She had been learning a new, delightful dance in which she had been skimming and flying about the room, like a large rose-colored butterfly, and the enjoyment and exercise had brought a brilliant, happy glow into her face.

When she entered the room, she floated in with a few of the butterfly steps—and there sat Becky, nodding her cap sideways off her head.

"Oh!" cried Sara, softly, when she saw her. "That poor thing!"

It did not occur to her to feel cross at finding her pet chair occupied by the small, dingy figure. To tell the truth, she was quite glad to find it there. When the ill-used heroine of her story wakened, she could talk to her. She crept toward her quietly, and stood looking at her. Becky gave a little snore.

"I wish she'd waken herself," Sara said. "I don't like to waken her. But Miss Minchin would be cross if she found out. I'll just wait a few minutes."

She took a seat on the edge of the table, and sat swinging her slim, rose-colored legs, and wondering what it would be best to do. Miss Amelia might come in at any moment, and if she did, Becky would be sure to be scolded.

"But she is so tired," she thought. "She *is* so tired!"

A piece of flaming coal ended her perplexity for her that very moment. It broke off from a large lump and fell on to the fender. Becky started, and opened her eyes with a frightened gasp. She did not know she had fallen asleep. She had only sat down for one moment and felt the beautiful glow—and here she found herself staring in wild alarm at the wonderful pupil, who sat perched quite near her, like a rose-colored fairy, with interested eyes.

She sprang up and clutched at her cap. She felt it dangling over her ear, and tried wildly to put it straight. Oh, she had got herself into trouble now with a vengeance! To have impudently fallen asleep on such a young lady's chair! She would be turned out of doors without wages.

She made a sound like a big breathless sob.

"Oh, miss! Oh, miss!" she stuttered. "I arst yer pardon, miss! Oh, I do, miss!"

Sara jumped down, and came quite close to her.

"Don't be frightened," she said, quite as if she had been speaking to a little girl like herself. "It doesn't matter the least bit."

"I didn't go to do it, miss," protested Becky. "It was the warm fire—an' me bein' so tired. It—it *wasn't* impertience!"

Sara broke into a friendly little laugh, and put her hand on her shoulder.

"You were tired," she said; "you could not help it. You are not really awake yet."

How poor Becky stared at her! In fact, she had never heard such a nice, friendly sound in anyone's voice before. She was used to being ordered about and scolded, and having her ears boxed. And this one—in her rose-colored dancing afternoon splendor—was looking at her as if she were not a culprit at all—as if she had a right to be tired—even to fall asleep! The touch of the soft, slim little paw on her shoulder was the most amazing thing she had ever known.

"Ain't—ain't yer angry, miss?" she gasped. "Ain't yer goin' to tell the missus?"

"No," cried out Sara. "Of course I'm not."

The woeful fright in the coal-smutted face made her suddenly so sorry that she could scarcely bear it. One of her queer thoughts rushed into her mind. She put her hand against Becky's cheek.

"Why," she said, "we are just the same—I am only a little girl like you. It's just an accident that I am not you, and you are not me!"

Becky did not understand in the least. Her mind could not grasp such amazing thoughts, and "an accident" meant to her a calamity in which some one was run over or fell off a ladder and was carried to "the 'orspital."

"A' accident, miss," she fluttered respectfully. "Is it?"

"Yes," Sara answered, and she looked at her dreamily for a moment. But the next she spoke in a different tone. She realized that Becky did not know what she meant.

"Have you done your work?" she asked. "Dare you stay here a few minutes?"

Becky lost her breath again.

"Here, miss? Me?"

Sara ran to the door, opened it, and looked out and listened.

"No one is anywhere about," she explained. "If your bedrooms are finished, perhaps you might stay a tiny while. I thought—perhaps—you might like a piece of cake."

The next ten minutes seemed to Becky like a sort of delirium. Sara opened a cupboard, and gave her a thick slice of cake. She seemed to rejoice when it was devoured in hungry bites. She talked and asked questions, and laughed until Becky's fears actually began to calm themselves, and she once or twice gathered boldness enough to ask a question or so herself, daring as she felt it to be.

"Is that—" she ventured, looking longingly at the rose-colored frock. And she asked it almost in a whisper. "Is that there your best?"

"It is one of my dancing frocks," answered Sara. "I like it, don't you?"

For a few seconds Becky was almost speechless with admiration. Then she said in an awed voice, "Once I see a princess. I was standin' in the street with the crowd outside Covin' Garden, watchin' the swells go inter the operer. An' there was one everyone stared at most. They ses to each other, 'That's the princess.' She was a growed-up young lady, but she was pink all over—gownd an' cloak, an' flowers an' all. I called her to mind the minnit I see you, sittin' there on the table, miss. You looked like her."

"I've often thought," said Sara, in her reflecting voice, "that I should like to be a princess; I wonder what it feels like. I believe I will begin pretending I am one."

Becky stared at her admiringly, and, as before, did not understand her in the least. She watched her with a sort of adoration. Very soon Sara left her reflections and turned to her with a new question.

"Becky," she said, "weren't you listening to that story?"

"Yes, miss," confessed Becky, a little alarmed again. "I knowed I hadn't orter, but it was that beautiful I—I couldn't help it."

"I liked you to listen to it," said Sara. "If you tell stories, you like nothing so much as to tell them to people who want to listen. I don't know why it is. Would you like to hear the rest?"

Becky lost her breath again.

"Me hear it?" she cried. "Like as if I was a pupil, miss! All about the Prince—and the little white Mer-babies swimming about laughing—with stars in their hair?"

Sara nodded.

"You haven't time to hear it now, I'm afraid," she said; "but if you will tell me just what time you come to do my rooms, I will try to be here and tell you a bit of it every day until it is finished. It's a lovely long one—and I'm always putting new bits to it."

"Then," breathed Becky, devoutly, "I wouldn't mind *how* heavy the coal boxes was—or *what* the cook done to me, if—if I might have that to think of."

"You may," said Sara. "I'll tell it *all* to you."

When Becky went downstairs, she was not the same Becky who had staggered up, loaded down by the weight of the coal scuttle. She had an extra piece of cake in her pocket, and she had been fed and warmed, but not only by cake and fire. Something else had warmed and fed her, and the something else was Sara.

When she was gone Sara sat on her favorite perch on the end of her table. Her feet were on a chair, her elbows on her knees, and her chin in her hands.

"If I *was* a princess—a *real* princess," she murmured, "I could scatter largess to the populace. But even if I am only a pretend princess, I can invent little things to do for people. Things like this. She was just as happy as if it was largess. I'll pretend that to do things people like is scattering largess. I've scattered largess."

6

The Diamond Mines

Not very long after this a very exciting thing happened. Not only Sara, but the entire school, found it exciting, and made it the chief subject of conversation for weeks after it occurred. In one of his letters Captain Crewe told a most interesting story. A friend who had been at school with him when he was a boy had unexpectedly come to see him in India. He was the owner of a large tract of land upon which diamonds had been found, and he was engaged in developing the mines. If all went as was confidently expected, he would become possessed of such wealth as it made one dizzy to think of; and because he was fond of the friend of his school days, he had given him an opportunity to share in this enormous fortune by becoming a partner in his scheme. This, at least, was what Sara gathered from his letters. It is true that any other business scheme, however magnificent, would have had but small attraction for her or for the schoolroom; but "diamond mines" sounded so like the Arabian Nights that no one could be indifferent. Sara thought them enchanting, and painted pictures, for Ermengarde and Lottie, of labyrinthine passages in the bowels of the earth, where sparkling stones studded the walls and roofs and ceilings, and strange, dark men dug them out with heavy picks. Ermengarde delighted in the story, and Lottie insisted on its being retold to her every evening. Lavinia was very spiteful about it, and told Jessie that she didn't believe such things as diamond mines existed.

"My mamma has a diamond ring which cost forty pounds," she said. "And it is not a big one, either. If there were mines full of diamonds, people would be so rich it would be ridiculous."

"Perhaps Sara will be so rich that she will be ridiculous," giggled Jessie.

"She's ridiculous without being rich," Lavinia sniffed.

"I believe you hate her," said Jessie.

"No, I don't," snapped Lavinia. "But I don't believe in mines full of diamonds."

"Well, people have to get them from somewhere," said Jessie. "Lavinia," with a new giggle, "what do you think Gertrude says?"

"I don't know, I'm sure; and I don't care if it's something more about that everlasting Sara."

"Well, it is. One of her 'pretends' is that she is a princess. She plays it all the time—even in school. She says it makes her learn her lessons better. She wants Ermengarde to be one, too, but Ermengarde says she is too fat."

"She *is* too fat," said Lavinia. "And Sara is too thin."

Naturally, Jessie giggled again.

"She says it has nothing to do with what you look like, or what you have. It has only to do with what you *think* of, and what you *do*."

"I suppose she thinks she could be a princess if she was a beggar," said Lavinia. "Let us begin to call her Your Royal Highness."

Lessons for the day were over, and they were sitting before the schoolroom fire, enjoying the time they liked best. It was the time when Miss Minchin and Miss Amelia were taking their tea in the sitting room sacred to themselves. At this hour a great deal of talking was done, and a great many secrets changed hands, particularly if the younger pupils behaved themselves well, and did not squabble or run about noisily, which it must be confessed they usually did. When they made an uproar the older girls usually interfered with scolding and shakes. They were expected to keep order, and there was danger that if they did not, Miss Minchin or Miss Amelia would appear and put an end to festivities. Even as Lavinia spoke the door opened and Sara entered with Lottie, whose habit was to trot everywhere after her like a little dog.

"There she is, with that horrid child!" exclaimed Lavinia in a whisper. "If she's so fond of her, why doesn't she keep her in her own room? She will begin howling about something in five minutes."

It happened that Lottie had been seized with a sudden desire to play in the schoolroom, and had begged her adopted parent to come with her. She joined a group of little ones who were playing in a corner. Sara curled herself up in the window-seat, opened a book, and began to read. It was a book about the French Revolution, and she was soon lost in a harrowing picture of the prisoners in the Bastille—men who had spent so many years in dungeons that when they were dragged out by those who rescued them, their long, gray hair and beards almost hid their faces, and they had forgotten that an outside world existed at all, and were like beings in a dream.

She was so far away from the schoolroom that it was not agreeable to be dragged back suddenly by a howl from Lottie. Never did she find anything so difficult as to keep herself from losing her temper when she was suddenly disturbed while absorbed in a book. People who are fond of books know the feeling of irritation which sweeps over them at such a moment. The temptation to be unreasonable and snappish is one not easy to manage.

"It makes me feel as if someone had hit me," Sara had told Ermengarde once in confidence. "And as if I want to hit back. I have to remember things quickly to keep from saying something ill-tempered."

She had to remember things quickly when she laid her book on the window-seat and jumped down from her comfortable corner.

Lottie had been sliding across the schoolroom floor, and, having first irritated Lavinia and Jessie by making a noise, had ended by falling down and hurting her fat knee. She was screaming and dancing up and down in the midst of a group of friends and enemies, who were alternately coaxing and scolding her.

"Stop this minute, you cry-baby! Stop this minute!" Lavinia commanded.

"I'm not a cry-baby . . . . I'm not!" wailed Lottie. "Sara, Sa—ra!"

"If she doesn't stop, Miss Minchin will hear her," cried Jessie. "Lottie darling, I'll give you a penny!"

"I don't want your penny," sobbed Lottie; and she looked down at the fat knee, and, seeing a drop of blood on it, burst forth again.

Sara flew across the room and, kneeling down, put her arms round her.

"Now, Lottie," she said. "Now, Lottie, you *promised* Sara."

"She said I was a cry-baby," wept Lottie.

Sara patted her, but spoke in the steady voice Lottie knew.

"But if you cry, you will be one, Lottie pet. You *promised*." Lottie remembered that she had promised, but she preferred to lift up her voice.

"I haven't any mamma," she proclaimed. "I haven't—a bit—of mamma."

"Yes, you have," said Sara, cheerfully. "Have you forgotten? Don't you know that Sara is your mamma? Don't you want Sara for your mamma?"

Lottie cuddled up to her with a consoled sniff.

"Come and sit in the window-seat with me," Sara went on, "and I'll whisper a story to you."

"Will you?" whimpered Lottie. "Will you—tell me—about the diamond mines?"

"The diamond mines?" broke out Lavinia. "Nasty, little spoiled thing, I should like to *slap* her!"

Sara got up quickly on her feet. It must be remembered that she had been very deeply absorbed in the book about the Bastille, and she had had to recall several things rapidly when she realized that she must go and take care of her adopted child. She was not an angel, and she was not fond of Lavinia.

"Well," she said, with some fire, "I should like to slap *you*—but I don't want to slap you!" restraining herself. "At least I both want to slap you—and I should *like* to slap you—but I *won't* slap you. We are not little gutter children. We are both old enough to know better."

Here was Lavinia's opportunity.

"Ah, yes, your royal highness," she said. "We are princesses, I believe. At least one of us is. The school ought to be very fashionable now Miss Minchin has a princess for a pupil."

Sara started toward her. She looked as if she were going to box her ears. Perhaps she was. Her trick of pretending things was the joy of her life. She never spoke of it to girls she was not fond of. Her new "pretend" about being a princess was very near to her heart, and she was shy and sensitive about it. She had meant it to be rather a secret, and here was Lavinia deriding it before nearly all the school. She felt the blood rush up into her face and tingle in her ears. She only just saved herself. If you were a princess, you did not fly into rages. Her hand dropped, and she stood quite still a moment. When she spoke it was in a quiet, steady voice; she held her head up, and everybody listened to her.

"It's true," she said. "Sometimes I do pretend I am a princess. I pretend I am a princess, so that I can try and behave like one."

Lavinia could not think of exactly the right thing to say. Several times she had found that she could not think of a satisfactory reply when she was dealing with Sara. The reason for this was that, somehow, the rest always seemed to be vaguely in sympathy with her opponent. She saw now that they were pricking up their ears interestedly. The truth was, they liked princesses, and they all hoped they might hear something more definite about this one, and drew nearer Sara accordingly.

Lavinia could only invent one remark, and it fell rather flat.

"Dear me," she said, "I hope, when you ascend the throne, you won't forget us!"

"I won't," said Sara, and she did not utter another word, but stood quite still, and stared at her steadily as she saw her take Jessie's arm and turn away.

After this, the girls who were jealous of her used to speak of her as "Princess Sara" whenever they wished to be particularly disdainful, and those who were fond of her gave her the name among themselves as a term of affection. No one called her "princess" instead of "Sara," but her adorers were much pleased with the picturesqueness and grandeur of the title, and Miss Minchin, hearing of it, mentioned it more than once to visiting parents, feeling that it rather suggested a sort of royal boarding school.

To Becky it seemed the most appropriate thing in the world. The acquaintance begun on the foggy afternoon when she had jumped up terrified from her sleep in the comfortable chair, had ripened and grown, though it must be confessed that Miss Minchin and Miss Amelia knew very little about it. They were aware that Sara was "kind" to the scullery maid, but they knew nothing of certain delightful moments snatched perilously when, the upstairs rooms being set in order with lightning rapidity, Sara's sitting room was reached, and the heavy coal box set down with a sigh of joy. At such times stories were told by installments, things of a satisfying nature were either produced and eaten or hastily tucked into pockets to be disposed of at night, when Becky went upstairs to her attic to bed.

"But I has to eat 'em careful, miss," she said once; "'cos if I leaves crumbs the rats come out to get 'em."

"Rats!" exclaimed Sara, in horror. "Are there *rats* there?"

"Lots of 'em, miss," Becky answered in quite a matter-of-fact manner. "There mostly is rats an' mice in attics. You gets used to the noise they makes scuttling about. I've got so I don't mind 'em s' long as they don't run over my piller."

"Ugh!" said Sara.

"You gets used to anythin' after a bit," said Becky. "You have to, miss, if you're born a scullery maid. I'd rather have rats than cockroaches."

"So would I," said Sara; "I suppose you might make friends with a rat in time, but I don't believe I should like to make friends with a cockroach."

Sometimes Becky did not dare to spend more than a few minutes in the bright, warm room, and when this was the case perhaps only a few words could be exchanged, and a small purchase slipped into the old-fashioned pocket Becky carried under her dress skirt, tied round her waist with a band of tape. The search for and discovery of satisfying things to eat which could be packed into small compass, added a new interest to Sara's existence. When she drove or walked out, she used to look into shop windows eagerly. The first time it occurred to her to bring home two or three little meat pies, she felt that she had hit upon a discovery. When she exhibited them, Becky's eyes quite sparkled.

"Oh, miss!" she murmured. "Them will be nice an' fillin'. It's fillin'ness that's best. Sponge cake's a 'evenly thing, but it melts away like—if you understand, miss. These'll just *stay* in yer stummick."

"Well," hesitated Sara, "I don't think it would be good if they stayed always, but I do believe they will be satisfying."

They were satisfying—and so were beef sandwiches, bought at a cook-shop—and so were rolls and Bologna sausage. In time, Becky began to lose her hungry, tired feeling, and the coal box did not seem so unbearably heavy.

However heavy it was, and whatsoever the temper of the cook, and the hardness of the work heaped upon her shoulders, she had always the chance of the afternoon to look forward to—the chance that Miss Sara would be able to be in her sitting room. In fact, the mere seeing of Miss Sara would have been enough without meat pies. If there was time only for a few words, they were always friendly, merry words that put heart into one; and if there was time for more, then there was an installment of a story to be told, or some other thing one remembered afterward and sometimes lay awake in one's bed in the attic to think over. Sara—who was only doing what she unconsciously liked better than anything else, Nature having made her for a giver—had not the least idea what she meant to poor Becky, and how wonderful a benefactor she seemed. If Nature has made you for a giver, your hands are born open, and so is your heart; and though there may be times when your hands are empty, your heart is always full, and you can give things out of that—warm things, kind things, sweet things—help and comfort and laughter—and sometimes gay, kind laughter is the best help of all.

Becky had scarcely known what laughter was through all her poor, little hard-driven life. Sara made her laugh, and laughed with her; and, though neither of them quite knew it, the laughter was as "fillin'" as the meat pies.

A few weeks before Sara's eleventh birthday a letter came to her from her father, which did not seem to be written in such boyish high spirits as usual. He was not very well, and was evidently overweighted by the business connected with the diamond mines.

"You see, little Sara," he wrote, "your daddy is not a businessman at all, and figures and documents bother him. He does not really understand them, and all this seems so enormous. Perhaps, if I was not feverish I should not be awake, tossing about, one half of the night and spend the other half in troublesome dreams. If my little missus were here, I dare say she would give me some solemn, good advice. You would, wouldn't you, Little Missus?"

One of his many jokes had been to call her his "little missus" because she had such an old-fashioned air.

He had made wonderful preparations for her birthday. Among other things, a new doll had been ordered in Paris, and her wardrobe was to be, indeed, a marvel of splendid perfection. When she had replied to the letter asking her if the doll would be an acceptable present, Sara had been very quaint.

"I am getting very old," she wrote; "you see, I shall never live to have another doll given me. This will be my last doll. There is something solemn about it. If I could write poetry, I am sure a poem about 'A Last Doll' would be very nice. But I cannot write poetry. I have tried, and it made me laugh. It did not sound like Watts or Coleridge or Shakespeare at all. No one could ever take Emily's place, but I should respect the Last Doll very much; and I am sure the school would love it. They all like dolls, though some of the big ones—the almost fifteen ones—pretend they are too grown up."

Captain Crewe had a splitting headache when he read this letter in his bungalow in India. The table before him was heaped with papers and letters which were alarming him and filling him with anxious dread, but he laughed as he had not laughed for weeks.

"Oh," he said, "she's better fun every year she lives. God grant this business may right itself and leave me free to run home and see her. What wouldn't I give to have her little arms round my neck this minute! What *wouldn't* I give!"

The birthday was to be celebrated by great festivities. The schoolroom was to be decorated, and there was to be a party. The boxes containing the presents were to be opened with great ceremony, and there was to be a glittering feast spread in Miss

Minchin's sacred room. When the day arrived the whole house was in a whirl of excitement. How the morning passed nobody quite knew, because there seemed such preparations to be made. The schoolroom was being decked with garlands of holly; the desks had been moved away, and red covers had been put on the forms which were arrayed round the room against the wall.

When Sara went into her sitting room in the morning, she found on the table a small, dumpy package, tied up in a piece of brown paper. She knew it was a present, and she thought she could guess whom it came from. She opened it quite tenderly. It was a square pincushion, made of not quite clean red flannel, and black pins had been stuck carefully into it to form the words, "Menny hapy returns."

"Oh!" cried Sara, with a warm feeling in her heart. "What pains she has taken! I like it so, it—it makes me feel sorrowful."

But the next moment she was mystified. On the under side of the pincushion was secured a card, bearing in neat letters the name "Miss Amelia Minchin."

Sara turned it over and over.

"Miss Amelia!" she said to herself "How *can* it be!"

And just at that very moment she heard the door being cautiously pushed open and saw Becky peeping round it.

There was an affectionate, happy grin on her face, and she shuffled forward and stood nervously pulling at her fingers.

"Do yer like it, Miss Sara?" she said. "Do yer?"

"Like it?" cried Sara. "You darling Becky, you made it all yourself."

Becky gave a hysteric but joyful sniff, and her eyes looked quite moist with delight.

"It ain't nothin' but flannin, an' the flannin ain't new; but I wanted to give yer somethin' an' I made it of nights. I knew yer could *pretend* it was satin with diamond pins in. *I* tried to when I was makin' it. The card, miss," rather doubtfully; "'t warn't wrong of me to pick it up out o' the dust-bin, was it? Miss 'Meliar had throwed it away. I hadn't no card o' my own, an' I knowed it wouldn't be a proper presink if I didn't pin a card on—so I pinned Miss 'Meliar's."

Sara flew at her and hugged her. She could not have told herself or anyone else why there was a lump in her throat.

"Oh, Becky!" she cried out, with a queer little laugh, "I love you, Becky—I do, I do!"

"Oh, miss!" breathed Becky. "Thank yer, miss, kindly; it ain't good enough for that. The—the flannin wasn't new."

7

The Diamond Mines Again

When Sara entered the holly-hung schoolroom in the afternoon, she did so as the head of a sort of procession. Miss Minchin, in her grandest silk dress, led her by the hand. A manservant followed, carrying the box containing the Last Doll, a housemaid carried a second box, and Becky brought up the rear, carrying a third and wearing a clean apron and a new cap. Sara would have much preferred to enter in the usual way, but Miss Minchin had sent for her, and, after an interview in her private sitting room, had expressed her wishes.

"This is not an ordinary occasion," she said. "I do not desire that it should be treated as one."

So Sara was led grandly in and felt shy when, on her entry, the big girls stared at her and touched each other's elbows, and the little ones began to squirm joyously in their seats.

"Silence, young ladies!" said Miss Minchin, at the murmur which arose. "James, place the box on the table and remove the lid. Emma, put yours upon a chair. Becky!" suddenly and severely.

Becky had quite forgotten herself in her excitement, and was grinning at Lottie, who was wriggling with rapturous expectation. She almost dropped her box, the disapproving voice so startled her, and her frightened, bobbing curtsy of apology was so funny that Lavinia and Jessie tittered.

"It is not your place to look at the young ladies," said Miss Minchin. "You forget yourself. Put your box down."

Becky obeyed with alarmed haste and hastily backed toward the door.

"You may leave us," Miss Minchin announced to the servants with a wave of her hand.

Becky stepped aside respectfully to allow the superior servants to pass out first. She could not help casting a longing glance at the box on the table. Something made of blue satin was peeping from between the folds of tissue paper.

"If you please, Miss Minchin," said Sara, suddenly, "mayn't Becky stay?"

It was a bold thing to do. Miss Minchin was betrayed into something like a slight jump. Then she put her eyeglass up, and gazed at her show pupil disturbedly.

"Becky!" she exclaimed. "My dearest Sara!"

Sara advanced a step toward her.

"I want her because I know she will like to see the presents," she explained. "She is a little girl, too, you know."

Miss Minchin was scandalized. She glanced from one figure to the other.

"My dear Sara," she said, "Becky is the scullery maid. Scullery maids—er—are not little girls."

It really had not occurred to her to think of them in that light. Scullery maids were machines who carried coal scuttles and made fires.

"But Becky is," said Sara. "And I know she would enjoy herself. Please let her stay—because it is my birthday."

Miss Minchin replied with much dignity:

"As you ask it as a birthday favor—she may stay. Rebecca, thank Miss Sara for her great kindness."

Becky had been backing into the corner, twisting the hem of her apron in delighted suspense. She came forward, bobbing curtsies, but between Sara's eyes and her own there passed a gleam of friendly understanding, while her words tumbled over each other.

"Oh, if you please, miss! I'm that grateful, miss! I did want to see the doll, miss, that I did. Thank you, miss. And thank you, ma'am,"—turning and making an alarmed bob to Miss Minchin—"for letting me take the liberty."

Miss Minchin waved her hand again—this time it was in the direction of the corner near the door.

"Go and stand there," she commanded. "Not too near the young ladies."

Becky went to her place, grinning. She did not care where she was sent, so that she might have the luck of being inside the room, instead of being downstairs in the scullery, while these delights were going on. She did not even mind when Miss Minchin cleared her throat ominously and spoke again.

"Now, young ladies, I have a few words to say to you," she announced.

"She's going to make a speech," whispered one of the girls. "I wish it was over."

Sara felt rather uncomfortable. As this was her party, it was probable that the speech was about her. It is not agreeable to stand in a schoolroom and have a speech made about you.

"You are aware, young ladies," the speech began—for it was a speech—"that dear Sara is eleven years old today."

"*Dear* Sara!" murmured Lavinia.

"Several of you here have also been eleven years old, but Sara's birthdays are rather different from other little girls' birthdays. When she is older she will be heiress to a large fortune, which it will be her duty to spend in a meritorious manner."

"The diamond mines," giggled Jessie, in a whisper.

Sara did not hear her; but as she stood with her green-gray eyes fixed steadily on Miss Minchin, she felt herself growing rather hot. When Miss Minchin talked about money, she felt somehow that she always hated her—and, of course, it was disrespectful to hate grown-up people.

"When her dear papa, Captain Crewe, brought her from India

and gave her into my care," the speech proceeded, "he said to me, in a jesting way, 'I am afraid she will be very rich, Miss Minchin.' My reply was, 'Her education at my seminary, Captain Crewe, shall be such as will adorn the largest fortune.' Sara has become my most accomplished pupil. Her French and her dancing are a credit to the seminary. Her manners—which have caused you to call her Princess Sara—are perfect. Her amiability she exhibits by giving you this afternoon's party. I hope you appreciate her generosity. I wish you to express your appreciation of it by saying aloud all together, 'Thank you, Sara!'"

The entire schoolroom rose to its feet as it had done the morning Sara remembered so well.

"Thank you, Sara!" it said, and it must be confessed that Lottie jumped up and down. Sara looked rather shy for a moment. She made a curtsy—and it was a very nice one.

"Thank you," she said, "for coming to my party."

"Very pretty, indeed, Sara," approved Miss Minchin. "That is what a real princess does when the populace applauds her. Lavinia"—scathingly—"the sound you just made was extremely like a snort. If you are jealous of your fellow-pupil, I beg you will express your feelings in some more lady-like manner. Now I will leave you to enjoy yourselves."

The instant she had swept out of the room the spell her presence always had upon them was broken. The door had scarcely closed before every seat was empty. The little girls jumped or tumbled out of theirs; the older ones wasted no time in deserting theirs. There was a rush toward the boxes. Sara had bent over one of them with a delighted face.

"These are books, I know," she said.

The little children broke into a rueful murmur, and Ermengarde looked aghast.

"Does your papa send you books for a birthday present?" she exclaimed. "Why, he's as bad as mine. Don't open them, Sara."

"I like them," Sara laughed, but she turned to the biggest box. When she took out the Last Doll it was so magnificent that the children uttered delighted groans of joy, and actually drew back to gaze at it in breathless rapture.

"She is almost as big as Lottie," someone gasped.

Lottie clapped her hands and danced about, giggling.

"She's dressed for the theater," said Lavinia. "Her cloak is lined with ermine."

"Oh," cried Ermengarde, darting forward, "she has an opera-glass in her hand—a blue-and-gold one!"

"Here is her trunk," said Sara. "Let us open it and look at her things."

She sat down upon the floor and turned the key. The children crowded clamoring around her, as she lifted tray after tray and revealed their contents. Never had the schoolroom been in such an uproar. There were lace collars and silk stockings and handkerchiefs; there was a jewel case containing a necklace and a tiara which looked quite as if they were made of real diamonds; there was a long sealskin and muff, there were ball dresses and walking dresses and visiting dresses; there were hats and tea gowns and fans. Even Lavinia and Jessie forgot that they were too elderly to care for dolls, and uttered exclamations of delight and caught up things to look at them.

"Suppose," Sara said, as she stood by the table, putting a large, black-velvet hat on the impassively smiling owner of all these splendors—"suppose she understands human talk and feels proud of being admired."

"You are always supposing things," said Lavinia, and her air was very superior.

"I know I am," answered Sara, undisturbedly. "I like it. There is nothing so nice as supposing. It's almost like being a fairy. If you suppose anything hard enough it seems as if it were real."

"It's all very well to suppose things if you have everything," said Lavinia. "Could you suppose and pretend if you were a beggar and lived in a garret?"

Sara stopped arranging the Last Doll's ostrich plumes, and looked thoughtful.

"I *believe* I could," she said. "If one was a beggar, one would have to suppose and pretend all the time. But it mightn't be easy."

She often thought afterward how strange it was that just as she had finished saying this—just at that very moment—Miss Amelia came into the room.

"Sara," she said, "your papa's solicitor, Mr. Barrow, has called to see Miss Minchin, and, as she must talk to him alone and the refreshments are laid in her parlor, you had all better come and have your feast now, so that my sister can have her interview here in the schoolroom."

Refreshments were not likely to be disdained at any hour, and many pairs of eyes gleamed. Miss Amelia arranged the procession into decorum, and then, with Sara at her side heading it, she led it away, leaving the Last Doll sitting upon a chair with the glories of her wardrobe scattered about her; dresses and coats hung upon chair backs, piles of lace-frilled petticoats lying upon their seats.

Becky, who was not expected to partake of refreshments, had the indiscretion to linger a moment to look at these beauties—it really was an indiscretion.

"Go back to your work, Becky," Miss Amelia had said; but she had stopped to pick up reverently first a muff and then a coat, and while she stood looking at them adoringly, she heard Miss Minchin upon the threshold, and, being smitten with terror at the thought of being accused of taking liberties, she rashly darted under the table, which hid her by its tablecloth.

Miss Minchin came into the room, accompanied by a sharp-featured, dry little gentleman, who looked rather disturbed. Miss Minchin herself also looked rather disturbed, it must be admitted, and she gazed at the dry little gentleman with an irritated and puzzled expression.

She sat down with stiff dignity, and waved him to a chair.

"Pray, be seated, Mr. Barrow," she said.

Mr. Barrow did not sit down at once. His attention seemed attracted by the Last Doll and the things which surrounded her. He settled his eyeglasses and looked at them in nervous disapproval. The Last Doll herself did not seem to mind this in the least. She merely sat upright and returned his gaze indifferently.

"A hundred pounds," Mr. Barrow remarked succinctly. "All expensive material, and made at a Parisian modiste's. He spent money lavishly enough, that young man."

Miss Minchin felt offended. This seemed to be a disparagement of her best patron and was a liberty.

Even solicitors had no right to take liberties.

"I beg your pardon, Mr. Barrow," she said stiffly. "I do not understand."

"Birthday presents," said Mr. Barrow in the same critical manner, "to a child eleven years old! Mad extravagance, I call it."

Miss Minchin drew herself up still more rigidly.

"Captain Crewe is a man of fortune," she said. "The diamond mines alone—"

Mr. Barrow wheeled round upon her. "Diamond mines!" he broke out. "There are none! Never were!"

Miss Minchin actually got up from her chair.

"What!" she cried. "What do you mean?"

"At any rate," answered Mr. Barrow, quite snappishly, "it would have been much better if there never had been any."

"Any diamond mines?" ejaculated Miss Minchin, catching at the back of a chair and feeling as if a splendid dream was fading away from her.

"Diamond mines spell ruin oftener than they spell wealth," said Mr. Barrow. "When a man is in the hands of a very dear friend and is not a businessman himself, he had better steer clear of the dear friend's diamond mines, or gold mines, or any other kind of mines dear friends want his money to put into. The late Captain Crewe—"

Here Miss Minchin stopped him with a gasp.

"The *late* Captain Crewe!" she cried out. "The *late*! You don't come to tell me that Captain Crewe is—"

"He's dead, ma'am," Mr. Barrow answered with jerky brusqueness. "Died of jungle fever and business troubles combined. The jungle fever might not have killed him if he had not been driven mad by the business troubles, and the business troubles might not have put an end to him if the jungle fever had not assisted. Captain Crewe is dead!"

Miss Minchin dropped into her chair again. The words he had spoken filled her with alarm.

"What *were* his business troubles?" she said. "What *were* they?"

"Diamond mines," answered Mr. Barrow, "and dear friends—and ruin."

Miss Minchin lost her breath.

"Ruin!" she gasped out.

"Lost every penny. That young man had too much money. The dear friend was mad on the subject of the diamond mine. He put all his own money into it, and all Captain Crewe's. Then the dear friend ran away—Captain Crewe was already stricken with fever when the news came. The shock was too much for him. He died delirious, raving about his little girl—and didn't leave a penny."

Now Miss Minchin understood, and never had she received such a blow in her life. Her show pupil, her show patron, swept away from the Select Seminary at one blow. She felt as if she had been outraged and robbed, and that Captain Crewe and Sara and Mr. Barrow were equally to blame.

"Do you mean to tell me," she cried out, "that he left *nothing*! That Sara will have no fortune! That the child is a beggar! That she is left on my hands a little pauper instead of an heiress?"

Mr. Barrow was a shrewd businessman, and felt it as well to make his own freedom from responsibility quite clear without any delay.

"She is certainly left a beggar," he replied. "And she is certainly left on your hands, ma'am—as she hasn't a relation in the world that we know of."

Miss Minchin started forward. She looked as if she was going to open the door and rush out of the room to stop the festivities going on joyfully and rather noisily that moment over the refreshments.

"It is monstrous!" she said. "She's in my sitting room at this moment, dressed in silk gauze and lace petticoats, giving a party at my expense."

"She's giving it at your expense, madam, if she's giving it," said Mr. Barrow, calmly. "Barrow & Skipworth are not responsible for anything. There never was a cleaner sweep made of a man's fortune. Captain Crewe died without paying *our* last bill—and it was a big one."

Miss Minchin turned back from the door in increased indignation. This was worse than anyone could have dreamed of its being.

"That is what has happened to me!" she cried. "I was always so sure of his payments that I went to all sorts of ridiculous expenses for the child. I paid the bills for that ridiculous doll and her ridiculous fantastic wardrobe. The child was to have anything she wanted. She has a carriage and a pony and a maid, and I've paid for all of them since the last cheque came."

Mr. Barrow evidently did not intend to remain to listen to the story of Miss Minchin's grievances after he had made the position of his firm clear and related the mere dry facts. He did not feel any particular sympathy for irate keepers of boarding schools.

"You had better not pay for anything more, ma'am," he remarked, "unless you want to make presents to the young lady. No one will remember you. She hasn't a brass farthing to call her own."

"But what am I to do?" demanded Miss Minchin, as if she felt it entirely his duty to make the matter right. "What am I to do?"

"There isn't anything to do," said Mr. Barrow, folding up his eyeglasses and slipping them into his pocket. "Captain Crewe is dead. The child is left a pauper. Nobody is responsible for her but you."

"I am not responsible for her, and I refuse to be made responsible!"

Miss Minchin became quite white with rage.

Mr. Barrow turned to go.

"I have nothing to do with that, madam," he said uninterestedly. "Barrow & Skipworth are not responsible. Very sorry the thing has happened, of course."

"If you think she is to be foisted off on me, you are greatly mistaken," Miss Minchin gasped. "I have been robbed and cheated; I will turn her into the street!"

If she had not been so furious, she would have been too discreet to say quite so much. She saw herself burdened with an extravagantly brought-up child whom she had always resented, and she lost all self-control.

Mr. Barrow undisturbedly moved toward the door.

"I wouldn't do that, madam," he commented; "it wouldn't look well. Unpleasant story to get about in connection with the establishment. Pupil bundled out penniless and without friends."

He was a clever business man, and he knew what he was saying. He also knew that Miss Minchin was a businesswoman, and would be shrewd enough to see the truth. She could not afford to do a thing which would make people speak of her as cruel and hard-hearted.

"Better keep her and make use of her," he added. "She's a clever child, I believe. You can get a good deal out of her as she grows older."

"I will get a good deal out of her before she grows older!" exclaimed Miss Minchin.

"I am sure you will, ma'am," said Mr. Barrow, with a little sinister smile. "I am sure you will. Good morning!"

He bowed himself out and closed the door, and it must be confessed that Miss Minchin stood for a few moments and glared at it. What he had said was quite true. She knew it. She had absolutely no redress. Her show pupil had melted into nothingness, leaving only a friendless, beggared little girl. Such money as she herself had advanced was lost and could not be regained.

And as she stood there breathless under her sense of injury, there fell upon her ears a burst of gay voices from her own sacred room, which had actually been given up to the feast. She could at least stop this.

But as she started toward the door it was opened by Miss Amelia, who, when she caught sight of the changed, angry face, fell back a step in alarm.

"What *is* the matter, sister?" she ejaculated.

Miss Minchin's voice was almost fierce when she answered:

"Where is Sara Crewe?"

Miss Amelia was bewildered.

"Sara!" she stammered. "Why, she's with the children in your room, of course."

"Has she a black frock in her sumptuous wardrobe?"—in bitter irony.

"A black frock?" Miss Amelia stammered again. "*A black* one?"

"She has frocks of every other color. Has she a black one?"

Miss Amelia began to turn pale.

"No—ye-es!" she said. "But it is too short for her. She has only the old black velvet, and she has outgrown it."

"Go and tell her to take off that preposterous pink silk gauze, and put the black one on, whether it is too short or not. She has done with finery!"

Then Miss Amelia began to wring her fat hands and cry.

"Oh, sister!" she sniffed. "Oh, sister! What *can* have happened?"

Miss Minchin wasted no words.

"Captain Crewe is dead," she said. "He has died without a penny. That spoiled, pampered, fanciful child is left a pauper on my hands."

Miss Amelia sat down quite heavily in the nearest chair.

"Hundreds of pounds have I spent on nonsense for her. And I shall never see a penny of it. Put a stop to this ridiculous party of hers. Go and make her change her frock at once."

"I?" panted Miss Amelia. "M-must I go and tell her now?"

"This moment!" was the fierce answer. "Don't sit staring like a goose. Go!"

Poor Miss Amelia was accustomed to being called a goose. She knew, in fact, that she was rather a goose, and that it was left to geese to do a great many disagreeable things. It was a somewhat embarrassing thing to go into the midst of a room full of delighted children, and tell the giver of the feast that she had suddenly been transformed into a little beggar, and must go upstairs and put on an old black frock which was too small for her. But the thing must be done. This was evidently not the time when questions might be asked.

She rubbed her eyes with her handkerchief until they looked quite red. After which she got up and went out of the room, without venturing to say another word. When her older sister looked and spoke as she had done just now, the wisest course to pursue was to obey orders without any comment. Miss Minchin walked across the room. She spoke to herself aloud without knowing that she was doing it. During the last year the story of the diamond mines had suggested all sorts of possibilities to her. Even proprietors of seminaries might make fortunes in stocks, with the aid of owners of mines. And now, instead of looking forward to gains, she was left to look back upon losses.

"The Princess Sara, indeed!" she said. "The child has been pampered as if she were a *queen*." She was sweeping angrily past the corner table as she said it, and the next moment she started at the sound of a loud, sobbing sniff which issued from under the cover.

"What is that!" she exclaimed angrily. The loud, sobbing sniff was heard again, and she stooped and raised the hanging folds of the table cover.

"How *dare* you!" she cried out. "*How dare* you! Come out immediately!"

It was poor Becky who crawled out, and her cap was knocked on one side, and her face was red with repressed crying.

"If you please, 'm—it's me, mum," she explained. "I know I hadn't ought to. But I was lookin' at the doll, mum—an' I was frightened when you come in—an' slipped under the table."

"You have been there all the time, listening," said Miss Minchin.

"No, mum," Becky protested, bobbing curtsies. "Not listenin'—I thought I could slip out without your noticin', but I couldn't an' I had to stay. But I didn't listen, mum—I wouldn't for nothin'. But I couldn't help hearin'."

Suddenly it seemed almost as if she lost all fear of the awful lady before her. She burst into fresh tears.

"Oh, please, 'm," she said; "I dare say you'll give me warnin', mum—but I'm so sorry for poor Miss Sara—I'm so sorry!"

"Leave the room!" ordered Miss Minchin.

Becky curtsied again, the tears openly streaming down her cheeks.

"Yes, 'm; I will, 'm," she said, trembling; "but oh, I just wanted to arst you: Miss Sara—she's been such a rich young lady, an' she's been waited on, 'and and foot; an' what will she do now, mum, without no maid? If—if, oh please, would you let me wait on her after I've done my pots an' kettles? I'd do 'em that quick—if you'd let me wait on her now she's poor. Oh," breaking out afresh, "poor little Miss Sara, mum—that was called a princess."

Somehow, she made Miss Minchin feel more angry than ever. That the very scullery maid should range herself on the side of this child—whom she realized more fully than ever that she had never liked—was too much. She actually stamped her foot.

"No—certainly not," she said. "She will wait on herself, and on other people, too. Leave the room this instant, or you'll leave your place."

Becky threw her apron over her head and fled. She ran out of the room and down the steps into the scullery, and there she sat down among her pots and kettles, and wept as if her heart would break.

"It's exactly like the ones in the stories," she wailed. "Them pore princess ones that was drove into the world."

Miss Minchin had never looked quite so still and hard as she did when Sara came to her, a few hours later, in response to a message she had sent her.

Even by that time it seemed to Sara as if the birthday party had either been a dream or a thing which had happened years ago, and had happened in the life of quite another little girl.

Every sign of the festivities had been swept away; the holly had been removed from the schoolroom walls, and the forms and desks put back into their places. Miss Minchin's sitting room looked as it always did—all traces of the feast were gone, and Miss Minchin had resumed her usual dress. The pupils had been ordered to lay aside their party frocks; and this having been done, they had returned to the schoolroom and huddled together in groups, whispering and talking excitedly.

"Tell Sara to come to my room," Miss Minchin had said to her sister. "And explain to her clearly that I will have no crying or unpleasant scenes."

"Sister," replied Miss Amelia, "she is the strangest child I ever saw. She has actually made no fuss at all. You remember she made none when Captain Crewe went back to India. When I told her what had happened, she just stood quite still and looked at me without making a sound. Her eyes seemed to get bigger and bigger, and she went quite pale. When I had finished, she still stood staring for a few seconds, and then her chin began to shake, and she turned round and ran out of the room and upstairs. Several of the other children began to cry, but she did not seem to hear them or to be alive to anything but just what I was saying. It made me feel quite queer not to be answered; and when you tell anything sudden and strange, you expect people will say *something*—whatever it is."

Nobody but Sara herself ever knew what had happened in her room after she had run upstairs and locked her door. In fact, she herself scarcely remembered anything but that she walked up and down, saying over and over again to herself in a voice which did not seem her own, "My papa is dead! My papa is dead!"

Once she stopped before Emily, who sat watching her from her chair, and cried out wildly, "Emily! Do you hear? Do you hear—papa is dead? He is dead in India—thousands of miles away."

When she came into Miss Minchin's sitting room in answer to her summons, her face was white and her eyes had dark rings around them. Her mouth was set as if she did not wish it to reveal what she had suffered and was suffering. She did not look in the least like the rose-colored butterfly child who had flown about from one of her treasures to the other in the decorated schoolroom. She looked instead a strange, desolate, almost grotesque little figure.

She had put on, without Mariette's help, the cast-aside black-velvet frock. It was too short and tight, and her slender legs looked long and thin, showing themselves from beneath the brief skirt. As she had not found a piece of black ribbon, her short, thick, black hair tumbled loosely about her face and contrasted strongly with its pallor. She held Emily tightly in one arm, and Emily was swathed in a piece of black material.

"Put down your doll," said Miss Minchin. "What do you mean by bringing her here?"

"No," Sara answered. "I will not put her down. She is all I have. My papa gave her to me."

She had always made Miss Minchin feel secretly uncomfortable, and she did so now. She did not speak with rudeness so much as with a cold steadiness with which Miss Minchin felt it difficult to cope—perhaps because she knew she was doing a heartless and inhuman thing.

"You will have no time for dolls in future," she said. "You will have to work and improve yourself and make yourself useful."

Sara kept her big, strange eyes fixed on her, and said not a word.

"Everything will be very different now," Miss Minchin went on. "I suppose Miss Amelia has explained matters to you."

"Yes," answered Sara. "My papa is dead. He left me no money. I am quite poor."

"You are a beggar," said Miss Minchin, her temper rising at the recollection of what all this meant. "It appears that you have no relations and no home, and no one to take care of you."

For a moment the thin, pale little face twitched, but Sara again said nothing.

"What are you staring at?" demanded Miss Minchin, sharply. "Are you so stupid that you cannot understand? I tell you that you are quite alone in the world, and have no one to do anything for you, unless I choose to keep you here out of charity."

"I understand," answered Sara, in a low tone; and there was a sound as if she had gulped down something which rose in her throat. "I understand."

"That doll," cried Miss Minchin, pointing to the splendid birthday gift seated near—"that ridiculous doll, with all her nonsensical, extravagant things—*I* actually paid the bill for her!"

Sara turned her head toward the chair.

"The Last Doll," she said. "The Last Doll." And her little mournful voice had an odd sound.

"The Last Doll, indeed!" said Miss Minchin. "And she is mine, not yours. Everything you own is mine."

"Please take it away from me, then," said Sara. "I do not want it."

If she had cried and sobbed and seemed frightened, Miss Minchin might almost have had more patience with her. She was a woman who liked to domineer and feel her power, and as she looked at Sara's pale little steadfast face and heard her proud little voice, she quite felt as if her might was being set at naught.

"Don't put on grand airs," she said. "The time for that sort of thing is past. You are not a princess any longer. Your carriage and your pony will be sent away—your maid will be dismissed. You will wear your oldest and plainest clothes—your extravagant ones are no longer suited to your station. You are like Becky—you must work for your living."

To her surprise, a faint gleam of light came into the child's eyes—a shade of relief.

"Can I work?" she said. "If I can work it will not matter so much. What can I do?"

"You can do anything you are told," was the answer. "You are a sharp child, and pick up things readily. If you make yourself useful I may let you stay here. You speak French well, and you can help with the younger children."

"May I?" exclaimed Sara. "Oh, please let me! I know I can teach them. I like them, and they like me."

"Don't talk nonsense about people liking you," said Miss Minchin. "You will have to do more than teach the little ones. You will run errands and help in the kitchen as well as in the schoolroom. If you don't please me, you will be sent away. Remember that. Now go."

Sara stood still just a moment, looking at her. In her young soul, she was thinking deep and strange things. Then she turned to leave the room.

"Stop!" said Miss Minchin. "Don't you intend to thank me?"

Sara paused, and all the deep, strange thoughts surged up in her breast.

"What for?" she said.

"For my kindness to you," replied Miss Minchin. "For my kindness in giving you a home."

Sara made two or three steps toward her. Her thin little chest heaved up and down, and she spoke in a strange un-childishly fierce way.

"You are not kind," she said. "You are *not* kind, and it is *not* a home." And she had turned and run out of the room before Miss Minchin could stop her or do anything but stare after her with stony anger.

She went up the stairs slowly, but panting for breath and she held Emily tightly against her side.

"I wish she could talk," she said to herself. "If she could speak—if she could speak!"

She meant to go to her room and lie down on the tiger-skin, with her cheek upon the great cat's head, and look into the fire and think and think and think. But just before she reached the landing Miss Amelia came out of the door and closed it behind her, and stood before it, looking nervous and awkward. The truth was that she felt secretly ashamed of the thing she had been ordered to do.

"You—you are not to go in there," she said.

"Not go in?" exclaimed Sara, and she fell back a pace.

"That is not your room now," Miss Amelia answered, reddening a little.

Somehow, all at once, Sara understood. She realized that this was the beginning of the change Miss Minchin had spoken of.

"Where is my room?" she asked, hoping very much that her voice did not shake.

"You are to sleep in the attic next to Becky."

Sara knew where it was. Becky had told her about it. She turned, and mounted up two flights of stairs. The last one was narrow, and covered with shabby strips of old carpet. She felt as if she were walking away and leaving far behind her the world in which that other child, who no longer seemed herself, had lived. This child, in her short, tight old frock, climbing the stairs to the attic, was quite a different creature.

When she reached the attic door and opened it, her heart gave a dreary little thump. Then she shut the door and stood against it and looked about her.

Yes, this was another world. The room had a slanting roof and was whitewashed. The whitewash was dingy and had fallen off in places. There was a rusty grate, an old iron bedstead, and a hard bed covered with a faded coverlet. Some pieces of furniture too much worn to be used downstairs had been sent up. Under the skylight in the roof, which showed nothing but an oblong piece of dull gray sky, there stood an old battered red footstool. Sara went to it and sat down. She seldom cried. She did not cry now. She laid Emily across her knees and put her face down upon her and her arms around her, and sat there, her little black head resting on the black draperies, not saying one word, not making one sound.

And as she sat in this silence there came a low tap at the door—such a low, humble one that she did not at first hear it, and, indeed, was not roused until the door was timidly pushed open and a poor tear-smeared face appeared peeping round it. It was Becky's face, and Becky had been crying furtively for hours and rubbing her eyes with her kitchen apron until she looked strange indeed.

"Oh, miss," she said under her breath. "Might I—would you allow me—jest to come in?"

Sara lifted her head and looked at her. She tried to begin a smile, and somehow she could not. Suddenly—and it was all through the loving mournfulness of Becky's streaming eyes—her face looked more like a child's not so much too old for her years. She held out her hand and gave a little sob.

"Oh, Becky," she said. "I told you we were just the same—only two little girls—just two little girls. You see how true it is. There's no difference now. I'm not a princess anymore."

Becky ran to her and caught her hand, and hugged it to her breast, kneeling beside her and sobbing with love and pain.

"Yes, miss, you are," she cried, and her words were all broken. "Whats'ever 'appens to you—whats'ever—you'd be a princess all the same—an' nothin' couldn't make you nothin' different."

8

In the Attic

The first night she spent in her attic was a thing Sara never forgot. During its passing she lived through a wild, unchildlike woe of which she never spoke to anyone about her. There was no one who would have understood. It was, indeed, well for her that as she lay awake in the darkness her mind was forcibly distracted, now and then, by the strangeness of her surroundings. It was, perhaps, well for her that she was reminded by her small body of material things. If this had not been so, the anguish of her young mind might have been too great for a child to bear. But, really, while the night was passing she scarcely knew that she had a body at all or remembered any other thing than one.

"My papa is dead!" she kept whispering to herself. "My papa is dead!"

It was not until long afterward that she realized that her bed had been so hard that she turned over and over in it to find a place to rest, that the darkness seemed more intense than any she had ever known, and that the wind howled over the roof among the chimneys like something which wailed aloud. Then there was something worse. This was certain scufflings and scratchings and squeakings in the walls and behind the skirting boards. She knew what they meant, because Becky had described them. They meant rats and mice who were either fighting with each other or playing together. Once or twice she even heard sharp-toed feet scurrying across the floor, and she remembered in those after days, when she recalled things, that when first she heard them she started up in bed and sat trembling, and when she lay down again covered her head with the bedclothes.

The change in her life did not come about gradually, but was made all at once.

"She must begin as she is to go on," Miss Minchin said to Miss Amelia. "She must be taught at once what she is to expect."

Mariette had left the house the next morning. The glimpse Sara caught of her sitting room, as she passed its open door, showed her that everything had been changed. Her ornaments and luxuries had been removed, and a bed had been placed in a corner to transform it into a new pupil's bedroom.

When she went down to breakfast she saw that her seat at Miss Minchin's side was occupied by Lavinia, and Miss Minchin spoke to her coldly.

"You will begin your new duties, Sara," she said, "by taking your seat with the younger children at a smaller table. You must keep them quiet, and see that they behave well and do not waste their food. You ought to have been down earlier. Lottie has already upset her tea."

That was the beginning, and from day to day the duties given to her were added to. She taught the younger children French and heard their other lessons, and these were the least of her labors. It was found that she could be made use of in numberless directions. She could be sent on errands at any time and in all weathers. She could be told to do things other people neglected. The cook and the housemaids took their tone from Miss Minchin, and rather enjoyed ordering about the "young one" who had been made so much fuss over for so long. They were not servants of the best class, and had neither good manners nor good tempers, and it was frequently convenient to have at hand someone on whom blame could be laid.

During the first month or two, Sara thought that her willingness to do things as well as she could, and her silence under reproof, might soften those who drove her so hard. In her proud little heart she wanted them to see that she was trying to earn her living and not accepting charity. But the time came when she saw that no one was softened at all; and the more willing she was to do as she was told, the more domineering and exacting careless housemaids became, and the more ready a scolding cook was to blame her.

If she had been older, Miss Minchin would have given her the bigger girls to teach and saved money by dismissing an instructress; but while she remained and looked like a child, she could be made more useful as a sort of little superior errand girl and maid of all work. An ordinary errand boy would not have been so clever and reliable. Sara could be trusted with difficult commissions and complicated messages. She could even go and pay bills, and she combined with this the ability to dust a room well and to set things in order.

Her own lessons became things of the past. She was taught nothing, and only after long and busy days spent in running here and there at everybody's orders was she grudgingly allowed to go into the deserted schoolroom, with a pile of old books, and study alone at night.

"If I do not remind myself of the things I have learned, perhaps I may forget them," she said to herself. "I am almost a scullery maid, and if I am a scullery maid who knows nothing, I shall be like poor Becky. I wonder if I could *quite* forget and begin to drop my *h's* and not remember that Henry the Eighth had six wives."

One of the most curious things in her new existence was her changed position among the pupils. Instead of being a sort of small royal personage among them, she no longer seemed to be one of their number at all. She was kept so constantly at work that she scarcely ever had an opportunity of speaking to any of them, and she could not avoid seeing that Miss Minchin preferred that she should live a life apart from that of the occupants of the schoolroom.

"I will not have her forming intimacies and talking to the other children," that lady said. "Girls like a grievance, and if she begins to tell romantic stories about herself, she will become an ill-used heroine, and parents will be given a wrong impression. It is better that she should live a separate life—one suited to her circumstances. I am giving her a home, and that is more than she has any right to expect from me."

Sara did not expect much, and was far too proud to try to continue to be intimate with girls who evidently felt rather awkward and uncertain about her. The fact was that Miss Minchin's pupils were a set of dull, matter-of-fact young people. They were accustomed to being rich and comfortable, and as Sara's frocks grew shorter and shabbier and queerer-looking, and it became an established fact that she wore shoes with holes in them and was sent out to buy groceries and carry them through the streets in a basket on her arm when the cook wanted them in a hurry, they felt rather as if, when they spoke to her, they were addressing an under servant.

"To think that she was the girl with the diamond mines," Lavinia commented. "She does look an object. And she's queerer than ever. I never liked her much, but I can't bear that way she has now of looking at people without speaking—just as if she was finding them out."

"I am," said Sara, promptly, when she heard of this. "That's what I look at some people for. I like to know about them. I think them over afterward."

The truth was that she had saved herself annoyance several times by keeping her eye on Lavinia, who was quite ready to make mischief, and would have been rather pleased to have made it for the ex-show pupil.

Sara never made any mischief herself, or interfered with anyone. She worked like a drudge; she tramped through the wet streets, carrying parcels and baskets; she labored with the childish inattention of the little ones' French lessons; as she became shabbier and more forlorn-looking, she was told that she had better take her meals downstairs; she was treated as if she was nobody's concern, and her heart grew proud and sore, but she never told anyone what she felt.

"Soldiers don't complain," she would say between her small, shut teeth, "I am not going to do it; I will pretend this is part of a war."

But there were hours when her child heart might almost have broken with loneliness but for three people.

The first, it must be owned, was Becky—just Becky. Throughout all that first night spent in the garret, she had felt a vague comfort in knowing that on the other side of the wall in which the rats scuffled and squeaked there was another young human creature. And during the nights that followed the sense of comfort grew. They had little chance to speak to each other during the day. Each had her own tasks to perform, and any attempt at conversation would have been regarded as a tendency to loiter and lose time. "Don't mind me, miss," Becky whispered during the first morning, "if I don't say nothin' polite. Some un'd be down on us if I did. I *means* 'please' an' 'thank you' an' 'beg pardon,' but I dassn't to take time to say it."

But before daybreak she used to slip into Sara's attic and button her dress and give her such help as she required before she went downstairs to light the kitchen fire. And when night came Sara always heard the humble knock at her door which meant that her handmaid was ready to help her again if she was needed. During the first weeks of her grief Sara felt as if she were too stupefied to talk, so it happened that some time passed before they saw each other much or exchanged visits. Becky's heart told her that it was best that people in trouble should be left alone.

The second of the trio of comforters was Ermengarde, but odd things happened before Ermengarde found her place.

When Sara's mind seemed to awaken again to the life about her, she realized that she had forgotten that an Ermengarde lived in the world. The two had always been friends, but Sara had felt as if she were years the older. It could not be contested that Ermengarde was as dull as she was affectionate. She clung to Sara in a simple, helpless way; she brought her lessons to her that she might be helped; she listened to her every word and besieged her with requests for stories. But she had nothing interesting to say herself, and she loathed books of every description. She was, in fact, not a person one would remember when one was caught in the storm of a great trouble, and Sara forgot her.

It had been all the easier to forget her because she had been suddenly called home for a few weeks. When she came back she did not see Sara for a day or two, and when she met her for the first time she encountered her coming down a corridor with her arms full of garments which were to be taken downstairs to be mended. Sara herself had already been taught to mend them. She looked pale and unlike herself, and she was attired in the queer, outgrown frock whose shortness showed so much thin black leg.

Ermengarde was too slow a girl to be equal to such a situation. She could not think of anything to say. She knew what had happened, but, somehow, she had never imagined Sara could look like this—so odd and poor and almost like a servant. It made her quite miserable, and she could do nothing but break into a short hysterical laugh and exclaim—aimlessly and as if without any meaning, "Oh, Sara, is that you?"

"Yes," answered Sara, and suddenly a strange thought passed through her mind and made her face flush. She held the pile of garments in her arms, and her chin rested upon the top of it to keep it steady. Something in the look of her straight-gazing eyes made Ermengarde lose her wits still more. She felt as if Sara had changed into a new kind of girl, and she had never known her before. Perhaps it was because she had suddenly grown poor and had to mend things and work like Becky.

"Oh," she stammered. "How—how are you?"

"I don't know," Sara replied. "How are you?"

"I'm—I'm quite well," said Ermengarde, overwhelmed with shyness. Then spasmodically she thought of something to say which seemed more intimate. "Are you—are you very unhappy?" she said in a rush.

Then Sara was guilty of an injustice. Just at that moment her torn heart swelled within her, and she felt that if anyone was as stupid as that, one had better get away from her.

"What do you think?" she said. "Do you think I am very happy?" And she marched past her without another word.

In course of time she realized that if her wretchedness had not made her forget things, she would have known that poor, dull Ermengarde was not to be blamed for her unready, awkward ways. She was always awkward, and the more she felt, the more stupid she was given to being.

But the sudden thought which had flashed upon her had made her over-sensitive.

"She is like the others," she had thought. "She does not really want to talk to me. She knows no one does."

So for several weeks a barrier stood between them. When they met by chance Sara looked the other way, and Ermengarde felt too stiff and embarrassed to speak. Sometimes they nodded to each other in passing, but there were times when they did not even exchange a greeting.

"If she would rather not talk to me," Sara thought, "I will keep out of her way. Miss Minchin makes that easy enough."

Miss Minchin made it so easy that at last they scarcely saw each other at all. At that time it was noticed that Ermengarde was more stupid than ever, and that she looked listless and unhappy. She used to sit in the window-seat, huddled in a heap, and stare out of the window without speaking. Once Jessie, who was passing, stopped to look at her curiously.

"What are you crying for, Ermengarde?" she asked.

"I'm not crying," answered Ermengarde, in a muffled, unsteady voice.

"You are," said Jessie. "A great big tear just rolled down the bridge of your nose and dropped off at the end of it. And there goes another."

"Well," said Ermengarde, "I'm miserable—and no one need interfere." And she turned her plump back and took out her handkerchief and boldly hid her face in it.

That night, when Sara went to her attic, she was later than usual. She had been kept at work until after the hour at which the pupils went to bed, and after that she had gone to her lessons in the lonely schoolroom. When she reached the top of the stairs, she was surprised to see a glimmer of light coming from under the attic door.

"Nobody goes there but myself," she thought quickly, "but someone has lighted a candle."

Someone had, indeed, lighted a candle, and it was not burning in the kitchen candlestick she was expected to use, but in one of those belonging to the pupils' bedrooms. The someone was sitting upon the battered footstool, and was dressed in her nightgown and wrapped up in a red shawl. It was Ermengarde.

"Ermengarde!" cried Sara. She was so startled that she was almost frightened. "You will get into trouble."

Ermengarde stumbled up from her footstool. She shuffled across the attic in her bedroom slippers, which were too large for her. Her eyes and nose were pink with crying.

"I know I shall—if I'm found out." she said. "But I don't care—I don't care a bit. Oh, Sara, please tell me. What is the matter? Why don't you like me any more?"

Something in her voice made the familiar lump rise in Sara's throat. It was so affectionate and simple—so like the old Ermengarde who had asked her to be "best friends." It sounded as if she had not meant what she had seemed to mean during these past weeks.

"I do like you," Sara answered. "I thought—you see, everything is different now. I thought you—were different."

Ermengarde opened her wet eyes wide.

"Why, it was you who were different!" she cried. "You didn't want to talk to me. I didn't know what to do. It was you who were different after I came back."

Sara thought a moment. She saw she had made a mistake.

"I *am* different," she explained, "though not in the way you think. Miss Minchin does not want me to talk to the girls. Most of them don't want to talk to me. I thought—perhaps—you didn't. So I tried to keep out of your way."

"Oh, Sara," Ermengarde almost wailed in her reproachful dismay. And then after one more look they rushed into each other's arms. It must be confessed that Sara's small black head lay for some minutes on the shoulder covered by the red shawl. When Ermengarde had seemed to desert her, she had felt horribly lonely.

Afterward they sat down upon the floor together, Sara clasping her knees with her arms, and Ermengarde rolled up in her shawl. Ermengarde looked at the odd, big-eyed little face adoringly.

"I couldn't bear it any more," she said. "I dare say you could live without me, Sara; but I couldn't live without you. I was nearly *dead*. So tonight, when I was crying under the bedclothes, I thought all at once of creeping up here and just begging you to let us be friends again."

"You are nicer than I am," said Sara. "I was too proud to try and make friends. You see, now that trials have come, they have shown that I am *not* a nice child. I was afraid they would. Perhaps"—wrinkling her forehead wisely—"that is what they were sent for."

"I don't see any good in them," said Ermengarde stoutly.

"Neither do I—to speak the truth," admitted Sara, frankly. "But I suppose there *might* be good in things, even if we don't see it. There *might*"—doubtfully—"be good in Miss Minchin."

Ermengarde looked round the attic with a rather fearsome curiosity.

"Sara," she said, "do you think you can bear living here?"

Sara looked round also.

"If I pretend it's quite different, I can," she answered; "or if I pretend it is a place in a story."

She spoke slowly. Her imagination was beginning to work for her. It had not worked for her at all since her troubles had come upon her. She had felt as if it had been stunned.

"Other people have lived in worse places. Think of the Count of Monte Cristo in the dungeons of the Chateau d'If. And think of the people in the Bastille!"

"The Bastille," half whispered Ermengarde, watching her and beginning to be fascinated. She remembered stories of the French Revolution which Sara had been able to fix in her mind by her dramatic relation of them. No one but Sara could have done it.

A well-known glow came into Sara's eyes.

"Yes," she said, hugging her knees, "that will be a good place to pretend about. I am a prisoner in the Bastille. I have been here for years and years—and years; and everybody has forgotten about me. Miss Minchin is the jailer—and Becky"—a sudden light adding itself to the glow in her eyes—"Becky is the prisoner in the next cell."

She turned to Ermengarde, looking quite like the old Sara.

"I shall pretend that," she said; "and it will be a great comfort."

Ermengarde was at once enraptured and awed.

"And will you tell me all about it?" she said. "May I creep up here at night, whenever it is safe, and hear the things you have made up in the day? It will seem as if we were more 'best friends' than ever."

"Yes," answered Sara, nodding. "Adversity tries people, and mine has tried you and proved how nice you are."

9

Melchisedec

The third person in the trio was Lottie. She was a small thing and did not know what adversity meant, and was much bewildered by the alteration she saw in her young adopted mother. She had heard it rumored that strange things had happened to Sara, but she could not understand why she looked different—why she wore an old black frock and came into the schoolroom only to teach instead of to sit in her place of honor and learn lessons herself. There had been much whispering among the little ones when it had been discovered that Sara no longer lived in the rooms in which Emily had so long sat in state. Lottie's chief difficulty was that Sara said so little when one asked her questions. At seven mysteries must be made very clear if one is to understand them.

"Are you very poor now, Sara?" she had asked confidentially the first morning her friend took charge of the small French class. "Are you as poor as a beggar?" She thrust a fat hand into the slim one and opened round, tearful eyes. "I don't want you to be as poor as a beggar."

She looked as if she was going to cry. And Sara hurriedly consoled her.

"Beggars have nowhere to live," she said courageously. "I have a place to live in."

"Where do you live?" persisted Lottie. "The new girl sleeps in your room, and it isn't pretty any more."

"I live in another room," said Sara.

"Is it a nice one?" inquired Lottie. "I want to go and see it."

"You must not talk," said Sara. "Miss Minchin is looking at us. She will be angry with me for letting you whisper."

She had found out already that she was to be held accountable for everything which was objected to. If the children were not attentive, if they talked, if they were restless, it was she who would be reproved.

But Lottie was a determined little person. If Sara would not tell her where she lived, she would find out in some other way. She talked to her small companions and hung about the elder girls and listened when they were gossiping; and acting upon certain information they had unconsciously let drop, she started late one afternoon on a voyage of discovery, climbing stairs she had never known the existence of, until she reached the attic floor. There she found two doors near each other, and opening one, she saw her beloved Sara standing upon an old table and looking out of a window.

"Sara!" she cried, aghast. "Mamma Sara!" She was aghast because the attic was so bare and ugly and seemed so far away from all the world. Her short legs had seemed to have been mounting hundreds of stairs.

Sara turned round at the sound of her voice. It was her turn to be aghast. What would happen now? If Lottie began to cry and any one chanced to hear, they were both lost. She jumped down from her table and ran to the child.

"Don't cry and make a noise," she implored. "I shall be scolded if you do, and I have been scolded all day. It's—it's not such a bad room, Lottie."

"Isn't it?" gasped Lottie, and as she looked round it she bit her lip. She was a spoiled child yet, but she was fond enough of her adopted parent to make an effort to control herself for her sake.

Then, somehow, it was quite possible that any place in which Sara lived might turn out to be nice. "Why isn't it, Sara?" she almost whispered.

Sara hugged her close and tried to laugh. There was a sort of comfort in the warmth of the plump, childish body. She had had a hard day and had been staring out of the windows with hot eyes.

"You can see all sorts of things you can't see downstairs," she said.

"What sort of things?" demanded Lottie, with that curiosity Sara could always awaken even in bigger girls.

"Chimneys—quite close to us—with smoke curling up in wreaths and clouds and going up into the sky—and sparrows hopping about and talking to each other just as if they were people—and other attic windows where heads may pop out any minute and you can wonder who they belong to. And it all feels as high up—as if it was another world."

"Oh, let me see it!" cried Lottie. "Lift me up!"

Sara lifted her up, and they stood on the old table together and leaned on the edge of the flat window in the roof, and looked out.

Anyone who has not done this does not know what a different world they saw. The slates spread out on either side of them and slanted down into the rain gutter-pipes. The sparrows, being at home there, twittered and hopped about quite without fear. Two of them perched on the chimney top nearest and quarrelled with each other fiercely until one pecked the other and drove him away. The garret window next to theirs was shut because the house next door was empty.

"I wish someone lived there," Sara said. "It is so close that if there was a little girl in the attic, we could talk to each other through the windows and climb over to see each other, if we were not afraid of falling."

The sky seemed so much nearer than when one saw it from the street, that Lottie was enchanted. From the attic window, among the chimney pots, the things which were happening in the world below seemed almost unreal. One scarcely believed in the existence of Miss Minchin and Miss Amelia and the schoolroom, and the roll of wheels in the square seemed a sound belonging to another existence.

"Oh, Sara!" cried Lottie, cuddling in her guarding arm. "I like this attic—I like it! It is nicer than downstairs!"

"Look at that sparrow," whispered Sara. "I wish I had some crumbs to throw to him."

"I have some!" came in a little shriek from Lottie. "I have part of a bun in my pocket; I bought it with my penny yesterday, and I saved a bit."

When they threw out a few crumbs the sparrow jumped and flew away to an adjacent chimney top. He was evidently not accustomed to intimates in attics, and unexpected crumbs startled him. But when Lottie remained quite still and Sara chirped very softly—almost as if she were a sparrow herself—he saw that the thing which had alarmed him represented hospitality, after all. He put his head on one side, and from his perch on the chimney looked down at the crumbs with twinkling eyes. Lottie could scarcely keep still.

"Will he come? Will he come?" she whispered.

"His eyes look as if he would," Sara whispered back. "He is thinking and thinking whether he dare. Yes, he will! Yes, he is coming!"

He flew down and hopped toward the crumbs, but stopped a few inches away from them, putting his head on one side again, as if reflecting on the chances that Sara and Lottie might turn out to be big cats and jump on him. At last his heart told him they were really nicer than they looked, and he hopped nearer and nearer, darted at the biggest crumb with a lightning peck, seized it, and carried it away to the other side of his chimney.

"Now he *knows*," said Sara. "And he will come back for the others."

He did come back, and even brought a friend, and the friend went away and brought a relative, and among them they made a hearty meal over which they twittered and chattered and exclaimed, stopping every now and then to put their heads on one side and examine Lottie and Sara. Lottie was so delighted that she quite forgot her first shocked impression of the attic. In fact, when she was lifted down from the table and returned to earthly things, as it were, Sara was able to point out to her many beauties in the room which she herself would not have suspected the existence of.

"It is so little and so high above everything," she said, "that it is almost like a nest in a tree. The slanting ceiling is so funny. See, you can scarcely stand up at this end of the room; and when the morning begins to come I can lie in bed and look right up into the sky through that flat window in the roof. It is like a square patch of light. If the sun is going to shine, little pink clouds float about, and I feel as if I could touch them. And if it rains, the drops patter and patter as if they were saying something nice. Then if there are stars, you can lie and try to count how many go into the patch. It takes such a lot. And just look at that tiny, rusty grate in the corner. If it was polished and there was a fire in it, just think how nice it would be. You see, it's really a beautiful little room."

She was walking round the small place, holding Lottie's hand and making gestures which described all the beauties she was making herself see. She quite made Lottie see them, too. Lottie could always believe in the things Sara made pictures of.

"You see," she said, "there could be a thick, soft blue Indian rug on the floor; and in that corner there could be a soft little sofa, with cushions to curl up on; and just over it could be a shelf full of books so that one could reach them easily; and there could be a fur rug before the fire, and hangings on the wall to cover up the whitewash, and pictures. They would have to be little ones, but they could be beautiful; and there could be a lamp with a deep rose-colored shade; and a table in the middle, with things to have tea with; and a little fat copper kettle singing on the hob; and the bed could be quite different. It could be made soft and covered with a lovely silk coverlet. It could be beautiful. And perhaps we could coax the sparrows until we made such friends with them that they would come and peck at the window and ask to be let in."

"Oh, Sara!" cried Lottie. "I should like to live here!"

When Sara had persuaded her to go downstairs again, and, after setting her on her way, had come back to her attic, she stood in the middle of it and looked about her. The enchantment of her imaginings for Lottie had died away. The bed was hard and covered with its dingy quilt. The whitewashed wall showed its broken patches, the floor was cold and bare, the grate was broken and rusty, and the battered footstool, tilted sideways on its injured leg, the only seat in the room. She sat down on it for a few minutes and let her head drop in her hands. The mere fact that Lottie had come and gone away again made things seem a little worse—just as perhaps prisoners feel a little more desolate after visitors come and go, leaving them behind.

"It's a lonely place," she said. "Sometimes it's the loneliest place in the world."

She was sitting in this way when her attention was attracted by a slight sound near her. She lifted her head to see where it came from, and if she had been a nervous child she would have left her seat on the battered footstool in a great hurry. A large rat was sitting up on his hind quarters and sniffing the air in an interested manner. Some of Lottie's crumbs had dropped upon the floor and their scent had drawn him out of his hole.

He looked so queer and so like a gray-whiskered dwarf or gnome that Sara was rather fascinated. He looked at her with his bright eyes, as if he were asking a question. He was evidently so doubtful that one of the child's queer thoughts came into her mind.

"I dare say it is rather hard to be a rat," she mused. "Nobody likes you. People jump and run away and scream out, 'Oh, a horrid rat!' I shouldn't like people to scream and jump and say, 'Oh, a horrid Sara!' the moment they saw me. And set traps for me, and pretend they were dinner. It's so different to be a sparrow. But nobody asked this rat if he wanted to be a rat when he was made. Nobody said, 'Wouldn't you rather be a sparrow?'"

She had sat so quietly that the rat had begun to take courage. He was very much afraid of her, but perhaps he had a heart like the sparrow and it told him that she was not a thing which pounced. He was very hungry. He had a wife and a large family in the wall, and they had had frightfully bad luck for several days. He had left the children crying bitterly, and felt he would risk a good deal for a few crumbs, so he cautiously dropped upon his feet.

"Come on," said Sara; "I'm not a trap. You can have them, poor thing! Prisoners in the Bastille used to make friends with rats. Suppose I make friends with you."

How it is that animals understand things I do not know, but it is certain that they do understand. Perhaps there is a language which is not made of words and everything in the world understands it. Perhaps there is a soul hidden in everything and it can always speak, without even making a sound, to another soul. But whatsoever was the reason, the rat knew from that moment that he was safe—even though he was a rat. He knew that this young human being sitting on the red footstool would not jump up and terrify him with wild, sharp noises or throw heavy objects at him which, if they did not fall and crush him, would send him limping in his scurry back to his hole. He was really a very nice rat, and did not mean the least harm. When he had stood on his hind legs and sniffed the air, with his bright eyes fixed on Sara, he had hoped that she would understand this, and would not begin by hating him as an enemy. When the mysterious thing which speaks without saying any words told him that she would not, he went softly toward the crumbs and began to eat them. As he did it he glanced every now and then at Sara, just as the sparrows had done, and his expression was so very apologetic that it touched her heart.

She sat and watched him without making any movement. One crumb was very much larger than the others—in fact, it could scarcely be called a crumb. It was evident that he wanted that piece very much, but it lay quite near the footstool and he was still rather timid.

"I believe he wants it to carry to his family in the wall," Sara thought. "If I do not stir at all, perhaps he will come and get it."

She scarcely allowed herself to breathe, she was so deeply interested. The rat shuffled a little nearer and ate a few more crumbs, then he stopped and sniffed delicately, giving a side glance at the occupant of the footstool; then he darted at the piece of bun with something very like the sudden boldness of the sparrow, and the instant he had possession of it fled back to the wall, slipped down a crack in the skirting board, and was gone.

"I knew he wanted it for his children," said Sara. "I do believe I could make friends with him."

A week or so afterward, on one of the rare nights when Ermengarde found it safe to steal up to the attic, when she tapped on the door with the tips of her fingers Sara did not come to her for two or three minutes. There was, indeed, such a silence in the room at first that Ermengarde wondered if she could have fallen asleep. Then, to her surprise, she heard her utter a little, low laugh and speak coaxingly to someone.

"There!" Ermengarde heard her say. "Take it and go home, Melchisedec! Go home to your wife!"

Almost immediately Sara opened the door, and when she did so she found Ermengarde standing with alarmed eyes upon the threshold.

"Who—who *are* you talking to, Sara?" she gasped out.

Sara drew her in cautiously, but she looked as if something pleased and amused her.

"You must promise not to be frightened—not to scream the least bit, or I can't tell you," she answered.

Ermengarde felt almost inclined to scream on the spot, but managed to control herself. She looked all round the attic and saw no one. And yet Sara had certainly been speaking *to* someone. She thought of ghosts.

"Is it—something that will frighten me?" she asked timorously.

"Some people are afraid of them," said Sara. "I was at first—but I am not now."

"Was it—a ghost?" quaked Ermengarde.

"No," said Sara, laughing. "It was my rat."

Ermengarde made one bound, and landed in the middle of the little dingy bed. She tucked her feet under her nightgown and the red shawl. She did not scream, but she gasped with fright.

"Oh! Oh!" she cried under her breath. "A rat! A rat!"

"I was afraid you would be frightened," said Sara. "But you needn't be. I am making him tame. He actually knows me and comes out when I call him. Are you too frightened to want to see him?"

The truth was that, as the days had gone on and, with the aid of scraps brought up from the kitchen, her curious friendship had developed, she had gradually forgotten that the timid creature she was becoming familiar with was a mere rat.

At first Ermengarde was too much alarmed to do anything but huddle in a heap upon the bed and tuck up her feet, but the sight of Sara's composed little countenance and the story of Melchisedec's first appearance began at last to rouse her curiosity, and she leaned forward over the edge of the bed and watched Sara go and kneel down by the hole in the skirting board.

"He—he won't run out quickly and jump on the bed, will he?" she said.

"No," answered Sara. "He's as polite as we are. He is just like a person. Now watch!"

She began to make a low, whistling sound—so low and coaxing that it could only have been heard in entire stillness. She did it several times, looking entirely absorbed in it. Ermengarde thought she looked as if she were working a spell. And at last, evidently in response to it, a gray-whiskered, bright-eyed head peeped out of the hole. Sara had some crumbs in her hand. She dropped them, and Melchisedec came quietly forth and ate them. A piece of larger size than the rest he took and carried in the most businesslike manner back to his home.

"You see," said Sara, "that is for his wife and children. He is very nice. He only eats the little bits. After he goes back I can always hear his family squeaking for joy. There are three kinds of squeaks. One kind is the children's, and one is Mrs. Melchisedec's, and one is Melchisedec's own."

Ermengarde began to laugh.

"Oh, Sara!" she said. "You *are* queer—but you are nice."

"I know I am queer," admitted Sara, cheerfully; "and I *try* to be nice." She rubbed her forehead with her little brown paw, and a puzzled, tender look came into her face. "Papa always laughed at me," she said; "but I liked it. He thought I was queer, but he liked me to make up things. I—I can't help making up things. If I didn't, I don't believe I could live." She paused and glanced around the attic. "I'm sure I couldn't live here," she added in a low voice.

Ermengarde was interested, as she always was. "When you talk about things," she said, "they seem as if they grew real. You talk about Melchisedec as if he was a person."

"He *is* a person," said Sara. "He gets hungry and frightened, just as we do; and he is married and has children. How do we know he doesn't think things, just as we do? His eyes look as if he was a person. That was why I gave him a name."

She sat down on the floor in her favorite attitude, holding her knees.

"Besides," she said, "he is a Bastille rat sent to be my friend. I can always get a bit of bread the cook has thrown away, and it is quite enough to support him."

"Is it the Bastille yet?" asked Ermengarde, eagerly. "Do you always pretend it is the Bastille?"

"Nearly always," answered Sara. "Sometimes I try to pretend it is another kind of place; but the Bastille is generally easiest—particularly when it is cold."

Just at that moment Ermengarde almost jumped off the bed, she was so startled by a sound she heard. It was like two distinct knocks on the wall.

"What is that?" she exclaimed.

Sara got up from the floor and answered quite dramatically:

"It is the prisoner in the next cell."

"Becky!" cried Ermengarde, enraptured.

"Yes," said Sara. "Listen; the two knocks meant, 'Prisoner, are you there?'"

She knocked three times on the wall herself, as if in answer.

"That means, 'Yes, I am here, and all is well.'"

Four knocks came from Becky's side of the wall.

"That means," explained Sara, "'Then, fellow-sufferer, we will sleep in peace. Goodnight.'"

Ermengarde quite beamed with delight.

"Oh, Sara!" she whispered joyfully. "It is like a story!"

"It *is* a story," said Sara. "*Everything's* a story. You are a story—I am a story. Miss Minchin is a story."

And she sat down again and talked until Ermengarde forgot that she was a sort of escaped prisoner herself, and had to be reminded by Sara that she could not remain in the Bastille all night, but must steal noiselessly downstairs again and creep back into her deserted bed.

10

The Indian Gentleman

But it was a perilous thing for Ermengarde and Lottie to make pilgrimages to the attic. They could never be quite sure when Sara would be there, and they could scarcely ever be certain that Miss Amelia would not make a tour of inspection through the bedrooms after the pupils were supposed to be asleep. So their visits were rare ones, and Sara lived a strange and lonely life. It was a lonelier life when she was downstairs than when she was in her attic. She had no one to talk to; and when she was sent out on errands and walked through the streets, a forlorn little figure carrying a basket or a parcel, trying to hold her hat on when the wind was blowing, and feeling the water soak through her shoes when it was raining, she felt as if the crowds hurrying past her made her loneliness greater. When she had been the Princess Sara, driving through the streets in her brougham, or walking, attended by Mariette, the sight of her bright, eager little face and picturesque coats and hats had often caused people to look after her. A happy, beautifully cared for little girl naturally attracts attention. Shabby, poorly dressed children are not rare enough and pretty enough to make people turn around to look at them and smile. No one looked at Sara in these days, and no one seemed to see her as she hurried along the crowded pavements. She had begun to grow very fast, and, as she was dressed only in such clothes as the plainer remnants of her wardrobe would supply, she knew she looked very queer, indeed. All her valuable garments had been disposed of, and such as had been left for her use she was expected to wear so long as she could put them on at all. Sometimes, when she passed a shop window with a mirror in it, she almost laughed outright on catching a glimpse of herself, and sometimes her face went red and she bit her lip and turned away.

In the evening, when she passed houses whose windows were lighted up, she used to look into the warm rooms and amuse herself by imagining things about the people she saw sitting before the fires or about the tables. It always interested her to catch glimpses of rooms before the shutters were closed. There were several families in the square in which Miss Minchin lived, with which she had become quite familiar in a way of her own. The one she liked best she called the Large Family. She called it the Large Family not because the members of it were big—for, indeed, most of them were little—but because there were so many of them. There were eight children in the Large Family, and a stout, rosy mother, and a stout, rosy father, and a stout, rosy grandmother, and any number of servants. The eight children were always either being taken out to walk or to ride in perambulators by comfortable nurses, or they were going to drive with their mamma, or they were flying to the door in the evening to meet their papa and kiss him and dance around him and drag off his overcoat and look in the pockets for packages, or they were crowding about the nursery windows and looking out and pushing each other and laughing—in fact, they were always doing something enjoyable and suited to the tastes of a large family. Sara was quite fond of them, and had given them names out of books—quite romantic names. She called them the Montmorencys when she did not call them the Large Family. The fat, fair baby with the lace cap was Ethelberta Beauchamp Montmorency; the next baby was Violet Cholmondeley Montmorency; the little boy who could just stagger and who had such round legs was Sydney Cecil Vivian

Montmorency; and then came Lilian Evangeline Maud Marion, Rosalind Gladys, Guy Clarence, Veronica Eustacia, and Claude Harold Hector.

One evening a very funny thing happened—though, perhaps, in one sense it was not a funny thing at all.

Several of the Montmorencys were evidently going to a children's party, and just as Sara was about to pass the door they were crossing the pavement to get into the carriage which was waiting for them. Veronica Eustacia and Rosalind Gladys, in white-lace frocks and lovely sashes, had just got in, and Guy Clarence, aged five, was following them. He was such a pretty fellow and had such rosy cheeks and blue eyes, and such a darling little round head covered with curls, that Sara forgot her basket and shabby cloak altogether—in fact, forgot everything but that she wanted to look at him for a moment. So she paused and looked.

It was Christmas time, and the Large Family had been hearing many stories about children who were poor and had no mammas and papas to fill their stockings and take them to the pantomime—children who were, in fact, cold and thinly clad and hungry. In the stories, kind people—sometimes little boys and girls with tender hearts—invariably saw the poor children and gave them money or rich gifts, or took them home to beautiful dinners. Guy Clarence had been affected to tears that very afternoon by the reading of such a story, and he had burned with a desire to find such a poor child and give her a certain sixpence he possessed, and thus provide for her for life. An entire sixpence, he was sure, would mean affluence for evermore. As he crossed the strip of red carpet laid across the pavement from the door to the carriage, he had this very sixpence in the pocket of his very short man-o'-war trousers; And just as Rosalind Gladys got into the vehicle and jumped on the seat in order to feel the cushions spring under her, he saw Sara standing on the wet pavement in her shabby frock and hat, with her old basket on her arm, looking at him hungrily.

He thought that her eyes looked hungry because she had perhaps had nothing to eat for a long time. He did not know that they looked so because she was hungry for the warm, merry life his home held and his rosy face spoke of, and that she had a hungry wish to snatch him in her arms and kiss him. He only knew that she had big eyes and a thin face and thin legs and a common basket and poor clothes. So he put his hand in his pocket and found his sixpence and walked up to her benignly.

"Here, poor little girl," he said. "Here is a sixpence. I will give it to you."

Sara started, and all at once realized that she looked exactly like poor children she had seen, in her better days, waiting on the pavement to watch her as she got out of her brougham. And she had given them pennies many a time. Her face went red and then it went pale, and for a second she felt as if she could not take the dear little sixpence.

"Oh, no!" she said. "Oh, no, thank you; I mustn't take it, indeed!"

Her voice was so unlike an ordinary street child's voice and her manner was so like the manner of a well-bred little person that Veronica Eustacia (whose real name was Janet) and Rosalind Gladys (who was really called Nora) leaned forward to listen.

But Guy Clarence was not to be thwarted in his benevolence. He thrust the sixpence into her hand.

"Yes, you must take it, poor little girl!" he insisted stoutly. "You can buy things to eat with it. It is a whole sixpence!"

There was something so honest and kind in his face, and he looked so likely to be heartbrokenly disappointed if she did not take it, that Sara knew she must not refuse him. To be as proud as that would be a cruel thing. So she actually put her pride in her pocket, though it must be admitted her cheeks burned.

"Thank you," she said. "You are a kind, kind little darling thing." And as he scrambled joyfully into the carriage she went away, trying to smile, though she caught her breath quickly and her eyes were shining through a mist. She had known that she looked odd and shabby, but until now she had not known that she might be taken for a beggar.

As the Large Family's carriage drove away, the children inside it were talking with interested excitement.

"Oh, Donald," (this was Guy Clarence's name), Janet exclaimed alarmedly, "why did you offer that little girl your sixpence? I'm sure she is not a beggar!"

"She didn't speak like a beggar!" cried Nora. "And her face didn't really look like a beggar's face!"

"Besides, she didn't beg," said Janet. "I was so afraid she might be angry with you. You know, it makes people angry to be taken for beggars when they are not beggars."

"She wasn't angry," said Donald, a trifle dismayed, but still firm. "She laughed a little, and she said I was a kind, kind little darling thing. And I was!"—stoutly. "It was my whole sixpence."

Janet and Nora exchanged glances.

"A beggar girl would never have said that," decided Janet. "She would have said, 'Thank yer kindly, little gentleman—thank yer, sir;' and perhaps she would have bobbed a curtsy."

Sara knew nothing about the fact, but from that time the Large Family was as profoundly interested in her as she was in it. Faces used to appear at the nursery windows when she passed, and many discussions concerning her were held round the fire.

"She is a kind of servant at the seminary," Janet said. "I don't believe she belongs to anybody. I believe she is an orphan. But she is not a beggar, however shabby she looks."

And afterward she was called by all of them, "The-little-girl-who-is-not-a-beggar," which was, of course, rather a long name, and sounded very funny sometimes when the youngest ones said it in a hurry.

Sara managed to bore a hole in the sixpence and hung it on an old bit of narrow ribbon round her neck. Her affection for the Large Family increased—as, indeed, her affection for everything she could love increased. She grew fonder and fonder of Becky, and she used to look forward to the two mornings a week when she went into the schoolroom to give the little ones their French lesson. Her small pupils loved her, and strove with each other for the privilege of standing close to her and insinuating their small hands into hers. It fed her hungry heart to feel them nestling up to her. She made such friends with the sparrows that when she stood upon the table, put her head and shoulders out of the attic window, and chirped, she heard almost immediately a flutter of wings and answering twitters, and a little flock of dingy town birds appeared and alighted on the slates to talk to her and make much of the crumbs she scattered.

With Melchisedec she had become so intimate that he actually brought Mrs. Melchisedec with him sometimes, and now and then one or two of his children. She used to talk to him, and, somehow, he looked quite as if he understood.

There had grown in her mind rather a strange feeling about Emily, who always sat and looked on at everything. It arose in one of her moments of great desolateness. She would have liked to believe or pretend to believe that Emily understood and sympathized with her. She did not like to own to herself that her only companion could feel and hear nothing. She used to put her in a chair sometimes and sit opposite to her on the old red footstool, and stare and pretend about her until her own eyes would grow large with something which was almost like fear—particularly at night when everything was so still, when the only sound in the attic was the occasional sudden scurry and squeak of Melchisedec's family in the wall. One of her "pretends" was that Emily was a kind of good witch who could protect her. Sometimes, after she had stared at her until she was wrought up to the highest pitch of fancifulness, she would ask her questions and find herself *almost* feeling as if she would presently answer. But she never did.

"As to answering, though," said Sara, trying to console herself, "I don't answer very often. I never answer when I can help it. When people are insulting you, there is nothing so good for them as not to say a word—just to look at them and *think*. Miss Minchin turns pale with rage when I do it, Miss Amelia looks frightened, and so do the girls. When you will not fly into a passion people know you are stronger than they are, because you are strong enough to hold in your rage, and they are not, and they say stupid things they wish they hadn't said afterward. There's nothing so strong as rage, except what makes you hold it in—that's stronger. It's a good thing not to answer your enemies. I scarcely ever do. Perhaps Emily is more like me than I am like myself. Perhaps she would rather not answer her friends, even. She keeps it all in her heart."

But though she tried to satisfy herself with these arguments, she did not find it easy. When, after a long, hard day, in which she had been sent here and there, sometimes on long errands through wind and cold and rain, she came in wet and hungry, and was sent out again because nobody chose to remember that she was only a child, and that her slim legs might be tired and her small body might be chilled; when she had been given only harsh words and cold, slighting looks for thanks; when the cook had been vulgar and insolent; when Miss Minchin had been in her worst mood, and when she had seen the girls sneering among themselves at her shabbiness—then she was not always able to comfort her sore, proud, desolate heart with fancies when Emily merely sat upright in her old chair and stared.

One of these nights, when she came up to the attic cold and hungry, with a tempest raging in her young breast, Emily's stare seemed so vacant, her sawdust legs and arms so inexpressive, that Sara lost all control over herself. There was nobody but Emily—no one in the world. And there she sat.

"I shall die presently," she said at first.

Emily simply stared.

"I can't bear this," said the poor child, trembling. "I know I shall die. I'm cold; I'm wet; I'm starving to death. I've walked a thousand miles today, and they have done nothing but scold me from morning until night. And because I could not find that last thing the cook sent me for, they would not give me any supper. Some men laughed at me because my old shoes made me slip down in the mud. I'm covered with mud now. And they laughed. Do you hear?"

She looked at the staring glass eyes and complacent face, and suddenly a sort of heartbroken rage seized her. She lifted her little savage hand and knocked Emily off the chair, bursting into a passion of sobbing—Sara who never cried.

"You are nothing but a *doll*!" she cried. "Nothing but a doll—doll—doll! You care for nothing. You are stuffed with sawdust. You never had a heart. Nothing could ever make you feel. You are a *doll*!" Emily lay on the floor, with her legs ignominiously doubled up over her head, and a new flat place on the end of her nose; but she was calm, even dignified. Sara hid her face in her arms. The rats in the wall began to fight and bite each other and squeak and scramble. Melchisedec was chastising some of his family.

Sara's sobs gradually quieted themselves. It was so unlike her to break down that she was surprised at herself. After a while she raised her face and looked at Emily, who seemed to be gazing at her round the side of one angle, and, somehow, by this time actually with a kind of glassy-eyed sympathy. Sara bent and picked her up. Remorse overtook her. She even smiled at herself a very little smile.

"You can't help being a doll," she said with a resigned sigh, "any more than Lavinia and Jessie can help not having any sense. We are not all made alike. Perhaps you do your sawdust best." And she kissed her and shook her clothes straight, and put her back upon her chair.

She had wished very much that some one would take the empty house next door. She wished it because of the attic window which was so near hers. It seemed as if it would be so nice to see it propped open someday and a head and shoulders rising out of the square aperture.

"If it looked a nice head," she thought, "I might begin by saying, 'Good morning,' and all sorts of things might happen. But, of course, it's not really likely that anyone but under servants would sleep there."

One morning, on turning the corner of the square after a visit to the grocer's, the butcher's, and the baker's, she saw, to her great delight, that during her rather prolonged absence, a van full of furniture had stopped before the next house, the front doors were thrown open, and men in shirt sleeves were going in and out carrying heavy packages and pieces of furniture.

"It's taken!" she said. "It really *is* taken! Oh, I do hope a nice head will look out of the attic window!"

She would almost have liked to join the group of loiterers who had stopped on the pavement to watch the things carried in. She had an idea that if she could see some of the furniture she could guess something about the people it belonged to.

"Miss Minchin's tables and chairs are just like her," she thought; "I remember thinking that the first minute I saw her, even though I was so little. I told papa afterward, and he laughed and said it was true. I am sure the Large Family have fat, comfortable armchairs and sofas, and I can see that their red-flowery wallpaper is exactly like them. It's warm and cheerful and kind-looking and happy."

She was sent out for parsley to the greengrocer's later in the day, and when she came up the area steps her heart gave quite a quick beat of recognition. Several pieces of furniture had been set out of the van upon the pavement. There was a beautiful table of elaborately wrought teakwood, and some chairs, and a screen covered with rich Oriental embroidery. The sight of them gave her a weird, homesick feeling. She had seen things so like them in India. One of the things Miss Minchin had taken from her was a carved teakwood desk her father had sent her.

"They are beautiful things," she said; "they look as if they ought to belong to a nice person. All the things look rather grand. I suppose it is a rich family."

The vans of furniture came and were unloaded and gave place to others all the day. Several times it so happened that Sara had an opportunity of seeing things carried in. It became plain that she had been right in guessing that the newcomers were people of large means. All the furniture was rich and beautiful, and a great deal of it was Oriental. Wonderful rugs and draperies and ornaments were taken from the vans, many pictures, and books enough for a library. Among other things there was a superb god Buddha in a splendid shrine.

"Someone in the family *must* have been in India," Sara thought. "They have got used to Indian things and like them. I *am* glad. I shall feel as if they were friends, even if a head never looks out of the attic window."

When she was taking in the evening's milk for the cook (there was really no odd job she was not called upon to do), she saw something occur which made the situation more interesting than ever. The handsome, rosy man who was the father of the Large Family walked across the square in the most matter-of-fact manner, and ran up the steps of the next-door house. He ran up them as if he felt quite at home and expected to run up and down them many a time in the future. He stayed inside quite a long time, and several times came out and gave directions to the workmen, as if he had a right to do so. It was quite certain that he was in some intimate way connected with the newcomers and was acting for them.

"If the new people have children," Sara speculated, "the Large Family children will be sure to come and play with them, and they *might* come up into the attic just for fun."

At night, after her work was done, Becky came in to see her fellow prisoner and bring her news.

"It's a' Nindian gentleman that's comin' to live next door, miss," she said. "I don't know whether he's a black gentleman or not, but he's a Nindian one. He's very rich, an' he's ill, an' the gentleman of the Large Family is his lawyer. He's had a lot of trouble, an' it's made him ill an' low in his mind. He worships idols, miss. He's an 'eathen an' bows down to wood an' stone. I seen a' idol bein' carried in for him to worship. Somebody had oughter send him a trac'. You can get a trac' for a penny."

Sara laughed a little.

"I don't believe he worships that idol," she said; "some people like to keep them to look at because they are interesting. My papa had a beautiful one, and he did not worship it."

But Becky was rather inclined to prefer to believe that the new neighbor was "an 'eathen." It sounded so much more romantic than that he should merely be the ordinary kind of gentleman who went to church with a prayer book. She sat and talked long that night of what he would be like, of what his wife would be like if he had one, and of what his children would be like if they had children. Sara saw that privately she could not help hoping very much that they would all be black, and would wear turbans, and, above all, that—like their parent—they would all be "'eathens."

"I never lived next door to no 'eathens, miss," she said; "I should like to see what sort o' ways they'd have."

It was several weeks before her curiosity was satisfied, and then it was revealed that the new occupant had neither wife nor children. He was a solitary man with no family at all, and it was evident that he was shattered in health and unhappy in mind.

A carriage drove up one day and stopped before the house. When the footman dismounted from the box and opened the door the gentleman who was the father of the Large Family got out first. After him there descended a nurse in uniform, then came down the steps two men-servants. They came to assist their master, who, when he was helped out of the carriage, proved to be a man with a haggard, distressed face, and a skeleton body wrapped in furs. He was carried up the steps, and the head of the Large Family went with him, looking very anxious. Shortly afterward a doctor's carriage arrived, and the doctor went in—plainly to take care of him.

"There is such a yellow gentleman next door, Sara," Lottie whispered at the French class afterward. "Do you think he is a Chinese? The geography says the Chinese men are yellow."

"No, he is not Chinese," Sara whispered back; "he is very ill. Go on with your exercise, Lottie. '*Non, monsieur. Je n'ai pas le canif de mon oncle.*'"

That was the beginning of the story of the Indian gentleman.

11

Ram Dass

There were fine sunsets even in the square, sometimes. One could only see parts of them, however, between the chimneys and over the roofs. From the kitchen windows one could not see them at all, and could only guess that they were going on because the bricks looked warm and the air rosy or yellow for a while, or perhaps one saw a blazing glow strike a particular pane of glass somewhere. There was, however, one place from which one could see all the splendor of them: the piles of red or gold clouds in the west; or the purple ones edged with dazzling brightness; or the little fleecy, floating ones, tinged with rose-color and looking like flights of pink doves scurrying across the blue in a great hurry if there was a wind. The place where one could see all this, and seem at the same time to breathe a purer air, was, of course, the attic window. When the square suddenly seemed to begin to glow in an enchanted way and look wonderful in spite of its sooty trees and railings, Sara knew something was going on in the sky; and when it was at all possible to leave the kitchen without being missed or called back, she invariably stole away and crept up the flights of stairs, and, climbing on the old table, got her head and body as far out of the window as possible. When she had accomplished this, she always drew a long breath and looked all round her. It used to seem as if she had all the sky and the world to herself. No one else ever looked out of the other attics. Generally the skylights were closed; but even if they were propped open to admit air, no one seemed to come near them. And there Sara would stand, sometimes turning her face upward to the blue which seemed so friendly and near—just like a lovely vaulted ceiling—sometimes watching the west and all the wonderful things that happened there: the clouds melting or drifting or waiting softly to be changed pink or crimson or snow-white or purple or pale dove-gray. Sometimes they made islands or great mountains enclosing lakes of deep turquoise-blue, or liquid amber, or chrysoprase-green; sometimes dark headlands jutted into strange, lost seas; sometimes slender strips of wonderful lands joined other wonderful lands together. There were places where it seemed that one could run or climb or stand and wait to see what next was coming—until, perhaps, as it all melted, one could float away. At least it seemed so to Sara, and nothing had ever been quite so beautiful to her as the things she saw as she stood on the table—her body half out of the skylight—the sparrows twittering with sunset softness on the slates. The sparrows always seemed to her to twitter with a sort of subdued softness just when these marvels were going on.

There was such a sunset as this a few days after the Indian gentleman was brought to his new home; and, as it fortunately happened that the afternoon's work was done in the kitchen and nobody had ordered her to go anywhere or perform any task, Sara found it easier than usual to slip away and go upstairs.

She mounted her table and stood looking out. It was a wonderful moment. There were floods of molten gold covering the west, as if a glorious tide was sweeping over the world. A deep, rich yellow light filled the air; the birds flying across the tops of the houses showed quite black against it.

"It's a Splendid one," said Sara, softly, to herself. "It makes me feel almost afraid—as if something strange was just going to happen. The Splendid ones always make me feel like that."

She suddenly turned her head because she heard a sound a few yards away from her. It was an odd sound like a queer little squeaky chattering. It came from the window of the next attic. Someone had come to look at the sunset as she had. There was a head and a part of a body emerging from the skylight, but it was not the head or body of a little girl or a housemaid; it was the picturesque white-swathed form and dark-faced, gleaming-eyed, white-turbaned head of a native Indian man-servant—"a Lascar," Sara said to herself quickly—and the sound she had heard came from a small monkey he held in his arms as if he were fond of it, and which was snuggling and chattering against his breast.

As Sara looked toward him he looked toward her. The first thing she thought was that his dark face looked sorrowful and homesick. She felt absolutely sure he had come up to look at the sun, because he had seen it so seldom in England that he longed for a sight of it. She looked at him interestedly for a second, and then smiled across the slates. She had learned to know how comforting a smile, even from a stranger, may be.

Hers was evidently a pleasure to him. His whole expression altered, and he showed such gleaming white teeth as he smiled back that it was as if a light had been illuminated in his dusky face. The friendly look in Sara's eyes was always very effective when people felt tired or dull.

It was perhaps in making his salute to her that he loosened his hold on the monkey. He was an impish monkey and always ready for adventure, and it is probable that the sight of a little girl excited him. He suddenly broke loose, jumped on to the slates, ran across them chattering, and actually leaped on to Sara's shoulder, and from there down into her attic room. It made her laugh and delighted her; but she knew he must be restored to his master—if the Lascar was his master—and she wondered how this was to be done. Would he let her catch him, or would he be naughty and refuse to be caught, and perhaps get away and run off over the roofs and be lost? That would not do at all. Perhaps he belonged to the Indian gentleman, and the poor man was fond of him.

She turned to the Lascar, feeling glad that she remembered still some of the Hindustani she had learned when she lived with her father. She could make the man understand. She spoke to him in the language he knew.

"Will he let me catch him?" she asked.

She thought she had never seen more surprise and delight than the dark face expressed when she spoke in the familiar tongue. The truth was that the poor fellow felt as if his gods had intervened, and the kind little voice came from heaven itself. At once Sara saw that he had been accustomed to European children. He poured forth a flood of respectful thanks. He was the servant of Missee Sahib. The monkey was a good monkey and would not bite; but, unfortunately, he was difficult to catch. He would flee from one spot to another, like the lightning. He was disobedient, though not evil. Ram Dass knew him as if he were his child, and Ram Dass he would sometimes obey, but not always. If Missee Sahib would permit Ram Dass, he himself could cross the roof to her room, enter the windows, and regain the unworthy little animal. But he was evidently afraid Sara might think he was taking a great liberty and perhaps would not let him come.

But Sara gave him leave at once.

"Can you get across?" she inquired.

"In a moment," he answered her.

"Then come," she said; "he is flying from side to side of the room as if he was frightened."

Ram Dass slipped through his attic window and crossed to hers as steadily and lightly as if he had walked on roofs all his life. He slipped through the skylight and dropped upon his feet without a sound. Then he turned to Sara and salaamed again. The monkey saw him and uttered a little scream. Ram Dass hastily took the precaution of shutting the skylight, and then went in chase of him. It was not a very long chase. The monkey prolonged it a few minutes evidently for the mere fun of it, but presently he sprang chattering on to Ram Dass's shoulder and sat there chattering and clinging to his neck with a weird little skinny arm.

Ram Dass thanked Sara profoundly. She had seen that his quick native eyes had taken in at a glance all the bare shabbiness of the room, but he spoke to her as if he were speaking to the little daughter of a rajah, and pretended that he observed nothing. He did not presume to remain more than a few moments after he had caught the monkey, and those moments were given to further deep and grateful obeisance to her in return for her indulgence. This little evil one, he said, stroking the monkey, was, in truth, not so evil as he seemed, and his master, who was ill, was sometimes amused by him. He would have been made sad if his favorite had run away and been lost. Then he salaamed once more and got through the skylight and across the slates again with as much agility as the monkey himself had displayed.

When he had gone Sara stood in the middle of her attic and thought of many things his face and his manner had brought back to her. The sight of his native costume and the profound reverence of his manner stirred all her past memories. It seemed a strange thing to remember that she—the drudge whom the cook had said insulting things to an hour ago—had only a few years ago been surrounded by people who all treated her as Ram Dass had treated her; who salaamed when she went by, whose foreheads almost touched the ground when she spoke to them, who were her servants and her slaves. It was like a sort of dream. It was all over, and it could never come back. It certainly seemed that there was no way in which any change could take place. She knew what Miss Minchin intended that her future should be. So long as she was too young to be used as a regular teacher, she would be used as an errand girl and servant and yet expected to remember what she had learned and in some mysterious way to learn more. The greater number of her evenings she was supposed to spend at study, and at various indefinite intervals she was examined and knew she would have been severely admonished if she had not advanced as was expected of her. The truth, indeed, was that Miss Minchin knew that she was too anxious to learn to require teachers. Give her books, and she would devour them and end by knowing them by heart. She might be trusted to be equal to teaching a good deal in the course of a few years. This was what would happen: when she was older she would be expected to drudge in the schoolroom as she drudged now in various parts of the house; they would be obliged to give her more respectable clothes, but they would be sure to be plain and ugly and to make her look somehow like a servant. That was all there seemed to be to look forward to, and Sara stood quite still for several minutes and thought it over.

Then a thought came back to her which made the color rise in her cheek and a spark light itself in her eyes. She straightened her thin little body and lifted her head.

"Whatever comes," she said, "cannot alter one thing. If I am a princess in rags and tatters, I can be a princess inside. It would be easy to be a princess if I were dressed in cloth of gold, but it is a great deal more of a triumph to be one all the time when no one knows it. There was Marie Antoinette when she was in prison and her throne was gone and she had only a black gown on, and her hair was white, and they insulted her and called her Widow Capet. She was a great deal more like a queen then than when she was so gay and everything was so grand. I like her best then. Those howling mobs of people did not frighten her. She was stronger than they were, even when they cut her head off."

This was not a new thought, but quite an old one, by this time. It had consoled her through many a bitter day, and she had gone about the house with an expression in her face which Miss Minchin could not understand and which was a source of great annoyance to her, as it seemed as if the child were mentally living a life which held her above the rest of the world. It was as if she scarcely heard the rude and acid things said to her; or, if she heard them, did not care for them at all. Sometimes, when she was in the midst of some harsh, domineering speech, Miss Minchin would find the still, unchildish eyes fixed upon her with something like a proud smile in them. At such times she did not know that Sara was saying to herself:

"You don't know that you are saying these things to a princess, and that if I chose I could wave my hand and order you to execution. I only spare you because I *am* a princess, and you are a poor, stupid, unkind, vulgar old thing, and don't know any better."

This used to interest and amuse her more than anything else; and queer and fanciful as it was, she found comfort in it and it was a good thing for her. While the thought held possession of her, she could not be made rude and malicious by the rudeness and malice of those about her.

"A princess must be polite," she said to herself.

And so when the servants, taking their tone from their mistress, were insolent and ordered her about, she would hold her head erect and reply to them with a quaint civility which often made them stare at her.

"She's got more airs and graces than if she come from Buckingham Palace, that young one," said the cook, chuckling a little sometimes. "I lose my temper with her often enough, but I will say she never forgets her manners. 'If you please, cook'; 'Will you be so kind, cook?' 'I beg your pardon, cook'; 'May I trouble you, cook?' She drops 'em about the kitchen as if they was nothing."

The morning after the interview with Ram Dass and his monkey, Sara was in the schoolroom with her small pupils. Having finished giving them their lessons, she was putting the French exercise-books together and thinking, as she did it, of the various things royal personages in disguise were called upon to do: Alfred the Great, for instance, burning the cakes and getting his ears boxed by the wife of the neat-herd. How frightened she must have been when she found out what she had done. If Miss Minchin should find out that she—Sara, whose toes were almost sticking out of her boots—was a princess—a real one! The look in her eyes was exactly the look which Miss Minchin most disliked. She would not have it; she was quite near her and was so enraged that she actually flew at her and boxed her ears—exactly as the neat-herd's wife had boxed King Alfred's. It made Sara start. She wakened from her dream at the shock, and, catching her breath, stood still a second. Then, not knowing she was going to do it, she broke into a little laugh.

"What are you laughing at, you bold, impudent child?" Miss Minchin exclaimed.

It took Sara a few seconds to control herself sufficiently to remember that she was a princess. Her cheeks were red and smarting from the blows she had received.

"I was thinking," she answered.

"Beg my pardon immediately," said Miss Minchin.

Sara hesitated a second before she replied.

"I will beg your pardon for laughing, if it was rude," she said then; "but I won't beg your pardon for thinking."

"What were you thinking?" demanded Miss Minchin. "How dare you think? What were you thinking?"

Jessie tittered, and she and Lavinia nudged each other in unison. All the girls looked up from their books to listen. Really, it always interested them a little when Miss Minchin attacked Sara. Sara always said something queer, and never seemed the least bit frightened. She was not in the least frightened now, though her boxed ears were scarlet and her eyes were as bright as stars.

"I was thinking," she answered grandly and politely, "that you did not know what you were doing."

"That I did not know what I was doing?" Miss Minchin fairly gasped.

"Yes," said Sara, "and I was thinking what would happen if I were a princess and you boxed my ears—what I should do to you. And I was thinking that if I were one, you would never dare to do it, whatever I said or did. And I was thinking how surprised and frightened you would be if you suddenly found out—"

She had the imagined future so clearly before her eyes that she spoke in a manner which had an effect even upon Miss Minchin. It almost seemed for the moment to her narrow, unimaginative mind that there must be some real power hidden behind this candid daring.

"What?" she exclaimed. "Found out what?"

"That I really was a princess," said Sara, "and could do anything—anything I liked."

Every pair of eyes in the room widened to its full limit. Lavinia leaned forward on her seat to look.

"Go to your room," cried Miss Minchin, breathlessly, "this instant! Leave the schoolroom! Attend to your lessons, young ladies!"

Sara made a little bow.

"Excuse me for laughing if it was impolite," she said, and walked out of the room, leaving Miss Minchin struggling with her rage, and the girls whispering over their books.

"Did you see her? Did you see how queer she looked?" Jessie broke out. "I shouldn't be at all surprised if she did turn out to be something. Suppose she should!"

12

The Other Side of the Wall

When one lives in a row of houses, it is interesting to think of the things which are being done and said on the other side of the wall of the very rooms one is living in. Sara was fond of amusing herself by trying to imagine the things hidden by the wall which divided the Select Seminary from the Indian gentleman's house. She knew that the schoolroom was next to the Indian gentleman's study, and she hoped that the wall was thick so that the noise made sometimes after lesson hours would not disturb him.

"I am growing quite fond of him," she said to Ermengarde; "I should not like him to be disturbed. I have adopted him for a friend. You can do that with people you never speak to at all. You can just watch them, and think about them and be sorry for them, until they seem almost like relations. I'm quite anxious sometimes when I see the doctor call twice a day."

"I have very few relations," said Ermengarde, reflectively, "and I'm very glad of it. I don't like those I have. My two aunts are always saying, 'Dear me, Ermengarde!

You are very fat. You shouldn't eat sweets,' and my uncle is always asking me things like, 'When did Edward the Third ascend the throne?' and, 'Who died of a surfeit of lampreys?'"

Sara laughed.

"People you never speak to can't ask you questions like that," she said; "and I'm sure the Indian gentleman wouldn't even if he was quite intimate with you. I am fond of him."

She had become fond of the Large Family because they looked happy; but she had become fond of the Indian gentleman because he looked unhappy. He had evidently not fully recovered from some very severe illness. In the kitchen—where, of course, the servants, through some mysterious means, knew everything—there was much discussion of his case. He was not an Indian gentleman really, but an Englishman who had lived in India. He had met with great misfortunes which had for a time so imperilled his whole fortune that he had thought himself ruined and disgraced forever. The shock had been so great that he had almost died of brain fever; and ever since he had been shattered in health, though his fortunes had changed and all his possessions had been restored to him. His trouble and peril had been connected with mines.

"And mines with diamonds in 'em!" said the cook. "No savin's of mine never goes into no mines—particular diamond ones"—with a side glance at Sara. "We all know somethin' of *them*."

"He felt as my papa felt," Sara thought. "He was ill as my papa was; but he did not die."

So her heart was more drawn to him than before. When she was sent out at night she used sometimes to feel quite glad, because there was always a chance that the curtains of the house next door might not yet be closed and she could look into the warm room and see her adopted friend. When no one was about she used sometimes to stop, and, holding to the iron railings, wish him goodnight as if he could hear her.

"Perhaps you can *feel* if you can't hear," was her fancy. "Perhaps kind thoughts reach people somehow, even through windows and doors and walls. Perhaps you feel a little warm and comforted, and don't know why, when I am standing here in the cold and hoping you will get well and happy again. I am so sorry for you," she would whisper in an intense little voice. "I wish you had a 'Little Missus' who could pet you as I used to pet papa when he had a headache. I should like to be your 'Little Missus' myself, poor dear! Goodnight—goodnight. God bless you!"

She would go away, feeling quite comforted and a little warmer herself. Her sympathy was so strong that it seemed as if it *must* reach him somehow as he sat alone in his armchair by the fire, nearly always in a great dressing gown, and nearly always with his forehead resting in his hand as he gazed hopelessly into the fire. He looked to Sara like a man who had a trouble on his mind still, not merely like one whose troubles lay all in the past.

"He always seems as if he were thinking of something that hurts him *now*," she said to herself, "but he has got his money back and he will get over his brain fever in time, so he ought not to look like that. I wonder if there is something else."

If there was something else—something even servants did not hear of—she could not help believing that the father of the Large Family knew it—the gentleman she called Mr. Montmorency. Mr. Montmorency went to see him often, and Mrs. Montmorency and all the little Montmorencys went, too, though less often. He seemed particularly fond of the two elder little girls—the Janet and Nora who had been so alarmed when their small brother Donald had given Sara his sixpence. He had, in fact, a very tender place in his heart for all children, and particularly for little girls. Janet and Nora were as fond of him as he was of them, and looked forward with the greatest pleasure to the afternoons when they were allowed to cross the square and make their well-behaved little visits to him. They were extremely decorous little visits because he was an invalid.

"He is a poor thing," said Janet, "and he says we cheer him up. We try to cheer him up very quietly."

Janet was the head of the family, and kept the rest of it in order. It was she who decided when it was discreet to ask the Indian gentleman to tell stories about India, and it was she who saw when he was tired and it was the time to steal quietly away and tell Ram Dass to go to him. They were very fond of Ram Dass. He could have told any number of stories if he had been able to speak anything but Hindustani. The Indian gentleman's real name was Mr. Carrisford, and Janet told Mr. Carrisford about the encounter with the little-girl-who-was-not-a-beggar. He was very much interested, and all the more so when he heard from Ram Dass of the adventure of the monkey on the roof. Ram Dass made for him a very clear picture of the attic and its desolateness—of the bare floor and broken plaster, the rusty, empty grate, and the hard, narrow bed.

"Carmichael," he said to the father of the Large Family, after he had heard this description, "I wonder how many of the attics in this square are like that one, and how many wretched little servant girls sleep on such beds, while I toss on my down pillows, loaded and harassed by wealth that is, most of it—not mine."

"My dear fellow," Mr. Carmichael answered cheerily, "the sooner you cease tormenting yourself the better it will be for you. If you possessed all the wealth of all the Indies, you could not set right all the discomforts in the world, and if you began to refurnish all the attics in this square, there would still remain all the attics in all the other squares and streets to put in order. And there you are!"

Mr. Carrisford sat and bit his nails as he looked into the glowing bed of coals in the grate.

"Do you suppose," he said slowly, after a pause—"do you think it is possible that the other child—the child I never cease thinking of, I believe—could be—could *possibly* be reduced to any such condition as the poor little soul next door?"

Mr. Carmichael looked at him uneasily. He knew that the worst thing the man could do for himself, for his reason and his health, was to begin to think in the particular way of this particular subject.

"If the child at Madame Pascal's school in Paris was the one you are in search of," he answered soothingly, "she would seem to be in the hands of people who can afford to take care of her. They adopted her because she had been the favorite companion of their little daughter who died. They had no other children, and Madame Pascal said that they were extremely well-to-do Russians."

"And the wretched woman actually did not know where they had taken her!" exclaimed Mr. Carrisford.

Mr. Carmichael shrugged his shoulders.

"She was a shrewd, worldly Frenchwoman, and was evidently only too glad to get the child so comfortably off her hands when the father's death left her totally unprovided for. Women of her type do not trouble themselves about the futures of children who might prove burdens. The adopted parents apparently disappeared and left no trace."

"But you say '*if*' the child was the one I am in search of. You say 'if.' We are not sure. There was a difference in the name."

"Madame Pascal pronounced it as if it were Carew instead of Crewe—but that might be merely a matter of pronunciation. The circumstances were curiously similar. An English officer in India had placed his motherless little girl at the school. He had died suddenly after losing his fortune." Mr. Carmichael paused a moment, as if a new thought had occurred to him. "Are you *sure* the child was left at a school in Paris? Are you sure it was Paris?"

"My dear fellow," broke forth Carrisford, with restless bitterness, "I am *sure* of nothing. I never saw either the child or her mother. Ralph Crewe and I loved each other as boys, but we had not met since our school days, until we met in India. I was absorbed in the magnificent promise of the mines. He became absorbed, too. The whole thing was so huge and glittering that we half lost our heads. When we met we scarcely spoke of anything else. I only knew that the child had been sent to school somewhere. I do not even remember, now, *how* I knew it."

He was beginning to be excited. He always became excited when his still weakened brain was stirred by memories of the catastrophes of the past.

Mr. Carmichael watched him anxiously. It was necessary to ask some questions, but they must be put quietly and with caution.

"But you had reason to think the school *was* in Paris?"

"Yes," was the answer, "because her mother was a Frenchwoman, and I had heard that she wished her child to be educated in Paris. It seemed only likely that she would be there."

"Yes," Mr. Carmichael said, "it seems more than probable."

The Indian gentleman leaned forward and struck the table with a long, wasted hand.

"Carmichael," he said, "I *must* find her. If she is alive, she is somewhere. If she is friendless and penniless, it is through my fault. How is a man to get back his nerve with a thing like that on his mind? This sudden change of luck at the mines has made realities of all our most fantastic dreams, and poor Crewe's child may be begging in the street!"

"No, no," said Carmichael. "Try to be calm. Console yourself with the fact that when she is found you have a fortune to hand over to her."

"Why was I not man enough to stand my ground when things looked black?" Carrisford groaned in petulant misery. "I believe I should have stood my ground if I had not been responsible for other people's money as well as my own. Poor Crewe had put into the scheme every penny that he owned. He trusted me—he *loved* me. And he died thinking I had ruined him—I—Tom Carrisford, who played cricket at Eton with him. What a villain he must have thought me!"

"Don't reproach yourself so bitterly."

"I don't reproach myself because the speculation threatened to fail—I reproach myself for losing my courage. I ran away like a swindler and a thief, because I could not face my best friend and tell him I had ruined him and his child."

The good-hearted father of the Large Family put his hand on his shoulder comfortingly.

"You ran away because your brain had given way under the strain of mental torture," he said. "You were half delirious already. If you had not been you would have stayed and fought it out. You were in a hospital, strapped down in bed, raving with brain fever, two days after you left the place. Remember that."

Carrisford dropped his forehead in his hands.

"Good God! Yes," he said. "I was driven mad with dread and horror. I had not slept for weeks. The night I staggered out of my house all the air seemed full of hideous things mocking and mouthing at me."

"That is explanation enough in itself," said Mr. Carmichael. "How could a man on the verge of brain fever judge sanely!"

Carrisford shook his drooping head.

"And when I returned to consciousness poor Crewe was dead—and buried. And I seemed to remember nothing. I did not remember the child for months and months. Even when I began to recall her existence everything seemed in a sort of haze."

He stopped a moment and rubbed his forehead. "It sometimes seems so now when I try to remember. Surely I must sometime have heard Crewe speak of the school she was sent to. Don't you think so?"

"He might not have spoken of it definitely. You never seem even to have heard her real name."

"He used to call her by an odd pet name he had invented. He called her his 'Little Missus.' But the wretched mines drove everything else out of our heads. We talked of nothing else. If he spoke of the school, I forgot—I forgot. And now I shall never remember."

"Come, come," said Carmichael. "We shall find her yet. We will continue to search for Madame Pascal's good-natured Russians. She seemed to have a vague idea that they lived in Moscow. We will take that as a clue. I will go to Moscow."

"If I were able to travel, I would go with you," said Carrisford; "but I can only sit here wrapped in furs and stare at the fire. And when I look into it I seem to see Crewe's gay young face gazing back at me. He looks as if he were asking me a question. Sometimes I dream of him at night, and he always stands before me and asks the same question in words. Can you guess what he says, Carmichael?"

Mr. Carmichael answered him in a rather low voice.

"Not exactly," he said.

"He always says, 'Tom, old man—Tom—where is the Little Missus?'" He caught at Carmichael's hand and clung to it. "I must be able to answer him—I must!" he said. "Help me to find her. Help me."

On the other side of the wall Sara was sitting in her garret talking to Melchisedec, who had come out for his evening meal.

"It has been hard to be a princess today, Melchisedec," she said. "It has been harder than usual. It gets harder as the weather grows colder and the streets get more sloppy. When Lavinia laughed at my muddy skirt as I passed her in the hall, I thought of something to say all in a flash—and I only just stopped myself in time. You can't sneer back at people like that—if you are a princess. But you have to bite your tongue to hold yourself in. I bit mine. It was a cold afternoon, Melchisedec. And it's a cold night."

Quite suddenly she put her black head down in her arms, as she often did when she was alone.

"Oh, papa," she whispered, "what a long time it seems since I was your 'Little Missus'!"

This was what happened that day on both sides of the wall.

13

One of the Populace

The winter was a wretched one. There were days on which Sara tramped through snow when she went on her errands; there were worse days when the snow melted and combined itself with mud to form slush; there were others when the fog was so thick that the lamps in the street were lighted all day and London looked as it had looked the afternoon, several years ago, when the cab had driven through the thoroughfares with Sara tucked up on its seat, leaning against her father's shoulder. On such days the windows of the house of the Large Family always looked delightfully cozy and alluring, and the study in which the Indian gentleman sat glowed with warmth and rich color. But the attic was dismal beyond words. There were no longer sunsets or sunrises to look at, and scarcely ever any stars, it seemed to Sara. The clouds hung low over the skylight and were either gray or mud-color, or dropping heavy rain. At four o'clock in the afternoon, even when there was no special fog, the daylight was at an end. If it was necessary to go to her attic for anything, Sara was obliged to light a candle. The women in the kitchen were depressed, and that made them more ill-tempered than ever. Becky was driven like a little slave.

"'Twarn't for you, miss," she said hoarsely to Sara one night when she had crept into the attic—"'twarn't for you, an' the Bastille, an' bein' the prisoner in the next cell, I should die. That there does seem real now, doesn't it? The missus is more like the head jailer every day she lives. I can jest see them big keys you say she carries. The cook she's like one of the under-jailers. Tell me some more, please, miss—tell me about the subt'ranean passage we've dug under the walls."

"I'll tell you something warmer," shivered Sara. "Get your coverlet and wrap it round you, and I'll get mine, and we will huddle close together on the bed, and I'll tell you about the tropical forest where the Indian gentleman's monkey used to live. When I see him sitting on the table near the window and looking out into the street with that mournful expression, I always feel sure he is thinking about the tropical forest where he used to swing by his tail from coconut trees. I wonder who caught him, and if he left a family behind who had depended on him for coconuts."

"That is warmer, miss," said Becky, gratefully; "but, someways, even the Bastille is sort of heatin' when you gets to tellin' about it."

"That is because it makes you think of something else," said Sara, wrapping the coverlet round her until only her small dark face was to be seen looking out of it. "I've noticed this. What you have to do with your mind, when your body is miserable, is to make it think of something else."

"Can you do it, miss?" faltered Becky, regarding her with admiring eyes.

Sara knitted her brows a moment.

"Sometimes I can and sometimes I can't," she said stoutly. "But when I *can* I'm all right. And what I believe is that we always could—if we practiced enough. I've been practicing a good deal lately, and it's beginning to be easier than it used to be. When things are horrible—just horrible—I think as hard as ever I can of being a princess. I say to myself, 'I am a princess, and I am a fairy one, and because I am a fairy nothing can hurt me or make me uncomfortable.' You don't know how it makes you forget"—with a laugh.

She had many opportunities of making her mind think of something else, and many opportunities of proving to herself whether or not she was a princess. But one of the strongest tests she was ever put to came on a certain dreadful day which, she often thought afterward, would never quite fade out of her memory even in the years to come.

For several days it had rained continuously; the streets were chilly and sloppy and full of dreary, cold mist; there was mud everywhere—sticky London mud—and over everything the pall of drizzle and fog. Of course there were several long and tiresome errands to be done—there always were on days like this—and Sara was sent out again and again, until her shabby clothes were damp through. The absurd old feathers on her forlorn hat were more draggled and absurd than ever, and her downtrodden shoes were so wet that they could not hold any more water. Added to this, she had been deprived of her dinner, because Miss Minchin had chosen to punish her. She was so cold and hungry and tired that her face began to have a pinched look, and now and then some kind-hearted person passing her in the street glanced at her with sudden sympathy. But she did not know that. She hurried on, trying to make her mind think of something else. It was really very necessary. Her way of doing it was to "pretend" and "suppose" with all the strength that was left in her. But really this time it was harder than she had ever found it, and once or twice she thought it almost made her more cold and hungry instead of less so. But she persevered obstinately, and as the muddy water squelched through her broken shoes and the wind seemed trying to drag her thin jacket from her, she talked to herself as she walked, though she did not speak aloud or even move her lips.

"Suppose I had dry clothes on," she thought. "Suppose I had good shoes and a long, thick coat and merino stockings and a whole umbrella. And suppose—suppose—just when I was near a baker's where they sold hot buns, I should find sixpence—which belonged to nobody. *Suppose* if I did, I should go into the shop and buy six of the hottest buns and eat them all without stopping."

Some very odd things happen in this world sometimes.

It certainly was an odd thing that happened to Sara. She had to cross the street just when she was saying this to herself. The mud was dreadful—she almost had to wade. She picked her way as carefully as she could, but she could not save herself much; only, in picking her way, she had to look down at her feet and the mud, and in looking down—just as she reached the pavement—she saw something shining in the gutter. It was actually a piece of silver—a tiny piece trodden upon by many feet, but still with spirit enough left to shine a little. Not quite a sixpence, but the next thing to it—a fourpenny piece.

In one second it was in her cold little red-and-blue hand.

"Oh," she gasped, "it is true! It is true!"

And then, if you will believe me, she looked straight at the shop directly facing her. And it was a baker's shop, and a cheerful, stout, motherly woman with rosy cheeks was putting into the window a tray of delicious newly baked hot buns, fresh from the oven—large, plump, shiny buns, with currants in them.

It almost made Sara feel faint for a few seconds—the shock, and the sight of the buns, and the delightful odors of warm bread floating up through the baker's cellar window.

She knew she need not hesitate to use the little piece of money. It had evidently been lying in the mud for some time, and its owner was completely lost in the stream of passing people who crowded and jostled each other all day long.

"But I'll go and ask the baker woman if she has lost anything," she said to herself, rather faintly. So she crossed the pavement and put her wet foot on the step. As she did so she saw something that made her stop.

It was a little figure more forlorn even than herself—a little figure which was not much more than a bundle of rags, from which small, bare, red muddy feet peeped out, only because the rags with which their owner was trying to cover them were not long enough. Above the rags appeared a shock head of tangled hair, and a dirty face with big, hollow, hungry eyes.

Sara knew they were hungry eyes the moment she saw them, and she felt a sudden sympathy.

"This," she said to herself, with a little sigh, "is one of the populace—and she is hungrier than I am."

The child—this "one of the populace"—stared up at Sara, and shuffled herself aside a little, so as to give her room to pass. She was used to being made to give room to everybody. She knew that if a policeman chanced to see her he would tell her to "move on."

Sara clutched her little fourpenny piece and hesitated for a few seconds. Then she spoke to her.

"Are you hungry?" she asked.

The child shuffled herself and her rags a little more.

"Ain't I jist?" she said in a hoarse voice. "Jist ain't I?"

"Haven't you had any dinner?" said Sara.

"No dinner," more hoarsely still and with more shuffling. "Nor yet no bre'fast—nor yet no supper. No nothin'.

"Since when?" asked Sara.

"Dunno. Never got nothin' today—nowhere. I've axed an' axed."

Just to look at her made Sara more hungry and faint. But those queer little thoughts were at work in her brain, and she was talking to herself, though she was sick at heart.

"If I'm a princess," she was saying, "if I'm a princess—when they were poor and driven from their thrones—they always shared—with the populace—if they met one poorer and hungrier than themselves. They always shared. Buns are a penny each. If it had been sixpence I could have eaten six. It won't be enough for either of us. But it will be better than nothing."

"Wait a minute," she said to the beggar child.

She went into the shop. It was warm and smelled deliciously. The woman was just going to put some more hot buns into the window.

"If you please," said Sara, "have you lost fourpence—a silver fourpence?" And she held the forlorn little piece of money out to her.

The woman looked at it and then at her—at her intense little face and draggled, once fine clothes.

"Bless us, no," she answered. "Did you find it?"

"Yes," said Sara. "In the gutter."

"Keep it, then," said the woman. "It may have been there for a week, and goodness knows who lost it. *You* could never find out."

"I know that," said Sara, "but I thought I would ask you."

"Not many would," said the woman, looking puzzled and interested and good-natured all at once.

"Do you want to buy something?" she added, as she saw Sara glance at the buns.

"Four buns, if you please," said Sara. "Those at a penny each."

The woman went to the window and put some in a paper bag.

Sara noticed that she put in six.

"I said four, if you please," she explained. "I have only fourpence."

"I'll throw in two for makeweight," said the woman with her good-natured look. "I dare say you can eat them sometime. Aren't you hungry?"

A mist rose before Sara's eyes.

"Yes," she answered. "I am very hungry, and I am much obliged to you for your kindness; and"—she was going to add—"there is a child outside who is hungrier than I am." But just at that moment two or three customers came in at once, and each one seemed in a hurry, so she could only thank the woman again and go out.

The beggar girl was still huddled up in the corner of the step. She looked frightful in her wet and dirty rags. She was staring straight before her with a stupid look of suffering, and Sara saw her suddenly draw the back of her roughened black hand across her eyes to rub away the tears which seemed to have surprised her by forcing their way from under her lids. She was muttering to herself.

Sara opened the paper bag and took out one of the hot buns, which had already warmed her own cold hands a little.

"See," she said, putting the bun in the ragged lap, "this is nice and hot. Eat it, and you will not feel so hungry."

The child started and stared up at her, as if such sudden, amazing good luck almost frightened her; then she snatched up the bun and began to cram it into her mouth with great wolfish bites.

"Oh, my! Oh, my!" Sara heard her say hoarsely, in wild delight. "*Oh my*!"

Sara took out three more buns and put them down.

The sound in the hoarse, ravenous voice was awful.

"She is hungrier than I am," she said to herself. "She's starving." But her hand trembled when she put down the fourth bun. "I'm not starving," she said—and she put down the fifth.

The little ravening London savage was still snatching and devouring when she turned away. She was too ravenous to give any thanks, even if she had ever been taught politeness—which she had not. She was only a poor little wild animal.

"Goodbye," said Sara.

When she reached the other side of the street she looked back. The child had a bun in each hand and had stopped in the middle of a bite to watch her. Sara gave her a little nod, and the child, after another stare—a curious lingering stare—jerked her shaggy head in response, and until Sara was out of sight she did not take another bite or even finish the one she had begun.

At that moment the baker-woman looked out of her shop window.

"Well, I never!" she exclaimed. "If that young un hasn't given her buns to a beggar child! It wasn't because she didn't want them, either. Well, well, she looked hungry enough. I'd give something to know what she did it for."

She stood behind her window for a few moments and pondered. Then her curiosity got the better of her. She went to the door and spoke to the beggar child.

"Who gave you those buns?" she asked her. The child nodded her head toward Sara's vanishing figure.

"What did she say?" inquired the woman.

"Axed me if I was 'ungry," replied the hoarse voice.

"What did you say?"

"Said I was jist."

"And then she came in and got the buns, and gave them to you, did she?"

The child nodded.

"How many?"

"Five."

The woman thought it over.

"Left just one for herself," she said in a low voice. "And she could have eaten the whole six—I saw it in her eyes."

She looked after the little draggled far-away figure and felt more disturbed in her usually comfortable mind than she had felt for many a day.

"I wish she hadn't gone so quick," she said. "I'm blest if she shouldn't have had a dozen." Then she turned to the child.

"Are you hungry yet?" she said.

"I'm allus hungry," was the answer, "but 't ain't as bad as it was."

"Come in here," said the woman, and she held open the shop door.

The child got up and shuffled in. To be invited into a warm place full of bread seemed an incredible thing. She did not know what was going to happen. She did not care, even.

"Get yourself warm," said the woman, pointing to a fire in the tiny back room. "And look here; when you are hard up for a bit of bread, you can come in here and ask for it. I'm blest if I won't give it to you for that young one's sake."

Sara found some comfort in her remaining bun. At all events, it was very hot, and it was better than nothing. As she walked along she broke off small pieces and ate them slowly to make them last longer.

"Suppose it was a magic bun," she said, "and a bite was as much as a whole dinner. I should be overeating myself if I went on like this."

It was dark when she reached the square where the Select Seminary was situated. The lights in the houses were all lighted. The blinds were not yet drawn in the windows of the room where she nearly always caught glimpses of members of the Large Family. Frequently at this hour she could see the gentleman she called Mr. Montmorency sitting in a big chair, with a small swarm round him, talking, laughing, perching on the arms of his seat or on his knees or leaning against them. This evening the swarm was about him, but he was not seated. On the contrary, there was a good deal of excitement going on. It was evident that a journey was to be taken, and it was Mr. Montmorency who was to take it. A brougham stood before the door, and a big portmanteau had been strapped upon it. The children were dancing about, chattering and hanging on to their father. The pretty rosy mother was standing near him, talking as if she was asking final questions. Sara paused a moment to see the little ones lifted up and kissed and the bigger ones bent over and kissed also.

"I wonder if he will stay away long," she thought. "The portmanteau is rather big. Oh, dear, how they will miss him! I shall miss him myself—even though he doesn't know I am alive."

When the door opened she moved away—remembering the sixpence—but she saw the traveler come out and stand against the background of the warmly-lighted hall, the older children still hovering about him.

"Will Moscow be covered with snow?" said the little girl Janet. "Will there be ice everywhere?"

"Shall you drive in a drosky?" cried another. "Shall you see the Czar?"

"I will write and tell you all about it," he answered, laughing. "And I will send you pictures of muzhiks and things. Run into the house. It is a hideous damp night. I would rather stay with you than go to Moscow. Goodnight! Goodnight, duckies! God bless you!" And he ran down the steps and jumped into the brougham.

"If you find the little girl, give her our love," shouted Guy Clarence, jumping up and down on the doormat.

Then they went in and shut the door.

"Did you see," said Janet to Nora, as they went back to the room—"the little-girl-who-is-not-a-beggar was passing? She looked all cold and wet, and I saw her turn her head over her shoulder and look at us. Mamma says her clothes always look as if they had been given her by someone who was quite rich—someone who only let her have them because they were too shabby to wear. The people at the school always send her out on errands on the horridest days and nights there are."

Sara crossed the square to Miss Minchin's area steps, feeling faint and shaky.

"I wonder who the little girl is," she thought—"the little girl he is going to look for."

And she went down the area steps, lugging her basket and finding it very heavy indeed, as the father of the Large Family drove quickly on his way to the station to take the train which was to carry him to Moscow, where he was to make his best efforts to search for the lost little daughter of Captain Crewe.

14

What Melchisedec Heard and Saw

On this very afternoon, while Sara was out, a strange thing happened in the attic. Only Melchisedec saw and heard it; and he was so much alarmed and mystified that he scuttled back to his hole and hid there, and really quaked and trembled as he peeped out furtively and with great caution to watch what was going on.

The attic had been very still all the day after Sara had left it in the early morning. The stillness had only been broken by the pattering of the rain upon the slates and the skylight. Melchisedec had, in fact, found it rather dull; and when the rain ceased to patter and perfect silence reigned, he decided to come out and reconnoiter, though experience taught him that Sara would not return for some time. He had been rambling and sniffing about, and had just found a totally unexpected and unexplained crumb left from his last meal, when his attention was attracted by a sound on the roof. He stopped to listen with a palpitating heart. The sound suggested that something was moving on the roof. It was approaching the skylight; it reached the skylight. The skylight was being mysteriously opened. A dark face peered into the attic; then another face appeared behind it, and both looked in with signs of caution and interest. Two men were outside on the roof, and were making silent preparations to enter through the skylight itself. One was Ram Dass and the other was a young man who was the Indian gentleman's secretary; but of course Melchisedec did not know this. He only knew that the men were invading the silence and privacy of the attic; and as the one with the dark face let himself down through the aperture with such lightness and dexterity that he did not make the slightest sound, Melchisedec turned tail and fled precipitately back to his hole. He was frightened to death. He had ceased to be timid with Sara, and knew she would never throw anything but crumbs, and would never make any sound other than the soft, low, coaxing whistling; but strange men were dangerous things to remain near. He lay close and flat near the entrance of his home, just managing to peep through the crack with a bright, alarmed eye. How much he understood of the talk he heard I am not in the least able to say; but, even if he had understood it all, he would probably have remained greatly mystified.

The secretary, who was light and young, slipped through the skylight as noiselessly as Ram Dass had done; and he caught a last glimpse of Melchisedec's vanishing tail.

"Was that a rat?" he asked Ram Dass in a whisper.

"Yes; a rat, Sahib," answered Ram Dass, also whispering. "There are many in the walls."

"Ugh!" exclaimed the young man. "It is a wonder the child is not terrified of them."

Ram Dass made a gesture with his hands. He also smiled respectfully. He was in this place as the intimate exponent of Sara, though she had only spoken to him once.

"The child is the little friend of all things, Sahib," he answered. "She is not as other children. I see her when she does not see me. I slip across the slates and look at her many nights to see that she is safe. I watch her from my window when she does not know I am near. She stands on the table there and looks out at the sky as if it spoke to her. The sparrows come at her call. The rat she has fed and tamed in her loneliness. The poor slave of the house comes to her for comfort. There is a little child who comes to her in secret; there is one older who worships her and would listen to her forever if she might. This I have seen when I have crept across the roof. By the mistress of the house—who is an evil woman—she is treated like a pariah; but she has the bearing of a child who is of the blood of kings!"

"You seem to know a great deal about her," the secretary said.

"All her life each day I know," answered Ram Dass. "Her going out I know, and her coming in; her sadness and her poor joys; her coldness and her hunger. I know when she is alone until midnight, learning from her books; I know when her secret friends steal to her and she is happier—as children can be, even in the midst of poverty—because they come and she may laugh and talk with them in whispers. If she were ill I should know, and I would come and serve her if it might be done."

"You are sure no one comes near this place but herself, and that she will not return and surprise us. She would be frightened if she found us here, and the Sahib Carrisford's plan would be spoiled."

Ram Dass crossed noiselessly to the door and stood close to it.

"None mount here but herself, Sahib," he said. "She has gone out with her basket and may be gone for hours. If I stand here I can hear any step before it reaches the last flight of the stairs."

The secretary took a pencil and a tablet from his breast pocket.

"Keep your ears open," he said; and he began to walk slowly and softly round the miserable little room, making rapid notes on his tablet as he looked at things.

First he went to the narrow bed. He pressed his hand upon the mattress and uttered an exclamation.

"As hard as a stone," he said. "That will have to be altered some day when she is out. A special journey can be made to bring it across. It cannot be done tonight." He lifted the covering and examined the one thin pillow.

"Coverlet dingy and worn, blanket thin, sheets patched and ragged," he said. "What a bed for a child to sleep in—and in a house which calls itself respectable! There has not been a fire in that grate for many a day," glancing at the rusty fireplace.

"Never since I have seen it," said Ram Dass. "The mistress of the house is not one who remembers that another than herself may be cold."

The secretary was writing quickly on his tablet. He looked up from it as he tore off a leaf and slipped it into his breast pocket.

"It is a strange way of doing the thing," he said. "Who planned it?"

Ram Dass made a modestly apologetic obeisance.

"It is true that the first thought was mine, Sahib," he said; "though it was naught but a fancy. I am fond of this child; we are both lonely. It is her way to relate her visions to her secret friends. Being sad one night, I lay close to the open skylight and listened. The vision she related told what this miserable room might be if it had comforts in it. She seemed to see it as she talked, and she grew cheered and warmed as she spoke. Then she came to this fancy; and the next day, the Sahib being ill and wretched, I told him of the thing to amuse him. It seemed then but a dream, but it pleased the Sahib. To hear of the child's doings gave him entertainment. He became interested in her and asked questions. At last he began to please himself with the thought of making her visions real things."

"You think that it can be done while she sleeps? Suppose she awakened," suggested the secretary; and it was evident that whatsoever the plan referred to was, it had caught and pleased his fancy as well as the Sahib Carrisford's.

"I can move as if my feet were of velvet," Ram Dass replied; "and children sleep soundly—even the unhappy ones. I could have entered this room in the night many times, and without causing her to turn upon her pillow. If the other bearer passes to me the things through the window, I can do all and she will not stir. When she awakens she will think a magician has been here."

He smiled as if his heart warmed under his white robe, and the secretary smiled back at him.

"It will be like a story from the *Arabian Nights*," he said. "Only an Oriental could have planned it. It does not belong to London fogs."

They did not remain very long, to the great relief of Melchisedec, who, as he probably did not comprehend their conversation, felt their movements and whispers ominous. The young secretary seemed interested in everything. He wrote down things about the floor, the fireplace, the broken footstool, the old table, the walls—which last he touched with his hand again and again, seeming much pleased when he found that a number of old nails had been driven in various places.

"You can hang things on them," he said.

Ram Dass smiled mysteriously.

"Yesterday, when she was out," he said, "I entered, bringing with me small, sharp nails which can be pressed into the wall without blows from a hammer. I placed many in the plaster where I may need them. They are ready."

The Indian gentleman's secretary stood still and looked round him as he thrust his tablets back into his pocket.

"I think I have made notes enough; we can go now," he said. "The Sahib Carrisford has a warm heart. It is a thousand pities that he has not found the lost child."

"If he should find her his strength would be restored to him," said Ram Dass. "His God may lead her to him yet."

Then they slipped through the skylight as noiselessly as they had entered it. And, after he was quite sure they had gone, Melchisedec was greatly relieved, and in the course of a few minutes felt it safe to emerge from his hole again and scuffle about in the hope that even such alarming human beings as these might have chanced to carry crumbs in their pockets and drop one or two of them.

15

The Magic

When Sara had passed the house next door she had seen Ram Dass closing the shutters, and caught her glimpse of this room also.

"It is a long time since I saw a nice place from the inside," was the thought which crossed her mind.

There was the usual bright fire glowing in the grate, and the Indian gentleman was sitting before it. His head was resting in his hand, and he looked as lonely and unhappy as ever.

"Poor man!" said Sara. "I wonder what *you* are supposing."

And this was what he was "supposing" at that very moment.

"Suppose," he was thinking, "suppose—even if Carmichael traces the people to Moscow—the little girl they took from Madame Pascal's school in Paris is *not* the one we are in search of. Suppose she proves to be quite a different child. What steps shall I take next?"

When Sara went into the house she met Miss Minchin, who had come downstairs to scold the cook.

"Where have you wasted your time?" she demanded. "You have been out for hours."

"It was so wet and muddy," Sara answered, "it was hard to walk, because my shoes were so bad and slipped about."

"Make no excuses," said Miss Minchin, "and tell no falsehoods."

Sara went in to the cook. The cook had received a severe lecture and was in a fearful temper as a result. She was only too rejoiced to have someone to vent her rage on, and Sara was a convenience, as usual.

"Why didn't you stay all night?" she snapped.

Sara laid her purchases on the table.

"Here are the things," she said.

The cook looked them over, grumbling. She was in a very savage humor indeed.

"May I have something to eat?" Sara asked rather faintly.

"Tea's over and done with," was the answer. "Did you expect me to keep it hot for you?"

Sara stood silent for a second.

"I had no dinner," she said next, and her voice was quite low. She made it low because she was afraid it would tremble.

"There's some bread in the pantry," said the cook. "That's all you'll get at this time of day."

Sara went and found the bread. It was old and hard and dry. The cook was in too vicious a humor to give her anything to eat with it. It was always safe and easy to vent her spite on Sara. Really, it was hard for the child to climb the three long flights of stairs leading to her attic. She often found them long and steep when she was tired; but tonight it seemed as if she would never reach the top. Several times she was obliged to stop to rest. When she reached the top landing she was glad to see the glimmer of a light coming from under her door. That meant that Ermengarde had managed to creep up to pay her a visit. There was some comfort in that. It was better than to go into the room alone and find it empty and desolate. The mere presence of plump, comfortable Ermengarde, wrapped in her red shawl, would warm it a little.

Yes; there Ermengarde was when she opened the door. She was sitting in the middle of the bed, with her feet tucked safely under her. She had never become intimate with Melchisedec and his family, though they rather fascinated her. When she found herself alone in the attic she always preferred to sit on the bed until Sara arrived. She had, in fact, on this occasion had time to become rather nervous, because Melchisedec had appeared and sniffed about a good deal, and once had made her utter a repressed squeal by sitting up on his hind legs and, while he looked at her, sniffing pointedly in her direction.

"Oh, Sara," she cried out, "I *am* glad you have come. Melchy *would* sniff about so. I tried to coax him to go back, but he wouldn't for such a long time. I like him, you know; but it does frighten me when he sniffs right at me. Do you think he ever *would* jump?"

"No," answered Sara.

Ermengarde crawled forward on the bed to look at her.

"You *do* look tired, Sara," she said; "you are quite pale."

"I *am* tired," said Sara, dropping on to the lopsided footstool. "Oh, there's Melchisedec, poor thing. He's come to ask for his supper."

Melchisedec had come out of his hole as if he had been listening for her footstep. Sara was quite sure he knew it. He came forward with an affectionate, expectant expression as Sara put her hand in her pocket and turned it inside out, shaking her head.

"I'm very sorry," she said. "I haven't one crumb left. Go home, Melchisedec, and tell your wife there was nothing in my pocket. I'm afraid I forgot because the cook and Miss Minchin were so cross."

Melchisedec seemed to understand. He shuffled resignedly, if not contentedly, back to his home.

"I did not expect to see you tonight, Ermie," Sara said. Ermengarde hugged herself in the red shawl.

"Miss Amelia has gone out to spend the night with her old aunt," she explained. "No one else ever comes and looks into the bedrooms after we are in bed. I could stay here until morning if I wanted to."

She pointed toward the table under the skylight. Sara had not looked toward it as she came in. A number of books were piled upon it. Ermengarde's gesture was a dejected one.

"Papa has sent me some more books, Sara," she said. "There they are."

Sara looked round and got up at once. She ran to the table, and picking up the top volume, turned over its leaves quickly. For the moment she forgot her discomforts.

"Ah," she cried out, "how beautiful! Carlyle's *French Revolution*. I have *so* wanted to read that!"

"I haven't," said Ermengarde. "And papa will be so cross if I don't. He'll expect me to know all about it when I go home for the holidays. What *shall* I do?"

Sara stopped turning over the leaves and looked at her with an excited flush on her cheeks.

"Look here," she cried, "if you'll lend me these books, *I'll* read them—and tell you everything that's in them afterward—and I'll tell it so that you will remember it, too."

"Oh, goodness!" exclaimed Ermengarde. "Do you think you can?"

"I know I can," Sara answered. "The little ones always remember what I tell them."

"Sara," said Ermengarde, hope gleaming in her round face, "if you'll do that, and make me remember, I'll—I'll give you anything."

"I don't want you to give me anything," said Sara. "I want your books—I want them!" And her eyes grew big, and her chest heaved.

"Take them, then," said Ermengarde. "I wish I wanted them—but I don't. I'm not clever, and my father is, and he thinks I ought to be."

Sara was opening one book after the other. "What are you going to tell your father?" she asked, a slight doubt dawning in her mind.

"Oh, he needn't know," answered Ermengarde. "He'll think I've read them."

Sara put down her book and shook her head slowly. "That's almost like telling lies," she said. "And lies—well, you see, they are not only wicked—they're *vulgar.* Sometimes"—reflectively—"I've thought perhaps I might do something wicked—I might suddenly fly into a rage and kill Miss Minchin, you know, when she was ill-treating me—but I *couldn't* be vulgar. Why can't you tell your father *I* read them?"

"He wants me to read them," said Ermengarde, a little discouraged by this unexpected turn of affairs.

"He wants you to know what is in them," said Sara. "And if I can tell it to you in an easy way and make you remember it, I should think he would like that."

"He'll like it if I learn anything in *any* way," said rueful Ermengarde. "You would if you were my father."

"It's not your fault that—" began Sara. She pulled herself up and stopped rather suddenly. She had been going to say, "It's not your fault that you are stupid."

"That what?" Ermengarde asked.

"That you can't learn things quickly," amended Sara. "If you can't, you can't. If I can—why, I can; that's all."

She always felt very tender of Ermengarde, and tried not to let her feel too strongly the difference between being able to learn anything at once, and not being able to learn anything at all. As she looked at her plump face, one of her wise, old-fashioned thoughts came to her.

"Perhaps," she said, "to be able to learn things quickly isn't everything. To be kind is worth a great deal to other people. If Miss Minchin knew everything on earth and was like what she is now, she'd still be a detestable thing, and everybody would hate her. Lots of clever people have done harm and have been wicked. Look at Robespierre—"

She stopped and examined Ermengarde's countenance, which was beginning to look bewildered. "Don't you remember?" she demanded. "I told you about him not long ago. I believe you've forgotten."

"Well, I don't remember *all* of it," admitted Ermengarde.

"Well, you wait a minute," said Sara, "and I'll take off my wet things and wrap myself in the coverlet and tell you over again."

She took off her hat and coat and hung them on a nail against the wall, and she changed her wet shoes for an old pair of slippers. Then she jumped on the bed, and drawing the coverlet about her shoulders, sat with her arms round her knees. "Now, listen," she said.

She plunged into the gory records of the French Revolution, and told such stories of it that Ermengarde's eyes grew round with alarm and she held her breath. But though she was rather terrified, there was a delightful thrill in listening, and she was not likely to forget Robespierre again, or to have any doubts about the Princesse de Lamballe.

"You know they put her head on a pike and danced round it," Sara explained. "And she had beautiful floating blonde hair; and when I think of her, I never see her head on her body, but always on a pike, with those furious people dancing and howling."

It was agreed that Mr. St. John was to be told the plan they had made, and for the present the books were to be left in the attic.

"Now let's tell each other things," said Sara. "How are you getting on with your French lessons?"

"Ever so much better since the last time I came up here and you explained the conjugations. Miss Minchin could not understand why I did my exercises so well that first morning."

Sara laughed a little and hugged her knees.

"She doesn't understand why Lottie is doing her sums so well," she said; "but it is because she creeps up here, too, and I help her." She glanced round the room. "The attic would be rather nice—if it wasn't so dreadful," she said, laughing again. "It's a good place to pretend in."

The truth was that Ermengarde did not know anything of the sometimes almost unbearable side of life in the attic and she had not a sufficiently vivid imagination to depict it for herself. On the rare occasions that she could reach Sara's room she only saw the side of it which was made exciting by things which were "pretended" and stories which were told. Her visits partook of the character of adventures; and though sometimes Sara looked rather pale, and it was not to be denied that she had grown very thin, her proud little spirit would not admit of complaints. She had never confessed that at times she was almost ravenous with hunger, as she was tonight. She was growing rapidly, and her constant walking and running about would have given her a keen appetite even if she had had abundant and regular meals of a much more nourishing nature than the unappetizing, inferior food snatched at such odd times as suited the kitchen convenience. She was growing used to a certain gnawing feeling in her young stomach.

"I suppose soldiers feel like this when they are on a long and weary march," she often said to herself. She liked the sound of the phrase, "long and weary march." It made her feel rather like a soldier. She had also a quaint sense of being a hostess in the attic.

"If I lived in a castle," she argued, "and Ermengarde was the lady of another castle, and came to see me, with knights and squires and vassals riding with her, and pennons flying, when I heard the clarions sounding outside the drawbridge I should go down to receive her, and I should spread feasts in the banquet hall and call in minstrels to sing and play and relate romances. When she comes into the attic I can't spread feasts, but I can tell stories, and not let her know disagreeable things. I dare say poor chatelaines had to do that in time of famine, when their lands had been pillaged." She was a proud, brave little chatelaine, and dispensed generously the one hospitality she could offer—the dreams she dreamed—the visions she saw—the imaginings which were her joy and comfort.

So, as they sat together, Ermengarde did not know that she was faint as well as ravenous, and that while she talked she now and then wondered if her hunger would let her sleep when she was left alone. She felt as if she had never been quite so hungry before.

"I wish I was as thin as you, Sara," Ermengarde said suddenly. "I believe you are thinner than you used to be. Your eyes look so big, and look at the sharp little bones sticking out of your elbow!"

Sara pulled down her sleeve, which had pushed itself up.

"I always was a thin child," she said bravely, "and I always had big green eyes."

"I love your queer eyes," said Ermengarde, looking into them with affectionate admiration. "They always look as if they saw such a long way. I love them—and I love them to be green—though they look black generally."

"They are cat's eyes," laughed Sara; "but I can't see in the dark with them—because I have tried, and I couldn't—I wish I could."

It was just at this minute that something happened at the skylight which neither of them saw. If either of them had chanced to turn and look, she would have been startled by the sight of a dark face which peered cautiously into the room and disappeared as quickly and almost as silently as it had appeared. Not *quite* as silently, however. Sara, who had keen ears, suddenly turned a little and looked up at the roof.

"That didn't sound like Melchisedec," she said. "It wasn't scratchy enough."

"What?" said Ermengarde, a little startled.

"Didn't you think you heard something?" asked Sara.

"N-no," Ermengarde faltered. "Did you?"

"Perhaps I didn't," said Sara; "but I thought I did. It sounded as if something was on the slates—something that dragged softly."

"What could it be?" said Ermengarde. "Could it be—robbers?"

"No," Sara began cheerfully. "There is nothing to steal—"

She broke off in the middle of her words. They both heard the sound that checked her. It was not on the slates, but on the stairs below, and it was Miss Minchin's angry voice. Sara sprang off the bed, and put out the candle.

"She is scolding Becky," she whispered, as she stood in the darkness. "She is making her cry."

"Will she come in here?" Ermengarde whispered back, panic-stricken.

"No. She will think I am in bed. Don't stir."

It was very seldom that Miss Minchin mounted the last flight of stairs. Sara could only remember that she had done it once before. But now she was angry enough to be coming at least part of the way up, and it sounded as if she was driving Becky before her.

"You impudent, dishonest child!" they heard her say. "Cook tells me she has missed things repeatedly."

"'T warn't me, mum," said Becky sobbing. "I was 'ungry enough, but 't warn't me—never!"

"You deserve to be sent to prison," said Miss Minchin's voice. "Picking and stealing! Half a meat pie, indeed!"

"'T warn't me," wept Becky. "I could 'ave eat a whole 'un—but I never laid a finger on it."

Miss Minchin was out of breath between temper and mounting the stairs. The meat pie had been intended for her special late supper. It became apparent that she boxed Becky's ears.

"Don't tell falsehoods," she said. "Go to your room this instant."

Both Sara and Ermengarde heard the slap, and then heard Becky run in her slipshod shoes up the stairs and into her attic. They heard her door shut, and knew that she threw herself upon her bed.

"I could 'ave e't two of 'em," they heard her cry into her pillow. "An' I never took a bite. 'Twas cook give it to her policeman."

Sara stood in the middle of the room in the darkness. She was clenching her little teeth and opening and shutting fiercely her outstretched hands. She could scarcely stand still, but she dared not move until Miss Minchin had gone down the stairs and all was still.

"The wicked, cruel thing!" she burst forth. "The cook takes things herself and then says Becky steals them. She *doesn't*! She *doesn't*! She's so hungry sometimes that she eats crusts out of the ash barrel!" She pressed her hands hard against her face and burst into passionate little sobs, and Ermengarde, hearing this unusual thing, was overawed by it. Sara was crying! The unconquerable Sara! It seemed to denote something new—some mood she had never known. Suppose—suppose—a new dread possibility presented itself to her kind, slow, little mind all at once. She crept off the bed in the dark and found her way to the table where the candle stood. She struck a match and lit the candle. When she had lighted it, she bent forward and looked at Sara, with her new thought growing to definite fear in her eyes.

"Sara," she said in a timid, almost awe-stricken voice, "are—are—you never told me—I don't want to be rude, but—are *you* ever hungry?"

It was too much just at that moment. The barrier broke down. Sara lifted her face from her hands.

"Yes," she said in a new passionate way. "Yes, I am. I'm so hungry now that I could almost eat *you*. And it makes it worse to hear poor Becky. She's hungrier than I am."

Ermengarde gasped.

"Oh, oh!" she cried woefully. "And I never knew!"

"I didn't want you to know," Sara said. "It would have made me feel like a street beggar. I know I look like a street beggar."

"No, you don't—you don't!" Ermengarde broke in. "Your clothes are a little queer—but you *couldn't* look like a street beggar. You haven't a street-beggar face."

"A little boy once gave me a sixpence for charity," said Sara, with a short little laugh in spite of herself. "Here it is." And she pulled out the thin ribbon from her neck. "He wouldn't have given me his Christmas sixpence if I hadn't looked as if I needed it."

Somehow the sight of the dear little sixpence was good for both of them. It made them laugh a little, though they both had tears in their eyes.

"Who was he?" asked Ermengarde, looking at it quite as if it had not been a mere ordinary silver sixpence.

"He was a darling little thing going to a party," said Sara. "He was one of the Large Family, the little one with the round legs—the one I call Guy Clarence. I suppose his nursery was crammed with Christmas presents and hampers full of cakes and things, and he could see I had nothing."

Ermengarde gave a little jump backward. The last sentences had recalled something to her troubled mind and given her a sudden inspiration.

"Oh, Sara!" she cried. "What a silly thing I am not to have thought of it!"

"Of what?"

"Something splendid!" said Ermengarde, in an excited hurry. "This very afternoon my nicest aunt sent me a box. It is full of good things. I never touched it, I had so much pudding at dinner, and I was so bothered about papa's books." Her words began to tumble over each other. "It's got cake in it, and little meat pies, and jam tarts and buns, and oranges and red-currant wine, and figs and chocolate. I'll creep back to my room and get it this minute, and we'll eat it now."

Sara almost reeled. When one is faint with hunger the mention of food has sometimes a curious effect. She clutched Ermengarde's arm.

"Do you think—you *could*?" she ejaculated.

"I know I could," answered Ermengarde, and she ran to the door—opened it softly—put her head out into the darkness, and listened. Then she went back to Sara. "The lights are out. Everybody's in bed. I can creep—and creep—and no one will hear."

It was so delightful that they caught each other's hands and a sudden light sprang into Sara's eyes.

"Ermie!" she said. "Let us *pretend*! Let us pretend it's a party! And oh, won't you invite the prisoner in the next cell?"

"Yes! Yes! Let us knock on the wall now. The jailer won't hear."

Sara went to the wall. Through it she could hear poor Becky crying more softly. She knocked four times.

"That means, 'Come to me through the secret passage under the wall,' she explained. 'I have something to communicate.'"

Five quick knocks answered her.

"She is coming," she said.

Almost immediately the door of the attic opened and Becky appeared. Her eyes were red and her cap was sliding off, and when she caught sight of Ermengarde she began to rub her face nervously with her apron.

"Don't mind me a bit, Becky!" cried Ermengarde.

"Miss Ermengarde has asked you to come in," said Sara, "because she is going to bring a box of good things up here to us."

Becky's cap almost fell off entirely, she broke in with such excitement.

"To eat, miss?" she said. "Things that's good to eat?"

"Yes," answered Sara, "and we are going to pretend a party."

"And you shall have as much as you *want* to eat," put in Ermengarde. "I'll go this minute!"

She was in such haste that as she tiptoed out of the attic she dropped her red shawl and did not know it had fallen. No one saw it for a minute or so. Becky was too much overpowered by the good luck which had befallen her.

"Oh, miss! oh, miss!" she gasped; "I know it was you that asked her to let me come. It—it makes me cry to think of it." And she went to Sara's side and stood and looked at her worshipingly.

But in Sara's hungry eyes the old light had begun to glow and transform her world for her. Here in the attic—with the cold night outside—with the afternoon in the sloppy streets barely passed—with the memory of the awful unfed look in the beggar child's eyes not yet faded—this simple, cheerful thing had happened like a thing of magic.

She caught her breath.

"Somehow, something always happens," she cried, "just before things get to the very worst. It is as if the Magic did it. If I could only just remember that always. The worst thing never *quite* comes."

She gave Becky a little cheerful shake.

"No, no! You mustn't cry!" she said. "We must make haste and set the table."

"Set the table, miss?" said Becky, gazing round the room. "What'll we set it with?"

Sara looked round the attic, too.

"There doesn't seem to be much," she answered, half laughing.

That moment she saw something and pounced upon it. It was Ermengarde's red shawl which lay upon the floor.

"Here's the shawl," she cried. "I know she won't mind it. It will make such a nice red tablecloth."

They pulled the old table forward, and threw the shawl over it. Red is a wonderfully kind and comfortable color. It began to make the room look furnished directly.

"How nice a red rug would look on the floor!" exclaimed Sara. "We must pretend there is one!"

Her eye swept the bare boards with a swift glance of admiration. The rug was laid down already.

"How soft and thick it is!" she said, with the little laugh which Becky knew the meaning of; and she raised and set her foot down again delicately, as if she felt something under it.

"Yes, miss," answered Becky, watching her with serious rapture. She was always quite serious.

"What next, now?" said Sara, and she stood still and put her hands over her eyes. "Something will come if I think and wait a little"—in a soft, expectant voice. "The Magic will tell me."

One of her favorite fancies was that on "the outside," as she called it, thoughts were waiting for people to call them. Becky had seen her stand and wait many a time before, and knew that in a few seconds she would uncover an enlightened, laughing face.

In a moment she did.

"There!" she cried. "It has come! I know now! I must look among the things in the old trunk I had when I was a princess."

She flew to its corner and kneeled down. It had not been put in the attic for her benefit, but because there was no room for it elsewhere. Nothing had been left in it but rubbish. But she knew she should find something. The Magic always arranged that kind of thing in one way or another.

In a corner lay a package so insignificant-looking that it had been overlooked, and when she herself had found it she had kept it as a relic. It contained a dozen small white handkerchiefs. She seized them joyfully and ran to the table. She began to arrange them upon the red table-cover, patting and coaxing them into shape with the narrow lace edge curling outward, her Magic working its spells for her as she did it.

"These are the plates," she said. "They are golden plates. These are the richly embroidered napkins. Nuns worked them in convents in Spain."

"Did they, miss?" breathed Becky, her very soul uplifted by the information.

"You must pretend it," said Sara. "If you pretend it enough, you will see them."

"Yes, miss," said Becky; and as Sara returned to the trunk she devoted herself to the effort of accomplishing an end so much to be desired.

Sara turned suddenly to find her standing by the table, looking very queer indeed. She had shut her eyes, and was twisting her face in strange convulsive contortions, her hands hanging stiffly clenched at her sides. She looked as if she was trying to lift some enormous weight.

"What is the matter, Becky?" Sara cried. "What are you doing?"

Becky opened her eyes with a start.

"I was a-'pretendin',' miss," she answered a little sheepishly; "I was tryin' to see it like you do. I almost did," with a hopeful grin. "But it takes a lot o' stren'th."

"Perhaps it does if you are not used to it," said Sara, with friendly sympathy; "but you don't know how easy it is when you've done it often. I wouldn't try so hard just at first. It will come to you after a while. I'll just tell you what things are. Look at these."

She held an old summer hat in her hand which she had fished out of the bottom of the trunk. There was a wreath of flowers on it. She pulled the wreath off.

"These are garlands for the feast," she said grandly. "They fill all the air with perfume. There's a mug on the wash-stand, Becky. Oh—and bring the soap dish for a centerpiece."

Becky handed them to her reverently.

"What are they now, miss?" she inquired. "You'd think they was made of crockery—but I know they ain't."

"This is a carven flagon," said Sara, arranging tendrils of the wreath about the mug. "And this"—bending tenderly over the soap dish and heaping it with roses—"is purest alabaster encrusted with gems."

She touched the things gently, a happy smile hovering about her lips which made her look as if she were a creature in a dream.

"My, ain't it lovely!" whispered Becky.

"If we just had something for bonbon dishes," Sara murmured. "There!"—darting to the trunk again. "I remember I saw something this minute."

It was only a bundle of wool wrapped in red and white tissue paper, but the tissue paper was soon twisted into the form of little dishes, and was combined with the remaining flowers to ornament the candlestick which was to light the feast. Only the Magic could have made it more than an old table covered with a red shawl and set with rubbish from a long-unopened trunk. But Sara drew back and gazed at it, seeing wonders; and Becky, after staring in delight, spoke with bated breath.

"This 'ere," she suggested, with a glance round the attic—"is it the Bastille now—or has it turned into somethin' different?"

"Oh, yes, yes!" said Sara. "Quite different. It is a banquet hall!"

"My eye, miss!" ejaculated Becky. "A blanket-'all!" and she turned to view the splendors about her with awed bewilderment.

"A banquet hall," said Sara. "A vast chamber where feasts are given. It has a vaulted roof, and a minstrels' gallery, and a huge chimney filled with blazing oaken logs, and it is brilliant with waxen tapers twinkling on every side."

"My eye, Miss Sara!" gasped Becky again.

Then the door opened, and Ermengarde came in, rather staggering under the weight of her hamper. She started back with an exclamation of joy. To enter from the chill darkness outside, and find one's self confronted by a totally unanticipated festal board, draped with red, adorned with white napery, and wreathed with flowers, was to feel that the preparations were brilliant indeed.

"Oh, Sara!" she cried out. "You are the cleverest girl I ever saw!"

"Isn't it nice?" said Sara. "They are things out of my old trunk. I asked my Magic, and it told me to go and look."

"But oh, miss," cried Becky, "wait till she's told you what they are! They ain't just—oh, miss, please tell her," appealing to Sara.

So Sara told her, and because her Magic helped her she made her *almost* see it all: the golden platters—the vaulted spaces—the blazing logs—the twinkling waxen tapers. As the things were taken out of the hamper—the frosted cakes—the fruits—the bonbons and the wine—the feast became a splendid thing.

"It's like a real party!" cried Ermengarde.

"It's like a queen's table," sighed Becky.

Then Ermengarde had a sudden brilliant thought.

"I'll tell you what, Sara," she said. "Pretend you are a princess now and this is a royal feast."

"But it's your feast," said Sara; "you must be the princess, and we will be your maids of honor."

"Oh, I can't," said Ermengarde. "I'm too fat, and I don't know how. *You* be her."

"Well, if you want me to," said Sara.

But suddenly she thought of something else and ran to the rusty grate.

"There is a lot of paper and rubbish stuffed in here!" she exclaimed. "If we light it, there will be a bright blaze for a few minutes, and we shall feel as if it was a real fire." She struck a match and lighted it up with a great specious glow which illuminated the room.

"By the time it stops blazing," Sara said, "we shall forget about its not being real."

She stood in the dancing glow and smiled.

"Doesn't it *look* real?" she said. "Now we will begin the party."

She led the way to the table. She waved her hand graciously to Ermengarde and Becky. She was in the midst of her dream.

"Advance, fair damsels," she said in her happy dream-voice, "and be seated at the banquet table. My noble father, the king, who is absent on a long journey, has commanded me to feast you." She turned her head slightly toward the corner of the room. "What, ho, there, minstrels! Strike up with your viols and bassoons. Princesses," she explained rapidly to Ermengarde and Becky, "always had minstrels to play at their feasts. Pretend there is a minstrel gallery up there in the corner. Now we will begin."

They had barely had time to take their pieces of cake into their hands—not one of them had time to do more, when—they all three sprang to their feet and turned pale faces toward the door—listening—listening.

Someone was coming up the stairs. There was no mistake about it. Each of them recognized the angry, mounting tread and knew that the end of all things had come.

"It's—the missus!" choked Becky, and dropped her piece of cake upon the floor.

"Yes," said Sara, her eyes growing shocked and large in her small white face. "Miss Minchin has found us out."

Miss Minchin struck the door open with a blow of her hand. She was pale herself, but it was with rage. She looked from the frightened faces to the banquet table, and from the banquet table to the last flicker of the burnt paper in the grate.

"I have been suspecting something of this sort," she exclaimed; "but I did not dream of such audacity. Lavinia was telling the truth."

So they knew that it was Lavinia who had somehow guessed their secret and had betrayed them. Miss Minchin strode over to Becky and boxed her ears for a second time.

"You impudent creature!" she said. "You leave the house in the morning!"

Sara stood quite still, her eyes growing larger, her face paler. Ermengarde burst into tears.

"Oh, don't send her away," she sobbed. "My aunt sent me the hamper. We're—only—having a party."

"So I see," said Miss Minchin, witheringly. "With the Princess Sara at the head of the table." She turned fiercely on Sara. "It is your doing, I know," she cried. "Ermengarde would never have thought of such a thing. You decorated the table, I suppose—with this rubbish." She stamped her foot at Becky. "Go to your attic!" she commanded, and Becky stole away, her face hidden in her apron, her shoulders shaking.

Then it was Sara's turn again.

"I will attend to you tomorrow. You shall have neither breakfast, dinner, nor supper!"

"I have not had either dinner or supper today, Miss Minchin," said Sara, rather faintly.

"Then all the better. You will have something to remember. Don't stand there. Put those things into the hamper again."

She began to sweep them off the table into the hamper herself, and caught sight of Ermengarde's new books.

"And you"—to Ermengarde—"have brought your beautiful new books into this dirty attic. Take them up and go back to bed. You will stay there all day tomorrow, and I shall write to your papa. What would *he* say if he knew where you are tonight?"

Something she saw in Sara's grave, fixed gaze at this moment made her turn on her fiercely.

"What are you thinking of?" she demanded. "Why do you look at me like that?"

"I was wondering," answered Sara, as she had answered that notable day in the schoolroom.

"What were you wondering?"

It was very like the scene in the schoolroom. There was no pertness in Sara's manner. It was only sad and quiet.

"I was wondering," she said in a low voice, "what *my* papa would say if he knew where I am tonight."

Miss Minchin was infuriated just as she had been before and her anger expressed itself, as before, in an intemperate fashion. She flew at her and shook her.

"You insolent, unmanageable child!" she cried. "How dare you! How dare you!"

She picked up the books, swept the rest of the feast back into the hamper in a jumbled heap, thrust it into Ermengarde's arms, and pushed her before her toward the door.

"I will leave you to wonder," she said. "Go to bed this instant." And she shut the door behind herself and poor stumbling Ermengarde, and left Sara standing quite alone.

The dream was quite at an end. The last spark had died out of the paper in the grate and left only black tinder; the table was left bare, the golden plates and richly embroidered napkins, and the garlands were transformed again into old handkerchiefs, scraps of red and white paper, and discarded artificial flowers all scattered on the floor; the minstrels in the minstrel gallery had stolen away, and the viols and bassoons were still. Emily was sitting with her back against the wall, staring very hard. Sara saw her, and went and picked her up with trembling hands.

"There isn't any banquet left, Emily," she said. "And there isn't any princess. There is nothing left but the prisoners in the Bastille." And she sat down and hid her face.

What would have happened if she had not hidden it just then, and if she had chanced to look up at the skylight at the wrong moment, I do not know—perhaps the end of this chapter might have been quite different—because if she had glanced at the skylight she would certainly have been startled by what she would have seen. She would have seen exactly the same face pressed against the glass and peering in at her as it had peered in earlier in the evening when she had been talking to Ermengarde.

But she did not look up. She sat with her little black head in her arms for some time. She always sat like that when she was trying to bear something in silence. Then she got up and went slowly to the bed.

"I can't pretend anything else—while I am awake," she said. "There wouldn't be any use in trying. If I go to sleep, perhaps a dream will come and pretend for me."

She suddenly felt so tired—perhaps through want of food—that she sat down on the edge of the bed quite weakly.

"Suppose there was a bright fire in the grate, with lots of little dancing flames," she murmured. "Suppose there was a comfortable chair before it—and suppose there was a small table near, with a little hot—hot supper on it. And suppose"—as she drew the thin coverings over her—"suppose this was a beautiful soft bed, with fleecy blankets and large downy pillows. Suppose—suppose—" And her very weariness was good to her, for her eyes closed and she fell fast asleep.

She did not know how long she slept. But she had been tired enough to sleep deeply and profoundly—too deeply and soundly to be disturbed by anything, even by the squeaks and scamperings of

Melchisedec's entire family, if all his sons and daughters had chosen to come out of their hole to fight and tumble and play.

When she awakened it was rather suddenly, and she did not know that any particular thing had called her out of her sleep. The truth was, however, that it was a sound which had called her back—a real sound—the click of the skylight as it fell in closing after a lithe white figure which slipped through it and crouched down close by upon the slates of the roof—just near enough to see what happened in the attic, but not near enough to be seen.

At first she did not open her eyes. She felt too sleepy and—curiously enough—too warm and comfortable. She was so warm and comfortable, indeed, that she did not believe she was really awake. She never was as warm and cozy as this except in some lovely vision.

"What a nice dream!" she murmured. "I feel quite warm. I—don't—want—to—wake—up."

Of course it was a dream. She felt as if warm, delightful bedclothes were heaped upon her. She could actually *feel* blankets, and when she put out her hand it touched something exactly like a satin-covered eider-down quilt. She must not awaken from this delight—she must be quite still and make it last.

But she could not—even though she kept her eyes closed tightly, she could not. Something was forcing her to awaken—something in the room. It was a sense of light, and a sound—the sound of a crackling, roaring little fire.

"Oh, I am awakening," she said mournfully. "I can't help it—I can't."

Her eyes opened in spite of herself. And then she actually smiled—for what she saw she had never seen in the attic before, and knew she never should see.

"Oh, I *haven't* awakened," she whispered, daring to rise on her elbow and look all about her. "I am dreaming yet." She knew it *must* be a dream, for if she were awake such things could not—could not be.

Do you wonder that she felt sure she had not come back to earth? This is what she saw. In the grate there was a glowing, blazing fire; on the hob was a little brass kettle hissing and boiling; spread upon the floor was a thick, warm crimson rug; before the fire a folding-chair, unfolded, and with cushions on it; by the chair a small folding-table, unfolded, covered with a white cloth, and upon it spread small covered dishes, a cup, a saucer, a teapot; on the bed were new warm coverings and a satin-covered down quilt; at the foot a curious wadded silk robe, a pair of quilted slippers, and some books. The room of her dream seemed changed into fairyland—and it was flooded with warm light, for a bright lamp stood on the table covered with a rosy shade.

She sat up, resting on her elbow, and her breathing came short and fast.

"It does not—melt away," she panted. "Oh, I never had such a dream before." She scarcely dared to stir; but at last she pushed the bedclothes aside, and put her feet on the floor with a rapturous smile.

"I am dreaming—I am getting out of bed," she heard her own voice say; and then, as she stood up in the midst of it all, turning slowly from side to side—"I am dreaming it stays—real! I'm dreaming it *feels* real. It's bewitched—or I'm bewitched. I only *think* I see it all." Her words began to hurry themselves. "If I can only keep on thinking it," she cried, "I don't care! I don't care!"

She stood panting a moment longer, and then cried out again.

"Oh, it isn't true!" she said. "It *can't* be true! But oh, how true it seems!"

The blazing fire drew her to it, and she knelt down and held out her hands close to it—so close that the heat made her start back.

"A fire I only dreamed wouldn't be *hot*," she cried.

She sprang up, touched the table, the dishes, the rug; she went to the bed and touched the blankets. She took up the soft wadded dressing-gown, and suddenly clutched it to her breast and held it to her cheek.

"It's warm. It's soft!" she almost sobbed. "It's real. It must be!"

She threw it over her shoulders, and put her feet into the slippers.

"They are real, too. It's all real!" she cried. "I am *not*—I am *not* dreaming!"

She almost staggered to the books and opened the one which lay upon the top. Something was written on the flyleaf—just a few words, and they were these:

"To the little girl in the attic. From a friend."

When she saw that—wasn't it a strange thing for her to do—she put her face down upon the page and burst into tears.

"I don't know who it is," she said; "but somebody cares for me a little. I have a friend."

She took her candle and stole out of her own room and into Becky's, and stood by her bedside.

"Becky, Becky!" she whispered as loudly as she dared. "Wake up!"

When Becky wakened, and she sat upright staring aghast, her face still smudged with traces of tears, beside her stood a little figure in a luxurious wadded robe of crimson silk. The face she saw was a shining, wonderful thing. The Princess Sara—as she remembered her—stood at her very bedside, holding a candle in her hand.

"Come," she said. "Oh, Becky, come!"

Becky was too frightened to speak. She simply got up and followed her, with her mouth and eyes open, and without a word.

And when they crossed the threshold, Sara shut the door gently and drew her into the warm, glowing midst of things which made her brain reel and her hungry senses faint. "It's true! It's true!" she cried. "I've touched them all. They are as real as we are. The Magic has come and done it, Becky, while we were asleep—the Magic that won't let those worst things *ever* quite happen."

16

The Visitor

Imagine, if you can, what the rest of the evening was like. How they crouched by the fire which blazed and leaped and made so much of itself in the little grate. How they removed the covers of the dishes, and found rich, hot, savory soup, which was a meal in itself, and sandwiches and toast and muffins enough for both of them. The mug from the washstand was used as Becky's tea cup, and the tea was so delicious that it was not necessary to pretend that it was anything but tea. They were warm and full-fed and happy, and it was just like Sara that, having found her strange good fortune real, she should give herself up to the enjoyment of it to the utmost. She had lived such a life of imaginings that she was quite equal to accepting any wonderful thing that happened, and almost to cease, in a short time, to find it bewildering.

"I don't know anyone in the world who could have done it," she said; "but there has been someone. And here we are sitting by their fire—and—and—it's *true*! And whoever it is—wherever they are—I have a friend, Becky—someone is my friend."

It cannot be denied that as they sat before the blazing fire, and ate the nourishing, comfortable food, they felt a kind of rapturous awe, and looked into each other's eyes with something like doubt.

"Do you think," Becky faltered once, in a whisper, "do you think it could melt away, miss? Hadn't we better be quick?" And she hastily crammed her sandwich into her mouth. If it was only a dream, kitchen manners would be overlooked.

"No, it won't melt away," said Sara. "I am *eating* this muffin, and I can taste it. You never really eat things in dreams. You only think you are going to eat them. Besides, I keep giving myself pinches; and I touched a hot piece of coal just now, on purpose."

The sleepy comfort which at length almost overpowered them was a heavenly thing. It was the drowsiness of happy, well-fed childhood, and they sat in the fire glow and luxuriated in it until Sara found herself turning to look at her transformed bed.

There were even blankets enough to share with Becky. The narrow couch in the next attic was more comfortable that night than its occupant had ever dreamed that it could be.

As she went out of the room, Becky turned upon the threshold and looked about her with devouring eyes.

"If it ain't here in the mornin', miss," she said, "it's been here tonight, anyways, an' I shan't never forget it." She looked at each particular thing, as if to commit it to memory. "The fire was *there*," pointing with her finger, "an' the table was before it; an' the lamp was there, an' the light looked rosy red; an' there was a satin cover on your bed, an' a warm rug on the floor, an' everythin' looked beautiful; an'"—she paused a second, and laid her hand on her stomach tenderly—"there *was* soup an' sandwiches an' muffins—there *was*." And, with this conviction a reality at least, she went away.

Through the mysterious agency which works in schools and among servants, it was quite well known in the morning that Sara Crewe was in horrible disgrace, that Ermengarde was under punishment, and that Becky would have been packed out of the house before breakfast, but that a scullery maid could not be dispensed with at once. The servants knew that she was allowed to stay because Miss Minchin could not easily find another creature helpless and humble enough to work like a bounden slave for so few shillings a week. The elder girls in the schoolroom knew that if Miss Minchin did not send Sara away it was for practical reasons of her own.

"She's growing so fast and learning such a lot, somehow," said Jessie to Lavinia, "that she will be given classes soon, and Miss Minchin knows she will have to work for nothing. It was rather nasty of you, Lavvy, to tell about her having fun in the garret. How did you find it out?"

"I got it out of Lottie. She's such a baby she didn't know she was telling me. There was nothing nasty at all in speaking to Miss Minchin. I felt it my duty"—priggishly. "She was being deceitful. And it's ridiculous that she should look so grand, and be made so much of, in her rags and tatters!"

"What were they doing when Miss Minchin caught them?"

"Pretending some silly thing. Ermengarde had taken up her hamper to share with Sara and Becky. She never invites us to share things. Not that I care, but it's rather vulgar of her to share with servant girls in attics. I wonder Miss Minchin didn't turn Sara out—even if she does want her for a teacher."

"If she was turned out where would she go?" inquired Jessie, a trifle anxiously.

"How do I know?" snapped Lavinia. "She'll look rather queer when she comes into the schoolroom this morning, I should think—after what's happened. She had no dinner yesterday, and she's not to have any today."

Jessie was not as ill-natured as she was silly. She picked up her book with a little jerk.

"Well, I think it's horrid," she said. "They've no right to starve her to death."

When Sara went into the kitchen that morning the cook looked askance at her, and so did the housemaids; but she passed them hurriedly. She had, in fact, overslept herself a little, and as Becky had done the same, neither had had time to see the other, and each had come downstairs in haste.

Sara went into the scullery. Becky was violently scrubbing a kettle, and was actually gurgling a little song in her throat. She looked up with a wildly elated face.

"It was there when I wakened, miss—the blanket," she whispered excitedly. "It was as real as it was last night."

"So was mine," said Sara. "It is all there now—all of it. While I was dressing I ate some of the cold things we left."

"Oh, laws! Oh, laws!" Becky uttered the exclamation in a sort of rapturous groan, and ducked her head over her kettle just in time, as the cook came in from the kitchen.

Miss Minchin had expected to see in Sara, when she appeared in the schoolroom, very much what Lavinia had expected to see. Sara had always been an annoying puzzle to her, because severity never made her cry or look frightened. When she was scolded she stood still and listened politely with a grave face; when she was punished she performed her extra tasks or went without her meals, making no complaint or outward sign of rebellion. The very fact that she never made an impudent answer seemed to Miss Minchin a kind of impudence in itself. But after yesterday's deprivation of meals, the violent scene of last night, the prospect of hunger today, she must surely have broken down. It would be strange indeed if she did not come downstairs with pale cheeks and red eyes and an unhappy, humbled face.

Miss Minchin saw her for the first time when she entered the schoolroom to hear the little French class recite its lessons and superintend its exercises. And she came in with a springing step, color in her cheeks, and a smile hovering about the corners of her mouth. It was the most astonishing thing Miss Minchin had ever known. It gave her quite a shock. What was the child made of? What could such a thing mean? She called her at once to her desk.

"You do not look as if you realize that you are in disgrace," she said. "Are you absolutely hardened?"

The truth is that when one is still a child—or even if one is grown up—and has been well fed, and has slept long and softly and warm; when one has gone to sleep in the midst of a fairy story, and has wakened to find it real, one cannot be unhappy or even look as if one were; and one could not, if one tried, keep a glow of joy out of one's eyes. Miss Minchin was almost struck dumb by the look of Sara's eyes when she made her perfectly respectful answer.

"I beg your pardon, Miss Minchin," she said; "I know that I am in disgrace."

"Be good enough not to forget it and look as if you had come into a fortune. It is an impertinence. And remember you are to have no food today."

"Yes, Miss Minchin," Sara answered; but as she turned away her heart leaped with the memory of what yesterday had been. "If the Magic had not saved me just in time," she thought, "how horrible it would have been!"

"She can't be very hungry," whispered Lavinia. "Just look at her. Perhaps she is pretending she has had a good breakfast"—with a spiteful laugh.

"She's different from other people," said Jessie, watching Sara with her class. "Sometimes I'm a bit frightened of her."

"Ridiculous thing!" ejaculated Lavinia.

All through the day the light was in Sara's face, and the color in her cheek. The servants cast puzzled glances at her, and whispered to each other, and Miss Amelia's small blue eyes wore an expression of bewilderment. What such an audacious look of well-being, under august displeasure could mean she could not understand. It was, however, just like Sara's singular obstinate way. She was probably determined to brave the matter out.

One thing Sara had resolved upon, as she thought things over. The wonders which had happened must be kept a secret, if such a thing were possible. If Miss Minchin should choose to mount to the attic again, of course all would be discovered. But it did not seem likely that she would do so for some time at least, unless she was led by suspicion. Ermengarde and Lottie would be watched with such strictness that they would not dare to steal out of their beds again. Ermengarde could be told the story and trusted to keep it secret. If Lottie made any discoveries, she could be bound to secrecy also. Perhaps the Magic itself would help to hide its own marvels.

"But whatever happens," Sara kept saying to herself all day—"*whatever* happens, somewhere in the world there is a heavenly kind person who is my friend—my friend. If I never know who it is—if I never can even thank him—I shall never feel quite so lonely. Oh, the Magic was *good* to me!"

If it was possible for weather to be worse than it had been the day before, it was worse this day—wetter, muddier, colder. There were more errands to be done, the cook was more irritable, and, knowing that Sara was in disgrace, she was more savage. But what does anything matter when one's Magic has just proved itself one's friend. Sara's supper of the night before had given her strength, she knew that she should sleep well and warmly, and, even though she had naturally begun to be hungry again before evening, she felt that she could bear it until breakfast-time on the following day, when her meals would surely be given to her again. It was quite late when she was at last allowed to go upstairs. She had been told to go into the schoolroom and study until ten o'clock, and she had become interested in her work, and remained over her books later.

When she reached the top flight of stairs and stood before the attic door, it must be confessed that her heart beat rather fast.

"Of course it *might* all have been taken away," she whispered, trying to be brave. "It might only have been lent to me for just that one awful night. But it *was* lent to me—I had it. It was real."

She pushed the door open and went in. Once inside, she gasped slightly, shut the door, and stood with her back against it looking from side to side.

The Magic had been there again. It actually had, and it had done even more than before. The fire was blazing, in lovely leaping flames, more merrily than ever. A number of new things had been brought into the attic which so altered the look of it that if she had not been past doubting she would have rubbed her eyes. Upon the low table another supper stood—this time with cups and plates for Becky as well as herself; a piece of bright, heavy, strange embroidery covered the battered mantel, and on it some ornaments had been placed. All the bare, ugly things which could be covered with draperies had been concealed and made to look quite pretty. Some odd materials of rich colors had been fastened against the wall with fine, sharp tacks—so sharp that they could be pressed into the wood and plaster without hammering. Some brilliant fans were pinned up, and there were several large cushions, big and substantial enough to use as seats. A wooden box was covered with a rug, and some cushions lay on it, so that it wore quite the air of a sofa.

Sara slowly moved away from the door and simply sat down and looked and looked again.

"It is exactly like something fairy come true," she said. "There isn't the least difference. I feel as if I might wish for anything—diamonds or bags of gold—and they would appear! *That* wouldn't be any stranger than this. Is this my garret? Am I the same cold, ragged, damp Sara? And to think I used to pretend and pretend and wish there were fairies! The one thing I always wanted was to see a fairy story come true. I am *living* in a fairy story. I feel as if I might be a fairy myself, and able to turn things into anything else."

She rose and knocked upon the wall for the prisoner in the next cell, and the prisoner came.

When she entered she almost dropped in a heap upon the floor. For a few seconds she quite lost her breath.

"Oh, laws!" she gasped. "Oh, laws, miss!"

"You see," said Sara.

On this night Becky sat on a cushion upon the hearth rug and had a cup and saucer of her own.

When Sara went to bed she found that she had a new thick mattress and big downy pillows. Her old mattress and pillow had been removed to Becky's bedstead, and, consequently, with these additions Becky had been supplied with unheard-of comfort.

"Where does it all come from?" Becky broke forth once. "Laws, who does it, miss?"

"Don't let us even *ask*," said Sara. "If it were not that I want to say, 'Oh, thank you,' I would rather not know. It makes it more beautiful."

From that time life became more wonderful day by day. The fairy story continued. Almost every day something new was done. Some new comfort or ornament appeared each time Sara opened the door at night, until in a short time the attic was a beautiful little room full of all sorts of odd and luxurious things. The ugly walls were gradually entirely covered with pictures and draperies, ingenious pieces of folding furniture appeared, a bookshelf was hung up and filled with books, new comforts and conveniences appeared one by one, until there seemed nothing left to be desired. When Sara went downstairs in the morning, the remains of the supper were on the table; and when she returned to the attic in the evening, the magician had removed them and left another nice little meal. Miss Minchin was as harsh and insulting as ever, Miss Amelia as peevish, and the servants were as vulgar and rude. Sara was sent on errands in all weathers, and scolded and driven hither and thither; she was scarcely allowed to speak to Ermengarde and Lottie; Lavinia sneered at the increasing shabbiness of her clothes; and the other girls stared curiously at her when she appeared in the schoolroom. But what did it all matter while she was living in this wonderful mysterious story? It was more romantic and delightful than anything she had ever invented to comfort her starved young soul and save herself from despair. Sometimes, when she was scolded, she could scarcely keep from smiling.

"If you only knew!" she was saying to herself. "If you only knew!"

The comfort and happiness she enjoyed were making her stronger, and she had them always to look forward to. If she came home from her errands wet and tired and hungry, she knew she would soon be warm and well fed after she had climbed the stairs. During the hardest day she could occupy herself blissfully by thinking of what she should see when she opened the attic door, and wondering what new delight had been prepared for her. In a very short time she began to look less thin. Color came into her cheeks, and her eyes did not seem so much too big for her face.

"Sara Crewe looks wonderfully well," Miss Minchin remarked disapprovingly to her sister.

"Yes," answered poor, silly Miss Amelia. "She is absolutely fattening. She was beginning to look like a little starved crow."

"Starved!" exclaimed Miss Minchin, angrily. "There was no reason why she should look starved. She always had plenty to eat!"

"Of—of course," agreed Miss Amelia, humbly, alarmed to find that she had, as usual, said the wrong thing.

"There is something very disagreeable in seeing that sort of thing in a child of her age," said Miss Minchin, with haughty vagueness.

"What—sort of thing?" Miss Amelia ventured.

"It might almost be called defiance," answered Miss Minchin, feeling annoyed because she knew the thing she resented was nothing like defiance, and she did not know what other unpleasant term to use. "The spirit and will of any other child would have been entirely humbled and broken by—by the changes she has had to submit to. But, upon my word, she seems as little subdued as if—as if she were a princess."

"Do you remember," put in the unwise Miss Amelia, "what she said to you that day in the schoolroom about what you would do if you found out that she was—"

"No, I don't," said Miss Minchin. "Don't talk nonsense." But she remembered very clearly indeed.

Very naturally, even Becky was beginning to look plumper and less frightened. She could not help it. She had her share in the secret fairy story, too. She had two mattresses, two pillows, plenty of bed-covering, and every night a hot supper and a seat on the cushions by the fire. The Bastille had melted away, the prisoners no longer existed. Two comforted children sat in the midst of delights. Sometimes Sara read aloud from her books, sometimes she learned her own lessons, sometimes she sat and looked into the fire and tried to imagine who her friend could be, and wished she could say to him some of the things in her heart.

Then it came about that another wonderful thing happened. A man came to the door and left several parcels. All were addressed in large letters, "To the Little Girl in the right-hand attic."

Sara herself was sent to open the door and take them in. She laid the two largest parcels on the hall table, and was looking at the address, when Miss Minchin came down the stairs and saw her.

"Take the things to the young lady to whom they belong," she said severely. "Don't stand there staring at them.

"They belong to me," answered Sara, quietly.

"To you?" exclaimed Miss Minchin. "What do you mean?"

"I don't know where they come from," said Sara, "but they are addressed to me. I sleep in the right-hand attic. Becky has the other one."

Miss Minchin came to her side and looked at the parcels with an excited expression.

"What is in them?" she demanded.

"I don't know," replied Sara.

"Open them," she ordered.

Sara did as she was told. When the packages were unfolded Miss Minchin's countenance wore suddenly a singular expression. What she saw was pretty and comfortable clothing—clothing of different kinds: shoes, stockings, and gloves, and a warm and beautiful coat. There were even a nice hat and an umbrella. They were all good and expensive things, and on the pocket of the coat was pinned a paper, on which were written these words: "To be worn every day. Will be replaced by others when necessary."

Miss Minchin was quite agitated. This was an incident which suggested strange things to her sordid mind. Could it be that she had made a mistake, after all, and that the neglected child had some powerful though eccentric friend in the background—perhaps some previously unknown relation, who had suddenly traced her whereabouts, and chose to provide for her in this mysterious and fantastic way? Relations were sometimes very odd—particularly rich old bachelor uncles, who did not care for having children near them. A man of that sort might prefer to overlook his young relation's welfare at a distance. Such a person, however, would be sure to be crotchety and hot-tempered enough to be easily offended. It would not be very pleasant if there were such a one, and he should learn all the truth about the thin, shabby clothes, the scant food, and the hard work. She felt very queer indeed, and very uncertain, and she gave a side glance at Sara.

"Well," she said, in a voice such as she had never used since the little girl lost her father, "someone is very kind to you. As the things have been sent, and you are to have new ones when they are worn out, you may as well go and put them on and look respectable. After you are dressed you may come downstairs and learn your lessons in the schoolroom. You need not go out on any more errands today."

About half an hour afterward, when the schoolroom door opened and Sara walked in, the entire seminary was struck dumb with amazement.

"My word!" ejaculated Jessie, jogging Lavinia's elbow. "Look at the Princess Sara!"

Everybody was looking, and when Lavinia looked she turned quite red.

It was the Princess Sara indeed. At least, since the days when she had been a princess, Sara had never looked as she did now. She did not seem the Sara they had seen come down the back stairs a few hours ago. She was dressed in the kind of frock Lavinia had been used to envying her the possession of. It was deep and warm in color, and beautifully made. Her slender feet looked as they had done when Jessie had admired them, and the hair, whose heavy locks had made her look rather like a Shetland pony when it fell loose about her small, odd face, was tied back with a ribbon.

"Perhaps someone has left her a fortune," Jessie whispered. "I always thought something would happen to her. She's so queer."

"Perhaps the diamond mines have suddenly appeared again," said Lavinia, scathingly. "Don't please her by staring at her in that way, you silly thing."

"Sara," broke in Miss Minchin's deep voice, "come and sit here."

And while the whole schoolroom stared and pushed with elbows, and scarcely made any effort to conceal its excited curiosity, Sara went to her old seat of honor, and bent her head over her books.

That night, when she went to her room, after she and Becky had eaten their supper she sat and looked at the fire seriously for a long time.

"Are you making something up in your head, miss?" Becky inquired with respectful softness. When Sara sat in silence and looked into the coals with dreaming eyes it generally meant that she was making a new story. But this time she was not, and she shook her head.

"No," she answered. "I am wondering what I ought to do."

Becky stared—still respectfully. She was filled with something approaching reverence for everything Sara did and said.

"I can't help thinking about my friend," Sara explained. "If he wants to keep himself a secret, it would be rude to try and find out who he is. But I do so want him to know how thankful I am to him—and how happy he has made me. Anyone who is kind wants to know when people have been made happy. They care for that more than for being thanked. I wish—I do wish—"

She stopped short because her eyes at that instant fell upon something standing on a table in a corner. It was something she had found in the room when she came up to it only two days before. It was a little writing-case fitted with paper and envelopes and pens and ink.

"Oh," she exclaimed, "why did I not think of that before?"

She rose and went to the corner and brought the case back to the fire.

"I can write to him," she said joyfully, "and leave it on the table. Then perhaps the person who takes the things away will take it, too. I won't ask him anything. He won't mind my thanking him, I feel sure."

So she wrote a note. This is what she said:

> I hope you will not think it is impolite that I should write this note to you when you wish to keep yourself a secret. Please believe I do not mean to be impolite or try to find out anything at all; only I want to thank you for being so kind to me—so heavenly kind—and making everything like a fairy story. I am so grateful to you, and I am so happy—and so is Becky. Becky feels just as thankful as I do—it is all just as beautiful and wonderful to her as it is to me. We used to be so lonely and cold and hungry, and now—oh, just think what you have done for us! Please let me say just these words. It seems as if I *ought* to say them. *Thank* you—*thank* you—*thank* you!
>
> THE LITTLE GIRL IN THE ATTIC.

The next morning she left this on the little table, and in the evening it had been taken away with the other things; so she knew the Magician had received it, and she was happier for the thought. She was reading one of her new books to Becky just before they went to their respective beds, when her attention was attracted by a sound at the skylight. When she looked up from her page she saw that Becky had heard the sound also, as she had turned her head to look and was listening rather nervously.

"Something's there, miss," she whispered.

"Yes," said Sara, slowly. "It sounds—rather like a cat—trying to get in."

She left her chair and went to the skylight. It was a queer little sound she heard—like a soft scratching. She suddenly remembered something and laughed. She remembered a quaint little intruder who had made his way into the attic once before. She had seen him that very afternoon, sitting disconsolately on a table before a window in the Indian gentleman's house.

"Suppose," she whispered in pleased excitement—"just suppose it was the monkey who got away again. Oh, I wish it was!"

She climbed on a chair, very cautiously raised the skylight, and peeped out. It had been snowing all day, and on the snow, quite near her, crouched a tiny, shivering figure, whose small black face wrinkled itself piteously at sight of her.

"It is the monkey," she cried out. "He has crept out of the Lascar's attic, and he saw the light."

Becky ran to her side.

"Are you going to let him in, miss?" she said.

"Yes," Sara answered joyfully. "It's too cold for monkeys to be out. They're delicate. I'll coax him in."

She put a hand out delicately, speaking in a coaxing voice—as she spoke to the sparrows and to Melchisedec—as if she were some friendly little animal herself.

"Come along, monkey darling," she said. "I won't hurt you."

He knew she would not hurt him. He knew it before she laid her soft, caressing little paw on him and drew him towards her. He had felt human love in the slim brown hands of Ram Dass, and he felt it in hers. He let her lift him through the skylight, and when he found himself in her arms he cuddled up to her breast and looked up into her face.

"Nice monkey! Nice monkey!" she crooned, kissing his funny head. "Oh, I do love little animal things."

He was evidently glad to get to the fire, and when she sat down and held him on her knee he looked from her to Becky with mingled interest and appreciation.

"He IS plain-looking, miss, ain't he?" said Becky.

"He looks like a very ugly baby," laughed Sara. "I beg your pardon, monkey; but I'm glad you are not a baby. Your mother *couldn't* be proud of you, and no one would dare to say you looked like any of your relations. Oh, I do like you!"

She leaned back in her chair and reflected.

"Perhaps he's sorry he's so ugly," she said, "and it's always on his mind. I wonder if he HAS a mind. Monkey, my love, have you a mind?"

But the monkey only put up a tiny paw and scratched his head.

"What shall you do with him?" Becky asked.

"I shall let him sleep with me tonight, and then take him back to the Indian gentleman tomorrow. I am sorry to take you back, monkey; but you must go. You ought to be fondest of your own family; and I'm not a *real* relation."

And when she went to bed she made him a nest at her feet, and he curled up and slept there as if he were a baby and much pleased with his quarters.

17

"It is the Child!"

The next afternoon three members of the Large Family sat in the Indian gentleman's library, doing their best to cheer him up. They had been allowed to come in to perform this office because he had specially invited them. He had been living in a state of suspense for some time, and today he was waiting for a certain event very anxiously. This event was the return of Mr. Carmichael from Moscow. His stay there had been prolonged from week to week. On his first arrival there, he had not been able satisfactorily to trace the family he had gone in search of. When he felt at last sure that he had found them and had gone to their house, he had been told that they were absent on a journey. His efforts to reach them had been unavailing, so he had decided to remain in Moscow until their return. Mr. Carrisford sat in his reclining chair, and Janet sat on the floor beside him. He was very fond of Janet. Nora had found a footstool, and Donald was astride the tiger's head which ornamented the rug made of the animal's skin. It must be owned that he was riding it rather violently.

"Don't chirrup so loud, Donald," Janet said. "When you come to cheer an ill person up you don't cheer him up at the top of your voice. Perhaps cheering up is too loud, Mr. Carrisford?" turning to the Indian gentleman.

But he only patted her shoulder.

"No, it isn't," he answered. "And it keeps me from thinking too much."

"I'm going to be quiet," Donald shouted. "We'll all be as quiet as mice."

"Mice don't make a noise like that," said Janet.

Donald made a bridle of his handkerchief and bounced up and down on the tiger's head.

"A whole lot of mice might," he said cheerfully. "A thousand mice might."

"I don't believe fifty thousand mice would," said Janet, severely; "and we have to be as quiet as *one* mouse."

Mr. Carrisford laughed and patted her shoulder again.

"Papa won't be very long now," she said. "May we talk about the lost little girl?"

"I don't think I could talk much about anything else just now," the Indian gentleman answered, knitting his forehead with a tired look.

"We like her so much," said Nora. "We call her the little *un*-fairy princess."

"Why?" the Indian gentleman inquired, because the fancies of the Large Family always made him forget things a little.

It was Janet who answered.

"It is because, though she is not exactly a fairy, she will be so rich when she is found that she will be like a princess in a fairy tale. We called her the fairy princess at first, but it didn't quite suit."

"Is it true," said Nora, "that her papa gave all his money to a friend to put in a mine that had diamonds in it, and then the friend thought he had lost it all and ran away because he felt as if he was a robber?"

"But he wasn't really, you know," put in Janet, hastily.

The Indian gentleman took hold of her hand quickly.

"No, he wasn't really," he said.

"I am sorry for the friend," Janet said; "I can't help it. He didn't mean to do it, and it would break his heart. I am sure it would break his heart."

"You are an understanding little woman, Janet," the Indian gentleman said, and he held her hand close.

"Did you tell Mr. Carrisford," Donald shouted again, "about the little-girl-who-isn't-a-beggar? Did you tell him she has new nice clothes? P'r'aps she's been found by somebody when she was lost."

"There's a cab!" exclaimed Janet. "It's stopping before the door. It is papa!"

They all ran to the windows to look out.

"Yes, it's papa," Donald proclaimed. "But there is no little girl."

All three of them incontinently fled from the room and tumbled into the hall. It was in this way they always welcomed their father. They were to be heard jumping up and down, clapping their hands, and being caught up and kissed.

Mr. Carrisford made an effort to rise and sank back again.

"It is no use," he said. "What a wreck I am!"

Mr. Carmichael's voice approached the door.

"No, children," he was saying; "you may come in after I have talked to Mr. Carrisford. Go and play with Ram Dass."

Then the door opened and he came in. He looked rosier than ever, and brought an atmosphere of freshness and health with him; but his eyes were disappointed and anxious as they met the invalid's look of eager question even as they grasped each other's hands.

"What news?" Mr. Carrisford asked. "The child the Russian people adopted?"

"She is not the child we are looking for," was Mr. Carmichael's answer. "She is much younger than Captain Crewe's little girl. Her name is Emily Carew. I have seen and talked to her. The Russians were able to give me every detail."

How wearied and miserable the Indian gentleman looked! His hand dropped from Mr. Carmichael's. "Then the search has to be begun over again," he said. "That is all. Please sit down."

Mr. Carmichael took a seat. Somehow, he had gradually grown fond of this unhappy man. He was himself so well and happy, and so surrounded by cheerfulness and love, that desolation and broken health seemed pitifully unbearable things. If there had been the sound of just one gay little high-pitched voice in the house, it would have been so much less forlorn. And that a man should be compelled to carry about in his breast the thought that he had seemed to wrong and desert a child was not a thing one could face.

"Come, come," he said in his cheery voice; "we'll find her yet."

"We must begin at once. No time must be lost," Mr. Carrisford fretted. "Have you any new suggestion to make—any whatsoever?"

Mr. Carmichael felt rather restless, and he rose and began to pace the room with a thoughtful, though uncertain face.

"Well, perhaps," he said. "I don't know what it may be worth. The fact is, an idea occurred to me as I was thinking the thing over in the train on the journey from Dover."

"What was it? If she is alive, she is somewhere."

"Yes; she is *somewhere.* We have searched the schools in Paris. Let us give up Paris and begin in London. That was my idea—to search London."

"There are schools enough in London," said Mr. Carrisford. Then he slightly started, roused by a recollection. "By the way, there is one next door."

"Then we will begin there. We cannot begin nearer than next door."

"No," said Carrisford. "There is a child there who interests me; but she is not a pupil. And she is a little dark, forlorn creature, as unlike poor Crewe as a child could be."

Perhaps the Magic was at work again at that very moment—the beautiful Magic. It really seemed as if it might be so. What was it that brought Ram Dass into the room—even as his master spoke—salaaming respectfully, but with a scarcely concealed touch of excitement in his dark, flashing eyes?

"Sahib," he said, "the child herself has come—the child the sahib felt pity for. She brings back the monkey who had again run away to her attic under the roof. I have asked that she remain. It was my thought that it would please the sahib to see and speak with her."

"Who is she?" inquired Mr. Carmichael.

"God knows," Mr. Carrrisford answered. "She is the child I spoke of. A little drudge at the school." He waved his hand to Ram Dass, and addressed him. "Yes, I should like to see her. Go and bring her in." Then he turned to Mr. Carmichael. "While you have been away," he explained, "I have been desperate. The days were so dark and long. Ram Dass told me of this child's miseries, and together we invented a romantic plan to help her. I suppose it was a childish thing to do; but it gave me something to plan and think of. Without the help of an agile, soft-footed Oriental like Ram Dass, however, it could not have been done."

Then Sara came into the room. She carried the monkey in her arms, and he evidently did not intend to part from her, if it could be helped. He was clinging to her and chattering, and the interesting excitement of finding herself in the Indian gentleman's room had brought a flush to Sara's cheeks.

"Your monkey ran away again," she said, in her pretty voice. "He came to my garret window last night, and I took him in because it was so cold. I would have brought him back if it had not been so late. I knew you were ill and might not like to be disturbed."

The Indian gentleman's hollow eyes dwelt on her with curious interest.

"That was very thoughtful of you," he said.

Sara looked toward Ram Dass, who stood near the door.

"Shall I give him to the Lascar?" she asked.

"How do you know he is a Lascar?" said the Indian gentleman, smiling a little.

"Oh, I know Lascars," Sara said, handing over the reluctant monkey. "I was born in India."

The Indian gentleman sat upright so suddenly, and with such a change of expression, that she was for a moment quite startled.

"You were born in India," he exclaimed, "were you? Come here." And he held out his hand.

Sara went to him and laid her hand in his, as he seemed to want to take it. She stood still, and her green-gray eyes met his wonderingly. Something seemed to be the matter with him.

"You live next door?" he demanded.

"Yes; I live at Miss Minchin's seminary."

"But you are not one of her pupils?"

A strange little smile hovered about Sara's mouth. She hesitated a moment.

"I don't think I know exactly *what* I am," she replied.

"Why not?"

"At first I was a pupil, and a parlor boarder; but now—"

"You were a pupil! What are you now?"

The queer little sad smile was on Sara's lips again.

"I sleep in the attic, next to the scullery maid," she said. "I run errands for the cook—I do anything she tells me; and I teach the little ones their lessons."

"Question her, Carmichael," said Mr. Carrisford, sinking back as if he had lost his strength. "Question her; I cannot."

The big, kind father of the Large Family knew how to question little girls. Sara realized how much practice he had had when he spoke to her in his nice, encouraging voice.

"What do you mean by 'At first,' my child?" he inquired.

"When I was first taken there by my papa."

"Where is your papa?"

"He died," said Sara, very quietly. "He lost all his money and there was none left for me. There was no one to take care of me or to pay Miss Minchin."

"Carmichael!" the Indian gentleman cried out loudly. "Carmichael!"

"We must not frighten her," Mr. Carmichael said aside to him in a quick, low voice. And he added aloud to Sara, "So you were sent up into the attic, and made into a little drudge. That was about it, wasn't it?"

"There was no one to take care of me," said Sara. "There was no money; I belong to nobody."

"How did your father lose his money?" the Indian gentleman broke in breathlessly.

"He did not lose it himself," Sara answered, wondering still more each moment. "He had a friend he was very fond of—he was *very* fond of him. It was his friend who took his money. He trusted his friend too much."

The Indian gentleman's breath came more quickly.

"The friend might have *meant* to do no harm," he said. "It might have happened through a mistake."

Sara did not know how unrelenting her quiet young voice sounded as she answered. If she had known, she would surely have tried to soften it for the Indian gentleman's sake.

"The suffering was just as bad for my papa," she said. "It killed him."

"What was your father's name?" the Indian gentleman said. "Tell me."

"His name was Ralph Crewe," Sara answered, feeling startled. "Captain Crewe. He died in India."

The haggard face contracted, and Ram Dass sprang to his master's side.

"Carmichael," the invalid gasped, "it is the child—the child!"

For a moment Sara thought he was going to die. Ram Dass poured out drops from a bottle, and held them to his lips. Sara stood near, trembling a little. She looked in a bewildered way at Mr. Carmichael.

"What child am I?" she faltered.

"He was your father's friend," Mr. Carmichael answered her. "Don't be frightened. We have been looking for you for two years."

Sara put her hand up to her forehead, and her mouth trembled. She spoke as if she were in a dream.

"And I was at Miss Minchin's all the while," she half whispered. "Just on the other side of the wall."

18

"I Tried Not to Be"

It was pretty, comfortable Mrs. Carmichael who explained everything. She was sent for at once, and came across the square to take Sara into her warm arms and make clear to her all that had happened. The excitement of the totally unexpected discovery had been temporarily almost overpowering to Mr. Carrisford in his weak condition.

"Upon my word," he said faintly to Mr. Carmichael, when it was suggested that the little girl should go into another room. "I feel as if I do not want to lose sight of her."

"I will take care of her," Janet said, "and mamma will come in a few minutes." And it was Janet who led her away.

"We're so glad you are found," she said. "You don't know how glad we are that you are found."

Donald stood with his hands in his pockets, and gazed at Sara with reflecting and self-reproachful eyes.

"If I'd just asked what your name was when I gave you my sixpence," he said, "you would have told me it was Sara Crewe, and then you would have been found in a minute."

Then Mrs. Carmichael came in. She looked very much moved, and suddenly took Sara in her arms and kissed her.

"You look bewildered, poor child," she said. "And it is not to be wondered at."

Sara could only think of one thing.

"Was he," she said, with a glance toward the closed door of the library—"was *he* the wicked friend? Oh, do tell me!"

Mrs. Carmichael was crying as she kissed her again. She felt as if she ought to be kissed very often because she had not been kissed for so long.

"He was not wicked, my dear," she answered. "He did not really lose your papa's money. He only thought he had lost it; and because he loved him so much his grief made him so ill that for a time he was not in his right mind. He almost died of brain fever, and long before he began to recover your poor papa was dead."

"And he did not know where to find me," murmured Sara. "And I was so near." Somehow, she could not forget that she had been so near.

"He believed you were in school in France," Mrs. Carmichael explained. "And he was continually misled by false clues. He has looked for you everywhere. When he saw you pass by, looking so sad and neglected, he did not dream that you were his friend's poor child; but because you were a little girl, too, he was sorry for you, and wanted to make you happier. And he told Ram Dass to climb into your attic window and try to make you comfortable."

Sara gave a start of joy; her whole look changed.

"Did Ram Dass bring the things?" she cried out. "Did he tell Ram Dass to do it? Did he make the dream that came true?"

"Yes, my dear—yes! He is kind and good, and he was sorry for you, for little lost Sara Crewe's sake."

The library door opened and Mr. Carmichael appeared, calling Sara to him with a gesture.

"Mr. Carrisford is better already," he said. "He wants you to come to him."

Sara did not wait. When the Indian gentleman looked at her as she entered, he saw that her face was all alight.

She went and stood before his chair, with her hands clasped together against her breast.

"You sent the things to me," she said, in a joyful emotional little voice, "the beautiful, beautiful things? *You* sent them!"

"Yes, poor, dear child, I did," he answered her. He was weak and broken with long illness and trouble, but he looked at her with the look she remembered in her father's eyes—that look of loving her and wanting to take her in his arms. It made her kneel down by him, just as she used to kneel by her father when they were the dearest friends and lovers in the world.

"Then it is you who are my friend," she said; "it is you who are my friend!" And she dropped her face on his thin hand and kissed it again and again.

"The man will be himself again in three weeks," Mr. Carmichael said aside to his wife. "Look at his face already."

In fact, he did look changed. Here was the "Little Missus," and he had new things to think of and plan for already. In the first place, there was Miss Minchin. She must be interviewed and told of the change which had taken place in the fortunes of her pupil.

Sara was not to return to the seminary at all. The Indian gentleman was very determined upon that point. She must remain where she was, and Mr. Carmichael should go and see Miss Minchin himself.

"I am glad I need not go back," said Sara. "She will be very angry. She does not like me; though perhaps it is my fault, because I do not like her."

But, oddly enough, Miss Minchin made it unnecessary for Mr. Carmichael to go to her, by actually coming in search of her pupil herself. She had wanted Sara for something, and on inquiry had heard an astonishing thing. One of the housemaids had seen her steal out of the area with something hidden under her cloak, and had also seen her go up the steps of the next door and enter the house.

"What does she mean!" cried Miss Minchin to Miss Amelia.

"I don't know, I'm sure, sister," answered Miss Amelia. "Unless she has made friends with him because he has lived in India."

"It would be just like her to thrust herself upon him and try to gain his sympathies in some such impertinent fashion," said Miss Minchin. "She must have been in the house for two hours. I will not allow such presumption. I shall go and inquire into the matter, and apologize for her intrusion."

Sara was sitting on a footstool close to Mr. Carrisford's knee, and listening to some of the many things he felt it necessary to try to explain to her, when Ram Dass announced the visitor's arrival.

Sara rose involuntarily, and became rather pale; but Mr. Carrisford saw that she stood quietly, and showed none of the ordinary signs of child terror.

Miss Minchin entered the room with a sternly dignified manner. She was correctly and well dressed, and rigidly polite.

"I am sorry to disturb Mr. Carrisford," she said; "but I have explanations to make. I am Miss Minchin, the proprietress of the Young Ladies' Seminary next door."

The Indian gentleman looked at her for a moment in silent scrutiny. He was a man who had naturally a rather hot temper, and he did not wish it to get too much the better of him.

"So you are Miss Minchin?" he said.

"I am, sir."

"In that case," the Indian gentleman replied, "you have arrived at the right time. My solicitor, Mr. Carmichael, was just on the point of going to see you."

Mr. Carmichael bowed slightly, and Miss Minchin looked from him to Mr. Carrisford in amazement.

"Your solicitor!" she said. "I do not understand. I have come here as a matter of duty. I have just discovered that you have been intruded upon through the forwardness of one of my pupils—a charity pupil. I came to explain that she intruded without my knowledge." She turned upon Sara. "Go home at once," she commanded indignantly. "You shall be severely punished. Go home at once."

The Indian gentleman drew Sara to his side and patted her hand. "She is not going."

Miss Minchin felt rather as if she must be losing her senses.

"Not going!" she repeated.

"No," said Mr. Carrisford. "She is not going *home*—if you give your house that name. Her home for the future will be with me."

Miss Minchin fell back in amazed indignation.

"With *you*! With *you* sir! What does this mean?"

"Kindly explain the matter, Carmichael," said the Indian gentleman; "and get it over as quickly as possible." And he made Sara sit down again, and held her hands in his—which was another trick of her papa's.

Then Mr. Carmichael explained—in the quiet, level-toned, steady manner of a man who knew his subject, and all its legal significance, which was a thing Miss Minchin understood as a business woman, and did not enjoy.

"Mr. Carrisford, madam," he said, "was an intimate friend of the late Captain Crewe. He was his partner in certain large investments. The fortune which Captain Crewe supposed he had lost has been recovered, and is now in Mr. Carrisford's hands."

"The fortune!" cried Miss Minchin; and she really lost color as she uttered the exclamation. "Sara's fortune!"

"It *will* be Sara's fortune," replied Mr. Carmichael, rather coldly. "It is Sara's fortune now, in fact. Certain events have increased it enormously. The diamond mines have retrieved themselves."

"The diamond mines!" Miss Minchin gasped out. If this was true, nothing so horrible, she felt, had ever happened to her since she was born.

"The diamond mines," Mr. Carmichael repeated, and he could not help adding, with a rather sly, unlawyer-like smile, "There are not many princesses, Miss Minchin, who are richer than your little charity pupil, Sara Crewe, will be. Mr. Carrisford has been searching for her for nearly two years; he has found her at last, and he will keep her."

After which he asked Miss Minchin to sit down while he explained matters to her fully, and went into such detail as was necessary to make it quite clear to her that Sara's future was an assured one, and that what had seemed to be lost was to be restored to her tenfold; also, that she had in Mr. Carrisford a guardian as well as a friend.

Miss Minchin was not a clever woman, and in her excitement she was silly enough to make one desperate effort to regain what she could not help seeing she had lost through her worldly folly.

"He found her under my care," she protested. "I have done everything for her. But for me she should have starved in the streets."

Here the Indian gentleman lost his temper.

"As to starving in the streets," he said, "she might have starved more comfortably there than in your attic."

"Captain Crewe left her in my charge," Miss Minchin argued. "She must return to it until she is of age. She can be a parlor boarder again. She must finish her education. The law will interfere in my behalf."

"Come, come, Miss Minchin," Mr. Carmichael interposed, "the law will do nothing of the sort. If Sara herself wishes to return to you, I dare say Mr. Carrisford might not refuse to allow it. But that rests with Sara."

"Then," said Miss Minchin, "I appeal to Sara. I have not spoiled you, perhaps," she said awkwardly to the little girl; "but you know that your papa was pleased with your progress. And—ahem—I have always been fond of you."

Sara's green-gray eyes fixed themselves on her with the quiet, clear look Miss Minchin particularly disliked.

"Have *you*, Miss Minchin?" she said. "I did not know that."

Miss Minchin reddened and drew herself up.

"You ought to have known it," said she; "but children, unfortunately, never know what is best for them. Amelia and I always said you were the cleverest child in the school. Will you not do your duty to your poor papa and come home with me?"

Sara took a step toward her and stood still. She was thinking of the day when she had been told that she belonged to nobody, and was in danger of being turned into the street; she was thinking of the cold, hungry hours she had spent alone with Emily and Melchisedec in the attic. She looked Miss Minchin steadily in the face.

"You know why I will not go home with you, Miss Minchin," she said; "you know quite well."

A hot flush showed itself on Miss Minchin's hard, angry face.

"You will never see your companions again," she began. "I will see that Ermengarde and Lottie are kept away—"

Mr. Carmichael stopped her with polite firmness.

"Excuse me," he said; "she will see anyone she wishes to see. The parents of Miss Crewe's fellow-pupils are not likely to refuse her invitations to visit her at her guardian's house. Mr. Carrisford will attend to that."

It must be confessed that even Miss Minchin flinched. This was worse than the eccentric bachelor uncle who might have a peppery temper and be easily offended at the treatment of his niece. A woman of sordid mind could easily believe that most people would not refuse to allow their children to remain friends with a little heiress of diamond mines. And if Mr. Carrisford chose to tell certain of her patrons how unhappy Sara Crewe had been made, many unpleasant things might happen.

"You have not undertaken an easy charge," she said to the Indian gentleman, as she turned to leave the room; "you will discover that very soon. The child is neither truthful nor grateful. I suppose"—to Sara—"that you feel now that you are a princess again."

Sara looked down and flushed a little, because she thought her pet fancy might not be easy for strangers—even nice ones—to understand at first.

"I—*tried* not to be anything else," she answered in a low voice—"even when I was coldest and hungriest—I *tried* not to be."

"Now it will not be necessary to try," said Miss Minchin, acidly, as Ram Dass salaamed her out of the room.

She returned home and, going to her sitting room, sent at once for Miss Amelia. She sat closeted with her all the rest of the afternoon, and it must be admitted that poor Miss Amelia passed through more than one bad quarter of an hour. She shed a good many tears, and mopped her eyes a good deal. One of her unfortunate remarks almost caused her sister to snap her head entirely off, but it resulted in an unusual manner.

"I'm not as clever as you, sister," she said, "and I am always afraid to say things to you for fear of making you angry. Perhaps if I were not so timid it would be better for the school and for both of us. I must say I've often thought it would have been better if you had been less severe on Sara Crewe, and had seen that she was decently dressed and more comfortable. I *know* she was worked too hard for a child of her age, and I know she was only half fed—"

"How dare you say such a thing!" exclaimed Miss Minchin.

"I don't know how I dare," Miss Amelia answered, with a kind of reckless courage; "but now I've begun I may as well finish, whatever happens to me. The child was a clever child and a good child—and she would have paid you for any kindness you had shown her. But you didn't show her any. The fact was, she was too clever for you, and you always disliked her for that reason. She used to see through us both—"

"Amelia!" gasped her infuriated elder, looking as if she would box her ears and knock her cap off, as she had often done to Becky.

But Miss Amelia's disappointment had made her hysterical enough not to care what occurred next.

"She did! She did!" she cried. "She saw through us both. She saw that you were a hard-hearted, worldly woman, and that I was a weak fool, and that we were both of us vulgar and mean enough to grovel on our knees for her money, and behave ill to her because it was taken from her—though she behaved herself like a little princess even when she was a beggar. She did—she did—like a little princess!" And her hysterics got the better of the poor woman, and she began to laugh and cry both at once, and rock herself backward and forward in such a way as made Miss Minchin stare aghast.

"And now you've lost her," she cried wildly; "and some other school will get her and her money; and if she were like any other child she'd tell how she's been treated, and all our pupils would be taken away and we should be ruined. And it serves us right; but it serves you right more than it does me, for you are a hard woman, Maria Minchin, you're a hard, selfish, worldly woman!"

And she was in danger of making so much noise with her hysterical chokes and gurgles that her sister was obliged to go to her and apply salts and sal volatile to quiet her, instead of pouring forth her indignation at her audacity.

And from that time forward, it may be mentioned, the elder Miss Minchin actually began to stand a little in awe of a sister who, while she looked so foolish, was evidently not quite so foolish as she looked, and might, consequently, break out and speak truths people did not want to hear.

That evening, when the pupils were gathered together before the fire in the schoolroom, as was their custom before going to bed, Ermengarde came in with a letter in her hand and a queer expression on her round face. It was queer because, while it was an expression of delighted excitement, it was combined with such amazement as seemed to belong to a kind of shock just received.

"What *is* the matter?" cried two or three voices at once.

"Is it anything to do with the row that has been going on?" said Lavinia, eagerly. "There has been such a row in Miss Minchin's room, Miss Amelia has had something like hysterics and has had to go to bed."

Ermengarde answered them slowly as if she were half stunned.

"I have just had this letter from Sara," she said, holding it out to let them see what a long letter it was.

"From Sara!" Every voice joined in that exclamation.

"Where is she?" almost shrieked Jessie.

"Next door," said Ermengarde, "with the Indian gentleman."

"Where? Where? Has she been sent away? Does Miss Minchin know? Was the row about that? Why did she write? Tell us! Tell us!"

There was a perfect babel, and Lottie began to cry plaintively.

Ermengarde answered them slowly as if she were half plunged out into what, at the moment, seemed the most important and self-explaining thing.

"There *were* diamond mines," she said stoutly; "there *were*!" Open mouths and open eyes confronted her.

"They were real," she hurried on. "It was all a mistake about them. Something happened for a time, and Mr. Carrisford thought they were ruined—"

"Who is Mr. Carrisford?" shouted Jessie.

"The Indian gentleman. And Captain Crewe thought so, too—and he died; and Mr. Carrisford had brain fever and ran away, and *he* almost died. And he did not know where Sara was. And it turned out that there were millions and millions of diamonds in the mines; and half of them belong to Sara; and they belonged to her when she was living in the attic with no one but Melchisedec for a friend, and the cook ordering her about. And Mr. Carrisford found her this afternoon, and he has got her in his home—and she will never come back—and she will be more a princess than she ever was—a hundred and fifty thousand times more. And I am going to see her tomorrow afternoon. There!"

Even Miss Minchin herself could scarcely have controlled the uproar after this; and though she heard the noise, she did not try. She was not in the mood to face anything more than she was facing in her room, while Miss Amelia was weeping in bed. She knew that the news had penetrated the walls in some mysterious manner, and that every servant and every child would go to bed talking about it.

So until almost midnight the entire seminary, realizing somehow that all rules were laid aside, crowded round Ermengarde in the schoolroom and heard read and re-read the letter containing a story which was quite as wonderful as any Sara herself had ever invented, and which had the amazing charm of having happened to Sara herself and the mystic Indian gentleman in the very next house.

Becky, who had heard it also, managed to creep up stairs earlier than usual. She wanted to get away from people and go and look at the little magic room once more. She did not know what would happen to it. It was not likely that it would be left to Miss Minchin. It would be taken away, and the attic would be bare and empty again. Glad as she was for Sara's sake, she went up the last flight of stairs with a lump in her throat and tears blurring her sight. There would be no fire tonight, and no rosy lamp; no supper, and no princess sitting in the glow reading or telling stories—no princess!

She choked down a sob as she pushed the attic door open, and then she broke into a low cry.

The lamp was flushing the room, the fire was blazing, the supper was waiting; and Ram Dass was standing smiling into her startled face.

"Missee sahib remembered," he said. "She told the sahib all. She wished you to know the good fortune which has befallen her. Behold a letter on the tray. She has written. She did not wish that you should go to sleep unhappy. The sahib commands you to come to him tomorrow. You are to be the attendant of missee sahib. Tonight I take these things back over the roof."

And having said this with a beaming face, he made a little salaam and slipped through the skylight with an agile silentness of movement which showed Becky how easily he had done it before.

19

Anne

Never had such joy reigned in the nursery of the Large Family. Never had they dreamed of such delights as resulted from an intimate acquaintance with the little-girl-who-was-not-a-beggar. The mere fact of her sufferings and adventures made her a priceless possession. Everybody wanted to be told over and over again the things which had happened to her. When one was sitting by a warm fire in a big, glowing room, it was quite delightful to hear how cold it could be in an attic. It must be admitted that the attic was rather delighted in, and that its coldness and bareness quite sank into insignificance when Melchisedec was remembered, and one heard about the sparrows and things one could see if one climbed on the table and stuck one's head and shoulders out of the skylight.

Of course the thing loved best was the story of the banquet and the dream which was true. Sara told it for the first time the day after she had been found. Several members of the Large Family came to take tea with her, and as they sat or curled up on the hearth-rug she told the story in her own way, and the Indian gentleman listened and watched her. When she had finished she looked up at him and put her hand on his knee.

"That is my part," she said. "Now won't you tell your part of it, Uncle Tom?" He had asked her to call him always "Uncle Tom." "I don't know your part yet, and it must be beautiful."

So he told them how, when he sat alone, ill and dull and irritable, Ram Dass had tried to distract him by describing the passers by, and there was one child who passed oftener than any one else; he had begun to be interested in her—partly perhaps because he was thinking a great deal of a little girl, and partly because Ram Dass had been able to relate the incident of his visit to the attic in chase of the monkey. He had described its cheerless look, and the bearing of the child, who seemed as if she was not of the class of those who were treated as drudges and servants. Bit by bit, Ram Dass had made discoveries concerning the wretchedness of her life. He had found out how easy a matter it was to climb across the few yards of roof to the skylight, and this fact had been the beginning of all that followed.

"Sahib," he had said one day, "I could cross the slates and make the child a fire when she is out on some errand. When she returned, wet and cold, to find it blazing, she would think a magician had done it."

The idea had been so fanciful that Mr. Carrisford's sad face had lighted with a smile, and Ram Dass had been so filled with rapture that he had enlarged upon it and explained to his master how simple it would be to accomplish numbers of other things. He had shown a childlike pleasure and invention, and the preparations for the carrying out of the plan had filled many a day with interest which would otherwise have dragged wearily. On the night of the frustrated banquet Ram Dass had kept watch, all his packages being in readiness in the attic which was his own; and the person who was to help him had waited with him, as interested as himself in the odd adventure. Ram Dass had been lying flat upon the slates, looking in at the skylight, when the banquet had come to its disastrous conclusion; he had been sure of the profoundness of Sara's wearied sleep; and then, with a dark lantern, he had crept into the room, while his companion remained outside and handed the things to him. When Sara had stirred ever so faintly, Ram Dass had closed the lantern-slide and lain flat upon the floor. These and many other exciting things the children found out by asking a thousand questions.

"I am so glad," Sara said. "I am so *glad* it was you who were my friend!"

There never were such friends as these two became. Somehow, they seemed to suit each other in a wonderful way. The Indian gentleman had never had a companion he liked quite as much as he liked Sara. In a month's time he was, as Mr. Carmichael had prophesied he would be, a new man. He was always amused and interested, and he began to find an actual pleasure in the possession of the wealth he had imagined that he loathed the burden of. There were so many charming things to plan for Sara. There was a little joke between them that he was a magician, and it was one of his pleasures to invent things to surprise her. She found beautiful new flowers growing in her room, whimsical little gifts tucked under pillows, and once, as they sat together in the evening, they heard the scratch of a heavy paw on the door, and when Sara went to find out what it was, there stood a great dog—a splendid Russian boarhound—with a grand silver and gold collar bearing an inscription. "I am Boris," it read; "I serve the Princess Sara."

There was nothing the Indian gentleman loved more than the recollection of the little princess in rags and tatters. The afternoons in which the Large Family, or Ermengarde and Lottie, gathered to rejoice together were very delightful. But the hours when Sara and the Indian gentleman sat alone and read or talked had a special charm of their own. During their passing many interesting things occurred.

One evening, Mr. Carrisford, looking up from his book, noticed that his companion had not stirred for some time, but sat gazing into the fire.

"What are you 'supposing,' Sara?" he asked.

Sara looked up, with a bright color on her cheek.

"I *was* supposing," she said; "I was remembering that hungry day, and a child I saw."

"But there were a great many hungry days," said the Indian gentleman, with rather a sad tone in his voice. "Which hungry day was it?"

"I forgot you didn't know," said Sara. "It was the day the dream came true."

Then she told him the story of the bun shop, and the fourpence she picked up out of the sloppy mud, and the child who was hungrier than herself. She told it quite simply, and in as few words as possible; but somehow the Indian gentleman found it necessary to shade his eyes with his hand and look down at the carpet.

"And I was supposing a kind of plan," she said, when she had finished. "I was thinking I should like to do something."

"What was it?" said Mr. Carrisford, in a low tone. "You may do anything you like to do, princess."

"I was wondering," rather hesitated Sara—"you know, you say I have so much money—I was wondering if I could go to see the bun-woman, and tell her that if, when hungry children—particularly on those dreadful days—come and sit on the steps, or look in at the window, she would just call them in and give them something to eat, she might send the bills to me. Could I do that?"

"You shall do it tomorrow morning," said the Indian gentleman.

"Thank you," said Sara. "You see, I know what it is to be hungry, and it is very hard when one cannot even *pretend* it away."

"Yes, yes, my dear," said the Indian gentleman. "Yes, yes, it must be. Try to forget it. Come and sit on this footstool near my knee, and only remember you are a princess."

"Yes," said Sara, smiling; "and I can give buns and bread to the populace." And she went and sat on the stool, and the Indian gentleman (he used to like her to call him that, too, sometimes) drew her small dark head down on his knee and stroked her hair.

The next morning, Miss Minchin, in looking out of her window, saw the things she perhaps least enjoyed seeing. The Indian gentleman's carriage, with its tall horses, drew up before the door of the next house, and its owner and a little figure, warm with soft, rich furs, descended the steps to get into it. The little figure was a familiar one, and reminded Miss Minchin of days in the past. It was followed by another as familiar—the sight of which she found very irritating. It was Becky, who, in the character of delighted attendant, always accompanied her young mistress to her carriage, carrying wraps and belongings. Already Becky had a pink, round face.

A little later the carriage drew up before the door of the baker's shop, and its occupants got out, oddly enough, just as the bun-woman was putting a tray of smoking-hot buns into the window.

When Sara entered the shop the woman turned and looked at her, and, leaving the buns, came and stood behind the counter. For a moment she looked at Sara very hard indeed, and then her good-natured face lighted up.

"I'm sure that I remember you, miss," she said. "And yet—"

"Yes," said Sara; "once you gave me six buns for fourpence, and—"

"And you gave five of 'em to a beggar child," the woman broke in on her. "I've always remembered it. I couldn't make it out at first." She turned round to the Indian gentleman and spoke her next words to him. "I beg your pardon, sir, but there's not many young people that notices a hungry face in that way; and I've thought of it many a time. Excuse the liberty, miss,"—to Sara—"but you look rosier and—well, better than you did that—that—"

"I am better, thank you," said Sara. "And—I am much happier—and I have come to ask you to do something for me."

"Me, miss!" exclaimed the bun-woman, smiling cheerfully. "Why, bless you! Yes, miss. What can I do?"

And then Sara, leaning on the counter, made her little proposal concerning the dreadful days and the hungry waifs and the buns.

The woman watched her, and listened with an astonished face.

"Why, bless me!" she said again when she had heard it all; "it'll be a pleasure to me to do it. I am a working-woman myself and cannot afford to do much on my own account, and there's sights of trouble on every side; but, if you'll excuse me, I'm bound to say I've given away many a bit of bread since that wet afternoon, just along o' thinking of you—an' how wet an' cold you was, an' how hungry you looked; an' yet you gave away your hot buns as if you was a princess."

The Indian gentleman smiled involuntarily at this, and Sara smiled a little, too, remembering what she had said to herself when she put the buns down on the ravenous child's ragged lap.

"She looked so hungry," she said. "She was even hungrier than I was."

"She was starving," said the woman. "Many's the time she's told me of it since—how she sat there in the wet, and felt as if a wolf was a-tearing at her poor young insides."

"Oh, have you seen her since then?" exclaimed Sara. "Do you know where she is?"

"Yes, I do," answered the woman, smiling more good-naturedly than ever. "Why, she's in that there back room, miss, an' has been for a month; an' a decent, well-meanin' girl she's goin' to turn out, an' such a help to me in the shop an' in the kitchen as you'd scarce believe, knowin' how she's lived."

She stepped to the door of the little back parlor and spoke; and the next minute a girl came out and followed her behind the counter. And actually it was the beggar-child, clean and neatly clothed, and looking as if she had not been hungry for a long time. She looked shy, but she had a nice face, now that she was no longer a savage, and the wild look had gone from her eyes. She knew Sara in an instant, and stood and looked at her as if she could never look enough.

"You see," said the woman, "I told her to come when she was hungry, and when she'd come I'd give her odd jobs to do; an' I found she was willing, and somehow I got to like her; and the end of it was, I've given her a place an' a home, and she helps me, an' behaves well, an' is as thankful as a girl can be. Her name's Anne. She has no other."

The children stood and looked at each other for a few minutes; and then Sara took her hand out of her muff and held it out across the counter, and Anne took it, and they looked straight into each other's eyes.

"I am so glad," Sara said. "And I have just thought of something. Perhaps Mrs. Brown will let you be the one to give the buns and bread to the children. Perhaps you would like to do it because you know what it is to be hungry, too."

"Yes, miss," said the girl.

And, somehow, Sara felt as if she understood her, though she said so little, and only stood still and looked and looked after her as she went out of the shop with the Indian gentleman, and they got into the carriage and drove away.

The Secret Garden

by Frances Hodgson Burnett

1

There is No One Left

When Mary Lennox was sent to Misselthwaite Manor to live with her uncle everybody said she was the most disagreeable-looking child ever seen. It was true, too. She had a little thin face and a little thin body, thin light hair and a sour expression. Her hair was yellow, and her face was yellow because she had been born in India and had always been ill in one way or another. Her father had held a position under the English Government and had always been busy and ill himself, and her mother had been a great beauty who cared only to go to parties and amuse herself with gay people. She had not wanted a little girl at all, and when Mary was born she handed her over to the care of an Ayah, who was made to understand that if she wished to please the Mem Sahib she must keep the child out of sight as much as possible. So when she was a sickly, fretful, ugly little baby she was kept out of the way, and when she became a sickly, fretful, toddling thing she was kept out of the way also. She never remembered seeing familiarly anything but the dark faces of her Ayah and the other native servants, and as they always obeyed her and gave her her own way in everything, because the Mem Sahib would be angry if she was disturbed by her crying, by the time she was six years old she was as tyrannical and selfish a little pig as ever lived. The young English governess who came to teach her to read and write disliked her so much that she gave up her place in three months, and when other governesses came to try to fill it they always went away in a shorter time than the first one. So if Mary had not chosen to really want to know how to read books she would never have learned her letters at all.

One frightfully hot morning, when she was about nine years old, she awakened feeling very cross, and she became crosser still when she saw that the servant who stood by her bedside was not her Ayah.

"Why did you come?" she said to the strange woman. "I will not let you stay. Send my Ayah to me."

The woman looked frightened, but she only stammered that the Ayah could not come and when Mary threw herself into a passion and beat and kicked her, she looked only more frightened and repeated that it was not possible for the Ayah to come to Missie Sahib.

There was something mysterious in the air that morning. Nothing was done in its regular order and several of the native servants seemed missing, while those whom Mary saw slunk or hurried about with ashy and scared faces. But no one would tell her anything and her Ayah did not come. She was actually left alone as the morning went on, and at last she wandered out into the garden and began to play by herself under a tree near the veranda. She pretended that she was making a flower-bed, and she stuck big scarlet hibiscus blossoms into little heaps of earth, all the time growing more and more angry and muttering to herself the things she would say and the names she would call Saidie when she returned.

"Pig! Pig! Daughter of Pigs!" she said, because to call a native a pig is the worst insult of all.

She was grinding her teeth and saying this over and over again when she heard her mother come out on the veranda with someone. She was with a fair young man and they stood talking together in low strange voices. Mary knew the fair young man who looked like a boy. She had heard that he was a very young officer who had just come from England. The child stared at him, but she stared most at her mother. She always did this when she had a chance to see her, because the Mem Sahib—Mary used to call her that oftener than anything else—was such a tall, slim, pretty person and wore such lovely clothes. Her hair was like curly silk and she had a delicate little nose which seemed to be disdaining things, and she had large laughing eyes. All her clothes were thin and floating, and Mary said they were "full of lace." They looked fuller of lace than ever this morning, but her eyes were not laughing at all. They were large and scared and lifted imploringly to the fair boy officer's face.

"Is it so very bad? Oh, is it?" Mary heard her say.

"Awfully," the young man answered in a trembling voice. "Awfully, Mrs. Lennox. You ought to have gone to the hills two weeks ago."

The Mem Sahib wrung her hands.

"Oh, I know I ought!" she cried. "I only stayed to go to that silly dinner party. What a fool I was!"

At that very moment such a loud sound of wailing broke out from the servants' quarters that she clutched the young man's arm, and Mary stood shivering from head to foot. The wailing grew wilder and wilder. "What is it? What is it?" Mrs. Lennox gasped.

"Someone has died," answered the boy officer. "You did not say it had broken out among your servants."

"I did not know!" the Mem Sahib cried. "Come with me! Come with me!" and she turned and ran into the house.

After that, appalling things happened, and the mysteriousness of the morning was explained to Mary. The cholera had broken out in its most fatal form and people were dying like flies. The Ayah had been taken ill in the night, and it was because she had just died that the servants had wailed in the huts. Before the next day three other servants were dead and others had run away in terror. There was panic on every side, and dying people in all the bungalows.

During the confusion and bewilderment of the second day Mary hid herself in the nursery and was forgotten by everyone. Nobody thought of her, nobody wanted her, and strange things happened of which she knew nothing. Mary alternately cried and slept through the hours. She only knew that people were ill and that she heard mysterious and frightening sounds. Once she crept into the dining room and found it empty, though a partly finished meal was on the table and chairs and plates looked as if they had been hastily pushed back when the diners rose suddenly for some reason. The child ate some fruit and biscuits, and being thirsty she drank a glass of wine which stood nearly filled. It was sweet, and she did not know how strong it was. Very soon it made her intensely drowsy, and she went back to her nursery and shut herself in again, frightened by cries she heard in the huts and by the hurrying sound of feet. The wine made her so sleepy that she could scarcely keep her eyes open and she lay down on her bed and knew nothing more for a long time.

Many things happened during the hours in which she slept so heavily, but she was not disturbed by the wails and the sound of things being carried in and out of the bungalow.

When she awakened she lay and stared at the wall. The house was perfectly still. She had never known it to be so silent before. She heard neither voices nor footsteps, and wondered if everybody had got well of the cholera and all the trouble was over. She wondered also who would take care of her now her Ayah was dead. There would be a new Ayah, and perhaps she would know some new stories. Mary had been rather tired of the old ones. She did not cry because her nurse had died. She was not an affectionate child and had never cared much for anyone. The noise and hurrying about and wailing over the cholera had frightened her, and she had been angry because no one seemed to remember that she was alive. Everyone was too panic-stricken to think of a little girl no one was fond of. When people had the cholera it seemed that they remembered nothing but themselves. But if everyone had got well again, surely someone would remember and come to look for her.

But no one came, and as she lay waiting the house seemed to grow more and more silent. She heard something rustling on the matting and when she looked down she saw a little snake gliding along and watching her with eyes like jewels. She was not frightened, because he was a harmless little thing who would not hurt her and he seemed in a hurry to get out of the room. He slipped under the door as she watched him.

"How queer and quiet it is," she said. "It sounds as if there were no one in the bungalow but me and the snake."

Almost the next minute she heard footsteps in the compound, and then on the veranda. They were men's footsteps, and the men entered the bungalow and talked in low voices. No one went to meet or speak to them and they seemed to open doors and look into rooms. "What desolation!" she heard one voice say. "That pretty, pretty woman! I suppose the child, too. I heard there was a child, though no one ever saw her."

Mary was standing in the middle of the nursery when they opened the door a few minutes later. She looked an ugly, cross little thing and was frowning because she was beginning to be hungry and feel disgracefully neglected. The first man who came in was a large officer she had once seen talking to her father. He looked tired and troubled, but when he saw her he was so startled that he almost jumped back.

"Barney!" he cried out. "There is a child here! A child alone! In a place like this! Mercy on us, who is she!"

"I am Mary Lennox," the little girl said, drawing herself up stiffly. She thought the man was very rude to call her father's bungalow "A place like this!" "I fell asleep when everyone had the cholera and I have only just wakened up. Why does nobody come?"

"It is the child no one ever saw!" exclaimed the man, turning to his companions. "She has actually been forgotten!"

"Why was I forgotten?" Mary said, stamping her foot. "Why does nobody come?"

The young man whose name was Barney looked at her very sadly. Mary even thought she saw him wink his eyes as if to wink tears away.

"Poor little kid!" he said. "There is nobody left to come."

It was in that strange and sudden way that Mary found out that she had neither father nor mother left; that they had died and been carried away in the night, and that the few native servants who had not died also had left the house as quickly as they could get out of it, none of them even remembering that there was a Missie Sahib. That was why the place was so quiet. It was true that there was no one in the bungalow but herself and the little rustling snake.

2

Mistress Mary Quite Contrary

Mary had liked to look at her mother from a distance and she had thought her very pretty, but as she knew very little of her she could scarcely have been expected to love her or to miss her very much when she was gone. She did not miss her at all, in fact, and as she was a self-absorbed child she gave her entire thought to herself, as she had always done. If she had been older she would no doubt have been very anxious at being left alone in the world, but she was very young, and as she had always been taken care of, she supposed she always would be. What she thought was that she would like to know if she was going to nice people, who would be polite to her and give her her own way as her Ayah and the other native servants had done.

She knew that she was not going to stay at the English clergyman's house where she was taken at first. She did not want to stay. The English clergyman was poor and he had five children nearly all the same age and they wore shabby clothes and were always quarreling and snatching toys from each other. Mary hated their untidy bungalow and was so disagreeable to them that after the first day or two nobody would play with her. By the second day they had given her a nickname which made her furious.

It was Basil who thought of it first. Basil was a little boy with impudent blue eyes and a turned-up nose, and Mary hated him. She was playing by herself under a tree, just as she had been playing the day the cholera broke out. She was making heaps of earth and paths for a garden and Basil came and stood near to watch her. Presently he got rather interested and suddenly made a suggestion.

"Why don't you put a heap of stones there and pretend it is a rockery?" he said. "There in the middle," and he leaned over her to point.

"Go away!" cried Mary. "I don't want boys. Go away!"

For a moment Basil looked angry, and then he began to tease. He was always teasing his sisters. He danced round and round her and made faces and sang and laughed.

"Mistress Mary, quite contrary,
How does your garden grow?
With silver bells, and cockle shells,
And marigolds all in a row."

He sang it until the other children heard and laughed, too; and the crosser Mary got, the more they sang "Mistress Mary, quite contrary"; and after that as long as she stayed with them they called her "Mistress Mary Quite Contrary" when they spoke of her to each other, and often when they spoke to her.

"You are going to be sent home," Basil said to her, "at the end of the week. And we're glad of it."

"I am glad of it, too," answered Mary. "Where is home?"

"She doesn't know where home is!" said Basil, with seven-year-old scorn. "It's England, of course. Our grandmama lives there and our sister Mabel was sent to her last year. You are not going to your grandmama. You have none. You are going to your uncle. His name is Mr. Archibald Craven."

"I don't know anything about him," snapped Mary.

"I know you don't," Basil answered. "You don't know anything. Girls never do. I heard father and mother talking about him. He lives in a great, big, desolate old house in the country and no one goes near him. He's so cross he won't let them, and they wouldn't come if he would let them. He's a hunchback, and he's horrid." "I don't believe you," said Mary; and she turned her back and stuck her fingers in her ears, because she would not listen any more.

But she thought over it a great deal afterward; and when Mrs. Crawford told her that night that she was going to sail away to England in a few days and go to her uncle, Mr. Archibald Craven, who lived at Misselthwaite Manor, she looked so stony and stubbornly uninterested that they did not know what to think about her. They tried to be kind to her, but she only turned her face away when Mrs. Crawford attempted to kiss her, and held herself stiffly when Mr. Crawford patted her shoulder.

"She is such a plain child," Mrs. Crawford said pityingly, afterward. "And her mother was such a pretty creature. She had a very pretty manner, too, and Mary has the most unattractive ways I ever saw in a child. The children call her 'Mistress Mary Quite Contrary,' and though it's naughty of them, one can't help understanding it."

"Perhaps if her mother had carried her pretty face and her pretty manners oftener into the nursery Mary might have learned some pretty ways too. It is very sad, now the poor beautiful thing is gone, to remember that many people never even knew that she had a child at all."

"I believe she scarcely ever looked at her," sighed Mrs. Crawford. "When her Ayah was dead there was no one to give a thought to the little thing. Think of the servants running away and leaving her all alone in that deserted bungalow. Colonel McGrew said he nearly jumped out of his skin when he opened the door and found her standing by herself in the middle of the room."

Mary made the long voyage to England under the care of an officer's wife, who was taking her children to leave them in a boarding-school. She was very much absorbed in her own little boy and girl, and was rather glad to hand the child over to the woman Mr. Archibald Craven sent to meet her, in London. The woman was his housekeeper at Misselthwaite Manor, and her name was Mrs. Medlock. She was a stout woman, with very red cheeks and sharp black eyes. She wore a very purple dress, a black silk mantle with jet fringe on it and a black bonnet with purple velvet flowers which stuck up and trembled when she moved her head. Mary did not like her at all, but as she very seldom liked people there was nothing remarkable in that; besides which it was very evident Mrs. Medlock did not think much of her.

"My word! she's a plain little piece of goods!" she said. "And we'd heard that her mother was a beauty. She hasn't handed much of it down, has she, ma'am?" "Perhaps she will improve as she grows older," the officer's wife said good-naturedly. "If she were not so sallow and had a nicer expression, her features are rather good. Children alter so much."

"She'll have to alter a good deal," answered Mrs. Medlock. "And, there's nothing likely to improve children at Misselthwaite—if you ask me!" They thought Mary was not listening because she was standing a little apart from them at the window of the private hotel they had gone to. She was watching the passing buses and cabs and people, but she heard quite well and was made very curious about her uncle and the place he lived in. What sort of a place was it, and what would he be like? What was a hunchback? She had never seen one. Perhaps there were none in India.

Since she had been living in other people's houses and had had no Ayah, she had begun to feel lonely and to think queer thoughts which were new to her. She had begun to wonder why she had never seemed to belong to anyone even when her father and mother had been alive. Other children seemed to belong to their fathers and mothers, but she had never seemed to really be anyone's little girl. She had had servants, and food and clothes, but no one had taken any notice of her. She did not know that this was because she was a disagreeable child; but then, of course, she did not know she was disagreeable. She often thought that other people were, but she did not know that she was so herself.

She thought Mrs. Medlock the most disagreeable person she had ever seen, with her common, highly colored face and her common fine bonnet. When the next day they set out on their journey to

Yorkshire, she walked through the station to the railway carriage with her head up and trying to keep as far away from her as she could, because she did not want to seem to belong to her. It would have made her angry to think people imagined she was her little girl.

But Mrs. Medlock was not in the least disturbed by her and her thoughts. She was the kind of woman who would "stand no nonsense from young ones." At least, that is what she would have said if she had been asked. She had not wanted to go to London just when her sister Maria's daughter was going to be married, but she had a comfortable, well-paid place as housekeeper at Misselthwaite Manor and the only way in which she could keep it was to do at once what Mr. Archibald Craven told her to do. She never dared even to ask a question.

"Captain Lennox and his wife died of the cholera," Mr. Craven had said in his short, cold way. "Captain Lennox was my wife's brother and I am their daughter's guardian. The child is to be brought here. You must go to London and bring her yourself."

So she packed her small trunk and made the journey.

Mary sat in her corner of the railway carriage and looked plain and fretful. She had nothing to read or to look at, and she had folded her thin little black-gloved hands in her lap. Her black dress made her look yellower than ever, and her limp light hair straggled from under her black crêpe hat.

"A more marred-looking young one I never saw in my life," Mrs. Medlock thought. (Marred is a Yorkshire word and means spoiled and pettish.) She had never seen a child who sat so still without doing anything; and at last she got tired of watching her and began to talk in a brisk, hard voice.

"I suppose I may as well tell you something about where you are going to," she said. "Do you know anything about your uncle?"

"No," said Mary.

"Never heard your father and mother talk about him?"

"No," said Mary frowning. She frowned because she remembered that her father and mother had never talked to her about anything in particular. Certainly they had never told her things.

"Humph," muttered Mrs. Medlock, staring at her queer, unresponsive little face. She did not say any more for a few moments and then she began again.

"I suppose you might as well be told something—to prepare you. You are going to a queer place."

Mary said nothing at all, and Mrs. Medlock looked rather discomfited by her apparent indifference, but, after taking a breath, she went on.

"Not but that it's a grand big place in a gloomy way, and Mr. Craven's proud of it in his way—and that's gloomy enough, too. The house is six hundred years old and it's on the edge of the moor, and there's near a hundred rooms in it, though most of them's shut up and locked. And there's pictures and fine old furniture and things that's been there for ages, and there's a big park round it and gardens and trees with branches trailing to the ground—some of them." She paused and took another breath. "But there's nothing else," she ended suddenly.

Mary had begun to listen in spite of herself. It all sounded so unlike India, and anything new rather attracted her. But she did not intend to look as if she were interested. That was one of her unhappy, disagreeable ways. So she sat still.

"Well," said Mrs. Medlock. "What do you think of it?"

"Nothing," she answered. "I know nothing about such places."

That made Mrs. Medlock laugh a short sort of laugh.

"Eh!" she said, "but you are like an old woman. Don't you care?"

"It doesn't matter" said Mary, "whether I care or not."

"You are right enough there," said Mrs. Medlock. "It doesn't. What you're to be kept at Misselthwaite Manor for I don't know, unless because it's the easiest way. He's not going to trouble himself about you, that's sure and certain. He never troubles himself about no one."

She stopped herself as if she had just remembered something in time.

"He's got a crooked back," she said. "That set him wrong. He was a sour young man and got no good of all his money and big place till he was married."

Mary's eyes turned toward her in spite of her intention not to seem to care. She had never thought of the hunchback's being married and she was a trifle surprised. Mrs. Medlock saw this, and as she was a talkative woman she continued with more interest. This was one way of passing some of the time, at any rate.

"She was a sweet, pretty thing and he'd have walked the world over to get her a blade o' grass she wanted. Nobody thought she'd marry him, but she did, and people said she married him for his money. But she didn't—she didn't," positively. "When she died—"

Mary gave a little involuntary jump.

"Oh! did she die!" she exclaimed, quite without meaning to. She had just remembered a French fairy story she had once read called *Riquet à la Houppe*. It had been about a poor hunchback and a beautiful princess and it had made her suddenly sorry for Mr. Archibald Craven.

"Yes, she died," Mrs. Medlock answered. "And it made him queerer than ever. He cares about nobody. He won't see people. Most of the time he goes away, and when he is at Misselthwaite he shuts himself up in the West Wing and won't let anyone but Pitcher see him. Pitcher's an old fellow, but he took care of him when he was a child and he knows his ways."

It sounded like something in a book and it did not make Mary feel cheerful. A house with a hundred rooms, nearly all shut up and with their doors locked—a house on the edge of a moor—whatsoever a moor was—sounded dreary. A man with a crooked back who shut himself up also! She stared out of the window with her lips pinched together, and it seemed quite natural that the rain should have begun to pour down in gray slanting lines and splash and stream down the window-panes. If the pretty wife had been alive she might have made things cheerful by being something like her own mother and by running in and out and going to parties as she had done in frocks "full of lace." But she was not there any more.

"You needn't expect to see him, because ten to one you won't," said Mrs. Medlock. "And you mustn't expect that there will be people to talk to you. You'll have to play about and look after yourself. You'll be told what rooms you can go into and what rooms you're to keep out of. There's gardens enough. But when you're in the house don't go wandering and poking about. Mr. Craven won't have it."

"I shall not want to go poking about," said sour little Mary and just as suddenly as she had begun to be rather sorry for Mr. Archibald Craven she began to cease to be sorry and to think he was unpleasant enough to deserve all that had happened to him.

And she turned her face toward the streaming panes of the window of the railway carriage and gazed out at the gray rain-storm which looked as if it would go on forever and ever. She watched it so long and steadily that the grayness grew heavier and heavier before her eyes and she fell asleep.

3

Across the Moor

She slept a long time, and when she awakened Mrs. Medlock had bought a lunch basket at one of the stations and they had some chicken and cold beef and bread and butter and some hot tea. The rain seemed to be streaming down more heavily than ever and everybody in the station wore wet and glistening waterproofs. The guard lighted the lamps in the carriage, and Mrs. Medlock cheered up very much over her tea and chicken and beef. She ate a great deal and afterward fell asleep herself, and Mary sat and stared at her and watched her fine bonnet slip on one side until she herself fell asleep once more in the corner of the carriage, lulled by the splashing of the rain against the windows. It was quite dark when she awakened again. The train had stopped at a station and Mrs. Medlock was shaking her.

"You have had a sleep!" she said. "It's time to open your eyes! We're at Thwaite Station and we've got a long drive before us."

Mary stood up and tried to keep her eyes open while Mrs. Medlock collected her parcels. The little girl did not offer to help her, because in India native servants always picked up or carried things and it seemed quite proper that other people should wait on one.

The station was a small one and nobody but themselves seemed to be getting out of the train. The station-master spoke to Mrs. Medlock in a rough, good-natured way, pronouncing his words in a queer broad fashion which Mary found out afterward was Yorkshire.

"I see tha's got back," he said. "An' tha's browt th' young 'un with thee."

"Aye, that's her," answered Mrs. Medlock, speaking with a Yorkshire accent herself and jerking her head over her shoulder toward Mary. "How's thy Missus?"

"Well enow. Th' carriage is waitin' outside for thee."

A brougham stood on the road before the little outside platform. Mary saw that it was a smart carriage and that it was a smart footman who helped her in. His long waterproof coat and the waterproof covering of his hat were shining and dripping with rain as everything was, the burly station-master included.

When he shut the door, mounted the box with the coachman, and they drove off, the little girl found herself seated in a comfortably cushioned corner, but she was not inclined to go to sleep again. She sat and looked out of the window, curious to see something of the road over which she was being driven to the queer place Mrs. Medlock had spoken of. She was not at all a timid child and she was not exactly frightened, but she felt that there was no knowing what might happen in a house with a hundred rooms nearly all shut up—a house standing on the edge of a moor.

"What is a moor?" she said suddenly to Mrs. Medlock.

"Look out of the window in about ten minutes and you'll see," the woman answered. "We've got to drive five miles across Missel Moor before we get to the Manor. You won't see much because it's a dark night, but you can see something."

Mary asked no more questions but waited in the darkness of her corner, keeping her eyes on the window. The carriage lamps cast rays of light a little distance ahead of them and she caught glimpses of the things they passed. After they had left the station they had driven through a tiny village and she had seen whitewashed cottages and the lights of a public house. Then they had passed a church and a vicarage and a little shop window or so in a cottage with toys and sweets and odd things set out for sale. Then they were on the highroad and she saw hedges and trees. After that there seemed nothing different for a long time—or at least it seemed a long time to her.

At last the horses began to go more slowly, as if they were climbing up-hill, and presently there seemed to be no more hedges and no more trees. She could see nothing, in fact, but a dense darkness on either side. She leaned forward and pressed her face against the window just as the carriage gave a big jolt.

"Eh! We're on the moor now sure enough," said Mrs. Medlock.

The carriage lamps shed a yellow light on a rough-looking road which seemed to be cut through bushes and low-growing things which ended in the great expanse of dark apparently spread out before and around them. A wind was rising and making a singular, wild, low, rushing sound.

"It's—it's not the sea, is it?" said Mary, looking round at her companion.

"No, not it," answered Mrs. Medlock. "Nor it isn't fields nor mountains, it's just miles and miles and miles of wild land that nothing grows on but heather and gorse and broom, and nothing lives on but wild ponies and sheep."

"I feel as if it might be the sea, if there were water on it," said Mary. "It sounds like the sea just now."

"That's the wind blowing through the bushes," Mrs. Medlock said. "It's a wild, dreary enough place to my mind, though there's plenty that likes it—particularly when the heather's in bloom."

On and on they drove through the darkness, and though the rain stopped, the wind rushed by and whistled and made strange sounds. The road went up and down, and several times the carriage passed over a little bridge beneath which water rushed very fast with a great deal of noise. Mary felt as if the drive would never come to an end and that the wide, bleak moor was a wide expanse of black ocean through which she was passing on a strip of dry land.

"I don't like it," she said to herself. "I don't like it," and she pinched her thin lips more tightly together.

The horses were climbing up a hilly piece of road when she first caught sight of a light. Mrs. Medlock saw it as soon as she did and drew a long sigh of relief.

"Eh, I am glad to see that bit o' light twinkling," she exclaimed. "It's the light in the lodge window. We shall get a good cup of tea after a bit, at all events."

It was "after a bit," as she said, for when the carriage passed through the park gates there was still two miles of avenue to drive through and the trees (which nearly met overhead) made it seem as if they were driving through a long dark vault.

They drove out of the vault into a clear space and stopped before an immensely long but low-built house which seemed to ramble round a stone court. At first Mary thought that there were no lights at all in the windows, but as she got out of the carriage she saw that one room in a corner upstairs showed a dull glow.

The entrance door was a huge one made of massive, curiously shaped panels of oak studded with big iron nails and bound with great iron bars. It opened into an enormous hall, which was so dimly lighted that the faces in the portraits on the walls and the figures in the suits of armor made Mary feel that she did not want to look at them. As she stood on the stone floor she looked a very small, odd little black figure, and she felt as small and lost and odd as she looked.

A neat, thin old man stood near the manservant who opened the door for them.

"You are to take her to her room," he said in a husky voice. "He doesn't want to see her. He's going to London in the morning."

"Very well, Mr. Pitcher," Mrs. Medlock answered. "So long as I know what's expected of me, I can manage."

"What's expected of you, Mrs. Medlock," Mr. Pitcher said, "is that you make sure that he's not disturbed and that he doesn't see what he doesn't want to see."

And then Mary Lennox was led up a broad staircase and down a long corridor and up a short flight of steps and through another corridor and another, until a door opened in a wall and she found herself in a room with a fire in it and a supper on a table.

Mrs. Medlock said unceremoniously:

"Well, here you are! This room and the next are where you'll live—and you must keep to them. Don't you forget that!"

It was in this way Mistress Mary arrived at Misselthwaite Manor and she had perhaps never felt quite so contrary in all her life.

4

Martha

When she opened her eyes in the morning it was because a young housemaid had come into her room to light the fire and was kneeling on the hearth-rug raking out the cinders noisily. Mary lay and watched her for a few moments and then began to look about the room. She had never seen a room at all like it and thought it curious and gloomy. The walls were covered with tapestry with a forest scene embroidered on it. There were fantastically dressed people under the trees and in the distance there was a glimpse of the turrets of a castle. There were hunters and horses and dogs and ladies. Mary felt as if she were in the forest with them. Out of a deep window she could see a great climbing stretch of land which seemed to have no trees on it, and to look rather like an endless, dull, purplish sea.

"What is that?" she said, pointing out of the window.

Martha, the young housemaid, who had just risen to her feet, looked and pointed also. "That there?" she said.

"Yes."

"That's th' moor," with a good-natured grin. "Does tha' like it?"

"No," answered Mary. "I hate it."

"That's because tha'rt not used to it," Martha said, going back to her hearth. "Tha' thinks it's too big an' bare now. But tha' will like it."

"Do you?" inquired Mary.

"Aye, that I do," answered Martha, cheerfully polishing away at the grate. "I just love it. It's none bare. It's covered wi' growin' things as smells sweet. It's fair lovely in spring an' summer when th' gorse an' broom an' heather's in flower. It smells o' honey an' there's such a lot o' fresh air—an' th' sky looks so high an' th' bees an' skylarks makes such a nice noise hummin' an' singin'. Eh! I wouldn't live away from th' moor for anythin'."

Mary listened to her with a grave, puzzled expression. The native servants she had been used to in India were not in the least like this. They were obsequious and servile and did not presume to talk to their masters as if they were their equals. They made salaams and called them "protector of the poor" and names of that sort. Indian servants were commanded to do things, not asked. It was not the custom to say "please" and "thank you" and Mary had always slapped her Ayah in the face when she was angry. She wondered a little what this girl would do if one slapped her in the face. She was a round, rosy, good-natured-looking creature, but she had a sturdy way which made Mistress Mary wonder if she might not even slap back—if the person who slapped her was only a little girl.

"You are a strange servant," she said from her pillows, rather haughtily.

Martha sat up on her heels, with her blacking-brush in her hand, and laughed, without seeming the least out of temper.

"Eh! I know that," she said. "If there was a grand Missus at Misselthwaite I should never have been even one of th' under-housemaids. I might have been let to be scullery maid but I'd never have been let upstairs. I'm too common an' I talk too much Yorkshire. But this is a funny house for all it's so grand. Seems like there's neither Master nor Mistress except Mr. Pitcher an' Mrs. Medlock.

Mr. Craven, he won't be troubled about anythin' when he's here, an' he's nearly always away. Mrs. Medlock gave me th' place out o' kindness. She told me she could never have done it if Misselthwaite had been like other big houses." "Are you going to be my servant?" Mary asked, still in her imperious little Indian way.

Martha began to rub her grate again.

"I'm Mrs. Medlock's servant," she said stoutly. "An' she's Mr. Craven's—but I'm to do the housemaid's work up here an' wait on you a bit. But you won't need much waitin' on."

"Who is going to dress me?" demanded Mary.

Martha sat up on her heels again and stared. She spoke in broad Yorkshire in her amazement.

"Canna' tha' dress thysen!" she said.

"What do you mean? I don't understand your language," said Mary.

"Eh! I forgot," Martha said. "Mrs. Medlock told me I'd have to be careful or you wouldn't know what I was sayin'. I mean can't you put on your own clothes?"

"No," answered Mary, quite indignantly. "I never did in my life. My Ayah dressed me, of course."

"Well," said Martha, evidently not in the least aware that she was impudent, "it's time tha' should learn. Tha' cannot begin younger. It'll do thee good to wait on thysen a bit. My mother always said she couldn't see why grand people's children didn't turn out fair fools—what with nurses an' bein' washed an' dressed an' took out to walk as if they was puppies!"

"It is different in India," said Mistress Mary disdainfully. She could scarcely stand this.

But Martha was not at all crushed.

"Eh! I can see it's different," she answered almost sympathetically. "I dare say it's because there's such a lot o' blacks there instead o' respectable white people. When I heard you was comin' from India I thought you was a black too."

Mary sat up in bed furious.

"What!" she said. "What! You thought I was a native. You—you daughter of a pig!"

Martha stared and looked hot.

"Who are you callin' names?" she said. "You needn't be so vexed. That's not th' way for a young lady to talk. I've nothin' against th' blacks. When you read about 'em in tracts they're always very religious. You always read as a black's a man an' a brother. I've never seen a black an' I was fair pleased to think I was goin' to see one close. When I come in to light your fire this mornin' I crep' up to your bed an' pulled th' cover back careful to look at you. An' there you was," disappointedly, "no more black than me—for all you're so yeller."

Mary did not even try to control her rage and humiliation. "You thought I was a native! You dared! You don't know anything about natives! They are not people—they're servants who must salaam to you. You know nothing about India. You know nothing about anything!"

She was in such a rage and felt so helpless before the girl's simple stare, and somehow she suddenly felt so horribly lonely and far away from everything she understood and which understood her, that she threw herself face downward on the pillows and burst into passionate sobbing. She sobbed so unrestrainedly that good-natured Yorkshire Martha was a little frightened and quite sorry for her. She went to the bed and bent over her.

"Eh! you mustn't cry like that there!" she begged. "You mustn't for sure. I didn't know you'd be vexed. I don't know anythin' about anythin'—just like you said. I beg your pardon, Miss. Do stop cryin'."

There was something comforting and really friendly in her queer Yorkshire speech and sturdy way which had a good effect on Mary. She gradually ceased crying and became quiet. Martha looked relieved.

"It's time for thee to get up now," she said. "Mrs. Medlock said I was to carry tha' breakfast an' tea an' dinner into th' room next to this. It's been made into a nursery for thee. I'll help thee on with thy clothes if tha'll get out o' bed. If th' buttons are at th' back tha' cannot button them up tha'self."

When Mary at last decided to get up, the clothes Martha took from the wardrobe were not the ones she had worn when she arrived the night before with Mrs. Medlock.

"Those are not mine," she said. "Mine are black."

She looked the thick white wool coat and dress over, and added with cool approval:

"Those are nicer than mine."

"These are th' ones tha' must put on," Martha answered. "Mr. Craven ordered Mrs. Medlock to get 'em in London. He said 'I won't have a child dressed in black wanderin' about like a lost soul,' he said. 'It'd make the place sadder than it is. Put color on her.' Mother she said she knew what he meant. Mother always knows what a body means. She doesn't hold with black hersel'."

"I hate black things," said Mary.

The dressing process was one which taught them both something. Martha had "buttoned up" her little sisters and brothers but she had never seen a child who stood still and waited for another person to do things for her as if she had neither hands nor feet of her own.

"Why doesn't tha' put on tha' own shoes?" she said when Mary quietly held out her foot.

"My Ayah did it," answered Mary, staring. "It was the custom."

She said that very often—"It was the custom." The native servants were always saying it. If one told them to do a thing their ancestors had not done for a thousand years they gazed at one mildly and said, "It is not the custom" and one knew that was the end of the matter.

It had not been the custom that Mistress Mary should do anything but stand and allow herself to be dressed like a doll, but before she was ready for breakfast she began to suspect that her life at Misselthwaite Manor would end by teaching her a number of things quite new to her—things such as putting on her own shoes and stockings, and picking up things she let fall. If Martha had been a well-trained fine young lady's maid she would have been more subservient and respectful and would have known that it was her business to brush hair, and button boots, and pick things up and lay them away. She was, however, only an untrained Yorkshire rustic who had been brought up in a moorland cottage with a swarm of little brothers and sisters who had never dreamed of doing anything but waiting on themselves and on the younger ones who were either babies in arms or just learning to totter about and tumble over things.

If Mary Lennox had been a child who was ready to be amused she would perhaps have laughed at Martha's readiness to talk, but Mary only listened to her coldly and wondered at her freedom of manner. At first she was not at all interested, but gradually, as the girl rattled on in her good-tempered, homely way, Mary began to notice what she was saying.

"Eh! you should see 'em all," she said. "There's twelve of us an' my father only gets sixteen shilling a week. I can tell you my mother's put to it to get porridge for 'em all. They tumble about on th' moor an' play there all day an' mother says th' air of th' moor fattens 'em. She says she believes they eat th' grass same as th' wild ponies do. Our Dickon, he's twelve years old and he's got a young pony he calls his own."

"Where did he get it?" asked Mary.

"He found it on th' moor with its mother when it was a little one an' he began to make friends with it an' give it bits o' bread an' pluck young grass for it. And it got to like him so it follows him about an' it lets him get on its back. Dickon's a kind lad an' animals likes him."

Mary had never possessed an animal pet of her own and had always thought she should like one. So she began to feel a slight interest in Dickon, and as she had never before been interested in anyone but herself, it was the dawning of a healthy sentiment. When she went into the room which had been made into a nursery for her, she found that it was rather like the one she had slept in. It was not a child's room, but a grown-up person's room, with gloomy old pictures on the walls and heavy old oak chairs. A table in the center was set with a good substantial breakfast. But she had always had a very small appetite, and she looked with something more than indifference at the first plate Martha set before her.

"I don't want it," she said.

"Tha' doesn't want thy porridge!" Martha exclaimed incredulously.

"No."

"Tha' doesn't know how good it is. Put a bit o' treacle on it or a bit o' sugar."

"I don't want it," repeated Mary.

"Eh!" said Martha. "I can't abide to see good victuals go to waste. If our children was at this table they'd clean it bare in five minutes."

"Why?" said Mary coldly. "Why!" echoed Martha. "Because they scarce ever had their stomachs full in their lives. They're as hungry as young hawks an' foxes."

"I don't know what it is to be hungry," said Mary, with the indifference of ignorance.

Martha looked indignant.

"Well, it would do thee good to try it. I can see that plain enough," she said outspokenly. "I've no patience with folk as sits an' just stares at good bread an' meat. My word! don't I wish Dickon and Phil an' Jane an' th' rest of 'em had what's here under their pinafores."

"Why don't you take it to them?" suggested Mary.

"It's not mine," answered Martha stoutly. "An' this isn't my day out. I get my day out once a month same as th' rest. Then I go home an' clean up for mother an' give her a day's rest."

Mary drank some tea and ate a little toast and some marmalade.

"You wrap up warm an' run out an' play you," said Martha. "It'll do you good and give you some stomach for your meat."

Mary went to the window. There were gardens and paths and big trees, but everything looked dull and wintry.

"Out? Why should I go out on a day like this?" "Well, if tha' doesn't go out tha'lt have to stay in, an' what has tha' got to do?"

Mary glanced about her. There was nothing to do. When Mrs. Medlock had prepared the nursery she had not thought of amusement. Perhaps it would be better to go and see what the gardens were like.

"Who will go with me?" she inquired.

Martha stared.

"You'll go by yourself," she answered. "You'll have to learn to play like other children does when they haven't got sisters and brothers. Our Dickon goes off on th' moor by himself an' plays for hours. That's how he made friends with th' pony. He's got sheep on th' moor that knows him, an' birds as comes an' eats out of his hand. However little there is to eat, he always saves a bit o' his bread to coax his pets."

It was really this mention of Dickon which made Mary decide to go out, though she was not aware of it. There would be, birds outside though there would not be ponies or sheep. They would be different from the birds in India and it might amuse her to look at them.

Martha found her coat and hat for her and a pair of stout little boots and she showed her her way downstairs.

"If tha' goes round that way tha'll come to th' gardens," she said, pointing to a gate in a wall of shrubbery. "There's lots o' flowers in summer-time, but there's nothin' bloomin' now." She seemed to hesitate a second before she added, "One of th' gardens is locked up. No one has been in it for ten years."

"Why?" asked Mary in spite of herself. Here was another locked door added to the hundred in the strange house.

"Mr. Craven had it shut when his wife died so sudden. He won't let no one go inside. It was her garden. He locked th' door an' dug a hole and buried th' key. There's Mrs. Medlock's bell ringing—I must run."

After she was gone Mary turned down the walk which led to the door in the shrubbery. She could not help thinking about the garden which no one had been into for ten years. She wondered what it would look like and whether there were any flowers still alive in it. When she had passed through the shrubbery gate she found herself in great gardens, with wide lawns and winding walks with clipped borders. There were trees, and flower-beds, and evergreens clipped into strange shapes, and a large pool with an old gray fountain in its midst. But the flower-beds were bare and wintry and the fountain was not playing. This was not the garden which was shut up. How could a garden be shut up? You could always walk into a garden.

She was just thinking this when she saw that, at the end of the path she was following, there seemed to be a long wall, with ivy growing over it. She was not familiar enough with England to know that she was coming upon the kitchen-gardens where the vegetables and fruit were growing. She went toward the wall and found that there was a green door in the ivy, and that it stood open. This was not the closed garden, evidently, and she could go into it.

She went through the door and found that it was a garden with walls all round it and that it was only one of several walled gardens which seemed to open into one another. She saw another open green door, revealing bushes and pathways between beds containing winter vegetables. Fruit-trees were trained flat against the wall, and over some of the beds there were glass frames. The place was bare and ugly enough, Mary thought, as she stood and stared about her. It might be nicer in summer when things were green, but there was nothing pretty about it now.

Presently an old man with a spade over his shoulder walked through the door leading from the second garden. He looked startled when he saw Mary, and then touched his cap. He had a surly old face, and did not seem at all pleased to see her—but then she was displeased with his garden and wore her "quite contrary" expression, and certainly did not seem at all pleased to see him.

"What is this place?" she asked.

"One o' th' kitchen-gardens," he answered.

"What is that?" said Mary, pointing through the other green door.

"Another of 'em," shortly. "There's another on t'other side o' th' wall an' there's th' orchard t'other side o' that."

"Can I go in them?" asked Mary.

"If tha' likes. But there's nowt to see."

Mary made no response. She went down the path and through the second green door. There, she found more walls and winter vegetables and glass frames, but in the second wall there was another green door and it was not open. Perhaps it led into the garden which no one had seen for ten years. As she was not at all a timid child and always did what she wanted to do, Mary went to the green door and turned the handle. She hoped the door would not open because she wanted to be sure she had found the mysterious garden—but it did open quite easily and she walked through it and found herself in an orchard. There were walls all round it also and trees trained against them, and there were bare fruit-trees growing in the winter-browned grass—but there was no green door to be seen anywhere. Mary looked for it, and yet when she had entered the upper end of the garden she had noticed that the wall did not seem to end with the orchard but to extend beyond it as if it enclosed a place at the other side. She could see the tops of trees above the wall, and when she stood still she saw a bird with a bright red breast sitting on the topmost branch of one of them, and suddenly he burst into his winter song—almost as if he had caught sight of her and was calling to her.

She stopped and listened to him and somehow his cheerful, friendly little whistle gave her a pleased feeling—even a disagreeable little girl may be lonely, and the big closed house and big bare moor and big bare gardens had made this one feel as if there was no one left in the world but herself. If she had been an affectionate child, who had been used to being loved, she would have broken her heart, but even though she was "Mistress Mary Quite Contrary" she was desolate, and the bright-breasted little bird brought a look into her sour little face which was almost a smile. She listened to him until he flew away. He was not like an Indian bird and she liked him and wondered if she should ever see him again. Perhaps he lived in the mysterious garden and knew all about it.

Perhaps it was because she had nothing whatever to do that she thought so much of the deserted garden. She was curious about it and wanted to see what it was like. Why had Mr. Archibald Craven buried the key? If he had liked his wife so much why did he hate her garden? She wondered if she should ever see him, but she knew that if she did she should not like him, and he would not like her, and that she should only stand and stare at him and say nothing, though she should be wanting dreadfully to ask him why he had done such a queer thing.

"People never like me and I never like people," she thought. "And I never can talk as the Crawford children could. They were always talking and laughing and making noises."

She thought of the robin and of the way he seemed to sing his song at her, and as she remembered the tree-top he perched on she stopped rather suddenly on the path.

"I believe that tree was in the secret garden—I feel sure it was," she said. "There was a wall round the place and there was no door."

She walked back into the first kitchen-garden she had entered and found the old man digging there. She went and stood beside him and watched him a few moments in her cold little way. He took no notice of her and so at last she spoke to him.

"I have been into the other gardens," she said.

"There was nothin' to prevent thee," he answered crustily.

"I went into the orchard."

"There was no dog at th' door to bite thee," he answered.

"There was no door there into the other garden," said Mary.

"What garden?" he said in a rough voice, stopping his digging for a moment.

"The one on the other side of the wall," answered Mistress Mary. "There are trees there—I saw the tops of them. A bird with a red breast was sitting on one of them and he sang."

To her surprise the surly old weather-beaten face actually changed its expression. A slow smile spread over it and the gardener looked quite different. It made her think that it was curious how much nicer a person looked when he smiled. She had not thought of it before.

He turned about to the orchard side of his garden and began to whistle—a low soft whistle. She could not understand how such a surly man could make such a coaxing sound. Almost the next moment a wonderful thing happened. She heard a soft little rushing flight through the air—and it was the bird with the red breast flying to them, and he actually alighted on the big clod of earth quite near to the gardener's foot.

"Here he is," chuckled the old man, and then he spoke to the bird as if he were speaking to a child.

"Where has tha' been, tha' cheeky little beggar?" he said. "I've not seen thee before today. Has tha, begun tha' courtin' this early in th' season? Tha'rt too forrad."

The bird put his tiny head on one side and looked up at him with his soft bright eye which was like a black dewdrop. He seemed quite familiar and not the least afraid. He hopped about and pecked the earth briskly, looking for seeds and insects. It actually gave Mary a queer feeling in her heart, because he was so pretty and cheerful and seemed so like a person. He had a tiny plump body and a delicate beak, and slender delicate legs.

"Will he always come when you call him?" she asked almost in a whisper.

"Aye, that he will. I've knowed him ever since he was a fledgling. He come out of th' nest in th' other garden an' when first he flew over th' wall he was too weak to fly back for a few days an' we got friendly. When he went over th' wall again th' rest of th' brood was gone an' he was lonely an' he come back to me."

"What kind of a bird is he?" Mary asked.

"Doesn't tha' know? He's a robin redbreast an' they're th' friendliest, curiousest birds alive. They're almost as friendly as dogs—if you know how to get on with 'em. Watch him peckin' about there an' lookin' round at us now an' again. He knows we're talkin' about him."

It was the queerest thing in the world to see the old fellow. He looked at the plump little scarlet-waistcoated bird as if he were both proud and fond of him.

"He's a conceited one," he chuckled. "He likes to hear folk talk about him. An' curious—bless me, there never was his like for curiosity an' meddlin'. He's always comin' to see what I'm plantin'. He knows all th' things Mester Craven never troubles hissel' to find out. He's th' head gardener, he is."

The robin hopped about busily pecking the soil and now and then stopped and looked at them a little. Mary thought his black dewdrop eyes gazed at her with great curiosity. It really seemed as if he were finding out all about her. The queer feeling in her heart increased. "Where did the rest of the brood fly to?" she asked.

"There's no knowin'. The old ones turn 'em out o' their nest an' make 'em fly an' they're scattered before you know it. This one was a knowin' one an' he knew he was lonely."

Mistress Mary went a step nearer to the robin and looked at him very hard.

"I'm lonely," she said.

She had not known before that this was one of the things which made her feel sour and cross. She seemed to find it out when the robin looked at her and she looked at the robin.

The old gardener pushed his cap back on his bald head and stared at her a minute.

"Art tha' th' little wench from India?" he asked.

Mary nodded.

"Then no wonder tha'rt lonely. Tha'lt be lonlier before tha's done," he said.

He began to dig again, driving his spade deep into the rich black garden soil while the robin hopped about very busily employed.

"What is your name?" Mary inquired.

He stood up to answer her.

"Ben Weatherstaff," he answered, and then he added with a surly chuckle, "I'm lonely mysel' except when he's with me," and he jerked his thumb toward the robin. "He's th' only friend I've got."

"I have no friends at all," said Mary. "I never had. My Ayah didn't like me and I never played with anyone."

It is a Yorkshire habit to say what you think with blunt frankness, and old Ben Weatherstaff was a Yorkshire moor man.

"Tha' an' me are a good bit alike," he said. "We was wove out of th' same cloth. We're neither of us good-lookin' an' we're both of us as sour as we look. We've got the same nasty tempers, both of us, I'll warrant."

This was plain speaking, and Mary Lennox had never heard the truth about herself in her life. Native servants always salaamed and submitted to you, whatever you did. She had never thought much about her looks, but she wondered if she was as unattractive as Ben Weatherstaff and she also wondered if she looked as sour as he had looked before the robin came. She actually began to wonder also if she was "nasty tempered." She felt uncomfortable.

Suddenly a clear rippling little sound broke out near her and she turned round. She was standing a few feet from a young apple-tree and the robin had flown on to one of its branches and had burst out into a scrap of a song. Ben Weatherstaff laughed outright.

"What did he do that for?" asked Mary.

"He's made up his mind to make friends with thee," replied Ben. "Dang me if he hasn't took a fancy to thee."

"To me?" said Mary, and she moved toward the little tree softly and looked up.

"Would you make friends with me?" she said to the robin just as if she was speaking to a person. "Would you?" And she did not say it either in her hard little voice or in her imperious Indian voice, but in a tone so soft and eager and coaxing that Ben Weatherstaff was as surprised as she had been when she heard him whistle.

"Why," he cried out, "tha' said that as nice an' human as if tha' was a real child instead of a sharp old woman. Tha' said it almost like Dickon talks to his wild things on th' moor."

"Do you know Dickon?" Mary asked, turning round rather in a hurry.

"Everybody knows him. Dickon's wanderin' about everywhere. Th' very blackberries an' heather-bells knows him. I warrant th' foxes shows him where their cubs lies an' th' skylarks doesn't hide their nests from him."

Mary would have liked to ask some more questions. She was almost as curious about Dickon as she was about the deserted garden. But just that moment the robin, who had ended his song, gave a little shake of his wings, spread them and flew away. He had made his visit and had other things to do.

"He has flown over the wall!" Mary cried out, watching him. "He has flown into the orchard—he has flown across the other wall—into the garden where there is no door!"

"He lives there," said old Ben. "He came out o' th' egg there. If he's courtin', he's makin' up to some young madam of a robin that lives among th' old rose-trees there."

"Rose-trees," said Mary. "Are there rose-trees?"

Ben Weatherstaff took up his spade again and began to dig.

"There was ten year' ago," he mumbled.

"I should like to see them," said Mary. "Where is the green door? There must be a door somewhere."

Ben drove his spade deep and looked as uncompanionable as he had looked when she first saw him.

"There was ten year' ago, but there isn't now," he said.

"No door!" cried Mary. "There must be." "None as anyone can find, an' none as is anyone's business. Don't you be a meddlesome wench an' poke your nose where it's no cause to go. Here, I must go on with my work. Get you gone an' play you. I've no more time."

And he actually stopped digging, threw his spade over his shoulder and walked off, without even glancing at her or saying goodbye.

5

The Cry in the Corridor

At first each day which passed by for Mary Lennox was exactly like the others. Every morning she awoke in her tapestried room and found Martha kneeling upon the hearth building her fire; every morning she ate her breakfast in the nursery which had nothing amusing in it; and after each breakfast she gazed out of the window across to the huge moor which seemed to spread out on all sides and climb up to the sky, and after she had stared for a while she realized that if she did not go out she would have to stay in and do nothing—and so she went out. She did not know that this was the best thing she could have done, and she did not know that, when she began to walk quickly or even run along the paths and down the avenue, she was stirring her slow blood and making herself stronger by fighting with the wind which swept down from the moor. She ran only to make herself warm, and she hated the wind which rushed at her face and roared and held her back as if it were some giant she could not see. But the big breaths of rough fresh air blown over the heather filled her lungs with something which was good for her whole thin body and whipped some red color into her cheeks and brightened her dull eyes when she did not know anything about it.

But after a few days spent almost entirely out of doors she wakened one morning knowing what it was to be hungry, and when she sat down to her breakfast she did not glance disdainfully at her porridge and push it away, but took up her spoon and began to eat it and went on eating it until her bowl was empty.

"Tha' got on well enough with that this mornin', didn't tha'?" said Martha.

"It tastes nice today," said Mary, feeling a little surprised her self.

"It's th' air of th' moor that's givin' thee stomach for tha' victuals," answered Martha. "It's lucky for thee that tha's got victuals as well as appetite. There's been twelve in our cottage as had th' stomach an' nothin' to put in it. You go on playin' you out o' doors every day an' you'll get some flesh on your bones an' you won't be so yeller."

"I don't play," said Mary. "I have nothing to play with."

"Nothin' to play with!" exclaimed Martha. "Our children plays with sticks and stones. They just runs about an' shouts an' looks at things." Mary did not shout, but she looked at things. There was nothing else to do. She walked round and round the gardens and wandered about the paths in the park. Sometimes she looked for Ben Weatherstaff, but though several times she saw him at work he was too busy to look at her or was too surly. Once when she was walking toward him he picked up his spade and turned away as if he did it on purpose.

One place she went to oftener than to any other. It was the long walk outside the gardens with the walls round them. There were bare flower-beds on either side of it and against the walls ivy grew thickly. There was one part of the wall where the creeping dark green leaves were more bushy than elsewhere. It seemed as if for a long time that part had been neglected. The rest of it had been clipped and made to look neat, but at this lower end of the walk it had not been trimmed at all.

A few days after she had talked to Ben Weatherstaff, Mary stopped to notice this and wondered why it was so. She had just paused and was looking up at a long spray of ivy swinging in the wind when she saw a gleam of scarlet and heard a brilliant chirp, and there, on the top of the wall, forward perched Ben Weatherstaff's robin redbreast, tilting forward to look at her with his small head on one side.

"Oh!" she cried out, "is it you—is it you?" And it did not seem at all queer to her that she spoke to him as if she were sure that he would understand and answer her.

He did answer. He twittered and chirped and hopped along the wall as if he were telling her all sorts of things. It seemed to Mistress Mary as if she understood him, too, though he was not speaking in words. It was as if he said:

"Good morning! Isn't the wind nice? Isn't the sun nice? Isn't everything nice? Let us both chirp and hop and twitter. Come on! Come on!"

Mary began to laugh, and as he hopped and took little flights along the wall she ran after him. Poor little thin, sallow, ugly Mary—she actually looked almost pretty for a moment.

"I like you! I like you!" she cried out, pattering down the walk; and she chirped and tried to whistle, which last she did not know how to do in the least. But the robin seemed to be quite satisfied and chirped and whistled back at her. At last he spread his wings and made a darting flight to the top of a tree, where he perched and sang loudly. That reminded Mary of the first time she had seen him. He had been swinging on a tree-top then and she had been standing in the orchard. Now she was on the other side of the orchard and standing in the path outside a wall—much lower down—and there was the same tree inside.

"It's in the garden no one can go into," she said to herself. "It's the garden without a door. He lives in there. How I wish I could see what it is like!"

She ran up the walk to the green door she had entered the first morning. Then she ran down the path through the other door and then into the orchard, and when she stood and looked up there was the tree on the other side of the wall, and there was the robin just finishing his song and, beginning to preen his feathers with his beak.

"It is the garden," she said. "I am sure it is."

She walked round and looked closely at that side of the orchard wall, but she only found what she had found before—that there was no door in it. Then she ran through the kitchen-gardens again and out into the walk outside the long ivy-covered wall, and she walked to the end of it and looked at it, but there was no door; and then she walked to the other end, looking again, but there was no door.

"It's very queer," she said. "Ben Weatherstaff said there was no door and there is no door. But there must have been one ten years ago, because Mr. Craven buried the key."

This gave her so much to think of that she began to be quite interested and feel that she was not sorry that she had come to Misselthwaite Manor. In India she had always felt hot and too languid to care much about anything. The fact was that the fresh wind from the moor had begun to blow the cobwebs out of her young brain and to waken her up a little.

She stayed out of doors nearly all day, and when she sat down to her supper at night she felt hungry and drowsy and comfortable. She did not feel cross when Martha chattered away. She felt as if she rather liked to hear her, and at last she thought she would ask her a question. She asked it after she had finished her supper and had sat down on the hearth-rug before the fire.

"Why did Mr. Craven hate the garden?" she said.

She had made Martha stay with her and Martha had not objected at all. She was very young, and used to a crowded cottage full of brothers and sisters, and she found it dull in the great servants' hall downstairs where the footman and upper-housemaids made fun of her Yorkshire speech and looked upon her as a common little thing, and sat and whispered among themselves. Martha liked to talk, and the strange child who had lived in India, and been waited upon by "blacks," was novelty enough to attract her.

She sat down on the hearth herself without waiting to be asked.

"Art tha' thinkin' about that garden yet?" she said. "I knew tha' would. That was just the way with me when I first heard about it."

"Why did he hate it?" Mary persisted.

Martha tucked her feet under her and made herself quite comfortable.

"Listen to th' wind wutherin' round the house," she said. "You could bare stand up on the moor if you was out on it tonight."

Mary did not know what "wutherin'" meant until she listened, and then she understood. It must mean that hollow shuddering sort of roar which rushed round and round the house as if the giant no one could see were buffeting it and beating at the walls and windows to try to break in. But one knew he could not get in, and somehow it made one feel very safe and warm inside a room with a red coal fire.

"But why did he hate it so?" she asked, after she had listened. She intended to know if Martha did.

Then Martha gave up her store of knowledge.

"Mind," she said, "Mrs. Medlock said it's not to be talked about. There's lots o' things in this place that's not to be talked over. That's Mr. Craven's orders. His troubles are none servants' business, he says. But for th' garden he wouldn't be like he is. It was Mrs. Craven's garden that she had made when first they were married an' she just loved it, an' they used to 'tend the flowers themselves. An' none o' th' gardeners was ever let to go in. Him an' her used to go in an' shut th' door an' stay there hours an' hours, readin' and talkin'. An' she was just a bit of a girl an' there was an old tree with a branch bent like a seat on it. An' she made roses grow over it an' she used to sit there. But one day when she was sittin' there th' branch broke an' she fell on th' ground an' was hurt so bad that next day she died. Th' doctors thought he'd go out o' his mind an' die, too. That's why he hates it. No one's never gone in since, an' he won't let anyone talk about it."

Mary did not ask any more questions. She looked at the red fire and listened to the wind "wutherin'." It seemed to be "wutherin'" louder than ever. At that moment a very good thing was happening to her. Four good things had happened to her, in fact, since she came to Misselthwaite Manor. She had felt as if she had understood a robin and that he had understood her; she had run in the wind until her blood had grown warm; she had been healthily hungry for the first time in her life; and she had found out what it was to be sorry for someone. She was getting on.

But as she was listening to the wind she began to listen to something else. She did not know what it was, because at first she could scarcely distinguish it from the wind itself. It was a curious sound—it seemed almost as if a child were crying somewhere. Sometimes the wind sounded rather like a child crying, but presently Mistress Mary felt quite sure this sound was inside the house, not outside it. It was far away, but it was inside. She turned round and looked at Martha.

"Do you hear anyone crying?" she said.

Martha suddenly looked confused.

"No," she answered. "It's th' wind. Sometimes it sounds like as if someone was lost on th' moor an' wailin'. It's got all sorts o' sounds."

"But listen," said Mary. "It's in the house—down one of those long corridors."

And at that very moment a door must have been opened somewhere downstairs; for a great rushing draft blew along the passage and the door of the room they sat in was blown open with a crash, and as they both jumped to their feet the light was blown out and the crying sound was swept down the far corridor so that it was to be heard more plainly than ever.

"There!" said Mary. "I told you so! It is someone crying—and it isn't a grown-up person."

Martha ran and shut the door and turned the key, but before she did it they both heard the sound of a door in some far passage shutting with a bang, and then everything was quiet, for even the wind ceased "wutherin'" for a few moments.

"It was th' wind," said Martha stubbornly. "An' if it wasn't, it was little Betty Butterworth, th' scullery-maid. She's had th' toothache all day."

But something troubled and awkward in her manner made Mistress Mary stare very hard at her. She did not believe she was speaking the truth.

6

"There Was Someone Crying—There Was!"

The next day the rain poured down in torrents again, and when Mary looked out of her window the moor was almost hidden by gray mist and cloud. There could be no going out today.

"What do you do in your cottage when it rains like this?" she asked Martha.

"Try to keep from under each other's feet mostly," Martha answered. "Eh! there does seem a lot of us then. Mother's a good-tempered woman but she gets fair moithered. The biggest ones goes out in th' cow-shed and plays there. Dickon he doesn't mind th' wet. He goes out just th' same as if th' sun was shinin'. He says he sees things on rainy days as doesn't show when it's fair weather. He once found a little fox cub half drowned in its hole and he brought it home in th' bosom of his shirt to keep it warm. Its mother had been killed nearby an' th' hole was swum out an' th' rest o' th' litter was dead. He's got it at home now. He found a half-drowned young crow another time an' he brought it home, too, an' tamed it. It's named Soot because it's so black, an' it hops an' flies about with him everywhere."

The time had come when Mary had forgotten to resent Martha's familiar talk. She had even begun to find it interesting and to be sorry when she stopped or went away. The stories she had been told by her Ayah when she lived in India had been quite unlike those Martha had to tell about the moorland cottage which held fourteen people who lived in four little rooms and never had quite enough to eat. The children seemed to tumble about and amuse themselves like a litter of rough, good-natured collie puppies. Mary was most attracted by the mother and Dickon. When Martha told stories of what "mother" said or did they always sounded comfortable.

"If I had a raven or a fox cub I could play with it," said Mary. "But I have nothing."

Martha looked perplexed.

"Can tha' knit?" she asked.

"No," answered Mary.

"Can tha' sew?"

"No."

"Can tha' read?"

"Yes."

"Then why doesn't tha, read somethin', or learn a bit o' spellin'? Tha'st old enough to be learnin' thy book a good bit now."

"I haven't any books," said Mary. "Those I had were left in India."

"That's a pity," said Martha. "If Mrs. Medlock'd let thee go into th' library, there's thousands o' books there."

Mary did not ask where the library was, because she was suddenly inspired by a new idea. She made up her mind to go and find it herself. She was not troubled about Mrs. Medlock. Mrs. Medlock seemed always to be in her comfortable housekeeper's sitting room downstairs. In this queer place one scarcely ever saw anyone at all. In fact, there was no one to see but the servants, and when their master was away they lived a luxurious life below stairs, where there was a huge kitchen hung about with shining brass and pewter, and a large servants' hall where there were four or five abundant meals eaten every day, and where a great deal of lively romping went on when Mrs. Medlock was out of the way.

Mary's meals were served regularly, and Martha waited on her, but no one troubled themselves about her in the least. Mrs. Medlock came and looked at her every day or two, but no one inquired what she did or told her what to do. She supposed that perhaps this was the English way of treating children. In India she had always been attended by her Ayah, who had followed her about and waited on her, hand and foot. She had often been tired of her company. Now she was followed by nobody and was learning to dress herself because Martha looked as though she thought she was silly and stupid when she wanted to have things handed to her and put on.

"Hasn't tha' got good sense?" she said once, when Mary had stood waiting for her to put on her gloves for her. "Our Susan Ann is twice as sharp as thee an' she's only four year' old. Sometimes tha' looks fair soft in th' head."

Mary had worn her contrary scowl for an hour after that, but it made her think several entirely new things.

She stood at the window for about ten minutes this morning after Martha had swept up the hearth for the last time and gone downstairs. She was thinking over the new idea which had come to her when she heard of the library. She did not care very much about the library itself, because she had read very few books; but to hear of it brought back to her mind the hundred rooms with closed doors. She wondered if they were all really locked and what she would find if she could get into any of them. Were there a hundred really? Why shouldn't she go and see how many doors she could count? It would be something to do on this morning when she could not go out. She had never been taught to ask permission to do things, and she knew nothing at all about authority, so she would not have thought it necessary to ask Mrs. Medlock if she might walk about the house, even if she had seen her.

She opened the door of the room and went into the corridor, and then she began her wanderings. It was a long corridor and it branched into other corridors and it led her up short flights of steps which mounted to others again. There were doors and doors, and there were pictures on the walls. Sometimes they were pictures of dark, curious landscapes, but oftenest they were portraits of men and women in queer, grand costumes made of satin and velvet. She found herself in one long gallery whose walls were covered with these portraits. She had never thought there could be so many in any house. She walked slowly down this place and stared at the faces which also seemed to stare at her. She felt as if they were wondering what a little girl from India was doing in their house. Some were pictures of children—little girls in thick satin frocks which reached to their feet and stood out about them, and boys with puffed sleeves and lace collars and long hair, or with big ruffs around their necks. She always stopped to look at the children, and wonder what their names were, and where they had gone, and why they wore such odd clothes. There was a stiff, plain little girl rather like herself. She wore a green brocade dress and held a green parrot on her finger. Her eyes had a sharp, curious look.

"Where do you live now?" said Mary aloud to her. "I wish you were here."

Surely no other little girl ever spent such a queer morning. It seemed as if there was no one in all the huge rambling house but her own small self, wandering about upstairs and down, through narrow passages and wide ones, where it seemed to her that no one but herself had ever walked. Since so many rooms had been built, people must have lived in them, but it all seemed so empty that she could not quite believe it true.

It was not until she climbed to the second floor that she thought of turning the handle of a door. All the doors were shut, as Mrs. Medlock had said they were, but at last she put her hand on the handle of one of them and turned it. She was almost frightened for a moment when she felt that it turned without difficulty and that when she pushed upon the door itself it slowly and heavily opened. It was a massive door and opened into a big bedroom. There were embroidered hangings on the wall, and inlaid furniture such as she had seen in India stood about the room. A broad window with leaded panes looked out upon the moor; and over the mantel was another portrait of the stiff, plain little girl who seemed to stare at her more curiously than ever.

"Perhaps she slept here once," said Mary. "She stares at me so that she makes me feel queer."

After that she opened more doors and more. She saw so many rooms that she became quite tired and began to think that there must be a hundred, though she had not counted them. In all of them there were old pictures or old tapestries with strange scenes worked on them. There were curious pieces of furniture and curious ornaments in nearly all of them.

In one room, which looked like a lady's sitting room, the hangings were all embroidered velvet, and in a cabinet were about a hundred little elephants made of ivory. They were of different sizes, and some had their mahouts or palanquins on their backs. Some were much bigger than the others and some were so tiny that they seemed only babies. Mary had seen carved ivory in India and she knew all about elephants. She opened the door of the cabinet and stood on a footstool and played with these for quite a long time. When she got tired she set the elephants in order and shut the door of the cabinet.

In all her wanderings through the long corridors and the empty rooms, she had seen nothing alive; but in this room she saw something. Just after she had closed the cabinet door she heard a tiny rustling sound. It made her jump and look around at the sofa by the fireplace, from which it seemed to come. In the corner of the sofa there was a cushion, and in the velvet which covered it there was a hole, and out of the hole peeped a tiny head with a pair of frightened eyes in it.

Mary crept softly across the room to look. The bright eyes belonged to a little gray mouse, and the mouse had eaten a hole into the cushion and made a comfortable nest there. Six baby mice were cuddled up asleep near her. If there was no one else alive in the hundred rooms there were seven mice who did not look lonely at all.

"If they wouldn't be so frightened I would take them back with me," said Mary.

She had wandered about long enough to feel too tired to wander any farther, and she turned back. Two or three times she lost her way by turning down the wrong corridor and was obliged to ramble up and down until she found the right one; but at last she reached her own floor again, though she was some distance from her own room and did not know exactly where she was.

"I believe I have taken a wrong turning again," she said, standing still at what seemed the end of a short passage with tapestry on the wall. "I don't know which way to go. How still everything is!"

It was while she was standing here and just after she had said this that the stillness was broken by a sound. It was another cry, but not quite like the one she had heard last night; it was only a short one, a fretful childish whine muffled by passing through walls.

"It's nearer than it was," said Mary, her heart beating rather faster. "And it is crying."

She put her hand accidentally upon the tapestry near her, and then sprang back, feeling quite startled. The tapestry was the covering of a door which fell open and showed her that there was another part of the corridor behind it, and Mrs. Medlock was coming up it with her bunch of keys in her hand and a very cross look on her face.

"What are you doing here?" she said, and she took Mary by the arm and pulled her away. "What did I tell you?"

"I turned round the wrong corner," explained Mary. "I didn't know which way to go and I heard someone crying." She quite hated Mrs. Medlock at the moment, but she hated her more the next.

"You didn't hear anything of the sort," said the housekeeper. "You come along back to your own nursery or I'll box your ears."

And she took her by the arm and half pushed, half pulled her up one passage and down another until she pushed her in at the door of her own room.

"Now," she said, "you stay where you're told to stay or you'll find yourself locked up. The master had better get you a governess, same as he said he would. You're one that needs someone to look sharp after you. I've got enough to do."

She went out of the room and slammed the door after her, and Mary went and sat on the hearth-rug, pale with rage. She did not cry, but ground her teeth.

"There *was* someone crying—there *was*—there *was*!" she said to herself.

She had heard it twice now, and sometime she would find out. She had found out a great deal this morning. She felt as if she had been on a long journey, and at any rate she had had something to amuse her all the time, and she had played with the ivory elephants and had seen the gray mouse and its babies in their nest in the velvet cushion.

7

The Key to the Garden

Two days after this, when Mary opened her eyes she sat upright in bed immediately, and called to Martha. "Look at the moor! Look at the moor!"

The rainstorm had ended and the gray mist and clouds had been swept away in the night by the wind. The wind itself had ceased and a brilliant, deep blue sky arched high over the moorland. Never, never had Mary dreamed of a sky so blue. In India skies were hot and blazing; this was of a deep cool blue which almost seemed to sparkle like the waters of some lovely bottomless lake, and here and there, high, high in the arched blueness floated small clouds of snow-white fleece. The far-reaching world of the moor itself looked softly blue instead of gloomy purple-black or awful dreary gray.

"Aye," said Martha with a cheerful grin. "Th' storm's over for a bit. It does like this at this time o' th' year. It goes off in a night like it was pretendin' it had never been here an' never meant to come again. That's because th' springtime's on its way. It's a long way off yet, but it's comin'."

"I thought perhaps it always rained or looked dark in England," Mary said.

"Eh! no!" said Martha, sitting up on her heels among her black lead brushes. "Nowt o' th' soart!"

"What does that mean?" asked Mary seriously. In India the natives spoke different dialects which only a few people understood, so she was not surprised when Martha used words she did not know.

Martha laughed as she had done the first morning.

"There now," she said. "I've talked broad Yorkshire again like Mrs. Medlock said I mustn't. 'Nowt o' th' soart' means 'nothin'-of-the-sort,'" slowly and carefully, "but it takes so long to say it. Yorkshire's th' sunniest place on earth when it is sunny. I told thee tha'd like th' moor after a bit. Just you wait till you see th' gold-colored gorse blossoms an' th' blossoms o' th' broom, an' th' heather flowerin', all purple bells, an' hundreds o' butterflies flutterin' an' bees hummin' an' skylarks soarin' up an' singin'. You'll want to get out on it as sunrise an' live out on it all day like Dickon does."

"Could I ever get there?" asked Mary wistfully, looking through her window at the far-off blue. It was so new and big and wonderful and such a heavenly color.

"I don't know," answered Martha. "Tha's never used tha' legs since tha' was born, it seems to me. Tha' couldn't walk five mile. It's five mile to our cottage."

"I should like to see your cottage."

Martha stared at her a moment curiously before she took up her polishing brush and began to rub the grate again. She was thinking that the small plain face did not look quite as sour at this moment as it had done the first morning she saw it. It looked just a trifle like little Susan Ann's when she wanted something very much.

"I'll ask my mother about it," she said. "She's one o' them that nearly always sees a way to do things. It's my day out today an' I'm goin' home. Eh! I am glad. Mrs. Medlock thinks a lot o' mother. Perhaps she could talk to her."

"I like your mother," said Mary.

"I should think tha' did," agreed Martha, polishing away.

"I've never seen her," said Mary.

"No, tha' hasn't," replied Martha.

She sat up on her heels again and rubbed the end of her nose with the back of her hand as if puzzled for a moment, but she ended quite positively.

"Well, she's that sensible an' hard workin' an' good-natured an' clean that no one could help likin' her whether they'd seen her or not. When I'm goin' home to her on my day out I just jump for joy when I'm crossin' the moor."

"I like Dickon," added Mary. "And I've never seen him."

"Well," said Martha stoutly, "I've told thee that th' very birds likes him an' th' rabbits an' wild sheep an' ponies, an' th' foxes themselves. I wonder," staring at her reflectively, "what Dickon would think of thee?"

"He wouldn't like me," said Mary in her stiff, cold little way. "No one does."

Martha looked reflective again.

"How does tha' like thysel'?" she inquired, really quite as if she were curious to know.

Mary hesitated a moment and thought it over.

"Not at all—really," she answered. "But I never thought of that before."

Martha grinned a little as if at some homely recollection.

"Mother said that to me once," she said. "She was at her wash-tub an' I was in a bad temper an' talkin' ill of folk, an' she turns round on me an' says: 'Tha' young vixen, tha'! There tha' stands sayin' tha' doesn't like this one an' tha' doesn't like that one. How does tha' like thysel'?' It made me laugh an' it brought me to my senses in a minute."

She went away in high spirits as soon as she had given Mary her breakfast. She was going to walk five miles across the moor to the cottage, and she was going to help her mother with the washing and do the week's baking and enjoy herself thoroughly.

Mary felt lonelier than ever when she knew she was no longer in the house. She went out into the garden as quickly as possible, and the first thing she did was to run round and round the fountain flower garden ten times. She counted the times carefully and when she had finished she felt in better spirits. The sunshine made the whole place look different. The high, deep, blue sky arched over Misselthwaite as well as over the moor, and she kept lifting her face and looking up into it, trying to imagine what it would be like to lie down on one of the little snow-white clouds and float about. She went into the first kitchen-garden and found Ben Weatherstaff working there with two other gardeners. The change in the weather seemed to have done him good. He spoke to her of his own accord. "Springtime's comin'," he said. "Cannot tha' smell it?"

Mary sniffed and thought she could.

"I smell something nice and fresh and damp," she said.

"That's th' good rich earth," he answered, digging away. "It's in a good humor makin' ready to grow things. It's glad when plantin' time comes. It's dull in th' winter when it's got nowt to do. In th' flower gardens out there things will be stirrin' down below in th' dark. Th' sun's warmin' 'em. You'll see bits o' green spikes stickin' out o' th' black earth after a bit."

"What will they be?" asked Mary.

"Crocuses an' snowdrops an' daffydowndillys. Has tha' never seen them?"

"No. Everything is hot, and wet, and green after the rains in India," said Mary. "And I think things grow up in a night."

"These won't grow up in a night," said Weatherstaff. "Tha'll have to wait for 'em. They'll poke up a bit higher here, an' push out a spike more there, an' uncurl a leaf this day an' another that. You watch 'em."

"I am going to," answered Mary.

Very soon she heard the soft rustling flight of wings again and she knew at once that the robin had come again. He was very pert and lively, and hopped about so close to her feet, and put his head on one side and looked at her so slyly that she asked Ben Weatherstaff a question.

"Do you think he remembers me?" she said.

"Remembers thee!" said Weatherstaff indignantly. "He knows every cabbage stump in th' gardens, let alone th' people. He's never seen a little wench here before, an' he's bent on findin' out all about thee. Tha's no need to try to hide anything from *him*."

"Are things stirring down below in the dark in that garden where he lives?" Mary inquired.

"What garden?" grunted Weatherstaff, becoming surly again.

"The one where the old rose-trees are." She could not help asking, because she wanted so much to know. "Are all the flowers dead, or do some of them come again in the summer? Are there ever any roses?"

"Ask him," said Ben Weatherstaff, hunching his shoulders toward the robin. "He's the only one as knows. No one else has seen inside it for ten years."

Ten years was a long time, Mary thought. She had been born ten years ago.

She walked away, slowly thinking. She had begun to like the garden just as she had begun to like the robin and Dickon and Martha's mother. She was beginning to like Martha, too. That seemed a good many people to like—when you were not used to liking. She thought of the robin as one of the people. She went to her walk outside the long, ivy-covered wall over which she could see the tree-tops; and the second time she walked up and down the most interesting and exciting thing happened to her, and it was all through Ben Weatherstaff's robin.

She heard a chirp and a twitter, and when she looked at the bare flower-bed at her left side there he was hopping about and pretending to peck things out of the earth to persuade her that he had not followed her. But she knew he had followed her and the surprise so filled her with delight that she almost trembled a little.

"You do remember me!" she cried out. "You do! You are prettier than anything else in the world!"

She chirped, and talked, and coaxed and he hopped, and flirted his tail and twittered. It was as if he were talking. His red waistcoat was like satin and he puffed his tiny breast out and was so fine and so grand and so pretty that it was really as if he were showing her how important and like a human person a robin could be. Mistress Mary forgot that she had ever been contrary in her life when he allowed her to draw closer and closer to him, and bend down and talk and try to make something like robin sounds.

Oh! to think that he should actually let her come as near to him as that! He knew nothing in the world would make her put out her hand toward him or startle him in the least tiniest way. He knew it because he was a real person—only nicer than any other person in the world. She was so happy that she scarcely dared to breathe.

The flower-bed was not quite bare. It was bare of flowers because the perennial plants had been cut down for their winter rest, but there were tall shrubs and low ones which grew together at the back of the bed, and as the robin hopped about under them she saw him hop over a small pile of freshly turned-up earth. He stopped on it to look for a worm. The earth had been turned up because a dog had been trying to dig up a mole and he had scratched quite a deep hole.

Mary looked at it, not really knowing why the hole was there, and as she looked she saw something almost buried in the newly-turned soil. It was something like a ring of rusty iron or brass and when the robin flew up into a tree nearby she put out her hand and picked the ring up. It was more than a ring, however; it was an old key which looked as if it had been buried a long time.

Mistress Mary stood up and looked at it with an almost frightened face as it hung from her finger.

"Perhaps it has been buried for ten years," she said in a whisper. "Perhaps it is the key to the garden!"

8

The Robin Who Showed the Way

She looked at the key quite a long time. She turned it over and over, and thought about it. As I have said before, she was not a child who had been trained to ask permission or consult her elders about things. All she thought about the key was that if it was the key to the closed garden, and she could find out where the door was, she could perhaps open it and see what was inside the walls, and what had happened to the old rose-trees. It was because it had been shut up so long that she wanted to see it. It seemed as if it must be different from other places and that something strange must have happened to it during ten years. Besides that, if she liked it she could go into it every day and shut the door behind her, and she could make up some play of her own and play it quite alone, because nobody would ever know where she was, but would think the door was still locked and the key buried in the earth. The thought of that pleased her very much.

Living as it were, all by herself in a house with a hundred mysteriously closed rooms and having nothing whatever to do to amuse herself, had set her inactive brain to working and was actually awakening her imagination. There is no doubt that the fresh, strong, pure air from the moor had a great deal to do with it. Just as it had given her an appetite, and fighting with the wind had stirred her blood, so the same things had stirred her mind. In India she had always been too hot and languid and weak to care much about anything, but in this place she was beginning to care and to want to do new things. Already she felt less "contrary," though she did not know why.

She put the key in her pocket and walked up and down her walk. No one but herself ever seemed to come there, so she could walk slowly and look at the wall, or, rather, at the ivy growing on it. The ivy was the baffling thing. Howsoever carefully she looked she could see nothing but thickly growing, glossy, dark green leaves. She was very much disappointed. Something of her contrariness came back to her as she paced the walk and looked over it at the tree-tops inside. It seemed so silly, she said to herself, to be near it and not be able to get in. She took the key in her pocket when she went back to the house, and she made up her mind that she would always carry it with her when she went out, so that if she ever should find the hidden door she would be ready.

Mrs. Medlock had allowed Martha to sleep all night at the cottage, but she was back at her work in the morning with cheeks redder than ever and in the best of spirits.

"I got up at four o'clock," she said. "Eh! it was pretty on th' moor with th' birds gettin' up an' th' rabbits scamperin' about an' th' sun risin'. I didn't walk all th' way. A man gave me a ride in his cart an' I did enjoy myself."

She was full of stories of the delights of her day out. Her mother had been glad to see her and they had got the baking and washing all out of the way. She had even made each of the children a dough-cake with a bit of brown sugar in it.

"I had 'em all pipin' hot when they came in from playin' on th' moor. An' th' cottage all smelt o' nice, clean hot bakin' an' there was a good fire, an' they just shouted for joy. Our Dickon he said our cottage was good enough for a king to live in."

In the evening they had all sat round the fire, and Martha and her mother had sewed patches on torn clothes and mended stockings and Martha had told them about the little girl who had come from India and who had been waited on all her life by what Martha called "blacks" until she didn't know how to put on her own stockings.

"Eh! they did like to hear about you," said Martha. "They wanted to know all about th' blacks an' about th' ship you came in. I couldn't tell 'em enough."

Mary reflected a little.

"I'll tell you a great deal more before your next day out," she said, "so that you will have more to talk about. I dare say they would like to hear about riding on elephants and camels, and about the officers going to hunt tigers."

"My word!" cried delighted Martha. "It would set 'em clean off their heads. Would tha' really do that, Miss? It would be same as a wild beast show like we heard they had in York once."

"India is quite different from Yorkshire," Mary said slowly, as she thought the matter over. "I never thought of that. Did Dickon and your mother like to hear you talk about me?"

"Why, our Dickon's eyes nearly started out o' his head, they got that round," answered Martha. "But mother, she was put out about your seemin' to be all by yourself like. She said, 'Hasn't Mr. Craven got no governess for her, nor no nurse?' and I said, 'No, he hasn't, though Mrs. Medlock says he will when he thinks of it, but she says he mayn't think of it for two or three years.'"

"I don't want a governess," said Mary sharply.

"But mother says you ought to be learnin' your book by this time an' you ought to have a woman to look after you, an' she says: 'Now, Martha, you just think how you'd feel yourself, in a big place like that, wanderin' about all alone, an' no mother. You do your best to cheer her up,' she says, an' I said I would."

Mary gave her a long, steady look.

"You do cheer me up," she said. "I like to hear you talk."

Presently Martha went out of the room and came back with something held in her hands under her apron.

"What does tha' think," she said, with a cheerful grin. "I've brought thee a present."

"A present!" exclaimed Mistress Mary. How could a cottage full of fourteen hungry people give anyone a present!

"A man was drivin' across the moor peddlin'," Martha explained. "An' he stopped his cart at our door. He had pots an' pans an' odds an' ends, but mother had no money to buy anythin'. Just as he was goin' away our 'Lizabeth Ellen called out, 'Mother, he's got skippin' ropes with red an' blue handles.' An' mother she calls out quite sudden, 'Here, stop, mister! How much are they?' An' he says 'Tuppence', an' mother she began fumblin' in her pocket an' she says to me, 'Martha, tha's brought me thy wages like a good lass, an' I've got four places to put every penny, but I'm just goin' to take tuppence out of it to buy that child a skippin'-rope,' an' she bought one an' here it is."

She brought it out from under her apron and exhibited it quite proudly. It was a strong, slender rope with a striped red and blue handle at each end, but Mary Lennox had never seen a skipping-rope before. She gazed at it with a mystified expression.

"What is it for?" she asked curiously.

"For!" cried out Martha. "Does tha' mean that they've not got skippin' ropes in India, for all they've got elephants and tigers and camels! No wonder most of 'em's black. This is what it's for; just watch me."

And she ran into the middle of the room and, taking a handle in each hand, began to skip, and skip, and skip, while Mary turned in her chair to stare at her, and the queer faces in the old portraits seemed to stare at her, too, and wonder what on earth this common little cottager had the impudence to be doing under their very noses. But Martha did not even see them. The interest and curiosity in Mistress Mary's face delighted her, and she went on skipping and counted as she skipped until she had reached a hundred.

"I could skip longer than that," she said when she stopped. "I've skipped as much as five hundred when I was twelve, but I wasn't as fat then as I am now, an' I was in practice."

Mary got up from her chair beginning to feel excited herself.

"It looks nice," she said. "Your mother is a kind woman. Do you think I could ever skip like that?"

"You just try it," urged Martha, handing her the skipping-rope. "You can't skip a hundred at first, but if you practice you'll mount up. That's what mother said. She says, 'Nothin' will do her more good than skippin' rope. It's th' sensiblest toy a child can have. Let her play out in th' fresh air skippin' an' it'll stretch her legs an' arms an' give her some strength in 'em.'"

It was plain that there was not a great deal of strength in Mistress Mary's arms and legs when she first began to skip. She was not very clever at it, but she liked it so much that she did not want to stop.

"Put on tha' things and run an' skip out o' doors," said Martha. "Mother said I must tell you to keep out o' doors as much as you could, even when it rains a bit, so as tha' wrap up warm."

Mary put on her coat and hat and took her skipping-rope over her arm. She opened the door to go out, and then suddenly thought of something and turned back rather slowly.

"Martha," she said, "they were your wages. It was your two-pence really. Thank you." She said it stiffly because she was not used to thanking people or noticing that they did things for her. "Thank you," she said, and held out her hand because she did not know what else to do.

Martha gave her hand a clumsy little shake, as if she was not accustomed to this sort of thing either. Then she laughed.

"Eh! th' art a queer, old-womanish thing," she said. "If tha'd been our 'Lizabeth Ellen tha'd have given me a kiss."

Mary looked stiffer than ever.

"Do you want me to kiss you?"

Martha laughed again.

"Nay, not me," she answered. "If tha' was different, p'raps tha'd want to thysel'. But tha' isn't. Run off outside an' play with thy rope."

Mistress Mary felt a little awkward as she went out of the room. Yorkshire people seemed strange, and Martha was always rather a puzzle to her. At first she had disliked her very much, but now she did not. The skipping-rope was a wonderful thing. She counted and skipped, and skipped and counted, until her cheeks were quite red, and she was more interested than she had ever been since she was born. The sun was shining and a little wind was blowing—not a rough wind, but one which came in delightful little gusts and brought a fresh scent of newly turned earth with it. She skipped round the fountain garden, and up one walk and down another. She skipped at last into the kitchen-garden and saw Ben Weatherstaff digging and talking to his robin, which was hopping about him. She skipped down the walk toward him and he lifted his head and looked at her with a curious expression. She had wondered if he would notice her. She wanted him to see her skip.

"Well!" he exclaimed. "Upon my word. P'raps tha' art a young 'un, after all, an' p'raps tha's got child's blood in thy veins instead of sour buttermilk. Tha's skipped red into thy cheeks as sure as my name's Ben Weatherstaff. I wouldn't have believed tha' could do it."

"I never skipped before," Mary said. "I'm just beginning. I can only go up to twenty."

"Tha' keep on," said Ben. "Tha' shapes well enough at it for a young 'un that's lived with heathen. Just see how he's watchin' thee," jerking his head toward the robin. "He followed after thee yesterday. He'll be at it again today. He'll be bound to find out what th' skippin'-rope is. He's never seen one. Eh!" shaking his head at the bird, "tha' curiosity will be th' death of thee sometime if tha' doesn't look sharp."

Mary skipped round all the gardens and round the orchard, resting every few minutes. At length she went to her own special walk and made up her mind to try if she could skip the whole length of it. It was a good long skip and she began slowly, but before she had gone half-way down the path she was so hot and breathless that she was obliged to stop. She did not mind much, because she had already counted up to thirty. She stopped with a little laugh of pleasure, and there, lo and behold, was the robin swaying on a long branch of ivy. He had followed her and he greeted her with a chirp. As Mary had skipped toward him she felt something heavy in her pocket strike against her at each jump, and when she saw the robin she laughed again.

"You showed me where the key was yesterday," she said. "You ought to show me the door today; but I don't believe you know!"

The robin flew from his swinging spray of ivy on to the top of the wall and he opened his beak and sang a loud, lovely trill, merely to show off. Nothing in the world is quite as adorably lovely as a robin when he shows off—and they are nearly always doing it.

Mary Lennox had heard a great deal about Magic in her Ayah's stories, and she always said that what happened almost at that moment was Magic.

One of the nice little gusts of wind rushed down the walk, and it was a stronger one than the rest. It was strong enough to wave the branches of the trees, and it was more than strong enough to sway the trailing sprays of untrimmed ivy hanging from the wall. Mary had stepped close to the robin, and suddenly the gust of wind swung aside some loose ivy trails, and more suddenly still she jumped toward it and caught it in her hand. This she did because she had seen something under it—a round knob which had been covered by the leaves hanging over it. It was the knob of a door.

She put her hands under the leaves and began to pull and push them aside. Thick as the ivy hung, it nearly all was a loose and swinging curtain, though some had crept over wood and iron. Mary's heart began to thump and her hands to shake a little in her delight and excitement. The robin kept singing and twittering away and tilting his head on one side, as if he were as excited as she was. What was this under her hands which was square and made of iron and which her fingers found a hole in?

It was the lock of the door which had been closed ten years and she put her hand in her pocket, drew out the key and found it fitted the keyhole. She put the key in and turned it. It took two hands to do it, but it did turn.

And then she took a long breath and looked behind her up the long walk to see if anyone was coming. No one was coming. No one ever did come, it seemed, and she took another long breath, because she could not help it, and she held back the swinging curtain of ivy and pushed back the door which opened slowly—slowly.

Then she slipped through it, and shut it behind her, and stood with her back against it, looking about her and breathing quite fast with excitement, and wonder, and delight.

She was standing *inside* the secret garden.

9

The Strangest House Anyone Ever Lived In

It was the sweetest, most mysterious-looking place anyone could imagine. The high walls which shut it in were covered with the leafless stems of climbing roses which were so thick that they were matted together. Mary Lennox knew they were roses because she had seen a great many roses in India. All the ground was covered with grass of a wintry brown and out of it grew clumps of bushes which were surely rosebushes if they were alive. There were numbers of standard roses which had so spread their branches that they were like little trees. There were other trees in the garden, and one of the things which made the place look strangest and loveliest was that climbing roses had run all over them and swung down long tendrils which made light swaying curtains, and here and there they had caught at each other or at a far-reaching branch and had crept from one tree to another and made lovely bridges of themselves. There were neither leaves nor roses on them now and Mary did not know whether they were dead or alive, but their thin gray or brown branches and sprays looked like a sort of hazy mantle spreading over everything, walls, and trees, and even brown grass, where they had fallen from their fastenings and run along the ground. It was this hazy tangle from tree to tree which made it all look so mysterious. Mary had thought it must be different from other gardens which had not been left all by themselves so long; and indeed it was different from any other place she had ever seen in her life.

"How still it is!" she whispered. "How still!"

Then she waited a moment and listened at the stillness. The robin, who had flown to his treetop, was still as all the rest. He did not even flutter his wings; he sat without stirring, and looked at Mary.

"No wonder it is still," she whispered again. "I am the first person who has spoken in here for ten years."

She moved away from the door, stepping as softly as if she were afraid of awakening someone. She was glad that there was grass under her feet and that her steps made no sounds. She walked under one of the fairy-like gray arches between the trees and looked up at the sprays and tendrils which formed them. "I wonder if they are all quite dead," she said. "Is it all a quite dead garden? I wish it wasn't."

If she had been Ben Weatherstaff she could have told whether the wood was alive by looking at it, but she could only see that there were only gray or brown sprays and branches and none showed any signs of even a tiny leaf-bud anywhere.

But she was *inside* the wonderful garden and she could come through the door under the ivy any time and she felt as if she had found a world all her own.

The sun was shining inside the four walls and the high arch of blue sky over this particular piece of Misselthwaite seemed even more brilliant and soft than it was over the moor. The robin flew down from his tree-top and hopped about or flew after her from one bush to another. He chirped a good deal and had a very busy air, as if he were showing her things. Everything was strange and silent and she seemed to be hundreds of miles away from anyone, but somehow she did not feel lonely at all. All that troubled her was her wish that she knew whether all the roses were dead, or if perhaps some of them had lived and might put out leaves and buds as the weather got warmer. She did not want it to be a quite dead garden. If it were a quite alive garden, how wonderful it would be, and what thousands of roses would grow on every side!

Her skipping-rope had hung over her arm when she came in and after she had walked about for a while she thought she would skip round the whole garden, stopping when she wanted to look at things. There seemed to have been grass paths here and there, and in one or two corners there were alcoves of evergreen with stone seats or tall moss-covered flower urns in them.

As she came near the second of these alcoves she stopped skipping. There had once been a flowerbed in it, and she thought she saw something sticking out of the black earth—some sharp little pale green points. She remembered what Ben Weatherstaff had said and she knelt down to look at them.

"Yes, they are tiny growing things and they *might* be crocuses or snowdrops or daffodils," she whispered.

She bent very close to them and sniffed the fresh scent of the damp earth. She liked it very much.

"Perhaps there are some other ones coming up in other places," she said. "I will go all over the garden and look."

She did not skip, but walked. She went slowly and kept her eyes on the ground. She looked in the old border beds and among the grass, and after she had gone round, trying to miss nothing, she had found ever so many more sharp, pale green points, and she had become quite excited again.

"It isn't a quite dead garden," she cried out softly to herself. "Even if the roses are dead, there are other things alive."

She did not know anything about gardening, but the grass seemed so thick in some of the places where the green points were pushing their way through that she thought they did not seem to have room enough to grow. She searched about until she found a rather sharp piece of wood and knelt down and dug and weeded out the weeds and grass until she made nice little clear places around them.

"Now they look as if they could breathe," she said, after she had finished with the first ones. "I am going to do ever so many more. I'll do all I can see. If I haven't time today I can come tomorrow."

She went from place to place, and dug and weeded, and enjoyed herself so immensely that she was led on from bed to bed and into the grass under the trees. The exercise made her so warm that she first threw her coat off, and then her hat, and without knowing it she was smiling down on to the grass and the pale green points all the time.

The robin was tremendously busy. He was very much pleased to see gardening begun on his own estate. He had often wondered at Ben Weatherstaff. Where gardening is done all sorts of delightful things to eat are turned up with the soil. Now here was this new kind of creature who was not half Ben's size and yet had had the sense to come into his garden and begin at once.

Mistress Mary worked in her garden until it was time to go to her midday dinner. In fact, she was rather late in remembering, and when she put on her coat and hat, and picked up her skipping-rope, she could not believe that she had been working two or three hours. She had been actually happy all the time; and dozens and dozens of the tiny, pale green points were to be seen in cleared places, looking twice as cheerful as they had looked before when the grass and weeds had been smothering them.

"I shall come back this afternoon," she said, looking all round at her new kingdom, and speaking to the trees and the rose-bushes as if they heard her.

Then she ran lightly across the grass, pushed open the slow old door and slipped through it under the ivy. She had such red cheeks and such bright eyes and ate such a dinner that Martha was delighted.

"Two pieces o' meat an' two helps o' rice puddin'!" she said. "Eh! mother will be pleased when I tell her what th' skippin'-rope's done for thee."

In the course of her digging with her pointed stick Mistress Mary had found herself digging up a sort of white root rather like an onion. She had put it back in its place and patted the earth carefully down on it and just now she wondered if Martha could tell her what it was.

"Martha," she said, "what are those white roots that look like onions?"

"They're bulbs," answered Martha. "Lots o' spring flowers grow from 'em. Th' very little ones are snowdrops an' crocuses an' th' big ones are narcissuses an' jonquils and daffydowndillys. Th' biggest of all is lilies an' purple flags. Eh! they are nice. Dickon's got a whole lot of 'em planted in our bit o' garden."

"Does Dickon know all about them?" asked Mary, a new idea taking possession of her.

"Our Dickon can make a flower grow out of a brick walk. Mother says he just whispers things out o' th' ground."

"Do bulbs live a long time? Would they live years and years if no one helped them?" inquired Mary anxiously.

"They're things as helps themselves," said Martha. "That's why poor folk can afford to have 'em. If you don't trouble 'em, most of 'em'll work away underground for a lifetime an' spread out an' have little 'uns. There's a place in th' park woods here where there's snowdrops by thousands. They're the prettiest sight in Yorkshire when th' spring comes. No one knows when they was first planted."

"I wish the spring was here now," said Mary. "I want to see all the things that grow in England."

She had finished her dinner and gone to her favorite seat on the hearth-rug.

"I wish—I wish I had a little spade," she said. "Whatever does tha' want a spade for?" asked Martha, laughing. "Art tha' goin' to take to diggin'? I must tell mother that, too."

Mary looked at the fire and pondered a little. She must be careful if she meant to keep her secret kingdom. She wasn't doing any harm, but if Mr. Craven found out about the open door he would be fearfully angry and get a new key and lock it up forevermore. She really could not bear that.

"This is such a big lonely place," she said slowly, as if she were turning matters over in her mind. "The house is lonely, and the park is lonely, and the gardens are lonely. So many places seem shut up. I never did many things in India, but there were more people to look at—natives and soldiers marching by—and sometimes bands playing, and my Ayah told me stories. There is no one to talk to here except you and Ben Weatherstaff. And you have to do your work and Ben Weatherstaff won't speak to me often. I thought if I had a little spade I could dig somewhere as he does, and I might make a little garden if he would give me some seeds."

Martha's face quite lighted up.

"There now!" she exclaimed, "if that wasn't one of th' things mother said. She says, 'There's such a lot o' room in that big place, why don't they give her a bit for herself, even if she doesn't plant nothin' but parsley an' radishes? She'd dig an' rake away an' be right down happy over it.' Them was the very words she said."

"Were they?" said Mary. "How many things she knows, doesn't she?"

"Eh!" said Martha. "It's like she says: 'A woman as brings up twelve children learns something besides her A B C. Children's as good as 'rithmetic to set you findin' out things.'"

"How much would a spade cost—a little one?" Mary asked.

"Well," was Martha's reflective answer, "at Thwaite village there's a shop or so an' I saw little garden sets with a spade an' a rake an' a fork all tied together for two shillings. An' they was stout enough to work with, too."

"I've got more than that in my purse," said Mary. "Mrs. Morrison gave me five shillings and Mrs. Medlock gave me some money from Mr. Craven."

"Did he remember thee that much?" exclaimed Martha.

"Mrs. Medlock said I was to have a shilling a week to spend. She gives me one every Saturday. I didn't know what to spend it on."

"My word! that's riches," said Martha. "Tha' can buy anything in th' world tha' wants. Th' rent of our cottage is only one an' threepence an' it's like pullin' eye-teeth to get it. Now I've just thought of somethin'," putting her hands on her hips.

"What?" said Mary eagerly.

"In the shop at Thwaite they sell packages o' flower-seeds for a penny each, and our Dickon he knows which is th' prettiest ones an' how to make 'em grow. He walks over to Thwaite many a day just for th' fun of it. Does tha' know how to print letters?" suddenly.

"I know how to write," Mary answered.

Martha shook her head.

"Our Dickon can only read printin'. If tha' could print we could write a letter to him an' ask him to go an' buy th' garden tools an' th' seeds at th' same time."

"Oh! you're a good girl!" Mary cried. "You are, really! I didn't know you were so nice. I know I can print letters if I try. Let's ask Mrs. Medlock for a pen and ink and some paper."

"I've got some of my own," said Martha. "I bought 'em so I could print a bit of a letter to mother of a Sunday. I'll go and get it." She ran out of the room, and Mary stood by the fire and twisted her thin little hands together with sheer pleasure.

"If I have a spade," she whispered, "I can make the earth nice and soft and dig up weeds. If I have seeds and can make flowers grow the garden won't be dead at all—it will come alive."

She did not go out again that afternoon because when Martha returned with her pen and ink and paper she was obliged to clear the table and carry the plates and dishes downstairs and when she got into the kitchen Mrs. Medlock was there and told her to do something, so Mary waited for what seemed to her a long time before she came back. Then it was a serious piece of work to write to Dickon. Mary had been taught very little because her governesses had disliked her too much to stay with her. She could not spell particularly well but she found that she could print letters when she tried. This was the letter Martha dictated to her:

"My Dear Dickon,

This comes hoping to find you well as it leaves me at present. Miss Mary has plenty of money and will you go to Thwaite and buy her some flower seeds and a set of garden tools to make a flower-bed. Pick the prettiest ones and easy to grow because she has never done it before and lived in India which is different. Give my love to mother and every one of you. Miss Mary is going to tell me a lot more so that on my next day out you can hear about elephants and camels and gentlemen going hunting lions and tigers.

Your loving sister,
Martha Phoebe Sowerby."

"We'll put the money in th' envelope an' I'll get th' butcher boy to take it in his cart. He's a great friend o' Dickon's," said Martha.

"How shall I get the things when Dickon buys them?" asked Mary

"He'll bring 'em to you himself. He'll like to walk over this way."

"Oh!" exclaimed Mary, "then I shall see him! I never thought I should see Dickon."

"Does tha' want to see him?" asked Martha suddenly, for Mary had looked so pleased.

"Yes, I do. I never saw a boy foxes and crows loved. I want to see him very much."

Martha gave a little start, as if she remembered something. "Now to think," she broke out, "to think o' me forgettin' that there; an' I thought I was goin' to tell you first thing this mornin'. I asked mother—and she said she'd ask Mrs. Medlock her own self."

"Do you mean—" Mary began.

"What I said Tuesday. Ask her if you might be driven over to our cottage some day and have a bit o' mother's hot oat cake, an' butter, an' a glass o' milk."

It seemed as if all the interesting things were happening in one day. To think of going over the moor in the daylight and when the sky was blue! To think of going into the cottage which held twelve children!

"Does she think Mrs. Medlock would let me go?" she asked, quite anxiously.

"Aye, she thinks she would. She knows what a tidy woman mother is and how clean she keeps the cottage."

"If I went I should see your mother as well as Dickon," said Mary, thinking it over and liking the idea very much. "She doesn't seem to be like the mothers in India."

Her work in the garden and the excitement of the afternoon ended by making her feel quiet and thoughtful. Martha stayed with her until tea-time, but they sat in comfortable quiet and talked very little. But just before Martha went downstairs for the tea-tray, Mary asked a question.

"Martha," she said, "has the scullery-maid had the toothache again today?"

Martha certainly started slightly.

"What makes thee ask that?" she said.

"Because when I waited so long for you to come back I opened the door and walked down the corridor to see if you were coming. And I heard that far-off crying again, just as we heard it the other night. There isn't a wind today, so you see it couldn't have been the wind."

"Eh!" said Martha restlessly. "Tha' mustn't go walkin' about in corridors an' listenin'. Mr. Craven would be that there angry there's no knowin' what he'd do."

"I wasn't listening," said Mary. "I was just waiting for you—and I heard it. That's three times."

"My word! There's Mrs. Medlock's bell," said Martha, and she almost ran out of the room.

"It's the strangest house anyone ever lived in," said Mary drowsily, as she dropped her head on the cushioned seat of the armchair near her. Fresh air, and digging, and skipping-rope had made her feel so comfortably tired that she fell asleep.

10

Dickon

The sun shone down for nearly a week on the secret garden. The Secret Garden was what Mary called it when she was thinking of it. She liked the name, and she liked still more the feeling that when its beautiful old walls shut her in no one knew where she was. It seemed almost like being shut out of the world in some fairy place. The few books she had read and liked had been fairy-story books, and she had read of secret gardens in some of the stories. Sometimes people went to sleep in them for a hundred years, which she had thought must be rather stupid. She had no intention of going to sleep, and, in fact, she was becoming wider awake every day which passed at Misselthwaite. She was beginning to like to be out of doors; she no longer hated the wind, but enjoyed it. She could run faster, and longer, and she could skip up to a hundred. The bulbs in the secret garden must have been much astonished. Such nice clear places were made round them that they had all the breathing space they wanted, and really, if Mistress Mary had known it, they began to cheer up under the dark earth and work tremendously. The sun could get at them and warm them, and when the rain came down it could reach them at once, so they began to feel very much alive.

Mary was an odd, determined little person, and now she had something interesting to be determined about, she was very much absorbed, indeed. She worked and dug and pulled up weeds steadily, only becoming more pleased with her work every hour instead of tiring of it. It seemed to her like a fascinating sort of play. She found many more of the sprouting pale green points than she had ever hoped to find. They seemed to be starting up everywhere and each day she was sure she found tiny new ones, some so tiny that they barely peeped above the earth. There were so many that she remembered what Martha had said about the "snowdrops by the thousands," and about bulbs spreading and making new ones. These had been left to themselves for ten years and perhaps they had spread, like the snowdrops, into thousands. She wondered how long it would be before they showed that they were flowers. Sometimes she stopped digging to look at the garden and try to imagine what it would be like when it was covered with thousands of lovely things in bloom. During that week of sunshine, she became more intimate with Ben Weatherstaff. She surprised him several times by seeming to start up beside him as if she sprang out of the earth. The truth was that she was afraid that he would pick up his tools and go away if he saw her coming, so she always walked toward him as silently as possible. But, in fact, he did not object to her as strongly as he had at first. Perhaps he was secretly rather flattered by her evident desire for his elderly company. Then, also, she was more civil than she had been. He did not know that when she first saw him she spoke to him as she would have spoken to a native, and had not known that a cross, sturdy old Yorkshire man was not accustomed to salaam to his masters, and be merely commanded by them to do things.

"Tha'rt like th' robin," he said to her one morning when he lifted his head and saw her standing by him. "I never knows when I shall see thee or which side tha'll come from."

"He's friends with me now," said Mary.

"That's like him," snapped Ben Weatherstaff. "Makin' up to th' women folk just for vanity an' flightiness. There's nothin' he wouldn't do for th' sake o' showin' off an' flirtin' his tail-feathers. He's as full o' pride as an egg's full o' meat."

He very seldom talked much and sometimes did not even answer Mary's questions except by a grunt, but this morning he said more than usual. He stood up and rested one hobnailed boot on the top of his spade while he looked her over.

"How long has tha' been here?" he jerked out.

"I think it's about a month," she answered.

"Tha's beginnin' to do Misselthwaite credit," he said. "Tha's a bit fatter than tha' was an' tha's not quite so yeller. Tha' looked like a young plucked crow when tha' first came into this garden. Thinks I to myself I never set eyes on an uglier, sourer-faced young 'un."

Mary was not vain and as she had never thought much of her looks she was not greatly disturbed.

"I know I'm fatter," she said. "My stockings are getting tighter. They used to make wrinkles. There's the robin, Ben Weatherstaff."

There, indeed, was the robin, and she thought he looked nicer than ever. His red waistcoat was as glossy as satin and he flirted his wings and tail and tilted his head and hopped about with all sorts of lively graces. He seemed determined to make Ben Weatherstaff admire him. But Ben was sarcastic.

"Aye, there tha' art!" he said. "Tha' can put up with me for a bit sometimes when tha's got no one better. Tha's been reddenin' up thy waistcoat an' polishin' thy feathers this two weeks. I know what tha's up to. Tha's courtin' some bold young madam somewhere tellin' thy lies to her about bein' th' finest cock robin on Missel Moor an' ready to fight all th' rest of 'em."

"Oh! look at him!" exclaimed Mary.

The robin was evidently in a fascinating, bold mood. He hopped closer and closer and looked at Ben Weatherstaff more and more engagingly. He flew on to the nearest currant bush and tilted his head and sang a little song right at him.

"Tha' thinks tha'll get over me by doin' that," said Ben, wrinkling his face up in such a way that Mary felt sure he was trying not to look pleased. "Tha' thinks no one can stand out against thee—that's what tha' thinks."

The robin spread his wings—Mary could scarcely believe her eyes. He flew right up to the handle of Ben Weatherstaff's spade and alighted on the top of it. Then the old man's face wrinkled itself slowly into a new expression. He stood still as if he were afraid to breathe—as if he would not have stirred for the world, lest his robin should start away. He spoke quite in a whisper.

"Well, I'm danged!" he said as softly as if he were saying something quite different. "Tha' does know how to get at a chap—tha' does! Tha's fair unearthly, tha's so knowin'."

And he stood without stirring—almost without drawing his breath—until the robin gave another flirt to his wings and flew away. Then he stood looking at the handle of the spade as if there might be Magic in it, and then he began to dig again and said nothing for several minutes.

But because he kept breaking into a slow grin now and then, Mary was not afraid to talk to him.

"Have you a garden of your own?" she asked.

"No. I'm bachelder an' lodge with Martin at th' gate."

"If you had one," said Mary, "what would you plant?"

"Cabbages an' 'taters an' onions."

"But if you wanted to make a flower garden," persisted Mary, "what would you plant?"

"Bulbs an' sweet-smellin' things—but mostly roses."

Mary's face lighted up.

"Do you like roses?" she said.

Ben Weatherstaff rooted up a weed and threw it aside before he answered.

"Well, yes, I do. I was learned that by a young lady I was gardener to. She had a lot in a place she was fond of, an' she loved 'em like they was children—or robins. I've seen her bend over an' kiss 'em." He dragged out another weed and scowled at it. "That were as much as ten year' ago."

"Where is she now?" asked Mary, much interested.

"Heaven," he answered, and drove his spade deep into the soil, "'cording to what parson says."

"What happened to the roses?" Mary asked again, more interested than ever.

"They was left to themselves."

Mary was becoming quite excited.

"Did they quite die? Do roses quite die when they are left to themselves?" she ventured.

"Well, I'd got to like 'em—an' I liked her—an' she liked 'em," Ben Weatherstaff admitted reluctantly. "Once or twice a year I'd go an' work at 'em a bit—prune 'em an' dig about th' roots. They run wild, but they was in rich soil, so some of 'em lived."

"When they have no leaves and look gray and brown and dry, how can you tell whether they are dead or alive?" inquired Mary.

"Wait till th' spring gets at 'em—wait till th' sun shines on th' rain and th' rain falls on th' sunshine an' then tha'll find out."

"How—how?" cried Mary, forgetting to be careful. "Look along th' twigs an' branches an' if tha' see a bit of a brown lump swelling here an' there, watch it after th' warm rain an' see what happens." He stopped suddenly and looked curiously at her eager face. "Why does tha' care so much about roses an' such, all of a sudden?" he demanded.

Mistress Mary felt her face grow red. She was almost afraid to answer.

"I—I want to play that—that I have a garden of my own," she stammered. "I—there is nothing for me to do. I have nothing—and no one."

"Well," said Ben Weatherstaff slowly, as he watched her, "that's true. Tha' hasn't."

He said it in such an odd way that Mary wondered if he was actually a little sorry for her. She had never felt sorry for herself; she had only felt tired and cross, because she disliked people and things so much. But now the world seemed to be changing and getting nicer. If no one found out about the secret garden, she should enjoy herself always.

She stayed with him for ten or fifteen minutes longer and asked him as many questions as she dared. He answered every one of them in his queer grunting way and he did not seem really cross and did not pick up his spade and leave her. He said something about roses just as she was going away and it reminded her of the ones he had said he had been fond of.

"Do you go and see those other roses now?" she asked.

"Not been this year. My rheumatics has made me too stiff in th' joints."

He said it in his grumbling voice, and then quite suddenly he seemed to get angry with her, though she did not see why he should.

"Now look here!" he said sharply. "Don't tha' ask so many questions. Tha'rt th' worst wench for askin' questions I've ever come across. Get thee gone an' play thee. I've done talkin' for today."

And he said it so crossly that she knew there was not the least use in staying another minute. She went skipping slowly down the outside walk, thinking him over and saying to herself that, queer as it was, here was another person whom she liked in spite of his crossness. She liked old Ben Weatherstaff. Yes, she did like him. She always wanted to try to make him talk to her. Also she began to believe that he knew everything in the world about flowers.

There was a laurel-hedged walk which curved round the secret garden and ended at a gate which opened into a wood, in the park. She thought she would slip round this walk and look into the wood and see if there were any rabbits hopping about. She enjoyed the skipping very much and when she reached the little gate she opened it and went through because she heard a low, peculiar whistling sound and wanted to find out what it was.

It was a very strange thing indeed. She quite caught her breath as she stopped to look at it. A boy was sitting under a tree, with his back against it, playing on a rough wooden pipe. He was a funny looking boy about twelve. He looked very clean and his nose turned up and his cheeks were as red as poppies and never had Mistress Mary seen such round and such blue eyes in any boy's face. And on the trunk of the tree he leaned against, a brown squirrel was clinging and watching him, and from behind a bush nearby a cock pheasant was delicately stretching his neck to peep out, and quite near him were two rabbits sitting up and sniffing with tremulous noses—and actually it appeared as if they were all drawing near to watch him and listen to the strange low little call his pipe seemed to make.

When he saw Mary he held up his hand and spoke to her in a voice almost as low as and rather like his piping.

"Don't tha' move," he said. "It'd flight 'em." Mary remained motionless. He stopped playing his pipe and began to rise from the ground. He moved so slowly that it scarcely seemed as though he were moving at all, but at last he stood on his feet and then the squirrel scampered back up into the branches of his tree, the pheasant withdrew his head and the rabbits dropped on all fours and began to hop away, though not at all as if they were frightened.

"I'm Dickon," the boy said. "I know tha'rt Miss Mary."

Then Mary realized that somehow she had known at first that he was Dickon. Who else could have been charming rabbits and pheasants as the natives charm snakes in India? He had a wide, red, curving mouth and his smile spread all over his face.

"I got up slow," he explained, "because if tha' makes a quick move it startles 'em. A body 'as to move gentle an' speak low when wild things is about."

He did not speak to her as if they had never seen each other before but as if he knew her quite well. Mary knew nothing about boys and she spoke to him a little stiffly because she felt rather shy.

"Did you get Martha's letter?" she asked.

He nodded his curly, rust-colored head. "That's why I come."

He stooped to pick up something which had been lying on the ground beside him when he piped.

"I've got th' garden tools. There's a little spade an' rake an' a fork an' hoe. Eh! they are good 'uns. There's a trowel, too. An' th' woman in th' shop threw in a packet o' white poppy an' one o' blue larkspur when I bought th' other seeds."

"Will you show the seeds to me?" Mary said.

She wished she could talk as he did. His speech was so quick and easy. It sounded as if he liked her and was not the least afraid she would not like him, though he was only a common moor boy, in patched clothes and with a funny face and a rough, rusty-red head. As she came closer to him she noticed that there was a clean fresh scent of heather and grass and leaves about him, almost as if he were made of them. She liked it very much and when she looked into his funny face with the red cheeks and round blue eyes she forgot that she had felt shy.

"Let us sit down on this log and look at them," she said.

They sat down and he took a clumsy little brown paper package out of his coat pocket. He untied the string and inside there were ever so many neater and smaller packages with a picture of a flower on each one.

"There's a lot o' mignonette an' poppies," he said. "Mignonette's th' sweetest smellin' thing as grows, an' it'll grow wherever you cast it, same as poppies will. Them as'll come up an' bloom if you just whistle to 'em, them's th' nicest of all." He stopped and turned his head quickly, his poppy-cheeked face lighting up.

"Where's that robin as is callin' us?" he said.

The chirp came from a thick holly bush, bright with scarlet berries, and Mary thought she knew whose it was.

"Is it really calling us?" she asked.

"Aye," said Dickon, as if it was the most natural thing in the world, "he's callin' someone he's friends with. That's same as sayin' 'Here I am. Look at me. I wants a bit of a chat.' There he is in the bush. Whose is he?"

"He's Ben Weatherstaff's, but I think he knows me a little," answered Mary.

"Aye, he knows thee," said Dickon in his low voice again. "An' he likes thee. He's took thee on. He'll tell me all about thee in a minute."

He moved quite close to the bush with the slow movement Mary had noticed before, and then he made a sound almost like the robin's own twitter. The robin listened a few seconds, intently, and then answered quite as if he were replying to a question.

"Aye, he's a friend o' yours," chuckled Dickon.

"Do you think he is?" cried Mary eagerly. She did so want to know. "Do you think he really likes me?"

"He wouldn't come near thee if he didn't," answered Dickon. "Birds is rare choosers an' a robin can flout a body worse than a man. See, he's making up to thee now. 'Cannot tha' see a chap?' he's sayin'."

And it really seemed as if it must be true. He so sidled and twittered and tilted as he hopped on his bush.

"Do you understand everything birds say?" said Mary.

Dickon's grin spread until he seemed all wide, red, curving mouth, and he rubbed his rough head.

"I think I do, and they think I do," he said. "I've lived on th' moor with 'em so long. I've watched 'em break shell an' come out an' fledge an' learn to fly an' begin to sing, till I think I'm one of 'em. Sometimes I think p'raps I'm a bird, or a fox, or a rabbit, or a squirrel, or even a beetle, an' I don't know it."

He laughed and came back to the log and began to talk about the flower seeds again. He told her what they looked like when they were flowers; he told her how to plant them, and watch them, and feed and water them.

"See here," he said suddenly, turning round to look at her. "I'll plant them for thee myself. Where is tha' garden?"

Mary's thin hands clutched each other as they lay on her lap. She did not know what to say, so for a whole minute she said nothing. She had never thought of this. She felt miserable. And she felt as if she went red and then pale.

"Tha's got a bit o' garden, hasn't tha'?" Dickon said.

It was true that she had turned red and then pale. Dickon saw her do it, and as she still said nothing, he began to be puzzled.

"Wouldn't they give thee a bit?" he asked. "Hasn't tha' got any yet?"

She held her hands tighter and turned her eyes toward him.

"I don't know anything about boys," she said slowly. "Could you keep a secret, if I told you one? It's a great secret. I don't know what I should do if anyone found it out. I believe I should die!" She said the last sentence quite fiercely.

Dickon looked more puzzled than ever and even rubbed his hand over his rough head again, but he answered quite good-humoredly. "I'm keepin' secrets all th' time," he said. "If I couldn't keep secrets from th' other lads, secrets about foxes' cubs, an' birds' nests, an' wild things' holes, there'd be naught safe on th' moor. Aye, I can keep secrets."

Mistress Mary did not mean to put out her hand and clutch his sleeve but she did it.

"I've stolen a garden," she said very fast. "It isn't mine. It isn't anybody's. Nobody wants it, nobody cares for it, nobody ever goes into it. Perhaps everything is dead in it already. I don't know."

She began to feel hot and as contrary as she had ever felt in her life.

"I don't care, I don't care! Nobody has any right to take it from me when I care about it and they don't. They're letting it die, all shut in by itself," she ended passionately, and she threw her arms over her face and burst out crying-poor little Mistress Mary.

Dickon's curious blue eyes grew rounder and rounder. "Eh-h-h!" he said, drawing his exclamation out slowly, and the way he did it meant both wonder and sympathy.

"I've nothing to do," said Mary. "Nothing belongs to me. I found it myself and I got into it myself. I was only just like the robin, and they wouldn't take it from the robin." "Where is it?" asked Dickon in a dropped voice.

Mistress Mary got up from the log at once. She knew she felt contrary again, and obstinate, and she did not care at all. She was imperious and Indian, and at the same time hot and sorrowful.

"Come with me and I'll show you," she said.

She led him round the laurel path and to the walk where the ivy grew so thickly. Dickon followed her with a queer, almost pitying, look on his face. He felt as if he were being led to look at some strange bird's nest and must move softly. When she stepped to the wall and lifted the hanging ivy he started. There was a door and Mary pushed it slowly open and they passed in together, and then Mary stood and waved her hand round defiantly.

"It's this," she said. "It's a secret garden, and I'm the only one in the world who wants it to be alive."

Dickon looked round and round about it, and round and round again.

"Eh!" he almost whispered, "it is a queer, pretty place! It's like as if a body was in a dream."

11

The Nest of the Missel Thrush

For two or three minutes he stood looking round him, while Mary watched him, and then he began to walk about softly, even more lightly than Mary had walked the first time she had found herself inside the four walls. His eyes seemed to be taking in everything—the gray trees with the gray creepers climbing over them and hanging from their branches, the tangle on the walls and among the grass, the evergreen alcoves with the stone seats and tall flower urns standing in them.

"I never thought I'd see this place," he said at last, in a whisper.

"Did you know about it?" asked Mary.

She had spoken aloud and he made a sign to her.

"We must talk low," he said, "or someone'll hear us an' wonder what's to do in here."

"Oh! I forgot!" said Mary, feeling frightened and putting her hand quickly against her mouth. "Did you know about the garden?" she asked again when she had recovered herself. Dickon nodded.

"Martha told me there was one as no one ever went inside," he answered. "Us used to wonder what it was like."

He stopped and looked round at the lovely gray tangle about him, and his round eyes looked queerly happy.

"Eh! the nests as'll be here come springtime," he said. "It'd be th' safest nestin' place in England. No one never comin' near an' tangles o' trees an' roses to build in. I wonder all th' birds on th' moor don't build here."

Mistress Mary put her hand on his arm again without knowing it.

"Will there be roses?" she whispered. "Can you tell? I thought perhaps they were all dead."

"Eh! No! Not them—not all of 'em!" he answered. "Look here!"

He stepped over to the nearest tree—an old, old one with gray lichen all over its bark, but upholding a curtain of tangled sprays and branches. He took a thick knife out of his Pocket and opened one of its blades.

"There's lots o' dead wood as ought to be cut out," he said. "An' there's a lot o' old wood, but it made some new last year. This here's a new bit," and he touched a shoot which looked brownish green instead of hard, dry gray. Mary touched it herself in an eager, reverent way.

"That one?" she said. "Is that one quite alive—quite?"

Dickon curved his wide smiling mouth.

"It's as wick as you or me," he said; and Mary remembered that Martha had told her that "wick" meant "alive" or "lively."

"I'm glad it's wick!" she cried out in her whisper. "I want them all to be wick. Let us go round the garden and count how many wick ones there are."

She quite panted with eagerness, and Dickon was as eager as she was. They went from tree to tree and from bush to bush. Dickon carried his knife in his hand and showed her things which she thought wonderful.

"They've run wild," he said, "but th' strongest ones has fair thrived on it. The delicatest ones has died out, but th' others has growed an' growed, an' spread an' spread, till they's a wonder. See here!" and he pulled down a thick gray, dry-looking branch. "A body might think this was dead wood, but I don't believe it is—down to th' root. I'll cut it low down an' see."

He knelt and with his knife cut the lifeless-looking branch through, not far above the earth.

"There!" he said exultantly. "I told thee so. There's green in that wood yet. Look at it."

Mary was down on her knees before he spoke, gazing with all her might.

"When it looks a bit greenish an' juicy like that, it's wick," he explained. "When th' inside is dry an' breaks easy, like this here piece I've cut off, it's done for. There's a big root here as all this live wood sprung out of, an' if th' old wood's cut off an' it's dug round, and took care of there'll be—" he stopped and lifted his face to look up at the climbing and hanging sprays above him—"there'll be a fountain o' roses here this summer."

They went from bush to bush and from tree to tree. He was very strong and clever with his knife and knew how to cut the dry and dead wood away, and could tell when an unpromising bough or twig had still green life in it. In the course of half an hour Mary thought she could tell too, and when he cut through a lifeless-looking branch she would cry out joyfully under her breath when she caught sight of the least shade of moist green. The spade, and hoe, and fork were very useful. He showed her how to use the fork while he dug about roots with the spade and stirred the earth and let the air in.

They were working industriously round one of the biggest standard roses when he caught sight of something which made him utter an exclamation of surprise.

"Why!" he cried, pointing to the grass a few feet away. "Who did that there?"

It was one of Mary's own little clearings round the pale green points.

"I did it," said Mary.

"Why, I thought tha' didn't know nothin' about gardenin'," he exclaimed.

"I don't," she answered, "but they were so little, and the grass was so thick and strong, and they looked as if they had no room to breathe. So I made a place for them. I don't even know what they are."

Dickon went and knelt down by them, smiling his wide smile.

"Tha' was right," he said. "A gardener couldn't have told thee better. They'll grow now like Jack's bean-stalk. They're crocuses an' snowdrops, an' these here is narcissuses," turning to another patch, "an here's daffydowndillys. Eh! they will be a sight."

He ran from one clearing to another.

"Tha' has done a lot o' work for such a little wench," he said, looking her over.

"I'm growing fatter," said Mary, "and I'm growing stronger. I used always to be tired. When I dig I'm not tired at all. I like to smell the earth when it's turned up."

"It's rare good for thee," he said, nodding his head wisely. "There's naught as nice as th' smell o' good clean earth, except th' smell o' fresh growin' things when th' rain falls on 'em. I get out on th' moor many a day when it's rainin' an' I lie under a bush an' listen to th' soft swish o' drops on th' heather an' I just sniff an' sniff. My nose end fair quivers like a rabbit's, mother says."

"Do you never catch cold?" inquired Mary, gazing at him wonderingly. She had never seen such a funny boy, or such a nice one.

"Not me," he said, grinning. "I never ketched cold since I was born. I wasn't brought up nesh enough. I've chased about th' moor in all weathers same as th' rabbits does. Mother says I've sniffed up too much fresh air for twelve year' to ever get to sniffin' with cold. I'm as tough as a white-thorn knobstick."

He was working all the time he was talking and Mary was following him and helping him with her fork or the trowel.

"There's a lot of work to do here!" he said once, looking about quite exultantly.

"Will you come again and help me to do it?" Mary begged. "I'm sure I can help, too. I can dig and pull up weeds, and do whatever you tell me. Oh! do come, Dickon!"

"I'll come every day if tha' wants me, rain or shine," he answered stoutly. "It's the best fun I ever had in my life—shut in here an' wakenin' up a garden."

"If you will come," said Mary, "if you will help me to make it alive I'll—I don't know what I'll do," she ended helplessly. What could you do for a boy like that?

"I'll tell thee what tha'll do," said Dickon, with his happy grin. "Tha'll get fat an' tha'll get as hungry as a young fox an' tha'll learn how to talk to th' robin same as I do. Eh! we'll have a lot o' fun."

He began to walk about, looking up in the trees and at the walls and bushes with a thoughtful expression.

"I wouldn't want to make it look like a gardener's garden, all clipped an' spick an' span, would you?" he said. "It's nicer like this with things runnin' wild, an' swingin' an' catchin' hold of each other."

"Don't let us make it tidy," said Mary anxiously. "It wouldn't seem like a secret garden if it was tidy."

Dickon stood rubbing his rusty-red head with a rather puzzled look. "It's a secret garden sure enough," he said, "but seems like someone besides th' robin must have been in it since it was shut up ten year' ago."

"But the door was locked and the key was buried," said Mary. "No one could get in."

"That's true," he answered. "It's a queer place. Seems to me as if there'd been a bit o' prunin' done here an' there, later than ten year' ago."

"But how could it have been done?" said Mary.

He was examining a branch of a standard rose and he shook his head.

"Aye! how could it!" he murmured. "With th' door locked an' th' key buried."

Mistress Mary always felt that however many years she lived she should never forget that first morning when her garden began to grow. Of course, it did seem to begin to grow for her that morning. When Dickon began to clear places to plant seeds, she remembered what Basil had sung at her when he wanted to tease her.

"Are there any flowers that look like bells?" she inquired.

"Lilies o' th' valley does," he answered, digging away with the trowel, "an' there's Canterbury bells, an' campanulas."

"Let's plant some," said Mary. "There's lilies o' th, valley here already; I saw 'em. They'll have growed too close an' we'll have to separate 'em, but there's plenty. Th' other ones takes two years to bloom from seed, but I can bring you some bits o' plants from our cottage garden. Why does tha' want 'em?"

Then Mary told him about Basil and his brothers and sisters in India and of how she had hated them and of their calling her "Mistress Mary Quite Contrary."

"They used to dance round and sing at me. They sang—

'Mistress Mary, quite contrary,
How does your garden grow?
With silver bells, and cockle shells,
And marigolds all in a row.'

I just remembered it and it made me wonder if there were really flowers like silver bells."

She frowned a little and gave her trowel a rather spiteful dig into the earth.

"I wasn't as contrary as they were."

But Dickon laughed.

"Eh!" he said, and as he crumbled the rich black soil she saw he was sniffing up the scent of it. "There doesn't seem to be no need for no one to be contrary when there's flowers an' such like, an' such lots o' friendly wild things runnin' about makin' homes for themselves, or buildin' nests an' singin' an' whistlin', does there?"

Mary, kneeling by him holding the seeds, looked at him and stopped frowning.

"Dickon," she said, "you are as nice as Martha said you were. I like you, and you make the fifth person. I never thought I should like five people."

Dickon sat up on his heels as Martha did when she was polishing the grate. He did look funny and delightful, Mary thought, with his round blue eyes and red cheeks and happy-looking turned-up nose.

"Only five folk as tha' likes?" he said. "Who is th' other four?"

"Your mother and Martha," Mary checked them off on her fingers, "and the robin and Ben Weatherstaff."

Dickon laughed so that he was obliged to stifle the sound by putting his arm over his mouth.

"I know tha' thinks I'm a queer lad," he said, "but I think tha' art th' queerest little lass I ever saw."

Then Mary did a strange thing. She leaned forward and asked him a question she had never dreamed of asking anyone before. And she tried to ask it in Yorkshire because that was his language, and in India a native was always pleased if you knew his speech.

"Does tha' like me?" she said.

"Eh!" he answered heartily, "that I does. I likes thee wonderful, an' so does th' robin, I do believe!"

"That's two, then," said Mary. "That's two for me."

And then they began to work harder than ever and more joyfully. Mary was startled and sorry when she heard the big clock in the courtyard strike the hour of her midday dinner.

"I shall have to go," she said mournfully. "And you will have to go too, won't you?"

Dickon grinned.

"My dinner's easy to carry about with me," he said. "Mother always lets me put a bit o' somethin' in my pocket."

He picked up his coat from the grass and brought out of a pocket a lumpy little bundle tied up in a quite clean, coarse, blue and white handkerchief. It held two thick pieces of bread with a slice of something laid between them.

"It's oftenest naught but bread," he said, "but I've got a fine slice o' fat bacon with it today."

Mary thought it looked a queer dinner, but he seemed ready to enjoy it.

"Run on an' get thy victuals," he said. "I'll be done with mine first. I'll get some more work done before I start back home."

He sat down with his back against a tree.

"I'll call th' robin up," he said, "and give him th' rind o' th' bacon to peck at. They likes a bit o' fat wonderful."

Mary could scarcely bear to leave him. Suddenly it seemed as if he might be a sort of wood fairy who might be gone when she came into the garden again. He seemed too good to be true. She went slowly half-way to the door in the wall and then she stopped and went back.

"Whatever happens, you—you never would tell?" she said.

His poppy-colored cheeks were distended with his first big bite of bread and bacon, but he managed to smile encouragingly.

"If tha' was a missel thrush an' showed me where thy nest was, does tha' think I'd tell anyone? Not me," he said. "Tha' art as safe as a missel thrush."

And she was quite sure she was.

12

"Might I Have a Bit of Earth?"

Mary ran so fast that she was rather out of breath when she reached her room. Her hair was ruffled on her forehead and her cheeks were bright pink. Her dinner was waiting on the table, and Martha was waiting near it.

"Tha's a bit late," she said. "Where has tha' been?"

"I've seen Dickon!" said Mary. "I've seen Dickon!"

"I knew he'd come," said Martha exultantly. "How does tha' like him?"

"I think—I think he's beautiful!" said Mary in a determined voice.

Martha looked rather taken aback but she looked pleased, too.

"Well," she said, "he's th' best lad as ever was born, but us never thought he was handsome. His nose turns up too much."

"I like it to turn up," said Mary.

"An' his eyes is so round," said Martha, a trifle doubtful. "Though they're a nice color." "I like them round," said Mary. "And they are exactly the color of the sky over the moor."

Martha beamed with satisfaction.

"Mother says he made 'em that color with always lookin' up at th' birds an' th' clouds. But he has got a big mouth, hasn't he, now?"

"I love his big mouth," said Mary obstinately. "I wish mine were just like it."

Martha chuckled delightedly.

"It'd look rare an' funny in thy bit of a face," she said. "But I knowed it would be that way when tha' saw him. How did tha' like th' seeds an' th' garden tools?"

"How did you know he brought them?" asked Mary.

"Eh! I never thought of him not bringin' 'em. He'd be sure to bring 'em if they was in Yorkshire. He's such a trusty lad."

Mary was afraid that she might begin to ask difficult questions, but she did not. She was very much interested in the seeds and gardening tools, and there was only one moment when Mary was frightened. This was when she began to ask where the flowers were to be planted.

"Who did tha' ask about it?" she inquired.

"I haven't asked anybody yet," said Mary, hesitating. "Well, I wouldn't ask th' head gardener. He's too grand, Mr. Roach is."

"I've never seen him," said Mary. "I've only seen under-gardeners and Ben Weatherstaff."

"If I was you, I'd ask Ben Weatherstaff," advised Martha. "He's not half as bad as he looks, for all he's so crabbed. Mr. Craven lets him do what he likes because he was here when Mrs. Craven was alive, an' he used to make her laugh. She liked him. Perhaps he'd find you a corner somewhere out o' the way."

"If it was out of the way and no one wanted it, no one *could* mind my having it, could they?" Mary said anxiously.

"There wouldn't be no reason," answered Martha. "You wouldn't do no harm."

Mary ate her dinner as quickly as she could and when she rose from the table she was going to run to her room to put on her hat again, but Martha stopped her.

"I've got somethin' to tell you," she said. "I thought I'd let you eat your dinner first. Mr. Craven came back this mornin' and I think he wants to see you."

Mary turned quite pale.

"Oh!" she said. "Why! Why! He didn't want to see me when I came. I heard Pitcher say he didn't." "Well," explained Martha, "Mrs. Medlock says it's because o' mother. She was walkin' to Thwaite village an' she met him. She'd never spoke to him before, but Mrs. Craven had been to our cottage two or three times. He'd forgot, but mother hadn't an' she made bold to stop him. I don't know what she said to him about you but she said somethin' as put him in th' mind to see you before he goes away again, tomorrow."

"Oh!" cried Mary, "is he going away tomorrow? I am so glad!"

"He's goin' for a long time. He mayn't come back till autumn or winter. He's goin' to travel in foreign places. He's always doin' it."

"Oh! I'm so glad—so glad!" said Mary thankfully.

If he did not come back until winter, or even autumn, there would be time to watch the secret garden come alive. Even if he found out then and took it away from her she would have had that much at least.

"When do you think he will want to see—"

She did not finish the sentence, because the door opened, and Mrs. Medlock walked in. She had on her best black dress and cap, and her collar was fastened with a large brooch with a picture of a man's face on it. It was a colored photograph of Mr. Medlock who had died years ago, and she always wore it when she was dressed up. She looked nervous and excited.

"Your hair's rough," she said quickly. "Go and brush it. Martha, help her to slip on her best dress. Mr. Craven sent me to bring her to him in his study."

All the pink left Mary's cheeks. Her heart began to thump and she felt herself changing into a stiff, plain, silent child again. She did not even answer Mrs. Medlock, but turned and walked into her bedroom, followed by Martha. She said nothing while her dress was changed, and her hair brushed, and after she was quite tidy she followed Mrs. Medlock down the corridors, in silence. What was there for her to say? She was obliged to go and see Mr. Craven and he would not like her, and she would not like him. She knew what he would think of her.

She was taken to a part of the house she had not been into before. At last Mrs. Medlock knocked at a door, and when someone said, "Come in," they entered the room together. A man was sitting in an armchair before the fire, and Mrs. Medlock spoke to him.

"This is Miss Mary, sir," she said.

"You can go and leave her here. I will ring for you when I want you to take her away," said Mr. Craven.

When she went out and closed the door, Mary could only stand waiting, a plain little thing, twisting her thin hands together. She could see that the man in the chair was not so much a hunchback as a man with high, rather crooked shoulders, and he had black hair streaked with white. He turned his head over his high shoulders and spoke to her.

"Come here!" he said.

Mary went to him.

He was not ugly. His face would have been handsome if it had not been so miserable. He looked as if the sight of her worried and fretted him and as if he did not know what in the world to do with her.

"Are you well?" he asked.

"Yes," answered Mary.

"Do they take good care of you?"

"Yes."

He rubbed his forehead fretfully as he looked her over.

"You are very thin," he said.

"I am getting fatter," Mary answered in what she knew was her stiffest way.

What an unhappy face he had! His black eyes seemed as if they scarcely saw her, as if they were seeing something else, and he could hardly keep his thoughts upon her.

"I forgot you," he said. "How could I remember you? I intended to send you a governess or a nurse, or someone of that sort, but I forgot."

"Please," began Mary. "Please—" and then the lump in her throat choked her.

"What do you want to say?" he inquired.

"I am—I am too big for a nurse," said Mary. "And please—please don't make me have a governess yet."

He rubbed his forehead again and stared at her.

"That was what the Sowerby woman said," he muttered absent-mindedly.

Then Mary gathered a scrap of courage.

"Is she—is she Martha's mother?" she stammered.

"Yes, I think so," he replied.

"She knows about children," said Mary. "She has twelve. She knows."

He seemed to rouse himself.

"What do you want to do?"

"I want to play out of doors," Mary answered, hoping that her voice did not tremble. "I never liked it in India. It makes me hungry here, and I am getting fatter."

He was watching her.

"Mrs. Sowerby said it would do you good. Perhaps it will," he said. "She thought you had better get stronger before you had a governess."

"It makes me feel strong when I play and the wind comes over the moor," argued Mary.

"Where do you play?" he asked next.

"Everywhere," gasped Mary. "Martha's mother sent me a skipping-rope. I skip and run—and I look about to see if things are beginning to stick up out of the earth. I don't do any harm."

"Don't look so frightened," he said in a worried voice. "You could not do any harm, a child like you! You may do what you like."

Mary put her hand up to her throat because she was afraid he might see the excited lump which she felt jump into it. She came a step nearer to him.

"May I?" she said tremulously.

Her anxious little face seemed to worry him more than ever.

"Don't look so frightened," he exclaimed. "Of course you may. I am your guardian, though I am a poor one for any child. I cannot give you time or attention. I am too ill, and wretched and distracted; but I wish you to be happy and comfortable. I don't know anything about children, but Mrs. Medlock is to see that you have all you need. I sent for you today because Mrs. Sowerby said I ought to see you. Her daughter had talked about you. She thought you needed fresh air and freedom and running about."

"She knows all about children," Mary said again in spite of herself.

"She ought to," said Mr. Craven. "I thought her rather bold to stop me on the moor, but she said—Mrs. Craven had been kind to her." It seemed hard for him to speak his dead wife's name. "She is a respectable woman. Now I have seen you I think she said sensible things. Play out of doors as much as you like. It's a big place and you may go where you like and amuse yourself as you like. Is there anything you want?" as if a sudden thought had struck him. "Do you want toys, books, dolls?"

"Might I," quavered Mary, "might I have a bit of earth?"

In her eagerness she did not realize how queer the words would sound and that they were not the ones she had meant to say. Mr. Craven looked quite startled.

"Earth!" he repeated. "What do you mean?"

"To plant seeds in—to make things grow—to see them come alive," Mary faltered.

He gazed at her a moment and then passed his hand quickly over his eyes.

"Do you—care about gardens so much," he said slowly.

"I didn't know about them in India," said Mary. "I was always ill and tired and it was too hot. I sometimes made little beds in the sand and stuck flowers in them. But here it is different."

Mr. Craven got up and began to walk slowly across the room.

"A bit of earth," he said to himself, and Mary thought that somehow she must have reminded him of something. When he stopped and spoke to her his dark eyes looked almost soft and kind.

"You can have as much earth as you want," he said. "You remind me of someone else who loved the earth and things that grow. When you see a bit of earth you want," with something like a smile, "take it, child, and make it come alive."

"May I take it from anywhere—if it's not wanted?"

"Anywhere," he answered. "There! You must go now, I am tired." He touched the bell to call Mrs. Medlock. "Goodbye. I shall be away all summer."

Mrs. Medlock came so quickly that Mary thought she must have been waiting in the corridor.

"Mrs. Medlock," Mr. Craven said to her, "now I have seen the child I understand what Mrs. Sowerby meant. She must be less delicate before she begins lessons. Give her simple, healthy food. Let her run wild in the garden. Don't look after her too much. She needs liberty and fresh air and romping about. Mrs. Sowerby is to come and see her now and then and she may sometimes go to the cottage."

Mrs. Medlock looked pleased. She was relieved to hear that she need not "look after" Mary too much. She had felt her a tiresome charge and had indeed seen as little of her as she dared. In addition to this she was fond of Martha's mother.

"Thank you, sir," she said. "Susan Sowerby and me went to school together and she's as sensible and good-hearted a woman as you'd find in a day's walk. I never had any children myself and she's had twelve, and there never was healthier or better ones. Miss Mary can get no harm from them. I'd always take Susan Sowerby's advice about children myself. She's what you might call healthy-minded—if you understand me."

"I understand," Mr. Craven answered. "Take Miss Mary away now and send Pitcher to me."

When Mrs. Medlock left her at the end of her own corridor Mary flew back to her room. She found Martha waiting there. Martha had, in fact, hurried back after she had removed the dinner service.

"I can have my garden!" cried Mary. "I may have it where I like! I am not going to have a governess for a long time! Your mother is coming to see me and I may go to your cottage! He says a little girl like me could not do any harm and I may do what I like—anywhere!"

"Eh!" said Martha delightedly, "that was nice of him wasn't it?"

"Martha," said Mary solemnly, "he is really a nice man, only his face is so miserable and his forehead is all drawn together."

She ran as quickly as she could to the garden. She had been away so much longer than she had thought she should and she knew Dickon would have to set out early on his five-mile walk. When she slipped through the door under the ivy, she saw he was not working where she had left him. The gardening tools were laid together under a tree. She ran to them, looking all round the place, but there was no Dickon to be seen. He had gone away and the secret garden was empty—except for the robin who had just flown across the wall and sat on a standard rose-bush watching her. "He's gone," she said woefully. "Oh! was he—was he—was he only a wood fairy?"

Something white fastened to the standard rose-bush caught her eye. It was a piece of paper, in fact, it was a piece of the letter she had printed for Martha to send to Dickon. It was fastened on the bush with a long thorn, and in a minute she knew Dickon had left it there. There were some roughly printed letters on it and a sort of picture. At first she could not tell what it was. Then she saw it was meant for a nest with a bird sitting on it. Underneath were the printed letters and they said:

"I will cum bak."

13

"I Am Colin"

Mary took the picture back to the house when she went to her supper and she showed it to Martha.

"Eh!" said Martha with great pride. "I never knew our Dickon was as clever as that. That there's a picture of a missel thrush on her nest, as large as life an' twice as natural."

Then Mary knew Dickon had meant the picture to be a message. He had meant that she might be sure he would keep her secret. Her garden was her nest and she was like a missel thrush. Oh, how she did like that queer, common boy!

She hoped he would come back the very next day and she fell asleep looking forward to the morning.

But you never know what the weather will do in Yorkshire, particularly in the springtime. She was awakened in the night by the sound of rain beating with heavy drops against her window. It was pouring down in torrents and the wind was "wuthering" round the corners and in the chimneys of the huge old house. Mary sat up in bed and felt miserable and angry.

"The rain is as contrary as I ever was," she said. "It came because it knew I did not want it."

She threw herself back on her pillow and buried her face. She did not cry, but she lay and hated the sound of the heavily beating rain, she hated the wind and its "wuthering." She could not go to sleep again. The mournful sound kept her awake because she felt mournful herself. If she had felt happy it would probably have lulled her to sleep. How it "wuthered" and how the big raindrops poured down and beat against the pane!

"It sounds just like a person lost on the moor and wandering on and on crying," she said.

*

She had been lying awake turning from side to side for about an hour, when suddenly something made her sit up in bed and turn her head toward the door listening. She listened and she listened.

"It isn't the wind now," she said in a loud whisper. "That isn't the wind. It is different. It is that crying I heard before."

The door of her room was ajar and the sound came down the corridor, a far-off faint sound of fretful crying. She listened for a few minutes and each minute she became more and more sure. She felt as if she must find out what it was. It seemed even stranger than the secret garden and the buried key. Perhaps the fact that she was in a rebellious mood made her bold. She put her foot out of bed and stood on the floor.

"I am going to find out what it is," she said. "Everybody is in bed and I don't care about Mrs. Medlock—I don't care!"

There was a candle by her bedside and she took it up and went softly out of the room. The corridor looked very long and dark, but she was too excited to mind that. She thought she remembered the corners she must turn to find the short corridor with the door covered with tapestry—the one Mrs. Medlock had come through the day she lost herself. The sound had come up that passage. So she went on with her dim light, almost feeling her way, her heart beating so loud that she fancied she could hear it. The far-off faint crying went on and led her. Sometimes it stopped for a moment or so and then began again. Was this the right corner to turn? She stopped and thought. Yes it was. Down this passage and then to the left, and then up two broad steps, and then to the right again. Yes, there was the tapestry door.

She pushed it open very gently and closed it behind her, and she stood in the corridor and could hear the crying quite plainly, though it was not loud. It was on the other side of the wall at her left and a few yards farther on there was a door. She could see a glimmer of light coming from beneath it. The Someone was crying in that room, and it was quite a young Someone.

So she walked to the door and pushed it open, and there she was standing in the room!

It was a big room with ancient, handsome furniture in it. There was a low fire glowing faintly on the hearth and a night light burning by the side of a carved four-posted bed hung with brocade, and on the bed was lying a boy, crying fretfully.

Mary wondered if she was in a real place or if she had fallen asleep again and was dreaming without knowing it.

The boy had a sharp, delicate face the color of ivory and he seemed to have eyes too big for it. He had also a lot of hair which tumbled over his forehead in heavy locks and made his thin face seem smaller. He looked like a boy who had been ill, but he was crying more as if he were tired and cross than as if he were in pain.

Mary stood near the door with her candle in her hand, holding her breath. Then she crept across the room, and, as she drew nearer, the light attracted the boy's attention and he turned his head on his pillow and stared at her, his gray eyes opening so wide that they seemed immense.

"Who are you?" he said at last in a half-frightened whisper. "Are you a ghost?"

"No, I am not," Mary answered, her own whisper sounding half-frightened. "Are you one?"

He stared and stared and stared. Mary could not help noticing what strange eyes he had. They were agate gray and they looked too big for his face because they had black lashes all round them.

"No," he replied after waiting a moment or so. "I am Colin."

"Who is Colin?" she faltered.

"I am Colin Craven. Who are you?"

"I am Mary Lennox. Mr. Craven is my uncle."

"He is my father," said the boy.

"Your father!" gasped Mary. "No one ever told me he had a boy! Why didn't they?"

"Come here," he said, still keeping his strange eyes fixed on her with an anxious expression.

She came close to the bed and he put out his hand and touched her.

"You are real, aren't you?" he said. "I have such real dreams very often. You might be one of them."

Mary had slipped on a woolen wrapper before she left her room and she put a piece of it between his fingers.

"Rub that and see how thick and warm it is," she said. "I will pinch you a little if you like, to show you how real I am. For a minute I thought you might be a dream too."

"Where did you come from?" he asked.

"From my own room. The wind wuthered so I couldn't go to sleep and I heard someone crying and wanted to find out who it was. What were you crying for?"

"Because I couldn't go to sleep either and my head ached. Tell me your name again."

"Mary Lennox. Did no one ever tell you I had come to live here?"

He was still fingering the fold of her wrapper, but he began to look a little more as if he believed in her reality.

"No," he answered. "They daren't."

"Why?" asked Mary.

"Because I should have been afraid you would see me. I won't let people see me and talk me over."

"Why?" Mary asked again, feeling more mystified every moment.

"Because I am like this always, ill and having to lie down. My father won't let people talk me over either. The servants are not allowed to speak about me. If I live I may be a hunchback, but I shan't live. My father hates to think I may be like him."

"Oh, what a queer house this is!" Mary said. "What a queer house! Everything is a kind of secret. Rooms are locked up and gardens are locked up—and you! Have you been locked up?"

"No. I stay in this room because I don't want to be moved out of it. It tires me too much."

"Does your father come and see you?" Mary ventured.

"Sometimes. Generally when I am asleep. He doesn't want to see me."

"Why?" Mary could not help asking again.

A sort of angry shadow passed over the boy's face.

"My mother died when I was born and it makes him wretched to look at me. He thinks I don't know, but I've heard people talking. He almost hates me."

"He hates the garden, because she died," said Mary half speaking to herself.

"What garden?" the boy asked.

"Oh! just—just a garden she used to like," Mary stammered. "Have you been here always?" "Nearly always. Sometimes I have been taken to places at the seaside, but I won't stay because people stare at me. I used to wear an iron thing to keep my back straight, but a grand doctor came from London to see me and said it was stupid. He told them to take it off and keep me out in the fresh air. I hate fresh air and I don't want to go out."

"I didn't when first I came here," said Mary. "Why do you keep looking at me like that?"

"Because of the dreams that are so real," he answered rather fretfully. "Sometimes when I open my eyes I don't believe I'm awake."

"We're both awake," said Mary. She glanced round the room with its high ceiling and shadowy corners and dim firelight. "It looks quite like a dream, and it's the middle of the night, and everybody in the house is asleep—everybody but us. We are wide awake."

"I don't want it to be a dream," the boy said restlessly.

Mary thought of something all at once.

"If you don't like people to see you," she began, "do you want me to go away?"

He still held the fold of her wrapper and he gave it a little pull.

"No," he said. "I should be sure you were a dream if you went. If you are real, sit down on that big footstool and talk. I want to hear about you."

Mary put down her candle on the table near the bed and sat down on the cushioned stool. She did not want to go away at all. She wanted to stay in the mysterious hidden-away room and talk to the mysterious boy.

"What do you want me to tell you?" she said.

He wanted to know how long she had been at Misselthwaite; he wanted to know which corridor her room was on; he wanted to know what she had been doing; if she disliked the moor as he disliked it; where she had lived before she came to Yorkshire. She answered all these questions and many more and he lay back on his pillow and listened. He made her tell him a great deal about India and about her voyage across the ocean. She found out that because he had been an invalid he had not learned things as other children had. One of his nurses had taught him to read when he was quite little and he was always reading and looking at pictures in splendid books.

Though his father rarely saw him when he was awake, he was given all sorts of wonderful things to amuse himself with. He never seemed to have been amused, however. He could have anything he asked for and was never made to do anything he did not like to do. "Everyone is obliged to do what pleases me," he said indifferently. "It makes me ill to be angry. No one believes I shall live to grow up."

He said it as if he was so accustomed to the idea that it had ceased to matter to him at all. He seemed to like the sound of Mary's voice. As she went on talking he listened in a drowsy, interested way. Once or twice she wondered if he were not gradually falling into a doze. But at last he asked a question which opened up a new subject.

"How old are you?" he asked.

"I am ten," answered Mary, forgetting herself for the moment, "and so are you."

"How do you know that?" he demanded in a surprised voice.

"Because when you were born the garden door was locked and the key was buried. And it has been locked for ten years."

Colin half sat up, turning toward her, leaning on his elbows.

"What garden door was locked? Who did it? Where was the key buried?" he exclaimed as if he were suddenly very much interested.

"It—it was the garden Mr. Craven hates," said Mary nervously. "He locked the door. No one—no one knew where he buried the key." "What sort of a garden is it?" Colin persisted eagerly.

"No one has been allowed to go into it for ten years," was Mary's careful answer.

But it was too late to be careful. He was too much like herself. He too had had nothing to think about and the idea of a hidden garden attracted him as it had attracted her. He asked question after question. Where was it? Had she never looked for the door? Had she never asked the gardeners?

"They won't talk about it," said Mary. "I think they have been told not to answer questions."

"I would make them," said Colin.

"Could you?" Mary faltered, beginning to feel frightened. If he could make people answer questions, who knew what might happen!

"Everyone is obliged to please me. I told you that," he said. "If I were to live, this place would sometime belong to me. They all know that. I would make them tell me."

Mary had not known that she herself had been spoiled, but she could see quite plainly that this mysterious boy had been. He thought that the whole world belonged to him. How peculiar he was and how coolly he spoke of not living.

"Do you think you won't live?" she asked, partly because she was curious and partly in hope of making him forget the garden.

"I don't suppose I shall," he answered as indifferently as he had spoken before. "Ever since I remember anything I have heard people say I shan't. At first they thought I was too little to understand and now they think I don't hear. But I do. My doctor is my father's cousin. He is quite poor and if I die he will have all Misselthwaite when my father is dead. I should think he wouldn't want me to live."

"Do you want to live?" inquired Mary.

"No," he answered, in a cross, tired fashion. "But I don't want to die. When I feel ill I lie here and think about it until I cry and cry."

"I have heard you crying three times," Mary said, "but I did not know who it was. Were you crying about that?" She did so want him to forget the garden.

"I dare say," he answered. "Let us talk about something else. Talk about that garden. Don't you want to see it?"

"Yes," answered Mary, in quite a low voice.

"I do," he went on persistently. "I don't think I ever really wanted to see anything before, but I want to see that garden. I want the key dug up. I want the door unlocked. I would let them take me there in my chair. That would be getting fresh air. I am going to make them open the door."

He had become quite excited and his strange eyes began to shine like stars and looked more immense than ever.

"They have to please me," he said. "I will make them take me there and I will let you go, too."

Mary's hands clutched each other. Everything would be spoiled—everything! Dickon would never come back. She would never again feel like a missel thrush with a safe-hidden nest.

"Oh, don't—don't—don't—don't do that!" she cried out.

He stared as if he thought she had gone crazy!

"Why?" he exclaimed. "You said you wanted to see it."

"I do," she answered almost with a sob in her throat, "but if you make them open the door and take you in like that it will never be a secret again."

He leaned still farther forward.

"A secret," he said. "What do you mean? Tell me."

Mary's words almost tumbled over one another.

"You see—you see," she panted, "if no one knows but ourselves—if there was a door, hidden somewhere under the ivy—if there was—and we could find it; and if we could slip through it together and shut it behind us, and no one knew anyone was inside and we called it our garden and pretended that—that we were missel thrushes and it was our nest, and if we played there almost every day and dug and planted seeds and made it all come alive—"

"Is it dead?" he interrupted her.

"It soon will be if no one cares for it," she went on. "The bulbs will live but the roses—"

He stopped her again as excited as she was herself.

"What are bulbs?" he put in quickly.

"They are daffodils and lilies and snowdrops. They are working in the earth now—pushing up pale green points because the spring is coming."

"Is the spring coming?" he said. "What is it like? You don't see it in rooms if you are ill."

"It is the sun shining on the rain and the rain falling on the sunshine, and things pushing up and working under the earth," said Mary. "If the garden was a secret and we could get into it we could watch the things grow bigger every day, and see how many roses are alive. Don't you see? Oh, don't you see how much nicer it would be if it was a secret?"

He dropped back on his pillow and lay there with an odd expression on his face.

"I never had a secret," he said, "except that one about not living to grow up. They don't know I know that, so it is a sort of secret. But I like this kind better."

"If you won't make them take you to the garden," pleaded Mary, "perhaps—I feel almost sure I can find out how to get in sometime. And then—if the doctor wants you to go out in your chair, and if you can always do what you want to do, perhaps—perhaps we might find some boy who would push you, and we could go alone and it would always be a secret garden."

"I should—like—that," he said very slowly, his eyes looking dreamy. "I should like that. I should not mind fresh air in a secret garden."

Mary began to recover her breath and feel safer because the idea of keeping the secret seemed to please him. She felt almost sure that if she kept on talking and could make him see the garden in his mind as she had seen it he would like it so much that he could not bear to think that everybody might tramp in to it when they chose.

"I'll tell you what I *think* it would be like, if we could go into it," she said. "It has been shut up so long things have grown into a tangle perhaps."

He lay quite still and listened while she went on talking about the roses which *might* have clambered from tree to tree and hung down—about the many birds which *might* have built their nests there because it was so safe. And then she told him about the robin and Ben Weatherstaff, and there was so much to tell about the robin and it was so easy and safe to talk about it that she ceased to be afraid. The robin pleased him so much that he smiled until he looked almost beautiful, and at first Mary had thought that he was even plainer than herself, with his big eyes and heavy locks of hair.

"I did not know birds could be like that," he said. "But if you stay in a room you never see things. What a lot of things you know. I feel as if you had been inside that garden."

She did not know what to say, so she did not say anything. He evidently did not expect an answer and the next moment he gave her a surprise.

"I am going to let you look at something," he said. "Do you see that rose-colored silk curtain hanging on the wall over the mantelpiece?"

Mary had not noticed it before, but she looked up and saw it. It was a curtain of soft silk hanging over what seemed to be some picture.

"Yes," she answered.

"There is a cord hanging from it," said Colin. "Go and pull it."

Mary got up, much mystified, and found the cord. When she pulled it the silk curtain ran back on rings and when it ran back it uncovered a picture. It was the picture of a girl with a laughing face. She had bright hair tied up with a blue ribbon and her gay, lovely eyes were exactly like Colin's unhappy ones, agate gray and looking twice as big as they really were because of the black lashes all round them.

"She is my mother," said Colin complainingly. "I don't see why she died. Sometimes I hate her for doing it."

"How queer!" said Mary.

"If she had lived I believe I should not have been ill always," he grumbled. "I dare say I should have lived, too. And my father would not have hated to look at me. I dare say I should have had a strong back. Draw the curtain again."

Mary did as she was told and returned to her footstool.

"She is much prettier than you," she said, "but her eyes are just like yours—at least they are the same shape and color. Why is the curtain drawn over her?"

He moved uncomfortably.

"I made them do it," he said. "Sometimes I don't like to see her looking at me. She smiles too much when I am ill and miserable. Besides, she is mine and I don't want everyone to see her." There were a few moments of silence and then Mary spoke.

"What would Mrs. Medlock do if she found out that I had been here?" she inquired.

"She would do as I told her to do," he answered. "And I should tell her that I wanted you to come here and talk to me every day. I am glad you came."

"So am I," said Mary. "I will come as often as I can, but"—she hesitated—"I shall have to look every day for the garden door."

"Yes, you must," said Colin, "and you can tell me about it afterward."

He lay thinking a few minutes, as he had done before, and then he spoke again.

"I think you shall be a secret, too," he said. "I will not tell them until they find out. I can always send the nurse out of the room and say that I want to be by myself. Do you know Martha?"

"Yes, I know her very well," said Mary. "She waits on me."

He nodded his head toward the outer corridor.

"She is the one who is asleep in the other room. The nurse went away yesterday to stay all night with her sister and she always makes Martha attend to me when she wants to go out. Martha shall tell you when to come here."

Then Mary understood Martha's troubled look when she had asked questions about the crying.

"Martha knew about you all the time?" she said.

"Yes; she often attends to me. The nurse likes to get away from me and then Martha comes."

"I have been here a long time," said Mary. "Shall I go away now? Your eyes look sleepy."

"I wish I could go to sleep before you leave me," he said rather shyly.

"Shut your eyes," said Mary, drawing her footstool closer, "and I will do what my Ayah used to do in India. I will pat your hand and stroke it and sing something quite low."

"I should like that perhaps," he said drowsily.

Somehow she was sorry for him and did not want him to lie awake, so she leaned against the bed and began to stroke and pat his hand and sing a very low little chanting song in Hindustani.

"That is nice," he said more drowsily still, and she went on chanting and stroking, but when she looked at him again his black lashes were lying close against his cheeks, for his eyes were shut and he was fast asleep. So she got up softly, took her candle and crept away without making a sound.

14

A Young Rajah

The moor was hidden in mist when the morning came, and the rain had not stopped pouring down. There could be no going out of doors. Martha was so busy that Mary had no opportunity of talking to her, but in the afternoon she asked her to come and sit with her in the nursery. She came bringing the stocking she was always knitting when she was doing nothing else.

"What's the matter with thee?" she asked as soon as they sat down. "Tha' looks as if tha'd somethin' to say."

"I have. I have found out what the crying was," said Mary.

Martha let her knitting drop on her knee and gazed at her with startled eyes.

"Tha' hasn't!" she exclaimed. "Never!"

"I heard it in the night," Mary went on. "And I got up and went to see where it came from. It was Colin. I found him."

Martha's face became red with fright.

"Eh! Miss Mary!" she said half crying. "Tha' shouldn't have done it—tha' shouldn't! Tha'll get me in trouble. I never told thee nothin' about him—but tha'll get me in trouble. I shall lose my place and what'll mother do!"

"You won't lose your place," said Mary. "He was glad I came. We talked and talked and he said he was glad I came."

"Was he?" cried Martha. "Art tha' sure? Tha' doesn't know what he's like when anything vexes him. He's a big lad to cry like a baby, but when he's in a passion he'll fair scream just to frighten us. He knows us daren't call our souls our own."

"He wasn't vexed," said Mary. "I asked him if I should go away and he made me stay. He asked me questions and I sat on a big footstool and talked to him about India and about the robin and gardens. He wouldn't let me go. He let me see his mother's picture. Before I left him I sang him to sleep."

Martha fairly gasped with amazement.

"I can scarcely believe thee!" she protested. "It's as if tha'd walked straight into a lion's den. If he'd been like he is most times he'd have throwed himself into one of his tantrums and roused th' house. He won't let strangers look at him."

"He let me look at him. I looked at him all the time and he looked at me. We stared!" said Mary.

"I don't know what to do!" cried agitated Martha. "If Mrs. Medlock finds out, she'll think I broke orders and told thee and I shall be packed back to mother."

"He is not going to tell Mrs. Medlock anything about it yet. It's to be a sort of secret just at first," said Mary firmly. "And he says everybody is obliged to do as he pleases."

"Aye, that's true enough—th' bad lad!" sighed Martha, wiping her forehead with her apron.

"He says Mrs. Medlock must. And he wants me to come and talk to him every day. And you are to tell me when he wants me."

"Me!" said Martha; "I shall lose my place—I shall for sure!"

"You can't if you are doing what he wants you to do and everybody is ordered to obey him," Mary argued.

"Does tha' mean to say," cried Martha with wide-open eyes, "that he was nice to thee!"

"I think he almost liked me," Mary answered.

"Then tha' must have bewitched him!" decided Martha, drawing a long breath.

"Do you mean Magic?" inquired Mary. "I've heard about Magic in India, but I can't make it. I just went into his room and I was so surprised to see him I stood and stared. And then he turned round and stared at me. And he thought I was a ghost or a dream and I thought perhaps he was. And it was so queer being there alone together in the middle of the night and not knowing about each other. And we began to ask each other questions. And when I asked him if I must go away he said I must not."

"Th' world's comin' to a end!" gasped Martha.

"What is the matter with him?" asked Mary.

"Nobody knows for sure and certain," said Martha. "Mr. Craven went off his head like when he was born. Th' doctors thought he'd have to be put in a 'sylum. It was because Mrs. Craven died like I told you. He wouldn't set eyes on th' baby. He just raved and said it'd be another hunchback like him and it'd better die."

"Is Colin a hunchback?" Mary asked. "He didn't look like one."

"He isn't yet," said Martha. "But he began all wrong. Mother said that there was enough trouble and raging in th' house to set any child wrong. They was afraid his back was weak an' they've always been takin' care of it—keepin' him lyin' down and not lettin' him walk. Once they made him wear a brace but he fretted so he was downright ill. Then a big doctor came to see him an' made them take it off. He talked to th' other doctor quite rough—in a polite way. He said there'd been too much medicine and too much lettin' him have his own way."

"I think he's a very spoiled boy," said Mary.

"He's th' worst young nowt as ever was!" said Martha. "I won't say as he hasn't been ill a good bit. He's had coughs an' colds that's nearly killed him two or three times. Once he had rheumatic fever an' once he had typhoid. Eh! Mrs. Medlock did get a fright then. He'd been out of his head an' she was talkin' to th' nurse, thinkin' he didn't know nothin', an' she said, 'He'll die this time sure enough, an' best thing for him an' for everybody.' An' she looked at him an' there he was with his big eyes open, starin' at her as sensible as she was herself. She didn't know wha'd happen but he just stared at her an' says, 'You give me some water an' stop talkin'.'"

"Do you think he will die?" asked Mary.

"Mother says there's no reason why any child should live that gets no fresh air an' doesn't do nothin' but lie on his back an' read picture books an' take medicine. He's weak and hates th' trouble o' bein' taken out o' doors, an' he gets cold so easy he says it makes him ill."

Mary sat and looked at the fire. "I wonder," she said slowly, "if it would not do him good to go out into a garden and watch things growing. It did me good."

"One of th' worst fits he ever had," said Martha, "was one time they took him out where the roses is by the fountain. He'd been readin' in a paper about people gettin' somethin' he called 'rose cold' an' he began to sneeze an' said he'd got it an' then a new gardener as didn't know th' rules passed by an' looked at him curious. He threw himself into a passion an' he said he'd looked at him because he was going to be a hunchback. He cried himself into a fever an' was ill all night."

"If he ever gets angry at me, I'll never go and see him again," said Mary.

"He'll have thee if he wants thee," said Martha. "Tha' may as well know that at th' start."

Very soon afterward a bell rang and she rolled up her knitting.

"I dare say th' nurse wants me to stay with him a bit," she said. "I hope he's in a good temper."

She was out of the room about ten minutes and then she came back with a puzzled expression.

"Well, tha' has bewitched him," she said. "He's up on his sofa with his picture books. He's told the nurse to stay away until six o'clock. I'm to wait in the next room. Th' minute she was gone he called me to him an' says, 'I want Mary Lennox to come and talk to me, and remember you're not to tell anyone.' You'd better go as quick as you can."

Mary was quite willing to go quickly. She did not want to see Colin as much as she wanted to see Dickon; but she wanted to see him very much.

There was a bright fire on the hearth when she entered his room, and in the daylight she saw it was a very beautiful room indeed. There were rich colors in the rugs and hangings and pictures and books on the walls which made it look glowing and comfortable even in spite of the gray sky and falling rain. Colin looked rather like a picture himself. He was wrapped in a velvet dressing-gown and sat against a big brocaded cushion. He had a red spot on each cheek.

"Come in," he said. "I've been thinking about you all morning."

"I've been thinking about you, too," answered Mary. "You don't know how frightened Martha is. She says Mrs. Medlock will think she told me about you and then she will be sent away."

He frowned.

"Go and tell her to come here," he said. "She is in the next room."

Mary went and brought her back. Poor Martha was shaking in her shoes. Colin was still frowning.

"Have you to do what I please or have you not?" he demanded.

"I have to do what you please, sir," Martha faltered, turning quite red.

"Has Medlock to do what I please?"

"Everybody has, sir," said Martha.

"Well, then, if I order you to bring Miss Mary to me, how can Medlock send you away if she finds it out?"

"Please don't let her, sir," pleaded Martha.

"I'll send *her* away if she dares to say a word about such a thing," said Master Craven grandly. "She wouldn't like that, I can tell you."

"Thank you, sir," bobbing a curtsy, "I want to do my duty, sir."

"What I want is your duty" said Colin more grandly still. "I'll take care of you. Now go away."

When the door closed behind Martha, Colin found Mistress Mary gazing at him as if he had set her wondering.

"Why do you look at me like that?" he asked her. "What are you thinking about?"

"I am thinking about two things."

"What are they? Sit down and tell me."

"This is the first one," said Mary, seating herself on the big stool. "Once in India I saw a boy who was a Rajah. He had rubies and emeralds and diamonds stuck all over him. He spoke to his people just as you spoke to Martha. Everybody had to do everything he told them—in a minute. I think they would have been killed if they hadn't."

"I shall make you tell me about Rajahs presently," he said, "but first tell me what the second thing was."

"I was thinking," said Mary, "how different you are from Dickon."

"Who is Dickon?" he said. "What a queer name!"

She might as well tell him, she thought she could talk about Dickon without mentioning the secret garden. She had liked to hear Martha talk about him. Besides, she longed to talk about him. It would seem to bring him nearer.

"He is Martha's brother. He is twelve years old," she explained. "He is not like anyone else in the world. He can charm foxes and squirrels and birds just as the natives in India charm snakes. He plays a very soft tune on a pipe and they come and listen."

There were some big books on a table at his side and he dragged one suddenly toward him. "There is a picture of a snake-charmer in this," he exclaimed. "Come and look at it."

The book was a beautiful one with superb colored illustrations and he turned to one of them.

"Can he do that?" he asked eagerly.

"He played on his pipe and they listened," Mary explained. "But he doesn't call it Magic. He says it's because he lives on the moor so much and he knows their ways. He says he feels sometimes as if he was a bird or a rabbit himself, he likes them so. I think he asked the robin questions. It seemed as if they talked to each other in soft chirps."

Colin lay back on his cushion and his eyes grew larger and larger and the spots on his cheeks burned.

"Tell me some more about him," he said.

"He knows all about eggs and nests," Mary went on. "And he knows where foxes and badgers and otters live. He keeps them secret so that other boys won't find their holes and frighten them. He knows about everything that grows or lives on the moor."

"Does he like the moor?" said Colin. "How can he when it's such a great, bare, dreary place?"

"It's the most beautiful place," protested Mary. "Thousands of lovely things grow on it and there are thousands of little creatures all busy building nests and making holes and burrows and chippering or singing or squeaking to each other. They are so busy and having such fun under the earth or in the trees or heather. It's their world."

"How do you know all that?" said Colin, turning on his elbow to look at her.

"I have never been there once, really," said Mary suddenly remembering. "I only drove over it in the dark. I thought it was hideous. Martha told me about it first and then Dickon. When Dickon talks about it you feel as if you saw things and heard them and as if you were standing in the heather with the sun shining and the gorse smelling like honey—and all full of bees and butterflies."

"You never see anything if you are ill," said Colin restlessly. He looked like a person listening to a new sound in the distance and wondering what it was.

"You can't if you stay in a room," said Mary.

"I couldn't go on the moor," he said in a resentful tone.

Mary was silent for a minute and then she said something bold.

"You might—sometime."

He moved as if he were startled.

"Go on the moor! How could I? I am going to die." "How do you know?" said Mary unsympathetically. She didn't like the way he had of talking about dying. She did not feel very sympathetic. She felt rather as if he almost boasted about it.

"Oh, I've heard it ever since I remember," he answered crossly. "They are always whispering about it and thinking I don't notice. They wish I would, too."

Mistress Mary felt quite contrary. She pinched her lips together.

"If they wished I would," she said, "I wouldn't. Who wishes you would?"

"The servants—and of course Dr. Craven because he would get Misselthwaite and be rich instead of poor. He daren't say so, but he always looks cheerful when I am worse. When I had typhoid fever his face got quite fat. I think my father wishes it, too."

"I don't believe he does," said Mary quite obstinately.

That made Colin turn and look at her again.

"Don't you?" he said.

And then he lay back on his cushion and was still, as if he were thinking. And there was quite a long silence. Perhaps they were both of them thinking strange things children do not usually think. "I like the grand doctor from London, because he made them take the iron thing off," said Mary at last "Did he say you were going to die?"

"No."

"What did he say?"

"He didn't whisper," Colin answered. "Perhaps he knew I hated whispering. I heard him say one thing quite aloud. He said, 'The lad might live if he would make up his mind to it. Put him in the humor.' It sounded as if he was in a temper."

"I'll tell you who would put you in the humor, perhaps," said Mary reflecting. She felt as if she would like this thing to be settled one way or the other. "I believe Dickon would. He's always talking about live things. He never talks about dead things or things that are ill. He's always looking up in the sky to watch birds flying—or looking down at the earth to see something growing. He has such round blue eyes and they are so wide open with looking about. And he laughs such a big laugh with his wide mouth—and his cheeks are as red—as red as cherries." She pulled her stool nearer to the sofa and her expression quite changed at the remembrance of the wide curving mouth and wide open eyes.

"See here," she said. "Don't let us talk about dying; I don't like it. Let us talk about living. Let us talk and talk about Dickon. And then we will look at your pictures."

It was the best thing she could have said. To talk about Dickon meant to talk about the moor and about the cottage and the fourteen people who lived in it on sixteen shillings a week—and the children who got fat on the moor grass like the wild ponies. And about Dickon's mother—and the skipping-rope—and the moor with the sun on it—and about pale green points sticking up out of the black sod. And it was all so alive that Mary talked more than she had ever talked before—and Colin both talked and listened as he had never done either before. And they both began to laugh over nothings as children will when they are happy together. And they laughed so that in the end they were making as much noise as if they had been two ordinary healthy natural ten-year-old creatures—instead of a hard, little, unloving girl and a sickly boy who believed that he was going to die.

They enjoyed themselves so much that they forgot the pictures and they forgot about the time. They had been laughing quite loudly over Ben Weatherstaff and his robin, and Colin was actually sitting up as if he had forgotten about his weak back, when he suddenly remembered something. "Do you know there is one thing we have never once thought of," he said. "We are cousins."

It seemed so queer that they had talked so much and never remembered this simple thing that they laughed more than ever, because they had got into the humor to laugh at anything. And in the midst of the fun the door opened and in walked Dr. Craven and Mrs. Medlock.

Dr. Craven started in actual alarm and Mrs. Medlock almost fell back because he had accidentally bumped against her.

"Good Lord!" exclaimed poor Mrs. Medlock with her eyes almost starting out of her head. "Good Lord!"

"What is this?" said Dr. Craven, coming forward. "What does it mean?"

Then Mary was reminded of the boy Rajah again. Colin answered as if neither the doctor's alarm nor Mrs. Medlock's terror were of the slightest consequence. He was as little disturbed or frightened as if an elderly cat and dog had walked into the room.

"This is my cousin, Mary Lennox," he said. "I asked her to come and talk to me. I like her. She must come and talk to me whenever I send for her."

Dr. Craven turned reproachfully to Mrs. Medlock. "Oh, sir" she panted. "I don't know how it's happened. There's not a servant on the place tha'd dare to talk—they all have their orders."

"Nobody told her anything," said Colin. "She heard me crying and found me herself. I am glad she came. Don't be silly, Medlock."

Mary saw that Dr. Craven did not look pleased, but it was quite plain that he dare not oppose his patient. He sat down by Colin and felt his pulse.

"I am afraid there has been too much excitement. Excitement is not good for you, my boy," he said.

"I should be excited if she kept away," answered Colin, his eyes beginning to look dangerously sparkling. "I am better. She makes me better. The nurse must bring up her tea with mine. We will have tea together."

Mrs. Medlock and Dr. Craven looked at each other in a troubled way, but there was evidently nothing to be done.

"He does look rather better, sir," ventured Mrs. Medlock. "But"—thinking the matter over—"he looked better this morning before she came into the room."

"She came into the room last night. She stayed with me a long time. She sang a Hindustani song to me and it made me go to sleep," said Colin. "I was better when I wakened up. I wanted my breakfast. I want my tea now. Tell nurse, Medlock."

Dr. Craven did not stay very long. He talked to the nurse for a few minutes when she came into the room and said a few words of warning to Colin. He must not talk too much; he must not forget that he was ill; he must not forget that he was very easily tired. Mary thought that there seemed to be a number of uncomfortable things he was not to forget.

Colin looked fretful and kept his strange black-lashed eyes fixed on Dr. Craven's face.

"I *want* to forget it," he said at last. "She makes me forget it. That is why I want her."

Dr. Craven did not look happy when he left the room. He gave a puzzled glance at the little girl sitting on the large stool. She had become a stiff, silent child again as soon as he entered and he could not see what the attraction was. The boy actually did look brighter, however—and he sighed rather heavily as he went down the corridor.

"They are always wanting me to eat things when I don't want to," said Colin, as the nurse brought in the tea and put it on the table by the sofa. "Now, if you'll eat I will. Those muffins look so nice and hot. Tell me about Rajahs."

15

Nest Building

After another week of rain the high arch of blue sky appeared again and the sun which poured down was quite hot. Though there had been no chance to see either the secret garden or Dickon, Mistress Mary had enjoyed herself very much. The week had not seemed long. She had spent hours of every day with Colin in his room, talking about Rajahs or gardens or Dickon and the cottage on the moor. They had looked at the splendid books and pictures and sometimes Mary had read things to Colin, and sometimes he had read a little to her. When he was amused and interested she thought he scarcely looked like an invalid at all, except that his face was so colorless and he was always on the sofa.

"You are a sly young one to listen and get out of your bed to go following things up like you did that night," Mrs. Medlock said once. "But there's no saying it's not been a sort of blessing to the lot of us. He's not had a tantrum or a whining fit since you made friends. The nurse was just going to give up the case because she was so sick of him, but she says she doesn't mind staying now you've gone on duty with her," laughing a little.

In her talks with Colin, Mary had tried to be very cautious about the secret garden. There were certain things she wanted to find out from him, but she felt that she must find them out without asking him direct questions. In the first place, as she began to like to be with him, she wanted to discover whether he was the kind of boy you could tell a secret to. He was not in the least like Dickon, but he was evidently so pleased with the idea of a garden no one knew anything about that she thought perhaps he could be trusted. But she had not known him long enough to be sure. The second thing she wanted to find out was this: If he could be trusted—if he really could—wouldn't it be possible to take him to the garden without having anyone find it out? The grand doctor had said that he must have fresh air and Colin had said that he would not mind fresh air in a secret garden. Perhaps if he had a great deal of fresh air and knew Dickon and the robin and saw things growing he might not think so much about dying. Mary had seen herself in the glass sometimes lately when she had realized that she looked quite a different creature from the child she had seen when she arrived from India. This child looked nicer. Even Martha had seen a change in her.

"Th' air from th' moor has done thee good already," she had said. "Tha'rt not nigh so yeller and tha'rt not nigh so scrawny. Even tha' hair doesn't slamp down on tha' head so flat. It's got some life in it so as it sticks out a bit."

"It's like me," said Mary. "It's growing stronger and fatter. I'm sure there's more of it."

"It looks it, for sure," said Martha, ruffling it up a little round her face. "Tha'rt not half so ugly when it's that way an' there's a bit o' red in tha' cheeks."

If gardens and fresh air had been good for her perhaps they would be good for Colin. But then, if he hated people to look at him, perhaps he would not like to see Dickon.

"Why does it make you angry when you are looked at?" she inquired one day.

"I always hated it," he answered, "even when I was very little. Then when they took me to the seaside and I used to lie in my carriage everybody used to stare and ladies would stop and talk to my nurse and then they would begin to whisper and I knew then they were saying I shouldn't live to grow up. Then sometimes the ladies would pat my cheeks and say 'Poor child!' Once when a lady did that I screamed out loud and bit her hand. She was so frightened she ran away."

"She thought you had gone mad like a dog," said Mary, not at all admiringly.

"I don't care what she thought," said Colin, frowning.

"I wonder why you didn't scream and bite me when I came into your room?" said Mary. Then she began to smile slowly.

"I thought you were a ghost or a dream," he said. "You can't bite a ghost or a dream, and if you scream they don't care."

"Would you hate it if—if a boy looked at you?" Mary asked uncertainly.

He lay back on his cushion and paused thoughtfully.

"There's one boy," he said quite slowly, as if he were thinking over every word, "there's one boy I believe I shouldn't mind. It's that boy who knows where the foxes live—Dickon."

"I'm sure you wouldn't mind him," said Mary.

"The birds don't and other animals," he said, still thinking it over, "perhaps that's why I shouldn't. He's a sort of animal charmer and I am a boy animal."

Then he laughed and she laughed too; in fact it ended in their both laughing a great deal and finding the idea of a boy animal hiding in his hole very funny indeed.

What Mary felt afterward was that she need not fear about Dickon.

*

On that first morning when the sky was blue again Mary wakened very early. The sun was pouring in slanting rays through the blinds and there was something so joyous in the sight of it that she jumped out of bed and ran to the window. She drew up the blinds and opened the window itself and a great waft of fresh, scented air blew in upon her. The moor was blue and the whole world looked as if something Magic had happened to it. There were tender little fluting sounds here and there and everywhere, as if scores of birds were beginning to tune up for a concert. Mary put her hand out of the window and held it in the sun.

"It's warm—warm!" she said. "It will make the green points push up and up and up, and it will make the bulbs and roots work and struggle with all their might under the earth."

She kneeled down and leaned out of the window as far as she could, breathing big breaths and sniffing the air until she laughed because she remembered what Dickon's mother had said about the end of his nose quivering like a rabbit's. "It must be very early," she said. "The little clouds are all pink and I've never seen the sky look like this. No one is up. I don't even hear the stable boys."

A sudden thought made her scramble to her feet.

"I can't wait! I am going to see the garden!"

She had learned to dress herself by this time and she put on her clothes in five minutes. She knew a small side door which she could unbolt herself and she flew downstairs in her stocking feet and put on her shoes in the hall. She unchained and unbolted and unlocked and when the door was open she sprang across the step with one bound, and there she was standing on the grass, which seemed to have turned green, and with the sun pouring down on her and warm sweet wafts about her and the fluting and twittering and singing coming from every bush and tree. She clasped her hands for pure joy and looked up in the sky and it was so blue and pink and pearly and white and flooded with springtime light that she felt as if she must flute and sing aloud herself and knew that thrushes and robins and skylarks could not possibly help it. She ran around the shrubs and paths towards the secret garden.

"It is all different already," she said. "The grass is greener and things are sticking up everywhere and things are uncurling and green buds of leaves are showing. This afternoon I am sure Dickon will come."

The long warm rain had done strange things to the herbaceous beds which bordered the walk by the lower wall. There were things sprouting and pushing out from the roots of clumps of plants and there were actually here and there glimpses of royal purple and yellow unfurling among the stems of crocuses. Six months before Mistress Mary would not have seen how the world was waking up, but now she missed nothing.

When she had reached the place where the door hid itself under the ivy, she was startled by a curious loud sound. It was the caw-caw of a crow and it came from the top of the wall, and when she looked up, there sat a big glossy-plumaged blue-black bird, looking down at her very wisely indeed. She had never seen a crow so close before and he made her a little nervous, but the next moment he spread his wings and flapped away across the garden. She hoped he was not going to stay inside and she pushed the door open wondering if he would. When she got fairly into the garden she saw that he probably did intend to stay because he had alighted on a dwarf apple-tree and under the apple-tree was lying a little reddish animal with a Bushy tail, and both of them were watching the stooping body and rust-red head of Dickon, who was kneeling on the grass working hard.

Mary flew across the grass to him.

"Oh, Dickon! Dickon!" she cried out. "How could you get here so early! How could you! The sun has only just got up!"

He got up himself, laughing and glowing, and tousled; his eyes like a bit of the sky.

"Eh!" he said. "I was up long before him. How could I have stayed abed! Th' world's all fair begun again this mornin', it has. An' it's workin' an' hummin' an' scratchin' an' pipin' an' nest-buildin' an' breathin' out scents, till you've got to be out on it 'stead o' lyin' on your back. When th' sun did jump up, th' moor went mad for joy, an' I was in the midst of th' heather, an' I run like mad myself, shoutin' an' singin'. An' I come straight here. I couldn't have stayed away. Why, th' garden was lyin' here waitin'!"

Mary put her hands on her chest, panting, as if she had been running herself.

"Oh, Dickon! Dickon!" she said. "I'm so happy I can scarcely breathe!"

Seeing him talking to a stranger, the little bushy-tailed animal rose from its place under the tree and came to him, and the rook, cawing once, flew down from its branch and settled quietly on his shoulder.

"This is th' little fox cub," he said, rubbing the little reddish animal's head. "It's named Captain. An' this here's Soot. Soot he flew across th' moor with me an' Captain he run same as if th' hounds had been after him. They both felt same as I did."

Neither of the creatures looked as if he were the least afraid of Mary. When Dickon began to walk about, Soot stayed on his shoulder and Captain trotted quietly close to his side.

"See here!" said Dickon. "See how these has pushed up, an' these an' these! An' Eh! Look at these here!"

He threw himself upon his knees and Mary went down beside him. They had come upon a whole clump of crocuses burst into purple and orange and gold. Mary bent her face down and kissed and kissed them.

"You never kiss a person in that way," she said when she lifted her head. "Flowers are so different."

He looked puzzled but smiled.

"Eh!" he said, "I've kissed mother many a time that way when I come in from th' moor after a day's roamin' an' she stood there at th' door in th' sun, lookin' so glad an' comfortable." They ran from one part of the garden to another and found so many wonders that they were obliged to remind themselves that they must whisper or speak low. He showed her swelling leaf buds on rose branches which had seemed dead. He showed her ten thousand new green points pushing through the mould. They put their eager young noses close to the earth and sniffed its warmed springtime breathing; they dug and pulled and laughed low with rapture until Mistress Mary's hair was as tumbled as Dickon's and her cheeks were almost as poppy red as his.

There was every joy on earth in the secret garden that morning, and in the midst of them came a delight more delightful than all, because it was more wonderful. Swiftly something flew across the wall and darted through the trees to a close-grown corner, a little flare of red-breasted bird with something hanging from its beak.

Dickon stood quite still and put his hand on Mary almost as if they had suddenly found themselves laughing in a church.

"We munnot stir," he whispered in broad Yorkshire. "We munnot scarce breathe. I knowed he was mate-huntin' when I seed him last. It's Ben Weatherstaff's robin. He's buildin' his nest. He'll stay here if us don't fight him." They settled down softly upon the grass and sat there without moving.

"Us mustn't seem as if us was watchin' him too close," said Dickon. "He'd be out with us for good if he got th' notion us was interferin' now. He'll be a good bit different till all this is over. He's settin' up housekeepin'. He'll be shyer an' readier to take things ill. He's got no time for visitin' an' gossipin'. Us must keep still a bit an' try to look as if us was grass an' trees an' bushes. Then when he's got used to seein' us I'll chirp a bit an' he'll know us'll not be in his way."

Mistress Mary was not at all sure that she knew, as Dickon seemed to, how to try to look like grass and trees and bushes. But he had said the queer thing as if it were the simplest and most natural thing in the world, and she felt it must be quite easy to him, and indeed she watched him for a few minutes carefully, wondering if it was possible for him to quietly turn green and put out branches and leaves. But he only sat wonderfully still, and when he spoke dropped his voice to such a softness that it was curious that she could hear him, but she could.

"It's part o' th' springtime, this nest-buildin' is," he said. "I warrant it's been goin' on in th' same way every year since th' world was begun. They've got their way o' thinkin' and doin' things an' a body had better not meddle. You can lose a friend in springtime easier than any other season if you're too curious."

"If we talk about him I can't help looking at him," Mary said as softly as possible. "We must talk of something else. There is something I want to tell you."

"He'll like it better if us talks o' somethin' else," said Dickon. "What is it tha's got to tell me?"

"Well—do you know about Colin?" she whispered.

He turned his head to look at her.

"What does tha' know about him?" he asked.

"I've seen him. I have been to talk to him every day this week. He wants me to come. He says I'm making him forget about being ill and dying," answered Mary.

Dickon looked actually relieved as soon as the surprise died away from his round face.

"I am glad o' that," he exclaimed. "I'm right down glad. It makes me easier. I knowed I must say nothin' about him an' I don't like havin' to hide things."

"Don't you like hiding the garden?" said Mary.

"I'll never tell about it," he answered. "But I says to mother, 'Mother,' I says, 'I got a secret to keep. It's not a bad 'un, tha' knows that. It's no worse than hidin' where a bird's nest is. Tha' doesn't mind it, does tha'?'"

Mary always wanted to hear about mother.

"What did she say?" she asked, not at all afraid to hear.

Dickon grinned sweet-temperedly.

"It was just like her, what she said," he answered. "She give my head a bit of a rub an' laughed an' she says, 'Eh, lad, tha' can have all th' secrets tha' likes. I've knowed thee twelve year.'"

"How did you know about Colin?" asked Mary.

"Everybody as knowed about Mester Craven knowed there was a little lad as was like to be a cripple, an' they knowed Mester Craven didn't like him to be talked about. Folks is sorry for Mester Craven because Mrs. Craven was such a pretty young lady an' they was so fond of each other. Mrs. Medlock stops in our cottage whenever she goes to Thwaite an' she doesn't mind talkin' to mother before us children, because she knows us has been brought up to be trusty. How did tha' find out about him? Martha was in fine trouble th' last time she came home. She said tha'd heard him frettin' an' tha' was askin' questions an' she didn't know what to say."

Mary told him her story about the midnight wuthering of the wind which had wakened her and about the faint far-off sounds of the complaining voice which had led her down the dark corridors with her candle and had ended with her opening of the door of the dimly lighted room with the carven four-posted bed in the corner. When she described the small ivory-white face and the strange black-rimmed eyes Dickon shook his head.

"Them's just like his mother's eyes, only hers was always laughin', they say," he said. "They say as Mr. Craven can't bear to see him when he's awake an' it's because his eyes is so like his mother's an' yet looks so different in his miserable bit of a face."

"Do you think he wants to die?" whispered Mary.

"No, but he wishes he'd never been born. Mother she says that's th' worst thing on earth for a child. Them as is not wanted scarce ever thrives. Mester Craven he'd buy anythin' as money could buy for th' poor lad but he'd like to forget as he's on earth. For one thing, he's afraid he'll look at him some day and find he's growed hunchback."

"Colin's so afraid of it himself that he won't sit up," said Mary. "He says he's always thinking that if he should feel a lump coming he should go crazy and scream himself to death."

"Eh! he oughtn't to lie there thinkin' things like that," said Dickon. "No lad could get well as thought them sort o' things."

The fox was lying on the grass close by him, looking up to ask for a pat now and then, and Dickon bent down and rubbed his neck softly and thought a few minutes in silence. Presently he lifted his head and looked round the garden.

"When first we got in here," he said, "it seemed like everything was gray. Look round now and tell me if tha' doesn't see a difference."

Mary looked and caught her breath a little.

"Why!" she cried, "the gray wall is changing. It is as if a green mist were creeping over it. It's almost like a green gauze veil."

"Aye," said Dickon. "An' it'll be greener and greener till th' gray's all gone. Can tha' guess what I was thinkin'?"

"I know it was something nice," said Mary eagerly. "I believe it was something about Colin."

"I was thinkin' that if he was out here he wouldn't be watchin' for lumps to grow on his back; he'd be watchin' for buds to break on th' rose-bushes, an' he'd likely be healthier," explained Dickon. "I was wonderin' if us could ever get him in th' humor to come out here an' lie under th' trees in his carriage."

"I've been wondering that myself. I've thought of it almost every time I've talked to him," said Mary. "I've wondered if he could keep a secret and I've wondered if we could bring him here without anyone seeing us. I thought perhaps you could push his carriage. The doctor said he must have fresh air and if he wants us to take him out no one dare disobey him. He won't go out for other people and perhaps they will be glad if he will go out with us. He could order the gardeners to keep away so they wouldn't find out."

Dickon was thinking very hard as he scratched Captain's back.

"It'd be good for him, I'll warrant," he said. "Us'd not be thinkin' he'd better never been born. Us'd be just two children watchin' a garden grow, an' he'd be another. Two lads an' a little lass just lookin' on at th' springtime. I warrant it'd be better than doctor's stuff."

"He's been lying in his room so long and he's always been so afraid of his back that it has made him queer," said Mary. "He knows a good many things out of books but he doesn't know anything else. He says he has been too ill to notice things and he hates going out of doors and hates gardens and gardeners. But he likes to hear about this garden because it is a secret. I daren't tell him much but he said he wanted to see it."

"Us'll have him out here sometime for sure," said Dickon. "I could push his carriage well enough. Has tha' noticed how th' robin an' his mate has been workin' while we've been sittin' here? Look at him perched on that branch wonderin' where it'd be best to put that twig he's got in his beak."

He made one of his low whistling calls and the robin turned his head and looked at him inquiringly, still holding his twig. Dickon spoke to him as Ben Weatherstaff did, but Dickon's tone was one of friendly advice.

"Wheres'ever tha' puts it," he said, "it'll be all right. Tha' knew how to build tha' nest before tha' came out o' th' egg. Get on with thee, lad. Tha'st got no time to lose."

"Oh, I do like to hear you talk to him!" Mary said, laughing delightedly. "Ben Weatherstaff scolds him and makes fun of him, and he hops about and looks as if he understood every word, and I know he likes it. Ben Weatherstaff says he is so conceited he would rather have stones thrown at him than not be noticed."

Dickon laughed too and went on talking.

"Tha' knows us won't trouble thee," he said to the robin. "Us is near bein' wild things ourselves. Us is nest-buildin' too, bless thee. Look out tha' doesn't tell on us." And though the robin did not answer, because his beak was occupied, Mary knew that when he flew away with his twig to his own corner of the garden the darkness of his dew-bright eye meant that he would not tell their secret for the world.

16

"I Won't!" Said Mary

They found a great deal to do that morning and Mary was late in returning to the house and was also in such a hurry to get back to her work that she quite forgot Colin until the last moment.

"Tell Colin that I can't come and see him yet," she said to Martha. "I'm very busy in the garden."

Martha looked rather frightened.

"Eh! Miss Mary," she said, "it may put him all out of humor when I tell him that."

But Mary was not as afraid of him as other people were and she was not a self-sacrificing person.

"I can't stay," she answered. "Dickon's waiting for me;" and she ran away.

The afternoon was even lovelier and busier than the morning had been. Already nearly all the weeds were cleared out of the garden and most of the roses and trees had been pruned or dug about. Dickon had brought a spade of his own and he had taught Mary to use all her tools, so that by this time it was plain that though the lovely wild place was not likely to become a "gardener's garden" it would be a wilderness of growing things before the springtime was over.

"There'll be apple blossoms an' cherry blossoms overhead," Dickon said, working away with all his might. "An' there'll be peach an' plum trees in bloom against th' walls, an' th' grass'll be a carpet o' flowers."

The little fox and the rook were as happy and busy as they were, and the robin and his mate flew backward and forward like tiny streaks of lightning. Sometimes the rook flapped his black wings and soared away over the tree-tops in the park. Each time he came back and perched near Dickon and cawed several times as if he were relating his adventures, and Dickon talked to him just as he had talked to the robin. Once when Dickon was so busy that he did not answer him at first, Soot flew on to his shoulders and gently tweaked his ear with his large beak. When Mary wanted to rest a little Dickon sat down with her under a tree and once he took his pipe out of his pocket and played the soft strange little notes and two squirrels appeared on the wall and looked and listened.

"Tha's a good bit stronger than tha' was," Dickon said, looking at her as she was digging. "Tha's beginning to look different, for sure."

Mary was glowing with exercise and good spirits.

"I'm getting fatter and fatter every day," she said quite exultantly. "Mrs. Medlock will have to get me some bigger dresses. Martha says my hair is growing thicker. It isn't so flat and stringy."

The sun was beginning to set and sending deep gold-colored rays slanting under the trees when they parted.

"It'll be fine tomorrow," said Dickon. "I'll be at work by sunrise."

"So will I," said Mary.

*

She ran back to the house as quickly as her feet would carry her. She wanted to tell Colin about Dickon's fox cub and the rook and about what the springtime had been doing. She felt sure he would like to hear. So it was not very pleasant when she opened the door of her room, to see Martha standing waiting for her with a doleful face.

"What is the matter?" she asked. "What did Colin say when you told him I couldn't come?"

"Eh!" said Martha, "I wish tha'd gone. He was nigh goin' into one o' his tantrums. There's been a nice to do all afternoon to keep him quiet. He would watch the clock all th' time."

Mary's lips pinched themselves together. She was no more used to considering other people than Colin was and she saw no reason why an ill-tempered boy should interfere with the thing she liked best. She knew nothing about the pitifulness of people who had been ill and nervous and who did not know that they could control their tempers and need not make other people ill and nervous, too. When she had had a headache in India she had done her best to see that everybody else also had a headache or something quite as bad. And she felt she was quite right; but of course now she felt that Colin was quite wrong.

He was not on his sofa when she went into his room. He was lying flat on his back in bed and he did not turn his head toward her as she came in. This was a bad beginning and Mary marched up to him with her stiff manner.

"Why didn't you get up?" she said.

"I did get up this morning when I thought you were coming," he answered, without looking at her. "I made them put me back in bed this afternoon. My back ached and my head ached and I was tired. Why didn't you come?" "I was working in the garden with Dickon," said Mary.

Colin frowned and condescended to look at her.

"I won't let that boy come here if you go and stay with him instead of coming to talk to me," he said.

Mary flew into a fine passion. She could fly into a passion without making a noise. She just grew sour and obstinate and did not care what happened.

"If you send Dickon away, I'll never come into this room again!" she retorted.

"You'll have to if I want you," said Colin.

"I won't!" said Mary.

"I'll make you," said Colin. "They shall drag you in."

"Shall they, Mr. Rajah!" said Mary fiercely. "They may drag me in but they can't make me talk when they get me here. I'll sit and clench my teeth and never tell you one thing. I won't even look at you. I'll stare at the floor!"

They were a nice agreeable pair as they glared at each other. If they had been two little street boys they would have sprung at each other and had a rough-and-tumble fight. As it was, they did the next thing to it.

"You are a selfish thing!" cried Colin.

"What are you?" said Mary. "Selfish people always say that. Anyone is selfish who doesn't do what they want. You're more selfish than I am. You're the most selfish boy I ever saw."

"I'm not!" snapped Colin. "I'm not as selfish as your fine Dickon is! He keeps you playing in the dirt when he knows I am all by myself. He's selfish, if you like!"

Mary's eyes flashed fire.

"He's nicer than any other boy that ever lived!" she said. "He's—he's like an angel!" It might sound rather silly to say that but she did not care.

"A nice angel!" Colin sneered ferociously. "He's a common cottage boy off the moor!"

"He's better than a common Rajah!" retorted Mary. "He's a thousand times better!"

Because she was the stronger of the two she was beginning to get the better of him. The truth was that he had never had a fight with anyone like himself in his life and, upon the whole, it was rather good for him, though neither he nor Mary knew anything about that. He turned his head on his pillow and shut his eyes and a big tear was squeezed out and ran down his cheek. He was beginning to feel pathetic and sorry for himself—not for anyone else.

"I'm not as selfish as you, because I'm always ill, and I'm sure there is a lump coming on my back," he said. "And I am going to die besides."

"You're not!" contradicted Mary unsympathetically.

He opened his eyes quite wide with indignation. He had never heard such a thing said before. He was at once furious and slightly pleased, if a person could be both at one time.

"I'm not?" he cried. "I am! You know I am! Everybody says so."

"I don't believe it!" said Mary sourly. "You just say that to make people sorry. I believe you're proud of it. I don't believe it! If you were a nice boy it might be true—but you're too nasty!"

In spite of his invalid back Colin sat up in bed in quite a healthy rage.

"Get out of the room!" he shouted and he caught hold of his pillow and threw it at her. He was not strong enough to throw it far and it only fell at her feet, but Mary's face looked as pinched as a nutcracker.

"I'm going," she said. "And I won't come back!" She walked to the door and when she reached it she turned round and spoke again.

"I was going to tell you all sorts of nice things," she said. "Dickon brought his fox and his rook and I was going to tell you all about them. Now I won't tell you a single thing!"

She marched out of the door and closed it behind her, and there to her great astonishment she found the trained nurse standing as if she had been listening and, more amazing still—she was laughing. She was a big handsome young woman who ought not to have been a trained nurse at all, as she could not bear invalids and she was always making excuses to leave Colin to Martha or anyone else who would take her place. Mary had never liked her, and she simply stood and gazed up at her as she stood giggling into her handkerchief.

"What are you laughing at?" she asked her.

"At you two young ones," said the nurse. "It's the best thing that could happen to the sickly pampered thing to have someone to stand up to him that's as spoiled as himself;" and she laughed into her handkerchief again. "If he'd had a young vixen of a sister to fight with it would have been the saving of him."

"Is he going to die?"

"I don't know and I don't care," said the nurse. "Hysterics and temper are half what ails him."

"What are hysterics?" asked Mary.

"You'll find out if you work him into a tantrum after this—but at any rate you've given him something to have hysterics about, and I'm glad of it."

Mary went back to her room not feeling at all as she had felt when she had come in from the garden. She was cross and disappointed but not at all sorry for Colin. She had looked forward to telling him a great many things and she had meant to try to make up her mind whether it would be safe to trust him with the great secret. She had been beginning to think it would be, but now she had changed her mind entirely. She would never tell him and he could stay in his room and never get any fresh air and die if he liked! It would serve him right! She felt so sour and unrelenting that for a few minutes she almost forgot about Dickon and the green veil creeping over the world and the soft wind blowing down from the moor.

Martha was waiting for her and the trouble in her face had been temporarily replaced by interest and curiosity. There was a wooden box on the table and its cover had been removed and revealed that it was full of neat packages.

"Mr. Craven sent it to you," said Martha. "It looks as if it had picture books in it."

Mary remembered what he had asked her the day she had gone to his room. "Do you want anything—dolls—toys—books?" She opened the package wondering if he had sent a doll, and also wondering what she should do with it if he had. But he had not sent one. There were several beautiful books such as Colin had, and two of them were about gardens and were full of pictures. There were two or three games and there was a beautiful little writing-case with a gold monogram on it and a gold pen and inkstand.

Everything was so nice that her pleasure began to crowd her anger out of her mind. She had not expected him to remember her at all and her hard little heart grew quite warm.

"I can write better than I can print," she said, "and the first thing I shall write with that pen will be a letter to tell him I am much obliged."

If she had been friends with Colin she would have run to show him her presents at once, and they would have looked at the pictures and read some of the gardening books and perhaps tried playing the games, and he would have enjoyed himself so much he would never once have thought he was going to die or have put his hand on his spine to see if there was a lump coming. He had a way of doing that which she could not bear. It gave her an uncomfortable frightened feeling because he always looked so frightened himself. He said that if he felt even quite a little lump some day he should know his hunch had begun to grow. Something he had heard Mrs. Medlock whispering to the nurse had given him the idea and he had thought over it in secret until it was quite firmly fixed in his mind. Mrs. Medlock had said his father's back had begun to show its crookedness in that way when he was a child. He had never told anyone but Mary that most of his "tantrums" as they called them grew out of his hysterical hidden fear. Mary had been sorry for him when he had told her.

"He always began to think about it when he was cross or tired," she said to herself. "And he has been cross today. Perhaps—perhaps he has been thinking about it all afternoon."

She stood still, looking down at the carpet and thinking.

"I said I would never go back again—" she hesitated, knitting her brows—"but perhaps, just perhaps, I will go and see—if he wants me—in the morning. Perhaps he'll try to throw his pillow at me again, but—I think—I'll go."

17

A Tantrum

She had got up very early in the morning and had worked hard in the garden and she was tired and sleepy, so as soon as Martha had brought her supper and she had eaten it, she was glad to go to bed. As she laid her head on the pillow she murmured to herself:

"I'll go out before breakfast and work with Dickon and then afterward—I believe—I'll go to see him."

She thought it was the middle of the night when she was awakened by such dreadful sounds that she jumped out of bed in an instant. What was it—what was it? The next minute she felt quite sure she knew. Doors were opened and shut and there were hurrying feet in the corridors and someone was crying and screaming at the same time, screaming and crying in a horrible way.

"It's Colin," she said. "He's having one of those tantrums the nurse called hysterics. How awful it sounds."

As she listened to the sobbing screams she did not wonder that people were so frightened that they gave him his own way in everything rather than hear them. She put her hands over her ears and felt sick and shivering.

"I don't know what to do. I don't know what to do," she kept saying. "I can't bear it."

Once she wondered if he would stop if she dared go to him and then she remembered how he had driven her out of the room and thought that perhaps the sight of her might make him worse. Even when she pressed her hands more tightly over her ears she could not keep the awful sounds out. She hated them so and was so terrified by them that suddenly they began to make her angry and she felt as if she should like to fly into a tantrum herself and frighten him as he was frightening her. She was not used to anyone's tempers but her own. She took her hands from her ears and sprang up and stamped her foot.

"He ought to be stopped! Somebody ought to make him stop! Somebody ought to beat him!" she cried out.

Just then she heard feet almost running down the corridor and her door opened and the nurse came in. She was not laughing now by any means. She even looked rather pale.

"He's worked himself into hysterics," she said in a great hurry. "He'll do himself harm. No one can do anything with him. You come and try, like a good child. He likes you."

"He turned me out of the room this morning," said Mary, stamping her foot with excitement.

The stamp rather pleased the nurse. The truth was that she had been afraid she might find Mary crying and hiding her head under the bedclothes.

"That's right," she said. "You're in the right humor. You go and scold him. Give him something new to think of. Do go, child, as quick as ever you can."

It was not until afterward that Mary realized that the thing had been funny as well as dreadful—that it was funny that all the grown-up people were so frightened that they came to a little girl just because they guessed she was almost as bad as Colin himself.

She flew along the corridor and the nearer she got to the screams the higher her temper mounted. She felt quite wicked by the time she reached the door. She slapped it open with her hand and ran across the room to the four-posted bed.

"You stop!" she almost shouted. "You stop! I hate you! Everybody hates you! I wish everybody would run out of the house and let you scream yourself to death! You *will* scream yourself to death in a minute, and I wish you would!" A nice sympathetic child could neither have thought nor said such things, but it just happened that the shock of hearing them was the best possible thing for this hysterical boy whom no one had ever dared to restrain or contradict.

He had been lying on his face beating his pillow with his hands and he actually almost jumped around, he turned so quickly at the sound of the furious little voice. His face looked dreadful, white and red and swollen, and he was gasping and choking; but savage little Mary did not care an atom.

"If you scream another scream," she said, "I'll scream too—and I can scream louder than you can and I'll frighten you, I'll frighten you!"

He actually had stopped screaming because she had startled him so. The scream which had been coming almost choked him. The tears were streaming down his face and he shook all over.

"I can't stop!" he gasped and sobbed. "I can't—I can't!"

"You can!" shouted Mary. "Half that ails you is hysterics and temper—just hysterics—hysterics—hysterics!" and she stamped each time she said it.

"I felt the lump—I felt it," choked out Colin. "I knew I should. I shall have a hunch on my back and then I shall die," and he began to writhe again and turned on his face and sobbed and wailed but he didn't scream.

"You didn't feel a lump!" contradicted Mary fiercely. "If you did it was only a hysterical lump. Hysterics makes lumps. There's nothing the matter with your horrid back—nothing but hysterics! Turn over and let me look at it!"

She liked the word "hysterics" and felt somehow as if it had an effect on him. He was probably like herself and had never heard it before.

"Nurse," she commanded, "come here and show me his back this minute!"

The nurse, Mrs. Medlock and Martha had been standing huddled together near the door staring at her, their mouths half open. All three had gasped with fright more than once. The nurse came forward as if she were half afraid. Colin was heaving with great breathless sobs.

"Perhaps he—he won't let me," she hesitated in a low voice.

Colin heard her, however, and he gasped out between two sobs: "Sh-show her! She-she'll see then!"

It was a poor thin back to look at when it was bared. Every rib could be counted and every joint of the spine, though Mistress Mary did not count them as she bent over and examined them with a solemn savage little face. She looked so sour and old-fashioned that the nurse turned her head aside to hide the twitching of her mouth. There was just a minute's silence, for even Colin tried to hold his breath while Mary looked up and down his spine, and down and up, as intently as if she had been the great doctor from London.

"There's not a single lump there!" she said at last. "There's not a lump as big as a pin—except backbone lumps, and you can only feel them because you're thin. I've got backbone lumps myself, and they used to stick out as much as yours do, until I began to get fatter, and I am not fat enough yet to hide them. There's not a lump as big as a pin! If you ever say there is again, I shall laugh!"

No one but Colin himself knew what effect those crossly spoken childish words had on him. If he had ever had anyone to talk to about his secret terrors—if he had ever dared to let himself ask questions—if he had had childish companions and had not lain on his back in the huge closed house, breathing an atmosphere heavy with the fears of people who were most of them ignorant and tired of him, he would have found out that most of his fright and illness was created by himself. But he had lain and thought of himself and his aches and weariness for hours and days and months and years. And now that an angry unsympathetic little girl insisted obstinately that he was not as ill as he thought he was he actually felt as if she might be speaking the truth.

"I didn't know," ventured the nurse, "that he thought he had a lump on his spine. His back is weak because he won't try to sit up. I could have told him there was no lump there." Colin gulped and turned his face a little to look at her.

"C-could you?" he said pathetically.

"Yes, sir."

"There!" said Mary, and she gulped too.

Colin turned on his face again and but for his long-drawn broken breaths, which were the dying down of his storm of sobbing, he lay still for a minute, though great tears streamed down his face and wet the pillow. Actually the tears meant that a curious great relief had come to him. Presently he turned and looked at the nurse again and strangely enough he was not like a Rajah at all as he spoke to her.

"Do you think—I could—live to grow up?" he said.

The nurse was neither clever nor soft-hearted but she could repeat some of the London doctor's words.

"You probably will if you will do what you are told to do and not give way to your temper, and stay out a great deal in the fresh air."

Colin's tantrum had passed and he was weak and worn out with crying and this perhaps made him feel gentle. He put out his hand a little toward Mary, and I am glad to say that, her own tantum having passed, she was softened too and met him half-way with her hand, so that it was a sort of making up.

"I'll—I'll go out with you, Mary," he said. "I shan't hate fresh air if we can find—" He remembered just in time to stop himself from saying "if we can find the secret garden" and he ended, "I shall like to go out with you if Dickon will come and push my chair. I do so want to see Dickon and the fox and the crow."

The nurse remade the tumbled bed and shook and straightened the pillows. Then she made Colin a cup of beef tea and gave a cup to Mary, who really was very glad to get it after her excitement. Mrs. Medlock and Martha gladly slipped away, and after everything was neat and calm and in order the nurse looked as if she would very gladly slip away also. She was a healthy young woman who resented being robbed of her sleep and she yawned quite openly as she looked at Mary, who had pushed her big footstool close to the four-posted bed and was holding Colin's hand.

"You must go back and get your sleep out," she said. "He'll drop off after a while—if he's not too upset. Then I'll lie down myself in the next room."

"Would you like me to sing you that song I learned from my Ayah?" Mary whispered to Colin.

His hand pulled hers gently and he turned his tired eyes on her appealingly.

"Oh, yes!" he answered. "It's such a soft song. I shall go to sleep in a minute."

"I will put him to sleep," Mary said to the yawning nurse. "You can go if you like."

"Well," said the nurse, with an attempt at reluctance. "If he doesn't go to sleep in half an hour you must call me."

"Very well," answered Mary.

The nurse was out of the room in a minute and as soon as she was gone Colin pulled Mary's hand again.

"I almost told," he said; "but I stopped myself in time. I won't talk and I'll go to sleep, but you said you had a whole lot of nice things to tell me. Have you—do you think you have found out anything at all about the way into the secret garden?"

Mary looked at his poor little tired face and swollen eyes and her heart relented.

"Ye-es," she answered, "I think I have. And if you will go to sleep I will tell you tomorrow." His hand quite trembled.

"Oh, Mary!" he said. "Oh, Mary! If I could get into it I think I should live to grow up! Do you suppose that instead of singing the Ayah song—you could just tell me softly as you did that first day what you imagine it looks like inside? I am sure it will make me go to sleep."

"Yes," answered Mary. "Shut your eyes."

He closed his eyes and lay quite still and she held his hand and began to speak very slowly and in a very low voice.

"I think it has been left alone so long—that it has grown all into a lovely tangle. I think the roses have climbed and climbed and climbed until they hang from the branches and walls and creep over the ground—almost like a strange gray mist. Some of them have died but many—are alive and when the summer comes there will be curtains and fountains of roses. I think the ground is full of daffodils and snowdrops and lilies and iris working their way out of the dark. Now the spring has begun—perhaps—perhaps—"

The soft drone of her voice was making him stiller and stiller and she saw it and went on.

"Perhaps they are coming up through the grass—perhaps there are clusters of purple crocuses and gold ones—even now. Perhaps the leaves are beginning to break out and uncurl—and perhaps—the gray is changing and a green gauze veil is creeping—and creeping over—everything. And the birds are coming to look at it—because it is—so safe and still. And perhaps—perhaps—perhaps—" very softly and slowly indeed, "the robin has found a mate—and is building a nest."

And Colin was asleep.

18

"Tha' Munnot Waste No Time"

Of course Mary did not waken early the next morning. She slept late because she was tired, and when Martha brought her breakfast she told her that though. Colin was quite quiet he was ill and feverish as he always was after he had worn himself out with a fit of crying. Mary ate her breakfast slowly as she listened.

"He says he wishes tha' would please go and see him as soon as tha' can," Martha said. "It's queer what a fancy he's took to thee. Tha' did give it him last night for sure—didn't tha? Nobody else would have dared to do it. Eh! poor lad! He's been spoiled till salt won't save him. Mother says as th' two worst things as can happen to a child is never to have his own way—or always to have it. She doesn't know which is th' worst. Tha' was in a fine temper tha'self, too. But he says to me when I went into his room, 'Please ask Miss Mary if she'll please come an' talk to me?' Think o' him saying please! Will you go, Miss?" "I'll run and see Dickon first," said Mary. "No, I'll go and see Colin first and tell him—I know what I'll tell him," with a sudden inspiration.

She had her hat on when she appeared in Colin's room and for a second he looked disappointed. He was in bed. His face was pitifully white and there were dark circles round his eyes.

"I'm glad you came," he said. "My head aches and I ache all over because I'm so tired. Are you going somewhere?"

Mary went and leaned against his bed.

"I won't be long," she said. "I'm going to Dickon, but I'll come back. Colin, it's—it's something about the garden."

His whole face brightened and a little color came into it.

"Oh! is it?" he cried out. "I dreamed about it all night I heard you say something about gray changing into green, and I dreamed I was standing in a place all filled with trembling little green leaves—and there were birds on nests everywhere and they looked so soft and still. I'll lie and think about it until you come back."

In five minutes Mary was with Dickon in their garden. The fox and the crow were with him again and this time he had brought two tame squirrels. "I came over on the pony this mornin'," he said. "Eh! he is a good little chap—Jump is! I brought these two in my pockets. This here one he's called Nut an' this here other one's called Shell."

When he said "Nut" one squirrel leaped on to his right shoulder and when he said "Shell" the other one leaped on to his left shoulder.

When they sat down on the grass with Captain curled at their feet, Soot solemnly listening on a tree and Nut and Shell nosing about close to them, it seemed to Mary that it would be scarcely bearable to leave such delightfulness, but when she began to tell her story somehow the look in Dickon's funny face gradually changed her mind. She could see he felt sorrier for Colin than she did. He looked up at the sky and all about him.

"Just listen to them birds—th' world seems full of 'em—all whistlin' an' pipin'," he said. "Look at 'em dartin' about, an' hearken at 'em callin' to each other. Come springtime seems like as if all th' world's callin'. The leaves is uncurlin' so you can see 'em—an', my word, th' nice smells there is about!" sniffing with his happy turned-up nose. "An' that poor lad lyin' shut up an' seein' so little that he gets to thinkin' o' things as sets him screamin'. Eh! my! we mun get him out here—we mun get him watchin' an listenin' an' sniffin' up th' air an' get him just soaked through wi' sunshine. An' we munnot lose no time about it."

When he was very much interested he often spoke quite broad Yorkshire though at other times he tried to modify his dialect so that Mary could better understand. But she loved his broad Yorkshire and had in fact been trying to learn to speak it herself. So she spoke a little now.

"Aye, that we mun," she said (which meant "Yes, indeed, we must"). "I'll tell thee what us'll do first," she proceeded, and Dickon grinned, because when the little wench tried to twist her tongue into speaking Yorkshire it amused him very much. "He's took a graidely fancy to thee. He wants to see thee and he wants to see Soot an' Captain. When I go back to the house to talk to him I'll ax him if tha' canna' come an' see him tomorrow mornin'—an'. bring tha' creatures wi' thee—an' then—in a bit, when there's more leaves out, an' happen a bud or two, we'll get him to come out an' tha' shall push him in his chair an' we'll bring him here an' show him everything."

When she stopped she was quite proud of herself. She had never made a long speech in Yorkshire before and she had remembered very well.

"Tha' mun talk a bit o' Yorkshire like that to Mester Colin," Dickon chuckled. "Tha'll make him laugh an' there's nowt as good for ill folk as laughin' is. Mother says she believes as half a hour's good laugh every mornin' 'ud cure a chap as was makin' ready for typhus fever."

"I'm going to talk Yorkshire to him this very day," said Mary, chuckling herself.

The garden had reached the time when every day and every night it seemed as if Magicians were passing through it drawing loveliness out of the earth and the boughs with wands. It was hard to go away and leave it all, particularly as Nut had actually crept on to her dress and Shell had scrambled down the trunk of the apple-tree they sat under and stayed there looking at her with inquiring eyes. But she went back to the house and when she sat down close to Colin's bed he began to sniff as Dickon did though not in such an experienced way.

"You smell like flowers and—and fresh things," he cried out quite joyously. "What is it you smell of? It's cool and warm and sweet all at the same time."

"It's th' wind from th' moor," said Mary. "It comes o' sittin' on th' grass under a tree wi' Dickon an' wi' Captain an' Soot an' Nut an' Shell. It's th' springtime an' out o' doors an' sunshine as smells so graidely."

She said it as broadly as she could, and you do not know how broadly Yorkshire sounds until you have heard someone speak it. Colin began to laugh.

"What are you doing?" he said. "I never heard you talk like that before. How funny it sounds."

"I'm givin' thee a bit o' Yorkshire," answered Mary triumphantly. "I canna' talk as graidely as Dickon an' Martha can but tha' sees I can shape a bit. Doesn't tha' understand a bit o' Yorkshire when tha' hears it? An' tha' a Yorkshire lad thysel' bred an' born! Eh! I wonder tha'rt not ashamed o' thy face."

And then she began to laugh too and they both laughed until they could not stop themselves and they laughed until the room echoed and Mrs. Medlock opening the door to come in drew back into the corridor and stood listening amazed.

"Well, upon my word!" she said, speaking rather broad Yorkshire herself because there was no one to hear her and she was so astonished. "Whoever heard th' like! Whoever on earth would ha' thought it!"

There was so much to talk about. It seemed as if Colin could never hear enough of Dickon and Captain and Soot and Nut and Shell and the pony whose name was Jump. Mary had run round into the wood with Dickon to see Jump. He was a tiny little shaggy moor pony with thick locks hanging over his eyes and with a pretty face and a nuzzling velvet nose. He was rather thin with living on moor grass but he was as tough and wiry as if the muscle in his little legs had been made of steel springs. He had lifted his head and whinnied softly the moment he saw Dickon and he had trotted up to him and put his head across his shoulder and then Dickon had talked into his ear and Jump had talked back in odd little whinnies and puffs and snorts. Dickon had made him give Mary his small front hoof and kiss her on her cheek with his velvet muzzle.

"Does he really understand everything Dickon says?" Colin asked.

"It seems as if he does," answered Mary. "Dickon says anything will understand if you're friends with it for sure, but you have to be friends for sure."

Colin lay quiet a little while and his strange gray eyes seemed to be staring at the wall, but Mary saw he was thinking.

"I wish I was friends with things," he said at last, "but I'm not. I never had anything to be friends with, and I can't bear people."

"Can't you bear me?" asked Mary.

"Yes, I can," he answered. "It's funny but I even like you."

"Ben Weatherstaff said I was like him," said Mary. "He said he'd warrant we'd both got the same nasty tempers. I think you are like him too. We are all three alike—you and I and Ben Weatherstaff. He said we were neither of us much to look at and we were as sour as we looked. But I don't feel as sour as I used to before I knew the robin and Dickon."

"Did you feel as if you hated people?"

"Yes," answered Mary without any affectation. "I should have detested you if I had seen you before I saw the robin and Dickon."

Colin put out his thin hand and touched her.

"Mary," he said, "I wish I hadn't said what I did about sending Dickon away. I hated you when you said he was like an angel and I laughed at you but—but perhaps he is."

"Well, it was rather funny to say it," she admitted frankly, "because his nose does turn up and he has a big mouth and his clothes have patches all over them and he talks broad Yorkshire, but—but if an angel did come to Yorkshire and live on the moor—if there was a Yorkshire angel—I believe he'd understand the green things and know how to make them grow and he would know how to talk to the wild creatures as Dickon does and they'd know he was friends for sure."

"I shouldn't mind Dickon looking at me," said Colin; "I want to see him."

"I'm glad you said that," answered Mary, "because—because—"

Quite suddenly it came into her mind that this was the minute to tell him. Colin knew something new was coming.

"Because what?" he cried eagerly.

Mary was so anxious that she got up from her stool and came to him and caught hold of both his hands.

"Can I trust you? I trusted Dickon because birds trusted him. Can I trust you—for sure—*for sure*?" she implored.

Her face was so solemn that he almost whispered his answer.

"Yes—yes!"

"Well, Dickon will come to see you tomorrow morning, and he'll bring his creatures with him."

"Oh! Oh!" Colin cried out in delight.

"But that's not all," Mary went on, almost pale with solemn excitement. "The rest is better. There is a door into the garden. I found it. It is under the ivy on the wall."

If he had been a strong healthy boy Colin would probably have shouted "Hooray! Hooray! Hooray!" but he was weak and rather hysterical; his eyes grew bigger and bigger and he gasped for breath.

"Oh! Mary!" he cried out with a half sob. "Shall I see it? Shall I get into it? Shall I *live* to get into it?" and he clutched her hands and dragged her toward him.

"Of course you'll see it!" snapped Mary indignantly. "Of course you'll live to get into it! Don't be silly!"

And she was so un-hysterical and natural and childish that she brought him to his senses and he began to laugh at himself and a few minutes afterward she was sitting on her stool again telling him not what she imagined the secret garden to be like but what it really was, and Colin's aches and tiredness were forgotten and he was listening enraptured.

"It is just what you thought it would be," he said at last. "It sounds just as if you had really seen it. You know I said that when you told me first."

Mary hesitated about two minutes and then boldly spoke the truth.

"I had seen it—and I had been in," she said. "I found the key and got in weeks ago. But I daren't tell you—I daren't because I was so afraid I couldn't trust you—*for sure*!"

19

"It Has Come!"

Of course Dr. Craven had been sent for the morning after Colin had had his tantrum. He was always sent for at once when such a thing occurred and he always found, when he arrived, a white shaken boy lying on his bed, sulky and still so hysterical that he was ready to break into fresh sobbing at the least word. In fact, Dr. Craven dreaded and detested the difficulties of these visits. On this occasion he was away from Misselthwaite Manor until afternoon.

"How is he?" he asked Mrs. Medlock rather irritably when he arrived. "He will break a blood-vessel in one of those fits some day. The boy is half insane with hysteria and self-indulgence."

"Well, sir," answered Mrs. Medlock, "you'll scarcely believe your eyes when you see him. That plain sour-faced child that's almost as bad as himself has just bewitched him. How she's done it there's no telling. The

Lord knows she's nothing to look at and you scarcely ever hear her speak, but she did what none of us dare do. She just flew at him like a little cat last night, and stamped her feet and ordered him to stop screaming, and somehow she startled him so that he actually did stop, and this afternoon—well just come up and see, sir. It's past crediting."

The scene which Dr. Craven beheld when he entered his patient's room was indeed rather astonishing to him. As Mrs. Medlock opened the door he heard laughing and chattering. Colin was on his sofa in his dressing-gown and he was sitting up quite straight looking at a picture in one of the garden books and talking to the plain child who at that moment could scarcely be called plain at all because her face was so glowing with enjoyment.

"Those long spires of blue ones—we'll have a lot of those," Colin was announcing. "They're called Del-phin-iums."

"Dickon says they're larkspurs made big and grand," cried Mistress Mary. "There are clumps there already."

Then they saw Dr. Craven and stopped. Mary became quite still and Colin looked fretful.

"I am sorry to hear you were ill last night, my boy," Dr. Craven said a trifle nervously. He was rather a nervous man.

"I'm better now—much better," Colin answered, rather like a Rajah. "I'm going out in my chair in a day or two if it is fine. I want some fresh air."

Dr. Craven sat down by him and felt his pulse and looked at him curiously.

"It must be a very fine day," he said, "and you must be very careful not to tire yourself."

"Fresh air won't tire me," said the young Rajah.

As there had been occasions when this same young gentleman had shrieked aloud with rage and had insisted that fresh air would give him cold and kill him, it is not to be wondered at that his doctor felt somewhat startled.

"I thought you did not like fresh air," he said.

"I don't when I am by myself," replied the Rajah; "but my cousin is going out with me."

"And the nurse, of course?" suggested Dr. Craven.

"No, I will not have the nurse," so magnificently that Mary could not help remembering how the young native Prince had looked with his diamonds and emeralds and pearls stuck all over him and the great rubies on the small dark hand he had waved to command his servants to approach with salaams and receive his orders.

"My cousin knows how to take care of me. I am always better when she is with me. She made me better last night. A very strong boy I know will push my carriage."

Dr. Craven felt rather alarmed. If this tiresome hysterical boy should chance to get well he himself would lose all chance of inheriting Misselthwaite; but he was not an unscrupulous man, though he was a weak one, and he did not intend to let him run into actual danger.

"He must be a strong boy and a steady boy," he said. "And I must know something about him. Who is he? What is his name?"

"It's Dickon," Mary spoke up suddenly. She felt somehow that everybody who knew the moor must know Dickon. And she was right, too. She saw that in a moment Dr. Craven's serious face relaxed into a relieved smile.

"Oh, Dickon," he said. "If it is Dickon you will be safe enough. He's as strong as a moor pony, is Dickon."

"And he's trusty," said Mary. "He's th' trustiest lad i' Yorkshire." She had been talking Yorkshire to Colin and she forgot herself.

"Did Dickon teach you that?" asked Dr. Craven, laughing outright.

"I'm learning it as if it was French," said Mary rather coldly. "It's like a native dialect in India. Very clever people try to learn them. I like it and so does Colin." "Well, well," he said. "If it amuses you perhaps it won't do you any harm. Did you take your bromide last night, Colin?"

"No," Colin answered. "I wouldn't take it at first and after Mary made me quiet she talked me to sleep—in a low voice—about the spring creeping into a garden."

"That sounds soothing," said Dr. Craven, more perplexed than ever and glancing sideways at Mistress Mary sitting on her stool and looking down silently at the carpet. "You are evidently better, but you must remember—"

"I don't want to remember," interrupted the Rajah, appearing again. "When I lie by myself and remember I begin to have pains everywhere and I think of things that make me begin to scream because I hate them so. If there was a doctor anywhere who could make you forget you were ill instead of remembering it I would have him brought here." And he waved a thin hand which ought really to have been covered with royal signet rings made of rubies. "It is because my cousin makes me forget that she makes me better."

Dr. Craven had never made such a short stay after a "tantrum"; usually he was obliged to remain a very long time and do a great many things. This afternoon he did not give any medicine or leave any new orders and he was spared any disagreeable scenes. When he went downstairs he looked very thoughtful and when he talked to Mrs. Medlock in the library she felt that he was a much puzzled man.

"Well, sir," she ventured, "could you have believed it?"

"It is certainly a new state of affairs," said the doctor. "And there's no denying it is better than the old one."

"I believe Susan Sowerby's right—I do that," said Mrs. Medlock. "I stopped in her cottage on my way to Thwaite yesterday and had a bit of talk with her. And she says to me, 'Well, Sarah Ann, she mayn't be a good child, an' she mayn't be a pretty one, but she's a child, an' children needs children.' We went to school together, Susan Sowerby and me."

"She's the best sick nurse I know," said Dr. Craven. "When I find her in a cottage I know the chances are that I shall save my patient."

Mrs. Medlock smiled. She was fond of Susan Sowerby.

"She's got a way with her, has Susan," she went on quite volubly. "I've been thinking all morning of one thing she said yesterday. She says, 'Once when I was givin' th' children a bit of a preach after they'd been fightin' I ses to 'em all, "When I was at school my jography told as th' world was shaped like a orange an' I found out before I was ten that th' whole orange doesn't belong to nobody. No one owns more than his bit of a quarter an' there's times it seems like there's not enow quarters to go round. But don't you—none o' you—think as you own th' whole orange or you'll find out you're mistaken, an' you won't find it out without hard knocks." 'What children learns from children,' she says, 'is that there's no sense in grabbin' at th' whole orange—peel an' all. If you do you'll likely not get even th' pips, an' them's too bitter to eat.'"

"She's a shrewd woman," said Dr. Craven, putting on his coat.

"Well, she's got a way of saying things," ended Mrs. Medlock, much pleased. "Sometimes I've said to her, 'Eh! Susan, if you was a different woman an' didn't talk such broad Yorkshire I've seen the times when I should have said you was clever.'"

*

That night Colin slept without once awakening and when he opened his eyes in the morning he lay still and smiled without knowing it—smiled because he felt so curiously comfortable. It was actually nice to be awake, and he turned over and stretched his limbs luxuriously. He felt as if tight strings which had held him had loosened themselves and let him go. He did not know that Dr. Craven would have said that his nerves had relaxed and rested themselves. Instead of lying and staring at the wall and wishing he had not awakened, his mind was full of the plans he and Mary had made yesterday, of pictures of the garden and of Dickon and his wild creatures. It was so nice to have things to think about. And he had not been awake more than ten minutes when he heard feet running along the corridor and Mary was at the door. The next minute she was in the room and had run across to his bed, bringing with her a waft of fresh air full of the scent of the morning.

"You've been out! You've been out! There's that nice smell of leaves!" he cried.

She had been running and her hair was loose and blown and she was bright with the air and pink-cheeked, though he could not see it.

"It's so beautiful!" she said, a little breathless with her speed. "You never saw anything so beautiful! It has *come*! I thought it had come that other morning, but it was only coming. It is here now! It has come, the Spring! Dickon says so!"

"Has it?" cried Colin, and though he really knew nothing about it he felt his heart beat. He actually sat up in bed.

"Open the window!" he added, laughing half with joyful excitement and half at his own fancy. "Perhaps we may hear golden trumpets!"

And though he laughed, Mary was at the window in a moment and in a moment more it was opened wide and freshness and softness and scents and birds' songs were pouring through.

"That's fresh air," she said. "Lie on your back and draw in long breaths of it. That's what Dickon does when he's lying on the moor. He says he feels it in his veins and it makes him strong and he feels as if he could live forever and ever. Breathe it and breathe it."

She was only repeating what Dickon had told her, but she caught Colin's fancy.

"'Forever and ever'! Does it make him feel like that?" he said, and he did as she told him, drawing in long deep breaths over and over again until he felt that something quite new and delightful was happening to him.

Mary was at his bedside again.

"Things are crowding up out of the earth," she ran on in a hurry. "And there are flowers uncurling and buds on everything and the green veil has covered nearly all the gray and the birds are in such a hurry about their nests for fear they may be too late that some of them are even fighting for places in the secret garden. And the rose-bushes look as wick as wick can be, and there are primroses in the lanes and woods, and the seeds we planted are up, and Dickon has brought the fox and the crow and the squirrels and a new-born lamb."

And then she paused for breath. The new-born lamb Dickon had found three days before lying by its dead mother among the gorse bushes on the moor. It was not the first motherless lamb he had found and he knew what to do with it. He had taken it to the cottage wrapped in his jacket and he had let it lie near the fire and had fed it with warm milk. It was a soft thing with a darling silly baby face and legs rather long for its body. Dickon had carried it over the moor in his arms and its feeding bottle was in his pocket with a squirrel, and when Mary had sat under a tree with its limp warmness huddled on her lap she had felt as if she were too full of strange joy to speak. A lamb—a lamb! A living lamb who lay on your lap like a baby!

She was describing it with great joy and Colin was listening and drawing in long breaths of air when the nurse entered. She started a little at the sight of the open window. She had sat stifling in the room many a warm day because her patient was sure that open windows gave people cold.

"Are you sure you are not chilly, Master Colin?" she inquired.

"No," was the answer. "I am breathing long breaths of fresh air. It makes you strong. I am going to get up to the sofa for breakfast. My cousin will have breakfast with me."

The nurse went away, concealing a smile, to give the order for two breakfasts. She found the servants' hall a more amusing place than the invalid's chamber and just now everybody wanted to hear the news from upstairs. There was a great deal of joking about the unpopular young recluse who, as the cook said, "had found his master, and good for him." The servants' hall had been very tired of the tantrums, and the butler, who was a man with a family, had more than once expressed his opinion that the invalid would be all the better "for a good hiding."

When Colin was on his sofa and the breakfast for two was put upon the table he made an announcement to the nurse in his most Rajah-like manner.

"A boy, and a fox, and a crow, and two squirrels, and a new-born lamb, are coming to see me this morning. I want them brought upstairs as soon as they come," he said. "You are not to begin playing with the animals in the servants' hall and keep them there. I want them here." The nurse gave a slight gasp and tried to conceal it with a cough.

"Yes, sir," she answered.

"I'll tell you what you can do," added Colin, waving his hand. "You can tell Martha to bring them here. The boy is Martha's brother. His name is Dickon and he is an animal charmer."

"I hope the animals won't bite, Master Colin," said the nurse.

"I told you he was a charmer," said Colin austerely. "Charmers' animals never bite."

"There are snake-charmers in India," said Mary. "And they can put their snakes' heads in their mouths."

"Goodness!" shuddered the nurse.

They ate their breakfast with the morning air pouring in upon them. Colin's breakfast was a very good one and Mary watched him with serious interest.

"You will begin to get fatter just as I did," she said. "I never wanted my breakfast when I was in India and now I always want it."

"I wanted mine this morning," said Colin. "Perhaps it was the fresh air. When do you think Dickon will come?"

He was not long in coming. In about ten minutes Mary held up her hand.

"Listen!" she said. "Did you hear a caw?"

Colin listened and heard it, the oddest sound in the world to hear inside a house, a hoarse "caw-caw."

"Yes," he answered.

"That's Soot," said Mary. "Listen again. Do you hear a bleat—a tiny one?"

"Oh, yes!" cried Colin, quite flushing.

"That's the new-born lamb," said Mary. "He's coming."

Dickon's moorland boots were thick and clumsy and though he tried to walk quietly they made a clumping sound as he walked through the long corridors. Mary and Colin heard him marching—marching, until he passed through the tapestry door on to the soft carpet of Colin's own passage.

"If you please, sir," announced Martha, opening the door, "if you please, sir, here's Dickon an' his creatures."

Dickon came in smiling his nicest wide smile. The new-born lamb was in his arms and the little red fox trotted by his side. Nut sat on his left shoulder and Soot on his right and Shell's head and paws peeped out of his coat pocket.

Colin slowly sat up and stared and stared—as he had stared when he first saw Mary; but this was a stare of wonder and delight. The truth was that in spite of all he had heard he had not in the least understood what this boy would be like and that his fox and his crow and his squirrels and his lamb were so near to him and his friendliness that they seemed almost to be part of himself. Colin had never talked to a boy in his life and he was so overwhelmed by his own pleasure and curiosity that he did not even think of speaking.

But Dickon did not feel the least shy or awkward. He had not felt embarrassed because the crow had not known his language and had only stared and had not spoken to him the first time they met. Creatures were always like that until they found out about you. He walked over to Colin's sofa and put the new-born lamb quietly on his lap, and immediately the little creature turned to the warm velvet dressing-gown and began to nuzzle and nuzzle into its folds and butt its tight-curled head with soft impatience against his side. Of course no boy could have helped speaking then.

"What is it doing?" cried Colin. "What does it want?"

"It wants its mother," said Dickon, smiling more and more. "I brought it to thee a bit hungry because I knowed tha'd like to see it feed."

He knelt down by the sofa and took a feeding-bottle from his pocket.

"Come on, little 'un," he said, turning the small woolly white head with a gentle brown hand. "This is what tha's after. Tha'll get more out o' this than tha' will out o' silk velvet coats. There now," and he pushed the rubber tip of the bottle into the nuzzling mouth and the lamb began to suck it with ravenous ecstasy.

After that there was no wondering what to say. By the time the lamb fell asleep questions poured forth and Dickon answered them all. He told them how he had found the lamb just as the sun was rising three mornings ago. He had been standing on the moor listening to a skylark and watching him swing higher and higher into the sky until he was only a speck in the heights of blue.

"I'd almost lost him but for his song an' I was wonderin' how a chap could hear it when it seemed as if he'd get out o' th' world in a minute—an' just then I heard somethin' else far off among th' gorse bushes. It was a weak bleatin' an' I knowed it was a new lamb as was hungry an' I knowed it wouldn't be hungry if it hadn't lost its mother somehow, so I set off searchin'. Eh! I did have a look for it. I went in an' out among th' gorse bushes an' round an' round an' I always seemed to take th' wrong turnin'. But at last I seed a bit o' white by a rock on top o' th' moor an' I climbed up an' found th' little 'un half dead wi' cold an' clemmin'." While he talked, Soot flew solemnly in and out of the open window and cawed remarks about the scenery while Nut and Shell made excursions into the big trees outside and ran up and down trunks and explored branches. Captain curled up near Dickon, who sat on the hearth-rug from preference.

They looked at the pictures in the gardening books and Dickon knew all the flowers by their country names and knew exactly which ones were already growing in the secret garden.

"I couldna' say that there name," he said, pointing to one under which was written "Aquilegia," "but us calls that a columbine, an' that there one it's a snapdragon and they both grow wild in hedges, but these is garden ones an' they're bigger an' grander. There's some big clumps o' columbine in th' garden. They'll look like a bed o' blue an' white butterflies flutterin' when they're out."

"I'm going to see them," cried Colin. "I am going to see them!"

"Aye, that tha' mun," said Mary quite seriously. "An' tha' munnot lose no time about it."

20

"I Shall Live Forever—and Ever—and Ever!"

But they were obliged to wait more than a week because first there came some very windy days and then Colin was threatened with a cold, which two things happening one after the other would no doubt have thrown him into a rage but that there was so much careful and mysterious planning to do and almost every day Dickon came in, if only for a few minutes, to talk about what was happening on the moor and in the lanes and hedges and on the borders of streams. The things he had to tell about otters' and badgers' and water-rats' houses, not to mention birds' nests and field-mice and their burrows, were enough to make you almost tremble with excitement when you heard all the intimate details from an animal charmer and realized with what thrilling eagerness and anxiety the whole busy underworld was working.

"They're same as us," said Dickon, "only they have to build their homes every year. An' it keeps 'em so busy they fair scuffle to get 'em done."

The most absorbing thing, however, was the preparations to be made before Colin could be transported with sufficient secrecy to the garden. No one must see the chair-carriage and Dickon and Mary after they turned a certain corner of the shrubbery and entered upon the walk outside the ivied walls. As each day passed, Colin had become more and more fixed in his feeling that the mystery surrounding the garden was one of its greatest charms. Nothing must spoil that. No one must ever suspect that they had a secret. People must think that he was simply going out with Mary and Dickon because he liked them and did not object to their looking at him. They had long and quite delightful talks about their route. They would go up this path and down that one and cross the other and go round among the fountain flower-beds as if they were looking at the "bedding-out plants" the head gardener, Mr. Roach, had been having arranged. That would seem such a rational thing to do that no one would think it at all mysterious. They would turn into the shrubbery walks and lose themselves until they came to the long walls. It was almost as serious and elaborately thought out as the plans of march made by great generals in time of war.

Rumors of the new and curious things which were occurring in the invalid's apartments had of course filtered through the servants' hall into the stable yards and out among the gardeners, but notwithstanding this, Mr. Roach was startled one day when he received orders from Master Colin's room to the effect that he must report himself in the apartment no outsider had ever seen, as the invalid himself desired to speak to him.

"Well, well," he said to himself as he hurriedly changed his coat, "what's to do now? His Royal Highness that wasn't to be looked at calling up a man he's never set eyes on."

Mr. Roach was not without curiosity. He had never caught even a glimpse of the boy and had heard a dozen exaggerated stories about his uncanny looks and ways and his insane tempers. The thing he had heard oftenest was that he might die at any moment and there had been numerous fanciful descriptions of a humped back and helpless limbs, given by people who had never seen him.

"Things are changing in this house, Mr. Roach," said Mrs. Medlock, as she led him up the back staircase to the corridor on to which opened the hitherto mysterious chamber.

"Let's hope they're changing for the better, Mrs. Medlock," he answered.

"They couldn't well change for the worse," she continued; "and queer as it all is there's them as finds their duties made a lot easier to stand up under. Don't you be surprised, Mr. Roach, if you find yourself in the middle of a menagerie and Martha Sowerby's Dickon more at home than you or me could ever be."

There really was a sort of Magic about Dickon, as Mary always privately believed. When Mr. Roach heard his name he smiled quite leniently.

"He'd be at home in Buckingham Palace or at the bottom of a coal mine," he said. "And yet it's not impudence, either. He's just fine, is that lad."

It was perhaps well he had been prepared or he might have been startled. When the bedroom door was opened a large crow, which seemed quite at home perched on the high back of a carven chair, announced the entrance of a visitor by saying "Caw-caw" quite loudly. In spite of Mrs. Medlock's warning, Mr. Roach only just escaped being sufficiently undignified to jump backward.

The young Rajah was neither in bed nor on his sofa. He was sitting in an armchair and a young lamb was standing by him shaking its tail in feeding-lamb fashion as Dickon knelt giving it milk from its bottle. A squirrel was perched on Dickon's bent back attentively nibbling a nut. The little girl from India was sitting on a big footstool looking on.

"Here is Mr. Roach, Master Colin," said Mrs. Medlock.

The young Rajah turned and looked his servitor over—at least that was what the head gardener felt happened.

"Oh, you are Roach, are you?" he said. "I sent for you to give you some very important orders."

"Very good, sir," answered Roach, wondering if he was to

receive instructions to fell all the oaks in the park or to transform the orchards into water-gardens.

"I am going out in my chair this afternoon," said Colin. "If the fresh air agrees with me I may go out every day. When I go, none of the gardeners are to be anywhere near the Long Walk by the garden walls. No one is to be there. I shall go out about two o'clock and everyone must keep away until I send word that they may go back to their work."

"Very good, sir," replied Mr. Roach, much relieved to hear that the oaks might remain and that the orchards were safe. "Mary," said Colin, turning to her, "what is that thing you say in India when you have finished talking and want people to go?"

"You say, 'You have my permission to go,'" answered Mary.

The Rajah waved his hand.

"You have my permission to go, Roach," he said. "But, remember, this is very important."

"Caw-caw!" remarked the crow hoarsely but not impolitely.

"Very good, sir. Thank you, sir," said Mr. Roach, and Mrs. Medlock took him out of the room.

Outside in the corridor, being a rather good-natured man, he smiled until he almost laughed.

"My word!" he said, "he's got a fine lordly way with him, hasn't he? You'd think he was a whole Royal Family rolled into one—Prince Consort and all.".

"Eh!" protested Mrs. Medlock, "we've had to let him trample all over every one of us ever since he had feet and he thinks that's what folks was born for."

"Perhaps he'll grow out of it, if he lives," suggested Mr. Roach.

"Well, there's one thing pretty sure," said Mrs. Medlock. "If he does live and that Indian child stays here I'll warrant she teaches him that the whole orange does not belong to him, as Susan Sowerby says. And he'll be likely to find out the size of his own quarter."

Inside the room Colin was leaning back on his cushions.

"It's all safe now," he said. "And this afternoon I shall see it—this afternoon I shall be in it!"

Dickon went back to the garden with his creatures and Mary stayed with Colin. She did not think he looked tired but he was very quiet before their lunch came and he was quiet while they were eating it. She wondered why and asked him about it.

"What big eyes you've got, Colin," she said. "When you are thinking they get as big as saucers. What are you thinking about now?"

"I can't help thinking about what it will look like," he answered.

"The garden?" asked Mary.

"The springtime," he said. "I was thinking that I've really never seen it before. I scarcely ever went out and when I did go I never looked at it. I didn't even think about it."

"I never saw it in India because there wasn't any," said Mary.

Shut in and morbid as his life had been, Colin had more imagination than she had and at least he had spent a good deal of time looking at wonderful books and pictures.

"That morning when you ran in and said 'It's come! It's come!', you made me feel quite queer. It sounded as if things were coming with a great procession and big bursts and wafts of music. I've a picture like it in one of my books—crowds of lovely people and children with garlands and branches with blossoms on them, everyone laughing and dancing and crowding and playing on pipes. That was why I said, 'Perhaps we shall hear golden trumpets' and told you to throw open the window."

"How funny!" said Mary. "That's really just what it feels like. And if all the flowers and leaves and green things and birds and wild creatures danced past at once, what a crowd it would be! I'm sure they'd dance and sing and flute and that would be the wafts of music."

They both laughed but it was not because the idea was laughable but because they both so liked it.

A little later the nurse made Colin ready. She noticed that instead of lying like a log while his clothes were put on he sat up and made some efforts to help himself, and he talked and laughed with Mary all the time.

"This is one of his good days, sir," she said to Dr. Craven, who dropped in to inspect him. "He's in such good spirits that it makes him stronger."

"I'll call in again later in the afternoon, after he has come in," said Dr. Craven. "I must see how the going out agrees with him. I wish," in a very low voice, "that he would let you go with him."

"I'd rather give up the case this moment, sir, than even stay here while it's suggested," answered the nurse. With sudden firmness.

"I hadn't really decided to suggest it," said the doctor, with his slight nervousness. "We'll try the experiment. Dickon's a lad I'd trust with a new-born child."

The strongest footman in the house carried Colin down stairs and put him in his wheeled chair near which Dickon waited outside. After the manservant had arranged his rugs and cushions the Rajah waved his hand to him and to the nurse.

"You have my permission to go," he said, and they both disappeared quickly and it must be confessed giggled when they were safely inside the house.

Dickon began to push the wheeled chair slowly and steadily. Mistress Mary walked beside it and Colin leaned back and lifted his face to the sky. The arch of it looked very high and the small snowy clouds seemed like white birds floating on outspread wings below its crystal blueness. The wind swept in soft big breaths down from the moor and was strange with a wild clear scented sweetness. Colin kept lifting his thin chest to draw it in, and his big eyes looked as if it were they which were listening—listening, instead of his ears.

"There are so many sounds of singing and humming and calling out," he said. "What is that scent the puffs of wind bring?"

"It's gorse on th' moor that's openin' out," answered Dickon. "Eh! th' bees are at it wonderful today."

Not a human creature was to be caught sight of in the paths they took. In fact every gardener or gardener's lad had been witched away. But they wound in and out among the shrubbery and out and round the fountain beds, following their carefully planned route for the mere mysterious pleasure of it. But when at last they turned into the Long Walk by the ivied walls the excited sense of an approaching thrill made them, for some curious reason they could not have explained, begin to speak in whispers.

"This is it," breathed Mary. "This is where I used to walk up and down and wonder and wonder." "Is it?" cried Colin, and his eyes began to search the ivy with eager curiousness. "But I can see nothing," he whispered. "There is no door."

"That's what I thought," said Mary.

Then there was a lovely breathless silence and the chair wheeled on.

"That is the garden where Ben Weatherstaff works," said Mary.

"Is it?" said Colin.

A few yards more and Mary whispered again.

"This is where the robin flew over the wall," she said.

"Is it?" cried Colin. "Oh! I wish he'd come again!"

"And that," said Mary with solemn delight, pointing under a big lilac bush, "is where he perched on the little heap of earth and showed me the key."

Then Colin sat up.

"Where? Where? There?" he cried, and his eyes were as big as the wolf's in Red Riding-Hood, when Red Riding-Hood felt called upon to remark on them. Dickon stood still and the wheeled chair stopped.

"And this," said Mary, stepping on to the bed close to the ivy, "is where I went to talk to him when he chirped at me from the top of the wall. And this is the ivy the wind blew back," and she took hold of the hanging green curtain.

"Oh! is it—is it!" gasped Colin.

"And here is the handle, and here is the door. Dickon push him in—push him in quickly!"

And Dickon did it with one strong, steady, splendid push.

But Colin had actually dropped back against his cushions, even though he gasped with delight, and he had covered his eyes with his hands and held them there shutting out everything until they were inside and the chair stopped as if by magic and the door was closed. Not till then did he take them away and look round and round and round as Dickon and Mary had done. And over walls and earth and trees and swinging sprays and tendrils the fair green veil of tender little leaves had crept, and in the grass under the trees and the gray urns in the alcoves and here and there everywhere were touches or splashes of gold and purple and white and the trees were showing pink and snow above his head and there were fluttering of wings and faint sweet pipes and humming and scents and scents. And the sun fell warm upon his face like a hand with a lovely touch. And in wonder Mary and Dickon stood and stared at him. He looked so strange and different because a pink glow of color had actually crept all over him—ivory face and neck and hands and all.

"I shall get well! I shall get well!" he cried out. "Mary! Dickon! I shall get well! And I shall live forever and ever and ever!"

21

Ben Weatherstaff

One of the strange things about living in the world is that it is only now and then one is quite sure one is going to live forever and ever and ever. One knows it sometimes when one gets up at the tender solemn dawn-time and goes out and stands alone and throws one's head far back and looks up and up and watches the pale sky slowly changing and flushing and marvelous unknown things happening until the East almost makes one cry out and one's heart stands still at the strange unchanging majesty of the rising of the sun—which has been happening every morning for thousands and thousands and thousands of years. One knows it then for a moment or so. And one knows it sometimes when one stands by oneself in a wood at sunset and the mysterious deep gold stillness slanting through and under the branches seems to be saying slowly again and again something one cannot quite hear, however much one tries. Then sometimes the immense quiet of the dark blue at night with millions of stars waiting and watching makes one sure; and sometimes a sound of far-off music makes it true; and sometimes a look in someone's eyes.

And it was like that with Colin when he first saw and heard and felt the Springtime inside the four high walls of a hidden garden. That afternoon the whole world seemed to devote itself to being perfect and radiantly beautiful and kind to one boy. Perhaps out of pure heavenly goodness the spring came and crowned everything it possibly could into that one place. More than once Dickon paused in what he was doing and stood still with a sort of growing wonder in his eyes, shaking his head softly.

"Eh! it is graidely," he said. "I'm twelve goin' on thirteen an' there's a lot o' afternoons in thirteen years, but seems to me like I never seed one as graidely as this 'ere."

"Aye, it is a graidely one," said Mary, and she sighed for mere joy. "I'll warrant it's the graidelest one as ever was in this world."

"Does tha' think," said Colin with dreamy carefulness, "as happen it was made loike this 'ere all o' purpose for me?"

"My word!" cried Mary admiringly, "that there is a bit o' good Yorkshire. Tha'rt shapin' first-rate—that tha' art."

And delight reigned. They drew the chair under the plum-tree, which was snow-white with blossoms and musical with bees. It was like a king's canopy, a fairy king's. There were flowering cherry-trees near and apple-trees whose buds were pink and white, and here and there one had burst open wide. Between the blossoming branches of the canopy bits of blue sky looked down like wonderful eyes.

Mary and Dickon worked a little here and there and Colin watched them. They brought him things to look at—buds which were opening, buds which were tight closed, bits of twig whose leaves were just showing green, the feather of a woodpecker which had dropped on the grass, the empty shell of some bird early hatched. Dickon pushed the chair slowly round and round the garden, stopping every other moment to let him look at wonders springing out of the earth or trailing down from trees. It was like being taken in state round the country of a magic king and queen and shown all the mysterious riches it contained.

"I wonder if we shall see the robin?" said Colin.

"Tha'll see him often enow after a bit," answered Dickon. "When th' eggs hatches out th' little chap he'll be kep' so busy it'll make his head swim. Tha'll see him flyin' backward an' for'ard carryin' worms nigh as big as himsel' an' that much noise goin' on in th' nest when he gets there as fair flusters him so as he scarce knows which big mouth to drop th' first piece in. An' gapin' beaks an' squawks on every side. Mother says as when she sees th' work a robin has to keep them gapin' beaks filled, she feels like she was a lady with nothin' to do. She says she's seen th' little chaps when it seemed like th' sweat must be droppin' off 'em, though folk can't see it."

This made them giggle so delightedly that they were obliged to cover their mouths with their hands, remembering that they must not be heard. Colin had been instructed as to the law of whispers and low voices several days before. He liked the mysteriousness of it and did his best, but in the midst of excited enjoyment it is rather difficult never to laugh above a whisper.

Every moment of the afternoon was full of new things and every hour the sunshine grew more golden. The wheeled chair had been drawn back under the canopy and Dickon had sat down on the grass and had just drawn out his pipe when Colin saw something he had not had time to notice before.

"That's a very old tree over there, isn't it?" he said. Dickon looked across the grass at the tree and Mary looked and there was a brief moment of stillness.

"Yes," answered Dickon, after it, and his low voice had a very gentle sound.

Mary gazed at the tree and thought.

"The branches are quite gray and there's not a single leaf anywhere," Colin went on. "It's quite dead, isn't it?"

"Aye," admitted Dickon. "But them roses as has climbed all over it will near hide every bit o' th' dead wood when they're full o' leaves an' flowers. It won't look dead then. It'll be th' prettiest of all."

Mary still gazed at the tree and thought.

"It looks as if a big branch had been broken off," said Colin. "I wonder how it was done."

"It's been done many a year," answered Dickon. "Eh!" with a

sudden relieved start and laying his hand on Colin. "Look at that robin! There he is! He's been foragin' for his mate."

Colin was almost too late but he just caught sight of him, the flash of red-breasted bird with something in his beak. He darted through the greenness and into the close-grown corner and was out of sight. Colin leaned back on his cushion again, laughing a little. "He's taking her tea to her. Perhaps it's five o'clock. I think I'd like some tea myself."

And so they were safe.

"It was Magic which sent the robin," said Mary secretly to Dickon afterward. "I know it was Magic." For both she and Dickon had been afraid Colin might ask something about the tree whose branch had broken off ten years ago and they had talked it over together and Dickon had stood and rubbed his head in a troubled way.

"We mun look as if it wasn't no different from th' other trees," he had said. "We couldn't never tell him how it broke, poor lad. If he says anything about it we mun—we mun try to look cheerful."

"Aye, that we mun," had answered Mary.

But she had not felt as if she looked cheerful when she gazed at the tree. She wondered and wondered in those few moments if there was any reality in that other thing Dickon had said. He had gone on rubbing his rust-red hair in a puzzled way, but a nice comforted look had begun to grow in his blue eyes.

"Mrs. Craven was a very lovely young lady," he had gone on rather hesitatingly. "An' mother she thinks maybe she's about Misselthwaite many a time lookin' after Mester Colin, same as all mothers do when they're took out o' th' world. They have to come back, tha' sees. Happen she's been in the garden an' happen it was her set us to work, an' told us to bring him here."

Mary had thought he meant something about Magic. She was a great believer in Magic. Secretly she quite believed that Dickon worked Magic, of course good Magic, on everything near him and that was why people liked him so much and wild creatures knew he was their friend. She wondered, indeed, if it were not possible that his gift had brought the robin just at the right moment when Colin asked that dangerous question. She felt that his Magic was working all the afternoon and making Colin look like an entirely different boy. It did not seem possible that he could be the crazy creature who had screamed and beaten and bitten his pillow. Even his ivory whiteness seemed to change. The faint glow of color which had shown on his face and neck and hands when he first got inside the garden really never quite died away. He looked as if he were made of flesh instead of ivory or wax.

They saw the robin carry food to his mate two or three times, and it was so suggestive of afternoon tea that Colin felt they must have some.

"Go and make one of the men servants bring some in a basket to the rhododendron walk," he said. "And then you and Dickon can bring it here."

It was an agreeable idea, easily carried out, and when the white cloth was spread upon the grass, with hot tea and buttered toast and crumpets, a delightfully hungry meal was eaten, and several birds on domestic errands paused to inquire what was going on and were led into investigating crumbs with great activity. Nut and Shell whisked up trees with pieces of cake and Soot took the entire half of a buttered crumpet into a corner and pecked at and examined and turned it over and made hoarse remarks about it until he decided to swallow it all joyfully in one gulp.

The afternoon was dragging towards its mellow hour. The sun was deepening the gold of its lances, the bees were going home and the birds were flying past less often. Dickon and Mary were sitting on the grass, the tea-basket was repacked ready to be taken back to the house, and Colin was lying against his cushions with his heavy locks pushed back from his forehead and his face looking quite a natural color.

"I don't want this afternoon to go," he said; "but I shall come back tomorrow, and the day after, and the day after, and the day after."

"You'll get plenty of fresh air, won't you?" said Mary. "I'm going to get nothing else," he answered. "I've seen the spring now and I'm going to see the summer. I'm going to see everything grow here. I'm going to grow here myself."

"That tha' will," said Dickon. "Us'll have thee walkin' about here an' diggin' same as other folk afore long."

Colin flushed tremendously.

"Walk!" he said. "Dig! Shall I?"

Dickon's glance at him was delicately cautious. Neither he nor Mary had ever asked if anything was the matter with his legs.

"For sure tha' will," he said stoutly. "Tha—tha's got legs o' thine own, same as other folks!"

Mary was rather frightened until she heard Colin's answer.

"Nothing really ails them," he said, "but they are so thin and weak. They shake so that I'm afraid to try to stand on them."

Both Mary and Dickon drew a relieved breath.

"When tha' stops bein' afraid tha'lt stand on 'em," Dickon said with renewed cheer. "An' tha'lt stop bein' afraid in a bit."

"I shall?" said Colin, and he lay still as if he were wondering about things.

They were really very quiet for a little while. The sun was dropping lower. It was that hour when everything stills itself, and they really had had a busy and exciting afternoon. Colin looked as if he were resting luxuriously. Even the creatures had ceased moving about and had drawn together and were resting near them. Soot had perched on a low branch and drawn up one leg and dropped the gray film drowsily over his eyes. Mary privately thought he looked as if he might snore in a minute.

In the midst of this stillness it was rather startling when Colin half lifted his head and exclaimed in a loud suddenly alarmed whisper:

"Who is that man?" Dickon and Mary scrambled to their feet.

"Man!" they both cried in low quick voices.

Colin pointed to the high wall. "Look!" he whispered excitedly. "Just look!"

Mary and Dickon wheeled about and looked. There was Ben Weatherstaff's indignant face glaring at them over the wall from the top of a ladder! He actually shook his fist at Mary.

"If I wasn't a bachelder, an' tha' was a wench o' mine," he cried, "I'd give thee a hidin'!"

He mounted another step threateningly as if it were his energetic intention to jump down and deal with her; but as she came toward him he evidently thought better of it and stood on the top step of his ladder shaking his fist down at her.

"I never thowt much o' thee!" he harangued. "I couldna' abide thee th' first time I set eyes on thee. A scrawny buttermilk-faced young besom, allus askin' questions an' pokin' tha' nose where it wasna, wanted. I never knowed how tha' got so thick wi' me. If it hadna' been for th' robin—Drat him—"

"Ben Weatherstaff," called out Mary, finding her breath. She stood below him and called up to him with a sort of gasp. "Ben Weatherstaff, it was the robin who showed me the way!"

Then it did seem as if Ben really would scramble down on her side of the wall, he was so outraged.

"Tha' young bad 'un!" he called down at her. "Layin' tha' badness on a robin—not but what he's impidint enow for anythin'. Him showin' thee th' way! Him! Eh! tha' young nowt"—she could see his next words burst out because he was overpowered by curiosity—"however i' this world did tha' get in?"

"It was the robin who showed me the way," she protested obstinately. "He didn't know he was doing it but he did. And I can't tell you from here while you're shaking your fist at me."

He stopped shaking his fist very suddenly at that very moment and his jaw actually dropped as he stared over her head at something he saw coming over the grass toward him.

At the first sound of his torrent of words Colin had been so surprised that he had only sat up and listened as if he were spellbound. But in the midst of it he had recovered himself and beckoned imperiously to Dickon.

"Wheel me over there!" he commanded. "Wheel me quite close and stop right in front of him!"

And this, if you please, this is what Ben Weatherstaff beheld and which made his jaw drop. A wheeled chair with luxurious cushions and robes which came toward him looking rather like some sort of State Coach because a young Rajah leaned back in it with royal command in his great black-rimmed eyes and a thin white hand extended haughtily toward him. And it stopped right under Ben Weatherstaff's nose. It was really no wonder his mouth dropped open.

"Do you know who I am?" demanded the Rajah.

How Ben Weatherstaff stared! His red old eyes fixed themselves on what was before him as if he were seeing a ghost. He gazed and gazed and gulped a lump down his throat and did not say a word. "Do you know who I am?" demanded Colin still more imperiously. "Answer!"

Ben Weatherstaff put his gnarled hand up and passed it over his eyes and over his forehead and then he did answer in a queer shaky voice.

"Who tha' art?" he said. "Aye, that I do—wi' tha' mother's eyes starin' at me out o' tha' face. Lord knows how tha' come here. But tha'rt th' poor cripple."

Colin forgot that he had ever had a back. His face flushed scarlet and he sat bolt upright.

"I'm not a cripple!" he cried out furiously. "I'm not!"

"He's not!" cried Mary, almost shouting up the wall in her fierce indignation. "He's not got a lump as big as a pin! I looked and there was none there—not one!"

Ben Weatherstaff passed his hand over his forehead again and gazed as if he could never gaze enough. His hand shook and his mouth shook and his voice shook. He was an ignorant old man and a tactless old man and he could only remember the things he had heard.

"Tha'—tha' hasn't got a crooked back?" he said hoarsely.

"No!" shouted Colin.

"Tha'—tha' hasn't got crooked legs?" quavered Ben more hoarsely yet. It was too much. The strength which Colin usually threw into his tantrums rushed through him now in a new way. Never yet had he been accused of crooked legs—even in whispers—and the perfectly simple belief in their existence which was revealed by Ben Weatherstaff's voice was more than Rajah flesh and blood could endure. His anger and insulted pride made him forget everything but this one moment and filled him with a power he had never known before, an almost unnatural strength.

"Come here!" he shouted to Dickon, and he actually began to tear the coverings off his lower limbs and disentangle himself. "Come here! Come here! This minute!"

Dickon was by his side in a second. Mary caught her breath in a short gasp and felt herself turn pale.

"He can do it! He can do it! He can do it! He can!" she gabbled over to herself under her breath as fast as ever she could.

There was a brief fierce scramble, the rugs were tossed on the ground, Dickon held Colin's arm, the thin legs were out, the thin feet were on the grass. Colin was standing upright—upright—as straight as an arrow and looking strangely tall—his head thrown back and his strange eyes flashing lightning. "Look at me!" he flung up at Ben Weatherstaff. "Just look at me—you! Just look at me!"

"He's as straight as I am!" cried Dickon. "He's as straight as any lad i' Yorkshire!"

What Ben Weatherstaff did Mary thought queer beyond measure. He choked and gulped and suddenly tears ran down his weather-wrinkled cheeks as he struck his old hands together.

"Eh!" he burst forth, "th' lies folk tells! Tha'rt as thin as a lath an' as white as a wraith, but there's not a knob on thee. Tha'lt make a mon yet. God bless thee!"

Dickon held Colin's arm strongly but the boy had not begun to falter. He stood straighter and straighter and looked Ben Weatherstaff in the face.

"I'm your master," he said, "when my father is away. And you are to obey me. This is my garden. Don't dare to say a word about it! You get down from that ladder and go out to the Long Walk and Miss Mary will meet you and bring you here. I want to talk to you. We did not want you, but now you will have to be in the secret. Be quick!"

Ben Weatherstaff's crabbed old face was still wet with that one queer rush of tears. It seemed as if he could not take his eyes from thin straight Colin standing on his feet with his head thrown back.

"Eh! lad," he almost whispered. "Eh! my lad!" And then remembering himself he suddenly touched his hat gardener fashion and said, "Yes, sir! Yes, sir!" and obediently disappeared as he descended the ladder.

22

When the Sun Went Down

When his head was out of sight Colin turned to Mary.

"Go and meet him," he said; and Mary flew across the grass to the door under the ivy.

Dickon was watching him with sharp eyes. There were scarlet spots on his cheeks and he looked amazing, but he showed no signs of falling.

"I can stand," he said, and his head was still held up and he said it quite grandly.

"I told thee tha' could as soon as tha' stopped bein' afraid," answered Dickon. "An' tha's stopped."

"Yes, I've stopped," said Colin.

Then suddenly he remembered something Mary had said.

"Are you making Magic?" he asked sharply.

Dickon's curly mouth spread in a cheerful grin.

"Tha's doin' Magic thysel'," he said. "It's same Magic as made these 'ere work out o' th' earth," and he touched with his thick boot a clump of crocuses in the grass. Colin looked down at them.

"Aye," he said slowly, "there couldna' be bigger Magic than that there—there couldna' be."

He drew himself up straighter than ever.

"I'm going to walk to that tree," he said, pointing to one a few feet away from him. "I'm going to be standing when Weatherstaff comes here. I can rest against the tree if I like. When I want to sit down I will sit down, but not before. Bring a rug from the chair."

He walked to the tree and though Dickon held his arm he was wonderfully steady. When he stood against the tree trunk it was not too plain that he supported himself against it, and he still held himself so straight that he looked tall.

When Ben Weatherstaff came through the door in the wall he saw him standing there and he heard Mary muttering something under her breath.

"What art sayin'?" he asked rather testily because he did not want his attention distracted from the long thin straight boy figure and proud face.

But she did not tell him. What she was saying was this:

"You can do it! You can do it! I told you you could! You can do it! You can do it! You *can*!" She was saying it to Colin because she wanted to make Magic and keep him on his feet looking like that. She could not bear that he should give in before Ben Weatherstaff. He did not give in. She was uplifted by a sudden feeling that he looked quite beautiful in spite of his thinness. He fixed his eyes on Ben Weatherstaff in his funny imperious way.

"Look at me!" he commanded. "Look at me all over! Am I a hunchback? Have I got crooked legs?"

Ben Weatherstaff had not quite got over his emotion, but he had recovered a little and answered almost in his usual way.

"Not tha'," he said. "Nowt o' th' sort. What's tha' been doin' with thysel'—hidin' out o' sight an' lettin' folk think tha' was cripple an' half-witted?"

"Half-witted!" said Colin angrily. "Who thought that?"

"Lots o' fools," said Ben. "Th' world's full o' jackasses brayin' an' they never bray nowt but lies. What did tha' shut thysel' up for?"

"Everyone thought I was going to die," said Colin shortly. "I'm not!"

And he said it with such decision Ben Weatherstaff looked him over, up and down, down and up.

"Tha' die!" he said with dry exultation. "Nowt o' th' sort! Tha's got too much pluck in thee. When I seed thee put tha' legs on th' ground in such a hurry I knowed tha' was all right. Sit thee down on th' rug a bit young Mester an' give me thy orders."

There was a queer mixture of crabbed tenderness and shrewd understanding in his manner. Mary had poured out speech as rapidly as she could as they had come down the Long Walk. The chief thing to be remembered, she had told him, was that Colin was getting well—getting well. The garden was doing it. No one must let him remember about having humps and dying.

The Rajah condescended to seat himself on a rug under the tree.

"What work do you do in the gardens, Weatherstaff?" he inquired.

"Anythin' I'm told to do," answered old Ben. "I'm kep' on by favor—because she liked me."

"She?" said Colin.

"Tha' mother," answered Ben Weatherstaff.

"My mother?" said Colin, and he looked about him quietly. "This was her garden, wasn't it?"

"Aye, it was that!" and Ben Weatherstaff looked about him too. "She were main fond of it."

"It is my garden now. I am fond of it. I shall come here every day," announced Colin. "But it is to be a secret. My orders are that no one is to know that we come here. Dickon and my cousin have worked and made it come alive. I shall send for you sometimes to help—but you must come when no one can see you."

Ben Weatherstaff's face twisted itself in a dry old smile.

"I've come here before when no one saw me," he said.

"What!" exclaimed Colin.

"When?"

"Th' last time I was here," rubbing his chin and looking round, "was about two year' ago."

"But no one has been in it for ten years!" cried Colin. "There was no door!"

"I'm no one," said old Ben dryly. "An' I didn't come through th' door. I come over th' wall. Th' rheumatics held me back th' last two year'."

"Tha' come an' did a bit o' prunin'!" cried Dickon. "I couldn't make out how it had been done."

"She was so fond of it—she was!" said Ben Weatherstaff slowly. "An' she was such a pretty young thing. She says to me once, 'Ben,' says she laughin', 'if ever I'm ill or if I go away you must take care of my roses.' When she did go away th' orders was no one was ever to come nigh. But I come," with grumpy obstinacy. "Over th' wall I come—until th' rheumatics stopped me—an' I did a bit o' work once a year. She'd gave her order first."

"It wouldn't have been as wick as it is if tha' hadn't done it," said Dickon. "I did wonder."

"I'm glad you did it, Weatherstaff," said Colin. "You'll know how to keep the secret."

"Aye, I'll know, sir," answered Ben. "An' it'll be easier for a man wi' rheumatics to come in at th' door."

On the grass near the tree Mary had dropped her trowel. Colin stretched out his hand and took it up. An odd expression came into his face and he began to scratch at the earth. His thin hand was weak enough but presently as they watched him—Mary with quite breathless interest—he drove the end of the trowel into the soil and turned some over.

"You can do it! You can do it!" said Mary to herself. "I tell you, you can!"

Dickon's round eyes were full of eager curiousness but he said not a word. Ben Weatherstaff looked on with interested face.

Colin persevered. After he had turned a few trowelfuls of soil he spoke exultantly to Dickon in his best Yorkshire.

"Tha' said as tha'd have me walkin' about here same as other folk—an' tha' said tha'd have me diggin'. I thowt tha' was just leein' to please me. This is only th' first day an' I've walked—an' here I am diggin'."

Ben Weatherstaff's mouth fell open again when he heard him, but he ended by chuckling.

"Eh!" he said, "that sounds as if tha'd got wits enow. Tha'rt a Yorkshire lad for sure. An' tha'rt diggin', too. How'd tha' like to plant a bit o' somethin'? I can get thee a rose in a pot."

"Go and get it!" said Colin, digging excitedly. "Quick! Quick!"

It was done quickly enough indeed. Ben Weatherstaff went his way forgetting rheumatics. Dickon took his spade and dug the hole deeper and wider than a new digger with thin white hands could make it. Mary slipped out to run and bring back a watering-can. When Dickon had deepened the hole Colin went on turning the soft earth over and over. He looked up at the sky, flushed and glowing with the strangely new exercise, slight as it was.

"I want to do it before the sun goes quite—quite down," he said.

Mary thought that perhaps the sun held back a few minutes just on purpose. Ben Weatherstaff brought the rose in its pot from the greenhouse. He hobbled over the grass as fast as he could. He had begun to be excited, too. He knelt down by the hole and broke the pot from the mould.

"Here, lad," he said, handing the plant to Colin. "Set it in the earth thysel' same as th' king does when he goes to a new place."

The thin white hands shook a little and Colin's flush grew deeper as he set the rose in the mould and held it while old Ben made firm the earth. It was filled in and pressed down and made steady. Mary was leaning forward on her hands and knees. Soot had flown down and marched forward to see what was being done. Nut and Shell chattered about it from a cherry-tree.

"It's planted!" said Colin at last. "And the sun is only slipping over the edge. Help me up, Dickon. I want to be standing when it goes. That's part of the Magic."

And Dickon helped him, and the Magic—or whatever it was—so gave him strength that when the sun did slip over the edge and end the strange lovely afternoon for them there he actually stood on his two feet—laughing.

23

Magic

Dr. Craven had been waiting some time at the house when they returned to it. He had indeed begun to wonder if it might not be wise to send someone out to explore the garden paths. When Colin was brought back to his room the poor man looked him over seriously.

"You should not have stayed so long," he said. "You must not overexert yourself."

"I am not tired at all," said Colin. "It has made me well. Tomorrow I am going out in the morning as well as in the afternoon."

"I am not sure that I can allow it," answered Dr. Craven. "I am afraid it would not be wise."

"It would not be wise to try to stop me," said Colin quite seriously. "I am going."

Even Mary had found out that one of Colin's chief peculiarities was that he did not know in the least what a rude little brute he was with his way of ordering people about. He had lived on a sort of desert island all his life and as he had been the king of it he had made his own manners and had had no one to compare himself with. Mary had indeed been rather like him herself and since she had been at Misselthwaite had gradually discovered that her own manners had not been of the kind which is usual or popular. Having made this discovery she naturally thought it of enough interest to communicate to Colin. So she sat and looked at him curiously for a few minutes after Dr. Craven had gone. She wanted to make him ask her why she was doing it and of course she did.

"What are you looking at me for?" he said.

"I'm thinking that I am rather sorry for Dr. Craven."

"So am I," said Colin calmly, but not without an air of some satisfaction. "He won't get Misselthwaite at all now I'm not going to die."

"I'm sorry for him because of that, of course," said Mary, "but I was thinking just then that it must have been very horrid to have had to be polite for ten years to a boy who was always rude. I would never have done it."

"Am I rude?" Colin inquired undisturbedly.

"If you had been his own boy and he had been a slapping sort of man," said Mary, "he would have slapped you."

"But he daren't," said Colin.

"No, he daren't," answered Mistress Mary, thinking the thing out quite without prejudice. "Nobody ever dared to do anything you didn't like—because you were going to die and things like that. You were such a poor thing."

"But," announced Colin stubbornly, "I am not going to be a poor thing. I won't let people think I'm one. I stood on my feet this afternoon."

"It is always having your own way that has made you so queer," Mary went on, thinking aloud.

Colin turned his head, frowning.

"Am I queer?" he demanded.

"Yes," answered Mary, "very. But you needn't be cross," she added impartially, "because so am I queer—and so is Ben Weatherstaff. But I am not as queer as I was before I began to like people and before I found the garden."

"I don't want to be queer," said Colin. "I am not going to be," and he frowned again with determination.

He was a very proud boy. He lay thinking for a while and then Mary saw his beautiful smile begin and gradually change his whole face.

"I shall stop being queer," he said, "if I go every day to the garden. There is Magic in there—good Magic, you know, Mary. I am sure there is." "So am I," said Mary.

"Even if it isn't real Magic," Colin said, "we can pretend it is. *Something* is there—*something*!"

"It's Magic," said Mary, "but not black. It's as white as snow."

They always called it Magic and indeed it seemed like it in the months that followed—the wonderful months—the radiant months—the amazing ones. Oh! the things which happened in that garden! If you have never had a garden you cannot understand, and if you have had a garden you will know that it would take a whole book to describe all that came to pass there. At first it seemed that green things would never cease pushing their way through the earth, in the grass, in the beds, even in the crevices of the walls. Then the green things began to show buds and the buds began to unfurl and show color, every shade of blue, every shade of purple, every tint and hue of crimson. In its happy days flowers had been tucked away into every inch and hole and corner. Ben Weatherstaff had seen it done and had himself scraped out mortar from between the bricks of the wall and made pockets of earth for lovely clinging things to grow on. Iris and white lilies rose out of the grass in sheaves, and the green alcoves filled themselves with amazing armies of the blue and white flower lances of tall delphiniums or columbines or campanulas.

"She was main fond o' them—she was," Ben Weatherstaff said. "She liked them things as was allus pointin' up to th' blue sky, she used to tell. Not as she was one o' them as looked down on th' earth—not her. She just loved it but she said as th' blue sky allus looked so joyful."

The seeds Dickon and Mary had planted grew as if fairies had tended them. Satiny poppies of all tints danced in the breeze by the score, gaily defying flowers which had lived in the garden for years and which it might be confessed seemed rather to wonder how such new people had got there. And the roses—the roses! Rising out of the grass, tangled round the sun-dial, wreathing the tree trunks and hanging from their branches, climbing up the walls and spreading over them with long garlands falling in cascades—they came alive day by day, hour by hour. Fair fresh leaves, and buds—and buds—tiny at first but swelling and working Magic until they burst and uncurled into cups of scent delicately spilling themselves over their brims and filling the garden air.

Colin saw it all, watching each change as it took place. Every morning he was brought out and every hour of each day when it didn't rain he spent in the garden. Even gray days pleased him. He would lie on the grass "watching things growing," he said. If you watched long enough, he declared, you could see buds unsheath themselves. Also you could make the acquaintance of strange busy insect things running about on various unknown but evidently serious errands, sometimes carrying tiny scraps of straw or feather or food, or climbing blades of grass as if they were trees from whose tops one could look out to explore the country. A mole throwing up its mound at the end of its burrow and making its way out at last with the long-nailed paws which looked so like elfish hands, had absorbed him one whole morning. Ants' ways, beetles' ways, bees' ways, frogs' ways, birds' ways, plants' ways, gave him a new world to explore and when Dickon revealed them all and added foxes' ways, otters' ways, ferrets' ways, squirrels' ways, and trout' and water-rats' and badgers' ways, there was no end to the things to talk about and think over.

And this was not the half of the Magic. The fact that he had really once stood on his feet had set Colin thinking tremendously and when Mary told him of the spell she had worked he was excited and approved of it greatly. He talked of it constantly.

"Of course there must be lots of Magic in the world," he said wisely one day, "but people don't know what it is like or how to make it. Perhaps the beginning is just to say nice things are going to happen until you make them happen. I am going to try and experiment."

The next morning when they went to the secret garden he sent at once for Ben Weatherstaff. Ben came as quickly as he could and found the Rajah standing on his feet under a tree and looking very grand but also very beautifully smiling.

"Good morning, Ben Weatherstaff," he said. "I want you and Dickon and Miss Mary to stand in a row and listen to me because I am going to tell you something very important."

"Aye, aye, sir!" answered Ben Weatherstaff, touching his forehead. (One of the long concealed charms of Ben Weatherstaff was that in his boyhood he had once run away to sea and had made voyages. So he could reply like a sailor.)

"I am going to try a scientific experiment," explained the Rajah. "When I grow up I am going to make great scientific discoveries and I am going to begin now with this experiment."

"Aye, aye, sir!" said Ben Weatherstaff promptly, though this was the first time he had heard of great scientific discoveries.

It was the first time Mary had heard of them, either, but even at this stage she had begun to realize that, queer as he was, Colin had read about a great many singular things and was somehow a very convincing sort of boy. When he held up his head and fixed his strange eyes on you it seemed as if you believed him almost in spite of yourself though he was only ten years old—going on eleven. At this moment he was especially convincing because he suddenly felt the fascination of actually making a sort of speech like a grown-up person.

"The great scientific discoveries I am going to make," he went on, "will be about Magic. Magic is a great thing and scarcely anyone knows anything about it except a few people in old books—and Mary a little, because she was born in India where there are fakirs. I believe Dickon knows some Magic, but perhaps he doesn't know he knows it. He charms animals and people. I would never have let him come to see me if he had not been an animal charmer—which is a boy charmer, too, because a boy is an animal. I am sure there is Magic in everything, only we have not sense enough to get hold of it and make it do things for us—like electricity and horses and steam."

This sounded so imposing that Ben Weatherstaff became quite excited and really could not keep still. "Aye, aye, sir," he said and he began to stand up quite straight.

"When Mary found this garden it looked quite dead," the orator proceeded. "Then something began pushing things up out of the soil and making things out of nothing. One day things weren't there and another they were. I had never watched things before and it made me feel very curious. Scientific people are always curious and I am going to be scientific. I keep saying to myself, 'What is it? What is it?' It's something. It can't be nothing! I don't know its name so I call it Magic. I have never seen the sun rise but Mary and Dickon have and from what they tell me I am sure that is Magic too. Something pushes it up and draws it. Sometimes since I've been in the garden I've looked up through the trees at the sky and I have had a strange feeling of being happy as if something were pushing and drawing in my chest and making me breathe fast. Magic is always pushing and drawing and making things out of nothing. Everything is made out of Magic, leaves and trees, flowers and birds, badgers and foxes and squirrels and people. So it must be all around us. In this garden—in all the places. The Magic in this garden has made me stand up and know I am going to live to be a man. I am going to make the scientific experiment of trying to get some and put it in myself and make it push and draw me and make me strong. I don't know how to do it but I think that if you keep thinking about it and calling it perhaps it will come. Perhaps that is the first baby way to get it. When I was going to try to stand that first time Mary kept saying to herself as fast as she could, 'You can do it! You can do it!' and I did. I had to try myself at the same time, of course, but her Magic helped me—and so did Dickon's. Every morning and evening and as often in the daytime as I can remember I am going to say, 'Magic is in me! Magic is making me well! I am going to be as strong as Dickon, as strong as Dickon!' And you must all do it, too. That is my experiment Will you help, Ben Weatherstaff?"

"Aye, aye, sir!" said Ben Weatherstaff. "Aye, aye!"

"If you keep doing it every day as regularly as soldiers go through drill we shall see what will happen and find out if the experiment succeeds. You learn things by saying them over and over and thinking about them until they stay in your mind forever and I think it will be the same with Magic. If you keep calling it to come to you and help you it will get to be part of you and it will stay and do things." "I once heard an officer in India tell my mother that there were fakirs who said words over and over thousands of times," said Mary.

"I've heard Jem Fettleworth's wife say th' same thing over thousands o' times—callin' Jem a drunken brute," said Ben Weatherstaff dryly. "Summat allus comes o' that, sure enough. He gave her a good hidin' an' went to th' Blue Lion an' got as drunk as a lord."

Colin drew his brows together and thought a few minutes. Then he cheered up.

"Well," he said, "you see something did come of it. She used the wrong Magic until she made him beat her. If she'd used the right Magic and had said something nice perhaps he wouldn't have got as drunk as a lord and perhaps—perhaps he might have bought her a new bonnet."

Ben Weatherstaff chuckled and there was shrewd admiration in his little old eyes.

"Tha'rt a clever lad as well as a straight-legged one, Mester Colin," he said. "Next time I see Bess Fettleworth I'll give her a bit of a hint o' what Magic will do for her. She'd be rare an' pleased if th' sinetifik 'speriment worked—an' so 'ud Jem."

Dickon had stood listening to the lecture, his round eyes shining with curious delight. Nut and Shell were on his shoulders and he held a long-eared white rabbit in his arm and stroked and stroked it softly while it laid its ears along its back and enjoyed itself.

"Do you think the experiment will work?" Colin asked him, wondering what he was thinking. He so often wondered what Dickon was thinking when he saw him looking at him or at one of his "creatures" with his happy wide smile.

He smiled now and his smile was wider than usual.

"Aye," he answered, "that I do. It'll work same as th' seeds do when th' sun shines on 'em. It'll work for sure. Shall us begin it now?"

Colin was delighted and so was Mary. Fired by recollections of fakirs and devotees in illustrations Colin suggested that they should all sit cross-legged under the tree which made a canopy.

"It will be like sitting in a sort of temple," said Colin. "I'm rather tired and I want to sit down."

"Eh!" said Dickon, "tha' mustn't begin by sayin' tha'rt tired. Tha' might spoil th' Magic."

Colin turned and looked at him—into his innocent round eyes.

"That's true," he said slowly. "I must only think of the Magic."

It all seemed most majestic and mysterious when they sat down in their circle. Ben Weatherstaff felt as if he had somehow been led into appearing at a prayer meeting. Ordinarily he was very fixed in being what he called "agen' prayer meetin's" but this being the Rajah's affair he did not resent it and was indeed inclined to be gratified at being called upon to assist. Mistress Mary felt solemnly enraptured. Dickon held his rabbit in his arm, and perhaps he made some charmer's signal no one heard, for when he sat down, cross-legged like the rest, the crow, the fox, the squirrels and the lamb slowly drew near and made part of the circle, settling each into a place of rest as if of their own desire.

"The 'creatures' have come," said Colin gravely. "They want to help us."

Colin really looked quite beautiful, Mary thought. He held his head high as if he felt like a sort of priest and his strange eyes had a wonderful look in them. The light shone on him through the tree canopy.

"Now we will begin," he said. "Shall we sway backward and forward, Mary, as if we were dervishes?"

"I canna' do no swayin' back'ard and for'ard," said Ben Weatherstaff. "I've got th' rheumatics."

"The Magic will take them away," said Colin in a High Priest tone, "but we won't sway until it has done it. We will only chant."

"I canna' do no chantin'" said Ben Weatherstaff a trifle testily. "They turned me out o' th' church choir th' only time I ever tried it."

No one smiled. They were all too much in earnest. Colin's face was not even crossed by a shadow. He was thinking only of the Magic.

"Then I will chant," he said. And he began, looking like a strange boy spirit. "The sun is shining—the sun is shining. That is the Magic. The flowers are growing—the roots are stirring. That is the Magic. Being alive is the Magic—being strong is the Magic. The Magic is in me—the Magic is in me. It is in me—it is in me. It's in every one of us. It's in Ben Weatherstaff's back. Magic! Magic! Come and help!"

He said it a great many times—not a thousand times but quite a goodly number. Mary listened entranced. She felt as if it were at once queer and beautiful and she wanted him to go on and on. Ben Weatherstaff began to feel soothed into a sort of dream which was quite agreeable. The humming of the bees in the blossoms mingled with the chanting voice and drowsily melted into a doze. Dickon sat cross-legged with his rabbit asleep on his arm and a hand resting on the lamb's back. Soot had pushed away a squirrel and huddled close to him on his shoulder, the gray film dropped over his eyes. At last Colin stopped.

"Now I am going to walk round the garden," he announced.

Ben Weatherstaff's head had just dropped forward and he lifted it with a jerk.

"You have been asleep," said Colin.

"Nowt o' th' sort," mumbled Ben. "Th' sermon was good enow—but I'm bound to get out afore th' collection."

He was not quite awake yet.

"You're not in church," said Colin.

"Not me," said Ben, straightening himself. "Who said I were? I heard every bit of it. You said th' Magic was in my back. Th' doctor calls it rheumatics."

The Rajah waved his hand.

"That was the wrong Magic," he said. "You will get better. You have my permission to go to your work. But come back tomorrow."

"I'd like to see thee walk round the garden," grunted Ben.

It was not an unfriendly grunt, but it was a grunt. In fact, being a stubborn old party and not having entire faith in Magic he had made up his mind that if he were sent away he would climb his ladder and look over the wall so that he might be ready to hobble back if there were any stumbling.

The Rajah did not object to his staying and so the procession was formed. It really did look like a procession. Colin was at its head with Dickon on one side and Mary on the other. Ben Weatherstaff walked behind, and the "creatures" trailed after them, the lamb and the fox cub keeping close to Dickon, the white rabbit hopping along or stopping to nibble and Soot following with the solemnity of a person who felt himself in charge.

It was a procession which moved slowly but with dignity. Every few yards it stopped to rest. Colin leaned on Dickon's arm and privately Ben Weatherstaff kept a sharp lookout, but now and then Colin took his hand from its support and walked a few steps alone. His head was held up all the time and he looked very grand.

"The Magic is in me!" he kept saying. "The Magic is making me strong! I can feel it! I can feel it!"

It seemed very certain that something was upholding and uplifting him. He sat on the seats in the alcoves, and once or twice he sat down on the grass and several times he paused in the path and leaned on Dickon, but he would not give up until he had gone all round the garden. When he returned to the canopy tree his cheeks were flushed and he looked triumphant.

"I did it! The Magic worked!" he cried. "That is my first scientific discovery."

"What will Dr. Craven say?" broke out Mary.

"He won't say anything," Colin answered, "because he will not be told. This is to be the biggest secret of all. No one is to know anything about it until I have grown so strong that I can walk and run like any other boy. I shall come here every day in my chair and I shall be taken back in it. I won't have people whispering and asking questions and I won't let my father hear about it until the experiment has quite succeeded. Then sometime when he comes back to Misselthwaite I shall just walk into his study and say 'Here I am; I am like any other boy. I am quite well and I shall live to be a man. It has been done by a scientific experiment.'"

"He will think he is in a dream," cried Mary. "He won't believe his eyes."

Colin flushed triumphantly. He had made himself believe that he was going to get well, which was really more than half the battle, if he had been aware of it. And the thought which stimulated him more than any other was this imagining what his father would look like when he saw that he had a son who was as straight and strong as other fathers' sons. One of his darkest miseries in the unhealthy morbid past days had been his hatred of being a sickly weak-backed boy whose father was afraid to look at him.

"He'll be obliged to believe them," he said.

"One of the things I am going to do, after the Magic works and before I begin to make scientific discoveries, is to be an athlete."

"We shall have thee takin' to boxin' in a week or so," said Ben Weatherstaff. "Tha'lt end wi' winnin' th' Belt an' bein' champion prize-fighter of all England."

Colin fixed his eyes on him sternly.

"Weatherstaff," he said, "that is disrespectful. You must not take liberties because you are in the secret. However much the Magic works I shall not be a prize-fighter. I shall be a Scientific Discoverer."

"Ax pardon—ax pardon, sir" answered Ben, touching his forehead in salute. "I ought to have seed it wasn't a jokin' matter," but his eyes twinkled and secretly he was immensely pleased. He really did not mind being snubbed since the snubbing meant that the lad was gaining strength and spirit.

24

"Let Them Laugh"

The secret garden was not the only one Dickon worked in. Round the cottage on the moor there was a piece of ground enclosed by a low wall of rough stones. Early in the morning and late in the fading twilight and on all the days Colin and Mary did not see him, Dickon worked there planting or tending potatoes and cabbages, turnips and carrots and herbs for his mother. In the company of his "creatures" he did wonders there and was never tired of doing them, it seemed. While he dug or weeded he whistled or sang bits of Yorkshire moor songs or talked to Soot or Captain or the brothers and sisters he had taught to help him.

"We'd never get on as comfortable as we do," Mrs. Sowerby said, "if it wasn't for Dickon's garden. Anything'll grow for him. His 'taters and cabbages is twice th' size of anyone else's an' they've got a flavor with 'em as nobody's has."

When she found a moment to spare she liked to go out and talk to him. After supper there was still a long clear twilight to work in and that was her quiet time. She could sit upon the low rough wall and look on and hear stories of the day. She loved this time. There were not only vegetables in this garden. Dickon had bought penny packages of flower seeds now and then and sown bright sweet-scented things among gooseberry bushes and even cabbages and he grew borders of mignonette and pinks and pansies and things whose seeds he could save year after year or whose roots would bloom each spring and spread in time into fine clumps. The low wall was one of the prettiest things in Yorkshire because he had tucked moorland foxglove and ferns and rock-cress and hedgerow flowers into every crevice until only here and there glimpses of the stones were to be seen.

"All a chap's got to do to make 'em thrive, mother," he would say, "is to be friends with 'em for sure. They're just like th' 'creatures.' If they're thirsty give 'em drink and if they're hungry give 'em a bit o' food. They want to live same as we do. If they died I should feel as if I'd been a bad lad and somehow treated them heartless."

It was in these twilight hours that Mrs. Sowerby heard of all that happened at Misselthwaite Manor. At first she was only told that "Mester Colin" had taken a fancy to going out into the grounds with Miss Mary and that it was doing him good. But it was not long before it was agreed between the two children that Dickon's mother might "come into the secret." Somehow it was not doubted that she was "safe for sure."

So one beautiful still evening Dickon told the whole story, with all the thrilling details of the buried key and the robin and the gray haze which had seemed like deadness and the secret Mistress Mary had planned never to reveal. The coming of Dickon and how it had been told to him, the doubt of Mester Colin and the final drama of his introduction to the hidden domain, combined with the incident of Ben Weatherstaff's angry face peering over the wall and Mester Colin's sudden indignant strength, made Mrs. Sowerby's nice-looking face quite change color several times.

"My word!" she said. "It was a good thing that little lass came to th' Manor. It's been th' makin' o' her an' th' savin, o' him. Standin' on his feet! An' us all thinkin' he was a poor half-witted lad with not a straight bone in him."

She asked a great many questions and her blue eyes were full of deep thinking.

"What do they make of it at th' Manor—him being so well an' cheerful an' never complainin'?" she inquired. "They don't know what to make of it," answered Dickon. "Every day as comes round his face looks different. It's fillin' out and doesn't look so sharp an' th' waxy color is goin'. But he has to do his bit o' complainin'," with a highly entertained grin.

"What for, i' Mercy's name?" asked Mrs. Sowerby.

Dickon chuckled.

"He does it to keep them from guessin' what's happened. If the doctor knew he'd found out he could stand on his feet he'd likely write and tell Mester Craven. Mester Colin's savin' th' secret to tell himself. He's goin' to practise his Magic on his legs every day till his father comes back an' then he's goin' to march into his room an' show him he's as straight as other lads. But him an' Miss Mary thinks it's best plan to do a bit o' groanin' an' frettin' now an' then to throw folk off th' scent."

Mrs. Sowerby was laughing a low comfortable laugh long before he had finished his last sentence.

"Eh!" she said, "that pair's enjoyin' theirselves I'll warrant. They'll get a good bit o' actin' out of it an' there's nothin' children likes as much as play-actin'. Let's hear what they do, Dickon lad." Dickon stopped weeding and sat up on his heels to tell her. His eyes were twinkling with fun.

"Mester Colin is carried down to his chair every time he goes out," he explained. "An' he flies out at John, th' footman, for not carryin' him careful enough. He makes himself as helpless lookin' as he can an' never lifts his head until we're out o' sight o' th' house. An' he grunts an' frets a good bit when he's bein' settled into his chair. Him an' Miss Mary's both got to enjoyin' it an' when he groans an' complains she'll say, 'Poor Colin! Does it hurt you so much? Are you so weak as that, poor Colin?'—but th' trouble is that sometimes they can scarce keep from burstin' out laughin'. When we get safe into the garden they laugh till they've no breath left to laugh with. An' they have to stuff their faces into Mester Colin's cushions to keep the gardeners from hearin', if any of, 'em's about."

"Th' more they laugh th' better for 'em!" said Mrs. Sowerby, still laughing herself. "Good healthy child laughin's better than pills any day o' th' year. That pair'll plump up for sure."

"They are plumpin' up," said Dickon. "They're that hungry they don't know how to get enough to eat without makin' talk. Mester Colin says if he keeps sendin' for more food they won't believe he's an invalid at all. Miss Mary says she'll let him eat her share, but he says that if she goes hungry she'll get thin an' they mun both get fat at once."

Mrs. Sowerby laughed so heartily at the revelation of this difficulty that she quite rocked backward and forward in her blue cloak, and Dickon laughed with her.

"I'll tell thee what, lad," Mrs. Sowerby said when she could speak. "I've thought of a way to help 'em. When tha' goes to 'em in th' mornin's tha' shall take a pail o' good new milk an' I'll bake 'em a crusty cottage loaf or some buns wi' currants in 'em, same as you children like. Nothin's so good as fresh milk an' bread. Then they could take off th' edge o' their hunger while they were in their garden an' th, fine food they get indoors 'ud polish off th' corners."

"Eh! mother!" said Dickon admiringly, "what a wonder tha' art! Tha' always sees a way out o' things. They was quite in a pother yesterday. They didn't see how they was to manage without orderin' up more food—they felt that empty inside."

"They're two young 'uns growin' fast, an' health's comin' back to both of 'em. Children like that feels like young wolves an' food's flesh an' blood to 'em," said Mrs. Sowerby. Then she smiled Dickon's own curving smile. "Eh! but they're enjoyin' theirselves for sure," she said.

She was quite right, the comfortable wonderful mother creature—and she had never been more so than when she said their "play-actin'" would be their joy. Colin and Mary found it one of their most thrilling sources of entertainment. The idea of protecting themselves from suspicion had been unconsciously suggested to them first by the puzzled nurse and then by Dr. Craven himself.

"Your appetite. Is improving very much, Master Colin," the nurse had said one day. "You used to eat nothing, and so many things disagreed with you."

"Nothing disagrees with me now" replied Colin, and then seeing the nurse looking at him curiously he suddenly remembered that perhaps he ought not to appear too well just yet. "At least things don't so often disagree with me. It's the fresh air."

"Perhaps it is," said the nurse, still looking at him with a mystified expression. "But I must talk to Dr. Craven about it."

"How she stared at you!" said Mary when she went away. "As if she thought there must be something to find out."

"I won't have her finding out things," said Colin. "No one must begin to find out yet." When Dr. Craven came that morning he seemed puzzled, also. He asked a number of questions, to Colin's great annoyance.

"You stay out in the garden a great deal," he suggested. "Where do you go?"

Colin put on his favorite air of dignified indifference to opinion.

"I will not let anyone know where I go," he answered. "I go to a place I like. Every one has orders to keep out of the way. I won't be watched and stared at. You know that!"

"You seem to be out all day but I do not think it has done you harm—I do not think so. The nurse says that you eat much more than you have ever done before."

"Perhaps," said Colin, prompted by a sudden inspiration, "perhaps it is an unnatural appetite."

"I do not think so, as your food seems to agree with you," said Dr. Craven. "You are gaining flesh rapidly and your color is better."

"Perhaps—perhaps I am bloated and feverish," said Colin, assuming a discouraging air of gloom. "People who are not going to live are often—different." Dr. Craven shook his head. He was holding Colin's wrist and he pushed up his sleeve and felt his arm.

"You are not feverish," he said thoughtfully, "and such flesh as you have gained is healthy. If you can keep this up, my boy, we need not talk of dying. Your father will be happy to hear of this remarkable improvement."

"I won't have him told!" Colin broke forth fiercely. "It will only disappoint him if I get worse again—and I may get worse this very night. I might have a raging fever. I feel as if I might be beginning to have one now. I won't have letters written to my father—I won't—I won't! You are making me angry and you know that is bad for me. I feel hot already. I hate being written about and being talked over as much as I hate being stared at!"

"Hush-h! my boy," Dr. Craven soothed him. "Nothing shall be written without your permission. You are too sensitive about things. You must not undo the good which has been done."

He said no more about writing to Mr. Craven and when he saw the nurse he privately warned her that such a possibility must not be mentioned to the patient.

"The boy is extraordinarily better," he said. "His advance seems almost abnormal. But of course he is doing now of his own free will what we could not make him do before. Still, he excites himself very easily and nothing must be said to irritate him." Mary and Colin were much alarmed and talked together anxiously. From this time dated their plan of "play-actin'."

"I may be obliged to have a tantrum," said Colin regretfully. "I don't want to have one and I'm not miserable enough now to work myself into a big one. Perhaps I couldn't have one at all. That lump doesn't come in my throat now and I keep thinking of nice things instead of horrible ones. But if they talk about writing to my father I shall have to do something."

He made up his mind to eat less, but unfortunately it was not possible to carry out this brilliant idea when he wakened each morning with an amazing appetite and the table near his sofa was set with a breakfast of home-made bread and fresh butter, snow-white eggs, raspberry jam and clotted cream. Mary always breakfasted with him and when they found themselves at the table—particularly if there were delicate slices of sizzling ham sending forth tempting odors from under a hot silver cover—they would look into each other's eyes in desperation.

"I think we shall have to eat it all this morning, Mary," Colin always ended by saying. "We can send away some of the lunch and a great deal of the dinner."

But they never found they could send away anything and the highly polished condition of the empty plates returned to the pantry awakened much comment.

"I do wish," Colin would say also, "I do wish the slices of ham were thicker, and one muffin each is not enough for anyone."

"It's enough for a person who is going to die," answered Mary when first she heard this, "but it's not enough for a person who is going to live. I sometimes feel as if I could eat three when those nice fresh heather and gorse smells from the moor come pouring in at the open window."

The morning that Dickon—after they had been enjoying themselves in the garden for about two hours—went behind a big rosebush and brought forth two tin pails and revealed that one was full of rich new milk with cream on the top of it, and that the other held cottage-made currant buns folded in a clean blue and white napkin, buns so carefully tucked in that they were still hot, there was a riot of surprised joyfulness. What a wonderful thing for Mrs. Sowerby to think of! What a kind, clever woman she must be! How good the buns were! And what delicious fresh milk!

"Magic is in her just as it is in Dickon," said Colin. "It makes her think of ways to do things—nice things. She is a Magic person. Tell her we are grateful, Dickon—extremely grateful." He was given to using rather grown-up phrases at times. He enjoyed them. He liked this so much that he improved upon it.

"Tell her she has been most bounteous and our gratitude is extreme."

And then forgetting his grandeur he fell to and stuffed himself with buns and drank milk out of the pail in copious draughts in the manner of any hungry little boy who had been taking unusual exercise and breathing in moorland air and whose breakfast was more than two hours behind him.

This was the beginning of many agreeable incidents of the same kind. They actually awoke to the fact that as Mrs. Sowerby had fourteen people to provide food for she might not have enough to satisfy two extra appetites every day. So they asked her to let them send some of their shillings to buy things.

Dickon made the stimulating discovery that in the wood in the park outside the garden where Mary had first found him piping to the wild creatures there was a deep little hollow where you could build a sort of tiny oven with stones and roast potatoes and eggs in it. Roasted eggs were a previously unknown luxury and very hot potatoes with salt and fresh butter in them were fit for a woodland king—besides being deliciously satisfying. You could buy both potatoes and eggs and eat as many as you liked without feeling as if you were taking food out of the mouths of fourteen people.

Every beautiful morning the Magic was worked by the mystic circle under the plum-tree which provided a canopy of thickening green leaves after its brief blossom-time was ended. After the ceremony Colin always took his walking exercise and throughout the day he exercised his newly found power at intervals. Each day he grew stronger and could walk more steadily and cover more ground. And each day his belief in the Magic grew stronger—as well it might. He tried one experiment after another as he felt himself gaining strength and it was Dickon who showed him the best things of all.

"Yesterday," he said one morning after an absence, "I went to Thwaite for mother an' near th' Blue Cow Inn I seed Bob Haworth. He's the strongest chap on th' moor. He's the champion wrestler an' he can jump higher than any other chap an' throw th' hammer farther. He's gone all th' way to Scotland for th' sports some years. He's knowed me ever since I was a little 'un an' he's a friendly sort an' I axed him some questions. Th' gentry calls him a athlete and I thought o' thee, Mester Colin, and I says, 'How did tha' make tha' muscles stick out that way, Bob? Did tha' do anythin' extra to make thysel' so strong?' An' he says 'Well, yes, lad, I did. A strong man in a show that came to Thwaite once showed me how to exercise my arms an' legs an' every muscle in my body. An' I says, 'Could a delicate chap make himself stronger with 'em, Bob?' an' he laughed an' says, 'Art tha' th' delicate chap?' an' I says, 'No, but I knows a young gentleman that's gettin' well of a long illness an' I wish I knowed some o' them tricks to tell him about.' I didn't say no names an' he didn't ask none. He's friendly same as I said an' he stood up an' showed me good-natured like, an' I imitated what he did till I knowed it by heart."

Colin had been listening excitedly.

"Can you show me?" he cried. "Will you?"

"Aye, to be sure," Dickon answered, getting up. "But he says tha' mun do 'em gentle at first an' be careful not to tire thysel'. Rest in between times an' take deep breaths an' don't overdo."

"I'll be careful," said Colin. "Show me! Show me! Dickon, you are the most Magic boy in the world!"

Dickon stood up on the grass and slowly went through a carefully practical but simple series of muscle exercises. Colin watched them with widening eyes. He could do a few while he was sitting down. Presently he did a few gently while he stood upon his already steadied feet. Mary began to do them also. Soot, who was watching the performance, became much disturbed and left his branch and hopped about restlessly because he could not do them too.

From that time the exercises were part of the day's duties as much as the Magic was. It became possible for both Colin and Mary to do more of them each time they tried, and such appetites were the results that but for the basket Dickon put down behind the bush each morning when he arrived they would have been lost. But the little oven in the hollow and Mrs. Sowerby's bounties were so satisfying that Mrs. Medlock and the nurse and Dr. Craven became mystified again. You can trifle with your breakfast and seem to disdain your dinner if you are full to the brim with roasted eggs and potatoes and richly frothed new milk and oatcakes and buns and heather honey and clotted cream.

"They are eating next to nothing," said the nurse. "They'll die of starvation if they can't be persuaded to take some nourishment. And yet see how they look."

"Look!" exclaimed Mrs. Medlock indignantly. "Eh! I'm moithered to death with them. They're a pair of young Satans. Bursting their jackets one day and the next turning up their noses at the best meals Cook can tempt them with. Not a mouthful of that lovely young fowl and bread sauce did they set a fork into yesterday—and the poor woman fair *invented* a pudding for them—and back it's sent. She almost cried. She's afraid she'll be blamed if they starve themselves into their graves."

Dr. Craven came and looked at Colin long and carefully, He wore an extremely worried expression when the nurse talked with him and showed him the almost untouched tray of breakfast she had saved for him to look at—but it was even more worried when he sat down by Colin's sofa and examined him. He had been called to London on business and had not seen the boy for nearly two weeks. When young things begin to gain health they gain it rapidly. The waxen tinge had left, Colins skin and a warm rose showed through it; his beautiful eyes were clear and the hollows under them and in his cheeks and temples had filled out. His once dark, heavy locks had begun to look as if they sprang healthily from his forehead and were soft and warm with life. His lips were fuller and of a normal color. In fact as an imitation of a boy who was a confirmed invalid he was a disgraceful sight. Dr. Craven held his chin in his hand and thought him over.

"I am sorry to hear that you do not eat anything," he said. "That will not do. You will lose all you have gained—and you have gained amazingly. You ate so well a short time ago."

"I told you it was an unnatural appetite," answered Colin.

Mary was sitting on her stool nearby and she suddenly made a very queer sound which she tried so violently to repress that she ended by almost choking.

"What is the matter?" said Dr. Craven, turning to look at her.

Mary became quite severe in her manner.

"It was something between a sneeze and a cough," she replied with reproachful dignity, "and it got into my throat."

"But," she said afterward to Colin, "I couldn't stop myself. It just burst out because all at once I couldn't help remembering that last big potato you ate and the way your mouth stretched when you bit through that thick lovely crust with jam and clotted cream on it."

"Is there any way in which those children can get food secretly?" Dr. Craven inquired of Mrs. Medlock.

"There's no way unless they dig it out of the earth or pick it off the trees," Mrs. Medlock answered. "They stay out in the grounds all day and see no one but each other. And if they want anything different to eat from what's sent up to them they need only ask for it."

"Well," said Dr. Craven, "so long as going without food agrees with them we need not disturb ourselves. The boy is a new creature."

"So is the girl," said Mrs. Medlock. "She's begun to be downright pretty since she's filled out and lost her ugly little sour look. Her hair's grown thick and healthy looking and she's got a bright color. The glummest, ill-natured little thing she used to be and now her and Master Colin laugh together like a pair of crazy young ones. Perhaps they're growing fat on that."

"Perhaps they are," said Dr. Craven. "Let them laugh."

25

The Curtain

And the secret garden bloomed and bloomed and every morning revealed new miracles. In the robin's nest there were Eggs and the robin's mate sat upon them keeping them warm with her feathery little breast and careful wings. At first she was very nervous and the robin himself was indignantly watchful. Even Dickon did not go near the close-grown corner in those days, but waited until by the quiet working of some mysterious spell he seemed to have conveyed to the soul of the little pair that in the garden there was nothing which was not quite like themselves—nothing which did not understand the wonderfulness of what was happening to them—the immense, tender, terrible, heart-breaking beauty and solemnity of Eggs. If there had been one person in that garden who had not known through all his or her innermost being that if an Egg were taken away or hurt the whole world would whirl round and crash through space and come to an end—if there had been even one who did not feel it and act accordingly there could have been no happiness even in that golden springtime air. But they all knew it and felt it and the robin and his mate knew they knew it.

At first the robin watched Mary and Colin with sharp anxiety. For some mysterious reason he knew he need not watch Dickon. The first moment he set his dew-bright black eye on Dickon he knew he was not a stranger but a sort of robin without beak or feathers. He could speak robin (which is a quite distinct language not to be mistaken for any other). To speak robin to a robin is like speaking French to a Frenchman. Dickon always spoke it to the robin himself, so the queer gibberish he used when he spoke to humans did not matter in the least. The robin thought he spoke this gibberish to them because they were not intelligent enough to understand feathered speech. His movements also were robin. They never startled one by being sudden enough to seem dangerous or threatening. Any robin could understand Dickon, so his presence was not even disturbing.

But at the outset it seemed necessary to be on guard against the other two. In the first place the boy creature did not come into the garden on his legs. He was pushed in on a thing with wheels and the skins of wild animals were thrown over him. That in itself was doubtful. Then when he began to stand up and move about he did it in a queer unaccustomed way and the others seemed to have to help him. The robin used to secrete himself in a bush and watch this anxiously, his head tilted first on one side and then on the other. He thought that the slow movements might mean that he was preparing to pounce, as cats do. When cats are preparing to pounce they creep over the ground very slowly. The robin talked this over with his mate a great deal for a few days but after that he decided not to speak of the subject because her terror was so great that he was afraid it might be injurious to the Eggs.

When the boy began to walk by himself and even to move more quickly it was an immense relief. But for a long time—or it seemed a long time to the robin—he was a source of some anxiety. He did not act as the other humans did. He seemed very fond of walking but he had a way of sitting or lying down for a while and then getting up in a disconcerting manner to begin again.

One day the robin remembered that when he himself had been made to learn to fly by his parents he had done much the same sort of thing. He had taken short flights of a few yards and then had been obliged to rest. So it occurred to him that this boy was learning to fly—or rather to walk. He mentioned this to his mate and when he told her that the Eggs would probably conduct themselves in the same way after they were fledged she was quite comforted and even became eagerly interested and derived great pleasure from watching the boy over the edge of her nest—though she always thought that the Eggs would be much cleverer and learn more quickly. But then she said indulgently that humans were always more clumsy and slow than Eggs and most of them never seemed really to learn to fly at all. You never met them in the air or on tree-tops.

After a while the boy began to move about as the others did, but all three of the children at times did unusual things. They would stand under the trees and move their arms and legs and heads about in a way which was neither walking nor running nor sitting down. They went through these movements at intervals every day and the robin was never able to explain to his mate what they were doing or tying to do. He could only say that he was sure that the Eggs would never flap about in such a manner; but as the boy who could speak robin so fluently was doing the thing with them, birds could be quite sure that the actions were not of a dangerous nature. Of course neither the robin nor his mate had ever heard of the champion wrestler, Bob Haworth, and his exercises for making the muscles stand out like lumps. Robins are not like human beings; their muscles are always exercised from the first and so they develop themselves in a natural manner. If you have to fly about to find every meal you eat, your muscles do not become atrophied (atrophied means wasted away through want of use).

When the boy was walking and running about and digging and weeding like the others, the nest in the corner was brooded over by a great peace and content. Fears for the Eggs became things of the past. Knowing that your Eggs were as safe as if they were locked in a bank vault and the fact that you could watch so many curious things going on made setting a most entertaining occupation. On wet days the Eggs' mother sometimes felt even a little dull because the children did not come into the garden.

But even on wet days it could not be said that Mary and Colin were dull. One morning when the rain streamed down unceasingly and Colin was beginning to feel a little restive, as he was obliged to remain on his sofa because it was not safe to get up and walk about, Mary had an inspiration.

"Now that I am a real boy," Colin had said, "my legs and arms and all my body are so full of Magic that I can't keep them still. They want to be doing things all the time. Do you know that when I waken in the morning, Mary, when it's quite early and the birds are just shouting outside and everything seems just shouting for joy—even the trees and things we can't really hear—I feel as if I must jump out of bed and shout myself. If I did it, just think what would happen!"

Mary giggled inordinately.

"The nurse would come running and Mrs. Medlock would come running and they would be sure you had gone crazy and they'd send for the doctor," she said.

Colin giggled himself. He could see how they would all look—how horrified by his outbreak and how amazed to see him standing upright.

"I wish my father would come home," he said. "I want to tell him myself. I'm always thinking about it—but we couldn't go on like this much longer. I can't stand lying still and pretending, and besides I look too different. I wish it wasn't raining today."

It was then Mistress Mary had her inspiration.

"Colin," she began mysteriously, "do you know how many rooms there are in this house?"

"About a thousand, I suppose," he answered.

"There's about a hundred no one ever goes into," said Mary. "And one rainy day I went and looked into ever so many of them. No one ever knew, though Mrs. Medlock nearly found me out. I lost my way when I was coming back and I stopped at the end of your corridor. That was the second time I heard you crying."

Colin started up on his sofa.

"A hundred rooms no one goes into," he said. "It sounds almost like a secret garden. Suppose we go and look at them. Wheel me in my chair and nobody would know we went."

"That's what I was thinking," said Mary. "No one would dare to follow us. There are galleries where you could run. We could do our exercises. There is a little Indian room where there is a cabinet full of ivory elephants. There are all sorts of rooms."

"Ring the bell," said Colin.

When the nurse came in he gave his orders.

"I want my chair," he said. "Miss Mary and I are going to look at the part of the house which is not used. John can push me as far as the picture-gallery because there are some stairs. Then he must go away and leave us alone until I send for him again."

Rainy days lost their terrors that morning. When the footman had wheeled the chair into the picture-gallery and left the two together in obedience to orders, Colin and Mary looked at each other delighted. As soon as Mary had made sure that John was really on his way back to his own quarters below stairs, Colin got out of his chair.

"I am going to run from one end of the gallery to the other," he said, "and then I am going to jump and then we will do Bob Haworth's exercises."

And they did all these things and many others. They looked at the portraits and found the plain little girl dressed in green brocade and holding the parrot on her finger.

"All these," said Colin, "must be my relations. They lived a long time ago. That parrot one, I believe, is one of my great, great, great, great aunts. She looks rather like you, Mary—not as you look now but as you looked when you came here. Now you are a great deal fatter and better looking."

"So are you," said Mary, and they both laughed.

They went to the Indian room and amused themselves with the ivory elephants. They found the rose-colored brocade boudoir and the hole in the cushion the mouse had left, but the mice had grown up and run away and the hole was empty. They saw more rooms and made more discoveries than Mary had made on her first pilgrimage. They found new corridors and corners and flights of steps and new old pictures they liked and weird old things they did not know the use of. It was a curiously entertaining morning and the feeling of wandering about in the same house with other people but at the same time feeling as if one were miles away from them was a fascinating thing.

"I'm glad we came," Colin said. "I never knew I lived in such a big queer old place. I like it. We will ramble about every rainy day. We shall always be finding new queer corners and things."

That morning they had found among other things such good appetites that when they returned to Colin's room it was not possible to send the luncheon away untouched.

When the nurse carried the tray downstairs she slapped it down on the kitchen dresser so that Mrs. Loomis, the cook, could see the highly polished dishes and plates.

"Look at that!" she said. "This is a house of mystery, and those two children are the greatest mysteries in it."

"If they keep that up every day," said the strong young footman John, "there'd be small wonder that he weighs twice as much today as he did a month ago. I should have to give up my place in time, for fear of doing my muscles an injury."

That afternoon Mary noticed that something new had happened in Colin's room. She had noticed it the day before but had said nothing because she thought the change might have been made by chance. She said nothing today but she sat and looked fixedly at the picture over the mantel. She could look at it because the curtain had been drawn aside. That was the change she noticed.

"I know what you want me to tell you," said Colin, after she had stared a few minutes. "I always know when you want me to tell you something. You are wondering why the curtain is drawn back. I am going to keep it like that."

"Why?" asked Mary.

"Because it doesn't make me angry any more to see her laughing. I wakened when it was bright moonlight two nights ago and felt as if the Magic was filling the room and making everything so splendid that I couldn't lie still. I got up and looked out of the window. The room was quite light and there was a patch of moonlight on the curtain and somehow that made me go and pull the cord. She looked right down at me as if she were laughing because she was glad I was standing there. It made me like to look at her. I want to see her laughing like that all the time. I think she must have been a sort of Magic person perhaps."

"You are so like her now," said Mary, "that sometimes I think perhaps you are her ghost made into a boy."

That idea seemed to impress Colin. He thought it over and then answered her slowly.

"If I were her ghost—my father would be fond of me," he said.

"Do you want him to be fond of you?" inquired Mary.

"I used to hate it because he was not fond of me. If he grew fond of me I think I should tell him about the Magic. It might make him more cheerful."

26

"It's Mother!"

Their belief in the Magic was an abiding thing. After the morning's incantations Colin sometimes gave them Magic lectures.

"I like to do it," he explained, "because when I grow up and make great scientific discoveries I shall be obliged to lecture about them and so this is practice. I can only give short lectures now because I am very young, and besides Ben Weatherstaff would feel as if he were in church and he would go to sleep."

"Th' best thing about lecturin'," said Ben, "is that a chap can get up an' say aught he pleases an' no other chap can answer him back. I wouldn't be agen' lecturin' a bit mysel' sometimes."

But when Colin held forth under his tree old Ben fixed devouring eyes on him and kept them there. He looked him over with critical affection. It was not so much the lecture which interested him as the legs which looked straighter and stronger each day, the boyish head which held itself up so well, the once sharp chin and hollow cheeks which had filled and rounded out and the eyes which had begun to hold the light he remembered in another pair. Sometimes when Colin felt Ben's earnest gaze meant that he was much impressed he wondered what he was reflecting on and once when he had seemed quite entranced he questioned him.

"What are you thinking about, Ben Weatherstaff?" he asked.

"I was thinkin'" answered Ben, "as I'd warrant tha's, gone up three or four pound this week. I was lookin' at tha' calves an' tha' shoulders. I'd like to get thee on a pair o' scales."

"It's the Magic and—and Mrs. Sowerby's buns and milk and things," said Colin. "You see the scientific experiment has succeeded."

That morning Dickon was too late to hear the lecture. When he came he was ruddy with running and his funny face looked more twinkling than usual. As they had a good deal of weeding to do after the rains they fell to work. They always had plenty to do after a warm deep sinking rain. The moisture which was good for the flowers was also good for the weeds which thrust up tiny blades of grass and points of leaves which must be pulled up before their roots took too firm hold. Colin was as good at weeding as anyone in these days and he could lecture while he was doing it. "The Magic works best when you work, yourself," he said this morning. "You can feel it in your bones and muscles. I am going to read books about bones and muscles, but I am going to write a book about Magic. I am making it up now. I keep finding out things."

It was not very long after he had said this that he laid down his trowel and stood up on his feet. He had been silent for several minutes and they had seen that he was thinking out lectures, as he often did. When he dropped his trowel and stood upright it seemed to Mary and Dickon as if a sudden strong thought had made him do it. He stretched himself out to his tallest height and he threw out his arms exultantly. Color glowed in his face and his strange eyes widened with joyfulness. All at once he had realized something to the full.

"Mary! Dickon!" he cried. "Just look at me!"

They stopped their weeding and looked at him.

"Do you remember that first morning you brought me in here?" he demanded.

Dickon was looking at him very hard. Being an animal charmer he could see more things than most people could and many of them were things he never talked about. He saw some of them now in this boy. "Aye, that we do," he answered.

Mary looked hard too, but she said nothing.

"Just this minute," said Colin, "all at once I remembered it myself—when I looked at my hand digging with the trowel—and I had to stand up on my feet to see if it was real. And it is real! I'm *well*—I'm *well*!"

"Aye, that th' art!" said Dickon.

"I'm well! I'm well!" said Colin again, and his face went quite red all over.

He had known it before in a way, he had hoped it and felt it and thought about it, but just at that minute something had rushed all through him—a sort of rapturous belief and realization and it had been so strong that he could not help calling out.

"I shall live forever and ever and ever!" he cried grandly. "I shall find out thousands and thousands of things. I shall find out about people and creatures and everything that grows—like Dickon—and I shall never stop making Magic. I'm well! I'm well! I feel—I feel as if I want to shout out something—something thankful, joyful!"

Ben Weatherstaff, who had been working near a rose-bush, glanced round at him.

"Tha' might sing th' Doxology," he suggested in his dryest grunt. He had no opinion of the Doxology and he did not make the suggestion with any particular reverence.

But Colin was of an exploring mind and he knew nothing about the Doxology.

"What is that?" he inquired.

"Dickon can sing it for thee, I'll warrant," replied Ben Weatherstaff.

Dickon answered with his all-perceiving animal charmer's smile.

"They sing it i' church," he said. "Mother says she believes th' skylarks sings it when they gets up i' th' mornin'."

"If she says that, it must be a nice song," Colin answered. "I've never been in a church myself. I was always too ill. Sing it, Dickon. I want to hear it."

Dickon was quite simple and unaffected about it. He understood what Colin felt better than Colin did himself. He understood by a sort of instinct so natural that he did not know it was understanding. He pulled off his cap and looked round still smiling.

"Tha' must take off tha' cap," he said to Colin, "an' so mun tha', Ben—an' tha' mun stand up, tha' knows."

Colin took off his cap and the sun shone on and warmed his thick hair as he watched Dickon intently. Ben Weatherstaff scrambled up from his knees and bared his head too with a sort of puzzled half-resentful look on his old face as if he didn't know exactly why he was doing this remarkable thing.

Dickon stood out among the trees and rose-bushes and began to sing in quite a simple matter-of-fact way and in a nice strong boy voice:

"Praise God from whom all blessings flow,
Praise Him all creatures here below,
Praise Him above ye Heavenly Host,
Praise Father, Son, and Holy Ghost.
Amen."

When he had finished, Ben Weatherstaff was standing quite still with his jaws set obstinately but with a disturbed look in his eyes fixed on Colin. Colin's face was thoughtful and appreciative.

"It is a very nice song," he said. "I like it. Perhaps it means just what I mean when I want to shout out that I am thankful to the Magic." He stopped and thought in a puzzled way. "Perhaps they are both the same thing. How can we know the exact names of everything? Sing it again, Dickon. Let us try, Mary. I want to sing it, too. It's my song. How does it begin? 'Praise God from whom all blessings flow'?"

And they sang it again, and Mary and Colin lifted their voices as musically as they could and Dickon's swelled quite loud and beautiful—and at the second line Ben Weatherstaff raspingly cleared his throat and at the third line he joined in with such vigor that it seemed almost savage and when the "Amen" came to an end Mary observed that the very same thing had happened to him which had happened when he found out that Colin was not a cripple—his chin was twitching and he was staring and winking and his leathery old cheeks were wet.

"I never seed no sense in th' Doxology afore," he said hoarsely, "but I may change my mind i' time. I should say tha'd gone up five pound this week Mester Colin—five on 'em!"

Colin was looking across the garden at something attracting his attention and his expression had become a startled one.

"Who is coming in here?" he said quickly. "Who is it?"

The door in the ivied wall had been pushed gently open and a woman had entered. She had come in with the last line of their song and she had stood still listening and looking at them. With the ivy behind her, the sunlight drifting through the trees and dappling her long blue cloak, and her nice fresh face smiling across the greenery she was rather like a softly colored illustration in one of Colin's books. She had wonderful affectionate eyes which seemed to take everything in—all of them, even Ben Weatherstaff and the "creatures" and every flower that was in bloom. Unexpectedly as she had appeared, not one of them felt that she was an intruder at all. Dickon's eyes lighted like lamps.

"It's mother—that's who it is!" he cried and went across the grass at a run.

Colin began to move toward her, too, and Mary went with him. They both felt their pulses beat faster.

"It's mother!" Dickon said again when they met halfway. "I knowed tha' wanted to see her an' I told her where th' door was hid."

Colin held out his hand with a sort of flushed royal shyness but his eyes quite devoured her face.

"Even when I was ill I wanted to see you," he said, "you and Dickon and the secret garden. I'd never wanted to see anyone or anything before."

The sight of his uplifted face brought about a sudden change in her own. She flushed and the corners of her mouth shook and a mist seemed to sweep over her eyes.

"Eh! dear lad!" she broke out tremulously. "Eh! dear lad!" as if she had not known she were going to say it. She did not say, "Mester Colin," but just "dear lad" quite suddenly. She might have said it to Dickon in the same way if she had seen something in his face which touched her. Colin liked it.

"Are you surprised because I am so well?" he asked. She put her hand on his shoulder and smiled the mist out of her eyes. "Aye, that I am!" she said; "but tha'rt so like thy mother tha' made my heart jump."

"Do you think," said Colin a little awkwardly, "that will make my father like me?"

"Aye, for sure, dear lad," she answered and she gave his shoulder a soft quick pat. "He mun come home—he mun come home."

"Susan Sowerby," said Ben Weatherstaff, getting close to her. "Look at th' lad's legs, wilt tha'? They was like drumsticks i' stockin' two month' ago—an' I heard folk tell as they was bandy an' knock-kneed both at th' same time. Look at 'em now!"

Susan Sowerby laughed a comfortable laugh.

"They're goin' to be fine strong lad's legs in a bit," she said. "Let him go on playin' an' workin' in the garden an' eatin' hearty an' drinkin' plenty o' good sweet milk an' there'll not be a finer pair i' Yorkshire, thank God for it."

She put both hands on Mistress Mary's shoulders and looked her little face over in a motherly fashion.

"An' thee, too!" she said. "Tha'rt grown near as hearty as our 'Lisabeth Ellen. I'll warrant tha'rt like thy mother too. Our Martha told me as Mrs. Medlock heard she was a pretty woman. Tha'lt be like a blush rose when tha' grows up, my little lass, bless thee."

She did not mention that when Martha came home on her "day out" and described the plain sallow child she had said that she had no confidence whatever in what Mrs. Medlock had heard. "It doesn't stand to reason that a pretty woman could be th' mother o' such a fou' little lass," she had added obstinately.

Mary had not had time to pay much attention to her changing face. She had only known that she looked "different" and seemed to have a great deal more hair and that it was growing very fast. But remembering her pleasure in looking at the Mem Sahib in the past she was glad to hear that she might some day look like her.

Susan Sowerby went round their garden with them and was told the whole story of it and shown every bush and tree which had come alive. Colin walked on one side of her and Mary on the other. Each of them kept looking up at her comfortable rosy face, secretly curious about the delightful feeling she gave them—a sort of warm, supported feeling. It seemed as if she understood them as Dickon understood his "creatures." She stooped over the flowers and talked about them as if they were children. Soot followed her and once or twice cawed at her and flew upon her shoulder as if it were Dickon's. When they told her about the robin and the first flight of the young ones she laughed a motherly little mellow laugh in her throat.

"I suppose learnin' 'em to fly is like learnin' children to walk, but I'm feared I should be all in a worrit if mine had wings instead o' legs," she said.

It was because she seemed such a wonderful woman in her nice moorland cottage way that at last she was told about the Magic.

"Do you believe in Magic?" asked Colin after he had explained about Indian fakirs. "I do hope you do."

"That I do, lad," she answered. "I never knowed it by that name but what does th' name matter? I warrant they call it a different name i' France an' a different one i' Germany. Th' same thing as set th' seeds swellin' an' th' sun shinin' made thee a well lad an' it's th' Good Thing. It isn't like us poor fools as think it matters if us is called out of our names. Th' Big Good Thing doesn't stop to worrit, bless thee. It goes on makin' worlds by th' million—worlds like us. Never thee stop believin' in th' Big Good Thing an' knowin' th' world's full of it—an' call it what tha' likes. Tha' wert singin' to it when I come into th' garden."

"I felt so joyful," said Colin, opening his beautiful strange eyes at her. "Suddenly I felt how different I was—how strong my arms and legs were, you know—and how I could dig and stand—and I jumped up and wanted to shout out something to anything that would listen."

"Th' Magic listened when tha' sung th' Doxology. It would ha' listened to anything tha'd sung. It was th' joy that mattered. Eh! lad, lad—what's names to th' Joy Maker," and she gave his shoulders a quick soft pat again.

She had packed a basket which held a regular feast this morning, and when the hungry hour came and Dickon brought it out from its hiding place, she sat down with them under their tree and watched them devour their food, laughing and quite gloating over their appetites. She was full of fun and made them laugh at all sorts of odd things. She told them stories in broad Yorkshire and taught them new words. She laughed as if she could not help it when they told her of the increasing difficulty there was in pretending that Colin was still a fretful invalid.

"You see we can't help laughing nearly all the time when we are together," explained Colin. "And it doesn't sound ill at all. We try to choke it back but it will burst out and that sounds worse than ever."

"There's one thing that comes into my mind so often," said Mary, "and I can scarcely ever hold in when I think of it suddenly. I keep thinking suppose Colin's face should get to look like a full moon. It isn't like one yet but he gets a tiny bit fatter every day—and suppose some morning it should look like one—what should we do!"

"Bless us all, I can see tha' has a good bit o' play-actin' to do," said Susan Sowerby. "But tha' won't have to keep it up much longer. Mester Craven'll come home."

"Do you think he will?" asked Colin. "Why?"

Susan Sowerby chuckled softly.

"I suppose it 'ud nigh break thy heart if he found out before tha' told him in tha' own way," she said. "Tha's laid awake nights plannin' it."

"I couldn't bear anyone else to tell him," said Colin. "I think about different ways every day, I think now I just want to run into his room." "That'd be a fine start for him," said Susan Sowerby. "I'd like to see his face, lad. I would that! He mun come back—that he mun."

One of the things they talked of was the visit they were to make to her cottage. They planned it all. They were to drive over the moor and lunch out of doors among the heather. They would see all the twelve children and Dickon's garden and would not come back until they were tired.

Susan Sowerby got up at last to return to the house and Mrs. Medlock. It was time for Colin to be wheeled back also. But before he got into his chair he stood quite close to Susan and fixed his eyes on her with a kind of bewildered adoration and he suddenly caught hold of the fold of her blue cloak and held it fast.

"You are just what I—what I wanted," he said. "I wish you were my mother—as well as Dickon's!"

All at once Susan Sowerby bent down and drew him with her warm arms close against the bosom under the blue cloak—as if he had been Dickon's brother. The quick mist swept over her eyes.

"Eh! dear lad!" she said. "Thy own mother's in this 'ere very garden, I do believe. She couldna' keep out of it. Thy father mun come back to thee—he mun!"

27

In the Garden

In each century since the beginning of the world wonderful things have been discovered. In the last century more amazing things were found out than in any century before. In this new century hundreds of things still more astounding will be brought to light. At first people refuse to believe that a strange new thing can be done, then they begin to hope it can be done, then they see it can be done—then it is done and all the world wonders why it was not done centuries ago. One of the new things people began to find out in the last century was that thoughts—just mere thoughts—are as powerful as electric batteries—as good for one as sunlight is, or as bad for one as poison. To let a sad thought or a bad one get into your mind is as dangerous as letting a scarlet fever germ get into your body. If you let it stay there after it has got in you may never get over it as long as you live.

So long as Mistress Mary's mind was full of disagreeable thoughts about her dislikes and sour opinions of people and her determination not to be pleased by or interested in anything, she was a yellow-faced, sickly, bored and wretched child. Circumstances, however, were very kind to her, though she was not at all aware of it. They began to push her about for her own good. When her mind gradually filled itself with robins, and moorland cottages crowded with children, with queer crabbed old gardeners and common little Yorkshire housemaids, with springtime and with secret gardens coming alive day by day, and also with a moor boy and his "creatures," there was no room left for the disagreeable thoughts which affected her liver and her digestion and made her yellow and tired.

So long as Colin shut himself up in his room and thought only of his fears and weakness and his detestation of people who looked at him and reflected hourly on humps and early death, he was a hysterical half-crazy little hypochondriac who knew nothing of the sunshine and the spring and also did not know that he could get well and could stand upon his feet if he tried to do it. When new beautiful thoughts began to push out the old hideous ones, life began to come back to him, his blood ran healthily through his veins and strength poured into him like a flood. His scientific experiment was quite practical and simple and there was nothing weird about it at all. Much more surprising things can happen to anyone who, when a disagreeable or discouraged thought comes into his mind, just has the sense to remember in time and push it out by putting in an agreeable determinedly courageous one. Two things cannot be in one place.

"Where, you tend a rose, my lad,
A thistle cannot grow."

While the secret garden was coming alive and two children were coming alive with it, there was a man wandering about certain far-away beautiful places in the Norwegian fiords and the valleys and mountains of Switzerland and he was a man who for ten years had kept his mind filled with dark and heart-broken thinking. He had not been courageous; he had never tried to put any other thoughts in the place of the dark ones. He had wandered by blue lakes and thought them; he had lain on mountain-sides with sheets of deep blue gentians blooming all about him and flower breaths filling all the air and he had thought them. A terrible sorrow had fallen upon him when he had been happy and he had let his soul fill itself with blackness and had refused obstinately to allow any rift of light to pierce through. He had forgotten and deserted his home and his duties. When he traveled about, darkness so brooded over him that the sight of him was a wrong done to other people because it was as if he poisoned the air about him with gloom. Most strangers thought he must be either half mad or a man with some hidden crime on his soul. He, was a tall man with a drawn face and crooked shoulders and the name he always entered on hotel registers was, "Archibald Craven, Misselthwaite Manor, Yorkshire, England."

He had traveled far and wide since the day he saw Mistress Mary in his study and told her she might have her "bit of earth." He had been in the most beautiful places in Europe, though he had remained nowhere more than a few days. He had chosen the quietest and remotest spots. He had been on the tops of mountains whose heads were in the clouds and had looked down on other mountains when the sun rose and touched them with such light as made it seem as if the world were just being born.

But the light had never seemed to touch himself until one day when he realized that for the first time in ten years a strange thing had happened. He was in a wonderful valley in the Austrian Tyrol and he had been walking alone through such beauty as might have lifted, any man's soul out of shadow. He had walked a long way and it had not lifted his. But at last he had felt tired and had thrown himself down to rest on a carpet of moss by a stream. It was a clear little stream which ran quite merrily along on its narrow way through the luscious damp greenness. Sometimes it made a sound rather like very low laughter as it bubbled over and round stones. He saw birds come and dip their heads to drink in it and then flick their wings and fly away. It seemed like a thing alive and yet its tiny voice made the stillness seem deeper. The valley was very, very still.

As he sat gazing into the clear running of the water, Archibald Craven gradually felt his mind and body both grow quiet, as quiet as the valley itself. He wondered if he were going to sleep, but he was not.

He sat and gazed at the sunlit water and his eyes began to see things growing at its edge. There was one lovely mass of blue forget-me-nots growing so close to the stream that its leaves were wet and at these he found himself looking as he remembered he had looked at such things years ago. He was actually thinking tenderly how lovely it was and what wonders of blue its hundreds of little blossoms were. He did not know that just that simple thought was slowly filling his mind—filling and filling it until other things were softly pushed aside. It was as if a sweet clear spring had begun to rise in a stagnant pool and had risen and risen until at last it swept the dark water away. But of course he did not think of this himself. He only knew that the valley seemed to grow quieter and quieter as he sat and stared at the bright delicate blueness. He did not know how long he sat there or what was happening to him, but at last he moved as if he were awakening and he got up slowly and stood on the moss carpet, drawing a long, deep, soft breath and wondering at himself. Something seemed to have been unbound and released in him, very quietly.

"What is it?" he said, almost in a whisper, and he passed his hand over his forehead. "I almost feel as if—I were alive!"

I do not know enough about the wonderfulness of undiscovered things to be able to explain how this had happened to him. Neither does anyone else yet. He did not understand at all himself—but he remembered this strange hour months afterward when he was at Misselthwaite again and he found out quite by accident that on this very day Colin had cried out as he went into the secret garden:

"I am going to live forever and ever and ever!"

The singular calmness remained with him the rest of the evening and he slept a new reposeful sleep; but it was not with him very long. He did not know that it could be kept. By the next night he had opened the doors wide to his dark thoughts and they had come trooping and rushing back. He left the valley and went on his wandering way again. But, strange as it seemed to him, there were minutes—sometimes half-hours—when, without his knowing why, the black burden seemed to lift itself again and he knew he was a living man and not a dead one. Slowly—slowly—for no reason that he knew of—he was "coming alive" with the garden.

As the golden summer changed into the deep golden autumn he went to the Lake of Como. There he found the loveliness of a dream. He spent his days upon the crystal blueness of the lake or he walked back into the soft thick verdure of the hills and tramped until he was tired so that he might sleep. But by this time he had begun to sleep better, he knew, and his dreams had ceased to be a terror to him.

"Perhaps," he thought, "my body is growing stronger."

It was growing stronger but—because of the rare peaceful hours when his thoughts were changed—his soul was slowly growing stronger, too. He began to think of Misselthwaite and wonder if he should not go home. Now and then he wondered vaguely about his boy and asked himself what he should feel when he went and stood by the carved four-posted bed again and looked down at the sharply chiseled ivory-white face while it slept and, the black lashes rimmed so startlingly the close-shut eyes. He shrank from it.

One marvel of a day he had walked so far that when he returned the moon was high and full and all the world was purple shadow and silver. The stillness of lake and shore and wood was so wonderful that he did not go into the villa he lived in. He walked down to a little bowered terrace at the water's edge and sat upon a seat and breathed in all the heavenly scents of the night. He felt the strange calmness stealing over him and it grew deeper and deeper until he fell asleep.

He did not know when he fell asleep and when he began to dream; his dream was so real that he did not feel as if he were dreaming. He remembered afterward how intensely wide awake and alert he had thought he was. He thought that as he sat and breathed in the scent of the late roses and listened to the lapping of the water at his feet he heard a voice calling. It was sweet and clear and happy and far away. It seemed very far, but he heard it as distinctly as if it had been at his very side.

"Archie! Archie! Archie!" it said, and then again, sweeter and clearer than before, "Archie! Archie!"

He thought he sprang to his feet not even startled. It was such a real voice and it seemed so natural that he should hear it.

"Lilias! Lilias!" he answered. "Lilias! where are you?"

"In the garden," it came back like a sound from a golden flute. "In the garden!"

And then the dream ended. But he did not awaken. He slept soundly and sweetly all through the lovely night. When he did awake at last it was brilliant morning and a servant was standing staring at him. He was an Italian servant and was accustomed, as all the servants of the villa were, to accepting without question any strange thing his foreign master might do. No one ever knew when he would go out or come in or where he would choose to sleep or if he would roam about the garden or lie in the boat on the lake all night. The man held a salver with some letters on it and he waited quietly until Mr. Craven took them. When he had gone away Mr. Craven sat a few moments holding them in his hand and looking at the lake. His strange calm was still upon him and something more—a lightness as if the cruel thing which had been done had not happened as he thought—as if something had changed. He was remembering the dream—the real—real dream.

"In the garden!" he said, wondering at himself. "In the garden! But the door is locked and the key is buried deep."

When he glanced at the letters a few minutes later he saw that the one lying at the top of the rest was an English letter and came from Yorkshire. It was directed in a plain woman's hand but it was not a hand he knew. He opened it, scarcely thinking of the writer, but the first words attracted his attention at once.

"Dear Sir,

I am Susan Sowerby that made bold to speak to you once on the moor. It was about Miss Mary I spoke. I will make bold to speak again. Please, sir, I would come home if I was you. I think you would be glad to come and—if you will excuse me, sir—I think your lady would ask you to come if she was here.

Your obedient servant,
Susan Sowerby."

Mr. Craven read the letter twice before he put it back in its envelope. He kept thinking about the dream.

"I will go back to Misselthwaite," he said. "Yes, I'll go at once."

And he went through the garden to the villa and ordered Pitcher to prepare for his return to England.

In a few days he was in Yorkshire again, and on his long railroad journey he found himself thinking of his boy as he had never thought in all the ten years past. During those years he had only wished to forget him. Now, though he did not intend to think about him, memories of him constantly drifted into his mind. He remembered the black days when he had raved like a madman because the child was alive and the mother was dead. He had refused to see it, and when he had gone to look at it at last it had been, such a weak wretched thing that everyone had been sure it would die in a few days. But to the surprise of those who took care of it the days passed and it lived and then everyone believed it would be a deformed and crippled creature.

He had not meant to be a bad father, but he had not felt like a father at all. He had supplied doctors and nurses and luxuries, but he had shrunk from the mere thought of the boy and had buried himself in his own misery. The first time after a year's absence he returned to Misselthwaite and the small miserable-looking thing languidly and indifferently lifted to his face the great gray eyes with black lashes round them, so like and yet so horribly unlike the happy eyes he had adored, he could not bear the sight of them and turned away pale as death. After that he scarcely ever saw him except when he was asleep, and all he knew of him was that he was a confirmed invalid, with a vicious, hysterical, half-insane temper. He could only be kept from furies dangerous to himself by being given his own way in every detail.

All this was not an uplifting thing to recall, but as the train whirled him through mountain passes and golden plains the man who was "coming alive" began to think in a new way and he thought long and steadily and deeply.

"Perhaps I have been all wrong for ten years," he said to himself. "Ten years is a long time. It may be too late to do anything—quite too late. What have I been thinking of!"

Of course this was the wrong Magic—to begin by saying "too late." Even Colin could have told him that. But he knew nothing of Magic—either black or white. This he had yet to learn. He wondered if Susan Sowerby had taken courage and written to him only because the motherly creature had realized that the boy was much worse—

was fatally ill. If he had not been under the spell of the curious calmness which had taken possession of him he would have been more wretched than ever. But the calm had brought a sort of courage and hope with it. Instead of giving way to thoughts of the worst he actually found he was trying to believe in better things.

"Could it be possible that she sees that I may be able to do him good and control him?" he thought. "I will go and see her on my way to Misselthwaite."

But when on his way across the moor he stopped the carriage at the cottage, seven or eight children who were playing about gathered in a group and bobbing seven or eight friendly and polite curtsies told him that their mother had gone to the other side of the moor early in the morning to help a woman who had a new baby. "Our Dickon," they volunteered, was over at the Manor working in one of the gardens where he went several days each week.

Mr. Craven looked over the collection of sturdy little bodies and round red-cheeked faces, each one grinning in its own particular way, and he awoke to the fact that they were a healthy likable lot. He smiled at their friendly grins and took a golden sovereign from his pocket and gave it to "our 'Lizabeth Ellen" who was the oldest.

"If you divide that into eight parts there will be half a crown for each of, you," he said.

Then amid grins and chuckles and bobbing of curtsies he drove away, leaving ecstasy and nudging elbows and little jumps of joy behind.

The drive across the wonderfulness of the moor was a soothing thing. Why did it seem to give him a sense of homecoming which he had been sure he could never feel again—that sense of the beauty of land and sky and purple bloom of distance and a warming of the heart at drawing, nearer to the great old house which had held those of his blood for six hundred years? How he had driven away from it the last time, shuddering to think of its closed rooms and the boy lying in the four-posted bed with the brocaded hangings. Was it possible that perhaps he might find him changed a little for the better and that he might overcome his shrinking from him? How real that dream had been—how wonderful and clear the voice which called back to him, "In the garden—In the garden!"

"I will try to find the key," he said. "I will try to open the door. I must—though I don't know why."

When he arrived at the Manor the servants who received him with the usual ceremony noticed that he looked better and that he did not go to the remote rooms where he usually lived attended by Pitcher. He went into the library and sent for Mrs. Medlock. She came to him somewhat excited and curious and flustered.

"How is Master Colin, Medlock?" he inquired. "Well, sir," Mrs. Medlock answered, "he's—he's different, in a manner of speaking."

"Worse?" he suggested.

Mrs. Medlock really was flushed.

"Well, you see, sir," she tried to explain, "neither Dr. Craven, nor the nurse, nor me can exactly make him out."

"Why is that?"

"To tell the truth, sir, Master Colin might be better and he might be changing for the worse. His appetite, sir, is past understanding—and his ways—"

"Has he become more—more peculiar?" her master, asked, knitting his brows anxiously.

"That's it, sir. He's growing very peculiar—when you compare him with what he used to be. He used to eat nothing and then suddenly he began to eat something enormous—and then he stopped again all at once and the meals were sent back just as they used to be. You never knew, sir, perhaps, that out of doors he never would let himself be taken. The things we've gone through to get him to go out in his chair would leave a body trembling like a leaf. He'd throw himself into such a state that Dr. Craven said he couldn't be responsible for forcing him. Well, sir, just without warning—not long after one of his worst tantrums he suddenly insisted on being taken out every day by Miss Mary and Susan Sowerby's boy Dickon that could push his chair. He took a fancy to both Miss Mary and Dickon, and Dickon brought his tame animals, and, if you'll credit it, sir, out of doors he will stay from morning until night."

"How does he look?" was the next question.

"If he took his food natural, sir, you'd think he was putting on flesh—but we're afraid it may be a sort of bloat. He laughs sometimes in a queer way when he's alone with Miss Mary. He never used to laugh at all. Dr. Craven is coming to see you at once, if you'll allow him. He never was as puzzled in his life."

"Where is Master Colin now?" Mr. Craven asked.

"In the garden, sir. He's always in the garden—though not a human creature is allowed to go near for fear they'll look at him."

Mr. Craven scarcely heard her last words.

"In the garden," he said, and after he had sent Mrs. Medlock away he stood and repeated it again and again. "In the garden!"

He had to make an effort to bring himself back to the place he was standing in and when he felt he was on earth again he turned and went out of the room. He took his way, as Mary had done, through the door in the shrubbery and among the laurels and the fountain beds. The fountain was playing now and was encircled by beds of brilliant autumn flowers. He crossed the lawn and turned into the Long Walk by the ivied walls. He did not walk quickly, but slowly, and his eyes were on the path. He felt as if he were being drawn back to the place he had so long forsaken, and he did not know why. As he drew near to it his step became still more slow. He knew where the door was even though the ivy hung thick over it—but he did not know exactly where it lay—that buried key.

So he stopped and stood still, looking about him, and almost the moment after he had paused he started and listened—asking himself if he were walking in a dream.

The ivy hung thick over the door, the key was buried under the shrubs, no human being had passed that portal for ten lonely years—and yet inside the garden there were sounds. They were the sounds of running scuffling feet seeming to chase round and round under the trees, they were strange sounds of lowered suppressed voices—exclamations and smothered joyous cries. It seemed actually like the laughter of young things, the uncontrollable laughter of children who were trying not to be heard but who in a moment or so—as their excitement mounted—would burst forth. What in heaven's name was he dreaming of—what in heaven's name did he hear? Was he losing his reason and thinking he heard things which were not for human ears? Was it that the far clear voice had meant?

And then the moment came, the uncontrollable moment when the sounds forgot to hush themselves. The feet ran faster and faster—they were nearing the garden door—there was quick strong young breathing and a wild outbreak of laughing shows which could not be contained—and the door in the wall was flung wide open, the sheet of ivy swinging back, and a boy burst through it at full speed and, without seeing the outsider, dashed almost into his arms.

Mr. Craven had extended them just in time to save him from falling as a result of his unseeing dash against him, and when he held him away to look at him in amazement at his being there he truly gasped for breath.

He was a tall boy and a handsomeone. He was glowing with life and his running had sent splendid color leaping to his face. He threw the thick hair back from his forehead and lifted a pair of strange gray eyes—eyes full of boyish laughter and rimmed with black lashes like a fringe. It was the eyes which made Mr. Craven gasp for breath. "Who—What? Who!" he stammered.

This was not what Colin had expected—this was not what he had planned. He had never thought of such a meeting. And yet to come dashing out—winning a race—perhaps it was even better. He drew himself up to his very tallest. Mary, who had been running with him and had dashed through the door too, believed that he managed to make himself look taller than he had ever looked before—inches taller.

"Father," he said, "I'm Colin. You can't believe it. I scarcely can myself. I'm Colin."

Like Mrs. Medlock, he did not understand what his father meant when he said hurriedly:

"In the garden! In the garden!"

"Yes," hurried on Colin. "It was the garden that did it—and Mary and Dickon and the creatures—and the Magic. No one knows. We kept it to tell you when you came. I'm well, I can beat Mary in a race. I'm going to be an athlete."

He said it all so like a healthy boy—his face flushed, his words tumbling over each other in his eagerness—that Mr. Craven's soul shook with unbelieving joy.

Colin put out his hand and laid it on his father's arm.

"Aren't you glad, Father?" he ended. "Aren't you glad? I'm going to live forever and ever and ever!"

Mr. Craven put his hands on both the boy's shoulders and held him still. He knew he dared not even try to speak for a moment.

"Take me into the garden, my boy," he said at last. "And tell me all about it."

And so they led him in.

The place was a wilderness of autumn gold and purple and violet blue and flaming scarlet and on every side were sheaves of late lilies standing together—lilies which were white or white and ruby. He remembered well when the first of them had been planted that just at this season of the year their late glories should reveal themselves. Late roses climbed and hung and clustered and the sunshine deepening the hue of the yellowing trees made one feel that one, stood in an embowered temple of gold. The newcomer stood silent just as the children had done when they came into its grayness. He looked round and round.

"I thought it would be dead," he said.

"Mary thought so at first," said Colin. "But it came alive."

Then they sat down under their tree—all but Colin, who wanted to stand while he told the story.

It was the strangest thing he had ever heard, Archibald Craven thought, as it was poured forth in headlong boy fashion. Mystery and Magic and wild creatures, the weird midnight meeting—the coming of the spring—the passion of insulted pride which had dragged the young Rajah to his feet to defy old Ben Weatherstaff to his face. The odd companionship, the play-acting, the great secret so carefully kept. The listener laughed until tears came into his eyes and sometimes tears came into his eyes when he was not laughing. The Athlete, the Lecturer, the Scientific Discoverer was a laughable, lovable, healthy young human thing.

"Now," he said at the end of the story, "it need not be a secret any more. I dare say it will frighten them nearly into fits when they see me—but I am never going to get into the chair again. I shall walk back with you, Father—to the house."

*

Ben Weatherstaff's duties rarely took him away from the gardens, but on this occasion he made an excuse to carry some vegetables to the kitchen and being invited into the servants' hall by Mrs. Medlock to drink a glass of beer he was on the spot—as he had hoped to be—when the most dramatic event Misselthwaite Manor had seen during the present generation actually took place. One of the windows looking upon the courtyard gave also a glimpse of the lawn. Mrs. Medlock, knowing Ben had come from the gardens, hoped that he might have caught sight of his master and even by chance of his meeting with Master Colin.

"Did you see either of them, Weatherstaff?" she asked.

Ben took his beer-mug from his mouth and wiped his lips with the back of his hand.

"Aye, that I did," he answered with a shrewdly significant air.

"Both of them?" suggested Mrs. Medlock.

"Both of 'em," returned Ben Weatherstaff. "Thank ye kindly, ma'am, I could sup up another mug of it."

"Together?" said Mrs. Medlock, hastily overfilling his beer-mug in her excitement.

"Together, ma'am," and Ben gulped down half of his new mug at one gulp.

"Where was Master Colin? How did he look? What did they say to each other?"

"I didna' hear that," said Ben, "along o' only bein' on th' stepladder lookin, over th' wall. But I'll tell thee this. There's been things goin' on outside as you house people knows nowt about. An' what tha'll find out tha'll find out soon."

And it was not two minutes before he swallowed the last of his beer and waved his mug solemnly toward the window which took in through the shrubbery a piece of the lawn.

"Look there," he said, "if tha's curious. Look what's comin' across th' grass."

When Mrs. Medlock looked she threw up her hands and gave a little shriek and every man and woman servant within hearing bolted across the servants' hall and stood looking through the window with their eyes almost starting out of their heads.

Across the lawn came the Master of Misselthwaite and he looked as many of them had never seen him. And by his, side with his head up in the air and his eyes full of laughter walked as strongly and steadily as any boy in Yorkshire—Master Colin.

Peter Pan

by J.M. Barrie

1

Peter Breaks Through

All children, except one, grow up. They soon know that they will grow up, and the way Wendy knew was this. One day when she was two years old she was playing in a garden, and she plucked another flower and ran with it to her mother. I suppose she must have looked rather delightful, for Mrs. Darling put her hand to her heart and cried, "Oh, why can't you remain like this for ever!" This was all that passed between them on the subject, but henceforth Wendy knew that she must grow up. You always know after you are two. Two is the beginning of the end.

Of course they lived at 14 [their house number on their street], and until Wendy came her mother was the chief one. She was a lovely lady, with a romantic mind and such a sweet mocking mouth. Her romantic mind was like the tiny boxes, one within the other, that come from the puzzling East, however many you discover there is always one more; and her sweet mocking mouth had one kiss on it that Wendy could never get, though there it was, perfectly conspicuous in the right-hand corner.

The way Mr. Darling won her was this: the many gentlemen who had been boys when she was a girl discovered simultaneously that they loved her, and they all ran to her house to propose to her except Mr. Darling, who took a cab and nipped in first, and so he got her. He got all of her, except the innermost box and the kiss. He never knew about the box, and in time he gave up trying for the kiss. Wendy thought Napoleon could have got it, but I can picture him trying, and then going off in a passion, slamming the door.

Mr. Darling used to boast to Wendy that her mother not only loved him but respected him. He was one of those deep ones who know about stocks and shares. Of course no one really knows, but he quite seemed to know, and he often said stocks were up and shares were down in a way that would have made any woman respect him.

Mrs. Darling was married in white, and at first she kept the books perfectly, almost gleefully, as if it were a game, not so much as a Brussels sprout was missing; but by and by whole cauliflowers dropped out, and instead of them there were pictures of babies without faces. She drew them when she should have been totting up. They were Mrs. Darling's guesses.

Wendy came first, then John, then Michael.

For a week or two after Wendy came it was doubtful whether they would be able to keep her, as she was another mouth to feed. Mr. Darling was frightfully proud of her, but he was very honourable, and he sat on the edge of Mrs. Darling's bed, holding her hand and calculating expenses, while she looked at him imploringly. She wanted to risk it, come what might, but that was not his way; his way was with a pencil and a piece of paper, and if she confused him with suggestions he had to begin at the beginning again.

"Now don't interrupt," he would beg of her.

"I have one pound seventeen here, and two and six at the office; I can cut off my coffee at the office, say ten shillings, making two nine and six, with your eighteen and three makes three nine seven, with five naught naught in my cheque-book makes eight nine seven—who is that moving?—eight nine seven, dot and carry seven—don't speak, my own—and the pound you lent to that man who came to the door—quiet, child—dot and carry child—there, you've done it!—did I say nine nine seven?

yes, I said nine nine seven; the question is, can we try it for a year on nine nine seven?"

"Of course we can, George," she cried. But she was prejudiced in Wendy's favour, and he was really the grander character of the two.

"Remember mumps," he warned her almost threateningly, and off he went again. "Mumps one pound, that is what I have put down, but I daresay it will be more like thirty shillings—don't speak—measles one five, German measles half a guinea, makes two fifteen six—don't waggle your finger—whooping-cough, say fifteen shillings"—and so on it went, and it added up differently each time; but at last Wendy just got through, with mumps reduced to twelve six, and the two kinds of measles treated as one.

There was the same excitement over John, and Michael had even a narrower squeak; but both were kept, and soon, you might have seen the three of them going in a row to Miss Fulsom's Kindergarten school, accompanied by their nurse.

Mrs. Darling loved to have everything just so, and Mr. Darling had a passion for being exactly like his neighbours; so, of course, they had a nurse. As they were poor, owing to the amount of milk the children drank, this nurse was a prim Newfoundland dog, called Nana, who had belonged to no one in particular until the Darlings engaged her. She had always thought children important, however, and the Darlings had become acquainted with her in Kensington Gardens, where she spent most of her spare time peeping into perambulators, and was much hated by careless nursemaids, whom she followed to their homes and complained of to their mistresses. She proved to be quite a treasure of a nurse. How thorough she was at bath-time, and up at any moment of the night if one of her charges made the slightest cry. Of course her kennel was in the nursery. She had a genius for knowing when a cough is a thing to have no patience with and when it needs stocking around your throat. She believed to her last day in old-fashioned remedies like rhubarb leaf, and made sounds of contempt over all this new-fangled talk about germs, and so on. It was a lesson in propriety to see her escorting the children to school, walking sedately by their side when they were well behaved, and butting them back into line if they strayed. On John's footer [in England soccer was called football, "footer" for short] days she never once forgot his sweater, and she usually carried an umbrella in her mouth in case of rain. There is a room in the basement of Miss Fulsom's school where the nurses wait. They sat on forms, while Nana lay on the floor, but that was the only difference. They affected to ignore her as of an inferior social status to themselves, and she despised their light talk. She resented visits to the nursery from Mrs. Darling's friends, but if they did come she first whipped off Michael's pinafore and put him into the one with blue braiding, and smoothed out Wendy and made a dash at John's hair.

No nursery could possibly have been conducted more correctly, and Mr. Darling knew it, yet he sometimes wondered uneasily whether the neighbours talked.

He had his position in the city to consider.

Nana also troubled him in another way. He had sometimes a feeling that she did not admire him. "I know she admires you tremendously, George," Mrs. Darling would assure him, and then she would sign to the children to be specially nice to father. Lovely dances followed, in which the only other servant, Liza, was sometimes allowed to join. Such a midget she looked in her long skirt and maid's cap, though she had sworn, when engaged, that she would never see ten again. The gaiety of those romps! And gayest of all was Mrs. Darling, who would pirouette so wildly that all you could see of her was the kiss, and then if you had dashed at her you might have got it. There never was a simpler happier family until the coming of Peter Pan.

Mrs. Darling first heard of Peter when she was tidying up her children's minds. It is the nightly custom of every good mother after her children are asleep to rummage in their minds and put things straight for next morning, repacking into their proper places the many articles that have wandered during the day. If you could keep awake (but of course you can't) you would see your own mother doing this, and you would find it very interesting to watch her. It is quite like tidying up drawers. You would see her on her knees, I expect, lingering humorously over some of your contents, wondering where on earth you had picked this thing up, making discoveries sweet and not so sweet, pressing this to her cheek as if it were as nice as a kitten, and hurriedly stowing that out of sight. When you wake in the morning, the naughtiness and evil passions with which you went to bed have been folded up small and placed at the bottom of your mind and on the top, beautifully aired, are spread out your prettier thoughts, ready for you to put on.

I don't know whether you have ever seen a map of a person's mind. Doctors sometimes draw maps of other parts of you, and your own map can become intensely interesting, but catch them trying to draw a map of a child's mind, which is not only confused, but keeps going round all the time. There are zigzag lines on it, just like your temperature on a card, and these are probably roads in the island, for the Neverland is always more or less an island, with astonishing splashes of colour here and there, and coral reefs and rakish-looking craft in the offing, and savages and lonely lairs, and gnomes who are mostly tailors, and caves through which a river runs, and princes with six elder brothers, and a hut fast going to decay, and one very small old lady with a hooked nose. It would be an easy map if that were all, but there is also first day at school, religion, fathers, the round pond, needlework, murders, hangings, verbs that take the dative, chocolate pudding day, getting into braces, say ninety-nine, three-pence for pulling out your tooth yourself, and so on, and either these are part of the island or they are another map showing through, and it is all rather confusing, especially as nothing will stand still.

Of course the Neverlands vary a good deal. John's, for instance, had a lagoon with flamingoes flying over it at which John was shooting, while Michael, who was very small, had a flamingo with lagoons flying over it. John lived in a boat turned upside down on the sands, Michael in a wigwam, Wendy in a house of leaves deftly sewn together. John had no friends, Michael had friends at night, Wendy had a pet wolf forsaken by its parents, but on the whole the Neverlands have a family resemblance, and if they stood still in a row you could say of them that they have each other's nose, and so forth. On these magic shores children at play are for ever beaching their coracles [simple boat]. We too have been there; we can still hear the sound of the surf, though we shall land no more.

Of all delectable islands the Neverland is the snuggest and most compact, not large and sprawly, you know, with tedious distances between one adventure and another, but nicely crammed. When you play at it by day with the chairs and table-cloth, it is not in the least alarming, but in the two minutes before you go to sleep it becomes very real. That is why there are night-lights.

Occasionally in her travels through her children's minds Mrs. Darling found things she could not understand, and of these quite the most perplexing was the word Peter. She knew of no Peter, and yet he was here and there in John and Michael's minds, while Wendy's began to be scrawled all over with him. The name stood out in bolder letters than any of the other words, and as Mrs. Darling gazed she felt that it had an oddly cocky appearance.

"Yes, he is rather cocky," Wendy admitted with regret. Her mother had been questioning her.

"But who is he, my pet?"

"He is Peter Pan, you know, mother."

At first Mrs. Darling did not know, but after thinking back into her childhood she just remembered a Peter Pan who was said to live with the fairies. There were odd stories about him, as that when children died he went part of the way with them, so that they should not be frightened. She had believed in him at the time, but now that she was married and full of sense she quite doubted whether there was any such person.

"Besides," she said to Wendy, "he would be grown up by this time."

"Oh no, he isn't grown up," Wendy assured her confidently, "and he is just my size." She meant that he was her size in both mind and body; she didn't know how she knew, she just knew it.

Mrs. Darling consulted Mr. Darling, but he smiled pooh-pooh. "Mark my words," he said, "it is some nonsense Nana has been putting into their heads; just the sort of idea a dog would have. Leave it alone, and it will blow over."

But it would not blow over and soon the troublesome boy gave Mrs. Darling quite a shock.

Children have the strangest adventures without being troubled by them. For instance, they may remember to mention, a week after the event happened, that when they were in the wood they had met their dead father and had a game with him. It was in this casual way that Wendy one morning made a disquieting revelation. Some leaves of a tree had been found on the nursery floor, which certainly were not there when the children went to bed, and Mrs. Darling was puzzling over them when Wendy said with a tolerant smile:

"I do believe it is that Peter again!"

"Whatever do you mean, Wendy?"

"It is so naughty of him not to wipe his feet," Wendy said, sighing. She was a tidy child.

She explained in quite a matter-of-fact way that she thought Peter sometimes came to the nursery in the night and sat on the foot of her bed and played on his pipes to her. Unfortunately she never woke, so she didn't know how she knew, she just knew.

"What nonsense you talk, precious. No one can get into the house without knocking."

"I think he comes in by the window," she said.

"My love, it is three floors up."

"Were not the leaves at the foot of the window, mother?"

It was quite true; the leaves had been found very near the window.

Mrs. Darling did not know what to think, for it all seemed so natural to Wendy that you could not dismiss it by saying she had been dreaming.

"My child," the mother cried, "why did you not tell me of this before?"

"I forgot," said Wendy lightly. She was in a hurry to get her breakfast.

Oh, surely she must have been dreaming.

But, on the other hand, there were the leaves. Mrs. Darling examined them very carefully; they were skeleton leaves, but she was sure they did not come from any tree that grew in England. She crawled about the floor, peering at it with a candle for marks of a strange foot. She rattled the poker up the chimney and tapped the walls. She let down a tape from the window to the pavement, and it was a sheer drop of thirty feet, without so much as a spout to climb up by.

Certainly Wendy had been dreaming.

But Wendy had not been dreaming, as the very next night showed, the night on which the extraordinary adventures of these children may be said to have begun.

On the night we speak of all the children were once more in bed. It happened to be Nana's evening off, and Mrs. Darling had bathed them and sung to them till one by one they had let go her hand and slid away into the land of sleep.

All were looking so safe and cosy that she smiled at her fears now and sat down tranquilly by the fire to sew.

It was something for Michael, who on his birthday was getting into shirts. The fire was warm, however, and the nursery dimly lit by three night-lights, and presently the sewing lay on Mrs. Darling's lap. Then her head nodded, oh, so gracefully. She was asleep. Look at the four of them, Wendy and Michael over there, John here, and Mrs. Darling by the fire. There should have been a fourth night-light.

While she slept she had a dream. She dreamt that the Neverland had come too near and that a strange boy had broken through from it. He did not alarm her, for she thought she had seen him before in the faces of many women who have no children. Perhaps he is to be found in the faces of some mothers also. But in her dream he had rent the film that obscures the Neverland, and she saw Wendy and John and Michael peeping through the gap.

The dream by itself would have been a trifle, but while she was dreaming the window of the nursery blew open, and a boy did drop on the floor. He was accompanied by a strange light, no bigger than your fist, which darted about the room like a living thing and I think it must have been this light that wakened Mrs. Darling.

She started up with a cry, and saw the boy, and somehow she knew at once that he was Peter Pan. If you or I or Wendy had been there we should have seen that he was very like Mrs. Darling's kiss. He was a lovely boy, clad in skeleton leaves and the juices that ooze out of trees but the most entrancing thing about him was that he had all his first teeth. When he saw she was a grown-up, he gnashed the little pearls at her.

2

The Shadow

Mrs. Darling screamed, and, as if in answer to a bell, the door opened, and Nana entered, returned from her evening out. She growled and sprang at the boy, who leapt lightly through the window. Again Mrs. Darling screamed, this time in distress for him, for she thought he was killed, and she ran down into the street to look for his little body, but it was not there; and she looked up, and in the black night she could see nothing but what she thought was a shooting star.

She returned to the nursery, and found Nana with something in her mouth, which proved to be the boy's shadow. As he leapt at the window Nana had closed it quickly, too late to catch him, but his shadow had not had time to get out; slam went the window and snapped it off.

You may be sure Mrs. Darling examined the shadow carefully, but it was quite the ordinary kind.

Nana had no doubt of what was the best thing to do with this shadow. She hung it out at the window, meaning "He is sure to come back for it; let us put it where he can get it easily without disturbing the children."

But unfortunately Mrs. Darling could not leave it hanging out at the window, it looked so like the washing and lowered the whole tone of the house. She thought of showing it to Mr. Darling, but he was totting up winter great-coats for John and Michael, with a wet towel around his head to keep his brain clear, and it seemed a shame to trouble him; besides, she knew exactly what he would say: "It all comes of having a dog for a nurse."

She decided to roll the shadow up and put it away carefully in a drawer, until a fitting opportunity came for telling her husband. Ah me!

The opportunity came a week later, on that never-to-be-forgotten Friday. Of course it was a Friday.

"I ought to have been specially careful on a Friday," she used to say afterwards to her husband, while perhaps Nana was on the other side of her, holding her hand.

"No, no," Mr. Darling always said, "I am responsible for it all. I, George Darling, did it. MEA CULPA, MEA CULPA." He had had a classical education.

They sat thus night after night recalling that fatal Friday, till every detail of it was stamped on their brains and came through on the other side like the faces on a bad coinage.

"If only I had not accepted that invitation to dine at 27," Mrs. Darling said.

"If only I had not poured my medicine into Nana's bowl," said Mr. Darling.

"If only I had pretended to like the medicine," was what Nana's wet eyes said.

"My liking for parties, George."

"My fatal gift of humour, dearest."

"My touchiness about trifles, dear master and mistress."

Then one or more of them would break down altogether; Nana at the thought, "It's true, it's true, they ought not to have had a dog for a nurse." Many a time it was Mr. Darling who put the handkerchief to Nana's eyes.

"That fiend!" Mr. Darling would cry, and Nana's bark was the echo of it, but Mrs. Darling never upbraided Peter; there was something in the right-hand corner of her mouth that wanted her not to call Peter names.

They would sit there in the empty nursery, recalling fondly every smallest detail of that dreadful evening. It had begun so uneventfully, so precisely like a hundred other evenings, with Nana putting on the water for Michael's bath and carrying him to it on her back.

"I won't go to bed," he had shouted, like one who still believed that he had the last word on the subject, "I won't, I won't. Nana, it isn't six o'clock yet. Oh dear, oh dear, I shan't love you any more, Nana. I tell you I won't be bathed, I won't, I won't!"

Then Mrs. Darling had come in, wearing her white evening-gown. She had dressed early because Wendy so loved to see her in her evening-gown, with the necklace George had given her. She was wearing Wendy's bracelet on her arm; she had asked for the loan of it. Wendy loved to lend her bracelet to her mother.

She had found her two older children playing at being herself and father on the occasion of Wendy's birth, and John was saying:

"I am happy to inform you, Mrs. Darling, that you are now a mother," in just such a tone as Mr. Darling himself may have used on the real occasion.

Wendy had danced with joy, just as the real Mrs. Darling must have done.

Then John was born, with the extra pomp that he conceived due to the birth of a male, and Michael came from his bath to ask to be born also, but John said brutally that they did not want any more.

Michael had nearly cried. "Nobody wants me," he said, and of course the lady in the evening-dress could not stand that.

"I do," she said, "I so want a third child."

"Boy or girl?" asked Michael, not too hopefully.

"Boy."

Then he had leapt into her arms. Such a little thing for Mr. and Mrs. Darling and Nana to recall now, but not so little if that was to be Michael's last night in the nursery.

They go on with their recollections.

"It was then that I rushed in like a tornado, wasn't it?" Mr. Darling would say, scorning himself; and indeed he had been like a tornado.

Perhaps there was some excuse for him. He, too, had been dressing for the party, and all had gone well with him until he came to his tie. It is an astounding thing to have to tell, but this man, though he knew about stocks and shares, had no real mastery of his tie. Sometimes the thing yielded to him without a contest, but there were occasions when it would have been better for the house if he had swallowed his pride and used a made-up tie.

This was such an occasion. He came rushing into the nursery with the crumpled little brute of a tie in his hand.

"Why, what is the matter, father dear?"

"Matter!" he yelled; he really yelled. "This tie, it will not tie." He became dangerously sarcastic. "Not round my neck! Round the bedpost! Oh yes, twenty times have I made it up round the bedpost, but round my neck, no! Oh dear no! begs to be excused!"

He thought Mrs. Darling was not sufficiently impressed, and he went on sternly, "I warn you of this, mother, that unless this tie is round my neck we don't go out to dinner tonight, and if I don't go out to dinner tonight, I never go to the office again, and if I don't go to the office again, you and I starve, and our children will be flung into the streets."

Even then Mrs. Darling was placid. "Let me try, dear," she said, and indeed that was what he had come to ask her to do, and with her nice cool hands she tied his tie for him, while the children stood around to see their fate decided. Some men would have resented her being able to do it so easily, but Mr. Darling had far too fine a nature for that; he thanked her carelessly, at once forgot his rage, and in another moment was dancing round the room with Michael on his back.

"How wildly we romped!" says Mrs. Darling now, recalling it.

"Our last romp!" Mr. Darling groaned.

"O George, do you remember Michael suddenly said to me, 'How did you get to know me, mother?'"

"I remember!"

"They were rather sweet, don't you think, George?"

"And they were ours, ours! and now they are gone."

The romp had ended with the appearance of Nana, and most unluckily Mr. Darling collided against her, covering his trousers with hairs. They were not only new trousers, but they were the first he had ever had with braid on them, and he had had to bite his lip to prevent the tears coming. Of course Mrs. Darling brushed him, but he began to talk again about its being a mistake to have a dog for a nurse.

"George, Nana is a treasure."

"No doubt, but I have an uneasy feeling at times that she looks upon the children as puppies."

"Oh no, dear one, I feel sure she knows they have souls."

"I wonder," Mr. Darling said thoughtfully, "I wonder." It was an opportunity, his wife felt, for telling him about the boy. At first he pooh-poohed the story, but he became thoughtful when she showed him the shadow.

"It is nobody I know," he said, examining it carefully, "but it does look a scoundrel."

"We were still discussing it, you remember," says Mr. Darling, "when Nana came in with Michael's medicine. You will never carry the bottle in your mouth again, Nana, and it is all my fault."

Strong man though he was, there is no doubt that he had behaved rather foolishly over the medicine. If he had a weakness, it was for thinking that all his life he had taken medicine boldly, and so now, when Michael dodged the spoon in Nana's mouth, he had said reprovingly, "Be a man, Michael."

"Won't; won't!" Michael cried naughtily. Mrs. Darling left the room to get a chocolate for him, and Mr. Darling thought this showed want of firmness.

"Mother, don't pamper him," he called after her. "Michael, when I was your age I took medicine without a murmur. I said, 'Thank you, kind parents, for giving me bottles to make me well.'"

He really thought this was true, and Wendy, who was now in her night-gown, believed it also, and she said, to encourage Michael, "That medicine you sometimes take, father, is much nastier, isn't it?"

"Ever so much nastier," Mr. Darling said bravely, "and I would take it now as an example to you, Michael, if I hadn't lost the bottle."

He had not exactly lost it; he had climbed in the dead of night to the top of the wardrobe and hidden it there. What he did not know was that the faithful Liza had found it, and put it back on his wash-stand.

"I know where it is, father," Wendy cried, always glad to be of service. "I'll bring it," and she was off before he could stop her. Immediately his spirits sank in the strangest way.

"John," he said, shuddering, "it's most beastly stuff. It's that nasty, sticky, sweet kind."

"It will soon be over, father," John said cheerily, and then in rushed Wendy with the medicine in a glass.

"I have been as quick as I could," she panted.

"You have been wonderfully quick," her father retorted, with a vindictive politeness that was quite thrown away upon her. "Michael first," he said doggedly.

"Father first," said Michael, who was of a suspicious nature.

"I shall be sick, you know," Mr. Darling said threateningly.

"Come on, father," said John.

"Hold your tongue, John," his father rapped out.

Wendy was quite puzzled. "I thought you took it quite easily, father."

"That is not the point," he retorted. "The point is, that there is more in my glass than in Michael's spoon." His proud heart was nearly bursting. "And it isn't fair: I would say it though it were with my last breath; it isn't fair."

"Father, I am waiting," said Michael coldly.

"It's all very well to say you are waiting; so am I waiting."

"Father's a cowardly custard."

"So are you a cowardly custard."

"I'm not frightened."

"Neither am I frightened."

"Well, then, take it."

"Well, then, you take it."

Wendy had a splendid idea. "Why not both take it at the same time?"

"Certainly," said Mr. Darling. "Are you ready, Michael?"

Wendy gave the words, one, two, three, and Michael took his medicine, but Mr. Darling slipped his behind his back.

There was a yell of rage from Michael, and "O father!" Wendy exclaimed.

"What do you mean by 'O father'?" Mr. Darling demanded. "Stop that row, Michael. I meant to take mine, but I—I missed it."

It was dreadful the way all the three were looking at him, just as if they did not admire him. "Look here, all of you," he said entreatingly, as soon as Nana had gone into the bathroom. "I have just thought of a splendid joke. I shall pour my medicine into Nana's bowl, and she will drink it, thinking it is milk!"

It was the colour of milk; but the children did not have their father's sense of humour, and they looked at him reproachfully as he poured the medicine into Nana's bowl. "What fun!" he said doubtfully, and they did not dare expose him when Mrs. Darling and Nana returned.

"Nana, good dog," he said, patting her, "I have put a little milk into your bowl, Nana."

Nana wagged her tail, ran to the medicine, and began lapping it. Then she gave Mr. Darling such a look, not an angry look: she showed him the great red tear that makes us so sorry for noble dogs, and crept into her kennel.

Mr. Darling was frightfully ashamed of himself, but he would not give in. In a horrid silence Mrs. Darling smelt the bowl. "O George," she said, "it's your medicine!"

"It was only a joke," he roared, while she comforted her boys, and Wendy hugged Nana. "Much good," he said bitterly, "my wearing myself to the bone trying to be funny in this house."

And still Wendy hugged Nana. "That's right," he shouted. "Coddle her! Nobody coddles me. Oh dear no! I am only the breadwinner, why should I be coddled—why, why, why!"

"George," Mrs. Darling entreated him, "not so loud; the servants will hear you." Somehow they had got into the way of calling Liza the servants.

"Let them!" he answered recklessly. "Bring in the whole world. But I refuse to allow that dog to lord it in my nursery for an hour longer."

The children wept, and Nana ran to him beseechingly, but he waved her back. He felt he was a strong man again. "In vain, in vain," he cried; "the proper place for you is the yard, and there you go to be tied up this instant."

"George, George," Mrs. Darling whispered, "remember what I told you about that boy."

Alas, he would not listen. He was determined to show who was master in that house, and when commands would not draw Nana from the kennel, he lured her out of it with honeyed words, and seizing her roughly, dragged her from the nursery. He was ashamed of himself, and yet he did it. It was all owing to his too affectionate nature, which craved for admiration. When he had tied her up in the backyard, the wretched father went and sat in the passage, with his knuckles to his eyes.

In the meantime Mrs. Darling had put the children to bed in unwonted silence and lit their night-lights. They could hear Nana barking, and John whimpered, "It is because he is chaining her up in the yard," but Wendy was wiser.

"That is not Nana's unhappy bark," she said, little guessing what was about to happen; "that is her bark when she smells danger."

Danger!

"Are you sure, Wendy?"

"Oh, yes."

Mrs. Darling quivered and went to the window. It was securely fastened. She looked out, and the night was peppered with stars. They were crowding round the house, as if curious to see what was to take place there, but she did not notice this, nor that one or two of the smaller ones winked at her. Yet a nameless fear clutched at her heart and made her cry, "Oh, how I wish that I wasn't going to a party tonight!"

Even Michael, already half asleep, knew that she was perturbed, and he asked, "Can anything harm us, mother, after the night-lights are lit?"

"Nothing, precious," she said; "they are the eyes a mother leaves behind her to guard her children."

She went from bed to bed singing enchantments over them, and little Michael flung his arms round her. "Mother," he cried, "I'm glad of you." They were the last words she was to hear from him for a long time.

No. 27 was only a few yards distant, but there had been a slight fall of snow, and Father and Mother Darling picked their way over it deftly not to soil their shoes. They were already the only persons in the street, and all the stars were watching them. Stars are beautiful, but they may not take an active part in anything, they must just look on for ever. It is a punishment put on them for something they did so long ago that no star now knows what it was. So the older ones have become glassy-eyed and seldom speak (winking is the star language), but the little ones still wonder. They are not really friendly to Peter, who had a mischievous way of stealing up behind them and trying to blow them out; but they are so fond of fun that they were on his side tonight, and anxious to get the grown-ups out of the way. So as soon as the door of 27 closed on Mr. and Mrs. Darling there was a commotion in the firmament, and the smallest of all the stars in the Milky Way screamed out:

"Now, Peter!"

3

Come Away, Come Away!

For a moment after Mr. and Mrs. Darling left the house the night-lights by the beds of the three children continued to burn clearly. They were awfully nice little night-lights, and one cannot help wishing that they could have kept awake to see Peter; but Wendy's light blinked and gave such a yawn that the other two yawned also, and before they could close their mouths all the three went out.

There was another light in the room now, a thousand times brighter than the night-lights, and in the time we have taken to say this, it had been in all the drawers in the nursery, looking for Peter's shadow, rummaged the wardrobe and turned every pocket inside out. It was not really a light; it made this light by flashing about so quickly, but when it came to rest for a second you saw it was a fairy, no longer than your hand, but still growing. It was a girl called Tinker Bell exquisitely gowned in a skeleton leaf, cut low and square, through which her figure could be seen to the best advantage. She was slightly inclined to EMBONPOINT. [plump hourglass figure]

A moment after the fairy's entrance the window was blown open by the breathing of the little stars, and Peter dropped in. He had carried Tinker Bell part of the way, and his hand was still messy with the fairy dust.

"Tinker Bell," he called softly, after making sure that the children were asleep, "Tink, where are you?" She was in a jug for the moment, and liking it extremely; she had never been in a jug before.

"Oh, do come out of that jug, and tell me, do you know where they put my shadow?"

The loveliest tinkle as of golden bells answered him. It is the fairy language. You ordinary children can never hear it, but if you were to hear it you would know that you had heard it once before.

Tink said that the shadow was in the big box. She meant the chest of drawers, and Peter jumped at the drawers, scattering their contents to the floor with both hands, as kings toss ha'pence to the crowd. In a moment he had recovered his shadow, and in his delight he forgot that he had shut Tinker Bell up in the drawer.

If he thought at all, but I don't believe he ever thought, it was that he and his shadow, when brought near each other, would join like drops of water, and when they did not he was appalled. He tried to stick it on with soap from the bathroom, but that also failed. A shudder passed through Peter, and he sat on the floor and cried.

His sobs woke Wendy, and she sat up in bed. She was not alarmed to see a stranger crying on the nursery floor; she was only pleasantly interested.

"Boy," she said courteously, "why are you crying?"

Peter could be exceeding polite also, having learned the grand manner at fairy ceremonies, and he rose and bowed to her beautifully. She was much pleased, and bowed beautifully to him from the bed.

"What's your name?" he asked.

"Wendy Moira Angela Darling," she replied with some satisfaction. "What is your name?"

"Peter Pan."

She was already sure that he must be Peter, but it did seem a comparatively short name.

"Is that all?"

"Yes," he said rather sharply. He felt for the first time that it was a shortish name.

"I'm so sorry," said Wendy Moira Angela.

"It doesn't matter," Peter gulped.

She asked where he lived.

"Second to the right," said Peter, "and then straight on till morning."

"What a funny address!"

Peter had a sinking. For the first time he felt that perhaps it was a funny address.

"No, it isn't," he said.

"I mean," Wendy said nicely, remembering that she was hostess, "is that what they put on the letters?"

He wished she had not mentioned letters.

"Don't get any letters," he said contemptuously.

"But your mother gets letters?"

"Don't have a mother," he said. Not only had he no mother, but he had not the slightest desire to have one. He thought them very over-rated persons. Wendy, however, felt at once that she was in the presence of a tragedy.

"O Peter, no wonder you were crying," she said, and got out of bed and ran to him.

"I wasn't crying about mothers," he said rather indignantly. "I was crying because I can't get my shadow to stick on. Besides, I wasn't crying."

"It has come off?"

"Yes."

Then Wendy saw the shadow on the floor, looking so draggled, and she was frightfully sorry for Peter. "How awful!" she said, but she could not help smiling when she saw that he had been trying to stick it on with soap. How exactly like a boy!

Fortunately she knew at once what to do. "It must be sewn on," she said, just a little patronisingly.

"What's sewn?" he asked.

"You're dreadfully ignorant."

"No, I'm not."

But she was exulting in his ignorance. "I shall sew it on for you, my little man," she said, though he was as tall as herself, and she got out her housewife [sewing bag], and sewed the shadow on to Peter's foot.

"I daresay it will hurt a little," she warned him.

"Oh, I shan't cry," said Peter, who was already of the opinion that he had never cried in his life. And he clenched his teeth and did not cry, and soon his shadow was behaving properly, though still a little creased.

"Perhaps I should have ironed it," Wendy said thoughtfully, but Peter, boylike, was indifferent to appearances, and he was now jumping about in the wildest glee. Alas, he had already forgotten that he owed his bliss to Wendy. He thought he had attached the shadow himself. "How clever I am!" he crowed rapturously, "oh, the cleverness of me!"

It is humiliating to have to confess that this conceit of Peter was one of his most fascinating qualities. To put it with brutal frankness, there never was a cockier boy.

But for the moment Wendy was shocked. "You conceit [braggart]," she exclaimed, with frightful sarcasm; "of course I did nothing!"

"You did a little," Peter said carelessly, and continued to dance.

"A little!" she replied with hauteur [pride]; "if I am no use I can at least withdraw," and she sprang in the most dignified way into bed and covered her face with the blankets.

To induce her to look up he pretended to be going away, and when this failed he sat on the end of the bed and tapped her gently with his foot. "Wendy," he said, "don't withdraw. I can't help crowing, Wendy, when I'm pleased with myself." Still she would not look up, though she was listening eagerly. "Wendy," he continued, in a voice that no woman has ever yet been able to resist, "Wendy, one girl is more use than twenty boys."

Now Wendy was every inch a woman, though there were not very many inches, and she peeped out of the bed-clothes.

"Do you really think so, Peter?"

"Yes, I do."

"I think it's perfectly sweet of you," she declared, "and I'll get up again," and she sat with him on the side of the bed. She also said she would give him a kiss if he liked, but Peter did not know what she meant, and he held out his hand expectantly.

"Surely you know what a kiss is?" she asked, aghast.

"I shall know when you give it to me," he replied stiffly, and not to hurt his feeling she gave him a thimble.

"Now," said he, "shall I give you a kiss?" and she replied with a slight primness, "If you please." She made herself rather cheap by inclining her face toward him, but he merely dropped an acorn button into her hand, so she slowly returned her face to where it had been before, and said nicely that she would wear his kiss on the chain around her neck. It was lucky that she did put it on that chain, for it was afterwards to save her life.

When people in our set are introduced, it is customary for them to ask each other's age, and so Wendy, who always liked to do the correct thing, asked Peter how old he was. It was not really a happy question to ask him; it was like an examination paper that asks grammar, when what you want to be asked is Kings of England.

"I don't know," he replied uneasily, "but I am quite young." He really knew nothing about it, he had merely suspicions, but he said at a venture, "Wendy, I ran away the day I was born."

Wendy was quite surprised, but interested; and she indicated in the charming drawing room manner, by a touch on her night-gown, that he could sit nearer her.

"It was because I heard father and mother," he explained in a low voice, "talking about what I was to be when I became a man." He was extraordinarily agitated now. "I don't want ever to be a man," he said with passion. "I want always to be a little boy and to have fun. So I ran away to Kensington Gardens and lived a long long time among the fairies."

She gave him a look of the most intense admiration, and he thought it was because he had run away, but it was really because he knew fairies. Wendy had lived such a home life that to know fairies struck her as quite delightful. She poured out questions about them, to his surprise, for they were rather a nuisance to him, getting in his way and so on, and indeed he sometimes had to give them a hiding [spanking]. Still, he liked them on the whole, and he told her about the beginning of fairies.

"You see, Wendy, when the first baby laughed for the first time, its laugh broke into a thousand pieces, and they all went skipping about, and that was the beginning of fairies."

Tedious talk this, but being a stay-at-home she liked it.

"And so," he went on good-naturedly, "there ought to be one fairy for every boy and girl."

"Ought to be? Isn't there?"

"No. You see children know such a lot now, they soon don't believe in fairies, and every time a child says, 'I don't believe in fairies,' there is a fairy somewhere that falls down dead."

Really, he thought they had now talked enough about fairies, and it struck him that Tinker Bell was keeping very quiet. "I can't think where she has gone to," he said, rising, and he called Tink by name. Wendy's heart went flutter with a sudden thrill.

"Peter," she cried, clutching him, "you don't mean to tell me that there is a fairy in this room!"

"She was here just now," he said a little impatiently. "You don't hear her, do you?" and they both listened.

"The only sound I hear," said Wendy, "is like a tinkle of bells."

"Well, that's Tink, that's the fairy language. I think I hear her too."

The sound came from the chest of drawers, and Peter made a merry face. No one could ever look quite so merry as Peter, and the loveliest of gurgles was his laugh. He had his first laugh still.

"Wendy," he whispered gleefully, "I do believe I shut her up in the drawer!"

He let poor Tink out of the drawer, and she flew about the nursery screaming with fury. "You shouldn't say such things," Peter retorted. "Of course I'm very sorry, but how could I know you were in the drawer?"

Wendy was not listening to him. "O Peter," she cried, "if she would only stand still and let me see her!"

"They hardly ever stand still," he said, but for one moment Wendy saw the romantic figure come to rest on the cuckoo clock. "O the lovely!" she cried, though Tink's face was still distorted with passion.

"Tink," said Peter amiably, "this lady says she wishes you were her fairy."

Tinker Bell answered insolently.

"What does she say, Peter?"

He had to translate. "She is not very polite. She says you are a great [huge] ugly girl, and that she is my fairy."

He tried to argue with Tink. "You know you can't be my fairy, Tink, because I am a gentleman and you are a lady."

To this Tink replied in these words, "You silly ass," and disappeared into the bathroom. "She is quite a common fairy," Peter explained apologetically, "she is called Tinker Bell because she mends the pots and kettles [tinker = tin worker]."

They were together in the armchair by this time, and Wendy plied him with more questions.

"If you don't live in Kensington Gardens now—"

"Sometimes I do still."

"But where do you live mostly now?"

"With the lost boys."

"Who are they?"

"They are the children who fall out of their perambulators when the nurse is looking the other way. If they are not claimed in seven days they are sent far away to the Neverland to defray expenses. I'm captain."

"What fun it must be!"

"Yes," said cunning Peter, "but we are rather lonely. You see we have no female companionship."

"Are none of the others girls?"

"Oh, no; girls, you know, are much too clever to fall out of their prams."

This flattered Wendy immensely. "I think," she said, "it is perfectly lovely the way you talk about girls; John there just despises us."

For reply Peter rose and kicked John out of bed, blankets and all; one kick. This seemed to Wendy rather forward for a first meeting, and she told him with spirit that he was not captain in her house. However, John continued to sleep so placidly on the floor that she allowed him to remain there. "And I know you meant to be kind," she said, relenting, "so you may give me a kiss."

For the moment she had forgotten his ignorance about kisses. "I thought you would want it back," he said a little bitterly, and offered to return her the thimble.

"Oh dear," said the nice Wendy, "I don't mean a kiss, I mean a thimble."

"What's that?"

"It's like this." She kissed him.

"Funny!" said Peter gravely. "Now shall I give you a thimble?"

"If you wish to," said Wendy, keeping her head erect this time.

Peter thimbled her, and almost immediately she screeched. "What is it, Wendy?"

"It was exactly as if someone were pulling my hair."

"That must have been Tink. I never knew her so naughty before."

And indeed Tink was darting about again, using offensive language.

"She says she will do that to you, Wendy, every time I give you a thimble."

"But why?"

"Why, Tink?"

Again Tink replied, "You silly ass." Peter could not understand why, but Wendy understood, and she was just slightly disappointed when he admitted that he came to the nursery window not to see her but to listen to stories.

"You see, I don't know any stories. None of the lost boys knows any stories."

"How perfectly awful," Wendy said.

"Do you know," Peter asked, "why swallows build in the eaves of houses? It is to listen to the stories. O Wendy, your mother was telling you such a lovely story."

"Which story was it?"

"About the prince who couldn't find the lady who wore the glass slipper."

"Peter," said Wendy excitedly, "that was Cinderella, and he found her, and they lived happily ever after."

Peter was so glad that he rose from the floor, where they had been sitting, and hurried to the window.

"Where are you going?" she cried with misgiving.

"To tell the other boys."

"Don't go Peter," she entreated, "I know such lots of stories."

Those were her precise words, so there can be no denying that it was she who first tempted him.

He came back, and there was a greedy look in his eyes now which ought to have alarmed her, but did not.

"Oh, the stories I could tell to the boys!" she cried, and then Peter gripped her and began to draw her toward the window.

"Let me go!" she ordered him.

"Wendy, do come with me and tell the other boys."

Of course she was very pleased to be asked, but she said, "Oh dear, I can't. Think of mummy! Besides, I can't fly."

"I'll teach you."

"Oh, how lovely to fly."

"I'll teach you how to jump on the wind's back, and then away we go."

"Oo!" she exclaimed rapturously.

"Wendy, Wendy, when you are sleeping in your silly bed you might be flying about with me saying funny things to the stars."

"Oo!"

"And, Wendy, there are mermaids."

"Mermaids! With tails?"

"Such long tails."

"Oh," cried Wendy, "to see a mermaid!"

He had become frightfully cunning. "Wendy," he said, "how we should all respect you."

She was wriggling her body in distress. It was quite as if she were trying to remain on the nursery floor.

But he had no pity for her.

"Wendy," he said, the sly one, "you could tuck us in at night."

"Oo!"

"None of us has ever been tucked in at night."

"Oo," and her arms went out to him.

"And you could darn our clothes, and make pockets for us. None of us has any pockets."

How could she resist. "Of course it's awfully fascinating!" she cried. "Peter, would you teach John and Michael to fly too?"

"If you like," he said indifferently, and she ran to John and Michael and shook them. "Wake up," she cried, "Peter Pan has come and he is to teach us to fly."

John rubbed his eyes. "Then I shall get up," he said. Of course he was on the floor already. "Hallo," he said, "I am up!"

Michael was up by this time also, looking as sharp as a knife with six blades and a saw, but Peter suddenly signed silence. Their faces assumed the awful craftiness of children listening for sounds from the grown-up world. All was as still as salt. Then everything was right. No, stop! Everything was wrong. Nana, who had been barking distressfully all the evening, was quiet now. It was her silence they had heard.

"Out with the light! Hide! Quick!" cried John, taking command for the only time throughout the whole adventure. And thus when Liza entered, holding Nana, the nursery seemed quite its old self, very dark, and you could have sworn you heard its three wicked inmates breathing angelically as they slept. They were really doing it artfully from behind the window curtains.

Liza was in a bad temper, for she was mixing the Christmas puddings in the kitchen, and had been drawn from them, with a raisin still on her cheek, by Nana's absurd suspicions. She thought the best way of getting a little quiet was to take Nana to the nursery for a moment, but in custody of course.

"There, you suspicious brute," she said, not sorry that Nana was in disgrace. "They are perfectly safe, aren't they? Every one of the little angels sound asleep in bed. Listen to their gentle breathing."

Here Michael, encouraged by his success, breathed so loudly that they were nearly detected. Nana knew that kind of breathing, and she tried to drag herself out of Liza's clutches.

But Liza was dense. "No more of it, Nana," she said sternly, pulling her out of the room. "I warn you if you bark again I shall go straight for master and missus and bring them home from the party, and then, oh, won't master whip you, just."

She tied the unhappy dog up again, but do you think Nana ceased to bark? Bring master and missus home from the party! Why, that was just what she wanted. Do you think she cared whether she was whipped so long as her charges were safe? Unfortunately Liza returned to her puddings, and Nana, seeing that no help would come from her, strained and strained at the chain until at last she broke it. In another moment she had burst into the dining room of 27 and flung up her paws to heaven, her most expressive way of making a communication. Mr. and Mrs. Darling knew at once that something terrible was happening in their nursery, and without a goodbye to their hostess they rushed into the street.

But it was now ten minutes since three scoundrels had been breathing behind the curtains, and Peter Pan can do a great deal in ten minutes.

We now return to the nursery.

"It's all right," John announced, emerging from his hiding-place. "I say, Peter, can you really fly?"

Instead of troubling to answer him Peter flew around the room, taking the mantelpiece on the way.

"How topping!" said John and Michael.

"How sweet!" cried Wendy.

"Yes, I'm sweet, oh, I am sweet!" said Peter, forgetting his manners again.

It looked delightfully easy, and they tried it first from the floor and then from the beds, but they always went down instead of up.

"I say, how do you do it?" asked John, rubbing his knee. He was quite a practical boy.

"You just think lovely wonderful thoughts," Peter explained, "and they lift you up in the air."

He showed them again.

"You're so nippy at it," John said, "couldn't you do it very slowly once?"

Peter did it both slowly and quickly. "I've got it now, Wendy!" cried John, but soon he found he had not. Not one of them could fly an inch, though even Michael was in words of two syllables, and Peter did not know A from Z.

Of course Peter had been trifling with them, for no one can fly unless the fairy dust has been blown on him. Fortunately, as we have mentioned, one of his hands was messy with it, and he blew some on each of them, with the most superb results.

"Now just wiggle your shoulders this way," he said, "and let go."

They were all on their beds, and gallant Michael let go first. He did not quite mean to let go, but he did it, and immediately he was borne across the room.

"I flewed!" he screamed while still in mid-air.

John let go and met Wendy near the bathroom.

"Oh, lovely!"

"Oh, ripping!"

"Look at me!"

"Look at me!"

"Look at me!"

They were not nearly so elegant as Peter, they could not help kicking a little, but their heads were bobbing against the ceiling, and there is almost nothing so delicious as that. Peter gave Wendy a hand at first, but had to desist, Tink was so indignant.

Up and down they went, and round and round. Heavenly was Wendy's word.

"I say," cried John, "why shouldn't we all go out?"

Of course it was to this that Peter had been luring them.

Michael was ready: he wanted to see how long it took him to do a billion miles. But Wendy hesitated.

"Mermaids!" said Peter again.

"Oo!"

"And there are pirates."

"Pirates," cried John, seizing his Sunday hat, "let us go at once."

It was just at this moment that Mr. and Mrs. Darling hurried with Nana out of 27. They ran into the middle of the street to look up at the nursery window; and, yes, it was still shut, but the room was ablaze with light, and most heart-gripping sight of all, they could see in shadow on the curtain three little figures in night attire circling round and round, not on the floor but in the air.

Not three figures, four!

In a tremble they opened the street door. Mr. Darling would have rushed upstairs, but Mrs. Darling signed him to go softly. She even tried to make her heart go softly.

Will they reach the nursery in time? If so, how delightful for them, and we shall all breathe a sigh of relief, but there will be no story. On the other hand, if they are not in time, I solemnly promise that it will all come right in the end.

They would have reached the nursery in time had it not been that the little stars were watching them. Once again the stars blew the window open, and that smallest star of all called out:

"Cave, Peter!"

Then Peter knew that there was not a moment to lose. "Come," he cried imperiously, and soared out at once into the night, followed by John and Michael and Wendy.

Mr. and Mrs. Darling and Nana rushed into the nursery too late. The birds were flown.

4

The Flight

"Second to the right, and straight on till morning."

That, Peter had told Wendy, was the way to the Neverland; but even birds, carrying maps and consulting them at windy corners, could not have sighted it with these instructions. Peter, you see, just said anything that came into his head.

At first his companions trusted him implicitly, and so great were the delights of flying that they wasted time circling round church spires or any other tall objects on the way that took their fancy.

John and Michael raced, Michael getting a start.

They recalled with contempt that not so long ago they had thought themselves fine fellows for being able to fly round a room.

Not long ago. But how long ago? They were flying over the sea before this thought began to disturb Wendy seriously. John thought it was their second sea and their third night.

Sometimes it was dark and sometimes light, and now they were very cold and again too warm. Did they really feel hungry at times, or were they merely pretending, because Peter had such a jolly new way of feeding them? His way was to pursue birds who had food in their mouths suitable for humans and snatch it from them; then the birds would follow and snatch it back; and they would all go chasing each other gaily for miles, parting at last with mutual expressions of good-will. But Wendy noticed with gentle concern that Peter did not seem to know that this was rather an odd way of getting your bread and butter, nor even that there are other ways.

Certainly they did not pretend to be sleepy, they were sleepy; and that was a danger, for the moment they popped off, down they fell. The awful thing was that Peter thought this funny.

"There he goes again!" he would cry gleefully, as Michael suddenly dropped like a stone.

"Save him, save him!" cried Wendy, looking with horror at the cruel sea far below. Eventually Peter would dive through the air, and catch Michael just before he could strike the sea, and it was lovely the way he did it; but he always waited till the last moment, and you felt it was his cleverness that interested him and not the saving of human life. Also he was fond of variety, and the sport that engrossed him one moment would suddenly cease to engage him, so there was always the possibility that the next time you fell he would let you go.

He could sleep in the air without falling, by merely lying on his back and floating, but this was, partly at least, because he was so light that if you got behind him and blew he went faster.

"Do be more polite to him," Wendy whispered to John, when they were playing "Follow my Leader."

"Then tell him to stop showing off," said John.

When playing Follow my Leader, Peter would fly close to the water and touch each shark's tail in passing, just as in the street you may run your finger along an iron railing. They could not follow him in this with much success, so perhaps it was rather like showing off, especially as he kept looking behind to see how many tails they missed.

"You must be nice to him," Wendy impressed on her brothers. "What could we do if he were to leave us!"

"We could go back," Michael said.

"How could we ever find our way back without him?"

"Well, then, we could go on," said John.

"That is the awful thing, John. We should have to go on, for we don't know how to stop."

This was true, Peter had forgotten to show them how to stop.

John said that if the worst came to the worst, all they had to do was to go straight on, for the world was round, and so in time they must come back to their own window.

"And who is to get food for us, John?"

"I nipped a bit out of that eagle's mouth pretty neatly, Wendy."

"After the twentieth try," Wendy reminded him. "And even though we became good at picking up food, see how we bump against clouds and things if he is not near to give us a hand."

Indeed they were constantly bumping. They could now fly strongly, though they still kicked far too much; but if they saw a cloud in front of them, the more they tried to avoid it, the more certainly did they bump into it. If Nana had been with them, she would have had a bandage round Michael's forehead by this time.

Peter was not with them for the moment, and they felt rather lonely up there by themselves. He could go so much faster than they that he would suddenly shoot out of sight, to have some adventure in which they had no share. He would come down laughing over something fearfully funny he had been saying to a star, but he had already forgotten what it was, or he would come up with mermaid scales still sticking to him, and yet not be able to say for certain what had been happening. It was really rather irritating to children who had never seen a mermaid.

"And if he forgets them so quickly," Wendy argued, "how can we expect that he will go on remembering us?"

Indeed, sometimes when he returned he did not remember them, at least not well. Wendy was sure of it. She saw recognition come into his eyes as he was about to pass them the time of day and go on; once even she had to call him by name.

"I'm Wendy," she said agitatedly.

He was very sorry. "I say, Wendy," he whispered to her, "always if you see me forgetting you, just keep on saying 'I'm Wendy,' and then I'll remember."

Of course this was rather unsatisfactory. However, to make amends he showed them how to lie out flat on a strong wind that was going their way, and this was such a pleasant change that they tried it several times and found that they could sleep thus with security. Indeed they would have slept longer, but Peter tired quickly of sleeping, and soon he would cry in his captain voice, "We get off here." So with occasional tiffs, but on the whole rollicking, they drew near the Neverland; for after many moons they did reach it, and, what is more, they had been going pretty straight all the time, not perhaps so much owing to the guidance of Peter or Tink as because the island was looking for them. It is only thus that any one may sight those magic shores.

"There it is," said Peter calmly.

"Where, where?"

"Where all the arrows are pointing."

Indeed a million golden arrows were pointing it out to the children, all directed by their friend the sun, who wanted them to be sure of their way before leaving them for the night.

Wendy and John and Michael stood on tip-toe in the air to get their first sight of the island. Strange to say, they all recognized it at once, and until fear fell upon them they hailed it, not as something long dreamt of and seen at last, but as a familiar friend to whom they were returning home for the holidays.

"John, there's the lagoon."

"Wendy, look at the turtles burying their eggs in the sand."

"I say, John, I see your flamingo with the broken leg!"

"Look, Michael, there's your cave!"

"John, what's that in the brushwood?"

"It's a wolf with her whelps. Wendy, I do believe that's your little whelp!"

"There's my boat, John, with her sides stove in!"

"No, it isn't. Why, we burned your boat."

"That's her, at any rate. I say, John, I see the smoke of the redskin camp!"

"Where? Show me, and I'll tell you by the way smoke curls whether they are on the war-path."

"There, just across the Mysterious River."

"I see now. Yes, they are on the war-path right enough."

Peter was a little annoyed with them for knowing so much, but if he wanted to lord it over them his triumph was at hand, for have I not told you that anon fear fell upon them?

It came as the arrows went, leaving the island in gloom.

In the old days at home the Neverland had always begun to look a little dark and threatening by bedtime. Then unexplored patches arose in it and spread, black shadows moved about in them, the roar of the beasts of prey was quite different now, and above all, you lost the certainty that you would win. You were quite glad that the night-lights were on. You even liked Nana to say that this was just the mantelpiece over here, and that the Neverland was all make-believe.

Of course the Neverland had been make-believe in those days, but it was real now, and there were no night-lights, and it was getting darker every moment, and where was Nana?

They had been flying apart, but they huddled close to Peter now. His careless manner had gone at last, his eyes were sparkling, and a tingle went through them every time they touched his body. They were now over the fearsome island, flying so low that sometimes a tree grazed their feet. Nothing horrid was visible in the air, yet their progress had become slow and laboured, exactly as if they were pushing their way through hostile forces. Sometimes they hung in the air until Peter had beaten on it with his fists.

"They don't want us to land," he explained.

"Who are they?" Wendy whispered, shuddering.

But he could not or would not say. Tinker Bell had been asleep on his shoulder, but now he wakened her and sent her on in front.

Sometimes he poised himself in the air, listening intently, with his hand to his ear, and again he would stare down with eyes so bright that they seemed to bore two holes to earth. Having done these things, he went on again.

His courage was almost appalling. "Would you like an adventure now," he said casually to John, "or would you like to have your tea first?"

Wendy said "tea first" quickly, and Michael pressed her hand in gratitude, but the braver John hesitated.

"What kind of adventure?" he asked cautiously.

"There's a pirate asleep in the pampas just beneath us," Peter told him. "If you like, we'll go down and kill him."

"I don't see him," John said after a long pause.

"I do."

"Suppose," John said, a little huskily, "he were to wake up."

Peter spoke indignantly. "You don't think I would kill him while he was sleeping! I would wake him first, and then kill him. That's the way I always do."

"I say! Do you kill many?"

"Tons."

John said "How ripping," but decided to have tea first. He asked if there were many pirates on the island just now, and Peter said he had never known so many.

"Who is captain now?"

"Hook," answered Peter, and his face became very stern as he said that hated word.

"Jas. Hook?"

"Ay."

Then indeed Michael began to cry, and even John could speak in gulps only, for they knew Hook's reputation.

"He was Blackbeard's bo'sun," John whispered huskily. "He is the worst of them all. He is the only man of whom Barbecue was afraid."

"That's him," said Peter.

"What is he like? Is he big?"

"He is not so big as he was."

"How do you mean?"

"I cut off a bit of him."

"You!"

"Yes, me," said Peter sharply.

"I wasn't meaning to be disrespectful."

"Oh, all right."

"But, I say, what bit?"

"His right hand."

"Then he can't fight now?"

"Oh, can't he just!"

"Left-hander?"

"He has an iron hook instead of a right hand, and he claws with it."

"Claws!"

"I say, John," said Peter.

"Yes."

"Say, 'Ay, ay, sir.'"

"Ay, ay, sir."

"There is one thing," Peter continued, "that every boy who serves under me has to promise, and so must you."

John paled.

"It is this, if we meet Hook in open fight, you must leave him to me."

"I promise," John said loyally.

For the moment they were feeling less eerie, because Tink was flying with them, and in her light they could distinguish each other. Unfortunately she could not fly so slowly as they, and so she had to go round and round them in a circle in which they moved as in a halo. Wendy quite liked it, until Peter pointed out the drawbacks.

"She tells me," he said, "that the pirates sighted us before the darkness came, and got Long Tom out."

"The big gun?"

"Yes. And of course they must see her light, and if they guess we are near it they are sure to let fly."

"Wendy!"

"John!"

"Michael!"

"Tell her to go away at once, Peter," the three cried simultaneously, but he refused.

"She thinks we have lost the way," he replied stiffly, "and she is rather frightened. You don't think I would send her away all by herself when she is frightened!"

For a moment the circle of light was broken, and something gave Peter a loving little pinch.

"Then tell her," Wendy begged, "to put out her light."

"She can't put it out. That is about the only thing fairies can't do. It just goes out of itself when she falls asleep, same as the stars."

"Then tell her to sleep at once," John almost ordered.

"She can't sleep except when she's sleepy. It is the only other thing fairies can't do."

"Seems to me," growled John, "these are the only two things worth doing."

Here he got a pinch, but not a loving one.

"If only one of us had a pocket," Peter said, "we could carry her in it." However, they had set off in such a hurry that there was not a pocket between the four of them.

He had a happy idea. John's hat!

Tink agreed to travel by hat if it was carried in the hand. John carried it, though she had hoped to be carried by Peter. Presently Wendy took the hat, because John said it struck against his knee as he flew; and this, as we shall see, led to mischief, for Tinker Bell hated to be under an obligation to Wendy.

In the black topper the light was completely hidden, and they flew on in silence. It was the stillest silence they had ever known, broken once by a distant lapping, which Peter explained was the wild beasts drinking at the ford, and again by a rasping sound that might have been the branches of trees rubbing together, but he said it was the redskins sharpening their knives.

Even these noises ceased. To Michael the loneliness was dreadful. "If only something would make a sound!" he cried.

As if in answer to his request, the air was rent by the most tremendous crash he had ever heard. The pirates had fired Long Tom at them.

The roar of it echoed through the mountains, and the echoes seemed to cry savagely, "Where are they, where are they, where are they?"

Thus sharply did the terrified three learn the difference between an island of make-believe and the same island come true.

When at last the heavens were steady again, John and Michael found themselves alone in the darkness. John was treading the air mechanically, and Michael without knowing how to float was floating.

"Are you shot?" John whispered tremulously.

"I haven't tried [myself out] yet," Michael whispered back.

We know now that no one had been hit. Peter, however, had

been carried by the wind of the shot far out to sea, while Wendy was blown upwards with no companion but Tinker Bell.

It would have been well for Wendy if at that moment she had dropped the hat.

I don't know whether the idea came suddenly to Tink, or whether she had planned it on the way, but she at once popped out of the hat and began to lure Wendy to her destruction.

Tink was not all bad; or, rather, she was all bad just now, but, on the other hand, sometimes she was all good. Fairies have to be one thing or the other, because being so small they unfortunately have room for one feeling only at a time. They are, however, allowed to change, only it must be a complete change. At present she was full of jealousy of Wendy. What she said in her lovely tinkle Wendy could not of course understand, and I believe some of it was bad words, but it sounded kind, and she flew back and forward, plainly meaning "Follow me, and all will be well."

What else could poor Wendy do? She called to Peter and John and Michael, and got only mocking echoes in reply. She did not yet know that Tink hated her with the fierce hatred of a very woman. And so, bewildered, and now staggering in her flight, she followed Tink to her doom.

5

The Island Come True

Feeling that Peter was on his way back, the Neverland had again woke into life. We ought to use the pluperfect and say wakened, but woke is better and was always used by Peter.

In his absence things are usually quiet on the island. The fairies take an hour longer in the morning, the beasts attend to their young, the redskins feed heavily for six days and nights, and when pirates and lost boys meet they merely bite their thumbs at each other. But with the coming of Peter, who hates lethargy, they are under way again: if you put your ear to the ground now, you would hear the whole island seething with life.

On this evening the chief forces of the island were disposed as follows. The lost boys were out looking for Peter, the pirates were out looking for the lost boys, the redskins were out looking for the pirates, and the beasts were out looking for the redskins. They were going round and round the island, but they did not meet because all were going at the same rate.

All wanted blood except the boys, who liked it as a

rule, but tonight were out to greet their captain. The boys on the island vary, of course, in numbers, according as they get killed and so on; and when they seem to be growing up, which is against the rules, Peter thins them out; but at this time there were six of them, counting the twins as two. Let us pretend to lie here among the sugar-cane and watch them as they steal by in single file, each with his hand on his dagger.

They are forbidden by Peter to look in the least like him, and they wear the skins of the bears slain by themselves, in which they are so round and furry that when they fall they roll. They have therefore become very sure-footed.

The first to pass is Tootles, not the least brave but the most unfortunate of all that gallant band. He had been in fewer adventures than any of them, because the big things constantly happened just when he had stepped round the corner; all would be quiet, he would take the opportunity of going off to gather a few sticks for firewood, and then when he returned the others would be sweeping up the blood. This ill-luck had given a gentle melancholy to his countenance, but instead of souring his nature had sweetened it, so that he was quite the humblest of the boys. Poor kind Tootles, there is danger in the air for you tonight. Take care lest an adventure is now offered you, which, if accepted, will plunge you in deepest woe. Tootles, the fairy Tink, who is bent on mischief this night is looking for a tool [for doing her mischief], and she thinks you are the most easily tricked of the boys. 'Ware Tinker Bell.

Would that he could hear us, but we are not really on the island, and he passes by, biting his knuckles.

Next comes Nibs, the gay and debonair, followed by Slightly, who cuts whistles out of the trees and dances ecstatically to his own tunes. Slightly is the most conceited of the boys. He thinks he remembers the days before he was lost, with their manners and customs, and this has given his nose an offensive tilt. Curly is fourth; he is a pickle, [a person who gets in pickles-predicaments] and so often has he had to deliver up his person when Peter said sternly, "Stand forth the one who did this thing," that now at the command he stands forth automatically whether he has done it or not. Last come the Twins, who cannot be described because we should be sure to be describing the wrong one. Peter never quite knew what twins were, and his band were not allowed to know anything he did not know, so these two were always vague about themselves, and did their best to give satisfaction by keeping close together in an apologetic sort of way.

The boys vanish in the gloom, and after a pause, but not a long pause, for things go briskly on the island, come the pirates on their track. We hear them before they are seen, and it is always the same dreadful song:

"Avast belay, yo ho, heave to,
A-pirating we go,
And if we're parted by a shot
We're sure to meet below!"

A more villainous-looking lot never hung in a row on Execution dock. Here, a little in advance, ever and again with his head to the ground listening, his great arms bare, pieces of eight in his ears as ornaments, is the handsome Italian Cecco, who cut his name in letters of blood on the back of the governor of the prison at Gao. That gigantic black behind him has had many names since he dropped the one with which dusky mothers still terrify their children on the banks of the Guidjo-mo. Here is Bill Jukes, every inch of him tattooed, the same Bill Jukes who got six dozen on the WALRUS from Flint before he would drop the bag of moidores [Portuguese gold pieces]; and Cookson, said to be Black Murphy's brother (but this was never proved), and Gentleman Starkey, once an usher in a public school and still dainty in his ways of killing; and Skylights (Morgan's Skylights); and the Irish bo'sun Smee, an oddly genial man who stabbed, so to speak, without offence, and was the only Non-conformist in Hook's crew; and Noodler, whose hands were fixed on backwards; and Robt. Mullins and Alf Mason and many another ruffian long known and feared on the Spanish Main.

In the midst of them, the blackest and largest jewel in that dark setting, reclined James Hook, or as he wrote himself, Jas. Hook, of whom it is said he was the only man that the Sea-Cook feared. He lay at his ease in a rough chariot drawn and propelled by his men, and instead of a right hand he had the iron hook with which ever and anon he encouraged them to increase their pace. As dogs this terrible man treated and addressed them, and as dogs they obeyed him. In person he was cadaverous [dead looking] and blackavized [dark faced], and his hair was dressed in long curls, which at a little distance looked like black candles, and gave a singularly threatening expression to his handsome countenance. His eyes were of the blue of the forget-me-not, and of a profound melancholy, save when he was plunging his hook into you, at which time two red spots appeared in them and lit them up horribly. In manner, something of the grand seigneur still clung to him, so that he even ripped you up with an air, and I have been told that he was a RACONTEUR [storyteller] of repute. He was never more sinister than when he was most polite, which is probably the truest test of breeding; and the elegance of his diction, even when he was swearing, no less than the distinction of his demeanour, showed him one of a different cast from his crew. A man of indomitable courage, it was said that the only thing he shied at was the sight of his own blood, which was thick and of an unusual colour. In dress he somewhat aped the attire associated with the name of Charles II, having heard it said in some earlier period of his career that he bore a strange resemblance to the ill-fated Stuarts; and in his mouth he had a holder of his own contrivance which enabled him to smoke two cigars at once. But undoubtedly the grimmest part of him was his iron claw.

Let us now kill a pirate, to show Hook's method. Skylights will do. As they pass, Skylights lurches clumsily against him, ruffling his lace collar; the hook shoots forth, there is a tearing sound and one screech, then the body is kicked aside, and the pirates pass on. He has not even taken the cigars from his mouth.

Such is the terrible man against whom Peter Pan is pitted. Which will win?

On the trail of the pirates, stealing noiselessly down the war-path, which is not visible to inexperienced eyes, come the redskins, every one of them with his eyes peeled. They carry tomahawks and knives, and their naked bodies gleam with paint and oil. Strung around them are scalps, of boys as well as of pirates, for these are the Piccaninny tribe, and not to be confused with the softer-hearted Delawares or the Hurons. In the van, on all fours, is Great Big Little Panther, a brave of so many scalps that in his present position they somewhat impede his progress. Bringing up the rear, the place of greatest danger, comes Tiger Lily, proudly erect, a princess in her own right. She is the most beautiful of dusky Dianas [Diana = goddess of the woods] and the belle of the Piccaninnies, coquettish [flirting], cold and amorous [loving] by turns; there is not a brave who would not have the wayward thing to wife, but she staves off the altar with a hatchet. Observe how they pass over fallen twigs without making the slightest noise. The only sound to be heard is their somewhat heavy breathing. The fact is that they are all a little fat just now after the heavy gorging, but in time they will work this off. For the moment, however, it constitutes their chief danger.

The redskins disappear as they have come like shadows, and soon their place is taken by the beasts, a great and motley procession: lions, tigers, bears, and the innumerable smaller savage things that flee from them, for every kind of beast, and, more particularly, all the man-eaters, live cheek by jowl on the favoured island. Their tongues are hanging out, they are hungry tonight.

When they have passed, comes the last figure of all, a gigantic crocodile. We shall see for whom she is looking presently.

The crocodile passes, but soon the boys appear again, for the procession must continue indefinitely until one of the parties stops or changes its pace. Then quickly they will be on top of each other.

All are keeping a sharp lookout in front, but none suspects that the danger may be creeping up from behind. This shows how real the island was.

The first to fall out of the moving circle was the boys. They flung themselves down on the sward [turf], close to their underground home.

"I do wish Peter would come back," every one of them said nervously, though in height and still more in breadth they were all larger than their captain.

"I am the only one who is not afraid of the pirates," Slightly said, in the tone that prevented his being a general favourite; but perhaps some distant sound disturbed him, for he added hastily, "but I wish he would come back, and tell us whether he has heard anything more about Cinderella."

They talked of Cinderella, and Tootles was confident that his mother must have been very like her.

It was only in Peter's absence that they could speak of mothers, the subject being forbidden by him as silly.

"All I remember about my mother," Nibs told them, "is that she often said to my father, 'Oh, how I wish I had a cheque-book of my own!' I don't know what a cheque-book is, but I should just love to give my mother one."

While they talked they heard a distant sound. You or I, not being wild things of the woods, would have heard nothing, but they heard it, and it was the grim song:

"Yo ho, yo ho, the pirate life,
The flag o' skull and bones,
A merry hour, a hempen rope,
And hey for Davy Jones."

At once the lost boys—but where are they? They are no longer there. Rabbits could not have disappeared more quickly.

I will tell you where they are. With the exception of Nibs, who has darted away to reconnoitre [look around], they are already in their home under the ground, a very delightful residence of which we shall see a good deal presently. But how have they reached it? for there is no entrance to be seen, not so much as a large stone, which if rolled away, would disclose the mouth of a cave. Look closely, however, and you may note that there are here seven large trees, each with a hole in its hollow trunk as large as a boy. These are the seven entrances to the home under the ground, for which Hook has been searching in vain these many moons. Will he find it tonight?

As the pirates advanced, the quick eye of Starkey sighted Nibs disappearing through the wood, and at once his pistol flashed out. But an iron claw gripped his shoulder.

"Captain, let go!" he cried, writhing.

Now for the first time we hear the voice of Hook. It was a black voice. "Put back that pistol first," it said threateningly.

"It was one of those boys you hate. I could have shot him dead."

"Ay, and the sound would have brought Tiger Lily's redskins upon us. Do you want to lose your scalp?"

"Shall I after him, Captain," asked pathetic Smee, "and tickle him with Johnny Corkscrew?" Smee had pleasant names for everything, and his cutlass was Johnny Corkscrew, because he wiggled it in the wound. One could mention many lovable traits in Smee. For instance, after killing, it was his spectacles he wiped instead of his weapon.

"Johnny's a silent fellow," he reminded Hook.

"Not now, Smee," Hook said darkly. "He is only one, and I want to mischief all the seven. Scatter and look for them."

The pirates disappeared among the trees, and in a moment their Captain and Smee were alone. Hook heaved a heavy sigh, and I know not why it was, perhaps it was because of the soft beauty of the evening, but there came over him a desire to confide to his faithful bo'sun the story of his life. He spoke long and earnestly, but what it was all about Smee, who was rather stupid, did not know in the least.

Anon [later] he caught the word Peter.

"Most of all," Hook was saying passionately, "I want their captain, Peter Pan. 'Twas he cut off my arm." He brandished the hook threateningly. "I've waited long to shake his hand with this. Oh, I'll tear him!"

"And yet," said Smee, "I have often heard you say that hook was worth a score of hands, for combing the hair and other homely uses."

"Ay," the captain answered, "if I was a mother I would pray to have my children born with this instead of that," and he cast a look of pride upon his iron hand and one of scorn upon the other. Then again he frowned.

"Peter flung my arm," he said, wincing, "to a crocodile that happened to be passing by."

"I have often," said Smee, "noticed your strange dread of crocodiles."

"Not of crocodiles," Hook corrected him, "but of that one crocodile." He lowered his voice. "It liked my arm so much, Smee, that it has followed me ever since, from sea to sea and from land to land, licking its lips for the rest of me."

"In a way," said Smee, "it's sort of a compliment."

"I want no such compliments," Hook barked petulantly. "I want Peter Pan, who first gave the brute its taste for me."

He sat down on a large mushroom, and now there was a quiver in his voice. "Smee," he said huskily, "that crocodile would have had me before this, but by a lucky chance it swallowed a clock which goes tick tick inside it, and so before it can reach me I hear the tick and bolt." He laughed, but in a hollow way.

"Some day," said Smee, "the clock will run down, and then he'll get you."

Hook wetted his dry lips. "Ay," he said, "that's the fear that haunts me."

Since sitting down he had felt curiously warm. "Smee," he said, "this seat is hot." He jumped up. "Odds bobs, hammer and tongs I'm burning."

They examined the mushroom, which was of a size and solidity unknown on the mainland; they tried to pull it up, and it came away at once in their hands, for it had no root. Stranger still, smoke began at once to ascend. The pirates looked at each other. "A chimney!" they both exclaimed.

They had indeed discovered the chimney of the home under the ground. It was the custom of the boys to stop it with a mushroom when enemies were in the neighbourhood.

Not only smoke came out of it. There came also children's voices, for so safe did the boys feel in their hiding-place that they were gaily chattering. The pirates listened grimly, and then replaced the mushroom. They looked around them and noted the holes in the seven trees.

"Did you hear them say Peter Pan's from home?" Smee whispered, fidgeting with Johnny Corkscrew.

Hook nodded. He stood for a long time lost in thought, and at last a curdling smile lit up his swarthy face. Smee had been waiting for it. "Unrip your plan, captain," he cried eagerly.

"To return to the ship," Hook replied slowly through his teeth, "and cook a large rich cake of a jolly thickness with green sugar on it. There can be but one room below, for there is but one chimney. The silly moles had not the sense to see that they did not need a door apiece. That shows they have no mother. We will leave the cake on the shore of the Mermaids' Lagoon. These boys are always swimming about there, playing with the mermaids. They will find the cake and they will gobble it up, because, having no mother, they don't know how dangerous 'tis to eat rich damp cake." He burst into laughter, not hollow laughter now, but honest laughter. "Aha, they will die."

Smee had listened with growing admiration.

"It's the wickedest, prettiest policy ever I heard of!" he cried, and in their exultation they danced and sang:

"Avast, belay, when I appear,
By fear they're overtook;
Nought's left upon your bones when you
Have shaken claws with Hook."

They began the verse, but they never finished it, for another sound broke in and stilled them. There was at first such a tiny sound that a leaf might have fallen on it and smothered it, but as it came nearer it was more distinct.

Tick tick tick tick!

Hook stood shuddering, one foot in the air.

"The crocodile!" he gasped, and bounded away, followed by his bo'sun.

It was indeed the crocodile. It had passed the redskins, who were now on the trail of the other pirates. It oozed on after Hook.

Once more the boys emerged into the open; but the dangers of the night were not yet over, for presently Nibs rushed breathless into their midst, pursued by a pack of wolves. The tongues of the pursuers were hanging out; the baying of them was horrible.

"Save me, save me!" cried Nibs, falling on the ground.

"But what can we do, what can we do?"

It was a high compliment to Peter that at that dire moment their thoughts turned to him.

"What would Peter do?" they cried simultaneously.

Almost in the same breath they cried, "Peter would look at them through his legs."

And then, "Let us do what Peter would do."

It is quite the most successful way of defying wolves, and as one boy they bent and looked through their legs. The next moment is the long one, but victory came quickly, for as the boys advanced upon them in the terrible attitude, the wolves dropped their tails and fled.

Now Nibs rose from the ground, and the others thought that his staring eyes still saw the wolves. But it was not wolves he saw.

"I have seen a wonderfuller thing," he cried, as they gathered round him eagerly. "A great white bird. It is flying this way."

"What kind of a bird, do you think?"

"I don't know," Nibs said, awestruck, "but it looks so weary, and as it flies it moans, 'Poor Wendy.'"

"Poor Wendy?"

"I remember," said Slightly instantly, "there are birds called Wendies."

"See, it comes!" cried Curly, pointing to Wendy in the heavens.

Wendy was now almost overhead, and they could hear her plaintive cry. But more distinct came the shrill voice of Tinker Bell. The jealous fairy had now cast off all disguise of friendship, and was darting at her victim from every direction, pinching savagely each time she touched.

"Hullo, Tink," cried the wondering boys.

Tink's reply rang out: "Peter wants you to shoot the Wendy."

It was not in their nature to question when Peter ordered. "Let us do what Peter wishes!" cried the simple boys. "Quick, bows and arrows!"

All but Tootles popped down their trees. He had a bow and arrow with him, and Tink noted it, and rubbed her little hands.

"Quick, Tootles, quick," she screamed. "Peter will be so pleased."

Tootles excitedly fitted the arrow to his bow. "Out of the way, Tink," he shouted, and then he fired, and Wendy fluttered to the ground with an arrow in her breast.

6

The Little House

Foolish Tootles was standing like a conqueror over Wendy's body when the other boys sprang, armed, from their trees.

"You are too late," he cried proudly, "I have shot the Wendy. Peter will be so pleased with me."

Overhead Tinker Bell shouted "Silly ass!" and darted into hiding. The others did not hear her. They had crowded round Wendy, and as they looked a terrible silence fell upon the wood. If Wendy's heart had been beating they would all have heard it.

Slightly was the first to speak. "This is no bird," he said in a scared voice. "I think this must be a lady."

"A lady?" said Tootles, and fell a-trembling.

"And we have killed her," Nibs said hoarsely.

They all whipped off their caps.

"Now I see," Curly said: "Peter was bringing her to us." He threw himself sorrowfully on the ground.

"A lady to take care of us at last," said one of the twins, "and you have killed her!"

They were sorry for him, but sorrier for themselves, and when he took a step nearer them they turned from him.

Tootles' face was very white, but there was a dignity about him now that had never been there before.

"I did it," he said, reflecting. "When ladies used to come to me in dreams, I said, 'Pretty mother, pretty mother.' But when at last she really came, I shot her."

He moved slowly away.

"Don't go," they called in pity.

"I must," he answered, shaking; "I am so afraid of Peter."

It was at this tragic moment that they heard a sound which made the heart of every one of them rise to his mouth. They heard Peter crow.

"Peter!" they cried, for it was always thus that he signalled his return.

"Hide her," they whispered, and gathered hastily around Wendy. But Tootles stood aloof.

Again came that ringing crow, and Peter dropped in front of them. "Greetings, boys," he cried, and mechanically they saluted, and then again was silence.

He frowned.

"I am back," he said hotly, "why do you not cheer?"

They opened their mouths, but the cheers would not come. He overlooked it in his haste to tell the glorious tidings.

"Great news, boys," he cried, "I have brought at last a mother for you all."

Still no sound, except a little thud from Tootles as he dropped on his knees.

"Have you not seen her?" asked Peter, becoming troubled. "She flew this way."

"Ah me!" one voice said, and another said, "Oh, mournful day."

Tootles rose. "Peter," he said quietly, "I will show her to you," and when the others would still have hidden her he said, "Back, twins, let Peter see."

So they all stood back, and let him see, and after he had looked for a little time he did not know what to do next.

"She is dead," he said uncomfortably. "Perhaps she is frightened at being dead."

He thought of hopping off in a comic sort of way till he was out of sight of her, and then never going near the spot any more. They would all have been glad to follow if he had done this.

But there was the arrow. He took it from her heart and faced his band.

"Whose arrow?" he demanded sternly.

"Mine, Peter," said Tootles on his knees.

"Oh, dastard hand," Peter said, and he raised the arrow to use it as a dagger.

Tootles did not flinch. He bared his breast. "Strike, Peter," he said firmly, "strike true."

Twice did Peter raise the arrow, and twice did his hand fall. "I cannot strike," he said with awe, "there is something stays my hand."

All looked at him in wonder, save Nibs, who fortunately looked at Wendy.

"It is she," he cried, "the Wendy lady, see, her arm!"

Wonderful to relate [tell], Wendy had raised her arm. Nibs bent over her and listened reverently. "I think she said, 'Poor Tootles,'" he whispered.

"She lives," Peter said briefly.

Slightly cried instantly, "The Wendy lady lives."

Then Peter knelt beside her and found his button. You remember she had put it on a chain that she wore round her neck.

"See," he said, "the arrow struck against this. It is the kiss I gave her. It has saved her life."

"I remember kisses," Slightly interposed quickly, "let me see it. Ay, that's a kiss."

Peter did not hear him. He was begging Wendy to get better quickly, so that he could show her the mermaids. Of course she could not answer yet, being still in a frightful faint; but from overhead came a wailing note.

"Listen to Tink," said Curly, "she is crying because the Wendy lives."

Then they had to tell Peter of Tink's crime, and almost never had they seen him look so stern.

"Listen, Tinker Bell," he cried, "I am your friend no more. Begone from me for ever."

She flew on to his shoulder and pleaded, but he brushed her off. Not until Wendy again raised her arm did he relent sufficiently to say, "Well, not for ever, but for a whole week."

Do you think Tinker Bell was grateful to Wendy for raising her arm? Oh dear no, never wanted to pinch her so much. Fairies indeed are strange, and Peter, who understood them best, often cuffed [slapped] them.

But what to do with Wendy in her present delicate state of health?

"Let us carry her down into the house," Curly suggested.

"Ay," said Slightly, "that is what one does with ladies."

"No, no," Peter said, "you must not touch her. It would not be sufficiently respectful."

"That," said Slightly, "is what I was thinking."

"But if she lies there," Tootles said, "she will die."

"Ay, she will die," Slightly admitted, "but there is no way out."

"Yes, there is," cried Peter. "Let us build a little house round her."

They were all delighted. "Quick," he ordered them, "bring me each of you the best of what we have. Gut our house. Be sharp."

In a moment they were as busy as tailors the night before a wedding. They skurried this way and that, down for bedding, up for firewood, and while they were at it, who should appear but John and Michael. As they dragged along the ground they fell asleep standing, stopped, woke up, moved another step and slept again.

"John, John," Michael would cry, "wake up! Where is Nana, John, and mother?"

And then John would rub his eyes and mutter, "It is true, we did fly."

You may be sure they were very relieved to find Peter.

"Hullo, Peter," they said.

"Hullo," replied Peter amicably, though he had quite forgotten them. He was very busy at the moment measuring Wendy with his feet to see how large a house she would need. Of course he meant to leave room for chairs and a table. John and Michael watched him.

"Is Wendy asleep?" they asked.

"Yes."

"John," Michael proposed, "let us wake her and get her to make supper for us," but as he said it some of the other boys rushed on carrying branches for the building of the house. "Look at them!" he cried.

"Curly," said Peter in his most captainy voice, "see that these boys help in the building of the house."

"Ay, ay, sir."

"Build a house?" exclaimed John.

"For the Wendy," said Curly.

"For Wendy?" John said, aghast. "Why, she is only a girl!"

"That," explained Curly, "is why we are her servants."

"You? Wendy's servants!"

"Yes," said Peter, "and you also. Away with them."

The astounded brothers were dragged away to hack and hew and carry. "Chairs and a fender [fireplace] first," Peter ordered. "Then we shall build a house round them."

"Ay," said Slightly, "that is how a house is built; it all comes back to me."

Peter thought of everything. "Slightly," he cried, "fetch a doctor."

"Ay, ay," said Slightly at once, and disappeared, scratching his head. But he knew Peter must be obeyed, and he returned in a moment, wearing John's hat and looking solemn.

"Please, sir," said Peter, going to him, "are you a doctor?"

The difference between him and the other boys at such a time was that they knew it was make-believe, while to him make-believe and true were exactly the same thing. This sometimes troubled them, as when they had to make-believe that they had had their dinners.

If they broke down in their make-believe he rapped them on the knuckles.

"Yes, my little man," Slightly anxiously replied, who had chapped knuckles.

"Please, sir," Peter explained, "a lady lies very ill."

She was lying at their feet, but Slightly had the sense not to see her.

"Tut, tut, tut," he said, "where does she lie?"

"In yonder glade."

"I will put a glass thing in her mouth," said Slightly, and he made-believe to do it, while Peter waited. It was an anxious moment when the glass thing was withdrawn.

"How is she?" inquired Peter.

"Tut, tut, tut," said Slightly, "this has cured her."

"I am glad!" Peter cried.

"I will call again in the evening," Slightly said; "give her beef tea out of a cup with a spout to it;" but after he had returned the hat to John he blew big breaths, which was his habit on escaping from a difficulty.

In the meantime the wood had been alive with the sound of axes; almost everything needed for a cosy dwelling already lay at Wendy's feet.

"If only we knew," said one, "the kind of house she likes best."

"Peter," shouted another, "she is moving in her sleep."

"Her mouth opens," cried a third, looking respectfully into it. "Oh, lovely!"

"Perhaps she is going to sing in her sleep," said Peter. "Wendy, sing the kind of house you would like to have."

Immediately, without opening her eyes, Wendy began to sing:

"I wish I had a pretty house,
The littlest ever seen,
With funny little red walls
And roof of mossy green."

They gurgled with joy at this, for by the greatest good luck the branches they had brought were sticky with red sap, and all the ground was carpeted with moss. As they rattled up the little house they broke into song themselves:

"We've built the little walls and roof
And made a lovely door,
So tell us, mother Wendy,
What are you wanting more?"

To this she answered rather greedily:

"Oh, really next I think I'll have
Gay windows all about,
With roses peeping in, you know,
And babies peeping out."

With a blow of their fists they made windows, and large yellow leaves were the blinds. But roses—?

"Roses," cried Peter sternly.

Quickly they made-believe to grow the loveliest roses up the walls.

Babies?

To prevent Peter ordering babies they hurried into song again:

"We've made the roses peeping out,
The babes are at the door,
We cannot make ourselves, you know,
'cos we've been made before."

Peter, seeing this to be a good idea, at once pretended that it was his own. The house was quite beautiful, and no doubt Wendy was very cosy within, though, of course, they could no longer see her. Peter strode up and down, ordering finishing touches. Nothing escaped his eagle eyes. Just when it seemed absolutely finished:

"There's no knocker on the door," he said.

They were very ashamed, but Tootles gave the sole of his shoe, and it made an excellent knocker.

Absolutely finished now, they thought.

Not of bit of it. "There's no chimney," Peter said; "we must have a chimney."

"It certainly does need a chimney," said John importantly. This gave Peter an idea. He snatched the hat off John's head, knocked out the bottom [top], and put the hat on the roof. The little house was so pleased to have such a capital chimney that, as if to say thank you, smoke immediately began to come out of the hat.

Now really and truly it was finished. Nothing remained to do but to knock.

"All look your best," Peter warned them; "first impressions are awfully important."

He was glad no one asked him what first impressions are; they were all too busy looking their best.

He knocked politely, and now the wood was as still as the children, not a sound to be heard except from Tinker Bell, who was watching from a branch and openly sneering.

What the boys were wondering was, would any one answer the knock? If a lady, what would she be like?

The door opened and a lady came out. It was Wendy. They all whipped off their hats.

She looked properly surprised, and this was just how they had hoped she would look.

"Where am I?" she said.

Of course Slightly was the first to get his word in. "Wendy lady," he said rapidly, "for you we built this house."

"Oh, say you're pleased," cried Nibs.

"Lovely, darling house," Wendy said, and they were the very words they had hoped she would say.

"And we are your children," cried the twins.

Then all went on their knees, and holding out their arms cried, "O Wendy lady, be our mother."

"Ought I?" Wendy said, all shining. "Of course it's frightfully fascinating, but you see I am only a little girl. I have no real experience."

"That doesn't matter," said Peter, as if he were the only person present who knew all about it, though he was really the one who knew least. "What we need is just a nice motherly person."

"Oh dear!" Wendy said, "you see, I feel that is exactly what I am."

"It is, it is," they all cried; "we saw it at once."

"Very well," she said, "I will do my best. Come inside at once, you naughty children; I am sure your feet are damp. And before I put you to bed I have just time to finish the story of Cinderella."

In they went; I don't know how there was room for them, but you can squeeze very tight in the Neverland. And that was the first of the many joyous evenings they had with Wendy. By and by she tucked them up in the great bed in the home under the trees, but she herself slept that night in the little house, and Peter kept watch outside with drawn sword, for the pirates could be heard carousing far away and the wolves were on the prowl. The little house looked so cosy and safe in the darkness, with a bright light showing through its blinds, and the chimney smoking beautifully, and Peter standing on guard. After a time he fell asleep, and some unsteady fairies had to climb over him on their way home from an orgy. Any of the other boys obstructing the fairy path at night they would have mischiefed, but they just tweaked Peter's nose and passed on.

7

The Home Under the Ground

One of the first things Peter did next day was to measure Wendy and John and Michael for hollow trees. Hook, you remember, had sneered at the boys for thinking they needed a tree apiece, but this was ignorance, for unless your tree fitted you it was difficult to go up and down, and no two of the boys were quite the same size. Once you fitted, you drew in [let out] your breath at the top, and down you went at exactly the right speed, while to ascend you drew in and let out alternately, and so wriggled up. Of course, when you have mastered the action you are able to do these things without thinking of them, and nothing can be more graceful.

But you simply must fit, and Peter measures you for your tree as carefully as for a suit of clothes: the only difference being that the clothes are made to fit you, while you have to be made to fit the tree. Usually it is done quite easily, as by your wearing too many garments or too few, but if you are bumpy in awkward places or the only available tree is an odd shape, Peter does some things to you, and after that you fit. Once you fit, great care must be taken to go on fitting, and this, as Wendy was to discover to her delight, keeps a whole family in perfect condition.

Wendy and Michael fitted their trees at the first try, but John had to be altered a little.

After a few days' practice they could go up and down as gaily as buckets in a well. And how ardently they grew to love their home under the ground; especially Wendy. It consisted of one large room, as all houses should do, with a floor in which you could dig [for worms] if you wanted to go fishing, and in this floor grew stout mushrooms of a charming colour, which were used as stools. A Never tree tried hard to grow in the centre of the room, but every morning they sawed the trunk through, level with the floor. By tea-time it was always about two feet high, and then they put a door on top of it, the whole thus becoming a table; as soon as they cleared away, they sawed off the trunk again, and thus there was more room to play. There was an enormous fireplace which was in almost any part of the room where you cared to light it, and across this Wendy stretched strings, made of fibre, from which she suspended her washing. The bed was tilted against the wall by day, and let down at 6:30, when it filled nearly half the room; and all the boys slept in it, except Michael, lying like sardines in a tin. There was a strict rule against turning round until one gave the signal, when all turned at once. Michael should have used it also, but Wendy would have [desired] a baby, and he was the littlest, and you know what women are, and the short and long of it is that he was hung up in a basket.

It was rough and simple, and not unlike what baby bears would have made of an underground house in the same circumstances. But there was one recess in the wall, no larger than a bird-cage, which was the private apartment of Tinker Bell. It could be shut off from the rest of the house by a tiny curtain, which Tink, who was most fastidious [particular], always kept drawn when dressing or undressing. No woman, however large, could have had a more exquisite boudoir [dressing room] and bedchamber combined. The couch, as she always called it, was a genuine Queen Mab, with club legs; and she varied the bedspreads according to what fruit-blossom was in season. Her mirror was a Puss-in-Boots, of which there are now only three, unchipped, known to fairy dealers; the washstand was Pie-crust and reversible, the chest of drawers an authentic Charming the Sixth, and the carpet and rugs the best (the early) period of Margery and Robin. There was a chandelier from Tiddlywinks for the look of the thing, but of course she lit the residence herself. Tink was very contemptuous of the rest of the house, as indeed was perhaps inevitable, and her chamber, though beautiful, looked rather conceited, having the appearance of a nose permanently turned up.

I suppose it was all especially entrancing to Wendy, because those rampagious boys of hers gave her so much to do. Really there were whole weeks when, except perhaps with a stocking in the evening, she was never above ground. The cooking, I can tell you, kept her nose to the pot, and even if there was nothing in it, even if there was no pot, she had to keep watching that it came aboil just the same. You never exactly knew whether there would be a real meal or just a make-believe, it all depended upon Peter's whim: he could eat, really eat, if it was part of a game, but he could not stodge [cram down the food] just to feel stodgy [stuffed with food], which is what most children like better than anything else; the next best thing being to talk about it. Make-believe was so real to him that during a meal of it you could see him getting rounder. Of course it was trying, but you simply had to follow his lead, and if you could prove to him that you were getting loose for your tree he let you stodge.

Wendy's favourite time for sewing and darning was after they had all gone to bed. Then, as she expressed it, she had a breathing time for herself; and she occupied it in making new things for them, and putting double pieces on the knees, for they were all most frightfully hard on their knees.

When she sat down to a basketful of their stockings, every heel with a hole in it, she would fling up her arms and exclaim, "Oh dear, I am sure I sometimes think spinsters are to be envied!"

Her face beamed when she exclaimed this.

You remember about her pet wolf. Well, it very soon discovered that she had come to the island and it found her out, and they just ran into each other's arms. After that it followed her about everywhere.

As time wore on did she think much about the beloved parents she had left behind her? This is a difficult question, because it is quite impossible to say how time does wear on in the Neverland, where it is calculated by moons and suns, and there are ever so many more of them than on the mainland. But I am afraid that Wendy did not really worry about her father and mother; she was absolutely confident that they would always keep the window open for her to fly back by, and this gave her complete ease of mind. What did disturb her at times was that John remembered his parents vaguely only, as people he had once known, while Michael was quite willing to believe that she was really his mother. These things scared her a little, and nobly anxious to do her duty, she tried to fix the old life in their minds by setting them examination papers on it, as like as possible to the ones she used to do at school. The other boys thought this awfully interesting, and insisted on joining, and they made slates for themselves, and sat round the table, writing and thinking hard about the questions she had written on another slate and passed round. They were the most ordinary questions—"What was the colour of Mother's eyes? Which was taller, Father or Mother? Was Mother blonde or brunette? Answer all three questions if possible." "(A) Write an essay of not less than 40 words on How I spent my last Holidays, or The Characters of Father and Mother compared. Only one of these to be attempted." Or "(1) Describe Mother's laugh; (2) Describe Father's laugh; (3) Describe Mother's Party Dress; (4) Describe the Kennel and its Inmate."

They were just everyday questions like these, and when you could not answer them you were told to make a cross; and it was really dreadful what a number of crosses even John made. Of course the only boy who replied to every question was Slightly, and no one could have been more hopeful of coming out first, but his answers were perfectly ridiculous, and he really came out last: a melancholy thing.

Peter did not compete. For one thing he despised all mothers except Wendy, and for another he was the only boy on the island who could neither write nor spell; not the smallest word. He was above all that sort of thing.

By the way, the questions were all written in the past tense. What was the colour of Mother's eyes, and so on. Wendy, you see, had been forgetting, too.

Adventures, of course, as we shall see, were of daily occurrence; but about this time Peter invented, with Wendy's help, a new game that fascinated him enormously, until he suddenly had no more interest in it, which, as you have been told, was what always happened with his games. It consisted in pretending not to have adventures, in doing the sort of thing John and Michael had been doing all their lives, sitting on stools flinging balls in the air, pushing each other, going out for walks and coming back without having killed so much as a grizzly. To see Peter doing nothing on a stool was a great sight; he could not help looking solemn at such times, to sit still seemed to him such a comic thing to do. He boasted that he had gone walking for the good of his health. For several suns these were the most novel of all adventures to him; and John and Michael had to pretend to be delighted also; otherwise he would have treated them severely.

He often went out alone, and when he came back you were never absolutely certain whether he had had an adventure or not. He might have forgotten it so completely that he said nothing about it; and then when you went out you found the body; and, on the other hand, he might say a great deal about it, and yet you could not find the body. Sometimes he came home with his head bandaged, and then Wendy cooed over him and bathed it in lukewarm water, while he told a dazzling tale. But she was never quite sure, you know. There were, however, many adventures which she knew to be true because she was in them herself, and there were still more that were at least partly true, for the other boys were in them and said they were wholly true. To describe them all would require a book as large as an English-Latin, Latin-English Dictionary, and the most we can do is to give one as a specimen of an average hour on the island. The difficulty is which one to choose. Should we take the brush with the redskins at Slightly Gulch? It was a sanguinary affair, and especially interesting as showing one of Peter's peculiarities, which was that in the middle of a fight he would suddenly change sides. At the Gulch, when victory was still in the balance, sometimes leaning this way and sometimes that, he called out, "I'm redskin today; what are you, Tootles?" And Tootles answered, "Redskin; what are you, Nibs?" and Nibs said, "Redskin; what are you Twin?" and so on; and they were all redskins; and of course this would have ended the fight had not the real redskins fascinated by Peter's methods, agreed to be lost boys for that once, and so at it they all went again, more fiercely than ever.

The extraordinary upshot of this adventure was—but we have not decided yet that this is the adventure we are to narrate. Perhaps a better one would be the night attack by the redskins on the house under the ground, when several of them stuck in the hollow trees and had to be pulled out like corks. Or we might tell how Peter saved Tiger Lily's life in the Mermaids' Lagoon, and so made her his ally.

Or we could tell of that cake the pirates cooked so that the boys might eat it and perish; and how they placed it in one cunning spot after another; but always Wendy snatched it from the hands of her children, so that in time it lost its succulence, and became as hard as a stone, and was used as a missile, and Hook fell over it in the dark.

Or suppose we tell of the birds that were Peter's friends, particularly of the Never bird that built in a tree overhanging the lagoon, and how the nest fell into the water, and still the bird sat on her eggs, and Peter gave orders that she was not to be disturbed. That is a pretty story, and the end shows how grateful a bird can be; but if we tell it we must also tell the whole adventure of the lagoon, which would of course be telling two adventures rather than just one. A shorter adventure, and quite as exciting, was Tinker Bell's attempt, with the help of some street fairies, to have the sleeping Wendy conveyed on a great floating leaf to the mainland. Fortunately the leaf gave way and Wendy woke, thinking it was bath-time, and swam back. Or again, we might choose Peter's defiance of the lions, when he drew a circle round him on the ground with an arrow and dared them to cross it; and though he waited for hours, with the other boys and Wendy looking on breathlessly from trees, not one of them dared to accept his challenge.

Which of these adventures shall we choose? The best way will be to toss for it.

I have tossed, and the lagoon has won. This almost makes one wish that the gulch or the cake or Tink's leaf had won. Of course I could do it again, and make it best out of three; however, perhaps fairest to stick to the lagoon.

8

The Mermaids' Lagoon

If you shut your eyes and are a lucky one, you may see at times a shapeless pool of lovely pale colours suspended in the darkness; then if you squeeze your eyes tighter, the pool begins to take shape, and the colours become so vivid that with another squeeze they must go on fire. But just before they go on fire you see the lagoon. This is the nearest you ever get to it on the mainland, just one heavenly moment; if there could be two moments you might see the surf and hear the mermaids singing.

The children often spent long summer days on this lagoon, swimming or floating most of the time, playing the mermaid games in the water, and so forth. You must not think from this that the mermaids were on friendly terms with them: on the contrary, it was among Wendy's lasting regrets that all the time she was on the island she never had a civil word from one of them. When she stole softly to the edge of the lagoon she might see them by the score, especially on Marooners' Rock, where they loved to bask, combing out their hair in a lazy way that quite irritated her; or she might even swim, on tiptoe as it were, to within a yard of them, but then they saw her and dived, probably splashing her with their tails, not by accident, but intentionally.

They treated all the boys in the same way, except of course Peter, who chatted with them on Marooners' Rock by the hour, and sat on their tails when they got cheeky. He gave Wendy one of their combs.

The most haunting time at which to see them is at the turn of the moon, when they utter strange wailing cries; but the lagoon is dangerous for mortals then, and until the evening of which we have now to tell, Wendy had never seen the lagoon by moonlight, less from fear, for of course Peter would have accompanied her, than because she had strict rules about every one being in bed by seven. She was often at the lagoon, however, on sunny days after rain, when the mermaids come up in extraordinary numbers to play with their bubbles. The bubbles of many colours made in rainbow water they treat as balls, hitting them gaily from one to another with their tails, and trying to keep them in the rainbow till they burst. The goals are at each end of the rainbow, and the keepers only are allowed to use their hands. Sometimes a dozen of these games will be going on in the lagoon at a time, and it is quite a pretty sight.

But the moment the children tried to join in they had to play by themselves, for the mermaids immediately disappeared. Nevertheless we have proof that they secretly watched the interlopers, and were not above taking an idea from them; for John introduced a new way of hitting the bubble, with the head instead of the hand, and the mermaids adopted it. This is the one mark that John has left on the Neverland.

It must also have been rather pretty to see the children resting on a rock for half an hour after their mid-day meal. Wendy insisted on their doing this, and it had to be a real rest even though the meal was make-believe. So they lay there in the sun, and their bodies glistened in it, while she sat beside them and looked important.

It was one such day, and they were all on Marooners' Rock. The rock was not much larger than their great bed, but of course they all knew how not to take up much room, and they were dozing, or at least lying with their eyes shut, and pinching occasionally when they thought Wendy was not looking. She was very busy, stitching.

While she stitched a change came to the lagoon. Little shivers ran over it, and the sun went away and shadows stole across the water, turning it cold. Wendy could no longer see to thread her needle, and when she looked up, the lagoon that had always hitherto been such a laughing place seemed formidable and unfriendly.

It was not, she knew, that night had come, but something as dark as night had come. No, worse than that. It had not come, but it had sent that shiver through the sea to say that it was coming. What was it?

There crowded upon her all the stories she had been told of Marooners' Rock, so called because evil captains put sailors on it and leave them there to drown. They drown when the tide rises, for then it is submerged.

Of course she should have roused the children at once; not merely because of the unknown that was stalking toward them, but because it was no longer good for them to sleep on a rock grown chilly. But she was a young mother and she did not know this; she thought you simply must stick to your rule about half an hour after the mid-day meal. So, though fear was upon her, and she longed to hear male voices, she would not waken them. Even when she heard the sound of muffled oars, though her heart was in her mouth, she did not waken them. She stood over them to let them have their sleep out. Was it not brave of Wendy?

It was well for those boys then that there was one among them who could sniff danger even in his sleep. Peter sprang erect, as wide awake at once as a dog, and with one warning cry he roused the others.

He stood motionless, one hand to his ear.

"Pirates!" he cried. The others came closer to him. A strange smile was playing about his face, and Wendy saw it and shuddered. While that smile was on his face no one dared address him; all they could do was to stand ready to obey. The order came sharp and incisive.

"Dive!"

There was a gleam of legs, and instantly the lagoon seemed deserted. Marooners' Rock stood alone in the forbidding waters as if it were itself marooned.

The boat drew nearer. It was the pirate dinghy, with three figures in her, Smee and Starkey, and the third a captive, no other than Tiger Lily. Her hands and ankles were tied, and she knew what was to be her fate. She was to be left on the rock to perish, an end to one of her race more terrible than death by fire or torture, for is it not written in the book of the tribe that there is no path through water to the happy hunting-ground? Yet her face was impassive; she was the daughter of a chief, she must die as a chief's daughter, it is enough.

They had caught her boarding the pirate ship with a knife in her mouth. No watch was kept on the ship, it being Hook's boast that the wind of his name guarded the ship for a mile around. Now her fate would help to guard it also. One more wail would go the round in that wind by night.

In the gloom that they brought with them the two pirates did not see the rock till they crashed into it.

"Luff, you lubber," cried an Irish voice that was Smee's; "here's the rock. Now, then, what we have to do is to hoist the redskin on to it and leave her here to drown."

It was the work of one brutal moment to land the beautiful girl on the rock; she was too proud to offer a vain resistance.

Quite near the rock, but out of sight, two heads were bobbing up and down, Peter's and Wendy's. Wendy was crying, for it was the first tragedy she had seen. Peter had seen many tragedies, but he had forgotten them all. He was less sorry than Wendy for Tiger Lily: it was two against one that angered him, and he meant to save her. An easy way would have been to wait until the pirates had gone, but he was never one to choose the easy way.

There was almost nothing he could not do, and he now imitated the voice of Hook.

"Ahoy there, you lubbers!" he called. It was a marvellous imitation.

"The captain!" said the pirates, staring at each other in surprise.

"He must be swimming out to us," Starkey said, when they had looked for him in vain.

"We are putting the redskin on the rock," Smee called out.

"Set her free," came the astonishing answer.

"Free!"

"Yes, cut her bonds and let her go."

"But, captain—"

"At once, d'ye hear," cried Peter, "or I'll plunge my hook in you."

"This is queer!" Smee gasped.

"Better do what the captain orders," said Starkey nervously.

"Ay, ay," Smee said, and he cut Tiger Lily's cords. At once like an eel she slid between Starkey's legs into the water.

Of course Wendy was very elated over Peter's cleverness; but she knew that he would be elated also and very likely crow and thus betray himself, so at once her hand went out to cover his mouth. But it was stayed even in the act, for "Boat ahoy!" rang over the lagoon in Hook's voice, and this time it was not Peter who had spoken.

Peter may have been about to crow, but his face puckered in a whistle of surprise instead.

"Boat ahoy!" again came the voice.

Now Wendy understood. The real Hook was also in the water.

He was swimming to the boat, and as his men showed a light to guide him he had soon reached them. In the light of the lantern Wendy saw his hook grip the boat's side; she saw his evil swarthy face as he rose dripping from the water, and, quaking, she would have liked to swim away, but Peter would not budge. He was tingling with life and also top-heavy with conceit. "Am I not a wonder, oh, I am a wonder!" he whispered to her, and though she thought so also, she was really glad for the sake of his reputation that no one heard him except herself.

He signed to her to listen.

The two pirates were very curious to know what had brought their captain to them, but he sat with his head on his hook in a position of profound melancholy.

"Captain, is all well?" they asked timidly, but he answered with a hollow moan.

"He sighs," said Smee.

"He sighs again," said Starkey.

"And yet a third time he sighs," said Smee.

"What's up, captain?"

Then at last he spoke passionately.

"The game's up," he cried, "those boys have found a mother."

Affrighted though she was, Wendy swelled with pride.

"O evil day!" cried Starkey.

"What's a mother?" asked the ignorant Smee.

Wendy was so shocked that she exclaimed. "He doesn't know!" and always after this she felt that if you could have a pet pirate Smee would be her one.

Peter pulled her beneath the water, for Hook had started up, crying, "What was that?"

"I heard nothing," said Starkey, raising the lantern over the waters, and as the pirates looked they saw a strange sight. It was the nest I have told you of, floating on the lagoon, and the Never bird was sitting on it.

"See," said Hook in answer to Smee's question, "that is a mother. What a lesson! The nest must have fallen into the water, but would the mother desert her eggs? No."

There was a break in his voice, as if for a moment he recalled innocent days when—but he brushed away this weakness with his hook.

Smee, much impressed, gazed at the bird as the nest was borne past, but the more suspicious Starkey said, "If she is a mother, perhaps she is hanging about here to help Peter."

Hook winced. "Ay," he said, "that is the fear that haunts me."

He was roused from this dejection by Smee's eager voice.

"Captain," said Smee, "could we not kidnap these boys' mother and make her our mother?"

"It is a princely scheme," cried Hook, and at once it took practical shape in his great brain. "We will seize the children and carry them to the boat: the boys we will make walk the plank, and Wendy shall be our mother."

Again Wendy forgot herself.

"Never!" she cried, and bobbed.

"What was that?"

But they could see nothing. They thought it must have been a leaf in the wind. "Do you agree, my bullies?" asked Hook.

"There is my hand on it," they both said.

"And there is my hook. Swear."

They all swore. By this time they were on the rock, and suddenly Hook remembered Tiger Lily.

"Where is the redskin?" he demanded abruptly.

He had a playful humour at moments, and they thought this was one of the moments.

"That is all right, captain," Smee answered complacently; "we let her go."

"Let her go!" cried Hook.

"'Twas your own orders," the bo'sun faltered.

"You called over the water to us to let her go," said Starkey.

"Brimstone and gall," thundered Hook, "what cozening [cheating] is going on here!" His face had gone black with rage, but he saw that they believed their words, and he was startled. "Lads," he said, shaking a little, "I gave no such order."

"It is passing queer," Smee said, and they all fidgeted uncomfortably. Hook raised his voice, but there was a quiver in it.

"Spirit that haunts this dark lagoon tonight," he cried, "dost hear me?"

Of course Peter should have kept quiet, but of course he did not. He immediately answered in Hook's voice:

"Odds, bobs, hammer and tongs, I hear you."

In that supreme moment Hook did not blanch, even at the gills, but Smee and Starkey clung to each other in terror.

"Who are you, stranger? Speak!" Hook demanded.

"I am James Hook," replied the voice, "captain of the JOLLY ROGER."

"You are not; you are not," Hook cried hoarsely.

"Brimstone and gall," the voice retorted, "say that again, and I'll cast anchor in you."

Hook tried a more ingratiating manner. "If you are Hook," he said almost humbly, "come tell me, who am I?"

"A codfish," replied the voice, "only a codfish."

"A codfish!" Hook echoed blankly, and it was then, but not till then, that his proud spirit broke. He saw his men draw back from him.

"Have we been captained all this time by a codfish!" they muttered. "It is lowering to our pride."

They were his dogs snapping at him, but, tragic figure though he had become, he scarcely heeded them. Against such fearful evidence it was not their belief in him that he needed, it was his own. He felt his ego slipping from him. "Don't desert me, bully," he whispered hoarsely to it.

In his dark nature there was a touch of the feminine, as in all the great pirates, and it sometimes gave him intuitions. Suddenly he tried the guessing game.

"Hook," he called, "have you another voice?"

Now Peter could never resist a game, and he answered blithely in his own voice, "I have."

"And another name?"

"Ay, ay."

"Vegetable?" asked Hook.

"No."

"Mineral?"

"No."

"Animal?"

"Yes."

"Man?"

"No!" This answer rang out scornfully.

"Boy?"

"Yes."

"Ordinary boy?"

"No!"

"Wonderful boy?"

To Wendy's pain the answer that rang out this time was "Yes."

"Are you in England?"

"No."

"Are you here?"

"Yes."

Hook was completely puzzled. "You ask him some questions," he said to the others, wiping his damp brow.

Smee reflected. "I can't think of a thing," he said regretfully.

"Can't guess, can't guess!" crowed Peter. "Do you give it up?"

Of course in his pride he was carrying the game too far, and the miscreants [villains] saw their chance.

"Yes, yes," they answered eagerly.

"Well, then," he cried, "I am Peter Pan."

Pan!

In a moment Hook was himself again, and Smee and Starkey were his faithful henchmen.

"Now we have him," Hook shouted. "Into the water, Smee. Starkey, mind the boat. Take him dead or alive!"

He leaped as he spoke, and simultaneously came the gay voice of Peter.

"Are you ready, boys?"

"Ay, ay," from various parts of the lagoon.

"Then lam into the pirates."

The fight was short and sharp. First to draw blood was John, who gallantly climbed into the boat and held Starkey. There was fierce struggle, in which the cutlass was torn from the pirate's grasp. He wriggled overboard and John leapt after him. The dinghy drifted away.

Here and there a head bobbed up in the water, and there was a flash of steel followed by a cry or a whoop. In the confusion some struck at their own side. The corkscrew of Smee got Tootles in the fourth rib, but he was himself pinked [nicked] in turn by Curly. Farther from the rock Starkey was pressing Slightly and the twins hard.

Where all this time was Peter? He was seeking bigger game.

The others were all brave boys, and they must not be blamed for backing from the pirate captain. His iron claw made a circle of dead water round him, from which they fled like affrighted fishes.

But there was one who did not fear him: there was one prepared to enter that circle.

Strangely, it was not in the water that they met. Hook rose to the rock to breathe, and at the same moment Peter scaled it on the opposite side. The rock was slippery as a ball, and they had to crawl rather than climb. Neither knew that the other was coming. Each feeling for a grip met the other's arm: in surprise they raised their heads; their faces were almost touching; so they met.

Some of the greatest heroes have confessed that just before they fell to [began combat] they had a sinking [feeling in the stomach].

Had it been so with Peter at that moment I would admit it. After all, he was the only man that the Sea-Cook had feared. But Peter had no sinking, he had one feeling only, gladness; and he gnashed his pretty teeth with joy. Quick as thought he snatched a knife from Hook's belt and was about to drive it home, when he saw that he was higher up the rock than his foe. It would not have been fighting fair. He gave the pirate a hand to help him up.

It was then that Hook bit him.

Not the pain of this but its unfairness was what dazed Peter. It made him quite helpless. He could only stare, horrified. Every child is affected thus the first time he is treated unfairly. All he thinks he has a right to when he comes to you to be yours is fairness. After you have been unfair to him he will love you again, but will never afterwards be quite the same boy. No one ever gets over the first unfairness; no one except Peter. He often met it, but he always forgot it. I suppose that was the real difference between him and all the rest.

So when he met it now it was like the first time; and he could just stare, helpless. Twice the iron hand clawed him.

A few moments afterwards the other boys saw Hook in the water striking wildly for the ship; no elation on the pestilent face now, only white fear, for the crocodile was in dogged pursuit of him. On ordinary occasions the boys would have swum alongside cheering; but now they were uneasy, for they had lost both Peter and Wendy, and were scouring the lagoon for them, calling them by name. They found the dinghy and went home in it, shouting "Peter, Wendy" as they went, but no answer came save mocking laughter from the mermaids. "They must be swimming back or flying," the boys concluded. They were not very anxious, because they had such faith in Peter. They chuckled, boylike, because they would be late for bed; and it was all mother Wendy's fault!

When their voices died away there came cold silence over the lagoon, and then a feeble cry.

"Help, help!"

Two small figures were beating against the rock; the girl had fainted and lay on the boy's arm. With a last effort Peter pulled her up the rock and then lay down beside her. Even as he also fainted he saw that the water was rising. He knew that they would soon be drowned, but he could do no more.

As they lay side by side a mermaid caught Wendy by the feet, and began pulling her softly into the water. Peter, feeling her slip from him, woke with a start, and was just in time to draw her back. But he had to tell her the truth.

"We are on the rock, Wendy," he said, "but it is growing smaller. Soon the water will be over it."

She did not understand even now.

"We must go," she said, almost brightly.

"Yes," he answered faintly.

"Shall we swim or fly, Peter?"

He had to tell her.

"Do you think you could swim or fly as far as the island, Wendy, without my help?"

She had to admit that she was too tired.

He moaned.

"What is it?" she asked, anxious about him at once.

"I can't help you, Wendy. Hook wounded me. I can neither fly nor swim."

"Do you mean we shall both be drowned?"

"Look how the water is rising."

They put their hands over their eyes to shut out the sight. They thought they would soon be no more. As they sat thus something brushed against Peter as light as a kiss, and stayed there, as if saying timidly, "Can I be of any use?"

It was the tail of a kite, which Michael had made some days before. It had torn itself out of his hand and floated away.

"Michael's kite," Peter said without interest, but next moment he had seized the tail, and was pulling the kite toward him.

"It lifted Michael off the ground," he cried; "why should it not carry you?"

"Both of us!"

"It can't lift two; Michael and Curly tried."

"Let us draw lots," Wendy said bravely.

"And you a lady; never." Already he had tied the tail round her. She clung to him; she refused to go without him; but with a "Goodbye,

Wendy," he pushed her from the rock; and in a few minutes she was borne out of his sight. Peter was alone on the lagoon.

The rock was very small now; soon it would be submerged. Pale rays of light tiptoed across the waters; and by and by there was to be heard a sound at once the most musical and the most melancholy in the world: the mermaids calling to the moon.

Peter was not quite like other boys; but he was afraid at last. A tremour ran through him, like a shudder passing over the sea; but on the sea one shudder follows another till there are hundreds of them, and Peter felt just the one. Next moment he was standing erect on the rock again, with that smile on his face and a drum beating within him. It was saying, "To die will be an awfully big adventure."

9

The Never Bird

The last sound Peter heard before he was quite alone were the mermaids retiring one by one to their bedchambers under the sea. He was too far away to hear their doors shut; but every door in the coral caves where they live rings a tiny bell when it opens or closes (as in all the nicest houses on the mainland), and he heard the bells.

Steadily the waters rose till they were nibbling at his feet; and to pass the time until they made their final gulp, he watched the only thing on the lagoon. He thought it was a piece of floating paper, perhaps part of the kite, and wondered idly how long it would take to drift ashore.

Presently he noticed as an odd thing that it was undoubtedly out upon the lagoon with some definite purpose, for it was fighting the tide, and sometimes winning; and when it won, Peter, always sympathetic to the weaker side, could not help clapping; it was such a gallant piece of paper.

It was not really a piece of paper; it was the Never bird, making desperate efforts to reach Peter on the nest. By working her wings, in a way she had learned since the nest fell into the water, she was able to some extent to guide her strange craft, but by the time Peter recognised her she was very exhausted. She had come to save him, to give him her nest, though there were eggs in it. I rather wonder at the bird, for though he had been nice to her, he had also sometimes tormented her. I can suppose only that, like Mrs. Darling and the rest of them, she was melted because he had all his first teeth.

She called out to him what she had come for, and he called out to her what she was doing there; but of course neither of them understood the other's language. In fanciful stories people can talk to the birds freely, and I wish for the moment I could pretend that this were such a story, and say that Peter replied intelligently to the Never bird; but truth is best, and I want to tell you only what really happened. Well, not only could they not understand each other, but they forgot their manners.

"I—want—you—to—get—into—the—nest," the bird called, speaking as slowly and distinctly as possible, "and—then—you—can—drift—ashore, but—I—am—too—tired—to—bring—it—any—nearer—so—you—must—try to—swim—to—it."

"What are you quacking about?" Peter answered. "Why don't you let the nest drift as usual?"

"I—want—you—" the bird said, and repeated it all over.

Then Peter tried slow and distinct.

"What—are—you—quacking—about?" and so on.

The Never bird became irritated; they have very short tempers.

"You dunderheaded little jay!" she screamed, "Why don't you do as I tell you?"

Peter felt that she was calling him names, and at a venture he retorted hotly:

"So are you!"

Then rather curiously they both snapped out the same remark:

"Shut up!"

"Shut up!"

Nevertheless the bird was determined to save him if she could, and by one last mighty effort she propelled the nest against the rock. Then up she flew; deserting her eggs, so as to make her meaning clear.

Then at last he understood, and clutched the nest and waved his thanks to the bird as she fluttered overhead. It was not to receive his thanks, however, that she hung there in the sky; it was not even to watch him get into the nest; it was to see what he did with her eggs.

There were two large white eggs, and Peter lifted them up and reflected. The bird covered her face with her wings, so as not to see the last of them; but she could not help peeping between the feathers.

I forget whether I have told you that there was a stave on the rock, driven into it by some buccaneers of long ago to mark the site of buried treasure. The children had discovered the glittering hoard, and when in a mischievous mood used to fling showers of moidores, diamonds, pearls and pieces of eight to the gulls, who pounced upon them for food, and then flew away, raging at the scurvy trick that had been played upon them. The stave was still there, and on it Starkey had hung his hat, a deep tarpaulin, watertight, with a broad brim. Peter put the eggs into this hat and set it on the lagoon. It floated beautifully.

The Never bird saw at once what he was up to, and screamed her admiration of him; and, alas, Peter crowed his agreement with her. Then he got into the nest, reared the stave in it as a mast, and hung up his shirt for a sail. At the same moment the bird fluttered down upon the hat and once more sat snugly on her eggs. She drifted in one direction, and he was borne off in another, both cheering.

Of course when Peter landed he beached his barque [small ship, actually the Never Bird's nest in this particular case in point] in a place where the bird would easily find it; but the hat was such a great success that she abandoned the nest. It drifted about till it went to pieces, and often Starkey came to the shore of the lagoon, and with many bitter feelings watched the bird sitting on his hat. As we shall not see her again, it may be worth mentioning here that all Never birds now build in that shape of nest, with a broad brim on which the youngsters take an airing.

Great were the rejoicings when Peter reached the home under the ground almost as soon as Wendy, who had been carried hither and thither by the kite. Every boy had adventures to tell; but perhaps the biggest adventure of all was that they were several hours late for bed. This so inflated them that they did various dodgy things to get staying up still longer, such as demanding bandages; but Wendy, though glorying in having them all home again safe and sound, was scandalised by the lateness of the hour, and cried, "To bed, to bed," in a voice that had to be obeyed. Next day, however, she was awfully tender, and gave out bandages to every one, and they played till bed-time at limping about and carrying their arms in slings.

10

The Happy Home

One important result of the brush [with the pirates] on the lagoon was that it made the redskins their friends. Peter had saved Tiger Lily from a dreadful fate, and now there was nothing she and her braves would not do for him. All night they sat above, keeping watch over the home under the ground and awaiting the big attack by the pirates which obviously could not be much longer delayed. Even by day they hung about, smoking the pipe of peace, and looking almost as if they wanted tit-bits to eat.

They called Peter the Great White Father, prostrating themselves [lying down] before him; and he liked this tremendously, so that it was not really good for him.

"The great white father," he would say to them in a very lordly manner, as they grovelled at his feet, "is glad to see the Piccaninny warriors protecting his wigwam from the pirates."

"Me Tiger Lily," that lovely creature would reply. "Peter Pan save me, me his velly nice friend. Me no let pirates hurt him."

She was far too pretty to cringe in this way, but Peter thought it his due, and he would answer condescendingly, "It is good. Peter Pan has spoken."

Always when he said, "Peter Pan has spoken," it meant that they must now shut up, and they accepted it humbly in that spirit; but they were by no means so respectful to the other boys, whom they looked upon as just ordinary braves. They said "How-do?" to them, and things like that; and what annoyed the boys was that Peter seemed to think this all right.

Secretly Wendy sympathised with them a little, but she was far too loyal a housewife to listen to any complaints against father. "Father knows best," she always said, whatever her private opinion must be. Her private opinion was that the redskins should not call her a squaw.

We have now reached the evening that was to be known among them as the Night of Nights, because of its adventures and their upshot. The day, as if quietly gathering its forces, had been almost uneventful, and now the redskins in their blankets were at their posts above, while, below, the children were having their evening meal; all except Peter, who had gone out to get the time. The way you got the time on the island was to find the crocodile, and then stay near him till the clock struck.

The meal happened to be a make-believe tea, and they sat around the board, guzzling in their greed; and really, what with their chatter and recriminations, the noise, as Wendy said, was positively deafening. To be sure, she did not mind noise, but she simply would not have them grabbing things, and then excusing themselves by saying that Tootles had pushed their elbow. There was a fixed rule that they must never hit back at meals, but should refer the matter of dispute to Wendy by raising the right arm politely and saying, "I complain of so-and-so;" but what usually happened was that they forgot to do this or did it too much.

"Silence," cried Wendy when for the twentieth time she had told them that they were not all to speak at once. "Is your mug empty, Slightly darling?"

"Not quite empty, mummy," Slightly said, after looking into an imaginary mug.

"He hasn't even begun to drink his milk," Nibs interposed.

This was telling, and Slightly seized his chance.

"I complain of Nibs," he cried promptly.

John, however, had held up his hand first.

"Well, John?"

"May I sit in Peter's chair, as he is not here?"

"Sit in father's chair, John!" Wendy was scandalised. "Certainly not."

"He is not really our father," John answered. "He didn't even know how a father does till I showed him."

This was grumbling. "We complain of John," cried the twins.

Tootles held up his hand. He was so much the humblest of them, indeed he was the only humble one, that Wendy was specially gentle with him.

"I don't suppose," Tootles said diffidently [bashfully or timidly], "that I could be father."

"No, Tootles."

Once Tootles began, which was not very often, he had a silly way of going on.

"As I can't be father," he said heavily, "I don't suppose, Michael, you would let me be baby?"

"No, I won't," Michael rapped out. He was already in his basket.

"As I can't be baby," Tootles said, getting heavier and heavier and heavier, "do you think I could be a twin?"

"No, indeed," replied the twins; "it's awfully difficult to be a twin."

"As I can't be anything important," said Tootles, "would any of you like to see me do a trick?"

"No," they all replied.

Then at last he stopped. "I hadn't really any hope," he said.

The hateful telling broke out again.

"Slightly is coughing on the table."

"The twins began with cheese-cakes."

"Curly is taking both butter and honey."

"Nibs is speaking with his mouth full."

"I complain of the twins."

"I complain of Curly."

"I complain of Nibs."

"Oh dear, oh dear," cried Wendy, "I'm sure I sometimes think that spinsters are to be envied."

She told them to clear away, and sat down to her work-basket, a heavy load of stockings and every knee with a hole in it as usual.

"Wendy," remonstrated [scolded] Michael, "I'm too big for a cradle."

"I must have somebody in a cradle," she said almost tartly, "and you are the littlest. A cradle is such a nice homely thing to have about a house."

While she sewed they played around her; such a group of happy faces and dancing limbs lit up by that romantic fire. It had become a very familiar scene, this, in the home under the ground, but we are looking on it for the last time.

There was a step above, and Wendy, you may be sure, was the first to recognize it.

"Children, I hear your father's step. He likes you to meet him at the door."

Above, the redskins crouched before Peter.

"Watch well, braves. I have spoken."

And then, as so often before, the gay children dragged him from his tree. As so often before, but never again.

He had brought nuts for the boys as well as the correct time for Wendy.

"Peter, you just spoil them, you know," Wendy simpered [exaggerated a smile].

"Ah, old lady," said Peter, hanging up his gun.

"It was me told him mothers are called old lady," Michael whispered to Curly.

"I complain of Michael," said Curly instantly.

The first twin came to Peter. "Father, we want to dance."

"Dance away, my little man," said Peter, who was in high good humour.

"But we want you to dance."

Peter was really the best dancer among them, but he pretended to be scandalised.

"Me! My old bones would rattle!"

"And mummy too."

"What," cried Wendy, "the mother of such an armful, dance!"

"But on a Saturday night," Slightly insinuated.

It was not really Saturday night, at least it may have been, for they had long lost count of the days; but always if they wanted to do anything special they said this was Saturday night, and then they did it.

"Of course it is Saturday night, Peter," Wendy said, relenting.

"People of our figure, Wendy!"

"But it is only among our own progeny [children]."

"True, true."

So they were told they could dance, but they must put on their nighties first.

"Ah, old lady," Peter said aside to Wendy, warming himself by the fire and looking down at her as she sat turning a heel, "there is nothing more pleasant of an evening for you and me when the day's toil is over than to rest by the fire with the little ones near by."

"It is sweet, Peter, isn't it?" Wendy said, frightfully gratified. "Peter, I think Curly has your nose."

"Michael takes after you."

She went to him and put her hand on his shoulder.

"Dear Peter," she said, "with such a large family, of course, I have now passed my best, but you don't want to [ex]change me, do you?"

"No, Wendy."

Certainly he did not want a change, but he looked at her uncomfortably, blinking, you know, like one not sure whether he was awake or asleep.

"Peter, what is it?"

"I was just thinking," he said, a little scared. "It is only make-believe, isn't it, that I am their father?"

"Oh yes," Wendy said primly [formally and properly].

"You see," he continued apologetically, "it would make me seem so old to be their real father."

"But they are ours, Peter, yours and mine."

"But not really, Wendy?" he asked anxiously.

"Not if you don't wish it," she replied; and she distinctly heard his sigh of relief. "Peter," she asked, trying to speak firmly, "what are your exact feelings for me?"

"Those of a devoted son, Wendy."

"I thought so," she said, and went and sat by herself at the extreme end of the room.

"You are so queer," he said, frankly puzzled, "and Tiger Lily is just the same. There is something she wants to be to me, but she says it is not my mother."

"No, indeed, it is not," Wendy replied with frightful emphasis. Now we know why she was prejudiced against the redskins.

"Then what is it?"

"It isn't for a lady to tell."

"Oh, very well," Peter said, a little nettled. "Perhaps Tinker Bell will tell me."

"Oh yes, Tinker Bell will tell you," Wendy retorted scornfully. "She is an abandoned little creature."

Here Tink, who was in her bedroom, eavesdropping, squeaked out something impudent.

"She says she glories in being abandoned," Peter interpreted.

He had a sudden idea. "Perhaps Tink wants to be my mother?"

"You silly ass!" cried Tinker Bell in a passion.

She had said it so often that Wendy needed no translation.

"I almost agree with her," Wendy snapped. Fancy Wendy snapping! But she had been much tried, and she little knew what was to happen before the night was out. If she had known she would not have snapped.

None of them knew. Perhaps it was best not to know. Their ignorance gave them one more glad hour; and as it was to be their last hour on the island, let us rejoice that there were sixty glad minutes in it. They sang and danced in their night-gowns. Such a deliciously creepy song it was, in which they pretended to be frightened at their own shadows, little witting that so soon shadows would close in upon them, from whom they would shrink in real fear. So uproariously gay was the dance, and how they buffeted each other on the bed and out of it! It was a pillow fight rather than a dance, and when it was finished, the pillows insisted on one bout more, like partners who know that they may never meet again. The stories they told, before it was time for Wendy's good-night story! Even Slightly tried to tell a story that night, but the beginning was so fearfully dull that it appalled not only the others but himself, and he said gloomily:

"Yes, it is a dull beginning. I say, let us pretend that it is the end."

And then at last they all got into bed for Wendy's story, the story they loved best, the story Peter hated. Usually when she began to tell this story he left the room or put his hands over his ears; and possibly if he had done either of those things this time they might all still be on the island. But tonight he remained on his stool; and we shall see what happened.

11

Wendy's Story

"Listen, then," said Wendy, settling down to her story, with Michael at her feet and seven boys in the bed. "There was once a gentleman—"

"I had rather he had been a lady," Curly said.

"I wish he had been a white rat," said Nibs.

"Quiet," their mother admonished [cautioned] them. "There was a lady also, and—"

"Oh, mummy," cried the first twin, "you mean that there is a lady also, don't you? She is not dead, is she?"

"Oh, no."

"I am awfully glad she isn't dead," said Tootles. "Are you glad, John?"

"Of course I am."

"Are you glad, Nibs?"

"Rather."

"Are you glad, Twins?"

"We are glad."

"Oh dear," sighed Wendy.

"Little less noise there," Peter called out, determined

that she should have fair play, however beastly a story it might be in his opinion.

"The gentleman's name," Wendy continued, "was Mr. Darling, and her name was Mrs. Darling."

"I knew them," John said, to annoy the others.

"I think I knew them," said Michael rather doubtfully.

"They were married, you know," explained Wendy, "and what do you think they had?"

"White rats," cried Nibs, inspired.

"No."

"It's awfully puzzling," said Tootles, who knew the story by heart.

"Quiet, Tootles. They had three descendants."

"What is descendants?"

"Well, you are one, Twin."

"Did you hear that, John? I am a descendant."

"Descendants are only children," said John.

"Oh dear, oh dear," sighed Wendy. "Now these three children had a faithful nurse called Nana; but Mr. Darling was angry with her and chained her up in the yard, and so all the children flew away."

"It's an awfully good story," said Nibs.

"They flew away," Wendy continued, "to the Neverland, where the lost children are."

"I just thought they did," Curly broke in excitedly. "I don't know how it is, but I just thought they did!"

"O Wendy," cried Tootles, "was one of the lost children called Tootles?"

"Yes, he was."

"I am in a story. Hurrah, I am in a story, Nibs."

"Hush. Now I want you to consider the feelings of the unhappy parents with all their children flown away."

"Oo!" they all moaned, though they were not really considering the feelings of the unhappy parents one jot.

"Think of the empty beds!"

"Oo!"

"It's awfully sad," the first twin said cheerfully.

"I don't see how it can have a happy ending," said the second twin. "Do you, Nibs?"

"I'm frightfully anxious."

"If you knew how great is a mother's love," Wendy told them triumphantly, "you would have no fear." She had now come to the part that Peter hated.

"I do like a mother's love," said Tootles, hitting Nibs with a pillow. "Do you like a mother's love, Nibs?"

"I do just," said Nibs, hitting back.

"You see," Wendy said complacently, "our heroine knew that the mother would always leave the window open for her children to fly back by; so they stayed away for years and had a lovely time."

"Did they ever go back?"

"Let us now," said Wendy, bracing herself up for her finest effort, "take a peep into the future;" and they all gave themselves the twist that makes peeps into the future easier. "Years have rolled by, and who is this elegant lady of uncertain age alighting at London Station?"

"O Wendy, who is she?" cried Nibs, every bit as excited as if he didn't know.

"Can it be—yes—no—it is—the fair Wendy!"

"Oh!"

"And who are the two noble portly figures accompanying her, now grown to man's estate? Can they be John and Michael? They are!"

"Oh!"

"'See, dear brothers,' says Wendy pointing upwards, 'there is the window still standing open. Ah, now we are rewarded for our sublime faith in a mother's love.' So up they flew to their mummy and daddy, and pen cannot describe the happy scene, over which we draw a veil."

That was the story, and they were as pleased with it as the fair narrator herself. Everything just as it should be, you see. Off we skip like the most heartless things in the world, which is what children are, but so attractive; and we have an entirely selfish time, and then when we have need of special attention we nobly return for it, confident that we shall be rewarded instead of smacked.

So great indeed was their faith in a mother's love that they felt they could afford to be callous for a bit longer.

But there was one there who knew better, and when Wendy finished he uttered a hollow groan.

"What is it, Peter?" she cried, running to him, thinking he was ill. She felt him solicitously, lower down than his chest. "Where is it, Peter?"

"It isn't that kind of pain," Peter replied darkly.

"Then what kind is it?"

"Wendy, you are wrong about mothers."

They all gathered round him in affright, so alarming was his agitation; and with a fine candour he told them what he had hitherto concealed.

"Long ago," he said, "I thought like you that my mother would always keep the window open for me, so I stayed away for moons and moons and moons, and then flew back; but the window was barred, for mother had forgotten all about me, and there was another little boy sleeping in my bed."

I am not sure that this was true, but Peter thought it was true; and it scared them.

"Are you sure mothers are like that?"

"Yes."

So this was the truth about mothers. The toads!

Still it is best to be careful; and no one knows so quickly as a child when he should give in. "Wendy, let us go home," cried John and Michael together.

"Yes," she said, clutching them.

"Not tonight?" asked the lost boys bewildered. They knew in what they called their hearts that one can get on quite well without a mother, and that it is only the mothers who think you can't.

"At once," Wendy replied resolutely, for the horrible thought had come to her: "Perhaps mother is in half mourning by this time."

This dread made her forgetful of what must be Peter's feelings, and she said to him rather sharply, "Peter, will you make the necessary arrangements?"

"If you wish it," he replied, as coolly as if she had asked him to pass the nuts.

Not so much as a sorry-to-lose-you between them! If she did not mind the parting, he was going to show her, was Peter, that neither did he.

But of course he cared very much; and he was so full of wrath against grown-ups, who, as usual, were spoiling everything, that as soon as he got inside his tree he breathed intentionally quick short breaths at the rate of about five to a second. He did this because there is a saying in the Neverland that, every time you breathe, a grown-up dies; and Peter was killing them off vindictively as fast as possible.

Then having given the necessary instructions to the redskins he returned to the home, where an unworthy scene had been enacted in his absence. Panic-stricken at the thought of losing Wendy the lost boys had advanced upon her threateningly.

"It will be worse than before she came," they cried.

"We shan't let her go."

"Let's keep her prisoner."

"Ay, chain her up."

In her extremity an instinct told her to which of them to turn.

"Tootles," she cried, "I appeal to you."

Was it not strange? She appealed to Tootles, quite the silliest one.

Grandly, however, did Tootles respond. For that one moment he dropped his silliness and spoke with dignity.

"I am just Tootles," he said, "and nobody minds me. But the first who does not behave to Wendy like an English gentleman I will blood him severely."

He drew back his hanger; and for that instant his sun was at noon. The others held back uneasily. Then Peter returned, and they saw at once that they would get no support from him. He would keep no girl in the Neverland against her will.

"Wendy," he said, striding up and down, "I have asked the redskins to guide you through the wood, as flying tires you so."

"Thank you, Peter."

"Then," he continued, in the short sharp voice of one accustomed to be obeyed, "Tinker Bell will take you across the sea. Wake her, Nibs."

Nibs had to knock twice before he got an answer, though Tink had really been sitting up in bed listening for some time.

"Who are you? How dare you? Go away," she cried.

"You are to get up, Tink," Nibs called, "and take Wendy on a journey."

Of course Tink had been delighted to hear that Wendy was going; but she was jolly well determined not to be her courier, and she said so in still more offensive language. Then she pretended to be asleep again.

"She says she won't!" Nibs exclaimed, aghast at such insubordination, whereupon Peter went sternly toward the young lady's chamber.

"Tink," he rapped out, "if you don't get up and dress at once I will open the curtains, and then we shall all see you in your negligee [nightgown]."

This made her leap to the floor. "Who said I wasn't getting up?" she cried.

In the meantime the boys were gazing very forlornly at Wendy, now equipped with John and Michael for the journey. By this time they were dejected, not merely because they were about to lose her, but also because they felt that she was going off to something nice to which they had not been invited. Novelty was beckoning to them as usual.

Crediting them with a nobler feeling Wendy melted.

"Dear ones," she said, "if you will all come with me I feel almost sure I can get my father and mother to adopt you."

The invitation was meant specially for Peter, but each of the boys was thinking exclusively of himself, and at once they jumped with joy.

"But won't they think us rather a handful?" Nibs asked in the middle of his jump.

"Oh no," said Wendy, rapidly thinking it out, "it will only mean having a few beds in the drawing room; they can be hidden behind the screens on first Thursdays."

"Peter, can we go?" they all cried imploringly. They took it for granted that if they went he would go also, but really they scarcely cared. Thus children are ever ready, when novelty knocks, to desert their dearest ones.

"All right," Peter replied with a bitter smile, and immediately they rushed to get their things.

"And now, Peter," Wendy said, thinking she had put everything right, "I am going to give you your medicine before you go." She loved to give them medicine, and undoubtedly gave them too much. Of course it was only water, but it was out of a bottle, and she always shook the bottle and counted the drops, which gave it a certain medicinal quality. On this occasion, however, she did not give Peter his draught [portion], for just as she had prepared it, she saw a look on his face that made her heart sink.

"Get your things, Peter," she cried, shaking.

"No," he answered, pretending indifference, "I am not going with you, Wendy."

"Yes, Peter."

"No."

To show that her departure would leave him unmoved, he skipped up and down the room, playing gaily on his heartless pipes. She had to run about after him, though it was rather undignified.

"To find your mother," she coaxed.

Now, if Peter had ever quite had a mother, he no longer missed her. He could do very well without one. He had thought them out, and remembered only their bad points.

"No, no," he told Wendy decisively; "perhaps she would say I was old, and I just want always to be a little boy and to have fun."

"But, Peter—"

"No."

And so the others had to be told.

"Peter isn't coming."

Peter not coming! They gazed blankly at him, their sticks over their backs, and on each stick a bundle. Their first thought was that if Peter was not going he had probably changed his mind about letting them go.

But he was far too proud for that. "If you find your mothers," he said darkly, "I hope you will like them."

The awful cynicism of this made an uncomfortable impression, and most of them began to look rather doubtful. After all, their faces said, were they not noodles to want to go?

"Now then," cried Peter, "no fuss, no blubbering; good-bye, Wendy;" and he held out his hand cheerily, quite as if they must really go now, for he had something important to do.

She had to take his hand, and there was no indication that he would prefer a thimble.

"You will remember about changing your flannels, Peter?" she said, lingering over him. She was always so particular about their flannels.

"Yes."

"And you will take your medicine?"

"Yes."

That seemed to be everything, and an awkward pause followed. Peter, however, was not the kind that breaks down before other people. "Are you ready, Tinker Bell?" he called out.

"Ay, ay."

"Then lead the way."

Tink darted up the nearest tree; but no one followed her, for it was at this moment that the pirates made their dreadful attack upon the redskins. Above, where all had been so still, the air was rent with shrieks and the clash of steel. Below, there was dead silence. Mouths opened and remained open. Wendy fell on her knees, but her arms were extended toward Peter. All arms were extended to him, as if suddenly blown in his direction; they were beseeching him mutely not to desert them. As for Peter, he seized his sword, the same he thought he had slain Barbecue with, and the lust of battle was in his eye.

12

The Children are Carried Off

The pirate attack had been a complete surprise: a sure proof that the unscrupulous Hook had conducted it improperly, for to surprise redskins fairly is beyond the wit of the white man.

By all the unwritten laws of savage warfare it is always the redskin who attacks, and with the wiliness of his race he does it just before the dawn, at which time he knows the courage of the whites to be at its lowest ebb. The white men have in the meantime made a rude stockade on the summit of yonder undulating ground, at the foot of which a stream runs, for it is destruction to be too far from water. There they await the onslaught, the inexperienced ones clutching their revolvers and treading on twigs, but the old hands sleeping tranquilly until just before the dawn. Through the long black night the savage scouts wriggle, snake-like, among the grass without stirring a blade. The brushwood closes behind them, as silently as sand into which a mole has dived. Not a sound is to be heard, save when they give vent to a wonderful imitation of the lonely call of the coyote. The cry is answered by other braves; and some of them do it even better than the coyotes, who are not very good at it. So the chill hours wear on, and the long suspense is horribly trying to the paleface who has to live through it for the first time; but to the trained hand those ghastly calls and still ghastlier silences are but an intimation of how the night is marching.

That this was the usual procedure was so well known to Hook that in disregarding it he cannot be excused on the plea of ignorance.

The Piccaninnies, on their part, trusted implicitly to his honour, and their whole action of the night stands out in marked contrast to his. They left nothing undone that was consistent with the reputation of their tribe. With that alertness of the senses which is at once the marvel and despair of civilised peoples, they knew that the pirates were on the island from the moment one of them trod on a dry stick; and in an incredibly short space of time the coyote cries began. Every foot of ground between the spot where Hook had landed his forces and the home under the trees was stealthily examined by braves wearing their moccasins with the heels in front. They found only one hillock with a stream at its base, so that Hook had no choice; here he must establish himself and wait for just before the dawn. Everything being thus mapped out with almost diabolical cunning, the main body of the redskins folded their blankets around them, and in the phlegmatic manner that is to them, the pearl of manhood squatted above the children's home, awaiting the cold moment when they should deal pale death.

Here dreaming, though wide-awake, of the exquisite tortures to which they were to put him at break of day, those confiding savages were found by the treacherous Hook. From the accounts afterwards supplied by such of the scouts as escaped the carnage, he does not seem even to have paused at the rising ground, though it is certain that in that grey light he must have seen it: no thought of waiting to be attacked appears from first to last to have visited his subtle mind; he would not even hold off till the night was nearly spent; on he pounded with no policy but to fall to [get into combat]. What could the bewildered scouts do, masters as they were of every war-like artifice save this one, but trot helplessly after him, exposing themselves fatally to view, while they gave pathetic utterance to the coyote cry.

Around the brave Tiger Lily were a dozen of her stoutest warriors, and they suddenly saw the perfidious pirates bearing down upon them. Fell from their eyes then the film through which they had looked at victory. No more would they torture at the stake. For them the happy hunting-grounds was now. They knew it; but as their father's sons they acquitted themselves. Even then they had time to gather in a phalanx [dense formation] that would have been hard to break had they risen quickly, but this they were forbidden to do by the traditions of their race. It is written that the noble savage must never express surprise in the presence of the white. Thus terrible as the sudden appearance of the pirates must have been to them, they remained stationary for a moment, not a muscle moving; as if the foe had come by invitation. Then, indeed, the tradition gallantly upheld, they seized their weapons, and the air was torn with the war-cry; but it was now too late.

It is no part of ours to describe what was a massacre rather than a fight. Thus perished many of the flower of the Piccaninny tribe. Not all unavenged did they die, for with Lean Wolf fell Alf Mason, to disturb the Spanish Main no more, and among others who bit the dust were Geo. Scourie, Chas. Turley, and the Alsatian Foggerty. Turley fell to the tomahawk of the terrible Panther, who ultimately cut a way through the pirates with Tiger Lily and a small remnant of the tribe.

To what extent Hook is to blame for his tactics on this occasion is for the historian to decide. Had he waited on the rising ground till the proper hour he and his men would probably have been butchered; and in judging him it is only fair to take this into account. What he should perhaps have done was to acquaint his opponents that he proposed to follow a new method. On the other hand, this, as destroying the element of surprise, would have made his strategy of no avail, so that the whole question is beset with difficulties. One cannot at least withhold a reluctant admiration for the wit that had conceived so bold a scheme, and the fell [deadly] genius with which it was carried out.

What were his own feelings about himself at that triumphant moment? Fain [gladly] would his dogs have known, as breathing heavily and wiping their cutlasses, they gathered at a discreet distance from his hook, and squinted through their ferret eyes at this extraordinary man. Elation must have been in his heart, but his face did not reflect it: ever a dark and solitary enigma, he stood aloof from his followers in spirit as in substance.

The night's work was not yet over, for it was not the redskins he had come out to destroy; they were but the bees to be smoked, so that he should get at the honey. It was Pan he wanted, Pan and Wendy and their band, but chiefly Pan.

Peter was such a small boy that one tends to wonder at the man's hatred of him. True he had flung Hook's arm to the crocodile, but even this and the increased insecurity of life to which it led, owing to the crocodile's pertinacity [persistance], hardly account for a vindictiveness so relentless and malignant. The truth is that there was a something about Peter which goaded the pirate captain to frenzy. It was not his courage, it was not his engaging appearance, it was not—. There is no beating about the bush, for we know quite well what it was, and have got to tell. It was Peter's cockiness.

This had got on Hook's nerves; it made his iron claw twitch, and at night it disturbed him like an insect. While Peter lived, the tortured man felt that he was a lion in a cage into which a sparrow had come.

The question now was how to get down the trees, or how to get his dogs down? He ran his greedy eyes over them, searching for the thinnest ones. They wriggled uncomfortably, for they knew he would not scruple [hesitate] to ram them down with poles.

In the meantime, what of the boys? We have seen them at the first clang of the weapons, turned as it were into stone figures, open-mouthed, all appealing with outstretched arms to Peter; and we return to them as their mouths close, and their arms fall to their sides. The pandemonium above has ceased almost as suddenly as it arose, passed like a fierce gust of wind; but they know that in the passing it has determined their fate.

Which side had won?

The pirates, listening avidly at the mouths of the trees, heard the question put by every boy, and alas, they also heard Peter's answer.

"If the redskins have won," he said, "they will beat the tom-tom; it is always their sign of victory."

Now Smee had found the tom-tom, and was at that moment sitting on it. "You will never hear the tom-tom again," he muttered, but inaudibly of course, for strict silence had been enjoined [urged]. To his amazement Hook signed him to beat the tom-tom, and slowly there came to Smee an understanding of the dreadful wickedness of the order. Never, probably, had this simple man admired Hook so much.

Twice Smee beat upon the instrument, and then stopped to listen gleefully.

"The tom-tom," the miscreants heard Peter cry; "an Indian victory!"

The doomed children answered with a cheer that was music to the black hearts above, and almost immediately they repeated their goodbyes to Peter. This puzzled the pirates, but all their other feelings were swallowed by a base delight that the enemy were about to come up the trees. They smirked at each other and rubbed their hands. Rapidly and silently Hook gave his orders: one man to each tree, and the others to arrange themselves in a line two yards apart.

13

Do You Believe in Fairies?

The more quickly this horror is disposed of the better. The first to emerge from his tree was Curly. He rose out of it into the arms of Cecco, who flung him to Smee, who flung him to Starkey, who flung him to Bill Jukes, who flung him to Noodler, and so he was tossed from one to another till he fell at the feet of the black pirate. All the boys were plucked from their trees in this ruthless manner; and several of them were in the air at a time, like bales of goods flung from hand to hand.

A different treatment was accorded to Wendy, who came last. With ironical politeness Hook raised his hat to her, and, offering her his arm, escorted her to the spot where the others were being gagged. He did it with such an air, he was so frightfully DISTINGUE [imposingly distinguished], that she was too fascinated to cry out. She was only a little girl.

Perhaps it is tell-tale to divulge that for a moment Hook entranced her, and we tell on her only because her slip led to strange results. Had she haughtily unhanded him (and we should have loved to write it of her), she would have been hurled through the air like the others, and then Hook would probably not have been present at the tying of the children; and had he not been at the tying he would not have discovered Slightly's secret, and without the secret he could not presently have made his foul attempt on Peter's life.

They were tied to prevent their flying away, doubled up with their knees close to their ears; and for the trussing of them the black pirate had cut a rope into nine equal pieces. All went well until Slightly's turn came, when he was found to be like those irritating parcels that use up all the string in going round and leave no tags [ends] with which to tie a knot. The pirates kicked him in their rage, just as you kick the parcel (though in fairness you should kick the string); and strange to say it was Hook who told them to belay their violence. His lip was curled with malicious triumph. While his dogs were merely sweating because every time they tried to pack the unhappy lad tight in one part he bulged out in another, Hook's master mind had gone far beneath Slightly's surface, probing not for effects but for causes; and his exultation showed that he had found them. Slightly, white to the gills, knew that Hook had surprised [discovered] his secret, which was this, that no boy so blown out could use a tree wherein an average man need stick. Poor Slightly, most wretched of all the children now, for he was in a panic about Peter, bitterly regretted what he had done. Madly addicted to the drinking of water when he was hot, he had swelled in consequence to his present girth, and instead of reducing himself to fit his tree he had, unknown to the others, whittled his tree to make it fit him.

Sufficient of this Hook guessed to persuade him that Peter at last lay at his mercy, but no word of the dark design that now formed in the subterranean caverns of his mind crossed his lips; he merely signed that the captives were to be conveyed to the ship, and that he would be alone.

How to convey them? Hunched up in their ropes they might indeed be rolled down hill like barrels, but most of the way lay through a morass. Again Hook's genius surmounted difficulties. He indicated that the little house must be used as a conveyance. The children were flung into it, four stout pirates raised it on their shoulders, the others fell in behind, and singing the hateful pirate chorus the strange procession set off through the wood. I don't know whether any of the children were crying; if so, the singing drowned the sound; but as the little house disappeared in the forest, a brave though tiny jet of smoke issued from its chimney as if defying Hook.

Hook saw it, and it did Peter a bad service. It dried up any trickle of pity for him that may have remained in the pirate's infuriated breast.

The first thing he did on finding himself alone in the fast-falling night was to tiptoe to Slightly's tree, and make sure that it provided him with a passage. Then for long he remained brooding; his hat of ill omen on the sward, so that any gentle breeze which had arisen might play refreshingly through his hair. Dark as were his thoughts his blue eyes were as soft as the periwinkle. Intently he listened for any sound from the nether world, but all was as silent below as above; the house under the ground seemed to be but one more empty tenement in the void. Was that boy asleep, or did he stand waiting at the foot of Slightly's tree, with his dagger in his hand?

There was no way of knowing, save by going down. Hook let his cloak slip softly to the ground, and then biting his lips till a lewd blood stood on them, he stepped into the tree. He was a brave man, but for a moment he had to stop there and wipe his brow, which was dripping like a candle. Then, silently, he let himself go into the unknown.

He arrived unmolested at the foot of the shaft, and stood still again, biting at his breath, which had almost left him. As his eyes became accustomed to the dim light various objects in the home under the trees took shape; but the only one on which his greedy gaze rested, long sought for and found at last, was the great bed. On the bed lay Peter fast asleep.

Unaware of the tragedy being enacted above, Peter had continued, for a little time after the children left, to play gaily on his pipes: no doubt rather a forlorn attempt to prove to himself that he did not care. Then he decided not to take his medicine, so as to grieve Wendy. Then he lay down on the bed outside the coverlet, to vex her still more; for she had always tucked them inside it, because you never know that you may not grow chilly at the turn of the night. Then he nearly cried; but it struck him how indignant she would be if he laughed instead; so he laughed a haughty laugh and fell asleep in the middle of it.

Sometimes, though not often, he had dreams, and they were more painful than the dreams of other boys. For hours he could not be separated from these dreams, though he wailed piteously in them. They had to do, I think, with the riddle of his existence. At such times it had been Wendy's custom to take him out of bed and sit with him on her lap, soothing him in dear ways of her own invention, and when he grew calmer to put him back to bed before he quite woke up, so that he should not know of the indignity to which she had subjected him. But on this occasion he had fallen at once into a dreamless sleep. One arm dropped over the edge of the bed, one leg was arched, and the unfinished part of his laugh was stranded on his mouth, which was open, showing the little pearls.

Thus defenceless Hook found him. He stood silent at the foot of the tree looking across the chamber at his enemy. Did no feeling of compassion disturb his sombre breast? The man was not wholly evil; he loved flowers (I have been told) and sweet music (he was himself no mean performer on the harpsichord); and, let it be frankly admitted, the idyllic nature of the scene stirred him profoundly. Mastered by his better self he would have returned reluctantly up the tree, but for one thing.

What stayed him was Peter's impertinent appearance as he slept. The open mouth, the drooping arm, the arched knee: they were such a personification of cockiness as, taken together, will never again, one may hope, be presented to eyes so sensitive to their offensiveness. They steeled Hook's heart. If his rage had broken him into a hundred pieces every one of them would have disregarded the incident, and leapt at the sleeper.

Though a light from the one lamp shone dimly on the bed, Hook stood in darkness himself, and at the first stealthy step forward he discovered an obstacle, the door of Slightly's tree. It did not entirely fill the aperture, and he had been looking over it. Feeling for the catch, he found to his fury that it was low down, beyond his reach. To his disordered brain it seemed then that the irritating quality in Peter's face and figure visibly increased, and he rattled the door and flung himself against it. Was his enemy to escape him after all?

But what was that? The red in his eye had caught sight of Peter's medicine standing on a ledge within easy reach. He fathomed what it was straightaway, and immediately knew that the sleeper was in his power.

Lest he should be taken alive, Hook always carried about his person a dreadful drug, blended by himself of all the death-dealing rings that had come into his possession. These he had boiled down into a yellow liquid quite unknown to science, which was probably the most virulent poison in existence.

Five drops of this he now added to Peter's cup. His hand shook, but it was in exultation rather than in shame. As he did it he avoided glancing at the sleeper, but not lest pity should unnerve him; merely to avoid spilling. Then one long gloating look he cast upon his victim, and turning, wormed his way with difficulty up the tree. As he emerged at the top he looked the very spirit of evil breaking from its hole. Donning his hat at its most rakish angle, he wound his cloak around him, holding one end in front as if to conceal his person from the night, of which it was the blackest part, and muttering strangely to himself, stole away through the trees.

Peter slept on. The light guttered [burned to edges] and went out, leaving the tenement in darkness; but still he slept. It must have been not less than ten o'clock by the crocodile, when he suddenly sat up in his bed, wakened by he knew not what. It was a soft cautious tapping on the door of his tree.

Soft and cautious, but in that stillness it was sinister. Peter felt for his dagger till his hand gripped it. Then he spoke.

"Who is that?"

For long there was no answer: then again the knock.

"Who are you?"

No answer.

He was thrilled, and he loved being thrilled. In two strides he reached the door. Unlike Slightly's door, it filled the aperture [opening], so that he could not see beyond it, nor could the one knocking see him.

"I won't open unless you speak," Peter cried.

Then at last the visitor spoke, in a lovely bell-like voice.

"Let me in, Peter."

It was Tink, and quickly he unbarred to her. She flew in excitedly, her face flushed and her dress stained with mud.

"What is it?"

"Oh, you could never guess!" she cried, and offered him three guesses. "Out with it!" he shouted, and in one ungrammatical sentence, as long as the ribbons that conjurers [magicians] pull from their mouths, she told of the capture of Wendy and the boys.

Peter's heart bobbed up and down as he listened. Wendy bound, and on the pirate ship; she who loved everything to be just so!

"I'll rescue her!" he cried, leaping at his weapons. As he leapt he thought of something he could do to please her. He could take his medicine.

His hand closed on the fatal draught.

"No!" shrieked Tinker Bell, who had heard Hook mutter about his deed as he sped through the forest.

"Why not?"

"It is poisoned."

"Poisoned? Who could have poisoned it?"

"Hook."

"Don't be silly. How could Hook have got down here?"

Alas, Tinker Bell could not explain this, for even she did not know the dark secret of Slightly's tree. Nevertheless Hook's words had left no room for doubt. The cup was poisoned.

"Besides," said Peter, quite believing himself, "I never fell asleep."

He raised the cup. No time for words now; time for deeds; and with one of her lightning movements Tink got between his lips and the draught, and drained it to the dregs.

"Why, Tink, how dare you drink my medicine?"

But she did not answer. Already she was reeling in the air.

"What is the matter with you?" cried Peter, suddenly afraid.

"It was poisoned, Peter," she told him softly; "and now I am going to be dead."

"O Tink, did you drink it to save me?"

"Yes."

"But why, Tink?"

Her wings would scarcely carry her now, but in reply she alighted on his shoulder and gave his nose a loving bite. She whispered in his ear "You silly ass," and then, tottering to her chamber, lay down on the bed.

His head almost filled the fourth wall of her little room as he knelt near her in distress. Every moment her light was growing fainter; and he knew that if it went out she would be no more. She liked his tears so much that she put out her beautiful finger and let them run over it.

Her voice was so low that at first he could not make out what she said. Then he made it out. She was saying that she thought she could get well again if children believed in fairies.

Peter flung out his arms. There were no children there, and it was night-time; but he addressed all who might be dreaming of the Neverland, and who were therefore nearer to him than you think: boys and girls in their nighties, and naked papooses in their baskets hung from trees.

"Do you believe?" he cried.

Tink sat up in bed almost briskly to listen to her fate.

She fancied she heard answers in the affirmative, and then again she wasn't sure.

"What do you think?" she asked Peter.

"If you believe," he shouted to them, "clap your hands; don't let Tink die."

Many clapped.

Some didn't.

A few beasts hissed.

The clapping stopped suddenly; as if countless mothers had rushed to their nurseries to see what on earth was happening; but already Tink was saved. First her voice grew strong, then she popped out of bed, then she was flashing through the room more merry and impudent than ever. She never thought of thanking those who believed, but she would have liked to get at the ones who had hissed.

"And now to rescue Wendy!"

The moon was riding in a cloudy heaven when Peter rose from his tree, begirt [belted] with weapons and wearing little else, to set out upon his perilous quest. It was not such a night as he would have chosen. He had hoped to fly, keeping not far from the ground so that nothing unwonted should escape his eyes; but in that fitful light to have flown low would have meant trailing his shadow through the trees, thus disturbing birds and acquainting a watchful foe that he was astir.

He regretted now that he had given the birds of the island such strange names that they are very wild and difficult of approach.

There was no other course but to press forward in redskin fashion, at which happily he was an adept [expert]. But in what direction, for he could not be sure that the children had been taken to the ship? A light fall of snow had obliterated all footmarks; and a deathly silence pervaded the island, as if for a space Nature stood still in horror of the recent carnage. He had taught the children something of the forest lore that he had himself learned from Tiger Lily and Tinker Bell, and knew that in their dire hour they were not likely to forget it. Slightly, if he had an opportunity, would blaze [cut a mark in] the trees, for instance, Curly would drop seeds, and Wendy would leave her handkerchief at some important place. But morning was needed to search for such guidance, and he could not wait. The upper world had called him, but would give no help.

The crocodile passed him, but not another living thing, not a sound, not a movement; and yet he knew well that sudden death might be at the next tree, or stalking him from behind.

He swore this terrible oath: "Hook or me this time."

Now he crawled forward like a snake, and again erect, he darted across a space on which the moonlight played, one finger on his lip and his dagger at the ready. He was frightfully happy.

14

The Pirate Ship

One green light squinting over Kidd's Creek, which is near the mouth of the pirate river, marked where the brig, the JOLLY ROGER, lay, low in the water; a rakish-looking [speedy-looking] craft foul to the hull, every beam in her detestable, like ground strewn with mangled feathers. She was the cannibal of the seas, and scarce needed that watchful eye, for she floated immune in the horror of her name.

She was wrapped in the blanket of night, through which no sound from her could have reached the shore. There was little sound, and none agreeable save the whir of the ship's sewing machine at which Smee sat, ever industrious and obliging, the essence of the commonplace, pathetic Smee. I know not why he was so infinitely pathetic, unless it were because he was so pathetically unaware of it; but even strong men had to turn hastily from looking at him, and more than once on summer evenings he had touched the fount of Hook's tears and made it flow. Of this, as of almost everything else, Smee was quite unconscious.

A few of the pirates leant over the bulwarks, drinking in the miasma [putrid mist] of the night; others sprawled by barrels over games of dice and cards; and the exhausted four who had carried the little house lay prone on the deck, where even in their sleep they rolled skillfully to this side or that out of Hook's reach, lest he should claw them mechanically in passing.

Hook trod the deck in thought. O man unfathomable. It was his hour of triumph. Peter had been removed for ever from his path, and all the other boys were on the brig, about to walk the plank. It was his grimmest deed since the days when he had brought Barbecue to heel; and knowing as we do how vain a tabernacle is man, could we be surprised had he now paced the deck unsteadily, bellied out by the winds of his success?

But there was no elation in his gait, which kept pace with the action of his sombre mind. Hook was profoundly dejected.

He was often thus when communing with himself on board ship in the quietude of the night. It was because he was so terribly alone. This inscrutable man never felt more alone than when surrounded by his dogs. They were socially inferior to him.

Hook was not his true name. To reveal who he really was would even at this date set the country in a blaze; but as those who read between the lines must already have guessed, he had been at a famous public school; and its traditions still clung to him like garments, with which indeed they are largely concerned. Thus it was offensive to him even now to board a ship in the same dress in which he grappled [attacked] her, and he still adhered in his walk to the school's distinguished slouch. But above all he retained the passion for good form.

Good form! However much he may have degenerated, he still knew that this is all that really matters.

From far within him he heard a creaking as of rusty portals, and through them came a stern tap-tap-tap, like hammering in the night when one cannot sleep. "Have you been good form today?" was their eternal question.

"Fame, fame, that glittering bauble, it is mine," he cried.

"Is it quite good form to be distinguished at anything?" the tap-tap from his school replied.

"I am the only man whom Barbecue feared," he urged, "and Flint feared Barbecue."

"Barbecue, Flint—what house?" came the cutting retort.

Most disquieting reflection of all, was it not bad form to think about good form?

His vitals were tortured by this problem. It was a claw within him sharper than the iron one; and as it tore him, the perspiration dripped down his sallow [waxy] countenance and streaked his doublet. Oft-times he drew his sleeve across his face, but there was no damming that trickle.

Ah, envy not Hook.

There came to him a presentiment of his early dissolution [death]. It was as if Peter's terrible oath had boarded the ship. Hook felt a gloomy desire to make his dying speech, lest presently there should be no time for it.

"Better for Hook," he cried, "if he had had less ambition!" It was in his darkest hours only that he referred to himself in the third person.

"No little children to love me!"

Strange that he should think of this, which had never troubled him before; perhaps the sewing machine brought it to his mind. For long he muttered to himself, staring at Smee, who was hemming placidly, under the conviction that all children feared him.

Feared him! Feared Smee! There was not a child on board the brig that night who did not already love him. He had said horrid things to them and hit them with the palm of his hand, because he could not hit with his fist, but they had only clung to him the more. Michael had tried on his spectacles.

To tell poor Smee that they thought him lovable! Hook itched to do it, but it seemed too brutal. Instead, he revolved this mystery in his mind: why do they find Smee lovable? He pursued the problem like the sleuth-hound that he was. If Smee was lovable, what was it that made him so? A terrible answer suddenly presented itself—"Good form?"

Had the bo'sun good form without knowing it, which is the best form of all?

He remembered that you have to prove you don't know you have it before you are eligible for Pop [an elite social club at Eton].

With a cry of rage he raised his iron hand over Smee's head; but he did not tear. What arrested him was this reflection:

"To claw a man because he is good form, what would that be?"

"Bad form!"

The unhappy Hook was as impotent [powerless] as he was damp, and he fell forward like a cut flower.

His dogs thinking him out of the way for a time, discipline instantly relaxed; and they broke into a bacchanalian [drunken] dance, which brought him to his feet at once, all traces of human weakness gone, as if a bucket of water had passed over him.

"Quiet, you scugs," he cried, "or I'll cast anchor in you;" and at once the din was hushed. "Are all the children chained, so that they cannot fly away?"

"Ay, ay."

"Then hoist them up."

The wretched prisoners were dragged from the hold, all except Wendy, and ranged in line in front of him. For a time he seemed unconscious of their presence. He lolled at his ease, humming, not unmelodiously, snatches of a rude song, and fingering a pack of cards. Ever and anon the light from his cigar gave a touch of colour to his face.

"Now then, bullies," he said briskly, "six of you walk the plank tonight, but I have room for two cabin boys. Which of you is it to be?"

"Don't irritate him unnecessarily," had been Wendy's instructions in the hold; so Tootles stepped forward politely. Tootles hated the idea of signing under such a man, but an instinct told him that it would be prudent to lay the responsibility on an absent person; and though a somewhat silly boy, he knew that mothers alone are always willing to be the buffer. All children know this about mothers, and despise them for it, but make constant use of it.

So Tootles explained prudently, "You see, sir, I don't think my mother would like me to be a pirate. Would your mother like you to be a pirate, Slightly?"

He winked at Slightly, who said mournfully, "I don't think so," as if he wished things had been otherwise. "Would your mother like you to be a pirate, Twin?"

"I don't think so," said the first twin, as clever as the others. "Nibs, would—"

"Stow this gab," roared Hook, and the spokesmen were dragged back. "You, boy," he said, addressing John, "you look as if you had a little pluck in you. Didst never want to be a pirate, my hearty?"

Now John had sometimes experienced this hankering at maths. prep.; and he was struck by Hook's picking him out.

"I once thought of calling myself Red-handed Jack," he said diffidently.

"And a good name too. We'll call you that here, bully, if you join."

"What do you think, Michael?" asked John.

"What would you call me if I join?" Michael demanded.

"Blackbeard Joe."

Michael was naturally impressed. "What do you think, John?" He wanted John to decide, and John wanted him to decide.

"Shall we still be respectful subjects of the King?" John inquired.

Through Hook's teeth came the answer: "You would have to swear, 'Down with the King.'"

Perhaps John had not behaved very well so far, but he shone out now.

"Then I refuse," he cried, banging the barrel in front of Hook.

"And I refuse," cried Michael.

"Rule Britannia!" squeaked Curly.

The infuriated pirates buffeted them in the mouth; and Hook roared out, "That seals your doom. Bring up their mother. Get the plank ready."

They were only boys, and they went white as they saw Jukes and Cecco preparing the fatal plank. But they tried to look brave when Wendy was brought up.

No words of mine can tell you how Wendy despised those pirates. To the boys there was at least some glamour in the pirate calling; but all that she saw was that the ship had not been tidied for years. There was not a porthole on the grimy glass of which you might not have written with your finger "Dirty pig"; and she had already written it on several. But as the boys gathered round her she had no thought, of course, save for them.

"So, my beauty," said Hook, as if he spoke in syrup, "you are to see your children walk the plank."

Fine gentlemen though he was, the intensity of his communings had soiled his ruff, and suddenly he knew that she was gazing at it. With a hasty gesture he tried to hide it, but he was too late.

"Are they to die?" asked Wendy, with a look of such frightful contempt that he nearly fainted.

"They are," he snarled. "Silence all," he called gloatingly, "for a mother's last words to her children."

At this moment Wendy was grand. "These are my last words, dear boys," she said firmly. "I feel that I have a message to you from your real mothers, and it is this: 'We hope our sons will die like English gentlemen.'"

Even the pirates were awed, and Tootles cried out hysterically, "I am going to do what my mother hopes. What are you to do, Nibs?"

"What my mother hopes. What are you to do, Twin?"

"What my mother hopes. John, what are—"

But Hook had found his voice again.

"Tie her up!" he shouted.

It was Smee who tied her to the mast. "See here, honey," he whispered, "I'll save you if you promise to be my mother."

But not even for Smee would she make such a promise. "I would almost rather have no children at all," she said disdainfully [scornfully].

It is sad to know that not a boy was looking at her as Smee tied her to the mast; the eyes of all were on the plank: that last little walk they were about to take. They were no longer able to hope that they would walk it manfully, for the capacity to think had gone from them; they could stare and shiver only.

Hook smiled on them with his teeth closed, and took a step toward Wendy. His intention was to turn her face so that she should see the boys walking the plank one by one. But he never reached her, he never heard the cry of anguish he hoped to wring from her. He heard something else instead.

It was the terrible tick-tick of the crocodile.

They all heard it—pirates, boys, Wendy; and immediately every head was blown in one direction; not to the water whence the sound proceeded, but toward Hook. All knew that what was about to happen concerned him alone, and that from being actors they were suddenly become spectators.

Very frightful was it to see the change that came over him. It was as if he had been clipped at every joint. He fell in a little heap.

The sound came steadily nearer; and in advance of it came this ghastly thought, "The crocodile is about to board the ship!"

Even the iron claw hung inactive; as if knowing that it was no intrinsic part of what the attacking force wanted. Left so fearfully alone, any other man would have lain with his eyes shut where he fell: but the gigantic brain of Hook was still working, and under its guidance he crawled on the knees along the deck as far from the sound as he could go. The pirates respectfully cleared a passage for him, and it was only when he brought up against the bulwarks that he spoke.

"Hide me!" he cried hoarsely.

They gathered round him, all eyes averted from the thing that was coming aboard. They had no thought of fighting it. It was Fate.

Only when Hook was hidden from them did curiosity loosen the limbs of the boys so that they could rush to the ship's side to see the crocodile climbing it. Then they got the strangest surprise of the Night of Nights; for it was no crocodile that was coming to their aid. It was Peter.

He signed to them not to give vent to any cry of admiration that might rouse suspicion. Then he went on ticking.

15

"Hook or Me this Time"

Odd things happen to all of us on our way through life without our noticing for a time that they have happened. Thus, to take an instance, we suddenly discover that we have been deaf in one ear for we don't know how long, but, say, half an hour. Now such an experience had come that night to Peter. When last we saw him he was stealing across the island with one finger to his lips and his dagger at the ready. He had seen the crocodile pass by without noticing anything peculiar about it, but by and by he remembered that it had not been ticking. At first he thought this eerie, but soon concluded rightly that the clock had run down.

Without giving a thought to what might be the feelings of a fellow-creature thus abruptly deprived of its closest companion, Peter began to consider how he could turn the catastrophe to his own use; and he decided to tick, so that wild beasts should believe he was the crocodile and let him pass unmolested. He ticked superbly, but with one unforeseen result. The crocodile was among those who heard the sound, and it followed him, though whether with the purpose of regaining what it had lost, or merely as a friend under the belief that it was again ticking itself, will never be certainly known, for, like slaves to a fixed idea, it was a stupid beast.

Peter reached the shore without mishap, and went straight on, his legs encountering the water as if quite unaware that they had entered a new element. Thus many animals pass from land to water, but no other human of whom I know. As he swam he had but one thought: "Hook or me this time." He had ticked so long that he now went on ticking without knowing that he was doing it. Had he known he would have stopped, for to board the brig by help of the tick, though an ingenious idea, had not occurred to him.

On the contrary, he thought he had scaled her side as noiseless as a mouse; and he was amazed to see the pirates cowering from him, with Hook in their midst as abject as if he had heard the crocodile.

The crocodile! No sooner did Peter remember it than he heard the ticking. At first he thought the sound did come from the crocodile, and he looked behind him swiftly. Then he realised that he was doing it himself, and in a flash he understood the situation. "How clever of me!" he thought at once, and signed to the boys not to burst into applause.

It was at this moment that Ed Teynte the quartermaster emerged from the forecastle and came along the deck. Now, reader, time what happened by your watch. Peter struck true and deep. John clapped his hands on the ill-fated pirate's mouth to stifle the dying groan. He fell forward. Four boys caught him to prevent the thud. Peter gave the signal, and the carrion was cast overboard. There was a splash, and then silence. How long has it taken?

"One!" (Slightly had begun to count.)

None too soon, Peter, every inch of him on tiptoe, vanished into the cabin; for more than one pirate was screwing up his courage to look round. They could hear each other's distressed breathing now, which showed them that the more terrible sound had passed.

"It's gone, captain," Smee said, wiping off his spectacles. "All's still again."

Slowly Hook let his head emerge from his ruff, and listened so intently that he could have caught the echo of the tick. There was not a sound, and he drew himself up firmly to his full height.

"Then here's to Johnny Plank!" he cried brazenly, hating the boys more than ever because they had seen him unbend. He broke into the villainous ditty:

"Yo ho, yo ho, the frisky plank,
You walks along it so,
Till it goes down and you goes down
To Davy Jones below!"

To terrorize the prisoners the more, though with a certain loss of dignity, he danced along an imaginary plank, grimacing at them as he sang; and when he finished he cried, "Do you want a touch of the cat before you walk the plank?"

At that they fell on their knees. "No, no!" they cried so piteously that every pirate smiled.

"Fetch the cat, Jukes," said Hook; "it's in the cabin."

The cabin! Peter was in the cabin! The children gazed at each other.

"Ay, ay," said Jukes blithely, and he strode into the cabin. They followed him with their eyes; they scarce knew that Hook had resumed his song, his dogs joining in with him:

"Yo ho, yo ho, the scratching cat,
Its tails are nine, you know,
And when they're writ upon your back—"

What was the last line will never be known, for of a sudden the song was stayed by a dreadful screech from the cabin. It wailed through the ship, and died away. Then was heard a crowing sound which was well understood by the boys, but to the pirates was almost more eerie than the screech.

"What was that?" cried Hook.

"Two," said Slightly solemnly.

The Italian Cecco hesitated for a moment and then swung into the cabin. He tottered out, haggard.

"What's the matter with Bill Jukes, you dog?" hissed Hook, towering over him.

"The matter wi' him is he's dead, stabbed," replied Cecco in a hollow voice.

"Bill Jukes dead!" cried the startled pirates.

"The cabin's as black as a pit," Cecco said, almost gibbering, "but there is something terrible in there: the thing you heard crowing."

The exultation of the boys, the lowering looks of the pirates, both were seen by Hook.

"Cecco," he said in his most steely voice, "go back and fetch me out that doodle-doo."

Cecco, bravest of the brave, cowered before his captain, crying "No, no"; but Hook was purring to his claw.

"Did you say you would go, Cecco?" he said musingly.

Cecco went, first flinging his arms despairingly. There was no more singing, all listened now; and again came a death-screech and again a crow.

No one spoke except Slightly. "Three," he said.

Hook rallied his dogs with a gesture. "'Sdeath and odds fish," he thundered, "who is to bring me that doodle-doo?"

"Wait till Cecco comes out," growled Starkey, and the others took up the cry.

"I think I heard you volunteer, Starkey," said Hook, purring again.

"No, by thunder!" Starkey cried.

"My hook thinks you did," said Hook, crossing to him. "I wonder if it would not be advisable, Starkey, to humour the hook?"

"I'll swing before I go in there," replied Starkey doggedly, and again he had the support of the crew.

"Is this mutiny?" asked Hook more pleasantly than ever. "Starkey's ringleader!"

"Captain, mercy!" Starkey whimpered, all of a tremble now.

"Shake hands, Starkey," said Hook, proffering his claw.

Starkey looked round for help, but all deserted him. As he backed up Hook advanced, and now the red spark was in his eye. With a despairing scream the pirate leapt upon Long Tom and precipitated himself into the sea.

"Four," said Slightly.

"And now," Hook said courteously, "did any other gentlemen say mutiny?" Seizing a lantern and raising his claw with a menacing gesture, "I'll bring out that doodle-doo myself," he said, and sped into the cabin.

"Five." How Slightly longed to say it. He wetted his lips to be ready, but Hook came staggering out, without his lantern.

"Something blew out the light," he said a little unsteadily.

"Something!" echoed Mullins.

"What of Cecco?" demanded Noodler.

"He's as dead as Jukes," said Hook shortly.

His reluctance to return to the cabin impressed them all unfavourably, and the mutinous sounds again broke forth. All pirates are superstitious, and Cookson cried, "They do say the surest sign a ship's accurst is when there's one on board more than can be accounted for."

"I've heard," muttered Mullins, "he always boards the pirate craft last. Had he a tail, captain?"

"They say," said another, looking viciously at Hook, "that when he comes it's in the likeness of the wickedest man aboard."

"Had he a hook, captain?" asked Cookson insolently; and one after another took up the cry, "The ship's doomed!" At this the children could not resist raising a cheer. Hook had well-nigh forgotten his prisoners, but as he swung round on them now his face lit up again.

"Lads," he cried to his crew, "now here's a notion. Open the cabin door and drive them in. Let them fight the doodle-doo for their lives. If they kill him, we're so much the better; if he kills them, we're none the worse."

For the last time his dogs admired Hook, and devotedly they did his bidding. The boys, pretending to struggle, were pushed into the cabin and the door was closed on them.

"Now, listen!" cried Hook, and all listened. But not one dared to face the door. Yes, one, Wendy, who all this time had been bound to the mast. It was for neither a scream nor a crow that she was watching, it was for the reappearance of Peter.

She had not long to wait. In the cabin he had found the thing for which he had gone in search: the key that would free the children of their manacles, and now they all stole forth, armed with such weapons as they could find. First signing them to hide, Peter cut Wendy's bonds, and then nothing could have been easier than for them all to fly off together; but one thing barred the way, an oath, "Hook or me this time." So when he had freed Wendy, he whispered for her to conceal herself with the others, and himself took her place by the mast, her cloak around him so that he should pass for her. Then he took a great breath and crowed.

To the pirates it was a voice crying that all the boys lay slain in the cabin; and they were panic-stricken. Hook tried to hearten them; but like the dogs he had made them they showed him their fangs, and he knew that if he took his eyes off them now they would leap at him.

"Lads," he said, ready to cajole or strike as need be, but never quailing for an instant, "I've thought it out. There's a Jonah aboard."

"Ay," they snarled, "a man wi' a hook."

"No, lads, no, it's the girl. Never was luck on a pirate ship wi' a woman on board. We'll right the ship when she's gone."

Some of them remembered that this had been a saying of Flint's. "It's worth trying," they said doubtfully.

"Fling the girl overboard," cried Hook; and they made a rush at the figure in the cloak.

"There's none can save you now, missy," Mullins hissed jeeringly.

"There's one," replied the figure.

"Who's that?"

"Peter Pan the avenger!" came the terrible answer; and as he spoke Peter flung off his cloak. Then they all knew who 'twas that had been undoing them in the cabin, and twice Hook essayed to speak and twice he failed. In that frightful moment I think his fierce heart broke.

At last he cried, "Cleave him to the brisket!" but without conviction.

"Down, boys, and at them!" Peter's voice rang out; and in another moment the clash of arms was resounding through the ship. Had the pirates kept together it is certain that they would have won; but the onset came when they were still unstrung, and they ran hither and thither, striking wildly, each thinking himself the last survivor of the crew. Man to man they were the stronger; but they fought on the defensive only, which enabled the boys to hunt in pairs and choose their quarry. Some of the miscreants leapt into the sea; others hid in dark recesses, where they were found by Slightly, who did not fight, but ran about with a lantern which he flashed in their faces, so that they were half blinded and fell as an easy prey to the reeking swords of the other boys. There was little sound to be heard but the clang of weapons, an occasional screech or splash, and Slightly monotonously counting—five—six—seven eight—nine—ten—eleven.

I think all were gone when a group of savage boys surrounded Hook, who seemed to have a charmed life, as he kept them at bay in that circle of fire. They had done for his dogs, but this man alone seemed to be a match for them all. Again and again they closed upon him, and again and again he hewed a clear space. He had lifted up one boy with his hook, and was using him as a buckler [shield], when another, who had just passed his sword through Mullins, sprang into the fray.

"Put up your swords, boys," cried the newcomer, "this man is mine."

Thus suddenly Hook found himself face to face with Peter. The others drew back and formed a ring around them.

For long the two enemies looked at one another, Hook shuddering slightly, and Peter with the strange smile upon his face.

"So, Pan," said Hook at last, "this is all your doing."

"Ay, James Hook," came the stern answer, "it is all my doing."

"Proud and insolent youth," said Hook, "prepare to meet thy doom."

"Dark and sinister man," Peter answered, "have at thee."

Without more words they fell to, and for a space there was no advantage to either blade. Peter was a superb swordsman, and parried with dazzling rapidity; ever and anon he followed up a feint with a lunge that got past his foe's defence, but his shorter reach stood him in ill stead, and he could not drive the steel home. Hook, scarcely his inferior in brilliancy, but not quite so nimble in wrist play, forced him back by the weight of his onset, hoping suddenly to end all with a favourite thrust, taught him long ago by Barbecue at Rio; but to his astonishment he found this thrust turned aside again and again. Then he sought to close and give the quietus with his iron hook, which all this time had been pawing the air; but Peter doubled under it and, lunging fiercely, pierced him in the ribs. At the sight of his own blood, whose peculiar colour, you remember, was offensive to him, the sword fell from Hook's hand, and he was at Peter's mercy.

"Now!" cried all the boys, but with a magnificent gesture Peter invited his opponent to pick up his sword. Hook did so instantly, but with a tragic feeling that Peter was showing good form.

Hitherto he had thought it was some fiend fighting him, but darker suspicions assailed him now.

"Pan, who and what art thou?" he cried huskily.

"I'm youth, I'm joy," Peter answered at a venture, "I'm a little bird that has broken out of the egg."

This, of course, was nonsense; but it was proof to the unhappy Hook that Peter did not know in the least who or what he was, which is the very pinnacle of good form.

"To't again," he cried despairingly.

He fought now like a human flail, and every sweep of that terrible sword would have severed in twain any man or boy who obstructed it; but Peter fluttered round him as if the very wind it made blew him out of the danger zone. And again and again he darted in and pricked.

Hook was fighting now without hope. That passionate breast no longer asked for life; but for one boon it craved: to see Peter show bad form before it was cold forever.

Abandoning the fight he rushed into the powder magazine and fired it.

"In two minutes," he cried, "the ship will be blown to pieces."

Now, now, he thought, true form will show.

But Peter issued from the powder magazine with the shell in his hands, and calmly flung it overboard.

What sort of form was Hook himself showing? Misguided man though he was, we may be glad, without sympathising with him, that in the end he was true to the traditions of his race. The other boys were flying around him now, flouting, scornful; and he staggered about the deck striking up at them impotently, his mind was no longer with them; it was slouching in the playing fields of long ago, or being sent up [to the headmaster] for good, or watching the wall-game from a famous wall. And his shoes were right, and his waistcoat was right, and his tie was right, and his socks were right.

James Hook, thou not wholly unheroic figure, farewell.

For we have come to his last moment.

Seeing Peter slowly advancing upon him through the air with dagger poised, he sprang upon the bulwarks to cast himself into the sea. He did not know that the crocodile was waiting for him; for we purposely stopped the clock that this knowledge might be spared him: a little mark of respect from us at the end.

He had one last triumph, which I think we need not grudge him. As he stood on the bulwark looking over his shoulder at Peter gliding through the air, he invited him with a gesture to use his foot. It made Peter kick instead of stab.

At last Hook had got the boon for which he craved.

"Bad form," he cried jeeringly, and went content to the crocodile.

Thus perished James Hook.

"Seventeen," Slightly sang out; but he was not quite correct in his figures. Fifteen paid the penalty for their crimes that night; but two reached the shore: Starkey to be captured by the redskins, who made him nurse for all their papooses, a melancholy come-down for a pirate; and Smee, who henceforth wandered about the world in his spectacles, making a precarious living by saying he was the only man that Jas. Hook had feared.

Wendy, of course, had stood by taking no part in the fight, though watching Peter with glistening eyes; but now that all was over she became prominent again. She praised them equally, and shuddered delightfully when Michael showed her the place where he had killed one; and then she took them into Hook's cabin and pointed to his watch which was hanging on a nail. It said "half past one!"

The lateness of the hour was almost the biggest thing of all. She got them to bed in the pirates' bunks pretty quickly, you may be sure; all but Peter, who strutted up and down on the deck, until at last he fell asleep by the side of Long Tom. He had one of his dreams that night, and cried in his sleep for a long time, and Wendy held him tightly.

16

The Return Home

By three bells that morning they were all stirring their stumps [legs]; for there was a big sea running; and Tootles, the bo'sun, was among them, with a rope's end in his hand and chewing tobacco. They all donned pirate clothes cut off at the knee, shaved smartly, and tumbled up, with the true nautical roll and hitching their trousers.

It need not be said who was the captain. Nibs and John were first and second mate. There was a woman aboard. The rest were tars [sailors] before the mast, and lived in the fo'c'sle. Peter had already lashed himself to the wheel; but he piped all hands and delivered a short address to them; said he hoped they would do their duty like gallant hearties, but that he knew they were the scum of Rio and the Gold Coast, and if they snapped at him he would tear them. The bluff strident words struck the note sailors understood, and they cheered him lustily. Then a few sharp orders were given, and they turned the ship round, and nosed her for the mainland.

Captain Pan calculated, after consulting the ship's chart, that if this weather lasted they should strike the Azores about the 21st of June, after which it would save time to fly.

Some of them wanted it to be an honest ship and others were in favour of keeping it a pirate; but the captain treated them as dogs, and they dared not express their wishes to him even in a round robin [one person after another, as they had to Cpt. Hook]. Instant obedience was the only safe thing. Slightly got a dozen for looking perplexed when told to take soundings. The general feeling was that Peter was honest just now to lull Wendy's suspicions, but that there might be a change when the new suit was ready, which, against her will, she was making for him out of some of Hook's wickedest garments. It was afterwards whispered among them that on the first night he wore this suit he sat long in the cabin with Hook's cigar-holder in his mouth and one hand clenched, all but for the forefinger, which he bent and held threateningly aloft like a hook.

Instead of watching the ship, however, we must now return to that desolate home from which three of our characters had taken heartless flight so long ago. It seems a shame to have neglected No. 14 all this time; and yet we may be sure that Mrs. Darling does not blame us. If we had returned sooner to look with sorrowful sympathy at her, she would probably have cried, "Don't be silly; what do I matter? Do go back and keep an eye on the children." So long as mothers are like this their children will take advantage of them; and they may lay to [bet on] that.

Even now we venture into that familiar nursery only because its lawful occupants are on their way home; we are merely hurrying on in advance of them to see that their beds are properly aired and that Mr. and Mrs. Darling do not go out for the evening. We are no more than servants. Why on earth should their beds be properly aired, seeing that they left them in such a thankless hurry? Would it not serve them jolly well right if they came back and found that their parents were spending the week-end in the country? It would be the moral lesson they have been in need of ever since we met them; but if we contrived things in this way Mrs. Darling would never forgive us.

One thing I should like to do immensely, and that is to tell her, in the way authors have, that the children are coming back, that indeed they will be here on Thursday week. This would spoil so completely the surprise to which Wendy and John and Michael are looking forward. They have been planning it out on the ship: mother's rapture, father's shout of joy, Nana's leap through the air to embrace them first, when what they ought to be prepared for is a good hiding. How delicious to spoil it all by breaking the news in advance; so that when they enter grandly Mrs. Darling may not even offer Wendy her mouth, and Mr. Darling may exclaim pettishly, "Dash it all, here are those boys again." However, we should get no thanks even for this. We are beginning to know Mrs. Darling by this time, and may be sure that she would upbraid us for depriving the children of their little pleasure.

"But, my dear madam, it is ten days till Thursday week; so that by telling you what's what, we can save you ten days of unhappiness."

"Yes, but at what a cost! By depriving the children of ten minutes of delight."

"Oh, if you look at it in that way!"

"What other way is there in which to look at it?"

You see, the woman had no proper spirit. I had meant to say extraordinarily nice things about her; but I despise her, and not one of them will I say now. She does not really need to be told to have things ready, for they are ready. All the beds are aired, and she never leaves the house, and observe, the window is open. For all the use we are to her, we might well go back to the ship. However, as we are here we may as well stay and look on. That is all we are, lookers-on. Nobody really wants us. So let us watch and say jaggy things, in the hope that some of them will hurt.

The only change to be seen in the night-nursery is that between nine and six the kennel is no longer there. When the children flew away, Mr. Darling felt in his bones that all the blame was his for having chained Nana up, and that from first to last she had been wiser than he. Of course, as we have seen, he was quite a simple man; indeed he might have passed for a boy again if he had been able to take his baldness off; but he had also a noble sense of justice and a lion's courage to do what seemed right to him; and having thought the matter out with anxious care after the flight of the children, he went down on all fours and crawled into the kennel. To all Mrs. Darling's dear invitations to him to come out he replied sadly but firmly:

"No, my own one, this is the place for me."

In the bitterness of his remorse he swore that he would never leave the kennel until his children came back. Of course this was a pity; but whatever Mr. Darling did he had to do in excess, otherwise he soon gave up doing it. And there never was a more humble man than the once proud George Darling, as he sat in the kennel of an evening talking with his wife of their children and all their pretty ways.

Very touching was his deference to Nana. He would not let her come into the kennel, but on all other matters he followed her wishes implicitly.

Every morning the kennel was carried with Mr. Darling in it to a cab, which conveyed him to his office, and he returned home in the same way at six. Something of the strength of character of the man will be seen if we remember how sensitive he was to the opinion of neighbours: this man whose every movement now attracted surprised attention. Inwardly he must have suffered torture; but he preserved a calm exterior even when the young criticised his little home, and he always lifted his hat courteously to any lady who looked inside.

It may have been Quixotic, but it was magnificent. Soon the inward meaning of it leaked out, and the great heart of the public was touched. Crowds followed the cab, cheering it lustily; charming girls scaled it to get his autograph; interviews appeared in the better class of papers, and society invited him to dinner and added, "Do come in the kennel."

On that eventful Thursday week, Mrs. Darling was in the night-nursery awaiting George's return home; a very sad-eyed woman. Now that we look at her closely and remember the gaiety of her in the old days, all gone now just because she has lost her babes, I find I won't be able to say nasty things about her after all. If she was too fond of her rubbishy children, she couldn't help it. Look at her in her chair, where she has fallen asleep. The corner of her mouth, where one looks first, is almost withered up. Her hand moves restlessly on her breast as if she had a pain there. Some like Peter best, and some like Wendy best, but I like her best. Suppose, to make her happy, we whisper to her in her sleep that the brats are coming back. They are really within two miles of the window now, and flying strong, but all we need whisper is that they are on the way. Let's.

It is a pity we did it, for she has started up, calling their names; and there is no one in the room but Nana.

"O Nana, I dreamt my dear ones had come back."

Nana had filmy eyes, but all she could do was put her paw gently on her mistress's lap; and they were sitting together thus when the kennel was brought back. As Mr. Darling puts his head out to kiss his wife, we see that his face is more worn than of yore, but has a softer expression.

He gave his hat to Liza, who took it scornfully; for she had no imagination, and was quite incapable of understanding the motives of such a man. Outside, the crowd who had accompanied the cab home were still cheering, and he was naturally not unmoved.

"Listen to them," he said; "it is very gratifying."

"Lots of little boys," sneered Liza.

"There were several adults today," he assured her with a faint flush; but when she tossed her head he had not a word of reproof for her. Social success had not spoilt him; it had made him sweeter. For some time he sat with his head out of the kennel, talking with Mrs. Darling of this success, and pressing her hand reassuringly when she said she hoped his head would not be turned by it.

"But if I had been a weak man," he said. "Good heavens, if I had been a weak man!"

"And, George," she said timidly, "you are as full of remorse as ever, aren't you?"

"Full of remorse as ever, dearest! See my punishment: living in a kennel."

"But it is punishment, isn't it, George? You are sure you are not enjoying it?"

"My love!"

You may be sure she begged his pardon; and then, feeling drowsy, he curled round in the kennel.

"Won't you play me to sleep," he asked, "on the nursery piano?" and as she was crossing to the day-nursery he added thoughtlessly, "And shut that window. I feel a draught."

"O George, never ask me to do that. The window must always be left open for them, always, always."

Now it was his turn to beg her pardon; and she went into the day-nursery and played, and soon he was asleep; and while he slept, Wendy and John and Michael flew into the room.

Oh no. We have written it so, because that was the charming arrangement planned by them before we left the ship; but something must have happened since then, for it is not they who have flown in, it is Peter and Tinker Bell.

Peter's first words tell all.

"Quick Tink," he whispered, "close the window; bar it! That's right. Now you and I must get away by the door; and when Wendy comes she will think her mother has barred her out; and she will have to go back with me."

Now I understand what had hitherto puzzled me, why when Peter had exterminated the pirates he did not return to the island and leave Tink to escort the children to the mainland. This trick had been in his head all the time.

Instead of feeling that he was behaving badly he danced with glee; then he peeped into the day-nursery to see who was playing. He whispered to Tink, "It's Wendy's mother! She is a pretty lady, but not so pretty as my mother. Her mouth is full of thimbles, but not so full as my mother's was."

Of course he knew nothing whatever about his mother; but he sometimes bragged about her.

He did not know the tune, which was "Home, Sweet Home," but he knew it was saying, "Come back, Wendy, Wendy, Wendy"; and he cried exultantly, "You will never see Wendy again, lady, for the window is barred!"

He peeped in again to see why the music had stopped, and now he saw that Mrs. Darling had laid her head on the box, and that two tears were sitting on her eyes.

"She wants me to unbar the window," thought Peter, "but I won't, not I!"

He peeped again, and the tears were still there, or another two had taken their place.

"She's awfully fond of Wendy," he said to himself. He was angry with her now for not seeing why she could not have Wendy.

The reason was so simple: "I'm fond of her too. We can't both have her, lady."

But the lady would not make the best of it, and he was unhappy. He ceased to look at her, but even then she would not let go of him. He skipped about and made funny faces, but when he stopped it was just as if she were inside him, knocking.

"Oh, all right," he said at last, and gulped. Then he unbarred the window. "Come on, Tink," he cried, with a frightful sneer at the laws of nature; "we don't want any silly mothers;" and he flew away.

Thus Wendy and John and Michael found the window open for them after all, which of course was more than they deserved. They alighted on the floor, quite unashamed of themselves, and the youngest one had already forgotten his home.

"John," he said, looking around him doubtfully, "I think I have been here before."

"Of course you have, you silly. There is your old bed."

"So it is," Michael said, but not with much conviction.

"I say," cried John, "the kennel!" and he dashed across to look into it.

"Perhaps Nana is inside it," Wendy said.

But John whistled. "Hullo," he said, "there's a man inside it."

"It's father!" exclaimed Wendy.

"Let me see father," Michael begged eagerly, and he took a good look. "He is not so big as the pirate I killed," he said with such frank disappointment that I am glad Mr. Darling was asleep; it would have been sad if those had been the first words he heard his little Michael say.

Wendy and John had been taken aback somewhat at finding their father in the kennel.

"Surely," said John, like one who had lost faith in his memory, "he used not to sleep in the kennel?"

"John," Wendy said falteringly, "perhaps we don't remember the old life as well as we thought we did."

A chill fell upon them; and serve them right.

"It is very careless of mother," said that young scoundrel John, "not to be here when we come back."

It was then that Mrs. Darling began playing again.

"It's mother!" cried Wendy, peeping.

"So it is!" said John.

"Then are you not really our mother, Wendy?" asked Michael, who was surely sleepy.

"Oh dear!" exclaimed Wendy, with her first real twinge of remorse [for having gone], "it was quite time we came back."

"Let us creep in," John suggested, "and put our hands over her eyes."

But Wendy, who saw that they must break the joyous news more gently, had a better plan.

"Let us all slip into our beds, and be there when she comes in, just as if we had never been away."

And so when Mrs. Darling went back to the night-nursery to see if her husband was asleep, all the beds were occupied. The children waited for her cry of joy, but it did not come. She saw them, but she did not believe they were there. You see, she saw them in their beds so often in her dreams that she thought this was just the dream hanging around her still.

She sat down in the chair by the fire, where in the old days she had nursed them.

They could not understand this, and a cold fear fell upon all the three of them.

"Mother!" Wendy cried.

"That's Wendy," she said, but still she was sure it was the dream.

"Mother!"

"That's John," she said.

"Mother!" cried Michael. He knew her now.

"That's Michael," she said, and she stretched out her arms for the three little selfish children they would never envelop again. Yes, they did, they went round Wendy and John and Michael, who had slipped out of bed and run to her.

"George, George!" she cried when she could speak; and Mr. Darling woke to share her bliss, and Nana came rushing in. There could not have been a lovelier sight; but there was none to see it except a little boy who was staring in at the window. He had had ecstasies innumerable that other children can never know; but he was looking through the window at the one joy from which he must be for ever barred.

17

When Wendy Grew Up

I hope you want to know what became of the other boys. They were waiting below to give Wendy time to explain about them; and when they had counted five hundred they went up. They went up by the stair, because they thought this would make a better impression. They stood in a row in front of Mrs. Darling, with their hats off, and wishing they were not wearing their pirate clothes. They said nothing, but their eyes asked her to have them. They ought to have looked at Mr. Darling also, but they forgot about him.

Of course Mrs. Darling said at once that she would have them; but Mr. Darling was curiously depressed, and they saw that he considered six a rather large number.

"I must say," he said to Wendy, "that you don't do things by halves," a grudging remark which the twins thought was pointed at them.

The first twin was the proud one, and he asked, flushing, "Do you think we should be too much of a handful, sir? Because, if so, we can go away."

"Father!" Wendy cried, shocked; but still the cloud was on him. He knew he was behaving unworthily, but he could not help it.

"We could lie doubled up," said Nibs.

"I always cut their hair myself," said Wendy.

"George!" Mrs. Darling exclaimed, pained to see her dear one showing himself in such an unfavourable light.

Then he burst into tears, and the truth came out. He was as glad to have them as she was, he said, but he thought they should have asked his consent as well as hers, instead of treating him as a cypher [zero] in his own house.

"I don't think he is a cypher," Tootles cried instantly. "Do you think he is a cypher, Curly?"

"No, I don't. Do you think he is a cypher, Slightly?"

"Rather not. Twin, what do you think?"

It turned out that not one of them thought him a cypher; and he was absurdly gratified, and said he would find space for them all in the drawing room if they fitted in.

"We'll fit in, sir," they assured him.

"Then follow the leader," he cried gaily. "Mind you, I am not sure that we have a drawing room, but we pretend we have, and it's all the same. Hoop la!"

He went off dancing through the house, and they all cried "Hoop la!" and danced after him, searching for the drawing room; and I forget whether they found it, but at any rate they found corners, and they all fitted in.

As for Peter, he saw Wendy once again before he flew away. He did not exactly come to the window, but he brushed against it in passing so that she could open it if she liked and call to him. That is what she did.

"Hullo, Wendy, goodbye," he said.

"Oh dear, are you going away?"

"Yes."

"You don't feel, Peter," she said falteringly, "that you would like to say anything to my parents about a very sweet subject?"

"No."

"About me, Peter?"

"No."

Mrs. Darling came to the window, for at present she was keeping a sharp eye on Wendy. She told Peter that she had adopted all the other boys, and would like to adopt him also.

"Would you send me to school?" he inquired craftily.

"Yes."

"And then to an office?"

"I suppose so."

"Soon I would be a man?"

"Very soon."

"I don't want to go to school and learn solemn things," he told her passionately. "I don't want to be a man. O Wendy's mother, if I was to wake up and feel there was a beard!"

"Peter," said Wendy the comforter, "I should love you in a beard;" and Mrs. Darling stretched out her arms to him, but he repulsed her.

"Keep back, lady, no one is going to catch me and make me a man."

"But where are you going to live?"

"With Tink in the house we built for Wendy. The fairies are to put it high up among the tree tops where they sleep at nights."

"How lovely," cried Wendy so longingly that Mrs. Darling tightened her grip.

"I thought all the fairies were dead," Mrs. Darling said.

"There are always a lot of young ones," explained Wendy, who was now quite an authority, "because you see when a new baby laughs for the first time a new fairy is born, and as there are always new babies there are always new fairies. They live in nests on the tops of trees; and the mauve ones are boys and the white ones are girls, and the blue ones are just little sillies who are not sure what they are."

"I shall have such fun," said Peter, with one eye on Wendy.

"It will be rather lonely in the evening," she said, "sitting by the fire."

"I shall have Tink."

"Tink can't go a twentieth part of the way round," she reminded him a little tartly.

"Sneaky tell-tale!" Tink called out from somewhere round the corner.

"It doesn't matter," Peter said.

"O Peter, you know it matters."

"Well, then, come with me to the little house."

"May I, mummy?"

"Certainly not. I have got you home again, and I mean to keep you."

"But he does so need a mother."

"So do you, my love."

"Oh, all right," Peter said, as if he had asked her from politeness merely; but Mrs. Darling saw his mouth twitch, and she made this handsome offer: to let Wendy go to him for a week every year to do his spring cleaning. Wendy would have preferred a more permanent arrangement; and it seemed to her that spring would be long in coming; but this promise sent Peter away quite gay again. He had no sense of time, and was so full of adventures that all I have told you about him is only a halfpenny-worth of them. I suppose it was because Wendy knew this that her last words to him were these rather plaintive ones:

"You won't forget me, Peter, will you, before spring-cleaning time comes?"

Of course Peter promised; and then he flew away. He took Mrs. Darling's kiss with him. The kiss that had been for no one else, Peter took quite easily. Funny. But she seemed satisfied.

Of course all the boys went to school; and most of them got into Class III, but Slightly was put first into Class IV and then into Class V. Class I is the top class. Before they had attended school a week they saw what goats they had been not to remain on the island; but it was too late now, and soon they settled down to being as ordinary as you or me or Jenkins minor [the younger Jenkins]. It is sad to have to say that the power to fly gradually left them. At first Nana tied their feet to the bedposts so that they should not fly away in the night; and one of their diversions by day was to pretend to fall off buses [the English double-deckers]; but by and by they ceased to tug at their bonds in bed, and found that they hurt themselves when they let go of the bus. In time they could not even fly after their hats. Want of practice, they called it; but what it really meant was that they no longer believed.

Michael believed longer than the other boys, though they jeered at him; so he was with Wendy when Peter came for her at the end of the first year. She flew away with Peter in the frock she had woven from leaves and berries in the Neverland, and her one fear was that he might notice how short it had become; but he never noticed, he had so much to say about himself.

She had looked forward to thrilling talks with him about old times, but new adventures had crowded the old ones from his mind.

"Who is Captain Hook?" he asked with interest when she spoke of the arch enemy.

"Don't you remember," she asked, amazed, "how you killed him and saved all our lives?"

"I forget them after I kill them," he replied carelessly.

When she expressed a doubtful hope that Tinker Bell would be glad to see her he said, "Who is Tinker Bell?"

"O Peter," she said, shocked; but even when she explained he could not remember.

"There are such a lot of them," he said. "I expect she is no more."

I expect he was right, for fairies don't live long, but they are so little that a short time seems a good while to them.

Wendy was pained too to find that the past year was but as yesterday to Peter; it had seemed such a long year of waiting to her. But he was exactly as fascinating as ever, and they had a lovely spring cleaning in the little house on the tree tops.

Next year he did not come for her. She waited in a new frock because the old one simply would not meet; but he never came.

"Perhaps he is ill," Michael said.

"You know he is never ill."

Michael came close to her and whispered, with a shiver, "Perhaps there is no such person, Wendy!" and then Wendy would have cried if Michael had not been crying.

Peter came next spring cleaning; and the strange thing was that he never knew he had missed a year.

That was the last time the girl Wendy ever saw him. For a little longer she tried for his sake not to have growing pains; and she felt she was untrue to him when she got a prize for general knowledge. But the years came and went without bringing the careless boy; and when they met again Wendy was a married woman, and Peter was no more to her than a little dust in the box in which she had kept her toys. Wendy was grown up. You need not be sorry for her. She was one of the kind that likes to grow up. In the end she grew up of her own free will a day quicker than other girls.

All the boys were grown up and done for by this time; so it is scarcely worth while saying anything more about them. You may see the twins and Nibs and Curly any day going to an office, each carrying a little bag and an umbrella. Michael is an engine-driver [train engineer]. Slightly married a lady of title, and so he became a lord. You see that judge in a wig coming out at the iron door? That used to be Tootles. The bearded man who doesn't know any story to tell his children was once John.

Wendy was married in white with a pink sash. It is strange to think that Peter did not alight in the church and forbid the banns [formal announcement of a marriage].

Years rolled on again, and Wendy had a daughter. This ought not to be written in ink but in a golden splash.

She was called Jane, and always had an odd inquiring look, as if from the moment she arrived on the mainland she wanted to ask questions. When she was old enough to ask them they were mostly about Peter Pan. She loved to hear of Peter, and Wendy told her all she could remember in the very nursery from which the famous flight had taken place. It was Jane's nursery now, for her father had bought it at the three per cents [mortgage rate] from Wendy's father, who was no longer fond of stairs. Mrs. Darling was now dead and forgotten.

There were only two beds in the nursery now, Jane's and her nurse's; and there was no kennel, for Nana also had passed away. She died of old age, and at the end she had been rather difficult to get on with; being very firmly convinced that no one knew how to look after children except herself.

Once a week Jane's nurse had her evening off; and then it was Wendy's part to put Jane to bed. That was the time for stories. It was Jane's invention to raise the sheet over her mother's head and her own, thus making a tent, and in the awful darkness to whisper:

"What do we see now?"

"I don't think I see anything tonight," says Wendy, with a feeling that if Nana were here she would object to further conversation.

"Yes, you do," says Jane, "you see when you were a little girl."

"That is a long time ago, sweetheart," says Wendy. "Ah me, how time flies!"

"Does it fly," asks the artful child, "the way you flew when you were a little girl?"

"The way I flew? Do you know, Jane, I sometimes wonder whether I ever did really fly."

"Yes, you did."

"The dear old days when I could fly!"

"Why can't you fly now, mother?"

"Because I am grown up, dearest. When people grow up they forget the way."

"Why do they forget the way?"

"Because they are no longer gay and innocent and heartless. It is only the gay and innocent and heartless who can fly."

"What is gay and innocent and heartless? I do wish I were gay and innocent and heartless."

Or perhaps Wendy admits she does see something.

"I do believe," she says, "that it is this nursery."

"I do believe it is," says Jane. "Go on."

They are now embarked on the great adventure of the night when Peter flew in looking for his shadow.

"The foolish fellow," says Wendy, "tried to stick it on with soap, and when he could not he cried, and that woke me, and I sewed it on for him."

"You have missed a bit," interrupts Jane, who now knows the story better than her mother. "When you saw him sitting on the floor crying, what did you say?"

"I sat up in bed and I said, 'Boy, why are you crying?'"

"Yes, that was it," says Jane, with a big breath.

"And then he flew us all away to the Neverland and the fairies and the pirates and the redskins and the mermaids' lagoon, and the home under the ground, and the little house."

"Yes! which did you like best of all?"

"I think I liked the home under the ground best of all."

"Yes, so do I. What was the last thing Peter ever said to you?"

"The last thing he ever said to me was, 'Just always be waiting for me, and then some night you will hear me crowing.'"

"Yes."

"But, alas, he forgot all about me," Wendy said it with a smile. She was as grown up as that.

"What did his crow sound like?" Jane asked one evening.

"It was like this," Wendy said, trying to imitate Peter's crow.

"No, it wasn't," Jane said gravely, "it was like this;" and she did it ever so much better than her mother.

Wendy was a little startled. "My darling, how can you know?"

"I often hear it when I am sleeping," Jane said.

"Ah yes, many girls hear it when they are sleeping, but I was the only one who heard it awake."

"Lucky you," said Jane.

And then one night came the tragedy. It was the spring of the year, and the story had been told for the night, and Jane was now asleep in her bed. Wendy was sitting on the floor, very close to the fire, so as to see to darn, for there was no other light in the nursery; and while she sat darning she heard a crow. Then the window blew open as of old, and Peter dropped in on the floor.

He was exactly the same as ever, and Wendy saw at once that he still had all his first teeth.

He was a little boy, and she was grown up. She huddled by the fire not daring to move, helpless and guilty, a big woman.

"Hullo, Wendy," he said, not noticing any difference, for he was thinking chiefly of himself; and in the dim light her white dress might have been the nightgown in which he had seen her first.

"Hullo, Peter," she replied faintly, squeezing herself as small as possible. Something inside her was crying "Woman, Woman, let go of me."

"Hullo, where is John?" he asked, suddenly missing the third bed.

"John is not here now," she gasped.

"Is Michael asleep?" he asked, with a careless glance at Jane.

"Yes," she answered; and now she felt that she was untrue to Jane as well as to Peter.

"That is not Michael," she said quickly, lest a judgment should fall on her.

Peter looked. "Hullo, is it a new one?"

"Yes."

"Boy or girl?"

"Girl."

Now surely he would understand; but not a bit of it.

"Peter," she said, faltering, "are you expecting me to fly away with you?"

"Of course; that is why I have come." He added a little sternly, "Have you forgotten that this is spring-cleaning time?"

She knew it was useless to say that he had let many spring-cleaning times pass.

"I can't come," she said apologetically, "I have forgotten how to fly."

"I'll soon teach you again."

"O Peter, don't waste the fairy dust on me."

She had risen; and now at last a fear assailed him. "What is it?" he cried, shrinking.

"I will turn up the light," she said, "and then you can see for yourself."

For almost the only time in his life that I know of, Peter was afraid. "Don't turn up the light," he cried.

She let her hands play in the hair of the tragic boy. She was not a little girl heart-broken about him; she was a grown woman smiling at it all, but they were wet-eyed smiles.

Then she turned up the light, and Peter saw. He gave a cry of pain; and when the tall beautiful creature stooped to lift him in her arms he drew back sharply.

"What is it?" he cried again.

She had to tell him.

"I am old, Peter. I am ever so much more than twenty. I grew up long ago."

"You promised not to!"

"I couldn't help it. I am a married woman, Peter."

"No, you're not."

"Yes, and the little girl in the bed is my baby."

"No, she's not."

But he supposed she was; and he took a step towards the sleeping child with his dagger upraised. Of course he did not strike. He sat down on the floor instead and sobbed; and Wendy did not know how to comfort him, though she could have done it so easily once. She was only a woman now, and she ran out of the room to try to think.

Peter continued to cry, and soon his sobs woke Jane. She sat up in bed, and was interested at once.

"Boy," she said, "why are you crying?"

Peter rose and bowed to her, and she bowed to him from the bed.

"Hullo," he said.

"Hullo," said Jane.

"My name is Peter Pan," he told her.

"Yes, I know."

"I came back for my mother," he explained, "to take her to the Neverland."

"Yes, I know," Jane said, "I have been waiting for you."

When Wendy returned diffidently she found Peter sitting on the bedpost crowing gloriously, while Jane in her nighty was flying round the room in solemn ecstasy.

"She is my mother," Peter explained; and Jane descended and stood by his side, with the look in her face that he liked to see on ladies when they gazed at him.

"He does so need a mother," Jane said.

"Yes, I know," Wendy admitted rather forlornly; "no one knows it so well as I."

"Goodbye," said Peter to Wendy; and he rose in the air, and the shameless Jane rose with him; it was already her easiest way of moving about.

Wendy rushed to the window.

"No, no," she cried.

"It is just for spring-cleaning time," Jane said, "he wants me always to do his spring cleaning."

"If only I could go with you," Wendy sighed.

"You see you can't fly," said Jane.

Of course in the end Wendy let them fly away together. Our last glimpse of her shows her at the window, watching them receding into the sky until they were as small as stars.

As you look at Wendy, you may see her hair becoming white, and her figure little again, for all this happened long ago. Jane is now a common grown-up, with a daughter called Margaret; and every spring-cleaning time, except when he forgets, Peter comes for Margaret and takes her to the Neverland, where she tells him stories about himself, to which he listens eagerly. When Margaret grows up she will have a daughter, who is to be Peter's mother in turn; and thus it will go on, so long as children are gay and innocent and heartless.